# Laffite's Lady
### An Epic Adventure

## Susan Elliston

Laffite's Lady. Copyright © 1998 by Susan Elliston.

Printed and bound in the United States of America. All rights reserved. No part of this book may be reproduced in any form or by any electronic or mechanical means including information storage and retrieval systems without permission in writing from the publisher, except by a reviewer, who may quote brief passages in a review.

Published by FirstPublish.COM, LLC
7512 Dr. Phillips Blvd., Suite 50-308
Orlando, FL 32819
(407) 827-7546

Photograph by Alexendrena Bathemess
Design by Dylan Daniels

email: info@firstpublish.com

Other fine books are available from FirstPublish.COM, LLC
Find us on the internet: http://www.firstpublish.com

ISBN 1-929925-00-X

Library of Congress Cataloging-in-Publication Data
9 9 - 0 6 6 9 1 9

Elliston, Susan
Laffite's Lady/ Susan Elliston – 1st ed.

First Edition

This book is dedicated with Love:

To Daniel my soul mate, who just happens to be my husband. His constant support and belief in my work, gave me the courage to write. Without him, Laffite's Lady would never have been born.

# Acknowledgments

I wish to thank:

First and foremost my family who have put up with me living in two worlds for the last fifteen years. Having a mom popping in and out of the past and present gave us all a few laughs. Daniel who took me to New Orleans countless times over the years to do the hours upon hours of research and always listened to me and on a few occasions got me to listen to him! I really want to thank Drena my daughter, David and Dylan my sons who have each in their own way helped me more than they know. For all the times they were dragged along to locations and took tours of plantations and battle sites, all without complaining. Drena for her spelling, research skills and love of reading. David for his laughter and support when I really needed it and Dylan for his constant help on the computer and finding my lost pages.

I want to thank the Louisiana Historical Association and the research center on Charter Street. The personnel there never let me down or ceased to amaze me.

The Destrehan Plantation was not open to the public when Daniel and I first came upon it. In fact they were battening down for an approaching hurricane when we pulled onto the grounds. Mr. Joseph Maddox listened to my husband's plea and was gracious enough to give us a personal tour and history of the place. We have since returned many times and though our paths have never crossed again, I just wanted Mr. Maddox to know that I did try my best to keep the historical facts correct as promised. From the shell of a neglected building now stands a proud and fine example of a historical plantation home. Its inspiration was invaluable.

I also wish to thank the fine people I have met in Laffite's Blacksmith Shop on Bourbon Street. It was because they were always willing to talk about the building and its history that I learned of the writing on the wall.

To my friends who were brave enough to read the first draft of the book and tell me what they thought. It was not because you said it was great that we are still friends, rather it's because you kept asking me when will it be published?

I would also like to thank Cindy Sosinski, for the countless hours that she put into editing and formatting my book.

Last of all I want to thank our friend Nick VandenBrekel, CEO of FirstPublish Corporation, for his help and determination that found the way to publish Laffite's Lady. I cannot thank him enough. Dan and I will always cherish both he and his wife's friendship.

My Lady,

Time is as fluid as the sea I sailed upon. Its currents like the days washing you along on life's journey. The kindest, most beautiful gift time ever deposited upon my shore was you. The cruelest its waves ever became was the day it swept you from my life. And now it seems in its grandest moment, I am to be put adrift in the mystery of its depths. Or rather set free to sail upon heaven's ocean above....

Upon which star I wonder will I wash ashore? Wherever time and tide take me, I go full of love and in peace. Let me no longer be an anchor to you. Instead let the memory of us calm your soul and set you free to sail the most glorious ocean of them all...the one called life.

Laffite

# Prologue

  Tori had been awake since before dawn. Once again the same haunting nightmare had slipped into her dreams, shattering her much-needed sleep. But this time it was no longer just fleeting shadows of the past that had reached out to her. She had seen so clearly all the people and places that meant so much. It had all seemed so very real, so clear, most of all Laffite. He had been so close, that she felt she could actually reach out and touch him.
  His image had made such an impression that even now wide awake, Tori could still see his face, the laughter behind his sparkling eyes. But it was those eyes that had upset her the most. The expression in them somehow had changed from the look she had grown to know as love, to one of hurt and pleading, tearing at her soul. In her dream she was unable to stare into those dark pools for fear of drowning in the terror they held. Always at this point she would wake. It would leave her torn emotionally; knowing it had only been a dream and nothing more. Yet she found herself dreading the next night, when she would have to face it all again. She shook her head as if trying to clear away the images. For months the dream had come only once or twice a week. Looking back, that had been somewhat manageable. But now it occurred each night, and it was getting difficult, if not impossible to bear. Then there was the knowledge that once she had gained control over the dream's residue, she would lie awake in the dark hours, knowing like now, that her sleep for the night was over...
  Tori lay still beside Dan and for a few minutes she listened to his slow rhythmic breathing. Cautiously she reached out to touch him, running her hand gently and lovingly up and down his naked back, feeling the strong muscles of his shoulders and the warmth of his skin. Just knowing that this protective man was within her reach, that she was not alone, helped calm her, enabling her to let some of the fear and loneliness slip away. It was almost as though by touching him she was drawing on his own strength for herself.
  Over the past few years Dan and she had grown very close. It had not been easy for her to allow him into her life. She had not wanted to ever feel the pain of losing someone again. If it had not been for his persistence and dedication to both her and Linni, she doubted that she would have ever given in. Now here she was with him firmly planted in her life as her lover, her constant companion, best friend and confidant. This big wonderful man had never given up, never allowed her to pull away. He had worked his way into her life and not just her life either. Dan had won the loyalty and love of her daughter Linni. He had from the very start filled that empty hole in Linni's life called father. Maybe it had been that unconditional love he shared with Linni, accepting her as his own child that had given him the key to reach herself.

Most important and right from the start, he had never doubted her or her story of what had happened on that summer morning two years ago. Never had he called her crazy or refused to discuss it at anytime. No, he was not like that. Instead he had become her lifeline in dealing with the emotional turmoil the experience had left her in.

Looking at Dan's sleeping form, his face lit softly by the light shining from the open bathroom door, filled her with mixed emotions. Both love and guilt flowed over her, as the past few weeks flashed in her mind. It hurt her to see the concern on his face grow each day. Like herself, he was worrying about her state of mind. She hated hurting either him or Linni by falling apart emotionally and had done her best to hide it from them. But it was becoming increasingly harder to act as if she had everything under control, when she knew damn well she was losing it. She stroked the side of his face, his lips twitched into a part smile and she withdrew her hand studying him. Tori knew she was not fooling him anymore, at least not all the time.

"I must get better at it," she said softly, "who knows, maybe it will all end soon."

Dan's sleepy voice broke the silence of the dark room. She had not meant to wake him. He would only worry about her and be full of questions she didn't want to answer through lies. He asked her if anything was wrong, then slowly turning over to face her, without even opening his eyes, asked again, in a voice slurred by sleep, "Is something wrong?"

She could smell the whiskey still on his breath. The sour odor was the result of the heavy drinking they had done that night. She reminded herself that she had best have the aspirin ready, because it was certain he would have a mean hangover come morning.

"No, just had one of my dreams. Nothing I can't handle. Go back to sleep." She watched him for a few minutes, holding her breath until she was sure he had indeed drifted back to sleep.

Handle it, that was a laugh. Sure she'd handle it the way she always did these days. Slowly so as not to disturb him, she slid out from beneath the covers and felt with her feet for her slippers. Not finding them and cursing softly to herself, she reached instead for her robe and cigarettes. Carrying both out to the other room, she slowly closed the door behind her.

Her skin that had been warm was now quickly chilling. The perspiration that covered her naked body was making her cool off even faster. Shuddering, Tori put on her robe. Then turning on a small lamp so she could find her matches, she lit a much-needed cigarette. Once she accomplished this, she put out the light and opened the curtains to the verandah. The pre-dawn light greeted her. She knew morning would soon be here, and that meant she wouldn't have to be alone with her thoughts and the ghosts of the past for long.

She opened the verandah door letting in a slight breeze from the courtyard below. It sent a chill through her as it blew around her head trying to lift her damp hair. Wet strands clung to the back of her neck and stuck firmly to her forehead, while the odd wisp of hair caught on the draft briefly took flight. She stepped out onto the verandah turning her head toward the cool air and its gentle gusts. The breeze was a welcome friend, so often she had felt its cooling touch like now. The moment made her think back in time to a memory of standing on a balcony just like this one, cooling off after making love with Jean.

She remembered those nights when she would stand and let the breeze blow over her naked body. A body that would be damp from perspiration and glistening in the moonlight. Of how he would gently reach up and push the damp hair away from her skin, letting his fingers slowly trace the outline of her face. She loved the touch of his hand, as it traced further down her body. The tingling sensation on her skin left a burning desire for more. She would stand there enjoying his caresses, until she could wait no longer. Then they'd leave the balcony, their sexual desire overcoming them both. Like a magnet it would draw them back to bed.

The memory sent a shiver through her and what a moment ago had been a beautiful daydream, now only filled her with a mixture of hurt and anger.

"Why won't you let me go? You had to know that I might find my way back someday day. Damn you Jean. I need peace in my life, not this walking from room to room, hour after hour, talking to no one but myself, myself and your ghost."

She shook her head slowly and rubbed at her tired eyes, her whole body felt exhausted and the day had not even begun. She needed more sleep but how? Even on those nights that Dan gave her a sleeping pill, rest seemed to avoid her. Those nights would be full of tossing and turning, and of images she couldn't run away from. Now day and night, the memories haunted her, leaving her wonder if she could ever learn to forget or live with what had happened?

For two years now Tori had been trying to put behind her what Dan had come to call her trip. Some trip she thought. Not only could she not explain to anyone what had happened, Dan had told her it would be best they kept it to themselves. She had trusted in that advice, after all who would ever believe in such an incredible story anyway? Trusted was the word wasn't it, she asked herself? Maybe that was what was wrong, she no longer trusted that was the right thing to do. She wanted to believe Dan was right, but he could be wrong, after all he based that conclusion on what she had told him. How would he feel, she asked herself, if he knew it all. So much of the story had been left untold. Secrets lay locked away deep down in her very soul, secrets that had smoldered, that could no longer be ignored. Now each one of them was rising up in her dreams, as if asking to be put to rest forever by their release.

She thought about the dreams and how this last one had changed and become a nightmare. Even in her waking hours Tori found herself struggling, with all that she had hidden so carefully away. She knew on some deep level, that it all had to come out if she were to ever let go of the past and go on with her future. She had to free herself from the pain, the memories, the guilt, but most of all from him, from the ghost of Jean Laffite.

"It's as if you're here reaching out to me. My God why is it that you're so strong. Is it because I'm here where it all happened? Or because I know what I'm going to do?" Her voice was shaking as she continued to mumble. "Talk and walk that's all I'm doing, all I've done but no more. It's going to end."

Tori wondered how could it be that after all those years of struggling to get back to her child, of finally succeeding, that she could not find peace. "Stupid question," she snapped. She knew the answer to that question only too well, she just didn't want to go there. It was not facing up to that answer that was tearing her apart, tearing them apart. Dan had brought her here, so she could come to grips with it all, and that was what she was about to do. She hugged herself as if trying to give herself strength. There was only one way to go about the healing, no matter what the consequences, and she would start today.

Reaching into the pocket of her robe, she felt for the piece of paper with the phone number on it. Finding it still safely where she had placed it the night before, she was able to relax a little. Tori knew all it would take would be one call and the courage to make it for the healing to begin.

Settling herself down on the verandah outside their room, her eyes began to wander. It was a beautiful sight from where she sat. The second floor of the hotel was high enough to let her view the whole courtyard without seeing over the vine-covered wall to the street. The sweet smell of jasmine and the colors of the flowers in their clay pots made her forget that she was in the heart of New Orleans, a modern fast-moving city of the 90's.

It was much lighter now and she noticed that even at this early hour someone had been busy. The tables were already set for breakfast. Just then the fountain off to the side turned on and the water could be heard splashing into the pool below. The pool itself was like a mirror reflecting the colors of the flowers that had opened and bloomed in the early morning sun. The tables below with their white cloths and table settings sat vacant at the moment waiting to be occupied by the guests. The only sound she could hear was of the occasional waiter placing some forgotten piece of silverware on the table, his steps on the flagstones echoing as he left the area.

Even the traffic in the city was light at this hour. The sound of a horse-drawn carriage, one of many that you see in the streets during the day, was passing by on the other side of the wall.

A small bird flew down among the tables hoping to find a crumb left there from the night before. He was just a little too early for breakfast. Watching the bird run from table to table, Tori found herself thinking back to another time, another courtyard and another New Orleans. The same sights, smells, oh yes, the aroma of fresh baked bread and strong black coffee, mixed in with the jasmine and the smell of the river carried on the soft morning breeze. Yes, they were all there. All she had to do was close her eyes and think back.

Slowly like a person in a trance not wanting to wake up, Tori lit another cigarette and inhaled deeply.

From off in the room a phone could be heard ringing followed by Dan's husky voice. She could hear him telling room service thanks, for the wake up call and asking for some coffee and rolls to be sent up.

Dan continued talking but Tori was no longer listening. She was submerged in remembering something that had long ago ceased to exist. She sat so still, that one might think she was a mannequin. It was not until you looked at her face, that you could see she was very much alive. For there, tears were falling freely down her cheeks. Her eyes had a great painful look about them, staring off into the distance, not really looking at anything and yet seeing something that was causing her all of the agony clearly etched there.

Tori had become so involved in her daydream that she was unaware of Dan who now stood in the doorway, his heart heavy as he looked upon the love of his life. He could see the tears streaming silently down her face and could only guess at the cause.

It had been his idea that she join him on this trip, to help her let go of what had happened. She had to come to grips with it once and for all, for both of their sakes. It had seemed like a good idea at the time. Hell, she had even seemed to welcome the chance. Yet, looking at her sitting there, so still and hurting with a pain that he couldn't begin to help cure, let alone understand, he wondered if he had done the right thing.

Dan had this overpowering feeling that even though she had told him her story of what had happened, that she had in fact, not told him everything she had been through. Either she could not because it was too painful for her, or better still maybe too painful for him? Could it be, he wondered, that the reason behind her not letting go had something, somehow to do with him?

Maybe Tori needed to talk to someone, other than himself, to really open up, but who in the hell would ever listen to her without thinking she had gone completely off the deep end. Who could they trust? Dan hit his fist into the doorframe. He himself had a hard time dealing with the story and he believed her. Incredible as it seemed the proof had been right before his very own eyes. But to talk about it now, no way! He had to think of her and what people would put her through if the tale ever got out. The headlines on those sleazy tabloids would read, "LOCAL WOMAN CLAIMS TIME TRAVEL." No, his way was best. She could not stand going through something like that. It was best to keep it to themselves. They just had to find another way to help her forget and heal, to put the whole episode behind her.

He had no doubt as to her feelings toward him. She trusted him and had grown to love him enough to say yes to his marriage proposal, but that was when things had really started to go wrong. Since that day, she had slipped deeper into her own tormented world. He realized if they were ever to have a chance at a future together she would have to let go of the past, for he knew she could not go on this way much longer.

Dan walked over to where she sat and not wanting to frighten her, he spoke her name softly. When that got him no reaction, he placed his hand gently on her shoulder. The touch was like giving her an electrical shock. She had been so deep in thought, that rushing back to reality caused her to let out a sound somewhere between a strangled cry and frightened whimper.

This reaction was totally unexpected on Dan's part and he acted instinctively, pulling her into his arms, as he would her daughter when she had a nightmare.

Tori fell into his embrace sobbing and clinging to him as if her very life depended on him. Her body shaking from the emotions brought on by the memories she had just relived, caused Dan to tighten his hold.

"That does it, I'm sending you back on the next available flight." His voice was calm, yet firm. "We were wrong bringing you back here, it's too painful for you and I can't see you suffer like this."

"No Dan! Please give me a day or two. I'll be fine. I know I will." She could still see he did not believe her and she had to stay no matter what. "You see I think it's going to get easier from now on." Tori forced a slight smile. She looked into his loving face and could see he still did not believe a word she was saying. She had to make him believe her. "All I need is some sleep. I couldn't last night you can understand that can't you? It's my first time back Dan. I won't lie to you. Sure it's hard, but tomorrow will be better. If I find I can't handle it, I'll go, no fighting, I promise."

Tori gave him one of her pleading looks, the one that he could never say no to. She watched his face soften and knew she had won her case. Tori decided not to push her luck. She reached up on tiptoe kissing his forehead lightly. "Thanks, now if you don't want to be late you had best get going." She turned him around and pushed him toward the open door.

"All right, all right. My, you can go on and on when you want woman. I will be out of here before you know it." He turned and kissed her on the cheek and headed inside. "I'll be out of the shower in a New York minute, that is if you don't join me."

She could hear his laughter in the room as he walked off in the direction of the bathroom. His jovial mood convinced Tori she had convinced him and gotten her way. Tori had at least one more day in the city, and one was all she needed, and she intended to keep it that way.

Joining him in the shower would only delay his departure and what she had to do. Thinking quickly for a reason other than being tired, she jumped on the first idea that came to mind, "I don't join people who have hangovers, but I will bring you two aspirin."

"Oh and just how many people do you join in their shower? And hangover, I doubt I would have one if you had not dragged me down Bourbon Street last night." He was really laughing now. Before she could reply, there came a knock on the door followed by a male voice saying "Room service."

"That will be your coffee, so if you don't want it cold you had better hurry." She pushed him into the bathroom against mock protesting on his part, and closed the door. Five minutes later she had a continental breakfast set up and waiting, as he stepped into the room.

Dan was still very much the jovial character, who had one thing on his mind, and it was far from eating breakfast. "Now that's a sight that could keep me here all day, you and breakfast in bed. Woman, you can do the damnedest things to me, one look at you and all thought of time and work just seem to vanish." Dropping his towel, his arousal very evident, he walked toward her with that determined look on his face.

Steam was still coming off his body. She noticed his brown curly hair combed back over his head was wet, depositing small drops of water on his shoulders. Tori could see a small patch of shaving cream just below his ear, and a few nicks still bled on his chin. He must have been in a big hurry she thought.

Before she could say a word, Dan had crossed the room and picked her up. He quickly carried her to the bed, where they both fell. Once there, they rolled about like a pair of young lovers just starting out, instead of a couple who had been together for a few years. True their sexual relationship had only been for half that time, but their body language spoke volumes of how deeply each cared.

"Dan stop it! I can't breath. Stop tickling, please. I'll scream." She could barely catch her breath let alone scream. He had her just where he wanted.

"For a kiss, a long loving one at that, I might stop." The creases around his eyes deepened giving him that impish look she had come to adore.

"Anything, anything," she said laughing so hard her sides hurt. Tori knew she would have agreed to anything at that point.

His face was full of mischief, as a husky voice spoke, "Anything? Hmm. Now let's see what can I think of."

His mouth came down slowly covering hers as he parted her lips with a soft loving kiss. She could feel him undoing her robe. Reaching inside, he cupped one of her breasts in his hand fondling the nipple between his fingers.

"I love you. You don't know how much I need you, to hold you, make love to you." He was kissing her neck now. The intimacy of the moment worked its magic on her, for the moment it washed away all sadness and awakened an overpowering desire in her. She needed him as much, if not more. Everything else could wait. She responded to his seduction. Her trembling hands pulled his head down to her. Tori kissed him with all the love she held for him. Her fingers wrapped themselves in his damp hair, twisting and sliding across his head. She guided his head toward her breast, where his mouth found her nipples. His tongue played with the pink tips, until they were taut peaks. He bit lightly, until she let out a soft moan of delight.

Tori's body was responding to his loving caresses and artful lovemaking. She was powerless to resist, slipping still deeper under his spell, when the phone rang loud and clear. Her body went rigid, followed by Dan's "God damn it," spoken through clenched teeth, shattering the moment.

Rolling off her and reaching for the phone, Dan's eyes did not lose contact with hers. "Don't move an inch. Hello, oh yes McDavid, no, no bother we were up," he winked at her. "Problem, no sir..."

Tori watched him as he talked and knew that the lovemaking would have to wait. He was already up, mouthing he was sorry and had to go, putting on his shirt as he talked.

Tori's trembling hand closed her robe. It would take time for the rest of her to calm down. The surge of excitement Dan had caused was like a smoldering fire that would take its own sweet time to die out. She walked to the coffeepot, pouring two cups. It was not his fault that he had to leave her feeling this way, so how could she get angry? She just wished that she could rid herself of the tingling feeling that was running up and down her body. Handing him a cup along with kissing him on the cheek, Tori whispered, "It's OK."

"Yes, of course, I'll be right over... No, we have to solve it now... Give me thirty minutes... Have the paperwork ready... No, tell him as long as it takes... Sometime late tonight or early tomorrow morning... Fine see you then bye." He hung up the phone and started cursing, saying how sorry he was he would have to miss dinner. He was explaining about how he was going to have to work late.

Tori was thinking everything happens for a reason. She now had all the time she needed, to do what she had to do, with no chance of Dan catching her. Strange how things work out.

"You will be all right now won't you?" Concern was written all over his face.

"I'm going to be fine honey. Like I told you before, all I need is some sleep." She smiled and then put on a stern face. "So don't you call to find out if I'm fine and wake me up. Or so help me I'll get even by keeping you up all night. Then you can see how it feels to be this tired."

"All night huh? Sounds like fun to me."

She could see his laugh lines deepening again; it was a sure giveaway that he was teasing her.

"You are impossible and you know what I mean. Now go on and get out of here, or you really will be late."

A few minutes later after several long kisses and more assurances that she was fine, Tori found herself alone at last...

It had been several hours since Dan left and still she had not made the phone call. She had found different things to do, keeping her busy. First she took a shower, followed by washing her hair. Then a quick phone call to her daughter, only to be told by her mother that Linni was at a friend's house. After writing a few post cards, Tori looked around for reason to delay further what she had been putting off all morning. But even she could only find so much to do in a hotel room. Now she sat with a fresh pot of coffee and no more excuses.

The phone was staring at her. The piece of paper with the number on it, felt as if it was burning her hand. Talking out loud to herself, a habit she had since childhood, she picked up the receiver. "All right I'll call, but please let him be there. Let him listen to me." The sound of the tones as she dialed seemed loud enough for the people in the next room to hear. So when she spoke, it was in a very shaky, quiet voice. The party at the other end had to tell her to talk louder.

"Is Tommy there? This is an old friend of his... I would like to talk to him if I may... Yes, I'll hold." The silence on the other end seemed to go on forever. With each minute Tori was losing her nerve. What if he does not remember me? No, he has to, if not me he will remember Linni... Such were the thoughts that were going through her head. She was just about to hang up, when a voice sounded on the other end.

"Yeah, Tom here. What can I do for you?"

"Tom, I don't know if you will remember me. My name is Tori, Tori Wilkinson. My daughter and I, we stayed at the campground this time two years ago."

"Yeah, sure I remember you Mam. How's that little one anyway?"

"She's fine thank you. Tommy. I mean Tom. It's Tom now isn't it? Tori could hear how shaky her own voice sounded as she rattled on. Was she making any sense she wondered? Tom on the other hand, sounded very calm. His Southern accent was strong and like music to listen to.

"Any ways you want it, Tom or Tommy, whatever. What can I do for you Mam? You want me to book you a cabin?"

Tori took in a big breath. This was it, the moment she had been dreading. "No nothing like that. Actually I have some news for you. Tom it's about your mother, I know who she is. I know where you come from." There, she said it. Tori waited for a response, but all she got was silence. "Tom, Tom you still there? Look I'm sorry I blurted it out like that. I'm just so nervous and all. Tom, Tom are you there? Hello."

"Yes, I'm still here. You say you know who my mother is? How do you know that? Is this some sort of joke? Cause if it is..."

"No Tom, it's no joke I promise you. I would never joke about something this serious. I do need to see you and tell you all I know though. Will you meet me? It's very important, please."

From there things happened fast. Tori told him where she was staying and that it would be fine for him to come over anytime that day. They ended up agreeing that he would come over and join her for lunch. She then called down to the desk, asking them to hold all calls. She told them she was going to rest and did not want to be disturbed. With that done, she settled back to wait for Tom. The wait was not a long one.

Tom had left the campground almost immediately after her call. He had waited all his life for this information. What puzzled him though, was just how did a white lady from California have information about his mother. It made no sense, but he sure as hell was going to find out. Shit, today just might be the day he had been waiting for, yes sir, it just might!

Tori had made another call to room service and had some fruit and a plate of sandwiches sent up. Not that she was hungry, that was far from the problem. Just what she was going to say to Tom and how, was the big problem. With very little time to figure it out, she just hoped she had done the right thing. It seemed to her that she had checked the small fridge a hundred times to make sure there were plenty of soft drinks and bottled water. She was about to check it yet again when the knock on the door made her jump. She opened the door and in those first few seconds of looking at Tommy she all but came unglued. Initially, she did not recognize him, but his voice was unforgettable.

"Mam, I hope I'm not too early? Just couldn't wait, you saying you had information on my mother and all."

Tori could see how in two years he had grown from the gangling teenager, awkward and a little shy, to a tall, self-assured young man. His hair was cut short, not too short though. It was still long enough for loose curls to form soft waves. The dark brown mass had just a hint of kink. Tori noticed his features definitely leaned toward his white genes. His father had given him his color of coffee au lait. He had skin too dark to be white, and too light to be passed off as pure black. Yet nothing had changed over the years, had it, she thought. For even today she knew he was judged by many because of his mixed blood.

"Mam," Tom broke the silence.

"Tommy, I'm sorry. Come in please. You have changed some. I would say you have grown by some two or three inches maybe."

"Close enough. Five to be exact," he laughed nervously. "Must be the Southern air." He was looking around the room as if his answers would somehow miraculously appear out of nowhere.

Lord she could see the resemblance to his father now. The way he was standing, legs slightly apart, his hands on his hips. The nose was there and the chin with that slight dimple. His skin was several shades lighter than his mother's. Yet even a part of her shone through. Maybe not in any physical way, as clear as his father's traits, but more in a spiritual sense. His soft spoken way, his gentle nature. She remembered the way he was good with children. He had been great with Linni and the other kids at the camp. Kate would have been proud of her son. More than that, happy because he was free...

"You changed yourself Mam. The tan's missing and you done something with your hair. You don't look none too well either, if you pardon me saying so. You sure you're all right?"

"Yes, Tommy, I'm fine. Just a little tired that's all, and maybe a little wound up. I will be a lot better after I unload on you." He smiled slightly. "It's not going to be easy for either one of us. You see Tommy, oh I forgot it's Tom now isn't it?" She did not give him a chance to answer as she rushed on. "See Tom, the only other person that knows the story I'm about to tell you is Dan. We live together. Have done for about two years. You might remember him. He was staying at the lake in one of the cabins not far from Linni and I. Loved fishing... Well, even he does not know it all, the story that is. I'm sure he would have a fit if he knew that I was going to tell someone, let alone you."

Tom's face flashed anger as he walked toward Tori. "You mean he's kept you from telling me information about my family. He had no right, why would he do something like that?" Tom was desperate now. He was afraid she would not tell him, afraid also of what it was she knew.

"Calm down Tom. It's not what you think. You will understand why he thinks the way he does once it all comes out. Look, sit down. It's going to be a long afternoon and I think it's best if I just start at the beginning." Twisting her hands together, her voice shaking, Tori started. "Tom, I was only going to tell you a little of it, just about background, and your mother. I can see now that won't work." He started to say something, but she cut him off. "No, wait, let me finish. The only way you are going to believe what I have to tell you is if I tell it all." Tori put her hand on her head and ran her fingers over her scalp and through her hair. "God help me it's not going to be easy. I ask only that you listen to me. Wait until I'm through before you ask any questions."

Tom studied her face. He could see that she was very upset. Indeed, more than that, she was scared to death of something.

"Look, I don't know what it is that you know, but I do think I should know it all. I have a right to. The good and the bad. I've waited all my life to find out who I am, and where I came from. If you know something, please, I need to hear it. I'm not going to judge you, or the information. If what you know turns out to be right and true, then I will always thank you. If it's not, well at least you cared enough and remembered me. You tried."

Tom reached out and took her hands. They were cold and clammy and the color had drained from her face. She smiled up at him, squeezing his hands; leaning over she hugged him. "Tom I can't rest until I tell you. You are tied into helping me as much as I am to helping you. I need to tell someone the whole story." She hesitated for a second. "I know that now, and you my friend are the one. I can see that so clearly. Will you listen?"

"I'll listen, don't you worry none. Seems like I don't have no choice in the matter if you ask me," he poked at her side trying to lighten the atmosphere. Then more seriously he softly added, "I'm here for you." The look on his face was a sincere one.

She knew he meant what he said. A grateful look crossed her face. Tori had expected he would understand all along. She spoke with love in her voice. "Just like your mother. She was a good listener and compassionate. You're very much like her. I knew I was right to come here to you." Tori saw the shock on his face; the realization of what she had just said to him was like a slap in his face, the shock quickly turning to questions.

"You knew her, my mother? How? When?"

Holding up her hand she stopped him. "This won't do. I'm sorry. I should think before I talk. I can explain it all and I will. Pour us some coffee and I will light a cigarette. You better listen because if I don't start now, I very well might lose my nerve."

Her hands were shaking as she reached for her cigarettes. Tom took the matches and lit it for her. This was not the happy-go-lucky woman of a few years ago he was looking at. The very fact that she was smoking again proved that. Tori had told him last time she was at the camp, how she herself had stopped the nasty habit. She had caught him sneaking one and given him that long lecture that he should never start. Then she had had him promise on his adoptive mother's life that he would never touch another one. He never forgot that day, or the fact that she never told on him, and he had never smoked after it either.

Tori took a long drag, blowing out the blue-colored smoke, and along with it all her doubts and nervousness. As she began to talk, he settled back to listen. Tom was the one now that was nervous. But listen he would, he would wait and hear what she had to say. He would judge the information later.

Tori's voice was soft, and had taken on a strong assured quality to it. She did not look toward Tom as she spoke. Instead her gaze was directed straight up toward the ceiling. She was staring without looking at anything, like a child in a daydream. She was not only telling the story, but was reliving it. Tori was seeing it as if it were all happening again. So intense was her mood, that Tom quickly became absorbed in the tale. He also would picture and relive the vision she was now describing. Hell, it had only been two years ago. How far away it all seemed and yet how close. Yes, he could see it, the campground, her cabin, himself...

# Chapter 1

Tori lay there for a few minutes listening to the crickets and wondering what time it was. She knew it was still quite early because the morning light creeping in between the curtains was not very bright.

What a night it had been! The wine and the crazy partying had gone on well into the early hours of the morning. The whole group from the camp had explored and occupied just about every bar the French Quarter had to offer, something she was sure she never would have attempted on her own. It had been that crazy English couple's idea. They had introduced them to, what did they call it, a pub crawl? The only thing being, they had no pubs, and no English beer. So they had improvised, until they found that Irish pub off Bourbon Street.

It had been while they were there, that Tori had started talking with Dan. She had finally given in and let him buy her a pint of beer. Dan was one of their group, tall, fair hair, with the bluest eyes she had ever seen. He like her was on vacation, doing some serious bass fishing. Only last night, his sport had taken on fishing for the two-legged kind. At first she had not been to happy with his constant attention but now lying in bed with just a slight hangover, she was glad they had become aquatinted. It had been his suggestion to take two aspirin before bed. She grinned as she recalled he had even added, "and call me in the morning," something she seriously intended to do.

A slow smile crept over her face as she turned over in bed. Across from her lay Linni. Her daughter was curled up in a small ball. She was tightly holding her ever-faithful teddybear Edmund. Tori frowned momentarily. Those two had been inseparable from the day she got him. She did not know if the attachment was a good thing or not. Some of her friends had told her that Linni was getting too old to be holding on to such a childish toy. There again, their children had not had a father who abandoned them at birth either. If her child found comfort in her bear, then that was just fine by her.

Tori climbed out of bed and slipped her robe on before reaching for Linni's covers, pulling them up. She kissed her lightly on the forehead and watched her sleep for a few minutes longer. The bond she felt to her daughter was in her mind, the driving force in her life. Linni was her world and she was the center of her daughter's, shared with good old Edmund of course. Dear old bear, he and his mistress could sleep on a while longer. She did not have the heart to wake them.

In the kitchen, Tori put the coffeepot on and took two more aspirin for the slight headache that she felt lingering in the background. The pot spluttered noisily, its antics sounding far too loud in the dim kitchen. She looked toward the other bedroom in the cabin where her daughter's best friend and mother were still sleeping. Knowing them, they would continue to do so for a few more hours. That was if the damn pot didn't explode and wake them, she thought.

Sara, Linni's friend, was spoiled and very much like her mother, who seemed to enjoy all activities that did not involve very much exertion. Something that she could just not fathom herself. But Sara had been the perfect match for Linni, who enjoyed reading and movies far more than what Tori would have considered normal for her age.

The coffeepot gurgled and stopped dripping its dark aromatic liquid into the glass container below. How people could add milk to such a wonderful beverage amazed her. Two sugars, a quick stir and you had what Tori would tell Linni was the nectar of the gods. The kickstart to each morning she could never do without.

Tori decided that her so-called kickstart would work better with a bit of fresh air. She needed to dust the cobwebs from her sleepy head if she were going to survive the day ahead. Looking at the clock on the wall which read 4:45, she grimaced. Only two and a half hours of sleep! Yes, it was going to be a long day indeed.

Tori had intended to sit and sip her coffee on the porch enjoying the view, but the quiet of the campground and its surroundings beckoned her forward. The mysterious atmosphere called out to her adventurous spirit, daring her to explore and experience what it had to offer. Normally from the porch, they could see the lake and its sandy shoreline. At this time of morning however, one could not see the lake. Its mirror-like surface was shrouded by ground fog, not yet disturbed by the heat of the sun's rays, or blown away by the light morning breeze.

The trees close to the cabin, draped in their gray Spanish moss stood silent, waiting for their tenants to stir. A few birds, the first to move among the large branches, were the only other living creatures sharing the tranquil moment. To Tori, if ever there were a time to take a walk, it was then. Slowly and without thinking much about what she was doing, Tori headed down the small path.

She could feel the cool damp mist on her face, and as she sipped her hot coffee, a slight chill ran up and down her body. She knew that walking around, in only her thin robe, was far from the proper thing to do. However, in the deserted campground at such an early hour, Tori could see no harm in walking just a little further. "It's not as if I'm parading around a crowded park," she chuckled to herself.

Just then, she heard someone headed her way humming. The tune was a haunting melody that she recognized immediately. The tune was known as Tommy's song. Everyone who visited here, would at sometime in their stay be exposed to it and learn its history. Tori herself had been moved to hear the story of its origin. Tommy himself had told her and the girls just a few days ago. It was that story that had bonded Linni's and his friendship. "Birds of a feather," she told herself, as she reflected on his story.

Tommy was the adoptive son of the campground owners. He had been abandoned and found as a toddler down by the lake one morning fifteen years ago. No one ever claimed him, nor did anyone ever learn who he was or where he came from. When found, it had been obvious to all that he was well cared for, even if from a poor home. The child was chubby, healthy and for the most part happy. He had been dressed in hand-made shorts and little shirt. His little feet were bare.

The only thing that they ever learned about him was from the child himself. When asked he told them his name, and he could hold up two, sometimes three fingers as to his age. After that he became withdrawn and frightened, happy only when humming or singing his song. A song that he did say once, his mamma taught him. It was that same song that he was humming now.

Tommy burst around the corner carrying his fishing pole. Upon seeing Tori, he stopped dead in his tracks. He just stood there staring at her. His eyes slowly running the length of her body, taking in every curve, every detail of the woman standing before him. Then seeing that she was watching him, he looked quickly away, turning crimson with embarrassment, wanting to run, yet stay at the same time.

It was Tori who broke the silence between them. She could see he was in an awkward situation and wanted to ease the tension between them. She liked this teenager. He had been so good with Linni, playing games with her and showing her around the camp. "Hi Tommy. I didn't expect to see anyone up so early. I guess you hadn't either."

"No Ma'am." He flashed her a quick look and once again turned bright red. Hell, he hated himself for being so embarrassed. What was wrong with him? He continued to look away.

"Tommy, it's all right. I won't bite you know. Look, it's only me, Tommy." She took a step toward him and he took one backwards away from her, almost stumbling over himself.

"Yes Ma'am, I know it's you Miss Tori Ma'am, but you're in your, ah, in your?" He wished he knew the word to describe what it was she had on. It was nothing like what his mother wore in the morning, that was for sure. Whatever it was called, wrapped around this women's shapely body, with the side slightly slipping open, was beyond him. The silky material was clinging to her every curve. Her breasts stood up firm and round. Their nipples were erect, pushing at the silk, making small peaks. The neckline dipped down exposing her cleavage, like a soft valley. Hell, he told himself he was having thoughts, just like what he read about in the girlie magazines he had hidden at home.

His dilemma suddenly became clear to Tori. It was the way she was dressed. She was standing there in a sexy robe designed to drive men wild. Of course it was more than this kid could endure. Here she was, talking to a teenage boy, who most likely only dreamed of a woman dressing in such a manner in public, let alone ever seeing one. She started to laugh.

Tommy looked at her now, failing to see what was so damn funny and thinking she was laughing at him, an angry glare flashed across his face.

Tori saw this and immediately replaced the laughter on her face with an understanding smile. "Look Tommy it's OK. I am dressed you know. Well, sort of I guess. You can't see anything you know. Heavens, you can see more at the lake. Those girls wear less than this to swim in."

It was Tommy's turn to laugh, partly at himself, partly at Tori. Why she was as flustered as he was. "They don't look half as good though. It's OK Ma'am really it is. I don't see anything wrong with what you have on now that you mention it. Nothing at all. I kind of like it if you want to know the truth." Realizing what he had just said, he panicked looking for a quick retreat. "Look,

I'd love to stay and talk and all. I mean it's not every morning I get to talk to a lady as hot looking as you."

"Well thank you Tommy, you sure know how to make an older woman feel good," she was laughing again.

If you're older, it's only in years, not looks. Wait till I tell the guys how my day started. They will all come out for early walks after this. You best be careful or you might find yourself the big attraction around here, not the French Quarter." Tommy was enjoying himself at last. "Oh! Get out of here you smooth talker. And don't you dare tell anyone. Remember you owe me a favor, I didn't tell on you the other day now did I big smoker?"

"Point well taken. Your identity will remain mine, but you have to let me have this one. The guys will be green, not that they will ever believe me and all. I better be off. Best fishing is about now and if I intend to catch something I'll have to be quick." He turned and was running off still shouting over his shoulder. "And if I was you, I'd head back to the cabin, before you catch something. Mr. Dan sees you like that and I'd bet it wouldn't be hell you'd catch if you get my point!"

"Just what do you mean by that?" She called out to him.

"Just that he's got the hots for you, plain as day!" He was laughing so hard he tripped and all but fell down, but managed to gain his balance and continue on, his laughter fading into the mist with him.

Tori found he had put her in a very good mood after all. He had a way of doing that with everyone he talked to. Some mother out there was missing out on a wonderful child she thought. What a shame.

It was still too peaceful and she felt too good to head back to the cabin. The aspirin had taken effect. There was no trace of the headache and her spirits were flying high. Taking a sip of her coffee and turning, Tori found herself headed toward the lake. It took her only a few minutes to walk down the narrow road to the shore, located at the opposite end of the camp.

The lake was a good size one. During the day, people could be found paddling the small brightly colored boats around on its clear spring-fed waters. The beach that the owners had made by trucking in sand from the gulf coast, was empty and somewhat eerie, making her feel slightly uncomfortable. Tori walked away from the abandoned tables and barbecues toward the end of the beach and the beginning of lush green foliage. Finding a small trail, she walked along just taking in the beauty of the sights and sounds. Tori had never noticed this path before, and guessed it went clear around to the other side. She had always assumed the fishermen on the other side of the lake traveled there by boat. The trail was well worn, twisting and winding its way by the water's edge. In a short distance Tori noticed the lush green grass gave way to a soft dirt track, well worn by the looks of it. So the fishermen did not need their boats after all, she had been right. All they needed was a good pair of walking shoes!

Stopping to look down at her bare feet, she told herself to watch where she was stepping. "I don't need to end up cutting myself on something sharp," she mumbled. Tori knew she was talking to herself again, it was a habit she was trying to stop. Linni would frequently catch her unaware, in full conversations, and tease her unmercifully. She grinned as another thought crossed her mind. How could she explain to Linni, that mother had not worn her shoes and hurt herself. After all, she was always telling the child to put something on her feet. She stood looking down at her toes as she wriggled them in the soft sand. The damp earth between them felt so cool and soft. Now she knew why children hated shoes. Exhilarated, she looked up and around at her surroundings and felt as if she were the only person in the world to have walked this way. She felt as carefree as a child in play and when she turned the next bend, she looked upon it in a child-like wonder.

There before her was a cove with a small sandy beach. The inlet was not a large one, but beautifully picturesque. The large moss-draped trees whose branches dipped down as if to kiss the water's surface, made the area appear like something from a movie set. The theme from Fantasy Island echoed in her mind briefly. It was truly magical. The beauty of the place held her in awe. She stood there looking at it, afraid to move, afraid that if she did, it would vanish.

Tori told herself tomorrow she would bring her Linni here. They could pretend they were on a deserted island. It would be their getaway spot, secret to them. Linni loved secrets. She would pack a small breakfast for the two of them to eat. Then they might take an early swim and still be back before Sara and her mother got up. A smile filled her face as a low chuckle escaped her. She could just see Linni's face as she asked her to swim with her. Linni would say they couldn't because they had no swimsuits. She would laugh at her daughter and then introduce her to the delight of skinny dipping in the wild.

A young deer bolted nearby, crashing through the underbrush, shattering her daydream. She only had a glimpse of the animal as it moved deeper into the surrounding terrain. Looking around, she could see that the tree-lined cove was very private, it would be the ideal spot to play in the water with her daughter, naked as the day they were born. Swimming in the nude was nothing new to her. For years she had gone to many free beaches in California and Hawaii, but never with Linni. Sure Linni and her would swim naked in the pool at grandma's but out in the wild like this, never. It would be an adventure she would relish.

Just standing there, Tori looked at the cool water, watching the mist slowly swirl around. It was being blown by a gentle morning breeze that would all to quickly disappear in the heat of the day. She thought of how hot the day would become when the sun finally burned off the mist. This cool tranquillity would be gone. The breeze would subside leaving only the heat and the distant sounds of people splashing in the lake to cool off. Yes, the calm and the beauty would soon be gone, that was until this time tomorrow. It was too much for her. She had to fully experience it today for herself.

Before Tori could think of any reason why she should wait, she placed her coffee cup upon the bank. She looked around to make sure she was not being watched, then she turned facing the lake. "Just one quick dip to test the water for tomorrow," she told herself. Untying the belt from around her waist, she let her robe fall to the ground. Stepping quickly to the edge of the water, Tori was once again spellbound by the vision before her.

The water's surface was like a mirror, so still and perfect. She sent several ripples across the top, when her toe tested the temperature. The small waves seemed to travel on forever, spreading out across the water, each pulse disturbing the glassy top. The water's temperature was not as cool as she thought it would be and once in the water, she knew it would feel warmer. Gingerly, trying not to disturb the glass-like effect, she entered the lake.

It was fantastic. Crisp and cool at first, then just plain stimulating, every nerve in her body responding, every inch of her naked body tingling and absorbing each sensation. The water slid by her as she swam using long slow strokes. How anyone could swim with a swimsuit on, was beyond her. Everyone should feel this freedom, the water caressing their bare bodies, she thought. It was like making love with nature.

After several minutes Tori stopped swimming and began treading water. She turned slowly and looked around surprised. She had not meant to swim out so far, but cutting through the water with such little effort, had resulted in the great distance she had covered so quickly.

The mist was swirling down, dipping as if to stroke the top of each wave that rippled out from her movements. The sight of the bank, could only be seen when the breeze cleared a pathway for her. Then, like curtains closing, that scene would disappear, another to begin as they parted again further along the shore. It was like watching a private show, put on by Mother Nature herself. The sound of the breeze in her ears, along with the gentle slosh of the water up against her, was broken only by birds diving into the lake, skimming the surface, catching whatever they fished for. The odd frog, could be heard croaking from the shoreline. Off to her right she could see a small rabbit drinking at the edge of the water, unaware of its human observer. He suddenly sat up, as if he had heard something or someone. Then, as if he had never been there, he was gone. This was far better than any TV show she had ever seen, talk about virtual reality. She felt as if she could spend hours treading water, just looking. "But all good things must end," she whispered. "Thank you Mother Nature for such a wonderful show. I shall return you can be sure of that." Tori meant it too. It was paradise and she would come back in the morning to share it with Linni. Right now her tiring legs told her she had best head back, besides it must be getting late and she would not want to worry the girls, she told herself.

It was then that she sensed a change. It was subtle at first, just an odd feeling, but one that was growing stronger every second. What was it? Slowly she spun around in the water. Something was definitely happening. The air had become very still, and she noticed even the mist had quit moving. It hung on top of the water blocking her view of the bank. Tori could not put her finger on it but something didn't feel right. Her thoughts were racing around. This is so weird. Something is going on here and I don't like it. In California strange things always started happening just before an earthquake. But she was not in earthquake country, was she? She had to stay calm. "Now don't panic," she said out loud, not caring she was talking to herself. "It's just a feeling. Get a hold of yourself. Your imagination could run away if you let it." Tori forced a laugh. Now you are talking to yourself, naked, swimming in the middle of a lake. People are going to call you crazy."

Staying calm however, was becoming increasingly difficult, as the minutes wore on. She was tiring rapidly, with the bank still hidden from view. If she swam the wrong way, further out into the lake as tired as she was, Tori knew she might not make it. Her heart was pounding and her arms had begun to feel very heavy.

Turning in circles she asked herself frantically, "Where is that damn breeze? Don't fail me now. Just one quick little puff to show me the shore, that's all I need."

Then it hit her. She had been so busy worrying about seeing her way back to land, that she had not noticed the silence. It was a silence as solid and thick as the wall of mist surrounding her. Total, absolute silence. Her ears suddenly blocked, as they often did when the plane she was flying in started to land. She could hear only her own breathing and the pounding sound of her heart in her ears. She held her nose closed and blew, resulting in the familiar pop inside her head. Her ears had cleared but the silence still held. It's impossible to have it this quiet she thought, swallowing down pure panic. She listened hard for any sound at all. Nothing, not a bird, frog, nothing. Not even the annoying crickets chirped and they always sang away.

Tori could stand it no longer and let out one very long loud call for help. The word echoed and then lost itself in the mist. It was simply swallowed up and smothered. Again she called, and again her plea was followed only by silence.

"My God what am I going to do? What in the hell is going on? Shit! I've got to get out of here," she cried out.

Then, just as she was going to gamble on which direction to start swimming, she felt it. The breeze was back. Like a message sent from above, the mist parted and she once again saw the shoreline. Then the mist swirled even further away and instantly she saw the woman. She was too far away to see her features clearly, but one thing was unmistakable. The woman was putting on her robe! Whoever she was she had her back to the lake and as she reached up, pulling her waist length hair around to her back, she turned.

Tori thought the woman was going to call out to her, but she did not have the chance. The mist lowered blocking her view. Maybe the woman had not seen her. No, that was crazy, she had to. Thinking of nothing else but to reach the shore and the stranger, Tori started swimming in that direction. She stopped only once to rest and catch her breath as a painful stitch in her side caused her to gasp for air. To panic now she knew could cost her her life, for she was growing ever weaker. Tori realized she was close to drowning. Encouragement came when the world woke up from its sleep. The birds sang, the crickets chirped, indeed the world exploded with sound, it was alive again. And with it so was her willpower to make the shore.

Tori only wanted one thing and that was the safety of solid ground under her feet again. With arms that felt as heavy as lead, she started her slow crawl-like strokes to safety. In her mind she coached herself. Forcing one stroke after another until exhausted, she crawled out on the bank, shaking uncontrollably with relief.

As she slowly regained her strength, she faced how lucky she had been. She reflected on how angry Linni would be if she knew her mom had done such a stupid thing. What had she been thinking she asked herself? Not being a strong swimmer, she had no business swimming alone in the lake. What had ever come over her?

The sun was warm but not very strong, and the light breeze that she had not so long ago begged for, was enough to chill her. At least her shoulder length hair would dry quickly she told herself. "One benefit to having it cut," she mused. The spiral perm had softened the past three months, so the result of letting it dry natural was quite acceptable. At least she would not look quite like the mess she felt, as she walked back to the cabin.

As the fear of nearly drowning subsided, anger quickly came over her. Why hadn't the woman she had seen tried to help her, she wondered. She would find that woman once back at the campground and demand an answer.

In a hurry now to get back before she was missed, she looked around for her robe and coffee cup. But now, only vacant ground greeted her gaze. The robe, along with the cup were nowhere in sight. Shocked Tori looked around the cove slowly. It seemed the same. Was it possible that she had gone in the wrong direction in her panicked state? Had she come out at another part of the lake? Was she even on the same side?

"Take a hold of yourself," she said out loud not caring who heard her. She looked around slowly and took in more detail. The shape of the cove was the same, but something was definately different. Then she realized what it was. The trees were not the large moss-draped ones she had admired. These were the same only a lot smaller. This was it then. She had her answer. She was not in her cove! The next problem for her to solve was which way was her cove? She looked both directions and thinking about it briefly, she headed off back toward the campground and her secret cove.

Walking at a good pace for ten minutes, Tori thought about the woman and her robe. Why was it that the lady had not headed toward her, bringing it to her? She herself would have run to help another in trouble. Tori stopped in her tracks, "She stole it! The bitch has taken my robe. You won't get away with it," she shouted, hoping to be heard. If you think for one second I won't follow you into the camp, well you're wrong. Just because I'm butt-ass naked, that won't stop me! I'm not bluffing." She listened, nothing. "I'm telling you, if you don't bring me my robe now, you are really going to pay!" Still nothing. "Right then, we will just see who's bluffing and who's not."

Once again Tori started walking in what she thought was toward the campground. Yet, as time and distance wore on, she began to realize she must have gone in the wrong direction after all. The camp was nowhere to be seen. Going back the other direction was one option, but at this point and with the morning growing later, she decided it would be quicker to continue on around. A frown crossed her face as she imagined the look on a fisherman's face, when he saw a naked lady walking up to him. "Excuse me, you don't know me, but can I borrow your shirt?" Then she broke into a smile as she thought what if that fisherman turned out to be her new friend Dan.

The hours wore on. The day slowly grew hotter and more unbearable. She would stop every now and then to put her feet into the water to ease their pain. This was not the kind of walk to take barefooted. Perspiration was running down her back, and her skin felt as if it were beginning to burn. Her throat had been dry and screaming for a cool drink for hours. Tori was a woman near tears. Desperate, she drank from the lake, convinced she would become ill with a good case of 'Montezuma's revenge'.

She estimated she had been walking around the lake for about four hours judging by the sun. That should have put it around ten in the morning, but the sun seemed much higher and far hotter than mid morning. Tori wearily rubbed her brow. Somehow she had lost track of time, and that was something which she never did. Of course the fact that she normally had her wristwatch on to help her, did not escape her thoughts either. "Damn it," she said angrily to her bare wrist. Tori looked up toward the sun once again. "How could it be past noon already?" It seemed highly unlikely that she had been walking that long without realizing it. "I'm just confused, damn hot and feeling stupid," she told herself. "I can't keep my thoughts clear and who could blame me, I ask you that?" She asked the sun. In answering her own question she quickly gave herself a logical explanation. She put it down to lack of sleep, exhaustion and just pure stress. Walking around the countryside, naked and lost was not her idea of a summer stroll in the park. She had to laugh a little at that thought.

Tori had given up all hope of sneaking into the camp unseen and really didn't care any more. Every so often she would call out for help and listen for a reply. It was not easy going, for there was little or no path to follow. This was another reason it was taking her so damn long she told herself. Finally, out of frustration and weariness she sank down on her knees by the water's edge. Never had she felt so alone and so foolish as she did right then. How could a grown woman lose her way? Worse than that, how could she have let this all happen to herself?

Slowly Tori looked out across the lake. The shoreline was near enough to see if there was any sight of a camp, but far enough away that she knew she could not swim over. So even if she did see it, she would have to stand up and wave her arms calling for help. Now that will be a sight to see she thought, and all at once she found herself laughing and crying.

"Oh Linni I'm sorry baby, you must be so worried about me. I'm trying to get home to you." She pictured Linni crying. Tori knew she would be so worried by now. It was not a nice thought. One good thing did come to mind though. By now the whole camp would know she was missing. They must have people looking for me. "Why didn't I just stay put instead of walking all these hours away from you?"

Tori rubbed at the tears on her cheeks with the back of her hand. In so doing, she left a long smudge of dirt across her face. Gone was the image of the beautiful woman, full of confidence and pride. In her place stood a dirty, sweating, pathetic lost child. She was just sitting there looking out to the opposite side of the lake, rocking back and forth holding herself and crying.

She stayed like this for sometime. Finally looking around her, she realized she had no idea of the time of day, or of how long she had wallowed in self pity. Taking hold of herself she uttered in a determined voice, "This won't do. If they won't find me, then by God I'll find them." Standing up and looking in both directions, Tori struggled to make up her mind what she should do next. To continue going on the way she had been going seemed stupid. After all she had no idea of the true size of the lake. Therefore it could take hours to reach the camp if she kept walking in the same direction, a direction that was obviously the wrong one. She should have been home a long time ago she told herself. If she had just gone the other way in the beginning. So she made the decision to go back in the other direction.

"One quick drink. Wash off some of this dirt and I'll be ready to start back," she said out loud.

What happened next, Tori would remember the rest of her life. It hit her with such force, as to make her physically ill with shock. Looking closer now at where she had been sitting, she realized that going anywhere was senseless. Tori without realizing it, had been the whole distance around the lake. She was already back where she started.

Her mind rejected this data right away. How could that be? Yet the more she looked, the more evident it became. The footprints by the water's edge. Her feet she told herself, had made those prints earlier in the morning, as she had climbed out of the water from her swim. How could this be possible? She could not have gone completely around the lake she reasoned. The camp, the people, where in the hell had everyone gone. It was just not possible.

"I'm going crazy," she cried out. "My God, maybe I drowned and I'm dead," she mumbled. This notion really frightened her. "Oh please someone, anyone, help me!" she screamed.

The scream was hysterical and Tori was violently shaking with fear. Something was very wrong, very wrong indeed. Sick to her stomach now, mind racing with all sorts of imaginings, Tori buckled over. Then with such force as to hurt her sides, she threw up, continuing until nothing was left but the dry heaves.

She walked to the water's edge and knelt down in the mud, too weak to stand. The world kept going in and out, graying around the edge. Sound was far away, then loud enough as to make her put her hands over her ears. It would have been a blessing at this point if she had fainted. Lord knows she was hoping it would happen, that or the awful sick feeling vanish.

The cold water she splashed on her face helped some. She told herself to calm down knowing there had to be a rational explanation. Something that could clarify everything that had happened this morning. She reasoned with herself. Once all the facts were known, she would solve it. The twisted events would fall into an orderly and fully understandable pattern. She started to pull herself together.

Tori had become so involved in her mixed-up train of thought, that she did not hear the sound of the horse at first. By the time it did register in her mind that someone was coming, it was too late.

"Well now, just what in the hell dew's have here? Looks as if I done gone and found me a runaway, and a fancy one at that. An none too bashful." With that the stranger turned his head slightly to one side, and while keeping his eyes fixed on Tori, he spit out a dark brown liquid, along with a wad of chewing tobacco. He almost accomplished this feat, without getting any of the vile substance on horse or himself, almost. Tori could see that a thin line of spit was slowly creeping down his chin. It started at the corner of his mouth and finished up dripping onto his already-stained shirt front. He noticed that she was looking at him disgustedly, while he wiped his mouth and chin with the corner of a what Tori assumed was meant to be a handkerchief. The cloth, like its owner, looked as though they could both use a good wash.

He just sat there up on his horse, leering down at her. His beady little eyes hungrily feasted on the sight before him. Slowly they roamed over her, taking in every inch of her body, stopping at her breasts for a second too long, causing him to unconsciously lick his lips, like an animal about to feed.

Tori became totally aware of her nakedness as never before. It was futile for her to try to shield herself from this man's lustful stares. The way he just continued to leer made her think that he was really enjoying watching her squirm. She had a dread deep down in her very soul, that this was a man capable of much more than just looking at her. Suddenly as if someone had just thrown a bucket of cold water on her, Tori knew she had to do something. She had to act fast, and take control of the situation.

"Look here you can stop staring at me like an animal in heat. Hand me something to cover up with before my friends find us like this." She watched as a look of astonishment crept over the stranger's face. He seemed to be holding his breath, his face turning the shade of her red hibiscus she had at home.

Never in his life had any Nigger dared to talk to him in such a tone. Just who in the hell did she think she was, lying to him and all? Friends find them? Hell, there weren't no one else around here for miles. The help at the house weren't allowed down here no more. The field hands, well they were clear away. No sir, there weren't no one here but that bitch and himself.

Tori could see that what she said had had an effect on him. She assumed that the mention of her friends finding them, along with her authoritative tone, had done the trick. At least he was not staring at her anymore. Slowly he turned his horse around, and walked it slowly away from her. Thinking he was going to leave her without even helping, she yelled at him.

"Hey you, whatever your name is, you could give me that blanket you have there before you go. I would be most grateful."

Damn that black bitch she did it again. Fancy or not, she needed to be taught a lesson on remembering how to address descent white folk. Looking at him like she did, eye to eye. Just who in the hell did she think she was anyway? He walked his horse over to a clump of bushes, and dismounted with a heavy thump as he hit the ground.

Once off the horse, Tori could see that he was a larger man than he had appeared. Not that he was tall, he was about average, but he was at least twice the weight he should be. He was getting the blanket off the back of the saddle and as he stood there untying the rope with one hand, Tori had a chance to look him over. Whoever he was, he really was in need of a good cleanup. A haircut and a shave would not hurt either. His collar-length hair was hanging in the back, clinging in strands held together by dirt, sweat and grease. His bloated red face was covered by pock marks giving it a blotched appearance. He was unshaven and dirt-smeared, rough and cruel looking. The shirt that she assumed had once been white, was gray in color and open down the front to what should have been his waist. His sweaty blubbery belly, which rose up and down with every breath he took, hung over a worn leather belt that had been pulled too tight. He probably did that to fool himself into thinking he was not that fat, she thought. Add that to the heat of the day and one knew it could only add to his discomfort. He was hot and filthy. No wonder he was in such a foul mood.

As if he had read her mind, he pulled at the leather buckle. Damn thing was digging into his belly again. Fact was, his belt was too small and he knew it. Sure he could save up and buy a new one. The idea had crossed his mind but somehow he never seemed to have enough money, what with the rising cost of liquor these days. Mix in the gambling losses, the whores and well there you had it.

Tori watched as he walked slowly toward her, noticing how his boots crunched the soil beneath his weight. God only knew what this sour individual had on his mind, but that was the least of her worries. She was so thankful that she would have something to cover herself with, that she really did not care what he thought of her. Her eyes were on the blanket in his hand as she reached out for it. When he was within reach, his slow steady movements ceased, and he suddenly struck like lightening. Never would she have thought that a man of his size could move with such speed. The power of his blow sent her reeling backwards, with a pain that she had trouble dealing with. The ringing in her ears brought flashes of light to her brain. Before she could fully register what had occurred, a large, rough hand was gripping her arm and angrily pulling her to her feet.

"You dare look and speak to me like that again you black bitch and I'll take those fancy looks of yours and make you as bout as purty as a field hand, d'ya hear me?"

Tori as hurt as she was and crying from the blow, was also fighting mad and scared out of her wits. Had she known the danger she was in, never would she had confronted him in the tone of voice that she did. She had always heard the best defense was a good offense. "Just who in the hell do you think you are? You're in big trouble now, you fat son of a bitch. And I'm telling you let go! Take you're filthy hands off of me you bastard!"

"What did you call me?" He spit the words out. "No one calls me that, specially a Nigger."

"Just who in the hell are you calling Nigger," she screamed back at him. "I think you have just made your second big mistake buster."

He could not believe his ears. This one had the fight of a wild cat and the temper the likes of which, could match is own. But call him a bastard, a son of a bitch, that was too much. Admire the fighting spirit he could, but no Nigger would ever talk to him like that. He would teach her, and with double the power he had used before, he raised his free hand and dealt her a blow that would have knocked most men out.

In the split second before his strike connected, Tori saw it coming. She saw everything in slow motion, as if watching it all on a movie screen, frame by frame. She heard a snapping sound as the slow hit, forced her head back and felt his iron grip hold fast as he pulled her forward. Something in her shoulder gave way, causing a searing pain. Then she felt her arm twisting, his fingers digging into her flesh, as she started to slip to the ground. Tori could see the blood from her head splatter onto his boots, boots that compared with the rest of him, were clean and shining. She could see the sun reflecting off them. Strange she thought, that a person dressed as he was, should have such clean boots. This was her final thought before blacking out.

Damn he had not meant to hit her that hard. Now he would have to bring her around and that might take some time. The man looked at her on the ground, lying there in a heap. He could see her breathing slowly. The blood was already drying on her face, caking in her hair and giving her a pitiful look. For an instant he found himself feeling sorry for her, then shook himself. Feel sorry for a Nigger, never and Nigger she was. She might have a lot of white in her, you could see that, but black blood always had a way of leaving its trace. He noticed how nowhere on her face did her black heritage show. In fact, if it was not for the color of her skin and that Nigger hair, why she might have passed herself for white. Just might at that. He shook his head in affirmation as he contemplated further. The Nigger blood in her had come out, just like it always did. That's why even if you only had a drop of black blood in your veins, you was black through and through. This one however, was the best looking Nigger wench he had ever seen. Sure he had heard about them fancies kept in New Orleans. Bought from their own mothers and then put up in one of them townhomes by their owners. They was there to serve them in the art of pleasing a man and how to be the best in everything. Hell yes, he'd heard the stories, even fancied owning such a wench one day, when he himself hit it big. Yes sir, he would go to New Orleans and buy himself the best that money could buy. She would be something and he would have her all to himself. He broke out of his daydream, as Tori moaned from the pain while she was still unconscious.

Who in the hell was he kidding? He would never have the chance to own such a wench as this. Life just wasn't fair, and never had been to him. He was stuck being an overseer, kissing the boss man's ass. He worked sun up, till sun down, making sure the fields was kept right, that the profits was big, the losses small. And all for what, he asked himself? For a place to live and what he considered a small salary, which he spent most each month on liquor and gambling. The liquor he drank trying to drown his misery and the gambling, to try and strike it rich. He didn't buy a woman often, being that it was too expensive to get a good whore. Anyway, the privilege of taking any wench from the plantation he wanted, whenever he wanted one, was his. Not that he was supposed to, just that he did and who in the hell would tell?

He laughed to himself as a sadistic smile crossed his face. Why the wenches all but begged him to take them, to become his bed mate. Take the one he had now. Missy was what, thirteen or fourteen? Not bad looking for a black, but she was black. Everything about that bitch was black. He put the blanket down and reached out his hand, stroking Tori's back. Bloody hell. It had been so long since he had had a white woman in his arms. Even then they had been the cheap riverfront whores. The ones he could afford were dogs you mounted, got your pleasure, and left.

But here laying at his feet, as if God himself had sent her to him, was a beautiful woman. Damn near white and skin as soft as a baby. How she came to be here naked, he could not imagine, unless she was one of the fancy whores from one of those fancy whorehouses. Maybe she had run away from the madam thinking she could pass herself off as white up North. He scratched his head, looking around puzzled. No, she had no clothes, and no sign of them anywhere. He looked back at Tori, kneeling down by her side. "Maybe," he said to her, "some dandy paid for your service, brought you here, had his way and left you naked." Once again it made no sense to him. He would just have to wait until she woke up, to find the answers. Yet chances were that she would lie to him anyway, so he might never know.

Trying to decide what to do with her, set his thinking off in a different direction. Now what do you suppose would happen if I took her to the big house? Maybe a reward? This possibility sounded good to him. But it had been such a long time since he had himself a good looking woman and he never had anything this good, ever. He could have his way for a while with her, then turn her over. Better still, if no one asked for her, he could take her down river in a few weeks and sell her for a good profit. There were those who bought blacks and no papers asked for. Yes sur, that's what he would do.

If Tori had known what he was thinking, she would have had a big clue as to her whereabouts and what had happened to her. She might have even acted differently, although that would not have helped her much.

With his mind made up, he reached down and picked her up as a child would a rag doll. He placed her on the blanket and slowly wrapped her up, and then lifted her up and placed her across his horse. He was more careful with her now. He told himself that from now on he would not hurt her in any way. At least in a way that it could mark her. Marks of any kind would take away from her value when it came time to sell. Hell he knew of ways to make her cooperate, ways to cause pain without leaving any signs. He spit again, smiling and nodding his head in agreement. Yes sur, that was his job. He did it all the time and that boss man thought he was good at his job because the slaves respected him. They did that all right, but fearing him was more the real reason. The boss man had said, "No violence, treat them fair, be understanding but firm." He threw back his head and laughed loudly. Understanding, hell! They were only dumb animals who understood one thing as far as he was concerned. Slowly, he mounted his horse, with Tori slumped over like a bag of potatoes in front of him. Then, easing the horse into a slow walk, he made his way carefully to his cabin.

It did not take them long to reach their destination. Its location was off by itself a good distance from the slave quarters and further still from the main house. The majority of the slaves were out in the fields working, so the overseer had no problem riding up to his front door without confronting anyone. Thus far, his plan seemed to be working out just fine for him. That was until, a slip of a girl pushed his cabin door open. Missy was on her way to help him unload whatever it was he had all wrapped up across his horse. Damn! He'd forgotten all about his bed wench Missy.

Normally, he would have been pleased to see her waiting for him like a faithful puppy. This time, however, she posed a threat to his secret. Knowing how these people talked among themselves, it would be only a matter of time before that interfering mammy up at the main house found out and put her black ugly face into his business.

"W'ad you gots there Massa Jack sur? You done got yo'self a sick un?"

Missy was up to the horse before he could stop the child. Curiosity pushing her, she raised the blanket to see which of her friends he had brought back. Missy expected to see anything because the truth was, the child had in her short fourteen years of life, seen more than most adults see in a lifetime. Exposed to life as a slave, she had learned to live by her cunning and wits. Unlike her mother, she was not content to work the fields from sun up to sun down. No sur, she'd seen the chance to please this master and become his wench. In so doing, it raised her status with the other slaves and kept her in the cool of the cabin with little to do most of the time.

It was not always easy living with him. The man drank too much and had a mean streak that made a mad dog look friendly. And he seemed to enjoy hitting her more than using her body for his own pleasure. But, life in his cabin was better than out in the cane fields, where she knew by listening to the others he was really cruel. Especially, they told her, when he had any reason to use that whip of his and if he could make up a reason, all the better.

Jack was too late to stop her from seeing Tori. Fear of losing control of the situation started a rage inside of him that took hold and threatened to cloud his thoughts and what to do next. All his life he had been a loser, but not this time he told himself. This time Jack Kane was going to win. He was going to show them all.

As Missy stood there staring at the lady hanging across the horse, she almost forgot her place. Many questions were right there on her lips. She was about to ask one, when his deep snarling voice commanded she git inside and quick like. The tone sent a warning to her; she knew this man well and found her feet flying across the short distance to the dim interior of the cabin. With her back up against the wall, her eyes cast down she heard him enter. The slam of the door caused her to physically jump, but raise up her head to see what he was doing, no sur, not her.

Jack put Tori down on his bed, turning her on her back. She was moving around a little, and a soft moan left her lips as he shifted her head to one side. She was coming around and would wake anytime now. Most likely she'd behave herself. But he remembered her fighting spirit, so he was not about to take any chances. First off, he had to deal with that stupid wench Missy. Jack turned to see her cowering in the corner, standing head down, waiting for his commands. She was always ready and eager to try and please him. Shame he'd have to let her go now, but he could not take the chance of her being here. But what to do with her was puzzling. He had to get her out first and deal with that problem later, not much later though...

"Missy," his voice was hard and cold.

"Yes, Massa sur," she answered looking up at him.

"You git your black ass back down them quarters and you stay there until I fetch you, you hear? You talk to no one bout this here wench, cause if you do, you'll be real sorry. You git me?" Jack shot her a look that would have terrified most.

"You want Missy to git out? What I'd do dat make you mad? I gonna be real good for you. I be one real sorry Missy."

Like a child, she was trying desperately to keep what she knew was hers. She wanted to stay, no matter what the price. In her eyes she had done nothing that wrong to be sent back to the quarters, had she?

His movement across the room was swift. Before she knew it he had a hold of her. His large hands on her slim frame seemed somehow grotesque in their size. Instantly he was shaking her so violently, that her head and body were rocking back and forth in opposite directions.

"Why you stupid little bitch, you dare question what I done told you to do? You don't dare do that again, or Jack will make sure your ass stays in them quarters and works in them fields till you is old and broken, like your mammy. Do you hear? Now you just do what I done told you. Move your black hide. And no one, you tell no one, or so help me I'll shake your head till it comes off and you won't ever talk again. Move!"

He pushed her toward the door, causing her to fall to her knees. Impatiently, Jack walked over to her and pulled her the rest of the way outside by her hair.

"Stop your sniveling and git going. I'll see to you later. Now git!"

With her knees bleeding and head hurting, Missy ran for all she was worth. The dirt under her bare feet left little clouds of dust as she passed. Jack watched her go until she was out of sight and the dust had settled. The quarters were about five minutes good walking distance, but running as she was, that time was cut in half. So it was the girl found herself at her mother's shack before she knew it. Letting herself in, and thankful to find no one there, she fell down on a grass mat, trying to make some sense of what had just happened. Just who in the world was that woman he had? Why did he have her? Was she going to replace her? So many unanswered questions filled her small head. But one thing was clear, she had to win her place back and somehow she'd find a way...

Tori's head felt as if it would burst, her whole body ached. In fact, she could not find a spot that did not feel sore. What a nightmare, it had seemed so real. The dream was still so vivid that she was half afraid to open her eyes. She might find herself back at the lake with that horrible fat man. But no, that was impossible. After all, she could feel that she was laying on her bed. God how she ached. "Linni honey, can you help me? Please I need some aspirin, I'm in really bad shape." No answer, nothing. Maybe she had not heard her. Damn she hurt. She simply had to do something. So she decided to try to reach the kitchen and the aspirin herself. Slowly with her eyes still closed, she pushed herself up on one arm. This took a lot of effort on her part. The stiffness in her shoulder, along with the sharp pain in her head, was enough to make her call out in agony.

"What in the hell have I done? Linni, do you hear me? I need some help." Still no answer. Slowly now she opened her eyes, shielding them from the sunlight. What greeted her was no morning sun. From what she could tell the sun was setting and casting an eerie light into the cabin from the small window. At first, she thought she was seeing things. It was hard to see through one eye, and she could make out only a little bit of her surroundings. Touching her eyes slowly with her hand, she found one painfully swollen. Realization of what was happening quickly took hold.

"Oh my God, it wasn't a dream. I really was hit... got to get out of here... got to find help," she mumbled.

"Ain't no one here going to help you any, an that you can be sure of. An if you smart and don't want more of what you got earlier, you'd best start acting like you supposed," Jack replied. "You can start by showing some respect to me, ain't ever had no black talk to me like you. And won't again, git me?"

Tori's blood ran cold at the sound of his voice. She turned her head and saw him sitting in a chair over in the corner of the room. He had been so quiet and still, that she had not seen him in the dim light. Panic and terror took hold as she pleaded helplessly.

"Please don't hurt me. You don't understand. I think you have mistaken me for someone else. I just need to get back to the campground and my daughter. Please help me by letting me go. I won't say a word to anyone about you. I'll say I fell. Yes, that's it. I'll tell everyone I fell."

"You ain't going nowhere and you ain't going to tell no one nothing. Not that it would matter anyway," he laughed. "You go ahead and tell em I hit you." He spit a wad of something out across the room, hitting a small round container. Slapping the side of his leg, and looking very pleased with himself, he smiled. "Hell, looks as if my luck's done gone and got better. Ain't hit that thing in months." He took a long drink from his mug and then topped it up again from a nearly empty bottle.

Tori could see there was going to be no reasoning with this madman. She would have to play it calm. Catch him off guard, and then make a run for it. Whatever she did, she knew deep down that she should not run the risk of making him angry again.

"Please Mr. ah?..."

"Jack Kane's the name, and you can forgit them fancy ways with me. You just watch that mouth of yours and do as I say ya hear?"

His English was uneducated to say the least. Tori had heard that there were people in the bayous and backwaters that lived most of their lives without much contact with the outside world. Could he be just such a person she wondered. An uneducated backwoods racist! Oh heaven help her if he was. And add those traits to his obvious drunken state and it could spell big trouble. He would have to be dealt with carefully.

"I only want a glass of water. Please, my head hurts so badly and some aspirin if you have any?"

"Water you can git for yourself over there," he jerked his head. "But ain't heard of no ass per rin. You kin eat in the morning when I do and be damn glad of it."

Tori sat up slowly, her whole body aching and protesting every move. His eyes bore into her, as she struggled with the blanket to hide herself from him.

"Ain't no need of no hiding neither. I done seen ya and I kind of like looking, just drop it."

She had to think fast. No way was she going to let that son of a bitch see her naked again, if she could help it. "I'm cold and I get sick easily, and you don't want me sick do you? I've gotten too much sun and I don't feel right." She did not look at him, but prayed her actions would work. Her head was down and she did indeed look a poor sight.

Jack in no way wanted her sick. Hell, he had heard how them fancies were a weak strain and died easy. No, he was not about to lose her to a simple chill. He would give in this once.

"Go on then and be quick." He motioned his head toward the far side of the small room.

As she struggled to the water, he sat and drank his rum, watching her every move. Once she got up, she could see that the place was tiny and dim inside. Nothing much in the way of furniture and even if it did not smell too good, it was clean and somewhat tidy. She was in the small bedroom. Through the doorway was the kitchen and living area. Although much larger and furnished, it was still a far cry from what she would ever have considered livable. But like the bedroom, this area too seemed very neat and well kept.

Little did she know Missy would have taken her observations as a compliment. She tried hard to keep the place clean. Not an easy job with a man like Jack.

The water was in a wooden tub, and was lukewarm. At this point Tori did not care, it was wet and she had a burning thirst. She did not want to talk to him anymore. She wanted to concentrate on remembering her surroundings. Everything she saw might hold a key to helping her out of this horrible hut and away from him. She spotted the door and turned her head just enough to see Jack out of the corner of her eye. He was watching her every move. Dare she chance it? She decided to bide her time. She reasoned that if she did make a dash for it, the chances of him, drunk or not, catching her were good. If he drank some more though, surely he would pass out. Then she could make her escape. The silence was broken by the sound of a chair being dragged across the floor.

"Ain't going to try to git by old Jack are Ya? Hell I'd be real upset if you even thought of that. I figures that I'd best just sit here tonight. Think yourself lucky, cause if I had me some good rope you'd be on the floor instead of in that bed. Best rest up, cause come tomorrow, I ain't sleeping here and I ain't sleeping alone either."

Tori panicked inside but kept it hidden. Her voice though a little shaky, answered him with a reply that even surprised herself. "Thanks, and I'll rest up real good for you. You'll see. I'll be good. Night."

With that she lay down, her back to the other room and him. She had one thought running through her mind. I've got to get out of here tonight. But how? How in the hell do I get away from this madman?"

# Chapter 2

Tori, feigning sleep, had kept her back to him for what seemed like hours. She had been too afraid to move, terrified of attracting unwanted attention from the crazed being that sat in the other room. The daylight in the cabin had completely disappeared leaving the interior in a darkness that to her amazement was not total.

Suddenly, the silence was broken by a growling voice. She slammed her eyes shut in terror and listened. She could hear Jack stumbling around angrily talking to himself. No matter what, he had to believe she was asleep in order to put him off guard. Forcibly fighting a rising panic, she told herself to wait patiently, and concentrated on breathing slowly and evenly.

Jack couldn't believe he was sitting in a hard chair, while she slept on his bed. He knew he couldn't trust her. Hell, if he slept on that bed with her, he'd pass out for sure and she'd be long gone by morning. He could kick himself for not thinking ahead. He'd started drinking early, just a few to clear his head and all. He realized that now it was too late, he was good and drunk. Reaching for the bottle and finding it empty, he made his way over to the cupboard for his last bottle of rum.

"Need a damn light in here, got it somewhere," he slurred. "Damn, where the hell she put the thing?" Jack fumbled some more. Then realizing it was a lost cause in the dark, stumbled back into his chair. He almost missed his seating and nearly fell to the floor. Trying to steady himself, the chair rocked off its two front legs, tipping over. Even if he had wanted, Jack didn't have a chance of stopping the fall. By the time his head hit the floor, he was out cold.

Tori heard all the commotion followed by silence and still she did not dare move. The urge to turn and see what had happened was strong, but fear still held her like a vice in its grip. He might be testing me she told herself. Instinctively she wanted to make a run for it, believing he had passed out but kept telling herself, just wait and listen.

The minutes seemed to drag by like hours, each crawling by uninterrupted. She found herself wishing he would say something, anything. Instead, only his snores assaulted her ears. To keep from losing her grip, she slowly formed a plan. Getting the courage up to attempt escape and run the risk of being caught, was far from easy. Thoughts raced through her mind one after the other. If only she had some way of reaching the outside for help. She wondered if there was another way out of the cabin, a back entrance maybe. If she did get outside, where would she go and which way to the road? Try as she might, she could hear no cars telling her that a highway was close by. In the dark it wouldn't be easy and she could get hopelessly lost. What if he woke up and caught her?

That thought scared the hell out of her. The idea of him in bed with her was even worse. Tori knew she had no choice. She would have to take her chance and make a run for it.

Slowly, she turned over, as if still asleep. Opening her eyes a fraction, she could make out his noisy form on the floor. No wonder she could hear no cars or anything else for that matter. His snoring was loud enough to wake the dead. It was the kind of noise that would make Linni laugh. The thought of Linni and how upset she must be by now had tears quickly filling her eyes.

"Stop it!" She quietly scolded herself. "You have to get away first and then, only then can you have a good cry." Gingerly she moved a leg, then the other, swinging them over the side of the bed. Jack appeared to be out cold but just for insurance she tested him by calling out his name.

"Jack, can I get some water? Mr. Kane?" He continued to snore and didn't even move. "Jack, do you hear me?" Still nothing. Tori's heart was pounding so hard that she thought it would come right out of her chest. The perspiration was dripping off her. Until that moment, she had not noticed how stifling it was in the small cabin. The oppressive heat was one thing to deal with, then there was the stench of foul body odor and bad breath. She felt a wave of revulsion followed rapidly by an overpowering need to throw up. She covered her mouth and nose with her hand in an attempt to stifle the foul odors. Tori looked longingly toward the little open window. She could see it was too high up for her to stick her head out. Looking at it, she realized it let in very little fresh air and the confinement of the place was getting to her. Her sunburn didn't help matters. Not only was she roasting from the heat radiating from her burned skin, but she found it hurt real bad every time she moved.

Tori had a deep desire to scream out as she tightened the rough blanket around her but the sleeping hulk on the floor held her silent. She was now so close to getting out that to slip up would be a disaster. Tori pulled at the blanket. This time at least she would have something to wear. Standing up, she wrapped the filthy blanket around her like a toga. Even with her spore ribs, she pulled the scratchy woolen cloth tighter around her. Pain or not she didn't want to lose it as she ran for safety.

At least the moon was on her side. Its silver rays shining through the window were enough to light the bedroom area, enabling her to pick her way toward the door without falling over anything. The main door, her route to freedom was right in front of her. She slowly crossed the room to it. All she had to do was pull it open. The chair was easy enough to move but Jack, damn him, he was passed out cold blocking her way.

Tori stood there for a minute looking at him, her hatred of the man written clearly on her face. Why did he have to pass out in the wrong spot? She would have to find a way to move the hulking lout. Her mind raced with different scenarios. He might wake up. What would she do if he woke? You must be very careful she told herself. Now think! What can I say to him? I could say I woke up when he fell and I was trying to help him. That's it! Hell, in his condition he would most likely pass out again anyway. Even if he didn't, he was not going to be in any shape to do much to her she rationalized.

"Here goes nothing," she whispered. If I pull you this way it should work." She tried to tug at him with no results. She was desperate to succeed so without realizing it she started talking even louder. "No, rolling you over is better, just a few inches. Come on Jack," she pleaded. "Move, damn it." All her pushing and pulling didn't move the sprawled mass one inch. By the time she gave up, Tori sat on the floor exhausted, sweating and breathing deeply, right next to his prostrate form.

It hurt to breathe and she found herself wondering just what had happened to cause her so much pain. It felt as if her whole body was badly bruised. Had he hit her while she lay unconscious she wondered? The man seemed capable of it. Panic rushed back. Her eyes flashed longingly again at the door. But all the looking in the world would not open it for her. The simple fact was that she was not strong enough to move him.

"Damn it. I won't quit. I can't not now. There has to be some way to move you." She looked around the room slowly trying to see anything in the gloom that could help her. She gazed at another window, but like the one in the bedroom, it was far too small to climb out. Tori had given up trying to be quiet. She knew that if he had not come around with her pulling and pushing, he most certainly would sleep through the sound of a chair being dragged across the floor. Immediately she was on her feet pulling the chair to the window. Standing on it put her shoulders level with the opening where she stared into the night. The cool fresh air felt good on her face. The night sky was clear and Tori could see every star. Out there someplace was her daughter. She couldn't be far away and Tori was determined to find a way to get back to her. She may have been kidnapped, but she would be damned if she would be raped!

"I'll do it. Somehow I'll get out of here tomorrow and get back to you."

Her eyes then traveled down from gazing at the heavens and scanned the dark surroundings. It was then she saw a small light off in the distance and her heart soared. It's not so far, she thought. Yet she knew at night distances could be deceiving. At least a light meant people, a gas station, a house or something. It was the first thing she had seen to give her hope and now at least she knew in which direction to run when the time came. All she had to do was keep her head and stay in a position to escape. There was no way she would make Jack mad enough to have him tie her up. No way! She would be very careful. If he liked thinking she was black, that was what she would be. He'd never believe her if she told him she was white anyway. He was a red neck hillbilly backwoods slob, who judged race by the way you looked period! But then come to think about it, she could understand how he came to the mistaken conclusion of her being black. It was easy enough to do what with the way she looked, with her dark all-over tan and her curly hair. If it wasn't so scary it would be funny, but this was no joking matter! For now, for her, it had become a frightening reality. Jack was convinced she was black, and they were in the deep south, a place where racism was alive and well! Well maybe not, she tried to tell herself. Maybe it was just a little stronger than other places she'd been, that was all. Oh, who was she kidding? He was probably a member of the KKK! It was obvious he had no love for the black race.

The light in the distance went out. "Tomorrow I'll find that house and the help I need," she whispered. Tori was just about to get down when she saw something else. At first, she did not want to trust her eyes. The full moon was right overhead, yet the shadows could still be playing tricks on her. Then the shadow moved, stepping out just far enough for her to distinguish the outline of person. Someone was out there! It was obvious to her that whoever it was, had been watching her.

"Hey you! Please help me," she called out. "I need help. Don't go please." Tori was shouting but the person had run off as soon as she had called out. Her frustration quickly turned to despair. It was all too much for her and she began to cry. Through her tears she watched and prayed for the person to come back...

After what seemed like hours Tori realized the stranger was not returning, not tonight anyway. The moon had sunk lower in the sky and with its light no longer coming in the window, the interior of the cabin was darker still. Slowly she started thinking clearly again. With some of her self-pity gone, the raw instinct of survival took over. She replaced the chair and stepped carefully back into the bedroom. He had to let her out sometime she told herself, like to go to the bathroom for one thing. Then she would find a way to escape. Sleeping with him would be a last resort, and she would delay that as long as possible. The thought of him even touching her, sent shivers through her.

Sitting in the underbrush not far away, was a very sad, confused young black girl. Missy had gone over to Jack's cabin, to see if she could find out what was going on. She hadn't learned anything at all, just got herself more questions. Why had that lady called out to her for help? If Jack found out she had been by the cabin, she would be whipped for sure....

How may hours had he been passed out on the floor? Once again that damn scrawny excuse for a wench had allowed him to spend the night sprawled out like a hound dog. He knew where he'd find her, in his bed no doubt. Hell, he'd teach her this time. Slowly with his head pounding and his temper rising, he pulled himself up and staggered toward the sleeping girl. He had every intention of beating the living daylights out of her. "Missy, you good for nothing black bitch. I'll show your lazy hide." Not another word left his mouth. Jack stood staring at his bed and the woman that lay on it. What he saw before him was a wench who was not his. He rubbed his eyes. She had to be a dream of some sort he reasoned.

Tori was awakened by the growling words coming her way. It took her a few seconds to realize where she was and who was coming at her with his hand raised, ready to strike. Then all too quickly it came flooding back. Instinctively she cowered back against the headboard, too frightened to move or talk. By the look on Jack's face, he was obviously shocked to see her. He just stood there with his mouth open, taking deep breaths and looking at her as if she were a ghost.

He dropped his hand and then slowly sat upon the end of the bed. His eyes held hers, revealing to her his struggle to recollect the happenings of the previous night.

Tori felt it best to say nothing and let him make the first move.

One word escaped his mouth causing her to jump. "Coffee." he ordered.

Pulling the blanket with her, she cringed trying to move away from him. His hand was on her wrist in a flash, his grip tight. Tori looked down at her arm and the searing pain. Jack's dirty finger nails were biting into her flesh. She looked back up and straight into his eyes just as recollection lit up his face.

"Now, I remember how your black ass found it's way here," he smirked. "What you don't seem to remember, is that you're staying and you're going to do as I say. I need coffee. Now move your lazy hide and get over there and start, cause I ain't fit for nothin a'fore I have my coffee." As an afterthought and with a dirty grin curling his lips he added, "I like my women like my coffee, strong and black. Get it?" His joke seemed to amuse him.

Tori's skin crawled as she was reminded once again of the danger she was in. Being raped by this lunatic had become even more of a possibility.

In a blind panic she tried to reach him. "Please you don't seem to understand. I'm not what you seem to think I am. Honestly, I'm not. I'm not black."

He laughed harshly, grabbing his crotch. "And I'm not a man either! Look I'm no fool. These eyes don't lie to old Jack. They see Nigger. Don't make no difference how much white you done got in you. You still a Nigger and I ain't going to tell you again how to act, cause you already knows your place. You might be a uppity fancy, used to a lot of nice things an all, but you be just a pretty Nigger to me and you best keep that tongue of yours in its place. Now move, get started on that coffee." He pulled Tori roughly off the bed and pushed her toward the outer room.

Trying to steady herself, Tori had no choice but to let the blanket fall, exposing her naked form clearly to his leering eyes. Quick as she was to retrieve the blanket and cover herself, his dirty laugh made her turn to face him. Lust was clearly written all over his face. He stood up slowly.

"Hell, I just might forget that coffee and take me a piece of that ass you just showed me."

For a few seconds Tori felt as if she would lose control and panic. She felt sick at the thought of him touching her and that thought was more than she could bear. She had to get away from this place and this maniac. But first she had to delay him, get his mind off her somehow. She desperately needed time. Time to find a way out without him catching her. All she could do for the moment was stall.

She forced a smile. "That's fine by me, but I should tell you that as long as you keep me here, I don't see how I can ever make you coffee. I just don't know how."

It had worked! Tori could see the change in him. The man was shocked. If she was a black fancy as he called her, it stood to reason that she might not know how to cook. If that was what he truly thought she was, then that was what she would be. She could delay him having her by very carefully using her wits.

"What the hell d'ya mean, you don't know how?"

"Just that. I have never been taught anything other than looking nice and all the finer things a lady learns. I am what I am and that won't be much use to you." She watched his eyes widen and his lips curl down in a scowl. She had to pacify him quickly. "Not that I don't want to, you understand. It's just that I can't do what I don't know how."

Jack just stood there thinking over what she had said. He seemed to be agreeing with her. "That's what I heard about your type. You have yourselves set up with Niggers working for you, just as if you was a white lady an all. Well, I guess if that's the way it is, it's a small price to pay for the pleasures you'll bring me. One of the wenches from down the way can do all you can't. You can just be here for me and what you be trained for. Pleasure, pure pleasure."

That look was back again, the one that filled his eyes with animal hunger. Tori knew she had to think quickly, and carefully. She'd been lucky so far, but shit she didn't know anything about what a fancy was, but she could guess. She had to change tactics.

"Well you might be able to take your pleasure, but I would be able to give you far more if I had something to eat and drink before. After all, why not get the best I can offer? You've waited this long and I was always told that a man does so much better on a full stomach. A large man such as yourself, needs his strength, has to have it to function fully." She could hardly believe herself. Just what in the hell was she babbling on about? Even to her own ears she sounded like a streetwalker not willing to put out.

"Now you wouldn't be trying to put me off would you? You're so willing now, when yesterday you was hell bent on running. You sure you not up to something? Cause if you are, you best put those thoughts right out of your head."

"No! no, it's just you reminded me of what I do, who I am. I had a long time to think about my situation last night, and well its not the best but I could be worse off." Tori lowered her eyes and prayed with all her heart that he would buy the lie and think she was indeed going to give him what he wanted... after they ate.

Tori continued to speak. "It's just I'm so weak from having nothing to eat. I have not eaten anything in a couple of days. I feel kind of faint."

Jack looked at her. He could jump her right now and it would give him satisfaction, just knowing he had mounted a wench such as her. On the other hand, what if she did pass out on him, hell, that would be no fun. He just couldn't function well unless they fought him. His stomach growled and he realized he himself could do with something hot in his belly. Yes, he could wait a few more hours. But he did not trust the bitch. She was lying through her teeth for sure. He bet she could be worse off, and he intended to get to the bottom of whatever it was she was keeping from him. She was smart this one. He could tell that. Jack would lay a bet that all she wanted right now was something to eat and drink and then run. She'd leave him here looking like a fool. He'd be damned if he'd let her. He would have to make sure she would not try to get away and that meant either taking her with him to get Missy and letting everyone see her, or leaving her in the cabin. One thing was certain, having her seen was not good. He would have to leave her here and that meant tying her up.

Tori had not looked up and she could not see what he was doing, she guessed he was trying to make up his mind whether or not to leave her alone for a while. She dared not move, if he came toward her with the intent of raping her, she could always delay again. She would ask him if she could clean up first. Who was she kidding, she thought. He probably wouldn't give a damn if she was clean or not. No, her best tactic would be to play up to him, and then pretend to get weak and sick. No one, not even that slob would like the idea of being thrown up on.

"Git you ass here wench."

Tori looked up and saw him pointing to the bed. Dread crept into her as she realized she had failed to persuade him to wait. She could not let him see that she was sickened by the mere thought of him, let alone of him touching her. She had to go along with her plan and just keep calm. Slowly she walked to the bed.

Turning to face him she sat down, making sure she swayed a little as she did so. She teetered just enough to show him she was in a weakened state.

As she sat there, looking at him, Jack was amazed by the fact that he had her in his cabin. She was one very good looking woman and he had her all to himself. Not to take her right now might be a mistake. However, he'd seen how she was almost too weak to walk, and like he told her, he liked his women strong. He almost wished she would show him some of that fighting spirit he'd seen yesterday. Hell, that got his blood flowing, aroused him just thinking of it. The bulge in his pants ached and it angered him that she was weak and would delay him taking her. Jack grabbed Tori's legs and swung them upon the bed, causing her to fall back upon the mattress.

While looking into his face, ready to go into the fainting sick act, she watched him remove his belt. It took all her will power to remain calm on the outside. Show him no emotion. Don't make your move yet. These were some of the things she told herself.

He had his belt in his hands and slapped it against his leg. Dear God! she thought. Was he going to beat her into submission? But why, when he was obviously so much stronger than her and could overcome her easily? Before she had time to think further, he rolled her over and was tying her hands with his belt. Next, and without warning came a gag. It was a dirty rolled up rag. She hoped it was not the same one she had seen the day before. The thought of that, made her retch. She didn't have to worry about acting sick. Tori was instantly ill.

She could feel the bile, burning the back of her throat. The acid stung coming up and burned worse going back down. She had to put the smell of the gag and the thought of it in her mouth right out of her mind, or she was going to choke to death. Tori knew it was no good fighting the man. She just had to concentrate on getting through whatever he had planned for her. Tori closed her eyes and tried hard to squelch the panic that was rapidly growing. By concentrating on keeping her breathing even, she was able to calm herself. For a few seconds nothing more happened, and Tori wondered what he was up to.

Jack's blood was running hot and his desire to take her was almost unbearable. He reached out and touched the calf of her leg. Her skin felt so soft and warm to his touch. Jack was always alert when sober, so his eyes did not miss the tensing of her body. Maybe she was not as willing as she'd said? Maybe she would fight him? She would have to if he was to get hard again. The sound of her being ill had deflated his cock, rendering it useless. He slid his hand higher up her leg, and then back down again. Jack was intrigued by what he found, a hairless leg, soft, smooth and silky. He'd never expected anything like that. He just sat stroking her slowly, enjoying the touch. Then he rolled her over exposing her breasts. The sight of them made him suck in his breath, and hold it a few seconds. Then he released it slowly as he licked his lips. Their eyes locked, his full of desire, hers full of terror.

"So the willing wench is not that willing. Could it be that you find me not to your liking? That I'm not good enough for you? Well bitch, I'll show you that I'm as good as any man you might have had. And the more you fight, the better you are going to give me what I want, when I want it and you better make it sweet.

She could not believe what she was hearing. She wished his voice was not real, that he himself was just a horrible dream. She wanted to wake up from this nightmare and be rid of him. Only trouble was, this was a living nightmare, it was very real and she couldn't stop it.

Jack's hands were all over her. She couldn't bear him touching her, but try as she might to squirm away from him, she could not. His fingers were playing roughly with her nipples, squeezing and pinching them. The pain was sharp. Her moaning and wincing, seemed to entice him even more. There was no escape and fighting him off was next to impossible.

Shaking her head no and crying out through the gag only seemed to arouse him more. She raised her legs and kicked him. It seemed somehow better than just laying there submissively, and gave her some satisfaction when he yelled out in pain.

Jack was enjoying himself, delighted at her futile attempts to escape. His cock had never been so hard and ready. He was going to enjoy every moment of pain he could inflict on her. Carefully planned pain, he told himself. He must be careful this time. No marks that would scar her unmarred skin. No death. He lowered his head and placed his mouth on one of her nipples, sucking and biting, thrilling to the discomfort he was causing her. Hell, this was better than he had imagined it would be.

His biting had brought tears to her eyes. Never had she felt such searing agony. When suddenly the assault stopped and she watched in disbelief as he rolled off her and stood up. For a brief second she hoped he had changed his mind, but his expression told her otherwise.

Jack's face was beet red where little rivers of sweat ran down the sides of his cheeks. These streams of sweat mixed with greasy grime disappeared in the dirty folds of fatty skin around his wet shirt collar. Jack removed his shirt leisurely, while watching her closely. He was scrutinizing her every reaction with great anticipation. Slowly, he started to remove his pants and was delighted when he saw her squeeze her eyes closed.

She realized what was about to happen. And there was no obvious way to prevent it, so Tori prepared herself to be taken by this evil maniac. I'll kill him! I swear I will she thought. I'll have my revenge. I'll get away from here and then the bastard will pay. I won't let myself think of what he's doing. Just concentrate on surviving she told herself.

His hot hands were again sadistically caressing her, his breath hot in her ear as he licked the side of her face. Jack had waited long enough. He had to have her now. "I'm about to give you a part of me you ain't ever gona forgit. Just spread those legs and fight Jack all you want, cause I ain't a waiting no more. You just..."

He got no further, for just then a loud male voice was calling his name from outside. Tori opened her eyes upon hearing Jack's fearful curse. The look of confusion as to what he should do, gave her hope.

His dirty hand covered her mouth, pushing the gag deeper, as she tried to call for help. He immediately hit her hard and though it did not render her unconscious, she was stilled just the same. Scared of another beating, she lay silent and frozen with fear. Jack raised his hand a second time, as if to hit her again. His message clear, she was to remain silent. Then he threw the blanket over her, covering her completely.

Tori lay very still as she listened to his growling obscenities while he dressed. Then close to her ear his foul hot breath penetrated the blanket with its stern warning.

"If you know what's good for you, you'll shut your mouth and stay still. I ain't in the mood to share you with no one. You do as I say." To back up this verbal instruction, he followed with a sharp blow to her head. Satisfied she would remain quiet he confidently strode across the wooden floor to the door.

She heard him open the cabin door then slam it shut, leaving her alone trying desperately to decide what to do. Tori could hear muffled voices but could not make out clearly what was being said. Could she make enough noise to draw attention to herself? Did she want to? He had made that remark about not wanting to share her. What if whoever called him was as bad, maybe worse than Jack. She just couldn't risk it, could she? Tori never got to make that choice. The cabin door opened and slammed shut again. Whoever had been outside with Jack was gone.

Jack had been lucky this time. His secret was still safe but for how long? The time had slipped away this morning and now he was late. The wench would have to wait until tonight. Then nothing and no one was going to stop him from having her. It was going to be a long day for him and all around him. His mood was infamous, and today as black as it was, it would stand up to its reputation. His head ached, and his nuts felt as if they had been kicked. Jack grabbed his crotch. His poor cock had gone hard and soft so many times in the past twelve hours, it was a wonder he could even walk.

He picked up his whip, a clean shirt and then marched over to the bed. He pulled back the blanket and rolled Tori over. He removed his belt and replaced it with a rope he had brought inside with him. Once this was done, he took a smaller piece and bound her legs together at the ankles. He tossed the blanket back over her body and then took what looked like a long strip of cloth torn from a shirt. He wrapped this around her head to hold the gag in place. All this he had done without uttering a word. To Tori he seemed to be in a hurry.

"I'll be gone for a while and you had better not get any ideas of calling for help. If I come by and hear one noise, you'll pay. You understand me?"

Tori, tears in her eyes, could only nod her head. She just wanted this beast to leave, to get out and stay out. As if guessing what she was thinking, he smiled at her. He placed a fresh wad of tobacco in his mouth, then spoke to her sarcastically.

"I ain't forgot where we was at and I aim to pick up where we was when I gits back. Keep still now and rest up for old Jack. You'll be a needing all your strength. I plan to ride you till I or my cock give out." He laughed. Last whore I rode said it cost her a weeks pay, said she couldn't do nothing after me. Told you I was good didn't I?" His laugh was harsh as he walked out, slamming the door behind him. Then at last the cabin fell silent broken only by Tori's sobbing.

Afraid that he might change his mind and come back, Tori lay still for sometime. Then as the minutes wore on, and no other sound could be heard, she knew he'd really gone. In the time that had passed she had done a lot of thinking. Even though her head had the worst headache ever, she could still think rationally. Staying calm and working one step at a time to escape now became her total focus. It was useless to try to shout for help with a mouth full of filthy rag. So the first thing she had to do was get rid of the thing. By laying on her side and rubbing her head against the mattress, she worked the cloth around her head down to her neck and with her tongue pushed out the rag.

Tori had her first success, and in between large gulps of air she repeated the word "Yes," out loud. Then came the realization that she had to escape or pay for this act of defiance. She just knew Jack would not hesitate to use it as an excuse to slap her around some more. The idea of feeling any more pain from his blows forced her to pull hard against the ropes that held her hands behind her. Yet the more she struggled the more the rough bindings cut into her skin. It soon became apparent to her that she just couldn't get them undone. If she could get her hands to the front however, she might have a chance.

"Come on now, if I keep talking to myself out loud and bend just a little more." Suddenly, the whole room spun around and a sharp pain tore at her shoulder as she hit the floor, causing her to scream. The blanket that had covered her was now wrapped around her, pinning her arms firmly to her sides. Instead of being closer to escape, she was now in a far worse situation. Defeated, Tori could not rally the strength to continue her attempt to escape. She just lay there...

Missy had stayed awake all night hiding in the small wooded area to avoid answering any questions from her family, as to why she was not at Jack's. She had left her hiding place before sunrise and stealthily walked in the direction of the overseer's cabin.

She had never considered her life to be one of misery. Sure she had been physically abused and unhappy at times but the way she felt at that moment was something she had never experienced. Missy had up until now considered herself very lucky indeed and was convinced that she had a good life. To lose her status as Kane's bed wench would not only be a big loss of face, but also the end to everything she had worked so hard to gain. In her one way, Missy had come to think of the cabin as her home and of Jack as hers. Now she stood outside the cabin thinking desperately to herself. A stranger was inside who had taken her place. Taken from her all that she held dear. Jack would have no use for Missy now he had himself a light-colored woman. How this had all happened she still could not understand, but she knew better than to go any closer to the cabin to find out. She wanted to approach the small abode and its occupants, to learn more of what was happening, but her built-in fear of Jack held her at bay.

She stood and watched the cabin and waited. Missy was not sure what she was looking for. One thing was clear in her mind though and that was she could not go back to the quarters and admit defeat. She would rather run! Why she might even have a chance at making it. No one would miss her for days. The others would think she was with Jack and he would not miss her as long as he had his new wench to keep him happy. She smiled to herself, as she daydreamed about Jack when he found her missing at last. How he would have no hope of finding her, the trail would be cold, she would be long gone.

What if he caught her a small voice in the back of her head asked? This thought made her hug herself as she shivered with the fear of that chance. Missy had seen what they did to runners. Most of the time the whip was used and if the slave lived from the lashing, they was scarred for life. If the Master was away, then the runner faced worse treatment. Oh yes, Master Jack could be very cruel and there were many who had not lived to tell of the hell he put them through.

It was getting late in the morning for Jack to still be inside. There was no sign of smoke from the fire telling Missy he was even up. She grinned slightly. The new wench would catch it for letting him sleep so late, that was for sure. A huge smug smile crossed her face, as Missy found herself hoping that he would miss her bringing him his first cup of coffee. Many other such thoughts passed through her mind, while she was staring at the quiet cabin. She was so preoccupied in the fantasies, that she was unaware that the Master of the plantation was riding up to the cabin. When she did hear his horse, it was too late for her to run off. All she could do was crouch down, and hide from sight.

Leon looked at Jack's horse saddled and ready to go, but still there was no sign of the overseer himself. Had he known Jack's animal had been there all night, unfed and unattended he would have been far from tolerant. Abuse of any kind was unacceptable. It did not matter if it was to animal or man, he would not permit it.

Missy was in a state as what to do. Her loyalty to Jack would not want the Master to find him with the wench inside, but how could she prevent it? There again did she want too, maybe if he found them together, he would make Jack send her away. Master Leon would have to, him being a God fearing man. The only female that would be allowed to stay in that cabin would be a wife! Ha! That was a good one that was, a wife! No way was that woman his wife. Just what she was still had to be found out. This could be interesting she told herself, as she leaned forward to get a better view.

The problem was solved when the Master's voice called out for Jack to join him, that they were running late. He did not even climb down off his horse. Leon would not be going inside after all.

Moments later Jack came out of the cabin closing the door behind him looking very humble and stood for a few minutes with his employer. Missy could hear nothing of what was said, and guessed Jack was lying to get out of being late. The way he was dressed told her why she had seen no smoke from the fire and why he was late. He had been laying with that bitch. Anger and jealousy were building inside of her.

She watched as Master Leon rode away toward the slave quarters. He often made rounds and looked in on his people. She supposed it made him feel good. He was most likely going to wait for his overseer there. This morning he and Jack were going out to see how the North fields were doing. Missy knew they would be gone the best part of the day. This raised another question, what was Jack going to do with that bitch while he was gone? Her cries for help last night had told Missy that she did not want to be with him. Things were one big mess that was for sure.

A short time later she saw Jack mount his horse and ride away. Still there was no sign of the woman he had in his cabin. Was she still inside Missy wondered? And if so, in what condition? She made up her mind to find out exactly what was going on. Missy had nothing to lose and maybe she could at least learn if the arrangement was going to be permanent or not.

She waited for a while, just to make sure that Jack had really gone and then slowly she made her way to the back of the cabin. Standing by the small open window she listened for any movement or sound coming from inside. There should be some sound, something to tell her what was going on she thought. By this time of the day, Missy would be busy cleaning or cooking. But no noise came from within indicating such an activity. Could she still be sleeping? No, that was impossible, for Jack would not stand for laziness. Even if Missy finished all her work, she still tried to look busy when he came home or suffer his abuse. No, it was just too quiet. The small girl could not stand not knowing and so she made up her mind to find out once and for all, she would go inside.

At first she saw nothing, the small living area was empty and pretty much the way she had left it the day before. Missy walked toward the bedroom door and could see that the bed was empty. For a brief second her spirits soared. Had she been wrong, could that woman have gone in the night? Then the movement on the floor caught her eyes. She saw Tori, lying face down, trying to get free from the blanket and the ropes that bound her.

Tori had heard the door open and thought it was Jack coming back to check on her. Fearing another beating, she tried with all her strength to break free. She would not give him the satisfaction of calling for help or begging to be let go but she would not give in either. The sound of the door shutting caused her to freeze and lie still awaiting what she was sure would be a very angry man. As the seconds ticked by, nothing happened. He did not come over to her. Panic took hold and Tori resumed her struggle. Then to her amazement, without a sound he had come to her and was untying the ropes!

"Look I don't know what you want me to do. I wish we could just talk things over. Really, I'm sure my friends have a lot of people searching for me by now. If you just let me go, I swear I will not tell a soul about you. Please can't you just let me go?" Damn she had not meant to do this, to beg like she was.

The ropes felt great off her legs, she could stretch them out and the tingling sensation of pins and needles quickly started to ease up, but nothing else happened. She waited for a few minutes to see what he would do next. Was this some kind of a twisted game he was playing with her? She knew he was still in the room because the door had not opened to let him out. Shit, if only the blanket was not over her head, she could see for herself. The silence was unnerving and Tori could not stand it any longer. She struggled to roll over. Anything was better than just laying there like she was. When she rolled over to face him, pushing her head free of the blanket at last, she was dumb struck. The two females just stared at each other, neither moving an inch. The shock of seeing a young black girl standing staring at her, instead of Jack, made her cry out in relief.

"Thank God. You must help me please. A man has me here and I need to get out before he comes back. Please finish untying me and I'll..."

Missy cut her short and feeling more in control and no longer afraid of the woman she screamed at her. "Shut up!"

Tori stopped to look at this child. She was young and not dressed too well. Just a slip of a girl really and one that should be in school judging by her age. She could not be more that thirteen she guessed, maybe a little older. Her child-like features gave her a somewhat friendly appearance but this girl was definitely hostile. And an enemy was not what Tori needed right now. What she needed was a friend. Tori would need her help to get out of his hell hole. She had to be very careful. The two of them just stared at each other again, each judging the other. It was Missy who broke the silence.

"You said your friends be looking for you? You means you don't wants him none? She jerked her head toward the door."

Tori was surprised by the girl's question. Shit, if she wanted him, why would she be tied up and held prisoner like she was. Was the girl stupid. "No, I don't want that bastard. All I want is to get out of here and get help. I must get back to where I belong. Please child."

"I ain't no child! And don't you be a callin me one neither, you hear? I's as much a woman as you." She stepped forward and angrily continued. "I'll be a dee'cide'n what to do. I ain'ts taking no orders from you. Specially cause you done took from me what be mine." She put her hands on her hips and looked hard at Tori. "If'n I sets you free and helps you git up yon to da house, you gots ta promise me dat you won't tell no one's hows you dun got dare. You gots to do dat or I's put some powerful "griss griss" on you."

A few moments later Tori was standing free and pulling the blanket once again around her bruised and battered body. The last few hours had left her shaking and looking too pale for Missy's likes. The blanket was soaked with urine, where Tori in desperation had relieved herself. She smelled and looked really sick and unsteady on her feet. If the woman fainted on her, she would not get her out of the cabin and away from Jack. Missy feared all of her efforts would be wasted and he would discover what she had attempted to do. She had to get her up to the main house one way or another and not before too long either. It was not out of kindness that she was now helping Tori. The water she brought her to drink, was only given to help revive her enough for the walk ahead.

Tori did not know this, she only knew the girl was helping her to escape and at some personal risk too by the way she was talking. Then it came to her. "You were the person last night weren't you? Thank you for coming back and helping me. I'll find a way to reward you."

Missy was horrified that she knew she was there last night. A voice screamed out in her brain. God if Jack ever found out... She looked at Tori and yelled at her. "No I weren't and don't you be a tell'n no ones. You done said you wouldn't. I helps you git out of here but you did it yo self, you hear. I's be Jack's woman and I wants it ta stay dat way. Now if'n we's don't want to gits ourselves caught we'd best be gitting."

Tori could not believe what she had just heard but she did not really care at that moment either. She would deal with it when she was safe and talked to the authorities.

The two of them made quite a sight as they walked toward the main house. Missy was always looking around to see if they had been observed by anyone, hurrying her nearly naked companion along. Although a lot smaller than Tori, she was the one who was clearly in charge.

Tori was being pushed by the girl, and did not protest or try to stop her. She was not really watching or caring where they were going. Her only goal was to put as much distance between herself and Jack Kane. To be free of that madman at last.

# Chapter 3

As Tori trudged along, she found herself thinking that soon she would get help and be on her way home to her daughter. By now, Linni would be worried sick about her. Sara's mom Jane would have her hands full with both girls, that was for sure. But it wouldn't stop her from having the whole campground and half the state out looking for her. This made her smile briefly. Seeing her friend and being with her daughter again was all she wanted. Then it hit her, what would she tell them when they found her? The time would come when she would have to tell about Jack and what he had done to her. That was going to be hard she told herself. She would like nothing better than to see Jack suffer, as she had the last twenty-four hours. But to do that, she would have to press charges and that meant a public trial! She pushed the thought away quickly. She had to focus on the positive as bad as the prospect of a trial seemed. It was far better than remaining Jack's prisoner.

The walk to the main house, their destination, was only about a half a mile from Jack's cabin. But in her physical and mental condition, Tori felt as if she would pass out when they were only halfway. Only the thought of Jack catching her again kept her going, as she tried to keep up with her prodding young guide.

Neither of them had spoken a word since starting out on the hike. So it surprised Tori when Missy finally broke the silence, telling her she would go no further. Tori's gaze went from Missy's face to the view that lay straight ahead of her. What greeted her eyes was a sight at once familiar to her and yet, somehow very different. Even all the books she had read and movies she had seen of the Old South, did nothing to compare with the splendor she was looking at. The plantation house standing before her, reminded her of some of the old homes she had visited along the River Road. None of those however had gone to such lengths to reconstruct the atmosphere and splendor as this one had done. What stood before her now appeared to be a fully restored plantation house. She couldn't deny her own eyes, nor could she explain it. From the magnificent manicured gardens, to the large open-aired porches, where splashes of colorful flowers hung from baskets, it all looked so authentic. Once again Tori felt the strange overpowering feeling that something was very wrong. It was the same odd feeling she had while walking around the lake. She thought she recognized the house as one she and Linni had toured two days ago but it couldn't be. There was no parking lot! Silly thing, she told herself, stop scaring yourself. If you would just stop jumping to conclusions. If it were the home you had toured, where is the main road that should be running in front of it? The river road. It had to be there somewhere cause she could see the dark flowing Mississippi off in the distance.

She was sure it was the Mississippi cause of its size. That prickling sensation at the back of her neck that put her nerves on edge returned. Terror gripped the pit of her stomach with a wave of nausea, joining the confusion that was rising in her mind. Part of her wanted to turn and run, while her mind just wanted to shut down. All of the confusion and fear were clearly visible on her face, as she frantically searched for any sign of anything familiar.

Recognizing the look on Tori's face, as one who was going to turn and run, Missy grabbed her hand and pulled her toward the house. It was clear to Missy that like it or not, she was going to have to take her the whole way, or risk her running back to Jack's cabin. She would just have to tell big Kate what little she knew about this woman and leave it at that. Missy knew if she could trust anyone, it was the mammy who ran things. She also knew Kate would keep her secret. She'd talk to no one. Missy smiled, no way would she tell who had brought the strange woman to the house, and where she came from. Yes um I's be safe, she told herself. Everyone knowd how much dat mammy hate Massa Jack. If'n she can git one over him, she sure'n go to like dat.

The day had been filled with so many emotional upheavals, that Tori found herself shutting things out that she could not explain. Like a lost child she let herself be led by Missy, who had taken her hand and was pulling her ever closer to the house. Up a pathway toward the back verandah they hurried toward an imposing black woman, who sat in the shade fanning herself from the heat.

At first Kate, so deep in thought, had not seen the two walking her way. Her face was filled with such sadness. Her demeanor however was in sharp contrast to her attire. On her head she wore a brightly colored cloth that was wrapped and tied neatly. Her bright blue dress was almost hidden by the white starched apron that covered her front. Large gold hoops hung from her ears, sparkling as they caught the sun's rays. She just sat there rocking seemingly unaware of the world around her.

Kate had worked hard all morning and felt that a few minutes alone on the verandah, to fight the heat and have a drink of cool water, was a well deserved break, and no one dare tell her different. Even the Master Leone like his father before him, let her run the house her way. She was as much a part of the plantation, as the land itself. She had raised its children black and white and seen the deaths of two generations, old and young dying alike, the last death being that of her friend, the wife of Master Leone. She had missed her Mistress dearly this last year, and somehow felt that the house would never recover the loss of such a dear person. The two women had in their own way, been far closer than they should have been. The status of slave and Mistress just never existed between them. It had never occurred to either of them from the moment they met, that they should act any other way but friends.

The wedding had taken place up North, when the Master Leone was on a trip. His young bride had come South to a new life and home. She had had no one other than her husband to help her understand how a plantation house was run. That was until Kate had stepped in, with her gentle guidance and understanding. She helped make the transition easier and less lonely.

As time wore on, a strong bond formed between the two women. The friendship became so close that the very idea of Kate being a slave upset the Mistress and became a main issue between her and her husband. She had begged him to free Kate to no avail. What came of the months of pleading was not Kate's freedom as she had hoped, but the promise that she and her youngest child would never be sold.

But from that day on, Kate was treated much more like a member of the family than a slave. Her power and position set her apart from the other slaves, who often unwittingly hurt her feelings. They treated her as an authority figure, no longer just a friend and one of them. Because of this, she was now left out of the happy events in the slave quarters. Her only comfort in this knowledge was that when any one of her people were in trouble, they would come to her with their problems. No matter how small or big, Mammy Kate would solve them fairly. To them she was the true heart of the plantation.

So it was that Kate was not surprised when she looked up from the verandah to see Missy dragging what appeared to be another slave behind her. It was however unusual for anyone to come to her at this time of the day with their problems. She shook her head mumbling to herself. This could only mean it would be a problem that would not be quickly solved. She had uneasy feelings about the situation, as she stood up and started to walk towards the two girls. One she knew well, but the other she had never laid eyes on and the state she was in was something awful. Just what kind of trouble had the wench Missy gone and got herself into this time? She bet it had something to do with that no-good overseer! Yes Sur, she just knew that for sure.

Missy had been watching the house, trying to decide how she was going to get Kate outside to meet them. The last thing she wanted was to enter Kate's kitchen. The last thing she wanted was to be overheard by the blabbermouth house Niggers. Those uppity no-goods, who thought because they worked in the house, they were better than the rest of them. She frowned at that thought. It seemed to Missy, that they just loved to spread gossip and cause trouble. To meet up with one of them before she had a chance to talk with Kate, could cause a lot of problems for her. Therefore, she was very relieved when she looked at the side of the house, to see the outline of Kate sitting in a chair watching them. Missy held on to Tori and stood her ground.

Slowly Kate made her way toward the pair. It was not until she emerged into the sunlight that Tori saw her. The very way she walked, head held high, hips swaying slowly from side to side, gave Tori the thought that they were about to meet someone with great authority. The manner in which this woman was dressed surprised her somewhat. From the brightly colored scarf wrapped around her head, the long dress and black lace-up boots, to the jewelry and lack of make-up, everything seemed out of place. As this woman got closer to Tori, her pace seemed to quicken with little effort. She seemed oblivious to the heat.

Missy was more than just a little uneasy as this powerful woman walked toward them. She found herself thinking that it had been a mistake to make Kate come to them. After all, she did not need to antagonize the only person that could at this point help her.

Kate stopped several feet from the odd-looking pair and her expression showed no surprise as she looked them over. It was almost as if she had been expecting them. Her hands went onto her hips, and her head nodded as if she was agreeing with something.

Missy did not give her a chance to talk. She pushed Tori toward the black woman, speaking to Tori in a rather shaky voice. "You best let's me talk to her if you know what's good fo you." She then looked Kate square in the face, determined to show no fear. She failed miserably when met by Kate's intimidating stare, which caused her to immediately lower her eyes. "I done know'd I's was wrong making you's walk out here in da heat and all Mizz Kate. But what I's got ta say, it needs ta be told ta you, without any of dem hearing." Her head nodded in the direction of the house. "Dem house Niggers don't need ta know's nothing bout dis. I's ain't gots no one else kin help. An I's know'd you be da only one. Dis one here, is a mess a trouble fo me. But I's aim ta tell you's and you kin makes up ya own thinking in it."

In the next few minutes that passed, Tori tried to interpret what was being said. However, she could only understand a word here and there. She knew they were discussing her and she understood that Missy was indeed trying to help her. But who was this person she had brought her to? And what language were they speaking? It sounded like English mixed in with what? She was trying hard to make sense of it when the conversation between the two stopped suddenly.

The pleading look on Missy's face, her hands twisting, told Tori that Kate was either going to help them, or send them on their way. She was about to speak for herself, when Kate spoke, looking not only at Missy but at Tori also. Her voice had a soft sing-song quality, with a heavy Southern drawl. Her grammar was no longer the same as she had just used in her conversation with Missy. Tori guessed what she was doing now, was projecting her authority, in a very subtle way. By talking to them in an educated manner, she confirmed to them both that she was in charge of the situation and that they had nothing to fear. Mammy Kate was going to help them.

"You don't have to worry about me saying anything girl. If'n you got this far without being seen and it seems to me that you have, your story is safe. You won't be mentioned none. Not that I'm going to lie for you mind, no sur! I'm just going to get around it for you. I'm only doing this for you, because it will give these old bones a good laugh to have pulled something over that Master Kane. Now you best be heading home before someone does see you. You hear me? Go on git."

Missy did not have to be told twice, she had done what she set out to do, and the joy of it sent her quickly and lightly on her feet back in the direction of the slave quarters. Kate however did not intend to let her off that easy and stopped her short.

"Missy!" The word sounded more like a command than a name and the young girl stopped but did not turn to face the older woman. "Girl, I've known your mammy for a long time. I've seen the work she does and that of your brothers in the fields. Your mammy's a good woman. She raised you child to be the same, did she not?" There was no answer. "So why, child, would you want to live with that man? You're going to wake up one day and see that hard work be a lot better than sleeping with the devil himself. That's what he is child, the devil."

Missy never said a word, just started running back down the trail. What did that woman know anyway, she asked herself? Sure she might be sleeping with him and hating herself for it, but she had power, like Kate had power. Other blacks envied her and feared her at the same time. Missy frowned, as her thoughts darkened. She was not afraid of work, that was not it. She slept with him because being his bed wench gave her the one thing she wanted most, to be like Kate and have authority over those that seemed to look down on her. Yes, she had authority through Jack. The blacks feared him and they feared his wench. She smiled, her mood lifting. She did not care what Kate or anyone else said for that matter. She was going to stay his wench and now that the fancy had been taken care of, she was going to be just that. Without her, Jack would want Missy back. She had won. All she had to do now, was get back to the quarters and wait. Wait and act dumb.

"I's know nothin, No sur, I's been here a waiting just like you says I's should. Dat what I's going to tell him. Yes sur," she told herself out loud laughing. "I's be one smart Nigger." The laughter that left her was one full of happiness and confidence. She felt as if her life was going to get back to the way it had been.

Kate just stood there listening to the child's laughter coming from down the trail and she shook her head. "That girl is heading for a heap of trouble. Seems that the more I or her mammy try to help, the worse it becomes. Now, let's see what we can do about you. Lord girl, you are a mess and by the looks of you, that so-called man gave you a real bad time." Kate took hold of Tori and the two of them started toward the side of the house. As they made their way, Kate was calling out orders to people that Tori could not even see. "You can put another glass with my lemon and then you best be cleaning them upstairs like I dun told you. If I get in there and find any of you sitting, you will answer to me!" The result of her orders was an empty kitchen when they entered. Kate helped her over to the table and sat her down. Waiting for them were two large glasses of water and a pitcher of lemonade. There wasn't another person to be seen. Kate had assured this by giving jobs in a part of the house far enough away, so that she and this stranger could talk without being overheard.

The kitchen itself was dim and even though it was cooler than outside, it was still uncomfortably warm. Tori gratefully drank the cup of water first as Kate instructed. She had not realized how thirsty she was, or how shaken up. Her hands could barely hold onto the cup for they were trembling so bad. As she sat there, Tori could not believe what she was looking at. Nothing she looked at seemed right somehow. A sinking feeling began to surface, as a horrible thought entered her mind. Something was telling her she was about to come face to face with the impossible.

Kate was watching this stranger and even though Tori had not said a word, Missy had called her a fancy and said that she talked like one. Kate sensed that something was odd about this woman who sat opposite her. Nothing she could really put her finger on, but it had something to do with the way she was acting. The way she was looking at everything around her with that puzzled look. She knew she had best find out all she could about her and fast.

Tori did not pay much attention to Kate at first, in fact her head was spinning with more questions than Kate could have imagined. Kate did however catch her attention when she reached across the table and took hold of her hand.

"Look at me girl. Let's start with, just who are you? That should be an easy enough question to answer. You can talk can't you?"

"Yes Mam, I can talk. Please, excuse me if I seem rude or ungrateful. I don't mean to be. It's just that so much has happened to me in such a short time."

She took a deep breath and with it control of herself and what to do. "I have to call the police, to let them know about that horrible man back there. I'm damn lucky you know, to have gotten away from the bastard." She started to cry. "I'm sorry. I was just so afraid of him. He hit me and..." she just cried harder.

"Nothing for you to be sorry about girl. If that animal had treated me as he obviously did you, I'd be a crying myself. Now just you go ahead cause it is nothing to be hiding. I know'd all about that man, a huh. I do that. But we'll deal with him later. Now as to your friend, I'm afraid I don't know this person, this Mr. Poleess. I doubt they be around here anyway, cause no one comes or goes around these parts without me knowing about it." She handed Tori a handkerchief. "So calling out to them will only be a waste of time, and upset you more I feel. Just dry those tears and let's see what we can do."

Tori stopped crying. She stared at Kate and then looked around the kitchen again. "You don't have a phone?"

Kate looked perplexed at her. "Can't say I do. Maybe I do, but then what is a phone?"

"Oh shit, this can't be happening. God help me, nothing is making any sense at all."

"I bet it isn't. With the lump on the side of your head like that, I say you be just a little mixed up that's all. You will be fine after a while, now just try and think slowly and things they'll come back to you."

Tori just shook her head as if she knew that was not going to happen. "Please, if you could just tell me where I am? Maybe that will help. In turn I will do my best to answer your questions."

Kate was stunned. This woman not only looked too good to be a fancy, her speech was educated as well. Her manners spoke for themselves. This was a fine lady sitting opposite her. One to be treated with respect as was only fitting. Missy had been wrong about her, or lied.

"You are in my kitchen, in the home of Monsieur Leone Duval."

Tori only shook her head no again. That was not what she meant. "I don't mean location Mam." Tori hesitated. "I know this might seem a little strange to you, but I need to know something else. What year is it? What is the date?"

If Kate was shocked by the question, Tori could not tell. She just sat back in her chair and after considering it for a moment, simply said, "1810. The year is 1810."

Tori had not wanted to hear what she had been told. Yet, in her heart, she knew it to be the only explanation for all that had happened to her. For everything she had been through and seen. The reason there had been no campground at the lake. Jack's actions. This house and Kate. It was no dream. It was a living nightmare.

To hear 1810 was a shock and almost too much for her to handle. All color drained from her face, as her mind reeled. The year 1810 echoed in her mind over and over. She felt as if she were a wild animal caged up against its will, desperately looking for a way out.

"It can't be true," she almost whispered. "Please tell me you're only pretending, acting or something. You made it up right?" She fell silent, her eyes doing the talking for her. They were pleading with Kate.

"Now why'd I go an make something like that up? You just all mixed up in the head right now that's all. It be one true fact, as sure as I am here and the good Lord is my witness. The year is 1810, yes sur it sure enough is."

Kate had watched as shock registered on the woman's face the first time she had told her. But this time it was like all the life was plumb taken away from her. She just sat there, acting as though she were terrified at the news, like she did not believe it to be true. The girl was just not acting right at all. She was sure it had to do with that lump on her head poor thing. Maybe she had forgotten things, like happened to Master Leone when he fell off his horse last year. A hit to the head could do that. Still, Kate remembered it didn't last long. If that was the problem, it would sort itself out in good time. One thing was very clear though and that was the girl had been through some sort of terrible ordeal. Not surprising if that Jack had anything to do with it. He must have been an animal. The bruises on her face and arms were evidence of that. No, she did not need to be pushed too much at this point. Kate was wise enough to know that she would have to move very carefully with her. The best thing for her at this point, was to get her cleaned up. A warm bath, along with something to wear and some food, yes sur, that should do the trick. Handle her like a fragile child and go slow. That is what she would do for now.

"Now you don't fret yourself. What you need, is to let Kate here take care of you. You just listen to me now. First thing we do is we will git you to feeling better."

Tori let herself be led from the kitchen to a small room off to one side. There she soon found herself in a warm tub of water, with Kate washing her as if she were a child. Slowly the shock eased and the reality of her situation began to sink in. Looking up into the older woman's face, she could see all the care and concern this stranger had for her.

"I want to thank you, for all your kindness Mam. You were right, I am feeling a bit better."

"Well now, I knew if you got cleaned up and all, you would feel like a new person." Kate stood back, her round face beaming. She did not seem to notice the fact that the front of her dress was splashed as she rolled down her long sleeves. Her bright smile left her face as she mused. "We can't have you getting yourself back into that piece of dirt you came wrapped up in. You need something decent to put on. Lord child, nothing I have will fit you for sure, Why, there isn't much to you at all." She was shaking her head, her face with a truly puzzled look about it. Then an idea hit her. "Why, you look to be the same size of Master Leone's late wife. God rest her soul. You just stay put for a while. Just lay back in the water and soak. I'll be right back. Don't you worry none. No one in this house dare come in my room, so you will be safe. Just you relax till Kate gets back."

Tori had nothing to lose and most certainly she had nowhere to go at this point. What she did have was time alone to think and take hold of herself and her situation.

"So this is a bath in the 1800's, a nice big tin can. Might as well enjoy it for now, who knows when the next one will come along," she murmured. She leaned back as well as she could, which was not as easy as it looked. If she put her head back, the rim of the tub cut into her neck and her legs were too long to stretch out. So in the end, she sat up and put her head on her knees, closing her eyes.

Relax, how could she do that? Here she was in a plantation home, miles, no, years away from her child and friends. How she needed them right now and how they must be worrying, not to mention the way her Linni must be crying for her. No one else could reach her daughter like she could. When she was upset she would always hold her and rock her. Then she would softly sing to her. Often Linni would fall asleep in her mother's arms this way, leaving her with a sense of peace and happiness that only a mother could understand. If she were with her daughter right now, she would sing her that new song that Tommy had taught them. Linni liked it so much.

She could hear the tune in her head, the way her daughter sang it. Softly at first, then as if she were singing to Linni, she found herself humming the song. She let herself dream that she was holding her child. As she did so she began to sing. The words came easy to her and mechanically she sang, as she tried to sort out how this had happened to her.

Time travel was something you saw in the movies, or read about in books. It was not something she had ever really considered to be a possibility. Yet, here she was and this was very real. Sure, like so many other people, she had wondered what it would be like to see the past, but to have it happen was another thing altogether. It was terrifying!

Kate had found what she was looking for and was pleased that she had not gotten rid of all the Mistress's dresses like Leone had wanted her to do. Holding the plain cotton day dress in her hands, she wondered if she should bring undergarments and other accessories downstairs. That thought soon left her mind as she remembered she would have to account to Leone. The dress would keep the girl covered, and she could at least have some dignity, far more than in that dirty rag of a blanket. But to take liberty of bringing more for her without asking, was something she knew she could not do, even with Leone.

"This will do just fine," she said. "Nothing fancy, just plain enough and fitting for her to wear." She was sure that Leone would not mind her having one plain dress. Such were the workings of her mind. She was just thinking to herself that she did not know the girl's name, when she came upon the two young slave girls she was training. She stopped long enough to inspect the work and gave them orders to keep them busy for a few more hours. She told them to do it all again as it was not to her liking.

Kate hurried toward her room. She knew she had been gone far longer than she had planned. Now nothing would stop her from the task at hand. She had to learn all she could about this girl before Leone returned. What brought her to a complete halt was the sound of a very familiar song, but one that she had not heard for a long time. Quietly, she made her way to her room. Opening the door very slowly, so as not to disturb the girl or her singing, she stood still and listened. She had to be sure she was hearing right.

There was no doubt about it. This stranger was singing her song, "Tommy's song." But how could this be? She had taught no one else the old song! No one but Kate and her son knew those words. Raw emotion took over. Kate could control herself no longer. Rushing toward Tori, throwing the dress on her cot, she reached Tori with such speed, that it caught both of them off guard.

Tori had no idea at first what was going on. She just knew that she was being handled violently by Kate, who was demanding something about giving her back her son.

Kate had reached down in the tub and pulled Tori to a standing position. She was screaming at her and shaking Tori so hard that they both nearly landed back in the water. The situation was definitely out of control. Tori was more afraid of falling, than of the woman who had a hold of her. She pushed away and quickly stepped out of the tub, putting it between her and Kate.

"Please Kate stop it. I don't know what it is I've done, or what it is your talking about. Let's calm down and talk this over. If you want me to go I will. Just please explain it to me."

Kate looked into Tori's eyes and could see that the girl was really confused. Could it be that she had no idea of the importance of the song, or was she playing some sort of a cruel joke? Either way she had to find out, for it was clear that Tori knew something.

Tori watched as Kate stood there with her tearing eyes boring into her. One minute the woman was kind and caring, next she was ranting and raving at her. It made no sense at all. Were all the people around here crazy?

Kate struggled to calm down, yelling at the woman was not the way to learn the answers to her questions. Taking in a deep breath and slowly exhaling she commanded, "The first thing is to git you dressed, then you and I have to talk, cause you have a lot of explaining to do." She handed the dress to Tori and left the room. Tori was trembling uncontrollably, her emotions in turmoil. Even in the warm room, a sudden chill ran up and down her body. Once again, she felt as if her world was spinning out of control. Nothing made any sense to her. But one thing was certain, she needed Kate's help. She also recognized that she would have to be very careful with what she said or did, very careful indeed.

Kate was waiting in the kitchen when Tori entered a short time later. The sound of the door being closed softly made Kate look up. Standing before her, was an entirely different woman than the one she had seen with Missy. That one had been nothing more than just another dirty pathetic wench, at best. Now, however, the beautiful woman who stood before her was a far cry from the earlier image. Even though the dress was a little tight in the bust, the length and waist were right. Kate found herself thinking that no matter what this woman wore she would look stunning. The bruised face and swollen eye did not take away from her beauty at all. Maybe that was because of the way she held herself, standing proud and defiant. Whatever it was, the woman was a true beauty and much more. In addition, she was a mystery, one that held information that Kate had to obtain.

"Come sits here and eat something. Den we'll talk." Kate inhaled deeply as if trying to calm down. I'm sorry if I upset you. I will try not to let it happen again. I said try mind you. Truth is all I want and that is what I will get." By her tone of voice it was clear that Kate meant what she said. In Kate's mind one thing was very clear. This stranger was a link to her son. This knowledge both excited and frightened her, "You best be sitting over there, so I kin git you something to eat and I kin git me a long cook drink of Lemon."

Tori could see Kate was in a very agitated state. A fact made evident by the way she was bouncing between the way she had spoken to Missy and the educated speech she had shown Tori. She watched as Kate prepared her a plate of cold meat and bread. This was placed in front of Tori, along with a fork and a glass. Kate poured Tori and herself a glass of the lemonade, then sat down opposite her.

Tori had forgotten how hungry she was, The food set her mouth to watering and her stomach growling. "You have to excuse me Kate. May I call you Kate? That is all right isn't it?"

"Yes um, I spect it is. What is it that I'm supposed to call you?"

"Tori will do just fine." She lowered her eyes and looked at the plate of food as she continued. "I doubt that my second name is of any importance now." Her glance from the plate to Kate's watchful eyes told her that some of the tension between them was easing. She was glad that the two of them seemed to be feeling each other out first instead of just reacting. At least the black woman was being kind again. Tori was trying to make up her mind on how much to tell Kate and how to go about it. The silence was broken by a rather firm but calm question from across the table. It not only interrupted her thoughts, it shattered them.

"I heard you singing my song. Only two people on this God's earth know's that song. That was up until you came along. It be me and my son Tommy. Now you sit there and you know's it. How can that be?"

Tori put down her fork, and swallowed a large mouthful of food. She washed this down with a drink and stared at Kate's face. All thought of hunger disappeared. Kate's eyes were glass-like in appearance and were brimming with tears, ready to flow at any second. The sadness behind those eyes, the loneliness and the love, she had seen before in someone else's eyes, in another time.

"Kate, you tell me I know a song that only you and your son know. Before you ask me where he is, please tell me, this Tommy you mentioned, is he really your son?"

"Yes um, he's my boy. He was the joy of my life. He is the only one of my chilen I was allowed to keep with me, The Mistress, God bless her, saw to that. The Master Leone, he is a good man really. Well, he told me that Tommy would never have to leave me here, that this would be his home until he died."

"If that's true, then why are you asking me where he is? I don't understand." Why did Tori hear those warning bells going off inside her head? She had that dreadful feeling deep down that she already knew the answer. Oh! How she wanted to wake up from this nightmare, if only it could be just that, a nightmare.

"You see child, last summer around this time of year I's took my son down to the lake. It's a cool spot, down there by the water in the early morning. He loved to go there. He would play and splash in the water and I could take's time out to thank the Lord for allowing me to keep him by my side. It's a place I could go to gather my thoughts."

The room went quiet for a moment as Kate seemed to be reliving those times, all the days she had gone to the lake. Her hands were busy, running a cloth from one to the other as she sat there. Every now and then she would use the cloth to mop her brow, to wipe the beads of perspiration away, or to dab at her eyes as large tears would appear on her long lashes.

"Tommy and I had a game that we'd play. We'd sometimes play as if we's were far away, in a place that my daddy came from, in a lands where we'd be free. We'd go down there's often as I could git away, without being missed and all. On Sunday afternoons we'd go down there sometimes. It was a very special place for my Tommy and me. It was our place. Yes um. Dat where I taught him our song, the song my daddy taught me."

The old woman fell silent again and was lost in a daydream as Tori studied her. Somehow she looked a lot older now than she had before, beaten, as if the will to live was slipping away. Tears were falling rapidly from her large brown eyes, eyes that never left Tori's face. Tori reached out and took hold of Kate's hand. She tried to comfort her by squeezing it gently. She had to do that for both of them. She had to touch something real because what she had just been told was becoming only too clear to her. Kate continued on with her story.

"Dis one morning, I had taken Tommy down to da lake. We had gone real early, so we could get back afore we was missed. Tommy was playing by da water, when I thought I heard somethin. I told him to stay put while his mammy took a look. I left him there. Lord how's I wish I could take back those few minutes. I was only gone for a few minutes, not long but when I got back, he was done gone. My baby child, was just gone. I called and looked. De Master he looked all day. Dey all looked and den dey come to me dat night and tells me, he dead. My boy's dead."

Kate was crying hard now, wailing in a strange sort of way, like a hurt animal. The pain was raw. It was as if she had just received the news, not something she had been living with for a year. Kate, in her despair was slipping back to a form of speaking that she seemed unaware of. Her grammar, her very accent, reminded Tori that this woman was indeed an uneducated slave of the South. She had to remind herself she was in time when slavery was a way of life. She knew that Kate must have seen many of her children sold and accepted it as the norm. But to lose the one child that she had been told she could keep. The one that she had allowed herself to become attached to…

"I know'd in my heart dat ain't so cause dey neber found no body of my boy. No sur, no body. So's I know's he be safe and I ain't sung dat song to no one's. Now you are here wid our song, wid Tommy's song. I need to know's how dat be? How you know's our song? You know's my baby? I think you know's where he be."

Tori was as upset as Kate at this point. Not for the same reason but just as upset. She had to tell this woman something but how could she explain that time had taken her son? How, when she herself found it hard to believe, let alone understand? Kate looked at her and pleaded.

"All I want is to hold my boy, my baby. You's can't understand that yet. But one day, when you's has a child of your own, you's will know'd the pain of needing to be wid dat child when you can't. It's been a year, one long year since I saw him. Next month's will be's his fourth birthday. He's so little and I had him such a short time. Lord child, if it be bad or good, the knowing can't be any worse den what I be a going through for all dee's months."

Tori was stunned. The Tommy she knew was a teen and the Tommy Kate talked of, was the Tommy that had been found all those years ago at the camp, when he had been found sobbing down by the lake calling for his mammy. But Kate said he was missing only a year, it made no sense to her. She desperately needed time to think this out before she said anything. She also needed Kate's help. She was now convinced that the lake was her key to getting home. Tori surmised that all she had to do was get back to the lake early in the morning to cross time. But she did not know where the lake was and Kate did. Tori had to tell her something and as crazy as it seemed, she decided to tell the woman some of the truth, slowly so as to test how she would react.

"Yes, Kate, I know your son. You're right. If the song is his and only he and you knew it, then it has to be him. Tommy taught my daughter the song." Tori caught the look of wonder on Kate's face.

"Yes, Kate, I have a child. So I can understand how you feel. I want to hold my Linni right now, as much as you want to hold your Tommy. That's the truth of it but you may not want to hear or believe the rest I have to tell you."

"Lord child, I know'd when I heard you singing, dat you was sent here by da good Lord. Dat you seen my baby boy. You was sent to me so I'd knowd he was fine." Her face was one big beaming grin. Gone were the tears of sadness as look of relief flooded her expression. It did not however hide the excitement that was about to overcome her. "He's fine isn't he?"

"Yes Kate, the last time I saw him, and that was yesterday morning, he was alive and well. But I feel I need to tell you that yesterday was not what it may seem. Yesterday has not even happened yet and won't for years to come."

Kate's face seemed to drop, then anger flashed across her eyes, the chair scraped across the floor as she leaned with her hands on the table. She stood bending forward so her face was only a few inches from Tori's, her voice shaking as she spoke.

"You's talking in circles and not making a lick oh sense. Dis old woman she ain't no dumb Nigger slave. She ain't stupid neither."

"Please, let me try to explain. Kate, as true as I'm sitting here, what I'm about to tell you, as God is my witness, is the truth as I know it. The best way I can explain it to you, is to say it right out." Tori looked Kate right in the eyes as she took a deep breath. Then she said out loud for the first time what she now realized beyond a shadow of doubt was the truth. "Yesterday when I got up, the year was 1999 and somehow when I took a swim in the lake, your lake, I ended up here in your time.

The two of them sat facing each other for some time. Kate had the strangest look on her face, one that Tori could not decipher. It was not a look of disbelief, nor was it one of acceptance either. Tori knew that what she had just said would seem totally outrageous, but she had to reach Kate and make her see that she was telling her the truth. "That must have been what happened to your son, why his body was never found. He must have somehow gone to my time where I met him."

Kate just sat back down staring at Tori. Was this woman being cruel by lying or was she mad, believing what she was saying? No matter which it was, this woman was her link to her son and she was not going to give up that easily.

"You says you are from the year 1999? How kin that be child? What proof can you give me? How can I believe you and Lord if it's true, how can I ever git my boy back?"

Tori could see what she was up against. She had to get Kate to believe her. The only way back to the lake was going to be with her help. "I know it's hard to believe and I know you might think I'm crazy. Proof you say, I have nothing I can show you but I can tell you things about my life, my time and history. Most of all, I think there is a chance we can both get what we want. I can go home and you can get Tommy. Don't you see? If I came here and your son went there, then it works both ways. Tommy can come home or you can come with me to find him. The link is the lake but I don't know how to find it. I do know where we need to be to cross over to my time. All we have to do is be there in the morning and we can be on our way."

Kate was worried now. She wanted her son but this could be some sort of trick. She nodded her head agreeing with herself. Yes sur, it sure could. Since her son's disappearance, the Master had banned anyone from going down there. Why the last black caught there, had been whipped by the overseer, who seemed to enjoy every minute of causing pain. She knew also that the overseer had it in for her and that it could be a plan he had hatched to catch her down by the lake. He would be well in his rights to punish her and punish her he would. She had no doubt in her mind that he would whip her. Yes sur, that evil man would whip with no stopping until her body lay lifeless. Yes sur, it could be a trick. Tori, after all, had been brought here by that Missy from the overseer's cabin. But what if, this story Tori told was the truth?

Kate had to be very careful. "I'm going to need some time to think about this story you told me. You can tell me more about this future you claim you're from. Maybe something you say to me will help me to believe you. Cause heavens child I wants to believe you so much. But before you and I can talk more on that, we have to think up what to tell the Master Leone when he gets home this evening. We has to keep you here somehow and that won't be easy. He's a fair man, but Lord he ain't never going to believe this. No way. I still don't know how you got to be at Jack Kane's and all. Oh we has so much to set straight and to decide what to do."

Tori was disappointed. She had hoped the two of them could have left right away for the lake. Once there, she would find a way home, she just knew it. She felt the longer she delayed the less chance she had. Still Tori could not blame the woman for not trusting her. She would have to gain her confidence first. "Very well Kate, we will do it your way. After all, I'm a stranger here and not just in this house, in your time also. I need you and all your help if I'm to stay here until we can get to the lake. I just hope it won't take us too long, that's all. As to what to tell this Master Leone? Well we could start by telling him that I'm white not black. I'm not a runaway or a fancy like that sadistic idiot thought. Heavens, I read enough in my time to know what they did to runaways and how they treated blacks. Kate, I'm telling you that I'm white, the trouble is how do we convince everyone else?"

Kate stared at her, Lord how this child could lie. Just how could she be white looking like she did? Sure her features were white but that was where it stopped. Kate could see how it would be to their advantage if she could prove she was white but that seemed unlikely. No harm in asking her though, see if she could lie her way out of this one. "How you going to prove to me you white? Cause if'n I don't believe you and I don't. I ain't going to be able to convince no one else, 'specially Master Leone."

Tori laughed, it seemed ridiculous that she should have to prove her race but she herself could see how in these times she could be mistaken for a woman of mixed blood. "You know, I worked hard on my tan and my hair seems to confirm that my tan, that's the color of my skin, is naturally my color, right? Well my hair is permed, something that I doubt has been invented yet, It will grow out in time but we don't have time do we? My tan will fade. That will take a shorter time but once again it seems I can't prove to you quickly enough that I am what I say. I'm really white. In a few weeks you would see for yourself, Kate, that I'm telling you the truth. You see, where I come from, an all over tan is considered good looking, very attractive."

The black woman sat across from her shaking her head from side to side.

"Is there nothing I can say or do to convince you I'm what I say?"

Kate looked at her and could see how desperately she wanted to prove she was telling the truth, or what she thought was the truth. "You say your skin, it will change color and your hair will grow different somehow? Next you will be telling me that your dark eyes will turn light!"

The shock and joy registered instantly on Tori's face as she laughed out loud. "That's it Kate! You've done it! I can prove to you that I'm white and that I'm from 1999. No I can't turn my dark eyes light. Well, I could if I were in my time, with things called contact lenses. People do it all the time now for fun. But I can show you contact lenses. I had completely forgotten about them being in. Look here I'll take them out and show you. It's like having glasses to read with, only they are right on your eyes." Tori laughed at the strange look Kate had on her face. She knew she must sound out of her mind. "Look here!"

Kate watched as Tori removed a small round clear glass-like object from her eye. Then as she held it in her fingers, the woman took another one out from the other eye. Kate didn't have to be told that what Tori was holding wasn't anything but glasses from the future. "May I hold them?" She reached out and took them from Tori. She held one up and tried to look through it, then she put them between her fingers and before Tori could stop her she rolled them up. The soft lenses were very quickly destroyed and became nothing more than small crumpled up pieces of plastic.

Kate looked up at Tori who sat looking distraught at her. God help them all, the woman was who she said she was. And better still, she could take her to Tommy! Then she looked at what she had done to the small glasses and she shamefully spoke. "I sorry child, I guess I have ruined them. Can you forgive me?" Then panic covered her face. "Oh, no! You can see can't you?" she hastily asked.

Tori smiled and tried to reassure her. "Don't worry Kate. It's all right, I can see just fine. I only need them to see off in the distance. I couldn't have put them back in if I had wanted to anyway. They are one shot deals. It is a shame though." She reached out and took one of them from Kate. "They were the only proof I had of where I came from." She looked back at Kate. "At least you believe me, that's the most important thing isn't it?"

# Chapter 4

It had been almost too much to hope for but there it was, the proof that she had wanted. Strange, Kate thought, but a calm had come over her with a new hope that she was going to get to her Tommy and that was all she really cared about. But Kate also realized she needed Tori's help and her wits about her if she was to succeed. "This time you come from, it must be very different from ours. I think I will enjoy hearing about it. But first, we must decide what to do about you. How can we explain how you got here?" Her calm attitude was slipping once again. "We's can't tell the Master what we know. Lord, he'd think us crazy. I know you is telling me the truth. You are white and dat be the way of it! I never would have thought so if'n I hadn't seen them things with my own eyes." She pointed at the two small crumpled contacts laying on the table between them. Kate looked toward Tori then with a puzzled expression, "You too dark for a white lady. Master Leone, he's only going to see you as I did." Kate was getting so worked up that she was ranting on and on. Her agitation was visibly clear, especially in the way her speech pattern alternated.

Tori thought that at any moment the old mammy would physically start jumping around the kitchen. "It's all right Kate, you don't have to be so flustered. Look I told you the truth and you believed me after you saw these." She held her contacts out toward her.

"Maybe that be so, but the ways I see's it is this. I'm just an old black fool with no education like the Master Leone has and all. He be real smart like and maybe too smart for his own thinking. He ain't a going to listen to what you done tell him unless it be plain and clear like. He ain't a going to think that you be from anyplace that he can't see. No sur, no way! Lord I knowd him all my life's and I be telling you we just can't tell him none of dis." Now Kate was pacing up and down the small kitchen shaking her head from side to side and really working herself up. "He a going to think you plumb crazy and me too for listening to you."

"Calm down Kate please, just come here and sit down for a second." She took Kate by the shoulders and pushed her back into her seat, sitting herself right next to the nanny. She took hold of her hands. Looking directly into her eyes she continued in a kind, understanding tone. "I understand that you know this Master of yours far better than I can even imagine. So if you think that we had best not tell him, well then I had better take your judgment to heart. You are not an old black fool regardless of how little education you have. It does not take book learning to understand people, it takes a thing called insight and gut instinct."

Kate looked at her, strangely cocking her head to one side, then as if understanding what it was Tori was trying to tell her she broke into a large grin. "I know my feelings is right, yes em I do." Her face then went serious, "but Lord child, that don't help us any, what we going to do now?"

Tori smiled at her. "I think that the two of us can come up with some sort of story. Maybe I could tell him I'm from a foreign land, that I got lost, something like that." God had she really said that? It sounded ridiculous even to her own ears.

The two women sat for the next hour putting together a story that they hoped would appear real enough and not raise undue suspicion. Then at the insistence of Kate, Tori was taken upstairs to a guest room, where Kate found all the necessary garments that a proper young lady of the day should wear.

The afternoon passed with the two of them talking and learning from each other. Of things neither had ever guessed existed. Kate spent a lot of time shaking her head and telling Tori to stop fooling her, that such things could not be, could they?

Tori found out that the clothes and conveniences of this age, compared to the modern way of life she was used to, were far harder to bear than she had imagined. "I'm telling you Kate, I can't breath in this thing and if you pull it any tighter, I will pop out the top or die from lack of air."

Kate just laughed at her and then they became serious again. Tori had a lot to learn in a short time if they were going to get away with their plan. After an hour of instructions on how to behave, the two sat down on the front verandah, mulling over what they were going to do until they could get to the lake.

For Tori it was going to be hard waiting. If it were up to her, the pair of them would have headed out for the lake hours ago. Kate had been the one to show her that it was impossible for her to just leave the house. It could not be done. She was needed here and would be missed immediately if they left. Her life was not her own to do with as she pleased. It might be different in the year that Tori was from, but right now they were in Kate's time and would have to do as she knew best.

At least Tori had a chance to glimpse life in the South in the year 1810. She was experiencing it first hand. She was actually living it. What some historians wouldn't give to trade places with her at this moment she thought.

It was going to be more difficult for Kate to deceive her Master. Never in her life had she lied to him about anything. He was almost like a son to her these days. She had watched him and his brother grow and had helped raise them. True, she was a few years older than him, but like Leone, to look at her now, she appeared far older than her years. Time had taken its toll on both of them. Leone had lost his wife and with her, his youth. Grief had aged him, and the plantation had become his life. In appearance he now looked years older than his late thirties. True, he was still dashing, his dark hair streaked here and there with silver. But he no longer had the sparkle of life behind his eyes. They seemed dead and vacant as the man himself felt.

Kate had also changed. Gone was the attractive carefree spirit, to be replaced by a more somber soul. Not always had she looked upon Leone as a son. When they were so much younger, it had been Kate he had bedded. She was his first. But from that day until many years later, he hadn't touched her again. It had not been because she was unattractive, far from it, for in her day Kate had turned quite a few heads. No, he had turned away from her because he had found his nights filled with courting a young lady, a true Southern belle, who he thought he would marry.

It was shortly before Leone was to announce their betrothal, that he found his young lady in what he referred to as a compromising situation, proving beyond a shadow of a doubt that she was not the virgin she claimed to be. With his heart broken, he had to run to Kate. That night produced Tommy. When Kate had told him she was with child, he made her promise no one was to know he was the father. After the birth of their son, Leone left for a trip up North. He returned, married to a frail and pretty woman.

To all who met her it was clear she loved her husband very much. To Kate it was evident that they were meant for each other. Because of his wife's love, Leone was able to mend his broken heart. And Kate knew he was truly glad that things had worked out as they had with one exception, his wife could bear no children. As much as she wanted to give him a son, it was not to be.

Kate knew the Mistress suspected who Tommy's father was. But never did Leone's wife ask her. This was something that a proper Mistress of a plantation would never do. How could she anyway? She dearly loved Kate and the child but would never go against her husband's wishes, She knew they were no threat to her marriage, it was just a part of plantation life. Besides the child brought so much laughter and love to them all, she could never see the place without him. It was because of her love for Kate and Leone that she made sure the child would stay forever on the plantation.

When Leone's wife died, it hurt not only him but Kate as well. Once again in despair, Leone had turned to Kate. This time however the two found friendship only. Never again would they share a bed. They had no need to. Kate and Leone could share the Mistress's memory and then they could share Tommy. It was the loss of Tommy, not long after, that hit them hard. They had both been irrevocably changed by the loss. Kate's life became the plantation house and taking care of Leone. He in turn had thrown himself into running the plantation to fill the void. Kate mothered Leone and fussed over him daily. So it was in this way they both had saved each other from self-destruction and managed to find the courage to go on. Now as she sat waiting for him to come home, she felt an overwhelming sadness that she would soon leave him. Kate would move heaven and earth to get her son back. Lying was a small price to pay she convinced herself. The good Lord would forgive her.

As the afternoon wore on and the sun set below the horizon, the sleepy plantation seemed to come alive. Tori could see more and more blacks walking in small groups toward the far side of the house. They began to sing, as they wound their way up the path that would take them to their quarters. A soft breeze blew in from the river, carrying on it the gentle rhythm of the slaves voices, soft and strangely hypnotic. Tori found herself wishing she could share this moment with Linni. She would have to remember just how everything was, so when she got home she could at least describe it to her. The sky was turning a deep rose color, enhancing the white of the jasmine whose scent filled the air. Everything around her created such a lazy atmosphere. Her emotions at that moment were different from anything she had ever felt before. She was sad and missing home, scared even, but a mood of serenity had enveloped her and with it came a certainty of the knowledge that she would be with Linni again.

Kate had left Tori every now and then to give instructions for the evening meal, and see to it that it was prepared exactly as she demanded. With the return of the field hands and the twilight of the evening, she knew it would not be long before Leone himself walked in the house.

The day had been hot, even sitting here on the verandah in the shade had been hard, not to mention the stifling confinement of all the clothes that Tori found herself in. The bruises and swelling on her face had subsided somewhat, but like the rest of her body, they remained sore. Still she had found it peaceful, fanning the warm air, sipping on lemonade and resting. Tori had to smile to herself. Her body was healing. She now had hope and with it returned a bit of her fighting spirit. Tori spoke softly to Kate, "This is a real 'Gone With The Wind' scene and I'm in it. It's exciting and yet very frightening Kate." Her smile faded. "Only because I know in my heart that I will find my way back to my own time, can I sit here so calmly. If I thought that I would have to stay though? Well, I just can't let myself think about that possibility or I'd be off to the loony bin for sure. You know what I mean?"

Kate did not understand everything Tori talked about. She was a strange one that was for sure. But sitting there, dressed as she was, Tori looked just like any other young lady in the South. Well almost, her color did stand out some. Kate knew also that she was as foreign to this place and time as anyone could be. Her thoughts were interrupted by the sight of her Master. "You best not think of anything but what we talked about girl, cause Master Leone, he be riding up yonder."

Tori looked out over the fields where she could see two people riding side by side. The pair stopped briefly and then parted, one headed off and the other rode in the direction of house. Tori's hands gripped Kate's, her stomach lurched in fear, as she realized who was riding off in the opposite direction.

"Kate! That must have been Kane! He's about to find I'm gone and I know he will come looking for me."

"Don't you fret none, by the time he finds where you are, you will be under this roof as a guest. The Master, he won't let nothing happen to you. Now you best git upstairs like we planned and don't come down till I dun come and gits you. You stay put."

Tori got to her feet and started to follow Kate's directions. Suddenly she stopped, turned and gave Kate a hug. "Thank you Kate. I'll see to it that I don't let you down. We both have a lot to lose but more to gain. I will never forget you or what you're doing for me."

Kate was moved by Tori. Once again this white woman was treating her as an equal, much as the Mistress had. It brought tears to her eyes. "Oh go on with you. You best git now or we's be in a heap ah trouble." With that she walked past Tori, out from under the verandah, to meet her Master. When she turned back, the verandah was empty.

It was early evening and all was quiet at the house. Things were cooling off at last. It had been a long hot workday out in the fields, made all the harder by his overseer's wandering mind. He had been distracted and difficult. Leone was glad it was over and looked forward to a quiet evening. To look at Kate though, standing there wringing her hands and sweating as if she had just run a mile, Leone knew something was up.

Kate watched as he approached the house, but try as she may, she could not calm herself down. So much depended on her and the conversation she was about to have. "Lord you best help me now, cause I be needing all da helps I kin git."

Leone's face darkened. The last thing he needed was another difficult confrontation, especially with Kate. His whole day had been filled with aggravation. Too many times he had to repeat himself because Jack had not been paying attention. Leone did not know why he put up with Jack Kane. He never would have thought he'd have someone such as him around, let alone working for him. But like it or not there was no denying it, Kane was good at his job. Leone knew he did not have to like him, just put up with him and pay his salary. Still, he found himself wishing that his overseer was more of a gentleman like himself. That he would clean himself up a little and look a bit more presentable. Leone had spoken to him once about his appearance but Jack had told him that it wasn't his looks that got the job done. He couldn't argue with the man about that and had dropped the subject. True he had tried some days to tidy himself up a bit after that discussion but today had not been one of them.

Now it looked as though his day might not have a peaceful end after all. Not that his nights were anything to look forward to. Damn, Leone thought, it was always the same old routine to look forward to. Kate would have his meal ready for him and even a bath would be waiting, but again he would be alone in that house and again the night would be long and empty. Even the day as bad as it had been, was far better than what faced him now. The long lonely night, in the shell of what had once been a home.

Leone had found that his days could be filled with work, but no amount of brandy could help the nights. His gaze again ran to the house, where he could see Kate anxiously awaiting him. It was unusual for her to be standing there like that. He knew something had to be very urgent, he only hoped that it was good news and not bad.

He reined his big black stallion to a stop and before Leone could dismount, a young boy appeared from nowhere to take hold of the animal. "You make sure that he's rubbed down good, boy, and see to it he gets extra oats." Without a word, just a nod of his head, the boy headed off in the direction of the stables. With three strides Leone was standing in front of Kate and simply stated. "If it's good news you have, let me hear it first. If it's bad, you best get my brandy and then I will listen."

"Oh, Master Leone it ain't…isn't bad news at all. No Sur, Lease wise, nothing dat you can't solve and it might even turn out to be good news and all. You best sits down, cause it's a going to take a spell to tell it."

Leone could see that Kate was a bundle of nerves and whatever it was she had to tell him, had her really worked up. He walked to the verandah and without looking at her took a seat. "Come now Kate, you can tell me anything, you do anyway," he chuckled.

His smile and his good nature did not fool Kate for one moment. She knew him to be fair, but he was also firm. If he found out she was lying… friendship or not, he would never stand for it and she dreaded to think what the outcome might be. "Master Leone it's like I done tol you, it ain't bad. This morning after you's left, a young lady done showed up here. She ain't from around these parts and she was a real mess, yes em, that she was. Seems that she was riding and her horse, it must have thrown her and all. Well, she got herself some nasty bruises, hits her head pretty bad. Seem's the only thing she members is her name and bits and pieces but nothing else. I done took it on myself to help her. To do what I'd know'd you would do. The hospitality of this here plantation has always been offered to all who needs it. So I well, she's upstairs in the guest room, resting. That be da one on the west wing. Anyways she be resting there. She ain't hurt bad like, just needed to rest some that's all."

Leone had listened and watched Kate closely as she had told her news. It all sounded innocent enough but Kate only reverted to slave-like dialect when she was upset or nervous about something. There was definitely something more to this tale and he would wait it out and see for himself just what it was. "Well, seems as if your day was a lot more interesting than mine. You say she does not know much other than her name? You did send out one of the boys to see if anyone else was hurt or looking for her I suppose?"

Kate had not expected this question and at first she was flustered. "No sur. I figured that if'n anyone was looking for her they's come here and ask. She didn't have no horse. Seems like he must have run off. She fell down by the lake. And I know'd your rule about anyone going there. Well, I didn't send no one out a looking."

Leone was intrigued not only by her story but by Kate's obvious agitation. This might not be a boring evening after all. Kate was definitely not herself for some reason or another and she seemed to be hiding something. "You have anything else to tell me Kate?"

Kate's nerves were calming a little, but Lord it had been hard lying to him at first. Once she had started though, she found it surprising how easy it was. The bit about her falling at the lake had been smart. Yes em it had but she must remember to clue Tori in on that. "No sur, there ain't nothing other than I made a few decisions on her clothing."

"Her clothing, what about it? She walked in here without any I suppose?" He was laughing now and was thoroughly enjoying himself. Had he guessed how close to the truth he had come, he would not have found it so amusing.

"No sur but da fall did make a mess of what she had. It plumb ruined her clothes. So I fetched a dress for her and let's her have it. One of the Mistress's old dresses. I know'd you told me to get rid of them but I just couldn't seem to get around to it and a good thing too, it seems."

My, things were getting better by the minute, far from the quiet evening he had envisioned. This latest bit of information could explain what had her so upset. He had told her to get rid of all his wife's things. Obviously she had disobeyed him, something he was unaccustomed to. "I won't discuss that with you right now. What I will do is go to the study, pour myself a brandy and meet this mystery lady. Kate, so far I don't see any reason for you to be so nervous and upset. You have done everything I would have if I had been here. Now you go and bring her down to the study and we will get to the bottom of this." With that he rose and walked down the verandah disappearing into his study. What Kate could not see as he left, was the smile on his face. Had she seen it, she would have been less worried. As it was, she had to reach Tori and tell her all that had happened so far, before she presented her to Leone...

The guest room that Tori found herself in was large and very well furnished. The French doors opened onto the balcony that overlooked the front gardens. A view of the river and the land around was hers to enjoy but that was the last thing she had on her mind at the moment. What was taking Kate so long? It seemed to her that she should have heard something by now. Pacing up and down was doing nothing but making her hot and very short-tempered. "God, how I could use a drink and a cigarette, and some light would be welcome," she told herself out loud. She realized that she must be really strung out to ever think of smoking again. It had been hell to stop and the best thing she had ever done. All in all though, she new she would still kill for one if it was available. Had they even invented cigarettes she wondered?

With the sun well below the horizon, the room was growing dark and just a little eerie. The shadows on the wall of the room grew larger each minute, and the whole world seemed so still and quiet. Only her voice broke the silence and that did not help her any. It just made her feel more lonely and lost. It was too hot to lie down on the bed, and the over-stuffed chair that sat in the corner did not appeal to her either.

Just about the time she had decided to go and see what was happening, the door opened and Kate all but ran into the room. "He wants to meet you. Tori I just don't know if he believes me or not. Look at you, just what have you been doing up here? You look's a mess, let's tidy you up some. Quick, let me help while I tell you what happened. You just listen cause it be up to you now. Lordy be. I done forgot to tell him about you being different, the color and all. What's we a going to do now?"

The first brandy went down so fast, that Leone decided he had best wait until he met this woman whoever she was, before pouring himself another. But he needed something to do while he waited for Kate to bring their guest. Walking over to his desk, Leone passed by the painting of his late wife. The memories of how things had been just a short time ago came to mind. There had always been laughter and people, yes, many people filling the rooms of their home. They always had guests to entertain, guests who filled their lives and often came to stay for long periods. They would enjoy the parties and long lazy summer days together.

It might be nice to have a guest he mused. It would be interesting if nothing else.

Reaching for a cigar and another brandy, Leone sat down behind his desk and waited for the knock announcing the meeting. He did not have to wait long before Kate's knock and entry, followed closely behind by quite a dark-skinned woman.

He hardly heard Kate as she introduced Tori, his shock over the fact that Kate had not told him that their guest was of mixed blood had thrown him. How Kate could allow this person into his home as a guest, let alone allow her to wear one of his wife's dresses, was beyond him. No wonder Kate had been acting strange. It was on the tip of his tongue to ask her just what in the hell was the meaning behind all of this, when he was cut short by Tori herself.

Tori walked from behind Kate, right up to Leone's desk. Holding out her hand, she spoke to him as any well bred Southern lady would, only her accent was not from the South. To him it sounded more like that of his dear wife, God rest her soul. Sounded like, he told himself, but not quite like it.

"How do you do Monsieur Duval. It is indeed a pleasure to meet with the owner of such a hospitable home as this. I want to thank you very much for all your help. I know I've put you to a lot of trouble, by my being here. I can assure you that I would not invade your home if circumstances were any different. I would fully understand sir, if you want me to vacate the premises but I ask that you would extend your hospitality for one night. I do indeed have nowhere else to go, as Kate must have explained to you, I'm sure."

Leone stood, quickly covering his shock. He walked around his desk and took hold of Tori's hand. He looked somewhat amused, if not pleased, as he spoke to her in a soft tone. "It is my pleasure I'm sure and the hospitality Madame is Southern and no Southern home would turn a lady out in the night, with nowhere to go, now would it?"

Tori liked Leone immediately. She felt very comfortable with him. He was just as Kate had told her, a true gentleman. Still she had to be very careful, not to reveal anything to him that would put Kate or her in jeopardy.

Leone's eyes had not left hers. Gone was the initial anger, left behind was an excitement, stirring emotions of younger years. She was standing there looking back at him, staring right into his eyes. No lady he knew of would act in such a manner, not even one from up North. The room was deathly quiet, the moment uncomfortable. He had to do something to break the spell along with the awkward situation.

"You may see to it the lamps are lit and bring something cool to drink for our guest and Kate set another place at the dining table. I hope it will be my pleasure to be joined by this charming lady."

Tori smiled and accepted, much to the dismay of Kate who had told her to complain of fatigue and ask to be allowed to retire for the night. Just what was she up to and what was she going to do? Kate did as she had been instructed and left hoping that Tori knew what she was getting herself into. Tori on the other hand had not stopped to think, she was just enjoying the company and the experience was a great opportunity to learn more about this lifestyle. She would have so much to tell when she got back! Her head was filling with all sorts of things when she realized what Leone was doing. He was pouring another brandy and automatically without thinking Tori asked him if she could join him. "It's been a very upsetting day and I could use a drink to calm my nerves and please, call me Tori. I hate being so formal it makes me feel uncomfortable."

My, this was a strange woman but amusing to say the least. He himself could not recall ever hearing or seeing a lady ask for a brandy. Wines and champagne yes, but brandy? He supposed there could be some who did, maybe... Leone poured her the drink and handing it to her, watched as she took a sip.

"This is excellent brandy Monsieur. I compliment you on your taste."

"You drink a lot of brandy madam?"

"Well no, just after a good meal sometimes."

"You can remember that fact. What else do you remember about your life?"

Tori realized her mistake right away. Damn, she would have to smooth talk her way out of this one and fast she thought. "It would seem so Monsieur. The fact that I enjoy brandy, not that I clearly remember much else. My memory seems to come in flashes, small bits and pieces. Nothing that makes much sense I'm afraid. I just saw you pouring and it made me remember. Can you forgive me Monsieur Duval?"

"Please call me Leone. It might make it easier for you." He was smiling at her as if he were enjoying this, making her squirm. "And I can assure you there is nothing to forgive, is there?"

"As I was saying, I seem to remember bits and pieces. Nothing much as to who I am, or where I'm from. I don't even remember where I was going." Tori forced herself to put tears in her eyes and to act very upset. Little did she know that if there was one thing that Leone could not cope with, it was a woman in distress. Seeing that he had upset her, Leone rushed to make amends.

"Please, you must excuse me. It was very callous of me, of course it must be very upsetting for you. Were you badly hurt in the fall?"

"No, other than hitting my head, which Kate thinks has caused me the loss of memory. I seem only to have a few bruises, as you can see."

Leone could very well see for himself that she had suffered injuries. Her beautiful face was still swollen on one side. Her one eye was blackened but there seemed to be nothing that wouldn't in time heal, leaving no scars. He could well imagine how she would look once healed. What in the hell was wrong with him, what was he thinking? "Well, let me assure you, that you may stay here at my home until we can locate your family or whoever. I will do everything to help you that I can. You just put yourself at ease my dear. I think under the circumstances, that it best if you rest up before dinner. You do still feel up to joining me don't you?" This afterthought came with dismay when he realized that he had just given her an opportunity to avoid the evening meal with him.

"Oh yes Leone, I would be delighted to join you. But maybe you are right, a short rest would be nice."

Leone called for Kate and told her to show Tori to her room, after which he wanted to speak with her. Left alone for a few minutes, Leone had time to collect himself and to think. This had been nothing like he had expected. In fact he found the whole situation rather stimulating. This Tori whoever she was, had set his heart pounding. He had to find out more about her. He needed to know, no, wanted to know all that there was. A soft knock at the door interrupted this train of thought. The one person who could help, entered the room.

"Kate, this Tori is indeed a mystery I might add, a very charming one, not to mention unusual. Just what do you think of her?"

"Master Leone, I not sure what it is you want to know."

"Damn it Kate you have been with her the better part of the day, did she say anything or do anything to give you a clue as to who she is or where she's from?"

"No sur."

"Well she is obviously educated and not from around here. I thought maybe for a while by her accent, she would be from up North." He rubbed his brow trying to remember his time up there. "The accent is not of any that I recall from up North. Oh hell Kate, I guess what I'm getting at is, this Tori is she somehow white or is she of mixed blood?" Leone could not believe what he had just asked. True, he was not sure himself. Even if all the signs pointed obviously one way, she was just so stunning, so different, he hoped that somehow she could... but what was he thinking of?

Kate had her chance now to tell him that she was indeed white, but how would she explain the color of her skin and all her crinkly hair. Tori could not explain that to him. Telling him she was from another country might have worked with someone else, yes em it might. But not him, no sur, Master Leone had traveled to many other countries as a young man. And to try and explain she was from another time now, when she should have told him right off. Oh dear, what was she to do she wondered? Then Kate made up her mind. She was going to have to lie again to cover herself.

Leone could see the look on Kate's face. He felt as if he should explain his question to her. Not that he had to, all he had to do was ask, she had to answer him. It was because of their unusual relationship that he felt so. "It's just that she is so, shall we say, white. No sign of any black in her face, her manners and speech, the way she holds herself, they are the actions of a lady of class are they not? It's her color and that hair, well what do you say, Kate?"

"Yes em, she seems to be of mixed blood as far as I kin see. You knows it can happen, that the blood turns up without any warning."

"Yes, I suppose you're right. Damn shame though. How am I going to ask her to leave, after I got carried away and offered my hospitality for as long as she needed? I don't want to offend her but I can't, in my position, have a Nigger as a house guest can I?'

This hurt Kate, when Leone acted the way he was expected, not how he really wanted. She knew him to be a caring person, one who would always try and help others. Right now however, he was acting like all the other whites. Tori was a Nigger in his eyes and she would have to go. It was too late now to go back and say that she was white, to admit that she had lied. He would never listen to her anyway, but it was not too late to change his mind. "Master Leone, you don't have to make her leave or put yourself in any position like. Don't a lot of your fine gentlemen friends, I mean you knows it is common knowledge, have them their fancies in New Orleans."

"Are you suggesting that I keep her in a house in New Orleans?"

"No sur! I don't mean that! Can't you tell anyone if they should find out that she is here, that she is staying here with you as your mistress. Tori don't have to know none about it. No one does. We's don't have many peoples stopping by now days. The cane need tending, people too busy to come anyway's. This way she could stay a few days and if'n someone did come by, that's something you could say. It would be proper then, yes?" Kate was willing to try anything at this point to keep Tori in the house. She knew it would not be proper by any stretch of the imagination, but she could try, couldn't she?

"Kate you might have something there but I won't lie. Can't stand lying. No, I will tell the truth as I see it. After all she could indeed be someone's mistress. I doubt it though. I think that I will tell anyone who may ask that she is staying here until her background can be found out. I will tell them that I am doing this for a friend. After all you are my friend and I'm doing it for you?" He took a long slow sip of his drink as he wondered. What if they could not find out who she was or where she was from? And just who was he doing this for, Kate or himself? These questions crossed his mind but he quickly put them aside.

Kate came into Tori's room, carrying with her a long gown of soft pink satin with velvet ribbons of fuchsia interlaced on the bodice and sleeves. In her other hand she saw small satin slippers the same color of the gown.

"I think if we spend this time getting you ready for dinner, the time will pass faster for you and give us more chance to talk without becoming too suspicious. I had to tell him you be black." Kate saw Tori's adverse reaction and held up her hand to silence her response. "Now don't go getting upset none. It was the only way. It will work out just listen."

"Kate how could you? What were you thinking of? I'm not black and we can prove that to him. We have my contacts right here." She was angry and desperate at the same time. No way did she want Leone to think of her as black.

"Miss Tori we can't show him those things. He would want to know what they was, them looking all funny and crumpled like. Sure they different but how you ever going to explain what they was and where they came from. We done talked on this and all. You agreed to listen to what this old fool knowd best, member?" Kate was just as upset as Tori. "Lord it be true" she muttered to herself, "the more one lies the harder it gets to get out of it, to not get caught. What is done is done, what we has to do is figure how not to get ourselves in a bigger mess. We had best get things right from now on."

The two talked while Kate helped Tori dress, something Tori was glad of as she could never have laced herself up and maneuvered into the swirls of material. Kate even pulled back her hair, fixing it in a way as to make it appear longer than it was. She gathered the tight curls in the back and held it all together with a mother of pearl comb. Fresh flowers added the final touch and when Tori stood before the mirror she could hardly believe the improvement. "Why Kate it's lovely, I feel like a Southern Belle." She stroked the satin skirt with her hands, "the gown is beautiful, a little tight maybe, in the top." She pulled at the low neckline trying to make an adjustment. "The way you have me laced in and pushed up, I'm afraid that I'll pop out if I take a deep breath," she laughed.

Kate rolled her eyes at this statement. "You be just fine if'n you leave it alone." She slapped Tori's hands away from the dress.

Tori turned slowly in front of the mirror. "You've worked wonders with my hair. My face though, and my arms, the bruises are so ugly."

"Nothing but time a gonna fix that. Yes um, but even with them black and blues, the truth is you are pretty as any lady I have seen."

Tori hugged Kate again. She was really grateful for all that the woman had done for her but she did wish there had been some way they could have told Leone the truth. She reluctantly realized Kate was right. Had Leone been told the truth and known she was from the future, he never would have let them near the lake out of fear of losing Kate. She had to lie, and now Tori would have to live with it.

Leone was heading for the dining room when he caught sight of Tori coming down the stairs. She was beautiful there was no doubt, standing there looking at him, the soft light of the oil lamps illuminating her whole face. The color of her skin did not seem to matter at that moment. She was a woman and a stunning one at that. Her hair had been pulled back making her face look somehow younger. She stood like a goddess, and never did her eyes leave his. Women of the South were always pretending to be shy and lowering their gaze. Not this woman however. She seemed to enjoy the effect she was having on him and watched him as he openly appraised her.

Being well endowed had only enhanced the cut of the gown and her figure. Tori's breasts were pushed up by the tight-fitting corset. But unlike the gown she had worn earlier, this one was low cut. Low enough that with every breath she took, one would think she was about to spill over the top. Her waist, small to begin with, was cut in by the tight fit of the garments. The fullness of the gown sweeping to the floor only made her look as if she had the hour-glass figure men only dream of seeing on a woman.

It was Leone who in the end looked away. He was stunned by her beauty and had to remind himself that she was black. Tori slowly continued down the stairs toward him, stopping at the bottom. He turned his eyes back toward her as she stood before him. She was looking up into his face, her dark eyes flashing, her skin smooth and golden, marred only from her fall. He felt as if she would take his breath away. The sound of her voice broke into his thoughts.

"I do hope I have not offended you by wearing this gown. Kate seemed to think it was all right, as I have no clothes of my own. If it upsets you too much, I will return to my room and change."

"On the contrary madam, you are a sight to behold. It would be my pleasure to have you join me as you are, for dinner. It has been a long time since I had such a charming and beautiful guest." Leone meant it and he found himself walking forward offering her his arm to escort Tori to dinner. He could not comprehend what had come over him. Why did his heart quicken as she took his arm? He would have to be very careful with his emotions. Had he been without a woman for too long he asked himself? That had to be the answer. As they walked toward the dining room it briefly flashed through his mind that he was supposed to be a grieving widower. But looking at her, he told himself maybe it was time to move on.

Up on the stairs watching the two, Kate smiled to herself and nodded her head. She knew that Tori would be staying. Leone could never turn away a pretty face. And to Kate it was obvious he was already taken by her beauty. Now all she had to do was wait until she could get Tori to the lake and that would not be long. No sur, with the cane needing to be cut soon and the busiest time of the year a coming up, Leone would be gone long hours, leaving them the perfect opportunity to make their move.

The dinner was wonderful and Tori was amazed by the amount, along with the variety of food that was served. It occurred to her, that she would have to see just how all of the dishes were cooked before leaving. She did not remember seeing an oven in the kitchen. That meant there had to be a cook house nearby. She had learned about the removed kitchen while she and Linni took the Oak Alley tour. Her daughter's sad face flashed briefly in her mind but Tori would not allow herself to take it further or to get upset. She couldn't do anything about it right now she told herself. She had to concentrate on something to take her mind off her daughter. She looked at the table. Tori could not imagine that Leone ate like this every night. There were dishes of rice and potatoes, salads and meats, fruits and rolls. Each dish set her head spinning. It seemed impossible to her, that such a layout of food could be presented as it was. Even the table settings were truly extravagant. In her own time, she had only seen such settings in first class restaurants.

The candles set a soft glow in the room, allowing her to see rainbows in the crystal glasses. The silver shone like new and the room was filled with the scent of gardenias that were floating in a bowl set at the center of the table. The only item she would have removed was the glass fly catcher. Like a large vase turned upside down, sitting in its own glass dish, it asked to be ignored. For already five large flies had found their way into the death trap and while one floated lifeless in the liquid, the others still struggled to find a way out. Tori decided to look away and put the ugly thing out of her mind.

She was well aware that Leone was staring at her far too much, but it seemed harmless enough. Their conversation was light and easy, indeed he seemed to be avoiding anything that might upset her and this made it simple for her. All through the meal Tori's glass was kept full of the best wine. The liquid slipped down so smoothly, leaving a warm glow that radiated from within, causing her cheeks to blush slightly. Her tongue began to feel thick when she spoke, and realizing just in time that she was becoming intoxicated, she excused herself for the evening. Tori had been afraid of slipping up, of saying something that she should not, so she feigned a headache and departed, leaving Leone with his thoughts.

Alone, Leone found himself hoping that Tori's stay would be more than just a few days. He had enjoyed her company so much, that he made his mind up to spend the next day at the house instead of out in the cane fields. It had been so long since he had enjoyed the presence of such a ravishing creature. Not only was she a mystery, she was refreshingly different from most other women who stopped by, or were introduced to him. Most of those had one thing on their minds, and that was how to snare him into a marriage. Chuckling to himself at the last thought, Leone sent for the stable boy and gave him a verbal message for Jack, then settled back for one last glass of wine before he himself retired for the evening.

Tori, with Kate's help, prepared for bed, even though she was sure sleep would avoid her. However, once she lay on the big soft mattress with the sound of the Southern countryside creeping in the open windows, it was not hard for her to relax. This along with the soft singing from the slave quarters carried on the evening breeze, soon lulled her into a blissful sleep...

Not far from this peaceful house was a far different scene. Sounds of a young girl's screams filled the air, sounds that would have turned Tori's blood cold.

Jack had received the message, along with a little bit of information that he had plied from the boy. It did not take him long to realize that their house guest was none other than the wench that had gotten away from him. He started drinking in his anger of not having had his way with the bitch before losing her. Then his wild imagination started taking over. Fear briefly gripped him. "She must have had a chance to tell the boss man what I done to her, bet she lied some too," he said out loud. Then thinking some on what he had just said, Jack realized that could not be. She had not told him he was sure of that. He was still here wasn't he? He had not been sent for had he? But why had she not told? He had to find out. Jack decided he would play her little game. One thing was certain though and that was he would have her yet.

Then he asked himself once again the one question that bothered him most. Just how in the hell had she escaped the cabin? How had she managed to get away? Those knots he tied were good ones. She must have had help and there was only one other person who knew she was there. Jack's temper began to simmer, and like a crazed man he headed down to the slave quarters, ordering Missy back up to his cabin. To all who saw him, he seemed like the same old Massa Kane, nothing wrong with him wanting Missy at his place.

Missy was so happy to see him, to know he wanted her back again, that she failed to see his cruel and calculating stare. His look was one that had she seen it, would have shattered her joy at once and replaced it with pure fear.

He would show the little black bitch what for. She caused him to lose the one chance he had at bedding a good looking piece of flesh and making some good money. Hell, he would teach her a lesson...

A few hours later Missy lay on the cabin floor, where Jack's whip had brutally taken her young life. Jack sat exhausted and breathing heavily, staring at the body. His face was covered with perspiration and splatters of blood. His bare arms also crimson splattered, were covered with flecks of the girl's skin. He had beaten the truth out of her, but instead of stopping, he had lost control. How many times he had hit her with his fists and the whip, which now lay heavy and blood-soaked in his hand, he did not know?

Sitting there in a daze, looking at his victim, a cruel smile crossed his lips at the recollection of the way she had begged him to stop. He had felt exhilarated as he dealt each blow, toying with her at first, then really hurting her, really beating at her naked flesh. He looked at her lying there, blood oozing from the open gashes, some so severe that he could see bone. He felt no remorse for what he had done. Hell, she had asked for it. He only wished he had taken more time. Her terrified screams still echoed in his head, the pleading, the whimpering, then ...as now, silence. It was this last state that aroused him, that caused him to sit up, and for a few minutes to panic. He had a dead slave before him, only one that was beaten very badly. Now how was he going to explain that?

Morning came and Tori woke slowly at first. Opening her eyes, she looked around the strange room for a few minutes trying to gain her whereabouts calmly, then in a flash it all came back to her. The sound of Kate mumbling to herself as she entered the room made Tori sit up in bed. "You look as if you are mad at the world Kate. Don't tell me I've done something wrong?"

"No child, it ain't you any. I'm mad that be the truth. Here drink yourself some of my coffee. I done brought you some breakfast. Not much, just some biscuits and jams. Master Leone, he said you should sleep in and rest, and not get up for breakfast.

"What time is it? It can't be that late."

"Well I don't know what late is to you but breakfast was hours ago. It's almost time for lunch. Now you eat that and I'll git you a bath filled and something to wear."

"Kate, you still haven't told me what has you so mad. Does my sleeping late have you this upset?"

Kate sat down on the end of the bed, her voice shaking. "You going to hear about it anyways, so I might as well be the one to tell you. That overseer, that debal of a man, he was here early this morning and asked to see da master. I don't trusts him none, so I stand outside the door while he meets with Master Leone. All the time I think he's here because of you. That he was going to say something, but what he says is worse and I know's it to be a lie. Bad thing is, I can't do nothing or say nothing, cause it ain't my place and even if I did, it's his white word against mine. You know whose side Master Leone going to have to take? Then that massa Kane, he be more cruel to my people's, they would pay." Kate was crying now, not hard, no noise, just large tears rolling down her face. She dabbed at them with the corner of her apron.

Tori did not speak as she sat in the big bed looking at Kate, not knowing what to do, or what she was going to say next. She had no idea what Kate was even getting at.

Kate continued, "You see that overseer, he done told that last night he found our Missy a running and he had to set an example and all, said she tried to run even after he caught her. He whipped her. Now she's dead! Dead at such a young age. I tried to tell that girl that Jack is the debal. He's evil that one. She just wouldn't listen. No sur, now look, she be dead and buried."

Tori was horrified, how could this be? Leone did not seem like the type of man to have such a punishment for such a crime. "But surely death is not the punishment for running? Kate, I can't believe that Leone would allow this? He does not seem to be that type of man."

"Oh, Lordy be no! Death is not the punishment on this plantation for running. We neber had no one run till that overseer came. He be real smart he be. Said he gave her the twenty lashes that he would have given any other slave but that she must have been sick or weak, cause he said she died and he was real sorry. Said he had to do it cause if'n he didn't, we would have more a running. Leone is going to listen to him cause that's the way, and because he thinks this here overseer be telling the truth, he be right. Just thank the Lord you found your way here before you ended up like our Missy."

Crying, Tori shook her head. Deep down she felt that somehow Missy's death was her fault. Missy had helped her. Jack must have found out how she got away, and must have killed Missy because of it. "One thing troubles me Kate. He must know I'm here, that Missy helped me, but why has he not said anything to Leone about me? He could blow the whole story we made up. What's he up to?"

Kate just shook her head from side to side. She had no answer for her.

This Jack frightened Tori and it made her all the more determined to get back to the lake. She had to get away from this mad world. Away from that madman and back to the safety of her time and into the small arms of her daughter.

"Ain't got no time to worry about that evil man. Can't worry none over Missy, she be with the Lord now. What I has to worry about is you and today." Kate got up and started laying out the clothes that she had found for Tori to wear.

Thinking she was referring to the escape plan Tori asked her, "What time are we going to the lake Kate?"

Kate turned her back on Tori. She could not answer her. What could she say? Tori looked at the dress on the end of the bed and then back at Kate who still stayed turned away from her.

"Don't you think that dress is a little too much for me to go walking in?"

Kate did not look up at Tori when she answered her, she was unsure as to how the girl would react to the news. "There will be no trip to the lake today, Mizz Tori. The Master has decided to stay home today. I think he wants to question you more. We can't go until we know'd he and that Jack are out in the South fields a cutting cane." Kate rushed on before Tori could talk. "You don't want's to get caught by that evil overseer do you?"

"No I don't, but Kate I don't want to wait forever. My family must be so upset as it is." Her disappointment was written all over her face. She knew Kate was right but that did not seem to help any.

"I know'd child, still we have no choice but to wait. Now come with me and I will show you where the bath is. We's best a be taking your mind off these bad things. You got plenty other thoughts to fill that head of yours. Dry them eyes and follow me." With that she left the bedroom with Tori following close behind.

Tori did not ask any questions or try to talk as they made their way down the large hallway. In looking around her as they walked, Tori was truly amazed at the fact that the upstairs was so large but even more surprising, was when she found herself in a bathroom.

"I thought that these weren't invented for years. Kate look! A huge bath. My God, it's marble'" Kate could see that this was a joy for Tori and that for the moment her worries were put aside.

"It was put here for the Mistress. She liked to take cool baths in the heat, and over there is the wash basin with clean water to rinse off your hair." Kate wrinkled her nose. "Neber smelled hair like yours."

"That's the color I put in it I told you about, but don't worry, it goes away." Tori was looking around for something as she spoke to Kate, "The one thing I need right now and don't see however, is the flush toilet. I'm sure it has not been invented yet has it?" She saw Kate's strange expression and had to laugh. No, all kidding aside, I'll explain a flush toilet to you later but right now I do need to relieve myself. I mean do I have to go outside and down the back somewhere?" She laughed.

Kate looked horrified. "Lordy be child no! You be a lady. Only the help go outside and down the back as you say. You just use that pot over there." She pointed. "It be in that cupboard. It's just like the one I showed you yesterday in your room, the same one that I put under your bed last night."

"Oh, thanks Kate. I don't think I could have held it a minute longer." Kate turned her back and busied herself by putting scents into the bath water. Tori hurried about her business while continuing to talk to her. "I wish you had told me about that pot being under the bed last night though. All yesterday it had been out where I could find it when I needed it. When I could not find it last night... never thought to look under the bed. Stupid me, I went downstairs and outside. That's not an easy thing to do in the dark. I was frightened to death someone would see me. Thank God those bushes are close to the house." The two of them laughed hysterically at this, while realizing that they did indeed have much to learn about each other.

Kate was all laughed out, her sides hurting from the experience. "Neber thought to have to tell you something like that. Most folks in this here time, they knowd the pot is under the bed. Where'd it be in your time, out the back?" She started chuckling.

"Oh Kate, really!" I guess it's time for lesson flush toilet. You might as well stay while I bathe and I'll try to explain it to you…"

It was noon when Tori came down the stairs. Unlike her dress of the night before, this one was made of cotton and had a high collar and long sleeves. However, what had seemed so feminine and grand at first, rapidly became uncomfortable and with its petticoats darned warm. She was about to turn around and head back to her room to remove them, when a voice stopped her.

"It seems that I am doomed to see you, always a vision of beauty, descending the staircase. Please come and join me. I have been waiting for you."

Tori smiled as she answered him. "I do hope I have not detained you."

"On the contrary Madame, let me assure you that I'm here awaiting only the pleasure of your company. If there is anything you would rather do, rest or remain in your room, I will of course understand? I do hope though, that you will excuse my presumption that you would like to go out. I have taken the liberty of having a light meal packed and my carriage awaits us."

"You may indeed," she beamed.

"Last night you showed such interest in the plantation and the running of it. Shall we say I have planned a short inspection of my land. I thought also that a ride might help you with your memory."

"Oh Leone, that would be lovely if you could just give me a minute to change."

"Change Madame? But you look so beautiful, as I said before. Not a prettier lady is there to be found. I am truly honored that you will accompany me."

"Leone you are a flatterer but I simply cannot go out in this dress, it's just too darn uncomfortable. And one more thing please, try to call me Tori, I'm not used to Madame."

She was gone from sight in a flash and Leone found that he had knots in his stomach once again. She was so different, so bold, yet such a lady at the same time. He was glad he had the idea to take her out. Maybe he could get her to talk about herself, or see if she could recall anything about what had happened to her. Either way it was bound to be a very interesting afternoon.

Tori had been impressed by what little she had seen of the inside of the house. Should it survive the ravages of time, there was no way in her opinion, that they would ever be able to restore it to this grandeur. The bedroom was wonderful and that bathroom, with the tile and inlaid marble. Tori had never dreamed that a house of this time could be anything close to this spectacular. The dining room last night, with its soft lights glowing from the chandelier, had made everything look so elegant. The mirrors on the walls opposite the windows had made the room look twice its size. Then the length of the table, what was it he had said? Twenty people had dined at it.

The food had been wonderful also. Tori had never thought that food could be that good without the modern ovens and conveniences. One meat would have been plenty but there had been two to choose from and fish if she wanted. Tonight Kate has said they were in for a treat, that the hunter had caught some game. She could see how they could make a whole evening eating and drinking. The china, the crystal, how was it possible to have so much in this time period? Her conclusion was that this must be a very wealthy plantation and she was fortunate to have this opportunity to view it.

Now, however, it was time to view the place from a different perspective and nothing would stop her from seeing it.

It took her only a minute to take the petticoats off and leave them on the floor. Kate might not like it but she had no choice in the matter, after all Tori thought, she didn't see Kate wearing them. It had only been a short time that she was gone but when Tori came back to the stairs, Leone was nowhere to be seen. She began talking to herself to help calm her nerves as she descended. "He must be in his study waiting for me. I'll just go and see. Now which room is it?" There weren't that many doors to choose from once she was down. The first she knew from the night before was the dining room. One quick look wouldn't hurt she told herself. "It isn't as if I'm prying, or such. I just want to see it for historical sake," she whispered. Tori slowly pushed open the heavy wooded doors, and looked inside. It was as grand as she remembered. As soon as she pushed the door open, the true size of the room hit her. The mirrors on the walls helped reflect the light and the doors to the verandah were all open, letting in a slight breeze. The table shone like new, it's wood almost red in color and the chairs were all upholstered in the same material that hung at the windows. Over toward the end, there was a large piece of matching furniture that looked somewhat like a large dry sink. Tori noticed the floors were of wood that also shone, and it occurred to her that she would hate to have to dust this room every day. Slowly she closed the door and headed for the next.

Knocking lightly, she entered and found it was the room she was looking for, but Leone was nowhere in sight. The room itself was of good size lined with many shelves of books. There were two overstuffed chairs sitting opposite a large fireplace and the desk that Leone had been sitting at when she first met him, was at the other end in front of the open doors. This room had carpet on the floor, thick and deep, in a rust color. She noticed a table that had bottles on it and a container of cigars. Funny but she seemed to remember the brandy bottle as half-empty, not full. "Oh the help is good. Like a five star hotel," she mumbled.

Her eyes fell on the box of cigars. "Such a shame cigarettes have not been invented," she whispered. I just might have to try one of those things, she thought. God, she could see their faces if she got caught. This made her smile. It would be just like one of those ads that used to show the lady being caught smoking, it made her shudder. "No, maybe not, after all I did give smoking up," she told herself firmly. Then looking around at the vacant room one last time, she tried to decide what to do. Quickly she made up her mind to keep looking, using it as an excuse of sorts. After all, she really did want to see the rest of the house. She didn't know if the people of this time gave tours of their homes or not and she hated to ask. The last door led into what she assumed to be the parlor, larger than the study and a lot warmer in looks. She could tell a woman's touch had been there. It was beautiful, cozy and inviting.

"Looking for me I hope?" Turning she saw Leone standing by his study door.

Embarrassed at the fact that she had been found snooping, Tori blushed slightly. "Forgive me but I was trying to find you. You weren't in your study a second ago I looked."

"You should have come out on the verandah. I was out there. I heard the door closing, and thought it might be you. Are you ready?"

Yes, Leone, quite ready thank you."

"Then madam, I mean Tori, shall we?"

The carriage was waiting for them in the front drive. Leone gave a few more instructions to Kate, then he told her where they were going so he could be reached if needed.

Tori did not want to look at Kate. She knew the woman would be upset with her for removing the petticoats, let alone going off with Leone for the afternoon.

"You be careful now Mizz Tori. Here, I have a hat for you to keep the sun off. It gets mighty hot and we don't need you getting sick on us."

"That's all right Kate, I'm used to the sun. I never have liked wearing hats." She looked at the black woman and gave her a wink. "I'll be just fine you'll see. I'm sure I'm in good hands." With that she turned and took Leone's hand as he helped her up into the carriage. Then Leone took a large wicker basket from Kate's hands, placing it in the back. He was looking so pleased with himself, almost like a young man out on his first date. Turning to face Kate after handling the basket, he asked in a joking manner, "I did say a light meal didn't I Kate?"

"Yes um, that's what it is, the weight might be from a bottle of wine that I took the liberty of putting in, as Mizz Tori seems to enjoy it so." Now it was Kate's turn to smile at Tori. She mumbled something to Leone before departing, some excuse of having a lot of work to do.

Leone climbed in next to Tori. The black man who was called Jobe took the reins. "Where's we be going to Massa?"

"That my friend is up to our guest, what would you like to see? The river road, or maybe the fields to the North?"

"I would love to see some of your plantation, where the workers are. That is if it's all right with you? But not too close, from a distance would be just fine."

"The cane fields to the North then. Though I must say not many woman care to see that side of plantation life."

They started out and Tori found she wished she had a camera to capture the view. Turning around as they left, she could see how magnificent the house was. They left the front driveway and headed out toward the back of the property and the slave quarters.

Leone was pointing and talking as they went. "Not many of the workers are here right now. Most are out in the fields where we are going." Those slaves that did remain in the quarters were working in small garden plots. Tori was fascinated.

"I had no idea that they had their own vegetable gardens, and chickens. Are they yours or do they belong to the slaves?"

"No, they're not mine. They bought the chickens from me."

"Bought, I thought slaves had no money?"

He smiled down at her. She had seemed so surprised by his answer.

"Well if they work for me on Sundays or on holidays I pay them a small amount. It is in the Code Noir, the black book."

"This Code Noir, what is that?"

"That my dear, is a book of laws that a slave owner like myself is supposed to follow. It states that the slaves are to be fed and clothed, that their days off are Sundays and holidays such as Christmas, and so forth. Unfortunately not all slave owners follow it. I however have found that they work better for me if I treat them fair."

"I had no idea anything such as that existed." She fell silent for a short time, thinking about what he had just said. Tori was surprised at the friendliness of the people. Some of the small children ran to the carriage and waved and danced around as they drove slowly by, their faces happy and not at all afraid. These people did not seem to fit at all what Tori had thought of as part of the slave system. They had all they needed and seemed to enjoy their life. But then these had it better than most she was sure. The children had no shoes, true, but they were not running naked, nor were they starving or dirty. The homes were not much more than shacks put together with what appeared to be leftover lumber. The two larger buildings at the far end seemed to be in far better shape. "What are those Leone, storage sheds of some sort?"

"No, those are the living quarters for the single slaves. Can't have them roaming free around here at night or staying with the families. They tend to be more like animals in their needs, if you will excuse my meaning." He seemed slightly uncomfortable with the discussion but continued. "They would take any woman, if they could." Leone could not believe he had just said what he had, but seeing that it had not embarrassed Tori, he relaxed. It was so good being able to talk to a lady without having to be careful as to what was said. In addition, to find out the lady was truly interested in the working side of his home and not just the comforts, was more than gratifying.

Tori on the other hand was getting just a little upset by Leone's attitude toward his slaves. He thought he was doing the best for his blacks, but in truth they were treated no better than animals with no rights. "But why don't they have families like these here, that we are seeing, I don't understand?"

"Tori, it takes food and money to keep my slaves healthy. It takes a lot more than you could know to feed, clothe them and see to their needs. When they do get together they breed like rabbits and that puts a burden on the plantation. The boys I can justify keeping. They can grow and work in the fields. As for the girls, well I just can't keep them all."

"You mean you sell them?"

"That's the way it has to be Tori. Now don't you go getting yourself upset. They don't seem to mind. That's simply the way it is. Let's move on before this place and these slaves blind you from the true beauty of the plantation." He looked away from her as he thought how very much alike his wife and Tori were. They would have liked each other and agreed on much. Why it seemed their feelings on slavery was identical.

Tori was glad somehow to be traveling on. She did not want to get into a fight with Leone on the evils of slavery. He would most certainly never see her point. It was just as well that she not try to make her position clear, knowing that she might let something slip in anger. She had to be very careful not to do that.

That afternoon Tori found herself lost in sights and sounds, in questions and answers. He answered all of her inquiries and showed her life on his plantation. What she learned in those few hours was more than she ever read in any book or saw in any movie. The day was not as hot as the last few had been. The air was still, but the building clouds hid the sun enough to offer some relief. The spot that Leone picked for the picnic had a view of the North cane fields and the blacks working them. They were singing as they worked. The music was a mixture of African rhythm with something she could not quite put her finger on. Once again it reminded her of Paul Simon's "Graceland." But how could she ask Leone to explain to her about music without getting into her knowledge of things not yet known to him. She decided to stick with subjects closer to home. "What is it that they are doing? I don't seem to see how moving the dirt can help the cane grow?"

"My dear, you are refreshing. Your constant inquiries truly amaze me. Why most women wouldn't even care. They would be more interested about what's in the basket at this point, than what's going on out there. I'll explain to you though, they are strengthening the levy over that way." He pointed toward the riverbank. "I suspect that we are in for some heavy rain soon and the river is not too mindful of where she runs when she is flooding. The levy is there so the water will stay out of the cane fields. Let us hope it works because the cane still has a while to go before it can be cut. The longer it stays in the field the better. Just as long as I time it right and beat the first frost. I have other fields that will need cutting far sooner but this is the area that needs to be watched for now."

"What happens then? When you cut the cane, how does it all get cut down? Oh come on. Do tell me please. I would love to know." She could see the puzzled look on his face, followed by a grin of sorts. So Tori went on trying to convince him she was truly interested." "I would like to know things like how many slaves work to cut it all. There seems to be so much."

"My, such a lot of questions, are you sure you just aren't trying to make me feel good?" His head was to one side and he had that suspicious look again. "You must have talked to Kate and she told you how I love to talk about the land."

"No, no really I just would love to know that's all."

"Well, have a glass of wine and I will try to explain it to you in a short time, so as not to bore you. First off, when the time comes it takes every man, woman and child to help. Over three hundred of them at last count. You were right, there is a lot of cane to cut. We work eighteen-hour days, and the mill goes nonstop day and night."

Leone talked and the hours passed. It was late afternoon before they headed back, something that he did not want to do. He had found someone he could talk to, someone he liked being with. By going back, he was afraid that somehow it would all change, that he would lose her.

The next few days were filled with even more questions, mostly from Tori to Leone about the plantation and his life. Tori continued to explain all her questions away with her amnesia, and how she hoped something would trigger her memory. "It's just like being a child, learning about everything from the beginning," she told him. If Leone found this strange he never said so, in fact he enjoyed her company more and more. She had brought life back into his everyday routine. He adored her company and found her such a refreshing change from his long and lonely days.

Leone began hoping that the inquiries he had sent out about Tori would all come back with no results. He wanted her to stay now more than ever. In just a few short days he had grown so fond of her, that he even began to fantasize what it would be like to make love to her. Leone was falling in love with Tori and did not realize until late on the fifth day when they had a visitor.

The afternoon had been a little cooler and Tori had accompanied Leone around the plantation gardens. True, the place was large but she had no idea that such an area could exist so close to the main house. Questions ran through her mind, like how did they manage to cut such perfect lawns without lawn mowers? Now she couldn't very well ask that could she. Her mind soon left that thought, as they came upon the most beautiful rose garden. A small path ran beside the flower beds, and planted on each side were more flowers than she could name. Leone led her down the stone-filled walkway toward the river. Turning here and there the path led between the largest oaks, draped in Spanish moss, which hung longer than she could ever remember seeing in her life. Then hidden off to one side of these magnificent trees was a gazebo. It sat in the shade of one of the giant oaks looking cool and inviting. Some chairs sat empty next to a small table. This was complete with a pitcher of lemon and small handmade cakes that she had seen Kate making the day before. She had to smile at Leone. He was always so thoughtful and kind, such a dear friend. Never did the thought cross her mind that it was anything more. Walking the grounds with Leone paying so much attention to her, she began to feel like a true lady of these times. "It's so kind of you to show me your home and to let me use all these beautiful clothes. You have been so very kind to me Leone. I'm not sure if I can ever repay all that you have done. Please know that it has meant so much to me and I will never forget you or your home."

"You talk as if you are leaving. Can it be that you are remembering?" His voice sounded anxious even to himself.

"No! No, I don't remember, but if something should happen, if someone should come and get me, or if I should leave without a chance to thank you, I wanted you to know that's all."

"Something is wrong isn't it? I've felt it more the past few days. Even though you seem to be recovering from your fall, the bruises are fading fast, you seem to be preoccupied. Are you not well?"

"I'm fine Leone. I guess I just tire easy that's all. It's the heat, I don't think I'm used to it."

"How rude of me, here I ask you to walk with me, to see the grounds. You will forgive me my dear, won't you?"

Leone had taken both her hands. Looking really concerned, he was blaming himself for something that Tori knew was not his fault at all. Looking at him right then, she almost wanted to tell him the whole story. Instead she stood there silently trying to decide what to do. The next thing she knew, he had taken her in his arms and was kissing her. Shocked, she pulled away from him, turning her back to him so he could not see her.

"Tori please my darling forgive an old fool. You are truly a beauty. Never would I hurt you. Please believe me. It's just that I have been so very lonely. There has been no one in my life since my wife died. Indeed, I thought there never could be anyone to take her place. That was until you came into my home. These past few days I have wanted to live again. Once again, I have wanted to get up each morning and face the day. You have done that my dear. I meant no harm or disrespect.

"Leone, I had no idea you felt this way. If I have done anything to lead you to think I..." she could not finish the sentence, turning to face him, she reached for his hands. "Please you don't know anything about me, my past or where I come from. I could even be married."

He turned her left hand over in his, "You have no ring, so I think that unlikely and woman in your position seldom marry."

"My position?"

"Forgive me my dear, but you are of, how do I say this? It means nothing to me, believe me." His gaze fell from hers as he mumbled, "Never would I have thought so myself in the past. Of that fact I am truly shamed. But you my dear, have come to show me in these few days by your actions, your beauty, it matters not that you are of mixed blood." There he had said it. Then afraid that she would take offense he hurriedly went on. "I have forgotten that you are what you are. To me you are just a wonderful, sensitive woman."

"Leone, that's one reason you should not let yourself get involved with me." Tori for once was thanking God that she could pass herself off as black. It was giving her a way out of what could become a difficult situation. She did not want to hurt him, as he had been so good to her. Looking at his somber face, and sad eyes she could see how very lonely he was.

A slight smile tugged at his lips as if in an attempt to conceal his pain. "Let us give each other some time. I give you my word, that as a gentleman, I will not let my emotions get out of control again. You must however agree to remain as my guest, until we can find something about you and your past." He hesitated slightly before going on. "If we can't, you will have nowhere to go. Tori my dear, I feel sure that if that should happen, in time I could convince you that this could become your home."

Tori was very moved by his offer, and his feelings toward her. She realized he must care for her a lot, enough to offer his home under the circumstances. Leone was so caring and sensitive, that she hated to think how he would feel or what he would wonder when she simply vanished into thin air, never to be heard from again. She would have to leave him a note and try to explain somehow. Looking at him and seeing the pleading in his eyes made her feel so guilty about all the lies. She wanted desperately to alleviate some of his anguish. What was one more small lie, she asked herself? "Oh Leone, you are so good-hearted. How could I not stay? But please, until we hear something, anything, let us just be friends."

Relief filled his expression. "I will try my dear, but it will not be too easy for me. For I must confess that my feelings toward you are already beyond me."

She could see that he did indeed care and her heart went out to this man. So it was easy for her to put her arms around him, to hug him and tell him thankyou. The two of them just stood silently in the shade of the gazebo holding one another. Each of them lost in their own thoughts and hopes. It was in this position that Edward Duval found them.

"Well, well, well! Seems the talk in town is right my dear brother. You have indeed taken yourself a beautiful mistress. Something I for one, never would have thought you had the courage to do. Amazing, truly amazing. I suppose even you have to bed a female once in a while, and darkie's just aren't good enough are they?"

Tori pulled away from Leone to get a better look at the man who had just called Leone his brother. And knowing Leone as she did, she never expected to see what greeted her eyes. Standing before her was a man much younger in age, with little or no family resemblance. The eyes that bore into hers were steel gray and close set, giving him a cold calculating appearance. His hair was longer than his brothers, and was several shades lighter in color. A light beard, showing he had not yet shaved for the day, covered his chiseled cheeks giving him a rugged appearance. She supposed one could say the man was quite dashing to look at, if it wasn't for the clothes he was wearing. His attire, obviously very expensive and somewhat colorful, was far from conservative. Tori found herself thinking that he either liked himself way too much, or was out to impress all those he met. The lace that hung on the front of the shirt fell in layer upon layer, leaving little room for the powder-blue jacket to button. And the lace did not stop there, no indeed, it came spilling out of each sleeve, and to add to that, the man was dabbing his brow with even more.

Tori wanted to laugh out loud at the spectacle he presented before her. The sight of this handsome man dressed up in all his ruffled splendor, looked so ridiculous to her. But looking back at Leone she quickly realized that he was trying hard to control his temper, and that laughing was the last thing on his mind. Leone's jaw was clenched tight, and the muscles in his neck were flexing ever so slightly. As she watched, harsh words escaped him in a deep angry growl.

"Edward! That is quite enough."

Her attention flashed back to the younger man, who rapidly was becoming no laughing matter. He was standing there acting like a gentleman of the day, but the way he spoke was ridiculing and sarcastic. But this was not a gentleman, she told herself. Tori had met his type before. This was a vindictive cruel son of a bitch.

Edward did not take his eyes off Tori as he addresses his brother. "My compliments to you. I must say your taste has somewhat improved. To obtain a fancy with such looks must have cost you, but oh my brother, from what I can see she's worth it. Is she as good in the bedroom as she looks?" Then noticing her bruises he added, "a little rough maybe?"

The blood drained from Leone's face and his temper causing him to visibly shake. Tori could see him stiffen with a look of disgust covering his face. But before he could speak his brother continued.

"Come now dear brother, you shouldn't get so upset. If I had such a mistress, I would most certainly wish to keep her by me at all times. But I might add, if I wanted to keep my reputation and I would, it would seem that the proper place for her would be a love nest in town…

"Edward!" shouted Leone. "I suggest that you hold your tongue at once, or I shall be forced, brother or not, to silence it for you. This lady is no mistress to me or to anyone else. Tori is my house guest, and as such will be treated with respect."

Edward laughed at him. "Oh come now Leone, a house guest? A fancy staying as your guest! You actually want me, along with half of New Orleans to believe that? Is that why you are asking all the questions in town about who might know her identity, so you can have people believe such a tale? Nice try, but don't bother. I must say though, quite clever of you to come up with that little story. But what bothers me is why? Really Leone, have you forgotten you can have her all you want in the city and still have your respectability…"

Edward was cut short at this point. Leone had had enough and was truly outraged. He lost control as his temper finally got the better of him. He acted swiftly with no warning. He hit his brother full force with his fist. The blow to Edward's chin sent him reeling backwards to the ground, and in a split second it was over.

Edward's pride hurt more than the blow, but being the coward that he was and seeing he had gone just a little too far, a humble man looked toward his brother asking forgiveness. "Ah, you should know me by now Leone. I was just joking. Come, you won't hold it against me will you?" He stood, brushing himself off and continued to talk without looking up. "It's just I'm under a lot of pressure with my business dealings. That is the reason why I'm here, to discuss business with you. Believe you me, I'm not here to spy on you and your lady." This last remark though spoken through a smile, sounded hollow.

"Gambling debts is more like it." Leone almost spit the words out. "You have acted intolerably in front of my guest. I shall have to ask you to leave at once, or apologize." Leone's arm came around Tori's waist protectively.

Edward fumed inside. Apologize to that bitch. Was his brother crazy? But the look on Leone's face showed him he had better comply! He told himself he could get thrown off the plantation without the money he needed. His debts were too large and they had to be paid off somehow, even if it meant apologizing to her. "My apologies madam and now if you will both excuse me, I will go and wait for you Leone, in the study. Good day madam. Leone?" With that he turned and headed for the house.

Tori watched the young man as he sauntered off, she could hardly believe the audacity of him, or what had just transpired. Turning her attention back to Leone she could see he was still very upset. "Leone are you all right? "If it's me you're worried about, please don't be. I'm fine. It's that insolent brother of mine you need to worry about. Edward never has been able to hold his tongue."

"He really did not mean what he said."

"On the contrary Tori, he meant every word of it. I had no idea that the people were talking in town. It would seem they have prejudged you and your stay here, before the facts are all known."

"It seems to me Leone, that they jumped to the only conclusion they could under the circumstances. Please don't be too upset with them. If it would help, I will leave."

"But where would you go? No, you have no place to go and I won't have you leaving. You will stay and I will handle my brother and anyone else. This has opened my eyes to one thing Tori, and that is that I want you, no I need you, to stay here with me. I will leave for New Orleans tomorrow myself and put my best people to work on finding your true identity. We will find out who you are and if it can't be done, then we will find a way to put things right. One thing is sure, you came into my life and one way or another I will do my best to see you stay. Now, if you will excuse me, I had better leave and see to my brother." He put his hands on her shoulders as he added softly, "You had best remain here for a while. I would not wish to expose you to any more of his foul mouth." Kissing her on the cheek Leone himself headed toward the house leaving a very guilt-ridden woman behind.

She had to put an end to this soon and the sooner the better. If in fact he was leaving for New Orleans in the morning, it meant the way would be clear at last for her to get to the lake and through the time door. What if it isn't there, a small voice in her head asked? A question she pushed away. "It will be, it has to be," she whispered. With that she herself headed toward the back of the house, and away from Edward. Tori did not like him and wanted to avoid running into him again at all costs. If he was going to stay the night, she would stay in her room she told herself.

Leone entered his study to find Edward drinking his brandy and smoking one of his cigars. "I see you helped yourself? Is the brandy to your liking?"

"Quite, you seem to have a good taste for the finer things in life."

"What is meant by that?"

"Nothing, just complimenting you that's all. Look, I'm sorry about what just happened out there."

"Sorry, you have never been sorry for anything a day in your life."

Edward spun around to face Leone spilling some of the golden liquid on his jacket. "That's where you are wrong my big brother, I'm truly sorry that I did not inherit the plantation, which should at least have been half mine."

"If it had you would have lost it by now to gambling. Just like everything else you've owned." Leone walked toward his younger brother. "You had a sizable income and the townhouse. And more than enough I might add to set yourself up in a good business."

The two were only inches apart, almost the same in height. Leone was heavier than Edward and this gave him the edge. Knowing this, Edward did not want to run the risk of getting physical again, so he stepped back and spoke more calmly to his big brother.

"Look I did not come here to argue. I came here to ask for an advance on my allowance. Will you give it to me? Or do I have to go back to the bank and let the whole damn world know I'm broke?"

"The whole damn world as you put it, can know for all I care. You will have to wait until the end of the month. I will not give you one dollar until then."

"You and your high and mighty ways, putting yourself above the rest of us. Why, you think you're so good, so well-liked. You bring that whore in here and bed her under this very roof and expect people to accept it. All because Monsieur Duval can do no wrong. Only his brother, the black sheep of the family, does wrong. Well, let me tell you Leone the respectable, that I have my woman.

A lot of them, but I do it with discretion. So you keep your money. I will wait until the mighty has fallen, and then Leone, I will have it all." He lowered his voice then to a deadly tone, "Or have you forgotten the provisions of father's will?"

Leone had been pushed to the limit. Edward had really done it this time. If he did not get him out of his sight, he knew he would lose all control again. "Why you bastard. Get out of my house and from now on you can get your money at the bank instead of from me. I will arrange it tomorrow when I'm in town. You are never to come back here again. Do you hear me? Never! Now get out before I have you thrown out."

Edward, seeing how angry his brother was and realizing too late he had pushed too far, was already on his way out the door and out of reach. His anger, though, gave him just enough courage to have the last say. "Suits me just fine, at least I won't be made to feel like a beggar in my own home." Then realizing he still had a drink in his hand, he walked back into the room toward Leone. He slammed the glass down on the table as he spoke. "I will come back mark my words. This will all be mine one day!"

"That Edward, will never happen, not as long as I'm alive." The two of them stood facing each other and then Leone turned his back on his brother and poured himself a drink. Slowly he drank the brandy, then put down the glass and walked out the verandah doors, leaving Edward standing alone.

Kate looked up from the table as Tori walked into the kitchen.

"Hell, I never will get used to these damn petticoats or whatever they are. Do you know that sitting down is a job in itself, not to mention trying to run with all this garb on?"

Kate laughed at her entrance. Oh she did look a sight. It would take quite a while for Tori to become a lady of the South. Why didn't she know that a lady was not meant to run? As for swearing, well that just plain was not done.

"Lord child, with a mouth like yours, it isn't a wonder that you can't act like a lady."

Exasperated and hot, not to mention uncomfortable, Tori just let go. "Oh, I am too a lady and what does saying a little word like damn have to do with it? I can say damn if I want to and damn it Kate, I want to. Damn! Damn! Damn!"

With that they both burst out laughing. Tori could just picture what she must look like, all dressed up prim and proper, swearing like a truck driver. Kate on the other hand had never met such a mess of a lady, and a Southern lady Tori was not. She had proven that. At least she was not a lady that could fit into this day and time. She could see that something had put Tori into a very agitated mood, and offered her a cool drink to calm her.

Exasperated, Tori snapped back, "If I drink one more glass of lemon I'll die. What I need is a real drink, and don't look at me like that Kate, if you can't get me one, then I'll find one."

Kate placed her hands on her hips and patiently answered, "Now just you calm yourself down some. I can get you a glass of wine but you best not let Leone know'd I got it for you, cause then he will find that I have some and all."

Tori grinned at her, "Why Kate, you sneak, you mean you have a nip every now and then?"

With a puzzled look Kate shook her head saying, "I don't know about nips but I do take a sip every now and then to help these old bones of mine. Now you go out to the back porch and we's will both have a nip, is it?"

Minutes later, Kate was telling Tori about Edward and how things had come to be. "You see the first born that always gits the land. It's just the way. It's not that Edward was left with nothing. He got a large amount of money when his folks died. They died of the fever you know? Well, he also got a townhome, no small home either. It was furnished grand too I'll tell you. Yes em, real grand. It's a good thing he got that and not this land, cause it didn't take him long to spend his money once he got his hands on it. Yes em, he be a real dandy that one. Could have married real well with his family name and all, but word soon got around of his woman and his ways. After that, no good family would ever allow their daughter near him. He lost the house, had to sell it for money he owed gambling, and ever since, Leone has paid for a small place and given him an allowance."

"Why doesn't he get a job or come home and help run this place? It seems big enough for both of them."

Kate laughed. "Him work that's funny. He ain't done a lick o' work in his life. No, he's a dandy, just dresses, and plays. That's all he's good for. Never was any good that one. Even as a child he had a lazy streak in him, and meeean," she stretched out the word.

The women sat in the shade finishing their wine. They were about to go in when Edward himself flew around the corner. Seeing them, he stopped and fumed, those gray eyes of his burning with hatred as he flashed a look of disgust from one to the other. Tori would not back down. She just stared right back into those cold eyes. Tori, who had been holding her breath, slowly let it out, making a hissing noise as she did. She was about ready to let the bastard have a bit of her mind, when Kate reached for Tori's hand and took hold. She was squeezing it, holding Tori to silence.

The air seemed to crackle with the tension that was building, and then his voice snarled across the space toward them both. "I will be back. You haven't seen the last of me." With that he headed for the stables yelling all the way for the lazy black bastards to move their hides.

Kate stood up, "I best go and see how Master Leone is."

"No Kate let me, please. I owe him that much. Let me try and make things better, he won't be here tomorrow, he's going to New Orleans." She softly smiled, "And you know what that means for us? For me anyway. I'm going home tomorrow and you, you get to see your son." She hugged Kate quickly and left before the black woman had a chance to say anything.

Kate sat down at this bit of news, the excitement and shock of realizing that she too might not be here after tomorrow, caused her legs to give in. She stared off into space, the dark brown eyes looking at the empty doorway that Tori had just gone through, and started talking as if Tori were still there. "What's a shame things ain't different, you'd be a fine lady for him, a good mistress for this here plantation. Why when he found out you be white he'd marry you for sure. But you don't belong with us do you child? Lordy, I hopes you get home. I hopes I gets my Tommy. Seems to me, I might fit some in your time, but sure will worry about Master Leone." She hung her head down, "yes em, he gonna be left all by his self."

## Chapter 5

No matter what Tori said to Leone, she could not seem to bring him out of his foul mood. He was reluctant to reveal what had transpired between his brother and himself, or anything else for that matter. Tori could read the pain in his eyes and knew he was hurt far more than angry. She realized he desperately needed to talk to someone, but his pride forced him to hold it within. Maybe a drink would help him relax and open up she thought. "Here, you look as if you could use a drink. I'll take the liberty of fixing myself one, hope you don't mind?"

He finally grinned lightening his mood. "You are a strange one Tori. One minute you can act every bit a lady, and the next you, well let's just say that you have a lot to learn about the way it is here in the South. Just where do you come from I wonder? Nothing about you makes sense to me. You are far too educated and know almost as much as I do when it comes to reading, and other such knowledge." He saw her eyes widen at this statement. "Now don't deny it. I overheard you the other day reading some poetry to Kate and very well I might add. Blacks are not educated, not even fancies. Nothing about you is real and yet I find I don't care. What I do care about is helping you. That is why I must do what I said earlier. I'll leave for New Orleans in the morning."

He sat there before her, with his head in his hands. He was confused and upset, and obviously torn emotionally inside out. His fight with his brother had only brought feelings long buried to the surface, and for the moment he was overwhelmed.

How she wished she could confide in him, to have him understand. This man was going to return and find her gone, and how would he cope with that? She had to think of something.

"Well then, when you return you will find that I can write also. I shall write a poem for you Leone, one that might help you understand me."

He looked up at her standing there before him. How was it she seemed to always know ahead of time just what he needed. She stood there with two drinks in her hands, trying to cheer him up. And God knows he needed cheering up. Reaching out he took one glass from her hand. "I shall look forward to returning then. But for now there is much for me to prepare. Kate will see to it that you have dinner. I'm afraid that you will have to dine alone this evening." He took a sip of his drink then added. "It is better if we say good-bye now, for the boat I catch passes by here long before you will awaken."

Leone rose from his seat and putting down his glass walked toward Tori. Very gently he took her in his arms, his whole body ached to kiss her, to take hold of her and make her his, but he had given his word. So with much effort on his part, he pushed her back gently and kissed her on her forehead as he would kiss a child. Just how much longer he could restrain himself he did not know.

Tori could see the struggle in his eyes, and she hurt deep inside. The guilt over what she was doing to him, was almost more that she could bear. She had to leave the room now or she would tell him everything. Tori stepped quickly toward the doorway, not even looking back toward him. She spoke, her voice quavering. "Good-bye Leone, and thank you."

She went straight to her room where she stayed the remainder of the day. That evening, she did not feel up to eating in the dining room all alone. She did not want to eat at all. It was Kate who brought a tray to her room long after the sun had set.

"Now it seems to me that you need to keep up your strength. You going to need it tomorrow. So I brought you some cold meats and a few slices of my bread. There be some fruit too, along with some wine. Thought you might be a needing a nip," she chuckled. "I be catching on to your ways real quick like, even if I don't understand them and all."

Tori smiled at her, "Kate you're a doll and I thank you but I don't feel like food. I will have a glass of wine though. Where is Leone?"

"He be out on the plantation giving orders as to what has to be done. He knowd he don't need to give me no orders. I know what's what around this here house. No sur, his worry's the fields and the cane."

Tori frowned, "Kate I've caused a lot of trouble haven't I, since I've been here? What with making you lie. Leone's fight with his brother, and even Missy's death. That was my fault."

"Now I don't want to hear nothing about this pity for yourself. This is not the Tori I knows. You done told me how women in your time are strong and stand up for their rights. Now you must stand strong child. None of anything was because of you. Missy was in a heap a trouble and would have ended up dead sooner or later. The boys been fighting all their days. No sur, if anything you been good. I know Tommy's well and alive and the Master Leone, he knows he ain't got to be sad no more. He can live again cause of you. He knows he can lets himself feel again."

"That's what I mean Kate, how is he going to feel when he gets back and I'm gone? I was going to write him but that won't do. He would never believe it."

Kate gave her a big smile, "Well I'll tell him and when he sees Tommy, he going to believe it sure enough will."

"But Kate, that's just it, you have to come with me to see Tommy. I don't think he will want to come here with you. It's like I told you. He is a free man in my time. There is no more slavery. If he came here with you he would be a slave again."

"What does a baby know of free. He aint a going to miss nothing." She dropped her head down and stood thinking for a brief time. To Tori it looked as if she were praying and she did not disturb her. She had her own thoughts to deal with. Kate suddenly lifted her head and spoke softly. "Tori if that really true, then I guess I have to stay in your time with him. It just don't seem right. Bring him back to…" the words would not come. She wanted the best for her son, even if it meant facing the unknown. "You's will help me won't you?"

Tori hugged the woman tightly. "Of course I will, and you will love it. Oh Kate, wait until you see what there is, how different things are." Tori started then to explain to Kate as much about her time as she could. She even threw in some history. The two women talked through the night without realizing it. Tori telling Kate as much as she could think of. And Kate, like a child hearing a story of fantasy, listened wide eyed, full of questions. The dawn was breaking when the two of them realized that the night was over.

In a way, Tori did not mind that she had talked to Kate so much. The woman had seen into the future with her help. It was just the boost Kate needed to get the courage to leave Leone and this life behind. To go to the lake and hopefully her new life with her son.

Realizing that morning was upon them Kate headed for downstairs and her duties. "You best try and rest some while I goes and gits Master Leone on his way."

Standing up quickly Tori shook her head no, "You have to be kidding me. You think that for one minute I will be able to rest? No Kate, I will get changed and come down to say good-bye to Leone myself."

Kate could not talk Tori into staying in her room, so she just told her that before a trip, Leone always took coffee in his study and that she should wait for him there.

The study was dim even with the large curtains pulled back and the French doors open. The light from outside was not yet sufficient to make the room come to life. It felt more like a morgue at the moment. Maybe it was just her down mood that made the room feel this way. However, she was determined to make Leone's farewell a pleasant experience, and not sorrowful.

Tori had the young black girl place the silver coffee pot and china, down on the table. Then she herself filled the cups and took them outside on the verandah instead of in the depressing room. Next she called out to a small black boy, whom she recognized as the stable boy, to run and pick one long red rose, which she placed next to the cups. Hearing footsteps coming down the hall, she stepped to one side out of view and waited.

Leone, accustomed to finding his coffee set up on the table, was at first angry to see it was not ready and waiting for him. Why, Kate always saw to it that it was there, he thought. She knew he would drink his coffee while the luggage for his trip was carried down to the river. He could see the coffee pot but no cups and he could smell coffee. But looking around he could swear it was coming from the verandah. Walking over to the open doors he spied the table. "What's going on?" He spoke to himself in French and spying the rose walked over to it passing right by Tori, not even realizing she was there. "Seems as if someone has left a calling card, or maybe a farewell?" His trembling hand picked up the flower. He held it to his lips as he spoke softly. "Am I a fool to hope that you Madame have arranged this for me?"

"Good morning Leone and you are right, I did arrange it for you. One should leave on a trip happy, no?"

Was that French he heard, how could it be? Leone spun around, and seeing her standing there he was overcome. It was not a dream, she was waiting for him and once again she had amazed him. "Not only do you surprise me by being here to see me on my way, but you also prove that you speak French very well indeed." Leone walked over to her, and presented the rose she had left for him with a bow. "You are truly a mystery lady, why did you not tell me you spoke French?"

"I had no idea that you would want to know, and it did not seem important."

Leone was unnerved by this latest development. Still he made up his mind not to show it. Casually now, as he poured two cups of coffee he asked, "Can I take it that you are regaining some of your memory then?'

"The only memory I have, is of how good you have been to me. I can't explain anything more than that." This was getting harder than she had thought it would be. Tori found herself turning away from him and his close scrutiny of her.

"I don't know who you are and indeed whoever you turn out to be will not matter to me, so long as you are not committed to anyone else. You know how I feel about you." He could see that she was becoming uneasy again and changed the subject. "I expect that you must be from Europe. You being able to speak French so well only serves to strengthen this theory.

Tori looked perplexed and spoke firmly. "Leone, the fact that I speak French does not prove I'm from Europe. Why you yourself speak the language very well and I am sure that you are not from Europe." He smiled at her.

"That is true but the French I speak is the same as most in this area. It is how can I say this? It is different, like the English that you speak. You talk in English and yet you speak a different version. Your French is that of France not New Orleans. Even the accent is correct." He looked truly happy as he continued. "So much could be explained, if it comes to light that you are from a distant land. It will be my advice to head the inquiries in that direction. When I return in a few days maybe you will trust in me and tell me more." He hesitated, "You could stop me from making this trip you know. If only you would open up to me, you do know more now don't you? I have seen it in your eyes."

How could she tell him her French sounded too good, because it was spoken without a Southern drawl. That her pronunciation was correct due to her studying the language in France itself. Turning to face him, she continued the conversation in English.

"Leone what you see in my eyes is concern that you will find out who I am or where I'm from and not like it at all. You have become a dear friend in such a short time and I would hate to see you disappointed. I have told you all that I can. I don't know what else I can tell you, I just don't know."

Leone misunderstood what she was saying, he took it that she could not remember anything, and seeing that she was upset he tried to calm her down. "You could never disappoint me Tori. Only intrigue me. The woman I know, is the one I will continue to hold dear. Nothing anyone says or does will sway me from that. Have no fear my dear."

Tori watched him anxiously, her pulse racing. He looked as if he were going to take her in his arms again. God, she hoped not. This lying to him was hard enough without that. Just then a long whistle blew from down by the river and Leone snapped out of his daze.

"It seems Madam, that you shall have to enjoy the coffee alone. My boat has arrived. You must take care of yourself while I'm gone. Kate has her orders. This is your home and you are to treat it as such. However, I do recommend caution. Stay close to the house. People around here may not have heard yet that you are my guest and that could be a problem for you, should you stray too far. Till my return then." With that he tipped his hat, turned and walked down the verandah to the awaiting horse in the garden.

Tori watched through tear-filled eyes as he mounted his stallion. "Goodbye my friend, and please forgive me for what I have done and am about to do. Never will I forget you, always I will be thankful."

Once up on his horse he turned toward her, "did you say something?"

She smiled and waved to him, "Nothing Leone, just wishing you a good trip and a safe one."

"Yea, Mister Duval, you have a safe trip and don't you worry none, I'll see that things run real smooth while you're gone."

Tori froze. Horrified she realized she recognized that voice without having to look at the person. Up until then, she had not realized that standing by the side of the house the whole time watching and listening, had been the overseer.

Leone was riding away calling over his shoulder, "Thank you Mr. Kane, I will do just that. You see to it for me that my guest stays close to the house and that no harm comes to her." With that he was riding fast and was quickly out of hearing range, or else he would have stopped and come back when Tori called out. Instead, he rode on unaware that he was leaving behind a very terrified woman.

Kate was at Tori's side in a second. She took her arm and pulled her back into the study, hastily closing the French doors behind them.

In a panicked voice Tori all but screamed, "I thought you told me that Kane would be off in the fields working. What in the hell is that man doing here?"

"Lordy I don't know. Seems as if Massa Leone, he done asked him to watch over you and the house and all. He must have put Jobe in charge down at the fields, we's got's ourselves a handful of problems now child."

"I can see that Kate. Ah shit! how in the hell are we going to get to the lake with him right outside? Tell me that? Just how in the hell do you expect us to get out of here?" her voice rising.

"Now I would say that the two of you ain't a going nowhere wouldn't you? Seems as the last words I heard from Mister Duval and all, was for you to stay put. Now ain't that a shame you having to stay here, in this big old house all by yourself."

Kate spun around, her dislike for the man evident in her tone of voice, "Just what do you think you're doing in here and who let you in? I'm gona skin some wench for opening dat door and letting you in here. You ain't got no rights to be here, lessan I says so. I say that you ain't supposed to be in da house with Master Leone gone. So's you just get out of my house, you hear?"

Tori watched in horror as Jack's face went from a smirk to the dark threatening scowl she remembered. "Why you black bitch, you don't ever talk to me that way or I'll see to it you get a taste of this here whip. I have every right to be here, cause I have been put in charge, of the plantation, this house, you and your fancy friend there." He pointed the whip in Tori's direction. "You move your black ass and get to the kitchen and git me some vittles and coffee, cause I ain't had none yet and I'm real mean without my coffee, ain't that right Tori?"

Kate moved quickly putting herself between the two of them. She could see how terrified Tori was of him and did not miss how the overseer was leering at her either. Kate knew she would have to do something and fast. Afraid of him she was not. Maybe out in the fields she would be, but not here in her house, the house she ran. "You done leave dis lady alone now you hear? She be real frail and if anything happened to her, the Master Leone would be real upset."

"Now ain't that just like a Nigger, sticking up and protecting another. I done told you what to do, now you move your hide bitch, or I'll move that lazy ass of yours myself." His whip hit the side of his leg and Kate had no doubt in her mind that if pushed he would indeed use it. Yet, she could not leave Tori alone with this animal.

Her predicament was clear to Tori, who after the initial shock of seeing the overseer again, felt a little more in control. After all, he could not, would not try anything in Leone's home with all the servants around would he? But she knew it was in his right as overseer if disobeyed, to take action.

"It's fine Kate. I'll be all right. After all, I'm sure that Mr. Kane will honor his boss's orders, not do anything, other than see I am well looked after. Isn't that right sir?"

Jack said nothing he just nodded his head and walked toward the desk. "You done heard the wench, Nigger. Now move and get me my breakfast. I'll eat it in here and bring two plates cause I hate to eat alone, get my meaning." He spit a wad of tobacco into the empty fireplace. His demeanor while walking around the room, told Tori that he was enjoying himself. "Now you wench, just sit down and wait nice like."

Tori nodded her head at Kate and the black woman slowly moved toward the door. She would leave all right but she would see to it that one of the small girls would stand outside and listen to all that went on. Yes em, Tori was not going to be left completely alone with him, not now or ever.

Once Kate had left, the room fell quiet. It was so quiet that Tori could hear Jack chewing on a new wad of tobacco, his teeth grinding, as he just sat there staring at her.

"I said sit down bitch," he growled spitting another mouthful of saliva toward the fireplace. It fell short and hit the floor. Jack stared at it as if contemplating where he went wrong. Tori chose the chair the farthest from him and the one closest to the door. Without even looking at her Jack started to chuckle. "There ain't no getting away from Jack this time. No Missy to help you either, no sur. You ain't a going nowhere."

"You had best let me be Jack, if you know what is good for you. I have done you no harm."

"No harm she says. Bitch!" he shouted, then lowering his voice he continued. "Ain't sure what your game is, but I knows one thing that's for sure, you and I, we still needs to finish something. And seems to me that I got all the time I needs to finish and in style."

"You touch me and I will see to it that Leone hears of it and you will be finished here, do you hear me?"

"Well now, Leone is it? He'll he be a good catch for you. Going to set you up purty like in New Orleans is he? Bets that's why he's gone, to get you a little house on Rampart next to them other fancy whores? Well I don't give a damn about this stinking job. Do you hear me? So now what are you going to say?"

Tori said nothing, she was well aware that this man intended to have her and he didn't give a damn about her threats. Her only hope was to keep him calm until Kate got back. She would run then and with Kate's help they might be able to do something.

Jack stood up and walked around the desk. He was looking for something. Not finding it he walked to the French doors, opened one and spit. Tori seeing her chance, got up to run.

"I don't think you best do that, cause the whip will reach you before you git to the door. Ain't missed yet with it and don't plan to, so sit."

Tori froze at his order with no doubt in her mind that he could indeed crack his whip as he said. She returned to her seat and sat there watching him. The door opened and a young girl entered with a pot of coffee and placed it on the small table. She looked at Tori and smiled nodding her head, as she left the room. Tori took this as a sign from Kate to hang in there and not panic... It was no such sign.

Kate was cooking in the kitchen house as Tori called it. Even though the small building was only two hundred feet from the back door with that evil man inside the house, it might as well have been a mile away. She worked as fast as she could, so she could get back to the study. She wanted to send for one of the blacks in the barn to come and help, but knew that they would not come. To go against any white man, good or bad, would bring a very severe punishment. No, she had to help Tori herself.

Tori sat waiting for Kate, trying to keep calm. She watched as Jack walked over to the where the coffee was. He had left his whip left laying on the desk. Seeing no cups he reached for a glass, and started to fill it up. Tori eyed his whip once again. Even without it he was still too close for her to try for the door. She remembered that he could move very fast for a man of his size. Watching him now, she could see that his hand was shaking as he poured the coffee. She surmised he was hung over. Probably feeling really sick, and that would mean that she just might have a chance. Before she could think further or lose her nerve, she was on her feet running for the door.

What happened next was pure hell. Jack seeing her move out of the corner of his eyes reacted fast. He caught her by surprise as he threw his cup of hot coffee at her. The scalding liquid hit her arm and caused her to stop momentarily giving Jack an edge. He was on her in a flash.

"I done told you Nigger not to try to get away from Jack. You ain't going no place, that is septing on the floor. I hoped to take you in a bed, like a man should a lady but hell, you ain't no lady, you're a Nigger through and through. The first time I laid eyes on you, I know'd I would take you and I ain't waiting no more."

Dragging her to the floor was easy, he was strong and his weight was on his side. His hands found her blouse and ripped it open exposing her breasts. His breath was vile but not as pungent as his body odor. The look on his face, was that of a deranged man intent on inflicting pain. Tori was fighting now for her very life. She would never let this pig have her she told herself over and over. Her screams could be heard all the way to the house kitchen, where Kate dropped what she was doing. Picking up a kitchen knife she ran for the study. The small girl who had been on her way to get Kate froze in her tracks at the sight of her large form running toward her. She took one look at Kate's face and the knife she held and ran. This was going to be bad for everyone she just knew it and she wanted no part in it. She was heading outside and away from here as fast as she could. She didn't want to know what was going to happen and she was sure that she was a going to tell everyone that she done knew nothing, nothing at all. She'd say she aint even been in da house all morning!

The door to the study burst open and Kate entered with the knife raised. Fearing she might harm Tori if she tried to use the knife on the struggling pair, Kate screamed at Jack to let her go. He looked up at the woman and seeing the knife did just that. Pushing Tori to the side, he freed himself from the tangle of torn material and kicking legs. Once she was free of him, Tori crawled on the floor toward the table, trying to cover herself as she went.

Jack stood up slowly, never looking away from the black mammy. "You just done made the biggest mistake of your life Nigger. I'm going to have to whoop you good, teach you whose Master round here."

Kate had had enough and Tori would never know if it was fear of the whip, or hate of the overseer, that made her charge him as she did. Screaming as she ran toward him, knife aimed at his gut, Kate saw only that it was the devil himself who she was going to kill.

Jack had been in many fights, and many of them with knives. This mammy was no match for him. Side stepping her quickly and turning as she passed him, he grabbed her from behind. Tori watched in horror as instantaneously Kane got Kate where he wanted.

Kate, however, had fear and anger on her side. She knew that if she did not stop him, he would rape Tori and end up killing them both. She twisted hard and managed to break free. She turned on him like a wildcat protecting her cubs. She once again tried to stab him in a move that cost her dearly. Kane grabbed her wrist and then tried to apply force to drop the weapon. The two of them wrestled furiously for control of the knife. Twice Jack hit her in the face with his free hand, as he held her knife hand away from him. Twisting her wrist and dealing the blows at the same time did the trick. Kate was losing her grip on the knife. In the next moment Tori watched, as she saw Kate make one last effort to get the knife into Jack. But a twist of her arm and a quick move of his body caused the knife to find a different target.

Kate did not scream she just stopped struggling. A look of horror filled her face as she realized that the knife was sticking in her middle and not Jack's. She released her grip but before she could take another breath Jack pulled the knife out and rammed at her again and again. Even as she was falling to the ground he kept stabbing her. Tori could hear the knife as it passed through Kate's clothes and into her body. She could see the blood coming out and covering Jack's hands, and she could hear screaming. It was her own voice that she heard filling the room. Instinctively she reached for something to protect herself with and grabbed the first thing she could. Without thinking, she took hold of the heavy silver coffee pot and attacked Jack before he had a chance to turn on her. The pot came down on his head and with a dull thud rendered him unconscious and the room deathly silent.

Jack and Kate had fallen almost side by side. There was one difference though Kate had been dead before she hit the floor. Tori went to her side crying for her to please be all right, yet knowing that her pleas were going to go unanswered.

Taking Kate's head in her lap and stroking her hair Tori rocked back and forth. "Oh Kate why?" Between soft sobs she continued to talk to the dead woman. "All because of me, you will never get to see your son now will you? He won't get to show you what a fine young man he is. I promise you Kate, on my own life, I swear to you that when I get back, I will tell him about you and your love for him. I will see that he knows the truth." Kate's empty eyes looked out and Tori somehow hoped that the woman could hear her. She spoke softly and lovingly to her companion. "Sleep now my friend, you are free and you will never again be sad." Tori sat there with Kate in her arms and cried for all she was worth. She cried for Kate and she cried for herself. The blood was smearing on her clothes and drying on her hands, but it was Kate's blood and she did not care. Deep down inside of her a rage was brewing. She looked at Kane with pure hatred in her heart.

He would pay for this. Jack would hang! The bastard would not get away with killing another black she would see to that. This time he had done his murdering in front of a witness. This time he would be the one with nowhere to go.

As the minutes slowly passed, the horror of what had just transpired slowly seeped into her grief stricken mind. Tori sat in total shock. Her confusion as to what she should do next, froze her in her present situation. She desperately needed Leone to walk in and take over, to tell her what she should do, to help her with Kate... But Leone was miles away by now, it was up to her to act. She closed her eyes and spoke out loud. "God help me. Somebody, anybody just help me please." Unaware of the figure behind her, Tori continued to plead over and over for help.

Edward stood in the open French doorway. Never had he expected to find what was now confronting him. He saw Tori mumbling to herself, tears flowing freely down her ashen face. In her lap was Kate's head, the rest of her body was sprawled out, laying lifeless in a pool of blood, the murderous knife still protruding from a deadly wound. And lastly the overseer lying not far from all this, with blood all over his hands, his body raising noisily up and down with every breath he was taking. Half to himself and half to Tori in a demanding voice he bellowed out, as if by doing so, the scene would somehow vanish.

"What in God's name happened here?"

Tori looked up from Kate and saw Edward walking toward her. Neither his sudden appearance nor his horrified expression did little to penetrate her mind. No words of explanation left her, as her whole body was constricted in grief. A large lump in her throat would not allow any sound to escape other than a soft whimper.

Suddenly there was movement off to her side and Tori turned to see Jack's large form shifting. Her fearful gaze did not escape Edward, who could plainly see the woman was terrified of the overseer. Fear was now covering her face, erasing the sadness that moments ago had been so visible.

Edward had always though Jack capable of murder but not stupid enough to get caught. Tori was telling him how they had to tie up Jack and how he must pay for murdering Kate. She just rambled on, about how he had tried to rape her.

And not once did she take her eyes off Jack's body. As Edward watched and listened to her, he became obsessed with her natural beauty, even through her tears distraught as she was, the woman mesmerized him. Somehow he could not blame Jack for wanting her. Did she realize that her blouse had been ripped and that she sat there with her breasts exposed? Even covered in blood they held his gaze. The fact that she was Leone's only added to Edward's own desire to taste for himself the joy of ravaging every inch of her. He wanted to destroy what his brother cherished! Suddenly he realized that she had stopped talking and was staring at him.

"I said, how will Leone ever accept Kate's murder?"

Edward turned away from her with a sadistic grin covering his face. My, how Leone is going to be shocked over this incident. It would give him the greatest pleasure to watch his brother grieve again. Then an idea occurred to him. He had a way to make his brother pay for all the groveling he had done, not to mention all the humiliation and suffering. It would be so easy to really make the mighty fall and end up with the grand prize, leaving his brother nothing. His mind was racing ahead with a plan he quickly put into action. "Tori, you poor soul. How callous of me to be only thinking of myself at a time when your shock and emotions must be in greater need of help than mine. Here, let me fix you a drink. It will help calm you. He handed her a glass. His face masked his true feelings as he poured the golden colored liquor. Edward's eyes were showing only concern and kindness. Then he handed her a small quilt that lay on top of one of the chairs. "Here cover yourself I don't think you realize quite what has happened yet." In order for his plan to succeed Tori had to remain unsuspecting of his true motives.

Thank you Edward, but before you do anything I think that you had better take care of Jack first, don't you?"

"Judging by the size of the lump on his head and the fact that you hit him with that," he pointed to the dented silver pot, I doubt that he will give us any trouble for a few hours at least. Come now, drink some brandy and we will figure out what to do."

Tori took a large drink before stating, "We have to report this to the authorities. He must be punished."

Edward's face changed visibly at the mention of the authorities. Tori looked puzzled. Was is possible he did not believe her?

"What do you mean? We have to report this to the authorities?" he asked.

"Jack must pay. He killed Kate. I saw him."

He could hear the panic in her voice. "Was there anyone else who saw this happen?"

"No, Why?" she whispered.

"Well, he hesitated, I believe you but it will be his word," he kicked at Jack's side with his foot, "against yours and quite frankly my dear, I feel as if the people will believe him before they believe you."

"But I saw him do it," she pleaded. "Look at the blood on his hands."

"You have blood on your hands, and he's hurt not you. Furthermore you are a stranger staying here. A person of shall we say, a questionable background. To most folks around here, if you beg my pardon in so saying, will believe a white man before a Nigger. And Nigger is how they will see you, no matter how much white's in you." Edward was quiet for a minute letting the thought sink in. He deliberately stood where she could study his face, while he supposedly planned how he could help her. "No, I think we had best try to figure out what we can do to help protect you."

His implications were very clear to her. She had flashes from books and movies, of what they did in this time to people accused of murder. He was right. Jack would say she did it, that she killed Kate along with attacking him. Panic took hold of her. All she knew at that moment was that she had to get away. "I could leave and you could pretend that you never found me here."

"There is not enough time I'm afraid. You would not get far. One of the servants will find this mess soon. Kate was loved by them all and they would hunt you down. I don't want to scare you but it might be best if you do not run."

Tori was really frightened now and Edward could see his plan was working. Of course he was lying through his teeth. He knew that Leone would get the truth out of Jack and Tori would be cleared but was not going to let her know that.

"I think it best if I lock up Jack and then you leave with me for New Orleans so we can reach Leone. He will believe you and I will see to it that he knows everything you have told me. He will know what to do."

"But to leave here now, it would be like running wouldn't it? Won't it make me look guilty? Won't they come after me like you said? How do I know you can find Leone? If we get caught, you will be in trouble." Tori was up, pacing back and forth in front of the desk, wringing her hands one minute and then rubbing her arms and pulling the quilt around her the next. She was really working herself up.

Edward cut in before she could continue. "Look I talked to Leone down by the boat this morning and he told me what he was going to do. I also apologized and explained about my unforgivable actions of yesterday. I was supposed to stay here and look after you for him. So if I don't take care of you now, he will never forgive me. I know where he is staying and we need his help, if we are to get you out of this mess. I don't know how else to keep them from hanging you! An angry mob is one thing, he is another," he pointed toward Kane. It was so easy for him to lie. Especially with such a trusting victim believing each and every word he uttered. Having her terrified and grief stricken at the same time, stopped her from thinking too clearly and only added to his control over her.

She had no choice in the matter. Tori saw that her only chance was to trust Edward and go with him. What else could she do? In her mind it was either she found Leone and together they prove her innocent or she slipped away from everyone right now, finding her way back to the lake and back home. But so many slaves would be after her like Edward said.

"Tori, are you listening to me? You had best go and clean up, change into something to travel in. I do hope you can ride?"

"Yes, I can ride, not side saddle though, it has to be like you ride." Then seeing the look on his face she went on. "It is how I learned."

Edward's look was somewhat amused. The resemblance to his brother was now astonishingly clear. They both had the same grin and way of holding their heads to one side when teasing. "You don't intend to ride in a skirt that way do you? I mean a lady can't do that, at least I doubt it can be done in comfort." Yes, he was teasing, but another thought quickly clouded the light moment. God, he hoped she wasn't beginning to think clearly, but then how clearly was riding like a man?

"Don't worry Edward I won't let you down." Turning, she looked once again at the form on the floor that belonged to her beloved Kate. The sorrow rushed back and with it the thought that to leave Kate like this was wrong. "We can't just leave Kate here like this. I can't stand the thought of her lying there on the floor."

Edward spoke in a kind but firm tone, "don't you worry about a thing. You just go and get ready. Stay in your room until I come for you. You'll be safe until we leave. We have to be fast Tori. If one of the servants finds this mess, or if Jack should awaken, I doubt that even I could help you then. I will take care of Kate and make sure Jack is out somewhere safe. Now do as I say, and hurry please."

Tori was scared. She had done nothing wrong but she could also see how things would go against her. Thank God Edward came along when he did. He knew what to do and how to find Leone. Quickly, she left the room and went to get ready for the ride to New Orleans. Those long bloomers would come in handy now after all. Riding pants would have been more to her liking though, even a good old pair of jeans.

Edward stood looking at the two bodies, seeing Kate lying there brought back childhood memories for him. She had been a good nanny. Kate had always been there, the girl who had gone into the kitchen at night to get more food for them. She had covered for the boys when they had slipped out at night to meet with some young ladies along the river to try their manhood. Generally she had been there for them, the whole family. Never did she deserve to end her days like this. Sure he and Kate had not liked each other the past few years. Things had changed with her always seeming to take Leone's side, but he never would have wished real harm on her, especially murder.

His gaze went toward Jack. He thought about the man laying on the floor. Edward had no hate for this man, he had no feeling one way or another at this time, he just knew what he had to do. He walked over to where Jack lay and stood looking down on him. The blow Tori had inflicted had been a good one but not good enough to do the job. He would survive and he would talk. Edward could not have that happening if his plan was to succeed. He had never killed a man before, but then he had never really had a reason to. Slowly now he moved toward Kate and wrapping his handkerchief around his hand so as not to get any blood on himself, he made his move. Taking hold of the knife, he closed his eyes, and withdrew the weapon. The knife did not leave Kate's back as easy as he thought it would and for a brief second he thought of not going through with his plan, but only for an instant. Once he had the knife he did not hesitate. Edward turned toward Jack and knelt down next to the unconscious man. Holding the knife in two hands with a death-like grip, he raised his arms. Taking in a deep breath and holding it, he started the downward motion with all the force he could muster. The blade came down swift and sure straight into the overseer's back.

It sunk in deep, almost to the handle and while blood oozed out of the wound around where the knife was planted, he twisted it back and forth pushing still deeper. It was not as much of a mess as Edward had anticipated. He looked at the handle and the handkerchief which had stayed fairly clean. Standing up Edward watched as Jack continued to breathe, something he found hard to believe considering the wound he had just inflicted. The thought of letting him alone to die slowly crossed his mind, however he had to make sure that the man did not live. He was about to remove the knife, to stab him again when Edward saw the bloody spittle that slipped slowly from Kane's open mouth. A strange rasping sound came wheezing out between his lips as he labored to breathe. Then the overseer's body shuddered as it gave up its life, and his breathing stopped. Jack lay dead.

With that accomplished he went next to Jack's hand, slowly now to avoid getting blood on himself, he picked it up putting Jack's finger in the pool of blood that covered the floor. He simply spelled out the word Tori on the wooded surface. That was his insurance should anything go wrong now. It would look as if Tori had killed both Kate and the overseer, but before his death Jack had spelled out the name of the killer. This would leave him in the clear, his ace in the hole so to speak. Carefully now he folded the handkerchief and placed it in the inside pocket of his jacket. Excitement ran through his body, as he realized he was well on his way. His plan was in motion.

He walked toward the open French doors and stepped outside. Gently he closed the glass doors on the macabre scene, smiling to himself how easy it had been. Thinking back over his actions of the last few minutes, he could not find one thing that he had left undone. Nothing could connect him in any way with the murder of Jack, even if the bodies were found right now. It would be his word against that of a Nigger.

Now there was only one thing left to do, finding a horse for Tori. This would have to be done as discreetly as possible, as the fewer people who saw him here now, the better. In fact he was about to have Tori ride with him rather than go to the barn to get her a horse, when off to the side of the house he spied exactly what he needed. Jack had left his horse tied up. He must have been in such a hurry to get into the house that he had forgotten to give orders for it to be taken to the stable. And with no orders the black stable boy would never have touched the animal. It was almost too good to be true. This was perfect. It would look as if Tori had taken Jack's horse to get away.

"So once again, Jack, you help me out, how considerate of you. Now to get that wench out of the house and away from here before anyone becomes suspicious or sees us together." He had been talking to himself, something he realized he had to stop doing in case someone should overhear him. Looking around, Edward knew that this was unlikely, it was still early and not a soul was in sight. Still he would not rest until they were well away from here. If they were to succeed, they needed not only luck but time.

Time surely would be cut short if one of the household's blacks went looking for Kate and find her. What if he could delay that for a while. Yes, that's what he would do. Edward headed toward the back and the kitchen where he knew he would find one of the small children playing. He would give them the message to tell all the others that Kate said for them to go to their rooms and wait for her there. It just might work. Hell he had nothing to lose, and as small as the little bastards were, he would have no trouble in convincing anyone in the days ahead that they were mistaken about it being him that gave the false message...

Upstairs, Tori had rushed, washing blood off her hands and changing into a skirt and top along with the long bloomers. The blood covered clothes that she took off, she threw under the bed, not really thinking what she was doing, just wanting to be rid of them. With this accomplished she was ready to ride. What was taking Edward so long she wondered? Should she go downstairs and see? Maybe she should even go into the study to leave Leone a note telling him that she was with Edward and that they had gone to New Orleans to find him. She would write that no matter what Jack had to say she was innocent of any crime. It could happen, she reasoned, that they would miss meeting him, and he would not know what happened to her or why she left. Yes, that's what she would do.

A cold shudder hit her as she walked down the stairs toward the study. She would have to go into that room because that was the only place that she knew of that had paper and ink.

"I hope Edward has taken Kate out of there," she told herself out loud. Oh stop being foolish, she thought, you are acting like a child. "You have to do it. Maybe I should have taken a sheet off the bed to cover Kate," she asked no one in particular. "If she is still laying there, that's what should be done." Talking to herself was a way of gaining courage, not that she felt any stronger. Tori went back into her room to get the sheet. "I will be able to see what Edward has done about Jack at the same time," she whispered as she stripped the top sheet off the bed and headed down toward the study. It was helping her now that she was doing something, giving her the added strength she needed. Tori found herself with tears in her eyes again, when she thought of Kate laying in there. It would be so easy just to go to pieces. "Keep busy, and try not to think about anything other than what you're doing," she told herself.

Heading down the stairs and toward the study she could hear her footsteps on the wooden floors. Not a sound came from anywhere else in the house. Not a soul was in sight. For the first time the hallway seemed so narrow and long. The study door was closed and no sound ushered from the other side. With her hand on the doorknob, her stomach twisted and bile rose up in her throat, warning her she was about to be ill. She would not be weak she told herself. Her hand squeezed the handle tight and as it did, she took a grip on her emotions. She simply had to do this. Taking a deep breath she began opening the door.

Edward's voice rang out in the silence making her jump. "Tori, what are you doing? I thought I told you to wait for me up in your room?"

Turning to look down the hall, she could see Edward hurrying toward her, his face grim with concern. His hands took hold of her and led her toward the far end of the hallway.

"I was only going in to cover Kate and leave a note for Leone, that's all. I didn't think there would be any harm in doing that." Crossing the hall and closing the study door, Edward knew that he had come very close to her finding out what he had done.

Tori could see the angry look on his face and asked, "is something wrong? You look as if you are angry with me. Why don't you want me to go into the study?"

He softened his scowl and answered her gently, "I feel it would be easier for you, Tori, not to have to face that room and it's contents again. Why look at you, even now the sorrow is almost too much for you to bear." Edward reached up and with his fingers, slowly touching one of the tears that lay on her face. He then took the sheet from her hands and dropped it. "I covered Kate's body but I fear just seeing that would overwhelm you. Tori you will need all your strength and all your wits about you for the ride."

"What about Jack?"

"The matter with Jack is solved. I have locked him up in the barn so he can't get to anyone. I tied him up and gagged him, and left orders that no one go near him. We will reach Leone and help before he will talk to anyone."

Tori could just see how mad Jack would be when he found himself tied up and gagged. See how he liked it! She thought. "But don't you think that we should leave a note for Leone in case he gets back here before we find him? I don't want him thinking that we ran out on him, or that I'm the one who did this."

"That has been taken care of. I myself left a note for Leone on his desk. That's what took me so much longer than I anticipated. A horse is waiting, so I think Madam that we had best depart before anything goes wrong." Giving her no chance to answer or to think about what she was doing, Edward hurried her outside to the waiting horses and helped her mount. She did look very strange seating a horse like a man, her skirt pulled up showing off her white bloomers, but it did not seem to bother her and if she could ride like that, all the better, because they had a long way to go in a short time.

It was early morning when the two of them set out. Not the best time of the day to travel together and not be seen. Edward had thought of that also. He explained to Tori along the way, it would be to her advantage if they stayed out of sight for a few hours, just in case something went wrong back at the plantation. The alarm could be raised and she would be hunted down he told her.

So it was a few hours later that they stopped at a small river road inn. They had been riding hard, staying clear of any fields where workers were too close or of any side roads that might be busy this time of the day. Edward knew his way around these parts well and it had paid off, so far. The place he had in mind for stopping was one that he had frequented now and then, when he was staying up at the plantation. The owner could be trusted to keep his mouth shut for a price. He was his kind of gentleman, see all and know nothing.

When they arrived outside of what Tori assumed was little more than a rundown shack, Edward had left her outside with the horses while he went in to make sure it was safe. Tori watched through the open door as money passed hands. If only she could have listened in on the conversation.

Edward was paying the owner of the establishment an extra sum of money to keep his mouth closed should anyone come around in the next few hours, or in the future, asking about him or the wench that was with him. He was speaking to him as if they were old friends who did business on a regular basis.

"You have not seen either of us. You have never been here n'est pas?"

The owner was what Edward considered a low life, someone to be used and then discarded. Under any other circumstances the two would never even have acknowledged one another. This was strictly business, nothing more. The owner saw his chance to earn a little more money for doing almost nothing and took it. He rather liked the idea of having some knowledge about this dandy, he thought to himself, as he was smiling his toothless grin. The day could come when maybe he could use the information for his own advantage. Looking out to the woman in question his grin subsided some as it became clear to him that she was a black. Good looking but black all the same. Hell, he had to be careful, if word got out that a Nigger had slept in one of his rooms, no amount of money would make up for the loss of business. He would stay where he was and send someone else to show them the room. After all, he could claim he did not know who was staying back there if he hadn't seen em, couldn't he?

The two were slipped in the back to a small room where Edward was told to keep the wench out of sight. Edward agreed to this, then handed the girl who had shown them the room some more money. It was for a bottle of cheap wine, red beans and rice along with some water for Tori.

The girl took the money into her dirty hand and grunted. After all, it was none of her business how this dandy wished to spend his money and his time. She just wished he could have been hers instead of that whores.

Once inside the room, Tori was afraid to touch anything. Unlike the plantation house that had been kept spotless, this place was filthy. Edward had told her they were going to stop at an out of the way inn, but this was far worse than anything that she had ever expected, or even seen in her life. It was dark, dirty and hot, not to mention the overpowering smell of mildew and other nasty odors she did not want to identify.

"Edward, how long are we going to stay here?"

"As long as it takes the animals to rest up. A few hours will do it. You should rest up yourself. We still have a long way to ride and I plan on making this the last stop until we reach the city."

Tori was relieved to hear their stay would not be overnight. "I'm glad of that, this place is awful and I doubt that I will be able to rest at all."

Edward was almost going to laugh but stopped himself. One minute she was the lady in manner and speech, and then she said or did the damnedest things. Either she was very clever or very cunning at some game she was playing. Right now she was standing there looking so beautiful and wild. Her full breasts were barely concealed beneath the fine clothing, taunting him, asking to be released and ravished. It was driving him crazy. She was brazen and yet not. He would have to get away from her or lose his self control. She was acting too much the part of a lady and he had the desire to show her just what she really was.

Edward however was smart enough to know that he had to keep her thinking she was being looked after, protected and helped in her time of need. In doing that, she would cooperate and things would go a lot easier. Once their destination was reached however... "I will send someone in to help you. You stay in here and do no not leave the room. I mean it this time, Tori. Do not leave. This is not the kind of place that you would be very safe in and I can't go on getting you out of trouble," he laughed. Then in a more subdued tone he added "I know it's not the best of places, it's just the best I can do right now. Please, forgive me."

Tori felt guilty, he was only trying to help her and she was not thinking of how he was putting himself on the line. "I promise Edward, you will not have to worry about me leaving the room, I'll do as you say. You are being so kind to me.

Leone will hear of all you have done. Edward I owe you an apology. I misjudged you. You are a true gentleman like your brother."

He had heard enough and had to get out. It was getting so he thought he would burst at the seams with laughter. He was so damn clever. She trusted him and was willing to go anywhere with him at this point. Without another word he left the room. Tori thought it was because of modesty and that she had embarrassed him.

A short time later a young girl of about eleven came and brought Tori a bowl of beans and rice along with more fresh water and a blanket for the bed. The last item she carried in was a chamber pot. She neither talked or looked at Tori, just did what she had to and left. The food Tori would not eat, it looked awful and she hated beans anyway. The thick grease floating on the top along with the bits of fatty meat turned her stomach. She took the mug and sat on the edge of the bed too drained to do anything else. After drinking some water she removed her skirt and shoes. Then she lay down on the bed to rest and cool down.

The mosquitoes whined in her ears and bit hungrily at her flesh. Slapping at them did not help any and in the end she reluctantly covered herself with the grimy blanket. This helped some but it did not help her with the black roaches and beetles. Bugs ran around the floor and up the walls disappearing for a while in the cracks only to reappear further along. This kept her squirming at the edge of her bed. As tired as she was, falling asleep was difficult. However, in the end, exhaustion took over. She just did not care. Today had been a nightmare and sleep was her only escape.

Tori's dreams were once again all mixed up. One minute she was with Linni, the next she was on a horse riding fast to get away from Jack. The ride from the plantation had been fast and long. Now her dream took her through the activities of the day in slow motion.

For three long hours they had pushed along the road leaving it to hide in the bushes or trees when they saw someone coming. Several times her heart had been in her throat. She had dreaded being found and captured. Tori had not much of a chance to enjoy the view of the river as they followed it downstream. Now in her dream it was a nightmarish blur. The road was twisty and in some places the going had not been that easy. She had thanked God that she had taken riding lessons and could handle the mount she was on. At any other time the ride would have been a great adventure. This time, it was a race for her life and she rode not seeing or caring just hoping that she got to New Orleans and Leone.

It had crossed her mind that she was riding further and further away from the lake, but she knew in her heart that she would be back with Leone on the plantation soon. Besides, she had no choice but to go with Edward. Without his help she might very well hang for a crime she did not commit. Then her dream took her back to the lake and back home. Slowly this vision faded as she slipped still deeper into a dreamless state.

Tori slept for the rest of the day. It was sunset when a knock at the door woke her from her dreams and the young girl entered carrying a bowl of hot soup. "You have to eat this and be ready to leave soon." No smile, just an order. She looked at Tori then. "My Pa ain't never had no Nigger stay here, and I hate Niggers. I got myself a lot more work cause of you. So's I think you best hurry and git yourself out of here, see." Even though she was a child, the hate in her eyes like an adults was very intense and mean, she meant what she had said.

Tori was shocked by her statement and felt sorry for her at the same time. "I'm sorry if I have made more work for you, please forgive me."

Angrily the young girl spat back, "Ain't going to. You just git out!" She left without another word.

Tori ate the soup, finding it was not as bad as she thought. It tasted like nothing she'd had before and looked like some sort of meat and fish. She ate fast, partly to be finished in time, partly out of hunger, but especially because she was sure if she investigated what it was she was eating, she would be ill. In minutes, she had dressed and was ready to go. If only the stiffness in her body would leave, she would be fine. Maybe by riding a little more it would help. That little more turned out to be all night long.

Edward had not spoken much in the first few hours. They had been traveling very fast and trying to cover as much ground as they could before darkness fell. Now the going would be slow.

"Edward, I want to thank you for letting me rest as long as you did and for sending the soup in before we left. It was really considerate of you."

"Not considerate at all, I knew this would be a long ride and you would do better if you had food in you. The girl told me you had not touched the beans, so I had her take you some of the soup they had."

"Well, it was very good of you to do that, in fact I quite enjoyed it. The flavor was like nothing I've had before. Do you know what it was?"

There she was at it again, playing her game. It was getting to him. How stupid did she think he was? "Most folks know that dish round here. You must have had gator sometime! Come now, Tori, you can fool Leone with that innocent act but I'm not as naïve as him. Just stop your talking and concentrate on the ride, the moon will be up soon and we should make better time."

Tori felt hurt, she knew it was not Edward's fault that he thought she was acting. How was he to know that she was really telling the truth. Still, it stung to have him think bad of her. She wanted so much to explain to him but then that was impossible. Even if she had wanted to tell him the truth about herself there and then, she could not have proved it to him. In her hurry to leave Leone's plantation she had forgotten her crumpled contacts. She had hidden them safely in the back of a drawer, but now she wondered if that had been a wise move?

Edward briefly broke the difficult silence that had developed between them. "It is best if we ride in silence so as not to draw any attention to ourselves. River pirates could be around. Need I say more?"

He didn't need to say anything more. The tone in his voice had done that. The silence that followed gave her time to ponder and her wandering thoughts caused her to fear for their safety. They must have found Kate's body by now and be looking for them, for her at least. Her leaving must make her look guilty. She only hoped she had done the right thing in running like she had.

The night in the beginning had been clear, letting the moon light their way. Now, however, clouds kept hiding the moon and blanketed the road with a darkness Tori had never experienced outside. Always in her time, there seemed to be a house or street lamp or lights from passing cars. Even driving home late at night, it had never seemed to be this black.

The shapes of the trees were frightening her, as if she were a small child. Sounds unfamiliar to her ears leapt up and grabbed at her senses. Whispers of the wind in the grass seemed to be talking to her, laughing in her face. Tori moved her horse up next to Edward's where he would protect her.

He must have sensed her uneasiness as he broke his silence, this time somewhat softer in tone as he spoke. "Looks like we are in for a storm. Let us just hope we get to town before it breaks."

She looked over at him, surprise sounding in her voice, "you can't mean that we will go on in the rain Edward? We will be soaked and I can't imagine what these roads would be like. The mud would be awful, not to mention dangerous to ride on."

She sounded like he was crazy to consider such a thing. Maybe he was crazy but hell he had to push on. There was no going back now. "You'll ride as long as I will. Don't worry, I think that if we keep going as fast as we are, we will make it before it breaks."

Tori had her doubts about that. The moon was coming out less and less and twice through the moss-covered trees she swore she saw lightening. She had not heard thunder yet, so that could mean she might be wrong. But she could feel the air beginning to move. The wind was picking up. The trees were moving and the Spanish moss that hung so still most of the time, seemed now to have come alive. The long tangles of moss, were like the long arms of an octopus reaching out to grab her. Leaning forward into the wind with her head down, she let her horse once again follow Edward's. Tori found herself hoping that Leone's people had finished the levee's and that they held. Leone had been right when he said it was going to storm and the lowlands flood. His fields would be saved, but what about the road they were on, so close to the water. This brought panic and the need to know if there was any possibility of such an occurrence. Lifting her head up and calling above the sound of the wind cracking through the branches, Tori was just able to make herself heard. "Edward if it rains, the river won't wash us off the road will it?"

He shouted back to her, "no, we are far enough inland for that not to happen but we had best hurry because it's not the river that has me worried. It's the wind and the lightening that gets the horses nervous and we won't have a chance of reaching the city unnoticed if we lose them."

With that, a crack of thunder rolled in the distance and the horse that Tori was on side stepped a little as if telling her that something was coming that he did not like.

"Easy boy it's fine, it's going to be just fine, I hope." She reached down on the horses neck to pat him, and her hand came away covered with white froth. She had not realized how hard they had been pushing the animals until that moment. The horses neck and sides were streaked with sweat. On looking closer she could see not only was her hand covered with the white salty sweat, but her own legs stuck to her soaked bloomers. The animals had to rest soon or they would not make it.

She was about to tell Edward of her concern, when she looked up and noticed that it was somewhat lighter. Was it a trick, could her eyes be wrong, or was it possible that the hours had passed and morning was near?

What she was seeing was the pre dawn light and a few lights from the outskirts of the city. Not many in the beginning, just an odd light in a window every now and then. However the sight was something to lift her spirits. She sat up and took notice, for the first time in hours, of her surroundings. They had made it. They were almost at the end of their journey, and soon Tori found herself following Edward down the streets of New Orleans.

The street names seemed to be jumping out at her. Some of them were unchanged from her time but that was all that was familiar. Gone were the paved roads, a few here and there did have cobble stones but all too soon they were dirt again. The smell in places was terrible and she could swear that the few people around the streets followed them every now and then. Pre dawn New Orleans seemed less friendly than the countryside she had just been in and that had been bad enough.

"Stay close to me," snapped Edward's voice. "I don't want you getting lost at this hour of the morning. It's still sometime before dawn and you would never find me or Leone if you got separated from me now."

Excitedly she asked, "are we going to meet Leone right away?"

He turned to her, with a look of concern on his face. "No, that's impossible. I think it best if I take you to a friend of mine. Don't worry. She will say nothing to anyone. You can't very well just walk into Leone's hotel dressed like you are and you would never be allowed in there anyway. Fancies just can't do as they please, even free ones or have you forgotten?"

Tori wanted once again to tell Edward the truth but decided that she would wait. She had to tell Leone first.

The houses and shops they passed were so small, nothing like the New Orleans they had built over the years. Every now and then they would pass a street that even at this hour had some activity. She was so involved with looking around at all they passed, that she did not realize at first that they were in the center of the French quarter. When she finally saw where they were, she longed to go slower so she could see for herself how much it had changed.

Tori's eyes had become accustomed to the light and it was easier to see. She wanted to ride down the main street but knew that the alleys and back streets were the safest way for them to proceed. Every now and then the storm that had been following them flashed a blue white streak across the sky, lighting the area around her. A roll of thunder would follow, faster now as the storm grew closer. So intent was Tori on seeing as much as she could, it surprised her when they stopped outside a tall wall and Edward dismounted.

"You can get down. We are here. Please let me do the talking and you just stay quiet. It's best if I handle this and you remain here to begin with."

Tori nodded her head and got down. He handed her the reins to his horse and then disappeared through a side gate. She could understand why he needed to go in first but why he would leave her out here by herself was beyond her? Then to make matters worse, it was beginning to rain. Large heavy spots of water hit the ground. It started slow and then the heavens opened up. Still holding on to the horses she was not sure what to do. Should she stay put or go in after him? He might not even be aware of the fact that she was getting soaked.

"You's best git inside Miz, afore you's catches a death, "a voice called out to her. "It be right through dem gates, an up to dat door. Da light be on, an peoples dey be a waitin for you's."

Tori did not have to be told twice. She gave up the horses and ran for the house. She ran as quick as she could through the pouring rain, that was coming down so hard, it made it difficult to see. Even with the back door open and a light shining out into the courtyard, she was not sure of her footing. The storm had made it dark again and only the brief flashes of lightning lit her way. Somehow, Tori was able to make it without stumbling and for that she was grateful. The room that she entered seemed full of people to her but on glancing around she counted only three, one of whom was Edward.

Standing there dripping wet, she was well aware that they were staring at her. Their obvious scrutiny of her made her uncomfortable. Especially knowing she was standing there in her dripping wet skirt and blouse. She noticed the way Edward's eyes, in particular, seemed glued to her. Did she look that awful she thought? Then running her hands down her skirt to try and straighten it out, it became only too obvious why Edward was scrutinizing her the way he was. The rain had rendered her blouse transparent and she was, of course, bra-less. Embarrassed she could feel the color climb into her face. Instinctively she raised her arms and covered herself, hugging the wet material to her body causing her to visibly shiver.

"You poor girl, please accept my apology for not sending my houseboy out to get you sooner. I was unaware that the rain had started. You must be frozen my dear and very tired after such a long ride. Lacy, take Miss Tori to the kitchen and see to it that she gets something warm and dry to wear. Some hot tea would be good for her too."

Tori looked at this woman whose home she had just entered and could see that it must be a home of prominence. The woman was taller than herself and very well endowed. She had the reddest hair that Tori had ever seen. This along with her heavily made-up face created an almost comical vision. The humorous sight was off-set however by the elegance of her low cut dress which was like something out of an old movie. It was truly beautiful and the jewelry that hung around her neck was exquisite. Tori found herself thinking that with a few lessons in the art of applying makeup and tinting of her hair, the woman would be very attractive. She found herself warming towards this person. Even the makeup could not hide the friendliness behind her eyes.

In the sudden silence that had developed, Tori suddenly became aware of male and female voices, mixed with laughter and soft piano music from somewhere off in the house. Judging by the way this woman was dressed and at the late hour it could only mean that a party was still going on from the night before.

Had she not read somewhere how the people of New Orleans loved to entertain, and that it was common for such evenings to go on well into the next day? How inconvenient their arrival must be. Yet this woman showed true Southern hospitality and had welcomed them. She felt as if she should make amends for their intrusion.

"You will please excuse how I look Mam, but as you said I am tired and have had a long journey. I do hope I am not being a nuisance to you. It sounds as if we have come at a bad time. Your guests must be wondering what had happened to you. Please, Mam, I will be fine if I can just get warm and dry. I will try not to be a bother."

The woman looked at Tori and smiled, stepping forward and taking hold of Tori's shoulders, "You will be no bother my dear, any friend of Edward's is welcome here in my house. You can stay as long as you need, and I will see to it that you feel at home in no time."

"Thank you very much Mam."

"Oh don't be so formal my dear. You may call me Aunt Salle, like most of my friends do. It comes from my given name, Madame Rose La Salle. Now off to the kitchen with you, I will join you in a short while. I must however see to my guests right now. You do understand I'm sure."

"Of course I do. Please don't let me detain you any longer. You have been so kind already." Tori followed the girl Lacy, out of the small entry hall and down a long dark passage way which she guessed to be well in the back of the house. There were several closed doors on each side and two more hallways leading in different directions. The size of the house seemed enormous to her and very well furnished from what she could tell.

Suddenly, Tori walked into the largest kitchen she had seen. Food was everywhere, and three large black women were baking bread and what she surmised to be breakfast. The kitchen was warm and it smelled like heaven. She was given a seat near the fire and a cup of hot tea. Lacy told her she would be right back with something for her to wear and with that she left Tori sitting there feeling very lucky to have come into such a grand home. Even with the thunder rolling outside and the lightening flashing in through the window, Tori felt relaxed and safe. Edward had kept his promise. Nothing had happened to them and now they were only hours away from Leone and his help. As the dawn slowly started over the horizon bringing with it a new day, Tori hoped it would also bring with it the help she so desperately needed.

# Chapter 6

As soon as Tori left the room, Rose turned toward Edward letting her benevolent look slip away. Uncontrollable laughter shook the women's large frame. Her whole torso seemed to jiggle as she tried to gain her composure. "Where did you say she came from?"

Edward was grinning as he spoke, "I didn't, not that that seems to be worrying you any. Why Aunt Rose, you seem to find your new guest very amusing."

His sarcastic use of Aunt Rose did little to bother her. She was very intrigued by this Tori. How had such a beauty fallen into the hands of such a fop as Edward she wondered. Her mirth gone, Rose suddenly became all business. Whenever there was money to be made she was always serious. And Rose's instincts were telling her that if she played her cards right she stood to gain much more than just money.

Edward sensed the change in her mood, and feared losing control of the situation. The woman who stood before him was going to have to follow his instructions for his plan to work. His terms had to be met. Knowing Rose as he did, he knew he had to handle her very diplomatically as he was well aware that she hated being told what to do under any circumstances. However in his haste to settle things quickly, he made a mistake in telling, not asking her. "You and I had better go into your parlor, to discuss the terms of her staying on."

My! How the timid can roar, she thought. How dare he have the audacity to tell me what to do. Unlike Edward though, experience had taught her how to hold her temper. She would hear him out after putting him in his place. With no trace of irritation showing on her face and in a calm voice she answered him. "This I can hardly wait to hear." She looked at him with a warning tone in her voice continuing. "I might add my dear Edward, that if I had not seen or heard her for myself, you would have been shown the door right now. No one tells me what to do in my own house!"

Realizing his blunder, Edward rapidly resorted to make amends. "I am truly hurt madam." He placed his hand over his heart. "If I sounded presumptuous or demanding, you misunderstood me." He leaned over to her and kissed her cheek lightly. Then whispering in her ear he added, "Would I ever offer you anything but the best?"

"You would cut your mother's throat if it would benefit you and we both know that don't we? Come, come Edward. Don't try to sweet talk your way into my good graces. There is still that little matter of some money you owe me, shall we say for past services rendered. Not to mention a certain lack of lady luck," she smiled knowingly. "It's only because I see the chance of recouping my losses, will I discuss this matter with you, and nothing more."

Edward followed her into the next room known as Rose's parlor. Only a select few had ever seen the inside of this chamber, such as the nobility and government officials, along with the very best of her clients. However, like the rest of her clientele, up until now, Edward only viewed the front and upstairs of the house.

Madame La Salle ran the most elite and expensive whorehouse in New Orleans, and she intended to keep it that way. Her girls were known to be the best and word was that if she did not have what you wanted, then for a certain amount of money she would get it for you. Only those who could afford her prices came here and they always got what they paid for. Privacy, discretion and the very best New Orleans would ever see as far as ladies of the night.

Some of Rose's regulars had certain girls booked from one week to the next. Others seemed to enjoy a variety. It was for her special clientele that Rose was always on the lookout for new and fresh talented young ladies. No one questioned whatever happened to the girls who left, and never feared any girl blackmailing them. After all, it was said that Madam La Salle paid off her girls and sent them up North, out of harms way. Not one of them had ever returned. Once they were gone they were truly gone. Still there were those who rumored, she was far too greedy to pay off any girl and that when a lady reached the end of her stay, she had in fact reached the end of her life! It was a rumor that had never been proven and never looked into.

Rose was not looking at Edward when she addressed him, "You would like something to drink, Edward, while I check my book to see just how much you owe me? We might be able to make a deal for your Tori." She flipped open a ledger as she talked. "Wipe the slate clean shall we say, with maybe a little credit on the side?"

Edward said nothing. He had no intention of wiping his slate clean by letting Rose get her hands on the wench. No, he would wait and see how much he owed and then he would make his deal. "I have written the amount down for you if you care to take a look. My, I must be a soft hearted old fool, to let you run up such a tab. Still all in all, I knew you would someday come through for me."

He knew being soft hearted was far from the reason she had allowed him to get into such a situation. His family name and fortune, not to mention the fact that he always brought the finer young gentlemen to her establishment, was closer to the truth.

Edward pulled the book across the table toward him and looked at the amount he owed. Some of which was for girls, but most he could see was a gambling debt. This he had run up on the many nights he had come in for a quick game. He swallowed hard, "I'll accept a Brandy if your offer still remains." He was biding his time, quickly going over the options in his mind. Edward knew he had to offer her a good deal, something that would be right for both of them, in order to get his way. He knew Rose was carefully watching him believing she had the upper hand. No matter what, he had to stay calm and not let her see his intentions he told himself. Stalling as if thinking, he let his eyes wonder around the room, which in his opinion was terribly overdone. The red velvet curtains, and gold brocade over-stuffed chairs clashed with the blue carpet. The room smelled too, with a mixture of Rose's heavy perfume and the smoke of her small strong cigars. Everything about the room was Rose, too much, too gaudy and very expensive.

"I did run up somewhat of a tab didn't I?" he laughed. "What would you say if I told you, I wish to pay it off in cash, right now?"

She smiled slyly, "I would say that I would have to see it to believe it." Her eyes sparkled at this prospect. He could be bluffing she told herself, or maybe not. "Did you finally get lucky in a game of chance? Or did one of your ladies take pity on you?" She was really enjoying watching him squirm. Her guess was that he was lying. Trying to bluff her now as always, and as usual he would lose. She smiled within, careful not to let him see her true emotions. Tori was getting closer and closer to being hers. She would become a working part of her organization very soon indeed.

Edward smirked, "A game, yes. You are nearly right, not of chance, but of skill and planning. I acted on an opportunity that paid off. It gave me what I wanted and will give you Tori in the end."

"In the end?" she questioned. Had he said the end, she asked herself again? This last statement had come as a shock to her and it took quite an effort to cover this fact, for it was she who was being closely observed now. Rose needed time to conceal her confusion and resume control.

"Edward, you had best explain to me this plan of yours and while you are doing so, please be a darling and pour me some brandy," she spoke as if nothing was bothering her. She sweetly added, "along with one for yourself of course."

Her actions did not fool him. Edward knew the tables had been turned. Now it was Rose who was trying to conceal that she was interested and intrigued. As Edward turned from her to pour the expensive brandy into the crystal glasses, his lips curled in an evil grin of victory. He finally had her where he wanted. He, Edward Duval, had the all powerful madam eating out of his hands. She was just about to find out who she was dealing with here! Of how brilliant he had been in his acquisition of such a beauty. Very slowly and carefully he explained to her the happenings of the last twenty-four hours, changing a few details of course. It would do him no good to have this woman know the whole truth now would it? He claimed that the overseer had attacked him and he of course had to kill him in self-defense. Of how he had plotted against Tori, so she would be blamed for it, thus giving him the hold that he and Rose would need to keep her. It was going to be nothing short of blackmail of the highest degree. Something he knew Rose would understand and accept.

Anticipating the questions before she could ask them, Edward continued laying out his plan. He wouldn't let Rose voice even the slightest opinion. He talked on, explaining how they both knew Tori would be of no use to Rose, until the scandal died down. Just in case someone should put two and two together and recognize her, she would have to be kept out of sight. In the meantime she would be for him only. He would pay for her upkeep until Rose took over. "You'll see, she will cooperate when she realizes she has no choice. Where could she go, who would listen to her? She is wanted for murder and there is no way she can prove her innocence."

Rose had seen and heard many things in her line of business, but this beat them all. Still she wondered, was there more here than meets the eye? She was curious. "I see, and you did all of this because you saw a chance at having her for a play thing?"

"What I did or why, is entirely my own matter. There are other reasons I wanted her away from the plantation. Far more personal matters that will remain my business. I will not now or ever indulge you or anyone with further explanations. Am I to assume madam that we have reached an agreement? You do after all stand to obtain one hell of a good looking wench. Unlike most of your ladies, this one is highly educated. She's bound to bring in lots of money, keeping your customers happy for some time to come."

Rose could see how this Dandy had come up with a very workable plan, but there were questions that remained unanswered. There were things she would have to find out for herself. Looking at him now, so sure of himself, she had the overpowering urge to knock some of the wind out of his sails. "If you can pay me what you owe me and pay for her keep for say six months, I will call it a deal."

"Done!" With that Edward reached into his pocket and removed a large amount of money from a leather pouch. The look of shock on the old madam's face was wonderful to Edward. "I took the liberty of removing this money from my brothers desk, or should I say Tori took it. Her escape will be well paid for don't you see? With this amount of money missing, people will say she could have traveled far away in her escape. They will have to give up searching for her and soon she will be forgotten, but always remain marked as guilty. This money seals her fate." Pleased with himself he chuckled as he waved the pouch at Rose. "Shall we say she is almost paying you for her stay here."

The two of them laughed, as Rose and Edward raised their glasses and toasted. Each with a new respect for the other! But Rose made a mental note. She would have to watch this Edward. He was not as stupid as she had assumed. He was in fact very clever and cunning! No, conniving was more the word that best fit him. These were all traits that she knew only too well, and like herself, she knew he was not to be trusted. Rose knew also that she had to gain a certain amount of control back and fast. "I do want to make one thing very clear to you Edward. This is my house and as such I intend to remain in full control of my new guest. You have to let me decide how to deal with her, starting right now."

Edward nodded in agreement, "She is in your hands, but she is for the next six months, mine exclusively. You agreed, no other man is to go near her."

"Yes, yes of course that is understood. What I'm getting at is gaining rapid and full control over the woman. I can't very well have her screaming to be let loose or trying to run now can I? I'm telling you this has to be settled very quickly."

So it was decided that they had best tell Tori of her new circumstances right away, rather than try to fool her. After all, it would not take her long to figure out for herself where she was and that no meeting with Leone was going to occur.

"We will take her upstairs to the back room, the luxury suite. By the look of the amount of money you have there you can well afford it." She hesitated as another thought came to mind. "It will be out of action for some time costing me a lot of money, so I believe a little extra is in order."

Edward knew she had him, after all where else could he keep her at this point? Besides it was a small price to pay to have her safely held captive.

Rose was still talking, her voice friendly and warm. "But the curiosity of who is in that room and what she is like, will in the end only serve to make me more money. So my dear Edward, you can keep the extra."

Surprise covered his face, and left him temporarily speechless.

She laughed at the expression. "My I must have a soft spot for you. But then we are partners now as well as friends are we not? She walked up to him and gave him a hug. Pushing him away, slightly she kissed him on the cheek as if sealing their agreement and friendship. Then the friendly Rose vanished and the business Rose took over. "Yes, we will take her to her room immediately but you will have to tell her! Not I, Edward darling! I think that I will be needed in the parlor."

"What and miss all the fun? Come Rose, I may need your help in convincing her the story is true. Along with calming her down if you understand my meaning. You don't want a fight on your hands do you? The screaming and carrying on she might do, could upset some of your present customers and cause inquiries that neither of us need or want."

She saw the sense in this. Edward was being very practical and this pleased her. "Very well, when you put it like that, I see that I had better come along. The sooner she knows that she has to follow orders the better! And my orders are always followed…"

Tori had never felt so frightened and betrayed in all her life. How could she have been so dumb, so utterly stupid? Looking back she could see for herself that she had made all the wrong moves. Edward had indeed manipulated her to do as he wanted. She clearly understood why he had not wanted her to go into the study. Sure, he had taken care of everything, and had set her up. She could never prove her innocence now and even Leone would have a hard time believing her. Tori knew she was alone and that it was up to her to figure a way out of the mess she had gotten into.

"Never again will I trust anyone! Do you hear me, never?" Shouting did little good. No one seemed to listen to her calls anyway, or come to her aid. The total silence only told her that the house and its contents were most likely asleep. It was well into the morning and not a sound came from the other side of the locked door. Twice she had gone to the window to see if she might find a way down but there was no way other than jumping and she knew that was out of the question. They knew she would not call for help from the window. After all they were right, if she were found, she would surely hang for the murders of both Kate and Jack. Funny, she had hated the man and remembered wishing him dead. Now however, she wished he was alive. He had been her only witness to what had happened and Leone would have gotten him to talk, she just knew it. Edward must have known it also, that's why he killed him.

Frustrated and angry she started talking out loud. "You have thought this out well and you might have me where you want me for now but not for long I promise you that. I will find a way to get out and back to the lake. I'll do whatever it takes to get away from here, and the both of you." She realized that talking to the door was stupid, and standing had become tiring. Tori had cried for hours leaving her exhausted, and finally she settled into a chair to think. She had to outsmart them she told herself and she knew that in the days ahead she would do just that.

For the first time she really looked around at her lavish furnishings. She had thought it was a room in a very well to do house and that Aunt Salle was a fine woman of wealth and standing. Some house, a whorehouse with Salle as the Madam! She had tried to reason with her, begging her to help, to listen to her pleas and only found an unresponsive, calculating bitch.

Edward had enjoyed telling her how he had set her up with every detail of his plan. How he was going to enjoy watching his brother suffer, and squirm under the guilt of having allowed Tori into his home without really knowing her. How, by doing so, he had allowed Tori to kill their beloved Kate. Oh yes, he had gone on and on explaining to her that she belonged to him now with nowhere to go, and had no one to help her, how screaming at him was useless and dangerous. She had best stay quiet and behave or risk being found and hung.

What was it, she wondered, with the men of this century that made them all want her? First Jack, then Leone and now Edward! Leone she reasoned had been different. His feelings for her had been the complete opposite of the other two. She could even sort of understand Jack's obsession, but Edward's? Tori hated him, and wanted to kill him at the moment he had finished explaining her situation. God Help Her! If she had had a chance and a weapon, she might very well have done it! Instead, all she did was land a hard slap across his face then turned her back on them, and walked to the other side of the room. Tori would not give them the satisfaction of seeing her cry, or letting them know they had her where they wanted her. Then the door closed and the key had turned in the lock.

That's how it stayed for hours, closed and locked. No one had come by and nothing had happened. She wondered how long the solitary confinement was going to continue. There was nothing to do, and no one to talk to. When would she eat? How was she going to keep her sanity? The room was large but held nothing in the way of entertainment. Not even any books, "Like they would read in a place like this stupid," she mumbled. She had explored her surroundings carefully, memorizing everything and its position. "You never know what can come in handy. If I'm to get out of this place I just might have to play McGuyver.

Off to one side was a small dressing room and opposite this she had found a bathroom. She noticed the size of the bath could easily fit two people. The large bedroom itself was divided into two areas, one sitting the other sleeping. The queensize canopy bed, had a large mosquito net hung from its sides giving it a romantic look. The carpet was thick and the prettiest pink salmon color she had ever seen. Two stuffed chairs covered in bright fabric that matched the curtains faced a fireplace. Between them, stood a table for eating she assumed, as nothing was placed on its shining wood surface. Everything was here that two people would need for an evening of pleasure.

"Must be pretty expensive even in these times to have a room like this. I wonder if I'm to be moved or worse, if I'm to be part of the entertainment," she asked herself softly. She shuddered at the thought. Sure Edward had said something about her being only for his use, but she had been too angry at that point to listen closely. Anyway, how could she believe him, the lying son of a bitch? Only time would tell if she was going to have to ... She shook her head violently no! One thing was certain she would not be the most willing of whores.

No. Sir! They were going to be in for a surprise if they thought she was going to be a willing part of all this!

It was then she heard the door being unlocked and the Madam walked in followed by the girl Lacy, whom Tori had met when she first arrived. She had not however noticed that Lacy was pregnant. How she missed that fact she did not know but then, she was not sure of much these days. She made up her mind right there and then to start paying more attention to detail, to listen and learn. It would be her only hope.

"I'm so glad to see you have calmed down my dear. Very sensible of you. Things will be so much nicer for us. Shall we talk?"

Aunt Salle was pointing to the chairs by the fireplace, "will you join me in a cup of coffee?"

"I could use a cup, and I do want to talk. I do however have a lot of questions concerning my stay here."

"I'm sure you do and I for one think it best if we get this little discussion out of the way, so we know where we stand. You seem to be a smart young lady and I hope you will give me your full cooperation. Not only as you are doing now but in the days that lay ahead."

"That depends on what cooperation you are talking about, Madam," the last word was spoken sarcastically.

"My name, dear girl, is Aunt Salle to you. Now sit down and let me explain a few things. I will only go over this once, so you will be well advised to pay attention. I am not an early riser and only because this talk has to be dealt with, am I here at this time."

Tori sat down feeling she was a student being talked to by the headmistress of a girl's school. She felt the same way years ago back in boarding school. As Rose spoke, the girl Lacy went back and fourth with buckets of water and was obviously filling the bath. Tori could not help but feel sorry for her in her condition, having to carry the heavy loads. She decided then to befriend her as soon as she had the chance.

"Now the rules for you are simple. You will be kept in this room at all times, that is until I feel you can be trusted. Don't try to fool me into believing you may be trusted, because you won't get far. You are to stay quiet at night. Do not try to call out to anyone outside the door. You will I'm sure hear people from time to time. If you were to call out, you may be reaching the one person whom you would not want to know of your whereabouts. A lot of well known clients come here my dear, people in authority. For instance the States Attorney, along with wealthy plantation owners who have undoubtedly heard of your crimes by now and they will be on the lookout for you. You will have Lacy here to bring you your food and take care of your needs. She is of no use to me in her present condition."

Tori's hate for the woman seated opposite her was growing rapidly. All she wanted to do at that second was lash out both physically and verbally. But common sense told her, it would be nothing more than a waste of time and effort. It would gain her little and most likely bring this woman's wrath down upon her. Watching, Aunt Salle sat sipping her coffee so calm and sure of herself, brought home the realization that she was really quite powerless to do anything. At this thought a cold fear crept deep down inside her, but she would not let it take hold.

There was going to be no reaching this heartless creature. One had to play by her rules, and Tori realized that the only chance she might have of getting out, would be to play along. She smiled inwardly to herself as she thought of how she was going to manipulate her way to freedom.

"That's fine and well Aunt Salle" the sarcasm oozed out sweetly. "I have only one question before I agree to stay and live by your rules. Am I to be one of your girls? Because, if you think I am, you can damn well think again."

Rose laughed at her. She was very amused by this show of defiance. Indeed, she had expected nothing less. The Madam could see the hate written all over Tori's face. The control she must have, to just sit there like that amazed her. Rose doubted that she herself could have done so. A sudden thought crossed her mind. Was that admiration she was feeling towards her? It couldn't be, because if it was, she was in trouble. She got where she was today by never allowing herself to feel anything for any of her girls. And that was not about to change. Placing the china cup she had been holding softly down, Rose made up her mind to leave. She had said just about all she was going to at this time. "You may rest for now, as you don't belong to me yet. When the time comes however, I have no doubt that you will cooperate fully."

The Madam was standing only inches away from Tori. A ray of sunlight filtered in the window illuminating her red hair and face. Tori could see in the sunlight that Rose's face was older and layered with heavy makeup. Layers of which were caking and cracking, leaving areas that seemed to be peeling away, exposing the monster hidden below. Only her eyes seemed human as they bore into Tori caring but firm. Rose's hand reached out and took hold of Tori's chin raising her face up toward the light.

"In the meantime you belong to Edward Duval. He has paid for your accommodation and has full rights to you. What he does is his business, so long as no harm comes to you and you remain as beautiful as you are." Rose's long fingers stroked the side of her face gently. "As soon as you are mine, and have no doubt I will own you, you will be outfitted with the best wardrobe and will only be with the most influential clientele. These Gentlemen, whom I have no doubt you will find pleasant to be with, will treat you like the lady you are. I have big plans for you Tori…" Her voice softened and trailed off as if the last statement had been for herself alone. She had made her point and without further delay, was making her way to the door.

"You and I will spend more time together soon. As for now, I will leave you to think over what I have said. Please cooperate because as Lacy can tell you, I never fail to have my way. Isn't that right Lacy?"

"Yes Aunt Salle." She was behind Rose saying yes but shaking her head no, with eyes as big as saucers. She rolled them looking from Rose towards the ceiling. This act of defiance sent Tori's hopes soaring. It was all she could do to keep her face straight. She felt that she would burst out laughing at any second. To hide her amusement she dropped her gaze quickly to the floor. Tori realized she had at least one friend in this hellhole and for that she was relieved.

Rose, was pleased with how the conversation had turned out and mistaking Tori's attitude as one of acceptance, she left the room.

The next few days slipped by very quietly. Lacy came by with food three times a day. She even brought up a decanter of wine that Tori had requested. It seemed the Madam was indeed trying to keep her content for the time being. With no sign of Edward or of the Madam, Tori could only wonder as to what they were up to. Days were coming and going, time was passing by and the lake and her twentieth century life seemed to be slipping further away than ever before.

The first few nights had been difficult. All Tori had to do was call out but fear and the fact that Aunt Salle had been telling the truth, kept her silent. She was wanted for murder, no matter which way she looked at it. Still the laughter and the sounds each night kept Tori on edge. Twice now her door had been knocked at, and she head held her breath, hoping against hope that whoever it was would not come in. She prayed that Rose had meant what she had said about her not having to take part...

As for Lacy, Tori could not make up her mind. She wanted to trust the girl and have her as a friend but she also knew that the girl was one of the whores who worked here and in doing so, could be reporting all she said to her boss. It was Lacy who did most of the talking when she came to Tori's room in the daylight hours. Nights were long and lonely, filled with anger that would slip into depression as she drank. The hours would pass and as the effects of the wine took hold, Tori would lay down upon the bed and cry herself to sleep.

Last night had been different though. Lacy, part out of loneliness and part out of kindness toward Tori, whom she genuinely liked, had slipped into the room to keep her company. Each of them seemed to sense some of the pain the other was feeling. It was this pain and need to talk to someone, that eventually broke down the barriers between them.

Lacy was easy to like and it did not take Tori long to feel comfortable around her. She realized that the fondness she felt for her was also mixed in with a lot of pity. Unbeknownst to Tori, Lacy so sad looking with her sulky mouth, kept her joy just below the surface. She had a secret that kept her going.

Lacy was sitting with Tori looking out at the night sky, when she decided she could really talk to this woman. "I'm not going back to work for Aunt Salle when this little one is born you know. It isn't going to be raised here or given away or sold either.

"What do you mean Lacy? Aren't you free to come or go? I mean, I thought that you worked for her because you wanted. That you were ... they just can't sell your baby can they.? It had never occurred to Tori that Lacy was anything but a young girl caught up in the wrong life. Now here she was telling her she was nothing more than a slave!

Lacy looked at her now, thinking this woman was the strangest person she had ever met. Not quite all in the head, she guessed. Or maybe she really did not know about such things. Maybe she was from some place where they did not have slavery, like her man was always telling her about.

"I'm not free. Will be soon though. Aunt Salle, she bought me at the auction to be a kitchen girl, but one of the men he done saw me and paid a lot of money to have me and all."

Shock ran though Tori as for the first time she really began to comprehend how Lacy lived. "How terrible for you. You can't be much older than sixteen?"

"Oh it ain't bad, and sixteen be plenty old enough. It was not the first time I laid with a man anyways. Just the first time I wanted to. He was so kind and good him paying all that money. Told me he cared. He could have got some cheap whore down the riverfront that know'd more an all. But no way, he wanted me and now I know my Robert he loves me. I ain't been with no other here septing him. He paid for me and them others. They don't want no girl with the looks of me. Too dark and all. Aunt Salle got it good until I got with child. I worked the kitchen and at night made her money by being with him." She wiped a tear from her cheek.

Tori said nothing. She just sat listening to her. This girl was little more than a child. A child who would believe anything and anyone, if what she was told made her happy.

"He wants me to be his an all. Tried to buy me, sept she said not yet, maybe one day. Never is more like it. She will never let me and Jim be together. It ain't the money either. Jim he got as much as he needs."

"So what do you and this Jim have planned, or should I ask?"

"We just a going to wait a while. I will be free one day and this here babe,' she rubbed her middle," is going to be free too."

Tori hoped for her sake that the girl was right but she could not see the Madame letting her go now or ever. This dusky colored girl was becoming quite a beauty and Tori guessed worth far more than her Jim could pay in the long run.

"You get to see this Jim of yours now? I thought that Rose said that you aren't working?"

"No, I have not seen him in a while, she would not let me see him even if he did come by, which he hasn't. I know where to find him if I have to and I know that he must be real busy not to come and see me."

Lacy just sat there looking out the window and Tori felt sorry for her. The man most likely had left her when she got pregnant and would not see her again. Damn him whoever he was. The girl was going to be really hurt when she found out the truth. No one wants a whore, that was the real truth. She felt a closeness for this girl and wanted to confide in her. Tonight seemed too soon however. Maybe tomorrow she would start talking a little bit more about herself. If she and Lacy could get close, well maybe just maybe, she would help her get away from here. She not only held the key to the door but it seemed that Lacy would play a major role in any escape plan.

That night was the first time Tori did not cry herself to sleep. Her Linni and her time seemed just a little closer and not so hopelessly out of reach. Little did she know her high spirits were to be short lived and reality would come knocking all too soon.

Lacy did not return the next morning, one of the other girls came by with her breakfast and she was far from friendly. "I fail to see why you have to be treated like some queen. Sitting up here getting waited on all the time and not even working. It's not fair! I'll tell you that the other girls and I, we don't like it." The girl put her tray down and faced Tori with open contempt.

How could Tori blame her for her actions? She could not get angry, but she was worried. Had Lacy been a plant and now Rose was replacing her with this? Her anger came out in her response.

"I'm sorry if you don't like it but that's the way it is thanks to Aunt Salle," she snapped. Then changing her tone she spoke softly. "Where is Lacy, has something happened to her?"

"Nothing that ain't natural. She is down in the back trying to bring her bastard into the world. So I got stuck waiting on you. I won't bring up bath water or empty the pot, so you had best make do." With that the woman left, and Tori felt abandoned without a friend in the world. She was also worried about Lacy. The girl had not seemed that far along. Was the baby coming early? Would she have a doctor she wondered? That was not likely she thought.

The rest of the day crawled by. Her lunch was brought in by the same sour girl, who was not in any mood to talk and left right away. Dinner was the same but a new decanter of wine had been added to the tray. Tori guessed that Rose kept tabs on every detail. She must have known or was told that her wine was running low.

Tori could not complain about the food, it was very good and despite how she felt, she ate it. This night was hard though, she had been thinking of Lacy and of how she herself had given birth to that squirming pink bundle of joy. Of how her sister had been at her side coaching her and how happy they had been. She doubted anyone would be with Lacy like that. She missed her daughter desperately. Why, she asked, had this happened to her? She wanted to get out of here, back to the lake, to her time and her family. How long had it been now since she crossed over? Four, or six weeks, she had lost count. Then there was the memory of what Kate had told her. It bothered her some, the fact that Tommy had been missing only a year and yet she knew him to be a teenager. That meant the time door was not the same. Somehow she could go in it and maybe go forward too much, or not enough. Now that made no sense, if she went forward too little she thought, there would be two Tori's. Her head was all mixed up, and nothing was clear.

She was drunk and depressed that was all. She stripped off her clothes and climbed under the mosquito netting to lay down. The room was spinning proving she had indeed consumed far too much wine. She closed her eyes to block out the spins. Then she blocked out the sounds of the night and concentrated on a friendly vision. In her mind she could see and hear her little girl calling "mummy." It was good she had drunk herself silly she told herself because she could at least sleep and for a short time and escape the hell house. Aunt Salle could not keep her here forever. She was going to try harder to get out, but that was tomorrow and right now all she wanted was oblivion far from Salle, the house and its sounds of the night.

# Chapter 7

The smoke filled room was crowded with well dressed gentlemen and beautifully attired women. Over to one side a black man was playing the piano and a young woman was singing, her voice husky and strangely provocative. Three gentlemen sat to one side at a table playing a game of cards. One of these had his lady standing by him for luck. Every now and then she would reach down and hug him, encouraging him, even though he was losing. The room was aglow with soft warm light, reflected here and there off crystal chandeliers and golden framed mirrors. The atmosphere was cheerful and friendly. The laughter and conversations were light, the food and wine good, the people happy and carefree.

Rose seemed to be everywhere, mingling with her clients. Chatting here and there, stopping only to arrange introductions between the single gentlemen and her young women. She was about to make one of these arrangements, when from the front entrance there came the sound of a disturbance, shattering the atmosphere.

A few of her clients shifted nervously in their chairs. Everybody's attention was directed toward the front entrance. One gentleman was actually standing as if intending to leave, rather than be found is such a compromising position. Rose, however, was the picture of calm and showing no sign of irritation whatsoever and in a calm and controlled manner, took immediate action.

"Gentlemen! Gentlemen! "Please let's not get upset over some small disturbance. I will see to this commotion personally. Please, relax and enjoy the company of my girls. I'm sure it's just some poor young man wanting to come in and join us, and poor is just the word to describe him if you know what I mean?"

The laughter came from around the room as they understood her meaning. Only those of wealth and standing entered this establishment. That fact was well known. Getting by Rose's doorman was an impossible task if you did not meet the proper criteria. Safety, and privacy were therefore guaranteed. The gentleman who had been standing, seated himself back down satisfied that Rose would handle the intruder. Quickly the previous atmosphere returned and people resumed their activities.

Rose turned from the room and went to take care of whatever was going on in her foyer to cause such a commotion. Only then letting the annoyance show clearly on her face. Why her man had not been able to prevent such as intrusion was foremost in her mind. He would most definitely have to do better than he was, or find himself working in the cane fields. She stopped dead in her tracks when the entrance hall came into view. Now she could understand why her doorman was having so much trouble. What she saw caused her to smile, something she quickly hid behind her lace trimmed fan. The gentleman causing all the commotion was well known to her and all of New Orleans itself, and always welcome no matter under what circumstances.

It was very evident that he was somewhat intoxicated, a condition not new to him, but easily managed. She approached the pair, watching as the two pushed apart, both stumbling to keep their balance. It was then she realized her visitor was in a far worse condition than merely angry and slightly intoxicated. He was as many would say, roaring drunk. Normally Rose would have anyone in such a state driven home and told to come back when they had sobered up. But this one man had always been such a good customer, that Rose herself had a soft spot for him. She knew she would not ask him to leave right away. He intrigued her, and she had to admit that to get him into her bed would not be an unpleasant adventure. Impossible as that was, it did cause her to visibly shiver at the thought.

Rose never slept with any of her customers. It was a house rule of hers, one that she never broke. However she knew in this one case had he ever asked her, she would have made an exception. Smart enough to know that it could never come about, Rose shook her head sadly. She was not his type. Young and pretty, were much to his liking and that was why he was here now, for his usual choice of her girls. Always the same girl and always willing to pay high for the privilege. Tonight, however, his choice was occupied and would be unavailable. This meant she would have to pacify him somehow, or face an even harder to get along with drunk.

"I'll take over Apollo. You go back outside and try to do the job I have for you. You can do that can't you? Because if you can't, then I'll sell your black hide and find me someone who can."

"Yes Mam. I's sure can do it." He looked toward the now slightly subdued drunk. "Dis Genalman pushed in like. Insisted dat you'd not mind none. Him be who's he is, an here so's much."

"Yes, yes I know. Now you just go and do what you're supposed to do and I mean now!"

Rose then dismisses him with a wave of her hand and turned to give her full attention to her visitor.

"You my dear friend, had best follow me into my parlor. I don't think you are in any condition to join my other guests this evening, friends of yours or not."

"Condition Madam? You should know what condition I'm in."

His chuckle and the fact that he had pulled himself upright swaying only slightly, alerted her to the fact that some of his drunken state could be an act, or he was trying very hard to act sober. This started her chuckling softly while she listened to him.

"I have come here this evening, to this fine establishment," he waved his hand around the air dramatically, "to help cure my woes. I am not in need of a game of cards, or sweet conversation. What I need is comfort Madam."

He had a grin that was inscrutable. The deep wrinkles around his flashing dark eyes gave him a roguish look and the weather beaten tan on his skin, told that he spent most of his time outside. He was well built for his height, and wore only the best that money could buy. His hair had just a hint of curl about it. It was pulled back in a ponytail at the base of his neck, where it fell softly just below the collar of his jacket. His jet black hair shone in the light like raven feathers in the sun. His skin, olive in complexion, had a flush about it that had nothing to do with the evening heat. Something or someone had gotten under his skin and the man was genuinely upset.

Once into her parlor, Rose closed the door and watched him as he made his way over to one of the chairs, swaying as if he were on the deck of a ship at sea.

"How about some of that fine brandy you keep hidden away for yourself, Rose, my love."

"I think, Mr. Laffite, you have a belly full, and I am not about to let you have one more drop," she said sternly. Then softening a little added, "Why, would I want to have you pass out on me? Just what would I do with you then might I ask?"

"That Madam is easy. Simply put me to bed with one of your lovelies so I will not wake up all alone."

She knew that he was going to be impossible. This was not the first time that he had turned up at her place in this condition. And like the times before she knew it could only mean one thing. A certain young plantation owner's daughter, was again angry with him. She had no doubt forgone their secretly meeting, something the two had been doing for quite a while on a regular basis.

Foolish girl, Rose thought, did she not realize that Jean was the type of man that had to have female companionship. To hold a woman in his arms and make love to her, was as much a part of his life as breathing. But marry! If she thought that her tantrums and denying him his needs, would get him to propose marriage, humph! Jean Laffite was not the marrying kind, not him. Didn't that silly little fool, realize that he was already married, to his freedom and the sea?

"Jean, I am afraid that all of my girls are occupied this evening, not that you could enjoy them in the state you're in. My don't you let me get my carriage and send you home to sleep it off? You can come back tomorrow as my guest. Have any young lady on the house, just for old times, because we are old and dear friends, who understand one another, do we not?"

The dashing figure sat across from her and looked straight at Rose. Then placing a look of great hurt and sorrow upon his face he spoke, "you mean Rose my love, you would send me out of here, without a care as to the fact that I am in desperate need of company? No not just company. I need something new and exciting in my life, especially this evening. Someone to distract my heart from other sad affairs. Madam, I have come here to you and your fine establishment because I know that you will not let an old friend down, would you?"

My, how she wished she were younger and free to play this game with him. To go after a night in the arms of a man such as he! His eyes alone could drive a woman crazy. Rose doubted there was a woman alive who would not give in to his gaze and his charm.

Jean sat up straight then and laughed at her. "Come now Rose old friend, how about it? All I require is one of your girls. She does not have to be the young lady that has entertained me in the past. As a matter of fact, I think it best if I not have her anymore. She seems to be, shall we say, a little too attached."

Rose could see that the only way to get him to leave, was to offer him something that would cost him way too much for his liking. Of course he would depart in a huff but he would be back. He always came back. Her mind was racing for an idea when it hit her, the perfect solution.

"Well I do have a new girl. She has not been out to meet anyone as of yet. She belongs to one of my clients, who will remain nameless for the time being. He is keeping here until he tires of her charms, then she will be joining my girls downstairs. She could be just what you are looking for but the risk I would be taking would be great. I have given my assurance that she would remain untouched and out of sight. I stand the chance of losing a good customer, not to mention my reputation as a lady who keeps her word. If this client were to find out that I let anyone have her at this point...well need I say more? It would have to be well worth my taking such a risk. Are you willing to pay me enough to encourage such a venture?

Jean was not looking forward to the idea of leaving Rose's or going back to an empty cabin aboard his ship. The idea of sailing on the afternoon tide without having had a woman before the long voyage did not sit well either. That thought was just too much. He reached into his coat and found his gambling winnings from John Davis's place and staggered over to Rose.

"This should more than cover any doubts you may have."

Rose had only been toying with him, not really meaning the offer. She had assumed incorrectly that he would have turned her down. But as she looked at Jean now, she could see he was very serious and the sum of gold that sat on the table in front of her was indeed impressive. It took her only a second to make up her mind as to what to do.

"Do I have your word that no harm will come to her? She is not too used to the company of gentlemen yet and may fight you somewhat. You will not get this back if she does not meet your needs Jean." Rose was enjoying watching his face as she handled his gold. The perplexed look was a new one for him, and she chuckled softly. "You will agree also that your evening with her will remain a secret between us."

Jean agreed with a nod of his head, covering his delight in the arrangement by hiding his smile with his hand. He played with his mustache twisting the ends as if pondering over his decision. He was truly intrigued by this mystery woman, whoever she was.

Rose could see the questions that were about to slip forth from Jean, but she had the gold in her hands, and did not want him changing his mind. Wasting no time she took his money and put it in her safe box as she talked. "Her name is Tori and I can tell you that she is in some trouble. She is of course innocent. You maybe have heard the rumors surrounding her circumstances. The fancy accused of trouble down at the Duval plantation?"

"No, I can't say that I have. We don't have much access to local gossip at sea. I have only been in port a short time, just long enough to earn a little, which I might add is now in your possession... and to be rejected?" At that last thought his brow went up and a scowl darkened his face. Then seeming to want to put the problem far from his mind, he quickly brought the conversation back to its present topic. "This trouble she is in, it is nothing that will stop her from being physical I suppose?"

"You are impossible. She is perfectly capable like I said. It is nothing you have to worry about. Now Jean, I don't talk about your comings and goings.

You can depend on my discretion at all times. I ask only the same of you in this matter. If you will follow me to the back stairs, I will give you the key to the suite and she is yours for the night. That is if she wants you! I want no trouble Jean, if the lady rejects you, then you must, I insist, be a true gentleman and abide by her wishes. Just please keep the door locked and do not let her out." She raised her finger to silence him. "No questions Jean, just do it and I'm sure you will not be disappointed. After all, has any lady not fallen victim to your charms? Rose was truly enjoying this game. Of course she knew that Tori would put up a fight. Just what the outcome would be she did not know. Her money was on Jean, but then this Tori was not one to be taken lightly either. "She is lucky to have you, if I were younger Jean my friend, you would not be free long," she joked.

"Ah, Rose my love! If I were not so set in my ways, it would be you who would be in trouble, n'est pas?"

She pushed at his broad shoulder, "Go on with you before I change my mind. Here, take the key. Have fun! You sure paid for it, and remember no matter the outcome, no refunds."

Rose left him standing outside the door to the upstair's most expensive suite, with the key in hand and anticipation clearly written all over his face. Not a sound ushered from within and he found himself excited, like a child at Christmas. No matter the outcome she had said. Well he had no doubt about that. As for his money, well it had been well worth every penny so far. The intrigue and anticipation alone. Now, to see if the mystery girl was worth his time.

Tori did not hear the door unlock or open. She lay in a deep sleep and even if she had heard the door open, she would have assumed it was one of the girls coming to get the dinner tray. She would have paid no attention to them or what they were doing.

The room was dimly lit, illuminated by two lamps that were burning low. Jean noticed the empty decanter on the table by one of them. On the floor by the table lay an empty glass, where it had fallen when Tori had been getting undressed. His quick eyes noticed only one glass. He smiled to himself, as he realized that like himself, she had been drinking alone this evening. Slowly now he closed the door and locked it, putting the key out of sight in his pants pocket.

He walked swaying slightly from side to side toward the four-poster bed. Mosquito netting hung from the ceiling, enveloped the whole structure. Its gauze-like material temporarily hid the person that lay within its confines sleeping. Upon reaching the foot of the bed Jean was able to gaze upon the beauty stretched out before him. Never in his life had he seen such a vision. He closed his eyes briefly thinking to himself that surely he was looking at a dream.

Gradually he opened them half expecting her to be gone. She was the color of gold in the lamplight. Her skin glistening, as if it were covered with a soft morning dew, beckoning to be touched. His eyes traveled the length of her naked body, nothing going undetected. Her hips were smooth and well rounded, followed by the tiniest waist. Her breasts from what he could see, were neither large nor small. Then his eyes fell upon her face. His left eyebrow rose a fraction in appreciation of what he saw. If ever there was a goddess on earth, truly he felt this had to be her. Whoever she belonged to, could never tire of her, for surely if he did, he must be blind or a fool.

Jean made a mental note to find out who she belonged to and see if there were a way he could continue to visit this vision, if not have her for his own. Once was not going to be enough for him he could already tell. Here before him lay many long nights filled with pleasure, and pure passion to make heaven on earth. All of this without the complications of a commitment. What more could a man ask for he questioned?

Jean studied her face closely now, etching forever in his mind, every curve and line. Her dark hair clustered in short curls around a goddess's face. Her facial bones were delicately shaped, the cheekbones were high, and between them was a Grecian nose. Suddenly she moved as if somehow sensing the scrutiny she was under. She turned her head on its side and raised her arm so that it lay above her. Her tongue slipped from between her full lips, sliding from one side to the other. She moistened them both, leaving a soft rosy shine. Jean blinked and rubbed his eyes with his thumb and finger, as if to reassure himself that what he saw before him had nothing to do with the amount of liquor he had consumed earlier.

There was one thing he did know was real, and that was the emotions this Tori stirred inside him. Like a hurricane coming on the horizon, it was a force to be reckoned with. One that could not be stopped or controlled. Such was his desire for her. To hold her in his arms and make passionate love till dawn's light, was all consuming. He simply had to have her.

Removing his jacket and dropping it to the floor, he started to take off his silk shirt. His buttons were fighting him, that or he was all thumbs! Damn the rum. He could not make his fingers work right or fast enough. Was the rum the reason she looked so good? Once again that thought passed through his mind. He doubted it. His eyes were not fooling him, his body was responding to what he saw and his instincts were seldom wrong.

"Damn these buttons," he growled.

His voice husky, even though spoken in such a low tone, was all it took to alert Tori that a man was in the room with her. Turning on her back, her long lashes lifted slowly, as she struggled to focus on the person who stood at the side of her bed. Slurred for the moment from her deep sleep and the wine she had drunk, she struggled to a semi-sitting position. It was then that she saw clearly, a man in what she judged to be his early thirties. His piercing dark eyes burning with desire, held her captivated. Stunned, she watched as slowly this stranger continued to remove his shirt.

Horrified she watched as instead of unfastening the buttons, he simply pulled the fabric apart, sending buttons flying across the room in different directions. He saw alarm fill her face causing an amused laugh to leave his lips.

Panicked, she all but shouted, as the words hissed out at him. "You had better get out of here now, before I call for Rose. I'm to be left alone, Sir! You must be in the wrong room."

"If you are right, and I am in the wrong room, then this is not a suite at Rose's," he cocked his head to one side, smiling softly at her. "This must be heaven, because I am gazing upon an angel." He had raised the netting on the side of her bed and was looking at her through eyes that seemed to twinkle with amusement.

Tori reached for the silk robe that lay on her side of the bed, hastily putting it on, covering her naked form with it.

"Rose! Someone! Please there's a man in here!" she called out.

"You can stop shouting for Rose. Not only does it hurt my head, but it will do you no good. She is well aware that I am here with you. Now if you hold your tongue and allow me to present myself. I am Jean Laffite, at your service. And you are Tori, oui?" She noticed that he was none too steady on his feet, his bow was short and shaky, and his words slightly slurred.

"Now that we have been introduced Mademoiselle, I shall join you oui?"

"You will do nothing of the sort! You can damn well get your ass out of my room and I mean now! I will not be a part of you or what you intend, is that clear?" Had she heard right? Jean Laffite? It couldn't be and if it was, that meant that the man standing before her laughing, was no more than a pirate, a blood thirsty, cold hearted, son of a bitching pirate!

Tori was off the bed in a flash. She ran to the door only to find it still locked. She placed her forehead against the door closing her eyes and taking in a deep breath. She had the sinking feeling that he was indeed telling the truth, that Rose did know that he was here. The bitch had lied after all, Of course she would let a pirate have her. After all, he was wanted by the law also. So, he could not tell on her and he would not care about what she was wanted for. Frantically looking around for somewhere to run, or something to protect herself with, she found her eyes drawn back to his.

Jean was watching her closely, this Tori was truly beautiful standing there with defiance in her eyes that did little to conceal the terror she was now feeling. The silk robe clung to her body, falling open slightly at the top, exposing just enough that the overall view of her was erotic as anything or anyone he had ever dreamed of. She was like a caged animal looking for some way of escape, revealing the fact that she was new to this way of life as Rose had said. Why else should she want to leave his company?

"You find me unpleasant, mon cherie? I have been told that I am not that bad to look at. Most have even said that I am quite a good lover. I will not harm you." He hiccuped. "It is not my wish to do so, to harm you that is. I will only give to you, pleasure. Now don't be foolish little one. Please, just come over here and sit with me." Jean had patted the bed and indicated where it was he wanted her to sit. It was those eyes of his that had said to her loud and clear, that sit was not what he had in mind.

"Like hell I will," she stormed.

"Such language from a lady. You sound more like a sailor or a common whore. Not one of Rose's girls," he playfully scolded.

"For the last time, I am not one of her girls!" she shouted. "Not now, not ever, do you hear me?"

"Ah, my love. If you fear your lover finding out that I was here, fear not, our secret will be safe."

"I have no lover and no man. Not you or anyone else is going to have me." Tori's voice was low now and full of determination to get her point across.

This pirate seemed educated and well mannered. Maybe she could reach him on some intellectual level. It was imperative that somehow she make him understand. If only her brain was not so muddled up. She wished desperately that she could remember more about him. But try as she might, nothing of what she had read or learned readily came to her.

"Madam, this is getting a little old. I have paid for the pleasure of your company and I'll have my money's worth. If you do not come here, I will be forced to come over there and get you!"

Tori just stood there frozen. By the tone of his voice and the steel hard glare that shot from his eyes, she knew that this man meant what he said and that there would be no reaching him on any level. Tears of frustration filled her eyes. She would however not make it pleasant for him or easy, the conceited bastard.

Jean had lost his patience with her. He marched over to where she stood and took hold of her hand.

"You will come with me," he demanded.

Tori would not give in, and as he pulled her in the direction of the bed, she stood firm grabbing hold of the doorknob.

"I do not find you my type. So if you don't mind, I prefer to stay where I am, until you leave."

"You Mademoiselle, have no choice in the matter." With that, he picked her up in his arms in one smooth move with very little effort and proceeded to carry her to the bed. It was not easy walking by himself, let alone carrying a struggling woman and Jean barely covered the distance without dropping her. They just reached the bed safely, when he lost his balance. They fell together landing side by side facing each other. Their faces were only inches apart and both were breathing heavily.

Tori looked into his coal black eyes. To her astonishment they were somehow warm and friendly. Weren't they supposed to be cold and bloodthirsty she thought? Jean looked into her eyes. They were flashing dark pools, mirror images of his own, with one exception. Her eyes were framed by soft long lashes that blinked as she fought her emotions. Large tears were slowly slipping from the corners of her eyes and sliding silently down her face. The look on her face was melting him and he felt for an instant that he had no right to take her. But damn it, his body was aching for her and he had paid, had he not? Besides this could be a trick of hers to sway him into pity and to leave.

Jean took her face into his hands and pulled it to him, his lips found hers and roughly now he parted them pushing his tongue into her mouth. The warm taste of wine still lingered there and for a brief instant he thought he had won, then she was like a wildcat fighting mad. What in the hell was the matter with her he thought? Pinning her down, he held her arms to her side. Even angry she was wonderful to look at, and the desire to have her only grew like the wind in a storm. Then instead of seeing one vision before him, he saw two. Then the two turned to three and all of them began to fade. He could feel himself slipping into a dark oblivion. He was passing out. Damn her, damn himself and the liqueur he had drunk earlier. These were the thoughts that echoed in his head as he fell unconscious.

Tori could not believe what had just happened. She was about to be ravished by him and now he lay out cold. Luck, was at last on her side. She knew he would be out for sometime. She just prayed that when he did come to, that he would be in no good mood to continue his advances. After all, this man was going to have one hell of a hangover, which she hoped would last for days. Pushing him to the side, she slowly got up and while pulling the robe around her she sat down in a chair watching him.

Jean Laffite. So this was the man she had read of in stories, had seen a movie of once. He looked nothing like the gentleman pirate they had portrayed him to be and worse he acted far from it. If only she could recall something about this man, something helpful.

Outside the door Rose stood and hearing no sound, smiled to herself. So this Tori who had said she would never be one of her girls, had succumbed to Jean and his ways. She could stand to make a lot of money out of this alliance. Yes she could. With Edward staying up river with his brother and out of harms way for a while, she could make use of his absence. All she had to do was persuade Jean not to leave so soon on his trip. She could continue to see to it that he could have Tori for a slight sum if he wanted her. She frowned knowing him as she did. Rose was sure of that answer. He would want her again and again, of that she was certain.

Tori dozed on and off, her eyes flashing toward him each time she woke up. It was hard to keep from staring at him. She told herself she was just watching him to see when he was going to wake. When in truth she was studying every aspect of him. His body was deeply tanned. His build was that of an athlete, his arms powerful and strong, the shoulders broad. His waist was slim and the way his pants fit him, was tight and smooth. She could easily imagine how he would look naked. What was wrong with her, thinking like she was? This was the man who had tried to rape her and would have done so without a second thought, if he had not passed out. Still she thought, tracing her lips with her finger, she could not forget or deny the feeling that had occurred for a split second when he had kissed her. The way his tongue had probed hungrily, his hands on her face. "Oh my God!" she uttered. She had not only enjoyed it, she had wanted him? Was that possible? Damn! What was wrong with her?

Her mind had shouted no. But her body seemed to have a way of its own. It had actually started to respond to him, to let her down. It had to be the drink, that and the fact that she was so alone. She just needed someone. She wanted to be held, that was all she reassured herself.

She had to confront her feelings trying to rationalize them. Was it purely physical? That had to be it. It had to be his charm and the way he smiled. His movie star looks could also be blamed. Even now as he lay there, with his hair curled down the back of his neck, and the one curl that fell over his left eye, his appearance drew her…Was she so alone and so afraid that even a pirate could be desired? Suddenly, he was stirring and she felt the overpowering urge to run. Panic was taking hold, but where could she go? He must not know how she was feeling, how a war of emotions was raging inside her, threatening to tear her apart. No, the best thing to do at this point was to pretend to sleep. Maybe he would leave her alone and just leave.

His head was pounding and it took him a few minutes to realize where he was. Then slowly like a vision emerging out of a fog, bits and pieces came back to him. Where was she, this beauty or had it been a dream he wondered. Sitting up he found himself half-dressed and alone in the bed but not the room. Asleep across in a chair was the woman in his dream. She had not been a product of his imagination after all. She was indeed very real.

It should be any other morning but this one, that he should find her. The way his head hurt and the way his stomach felt, he was in no shape to make any further advances other than look. What a shame he would have to wait until his return, but at least he had something to look forward to. The conquest of this woman would indeed be a sweet victory. A grin crossed his face at this thought. The morning however was growing late and he had so much to do. The tide would not wait and as much as he hated to, he left the bed and proceeded to dress. Finding his shirt buttons all ripped off he silently cursed, his jacket however would cover this and he could change once on board his ship.

He walked toward the door, but before he left, he looked upon Tori once more. Was that her eyes he saw move? Why, the minx was only pretending to sleep. His lips twitched in amusement.

"I want to thank you for an enjoyable time Tori. You can be assured that I will come in better condition next time I visit. I ask your pardon for my state last night. You have my humble apologies and assurance it will not occur again. I will not let you slip so easily through my fingers again." He walked over to her and took her chin in his hand raising her face toward his. Still her eyes did not open, and he let her go, walking toward the door.

Tori was watching him through her lashes and could see him quite clearly. His next move caused her to sit up and stare. He had reached into his pants pocket and removed the key to the door. Her way out had been in her reach all night long and she like a fool had let it slip by.

Jean laughed at her, thinking her reaction was to what he had said, not to the sight of the key. His bow to her hurt his aching head, yet only a smile crossed his face regardless of the pain. "Bonjour Mademoiselle." Then he was gone.

Tori sat there for a time staring at the door. She could not believe the audacity of the man. Worse yet, she knew he would be back and her guess was it would be soon, maybe even tonight. She had to get out of there and it had to be today.

Her meal would be brought up soon and Tori knew it would be then that she would have her only chance of escape. She would have to overpower the whore that brought her her tray, then get out. "But how?" she asked herself out loud. Then as if someone answered her, an idea came clearly to mind. She would simply surprise her. She would knock her out. After all she had knocked Jack on the head. That had been easy enough to do. She had simply done it on the spur of the moment. This time however she had to plan it, think it through. She would have only one chance to get it right. She must remember to hit hard but not as hard as she struck Jack. Oh God! Could she do it and get it right?

Her breakfast was on its way, the footsteps had stopped by the door and she could hear the key turning. Quickly she ran over to where the vase sat on the fireplace. It sat empty with not even a drop of water in it. She picked it up and weighed it in her hand. The vase would be the perfect weapon. She just hoped it would be heavy enough to do the job.

The same girl who had taken over Lacy's chores entered the room. She seemed even less friendly than before, slamming the tray down on the table. She looked over at the unmade bed, then turned toward Tori, her face full of pure hate.

"You won't keep him you know, even with your looks. Jean always comes back to me in the end. I know how to please him the best and he will be mine again." If looks could kill, Tori felt she would have died right then and there. Worse than that, this woman hated her so much right now, that Tori found herself thinking that she might even try to harm her. She looked as if she might physically fight her for what she thought of as her right to Jean.

Tori knew she could alleviate some of the hatred by clarifying just what had gone on between her and Jean. There again she found she was getting great pleasure in not telling her that nothing had happened between her and that damned pirate. Besides this woman's attitude, along with the mention of Jean, made it easier for her to vent her anger with one swift blow. The sound of the vase breaking over the girls head was horrible and Tori only just had enough time to break her fall to the ground before she made any further noise.

"I'm getting good at this you know, and you did ask for it," she told her as if she was listening. "The best part is I really enjoyed it. The worst is, I won't be here to see your conceited face when you come too and have to explain to Aunt Salle where I am. Now to add insult to injury, off with your clothes bitch." She had to smile to herself, she always seemed to talk out loud when she was nervous or better yet, when she was excited and happy.

It was not as easy a job stripping the clothes off a limp body and it took up precious time. In the end, she had the girl's dress and that was what she wanted, nothing more. Tori felt a little guilty as she noticed the lump on the girls head, but only a little. She had no time for the luxury of feelings right now, no matter what they would be. Quickly she put the dress on. She had no shoes and knew there were none in the room. Tori looked at her victim's feet. Her slippers were way too large for her. There was nothing else she could do. She would have to go barefoot for now and deal with it later. The important thing at that instant was to get out and fast.

With the key in hand, she opened the door and stepped out. No mistakes this time, she had to do it right. With the door closed and locked, she headed down the hall and down the back stairs. It was still quiet and she hoped everyone was asleep or just going to sleep, if not all hell was going to break loose. The hall at the bottom was very dim and there was only one way she could go straight toward the end and the last door. Almost there she thought. The door to freedom was within her reach when suddenly, a side door opened. With no time to hide, Tori watched horrified as the person stepped into the hall between her and her goal, blocking her escape.

The two locked eyes and for a second nothing was said, neither moved as both were just as shocked to see the other. Lacy put her finger to her mouth, indicating that they should stay silent, then motioned her to follow. Tori had no choice but to do so. She had to trust this young girl and pray she would not turn her in. It was a good choice on her part. The door she would have opened went into Rose's parlor, not the outside as she had thought, and the parlor was not empty. Rose's voice could be heard from behind the closed door shouting angrily at someone. Neither of them stayed long enough to hear who. They hurried through the small door on the side and into the area Tori had first arrived.

The two made their way without a word to the gate and out into the alley. Tori started to run but Lacy's hand reached out and held her back. Quickly they walked down to the first turn and around the corner. Really not wanting to stop

Tori waited as Lacy pulled her to one side. Both were short of breath and leaning against each other they hugged, laughed and then briefly fell silent.

"Where you going? I mean do you have any place to head for that will be safe like? They's going to miss you real soon and start a looking. No one's ever gotten away from her," she jerked her head back towards the house.

"I have to head North, up the river road, how about you Lacy, where are you going?"

"I'm going to get my son to his daddy and I will be safe once I get there. You can come with me if you want Tori. They will help you. I know they will. You don't have no chance without help."

"No, I think I had better go this one on my own. You had best get going now or you won't make it. Don't you shake your head, and don't you look so worried. I would only bring more attention to you and your son. It's me they are going to be hunting, not you. Tori smiled at her then and looking for the first time at the small bundle Lacy held close to her, Tori reached up and pulled the cloth away exposing the small face pushed close to it's mothers chest.

"You had best be going, or you won't make it. Good luck Lacy and I mean that. I hope you find what you're looking for. Take care of yourself and your son, and thanks for helping me."

The two looked at each other briefly, each knowing they had no choice and every second wasted could mean the difference between escape and capture. Lacy was driven by her love for her child and the overpowering need to flee. She simply nodded her head and smiled. No more words were necessary between them. She turned and continued her escape, walking fast but not drawing undue attention to herself. Tori watched her leave until she turned out of sight and then she herself turned in the direction she hoped was North. But fear of being caught and of being alone drove her to quicken her step.

Terror and panic gripped at her, blinding her and blocking all thinking other than run. His fast-walking pace quickly turned into a slow jog which in turn picked up its own speed. She ran for all she was worth, turning this way and that, not caring or knowing which direction, she just had to put distance between her and that house fast.

The sudden sharp pain in her side like a knife ripping her open, brought her to a stop. Gasping for air she looked around and even though the alley was empty of humans black or white, she felt crowded. Slowly taking hold of the situation, she knew what she had to do. The back alleys all looked the same, she could get very lost or worse go in one big circle. She had to find out where she was, and she would have to stop running, because it would only draw attention to her.

"Calm down and think before you get yourself caught. And better if you should get caught, it be by Rose, not the authorities, cause with her there would be a second chance of escape," she told herself.

The morning was early yet, at least by Edward's standards. Very seldom would he rise before noon. He was to have morning coffee and Calas, the sweet rice fritters, a delicacy of New Orleans, with friends. They were meeting to discuss the social plans for the remainder of the week. Edward felt as if things were really going his way at last. Not only had he spent the last few days goading

Leone, he had enjoyed himself tremendously watching his brother suffer over the fact that his precious Tori was still missing.

True it had not all gone according to his plan. Tori was not wanted for murder as he had hoped but was instead considered kidnapped by whomever had committed the crime. He had tried to convince Leone that she was the guilty party but he would hear nothing of the sort. Then the plot exploded, unraveling Edward's plan. What had seemed brilliant to him had backfired and saved Tori. The one bit of evidence in her favor it seemed, was the fact that the overseer had written her name in blood. Leone had asked Edward what he thought about that fact. But no matter what he said, it did not sway his brothers interpretation of what had happened.

"No Edward! Someone wants us to believe that Tori was involved. I think whomever she was running from when she was first found and brought here, came for her and she did not want to go with them. Kate must have tried to stop them, as did Jack. What happened next, well I just have to think she is all right.

Even when the blood-stained clothes were discovered under her bed, it was assumed it was her blood and that she was hurt fighting off whomever. Edward had been unable to change his brother's mind on this and because Leone was respected and trusted by so many, this is the story that went out.

Edward groaned, then told himself to cheer up. It had not been all a failure had it? Leone in his grief had given him the money he needed to pay off his debts and Edward still had Tori for himself, while his brother agonized over her loss. Tori however would not be told that she was not wanted for murder. On the contrary, after all, this was his one hold over her, to keep her in line. He was sure Rose would agree with him. He would pay a visit to Rose's this very evening and see how Tori had adjusted to her new surroundings. After all, he had only stayed away this long hoping that time had found a way of taming the vixen. She had plenty of it to sit and think about her situation. He grinned to himself. Maybe now she would be agreeable to showing him some of the pleasures she had shared with his brother. He just knew she must be really special in bed. Why else would his older brother be so fixated by her? He could only imagine the nights about that lay ahead and how they would be filled. Edward made up his mind to leave before his friends arrived and send his regrets with some excuse or other. This itch he had, needed satisfying. Quickly he stood and started out in the direction of Madame La Salle's, only to be completely stunned by who he saw standing across the street. Surely his eyes were playing some kind of a trick on him, because there was no way she could be standing there. No way in hell!

Tori saw Edward at the same instant he spied her and the two looked at each other with alarm as they realized who they were staring at. Tori was instantly terrified that he would catch her, or worse yet call out to the people around her to help him. She felt paralyzed to the spot not knowing what he was thinking and watched as he slowly stood up from his chair.

Edward was furious at the fact that she had escaped Rose's. He would now have to catch her and fast without drawing any undue attention. Two other thoughts immediately entered his mind. How long she had been free and had she found out that she was not wanted for murder? If the later was the case, she could easily turn the tables on him and Rose. After all, she was the only one besides them, that knew he had killed Kane. She had to be caught at any cost. He had to get her back to Rose's before she could do any thing to cause trouble.

The chase was on in an instant. Tori saw him coming for her and she turned and ran. She had no idea where she was going, her only thought was to get as far away from him as she could and fast. As she ran not caring what people thought of her, she would turn her head back to see Edward slowly closing the gap between them. She realized that she would have to quickly hide somewhere, because she knew she could not out run him for long.

First down one street then the next, always looking for someway to lose Edward, Tori blindly came around a corner and into a small market area. The people there were free mulattos, poor whites or blacks who had set up their own small businesses. Their stalls were mostly food stalls, with breads, hot gumbo, shell fish, and vegetables. Without realizing it she had chosen the most opportune route. For these people were Tori's best chance of escape. The merchants could not risk getting involved directly but a bump or an accident here and a spilled cart of fish there, gave Tori a much needed lead in the deadly pursuit. Some of the blacks would even point briefly the way for her to run. To them all they saw was one of their own been chased by a well-dressed white man, who was screaming for anyone to stop her. It gave them great pleasure to be able to aid her, to keep the so-called Gentleman from getting his hands on her. Down one aisle of stalls she flew, behind her a hand cart was pushed into the pathway temporarily blocking it. Someone grabbed her arm and turned her toward the opening between two large buildings and before she knew it she found herself dashing out onto the river front.

Even at this early hour of the day the dockside was a hive of activity. Boats were being loaded and unloaded. Everywhere people were selling and buying all sorts of merchandise. There were horse drawn carts, and hand pushed wagons loaded down with a variety of wares. And every direction she looked there were people, hundreds of people! It was a heaven-sent answer to her plight. Looking around behind her, she could see no sign of Edward yet and now would be her only chance to disappear into the crowd and slip away. Into the throng of people she went, not running any more but rather walking and pushing by like most of the others. If she was careful and stayed in amongst the sway of people she just might have a chance, she told herself, but for how long? Edward knew these docks she was sure, and she did not. She would have to make her way cautiously, watching for a chance to head out of this swarm and back into the French Quarter. It was not easy going and twice someone had stepped on her bare feet. Try as she might to watch her way, she soon became aware that her initial goal of a side street was not going to be easy to find.

Instead, she found herself walking at the dock's edge along the riverbank itself. She looked ahead, along the water's edge, and there she could see steps going down to the water. Looking back to see if she could catch a glimpse of Edward, her heart sank as she did indeed spot him. He was paying some men and pointing up and down the wharf. Running from him was hard enough, but running from men she had no idea were looking for her was impossible. Her only chance now was to get out of sight and fast. So at the first set of stone steps she came to she turned and headed down to the water.

Once below the top of the wharf she was momentarily out of sight. She looked back up the steps and along the top of the stone wall in both directions. But from her vantage point she couldn't see anyone or anything. Then her error in judgment of a secure hiding place reviled itself. Wouldn't they look over the edge for her she asked herself? Too late now to go back up and find somewhere else to hide, she looked around seeing only one place she could at that moment go. So into the murky water she slipped. It was cool but not cold, the water was not even that dirty as far as she could tell. A little muddy but that was it.

"Good thing pollution has a hundred years to wait," she told herself out loud. There she went, talking to herself again. Tori held her hand over her mouth. It could give her away she reasoned. Still she doubted that anyone could hear her over all the noise above her on the wharf.

Making her way in the water, along the stone wall, was no easy task in the long dress. She could not let go as she knew that swimming would be next to impossible. So she squeezed into a small gap in between a large boat and the wall. Then finding a place in the wall to hang on and finding a footing, she held fast.

"I'll give them time to think I got away. An hour maybe or as long as I can," she murmured. It was not going to be easy, but then nothing had been, since she came into this century.

It had been at least two hours and not one of the men had come up with anything. It was as if she had vanished into thin air. Hell, she most likely had left the dock area and doubled back on him. Well, he would not give up and if Tori thought he had, she did not know him at all. He gave the men each some more money and told them to search the market.

"There will be a reward to whomever can bring her to me at Madam La Salle's. I mean discreetly and not harmed do you understand?"

To the sound of cheers the men were off like bloodhounds. The chance to catch one of Madam La Salle's girls was more than enough reward for them. Hell, the last girl that had run and been brought back, came with a reward all right. It was told that the Madam gave the bloke who did it, a night on the house and what a house that was supposed to be. Then the next day she had sent him happily home with a pocket full of gold!

Edward headed off toward Rose's as his anger soared. How in the hell had she let her get away? She had a lot of explaining to do. More than that she could damn well help him get her back, no matter the cost.

Tori was numb to the bone, she could no longer feel her feet and her hands were finding it harder and harder to hang on. Her fingers were blistered and bleeding, her nails broken and torn. As her hands had weakened, her feet had desperately tried to take the weight and hold her up. Now, even without seeing them, she knew the state they too must be in. The pain she felt throughout her body and the weakness in her limbs, signaled to her only too clearly that she would have to get out of the water or slip beneath its surface for good.

Slowly she pulled herself painfully back along the wall to the steps and climbed up out of the river. Her dress hung heavily with the weight of so much water that it was hard to stand. Tori painfully wrung out as much as she could. This left streaks of blood here and there from her wounded hands and there was nothing she could do to prevent it. She realized also that wringing the cotton material dry crinkled the garment, as if that really mattered. With or without wrinkles and blood stains she knew she was a hopeless mess.

Finding a small patch of sun, she sat down too afraid to go up and be seen. How could she anyway, dripping wet like she was? People would think she had fallen in the river and that she might need help. She would become the center of attention. And that was the one thing she most wanted to avoid. No, she would have to stay put until she dried off, or better still until night fall.

It soon became obvious to her that time was not what she needed. All too quickly the sun moved across the sky, taking with it the small patch of warmth. In the shade with the wind picking up, it felt to her as if she had stepped into an ice box.

Wrapping her arms around her cold body and rocking back and forth did little to alleviate the situation and it was the knowledge that the afternoon was going to stretch into hours of torment like this, that forced her to act.

Slowly with her head down, she climbed the stairs toward the dock. Her teeth were chattering hard, as she shivered violently. She just had to get warm. She pulled herself up eye level, daring only to peer briefly before slipping back out of sight. Tori could see that the crowds had thinned out but still far too many people roamed about for her to go unnoticed for long. She knew she would have to move soon or run the risk of being spotted, when she remembered something someone had once told her. If you want to hide something do it right in the open, under everyone's noses. If she just walked up as if she knew what she was about and went straight to a side street leading out of the area, it just might work. Her sore hands smoothed out the skirt part of her dress. It was not totally dry, nor was it dripping wet either, just damp and damn cold. At least it was not torn or too filthy and the fact that it was just a little too long hid her cut and bleeding feet. She knew she would not look that good but she certainly had seen worse looking where she was about to go.

Pushing her hair back and standing straight she walked up onto the dockside. No one seemed to notice her, or care much, so involved were they in their own lives. One well dressed woman did gaze her way and shake her head sadly before looking away. She was pulled along by the hand of a small boy, who also kept looking back towards her. It was then that Tori realized she could not blend in with this crowd. She felt so out of place and so hunted that she was sure it was written clearly on her face. What had she been thinking? Looking frantically up and down the wharf, it was clear that hiding in amongst the people either here or on one of the city streets would be impossible. Just where in the hell she could go in the middle of the afternoon was a question she had no answer for. "Oh dear God help me," she pleaded.

Her eyes caught the ship off to her right, the gang plank was in place and not a soul was around. There was no sign of loading or unloading, no activity at all. It could be the very place she was looking for until dark she told herself. Then as if a miracle was happening just for her, a brawl broke out, which drew everyone's attention. The crowd grew around the fight and the people cheered and shouted at the pair as slowly they moved down and away from Tori.

Her move was accomplished in a heartbeat. Tori was up the gangplank onto the deck and along to a door that had steps leading down into its hold. She had only meant to hide some place on deck in the sun, but the open doorway was indeed more than she had hoped for. Down the few steps she went and standing still she listened for any sound alerting her to anyone down the dim lit passageway.

All was quiet, so she walked to the first door and tried it. Pushing it open slowly with her shaking hands she looked inside.

It was a cabin, not too large but comfortable just the same. What was more important, was the fact that it was empty. Tori entered and softy closed the door behind her closing her eyes and leaning back against it. She was just so relieved and thankful she had not been found so far. Opening her eyes and adjusting to the gloomy light, she looked around at her new surroundings. The cabin had a small window which was open, letting in the fresh air and a small amount of light. On the side by the window, was a large desk with papers spread out all over it and an ink well with a pen in it. Across was a bed, not big but it could sleep one comfortably. A large leather chair and a small book case with rolled up parchments, which she assumed would have to be maps, was at the end of the bed. Next to the chair was a large trunk. It would most likely contain the clothes and personal belongings of the owner of the cabin. Dry clothes came to mind and not caring about the circumstances she went to the trunk to help herself. The trunk however was locked and no amount of prying or pulling would open it.

Then she heard footsteps slow and heavy coming from the passageway and headed in her direction. How would she ever explain what she was doing there? A cold dread came over her. She simply was not prepared to face anyone, not without thinking her situation out. Going at once behind the chair and sitting down on the floor so her legs were concealed by the trunk, she waited.

Whoever it was, came nowhere near the cabin and for that she was grateful. It would be getting dark in a few hours and she could get off the ship and hopefully find her way to the other side of New Orleans and the river road. Then maybe, she could get some help. The vendors in the market place, they had helped her she was sure, how else had she gained such a head start onto the dock?

Feeling warm Tori soon drifted off in exhaustion but not before tears fell down her dirt covered face, leaving tracks as they made their way down her cheeks. Her last thought was how would she ever get back to the lake? It seemed to her, that she was getting herself deeper and deeper in trouble.

# Chapter 8

The air in the cabin was stifling hot. Tori's body ached and her head was swimming, not to mention how her stomach was churning. She felt this nauseated feeling would cause her to heave for all she was worth. At this point two more facts hit her simultaneously. First, the ship was rocking gently back and forth, which obviously was the major contributor of her green condition. She had never been a good sailor, but the movement of the boat told her that they were at sea. Secondly she realized she was no longer alone in the cabin! She could hear the scratching of a quill pen on parchment and the mumbling of a voice.

Panic like waves, rode through her thoughts driving home the realization that she was a stowaway on a boat sailing away from New Orleans. It was taking her from her way home. She rubbed her brow and squeezed her eyes closed as she tried to think clearly. Not only was she a stowaway but she would most likely be handled as a runaway again. Even if she could convince them she was not a black what good would it do. What lay in store for her now? She hated to think of the punishment for stowaways in this time. Whatever it was, it was not going to be good that was for sure.

Feeling as sick as she was, Tori knew that she had only minutes before she would be found out. Rather than be discovered emptying the contents of her stomach on the cabin floor, she decided to assess her situation and then make herself known.

Gingerly she peeked around the side of the chair, praying that she would not be seen just yet. Hoping against hope, that whoever was occupying the cabin would take pity on her when she asked for their help. What other choice do I have? She thought.

Slowly now, so as not to give herself away, Tori moved her head still further around the chair, until she could peer over the chest. She saw the back of a man, working on something at the large desk, most likely maps she told herself. The man was totally unaware of the scrutiny he and his surroundings were under. Nothing else had been brought into the cabin. Tori could see no additional trucks. Maybe he was not a passenger. This person could be someone who worked on the boat? Tori strained her head still further to try and get a better look at the man and in so doing she moved her legs over slowly. Not slow enough though.

The pain that ran up them was excruciating. It caused her to take in a loud deep breath and let out a deep moan. Instantly, the man stopped writing. Tori watched in dismay as he spun around to face her.

Recognition was instant, as their eyes met. To Tori it was a sinking cold dread that ran up and down her body, as she looked into the face of the one person she had never expected to see again.

To Jean, it was a combination of amusement and anger to see Rose's girl staring at him, over his trunk. She was a dismal sight; a far cry from the beauty he had left early that morning, yet there was no doubting it was she. Under any other circumstances he would have enjoyed whatever game this particular delight was playing at, but his men would consider a woman on board the ship bad luck. Even looking the way she looked now which was far from attractive, she was most definitely a woman; there would be no hiding that fact. This could only mean trouble for him in a big way!

The two just stared at each other, waiting to see who would talk first. Tori, anxiously decided that she would stay quiet and see just what this pirate would do. At least she knew one thing, thank God; he would turn his boat around and take her back to La Salle's. She hated boats, the motion of the ocean, seasickness and drunken pirates a hell of a lot more than Rose La Salles. No, she would be back on dry land very quickly thank God. After all, there must be a big reward out for her and he would be wanting the money wouldn't he?

Jean studied her carefully, weighing what to do next. She was staring at him with her large dark eyes as if trying to read his mind, yet something was very wrong. Her eyes, they seemed too glassy and she looked ill, from what little he could see of her. In all she was a pitiful sight, one that tugged at his heartstrings. But, damn it to hell, she had no right to be on his ship, none whatsoever. His anger was visible on his face as he spoke. His tone was firm yet sarcastic, his eyes cold and much darker than she remembered. They reminded her of the color of the North Atlantic. It's deep seas raging in a winter's storm were warmer looking.

"So my lady, you could not wait for Jean Laffite's return? You were so anxious to be once again in my arms, that you came to me, yes?" Jean had spoken to her in French and even though Tori could understand him very well, she still did not respond.

To Tori it felt as if the room was swaying more but she could not be certain, her vision blurred one second and cleared the next. His words seemed to be coming from far away and had an echo to them. Each syllable ringing in her ears, growing louder and louder. Tori knew this feeling only too well. She was on the verge of passing out and she didn't care.

Jean mistook her silence, believing that she did not understand French, he switched to English, repeating his question. Still he got no response from the woman. His temper raising, his patience growing shorter by the second he snapped at her.

"Come now has the cat got your tongue? Maybe the fact that you have changed your mind and don't wish to be here on my ship, holds you silent?" Still nothing, she just stared at him. This enraged him, as Jean was not in the mood to play games. He could stand it no longer; he would shake an answer from the whore if he had to. He moved quickly toward Tori. His hands, none too gently, pulled her to a standing position before Tori had a chance to utter a word.

Her body had been cramped in the small area for hours; her clothes had dried on her. They were stained and crumpled. She hurt all the way from her bloody feet, to her aching head and she cared not.

"Please, I am sorry. I never meant to stay, just to hide. It is so hot in here, could you turn on the air?"

This last remark caused his eyebrow to raise on one side as he questioned in his mind once again; just what was she was up to.

"So you can talk. That's good, because you have a lot of explaining to do."

Jean pulled her around the chest and she stood for a few seconds in front of him. Only one more word left her as she slipped into oblivion. It was a pitiful, "help," that she whimpered.

Jean caught her as she passed out. Thinking at first that she was only acting, he picked her up and carried her over to his bed, putting her down simply by dropping her.

"Turn on the air indeed! Madam, you can stop with your acting. I am not one to be so easily toyed with."

She did not move. Her whole body just lay there motionless, while her breathing was wheezy, rapid and shallow. Her face was as pale as the sheet that covered the bed. After several minutes of waiting for a response and the fact that her eyes did not flutter open, Jean reached down and touched her forehead. He found it burning hot with not a drop of perspiration. This woman definitely had a dangerously high fever. She was indeed very ill. Damn it the last thing he needed was a sick woman on board his ship sailing on a schedule that had to be met. There would be no way of turning back to New Orleans and help and still maintain the integrity of the mission. Jean knew he had no choice but to go on at this point. He looked toward the cabin door. If his men found out that a woman was on board, and a sick one at that all hell would break loose. Could he control them if that were to happen? He doubted it.

He could not risk upsetting his men. They were a good lot who stood ready day and night for his command, ready to follow him into anything. For the most part uneducated rough rogues, afraid of no man, so long as they got what they wanted. Yet some silly superstition could drive any one of them into terror, reducing them into nothing more than overgrown children lashing out against whatever and whomever. He looked back at Tori. This time it would be this beauty that lay before him. Once word got around that she was sick with who knows what, all out panic would take over. He knew that he had to deal with the situation at once. Without hesitating, Jean put a plan into immediate action. He opened the door and yelled out for his trusted lieutenant and closest friend Dominique You.

Dominique entered the cabin and saw at once the woman lying on Jean's bed. A thousand questions formed in his mind as he turned in surprise towards Jean. Before he could question him however, orders were flying his way. First he was told to take command of the ship for the time being. Then while this order was sinking in, Jean added a few more.

"I want you to bring me my food here to the cabin, say nothing to the men at this time and under no circumstances is anyone but you to enter. Tell the men that this end of the ship is off limits. Give them any excuse you can think of, anything that is but the real reason." He turned and looked back at Tori as he continued, "And my friend, ask me no questions at this time. He shook his head, I am not sure I even have any answers."

Dominique looked at Jean and seeing that familiar stubborn look, he knew that to stay and talk with him at this point was useless. So with a simple nod of his head he turned to leave.

"You will have to talk to me sometime Jean, and I will be waiting. It will be interesting to see how you explain this." The older man had somehow found some humor in the predicament and was joyfully chuckling to himself.

He left the cabin closing the door softly behind him. To Jean's dismay his laughter could be heard as he headed down the passage. It looked like Jean had his hands full and in more ways than one! Jean scowled. He knew that he could trust his friend beyond anything else. He could trust him with his life and feel safe but with a good story, never! Dominique You loved to tell a good story and this would be a good one to tell his shipmates in the days to come. He knew he would never go against an order, on purpose anyway. Jean just hoped that Dominique could hold his rum and his tongue for a little while, at least until he could come up with some explanation for his crew. One that they would believe and if not at least accept.

Jean spent the next five days by Tori's side. He had moved his chair over to the bedside and nursed her as best he could. His food was brought to the cabin by Dominique, who after the first day simply left it outside the cabin door. Sometimes when he returned it was gone, other times it was still there untouched. Just what was going on in that cabin, he did not know? And by the sounds of it, he really was glad he did not.

Tori was raving in delirium, about things that made very little sense to Jean. He listened as she called out to the ghosts that haunted her dreams. Often she would look to him and call him Linni. The tales that she spun about a land that he had never heard of before were beyond his understanding. Often he found himself thinking she was going mad, if she was not already.

Then there were the things she talked of, that he could understand. To this he listened closely and learned for himself in part, who she was and how she came to be with him on his ship.

As the days and nights passed and Tori became weaker and weaker, Jean worried more. He knew that the longer she went without her fever breaking, the closer she inched towards death. The vision of the golden goddess was still so fresh in his mind that he couldn't accept that she lay slipping away. So it was, he would talk to her, willing her back to life.

"You really are quite something, you know? You are a fighter Tori. You have a combination I have never found in a woman. Looks of an angel with a fiery spirit in your soul who knows what it wants and always gets it. You are like me in many ways. It will be interesting indeed, getting to know you better. Now just fight and win this time. You are safe here; all you have to do is get well. Can you hear me Tori? Can you understand? You have to fight."

Tori could hear him all right but she was so weak and confused. She did not even know who he was, or where she was. Where did Linni go? Why did she keep seeing Jack? He was dead. He could not hurt her. No, it was Edward she had to get away from. She just wanted to be left alone. She just wanted to rest.

By the fifth day Jean was exhausted, he had little or no sleep and felt he was losing the battle. His guilt of not turning back to New Orleans for a doctor was overcoming him. If she did not make it, then it would be as if he himself had killed her. Jean had never harmed a lady and never would. How could he live with this? The man reached out gently to wipe away the perspiration from her forehead, not realizing what he was doing at first. Then, it dawned on him she was sweating. They had done it. Tears filled his eyes as he looked at her gratefully.

"Tori you will be all right, can you hear me? The fever has broken. Tori, you will do nothing but get better now. Tori can you hear?"

Her head hurt and the light was too bright to open her eyes but she could hear him. Yes, she did understand. Weakly she reached for his hand.

"Yes, I hear you."

Her answer was softly spoken but he had heard it clear enough. Jean had heard a lot in the time they had spent together and he had a lot of questions for her, when she was well enough. He had here in his cabin the most fascinating lady he had ever met. She was an enigma. One that he would solve in time, and they had a lot of that left before reaching port...

Tori slowly opened her eyes and for the first time in days it did not hurt her to do so. She had no fever. The burning heat had left her body and now she felt a little chilled. How long she had been sick she did not know. Thinking back, she could remember a little, of how someone had taken care of her. Who, she was not sure. Some of the times she had seen her mother, other times it had been her father. Both of which she knew to be impossible.

She turned her head and looked around the cabin. Jean was asleep at his desk. His head rested on his arms, a tray was on the table to the side and the food on it lay untouched. Tori looked closer at the pirate. The stubble on his face replaced his tan with a dark shadow. She could not imagine why he had not shaved? Maybe he did not bother while he was at sea she thought. At sea, the thought caught her off guard, how far had they sailed? Where were they going? Just what was this man going to do to her? She had so many questions.

First off, she wanted to offer her thanks to whoever had taken care of her. They could be her only ally. But the fact that Jean had allowed someone to come in and help her through her sickness, was a good sign wasn't it? She asked herself. After all he could not really be that bad could he? They must have a ships doctor on board, or someone like that she thought. She was grateful that whoever it was, had gotten her over the worst. Tori knew she had been really ill and could never remember having been that bad before in her life. Something to be said for modern medicines she told herself.

If only she could get up and go and get some of that water she could see on the table. Lifting her head was too much of an effort let alone getting out of bed. She might be feeling better but whatever she had been through had left her very weak.

"Monsieur Laffite," she whispered, "could I please have something to drink? If you would please wake up, monsieur, please."

Jean was instantly awake and sat up. His surprise at hearing his name leave her lips and the fact she was asking for water just made his face light up.

"You may have all the water you wish my lady even something light to eat, maybe some broth?"

Jean carried the water towards her and then raised her head to the glass, as she took a small drink.

"You are going to be weak for sometime, so just rest and let me bring you whatever you may need."

Was she hearing right? Was this man actually being nice to her? Was that genuine concern written on his face or was it an act? Why the man she last remembered seeing was anything but glad to see her. He was very angry if her recollection was right. Still not wanting to upset him, she just nodded her head yes and let him hold her head up to drink. When she had finished he gently lay her head down and smiled at her. The weary lines around his eyes deepened, as he grinned. Even unshaven he was a very attractive man to look at.

"Thank you Monsieur."

"Please call me Jean. We are, after all, old friends aren't we?"

She could see he was in a good mood and meant nothing by this last statement, other than to cheer her up.

"All right, Jean."

It was becoming an effort to stay awake let alone talk.

"I am so tired. Seems funny that I should want to sleep after all the sleep I have had lately."

"Don't you worry. You have been through much, and need rest. I don't want you getting sick again; after all I need my sleep too. You just sleep and when you wake up, then you will feel like eating, oui?"

Tori did not answer; she was exhausted. Her eyes got suddenly very heavy as she drifted off into a deep and restful sleep. When next she awoke it was to the smell of something good to eat and the ever-watchful eyes of Jean. He was clean-shaven and freshly dressed in a nice white silk shirt that lay open halfway down his chest. He was drinking something and just sat looking at her.

"So you finally awaken? The smell of the food or the need to see me perhaps?" He was impossible, his constant kidding around, or was he? She could not be sure.

"It was the smell of the food, and it seems that I am very hungry. So if you don't mind, I would like to try to sit up and have some."

With that she started to push herself up, and in so doing the sheets slipped down. Then for the first time Tori realized that she had nothing on. Pulling up the sheets she shot Jean a disgusted look. Anger gave her strength enough to hiss at him.

"You might have told me that I was naked, or do you enjoy taking advantage of a helpless woman?"

Jean put back his head and laughed. He knew now that she really would make it because her fighting spirit had returned.

"You don't seem to be the helpless lady type and don't worry I am not about to take advantage of you, yet!"

"And just what in the hell does that mean?"

"Nothing, nothing at all. Look, let us not argue. The most important thing for you to do at this moment is eat and get back your strength. Now my lady, if you will allow me I will help you."

"You most certainly will not help me. I am quite capable of helping myself and I am not your lady! Get that fact right. Now if you will give me something to put on and leave the room, I will get dressed."

"You are far too weak to get dressed, even if you had something to put on, which you don't. What you had on when I found you hiding was ruined, so it was disposed of and you didn't actually come on board with trunks did you?"

"Well you could let me have one of your shirts to start with. Please Jean it would make me feel a lot better? You could let the doctor help me of you really think I can't do it by myself."

"The what?"

"The doctor, the person who nursed me, who helped me."

Once again he was laughing. She however could not see what was so hilarious.

"Now what is so damned funny?"

"You, you think that this ship has a doctor on board? Tori you are on my ship and we need good sailing men, not doctors for fragile ladies."

"Well who in the hell did take care of me then?"

"I did."

Stunned she could not believe it but then why would he lie and if he did take care of her, she owed him her life.

"I did not know...Jean if it were you, then I owe you an apology and my thanks."

"I can assure you that it was I and no one else. Only one other person even knows you are on board and he would never be able to nurse himself, let alone a lady. So you see, you can let me help you after all. You have nothing to hide, nothing that I have not already seen," he said letting a roguish smile sparkle from his eyes.

Jean was pouring himself more wine, thoroughly enjoying the moment. He knew he should not tease her so but then he could not help himself. Something in her just brought out the worst in him.

"It was you who undressed me?"

"One and only. But next time I hope you will be, shall we say, more willing and less sick?"

"You are unbelievable, how can you be so, so..." Tori was lost for words, her anger and frustration showing on her face.

Jean ignored her and simply went to his chest, opened it and pulled out another silk shirt. Walking towards Tori with a look of determination on his face, he simply paid no heed to her protests, visual or verbal. It was no use fighting him; she was just too weak. Still, it was a very reluctant Tori who allowed his help, in putting on the shirt. When it was done, he filled a mug with some hot soup and handed it to her.

It infuriated her being so helpless, and him so sure of himself. She had to put him in his place and right away. Heaven help her if she did not, the possibilities caused her to shiver.

"Thank you for the soup, but I warn you now Jean, that was the last time that you will help me with my clothes, do I make myself clear? The last."

"Whatever you wish to think."

"Not think, I know."

"And I know my lady, that you are wrong! You will see in time. Now eat and rest. I had best go and attend my duties, duties that I have let slip since you came on board my vessel. Sleep well."

With that he left and Tori heard the key turn in the lock as he did, as if she had some place to escape to she angrily thought. He was arrogant and impossible and she was glad he was gone.

The next few days Tori spent sleeping and gaining back her strength. She was glad that she saw little of Jean. The man was far too difficult to talk to, as far as she was concerned.

Her food was now being brought to her by a young boy of about eighteen. Through him she learned that Jean had let his men know that they had a female passenger and that she was remaining in his cabin, not to be disturbed. At first the men had not liked the idea of a woman on board but then they trusted their captain, at least for the time being. Until something really went wrong, they had no proof that Tori was bad luck, now did they? In fact they were making great time on this trip and the weather had been perfect. It would seem therefore she was good luck, at least that was what Jean had them believing.

He himself could not get her out of his mind. The things she had talked about, the questions he had for her. So at last after a week of self-imposed exile, he made up his mind to return to his cabin to pay her a visit.

The breeze that came in from the small window was a blessing. Tori sat in the small patch of sun and let the wind blow through her damp hair. She had rinsed her hair with the bowl of fresh water that the boy had brought her and indeed managed to sponge bath some of the grime away. Feeling a lot better, yet not quite herself, she sat thinking of her daughter and family. Would she ever get back to them or was it her fate to remain forever in this time? Her thoughts were disturbed when a knock came on the cabin door followed by Jean's deep voice.

"Tori, may I enter?"

"I suppose if I said no," she said sounding resigned to the inevitable, "it would not matter anyway, so you might as well come in."

Jean entered with a smile on his face. "I see you have much improved in my absence. Is it wise to be out of bed so soon though?"

"I feel a lot better and what I do is really no concern of yours."

"Ah my lady," he placed his hand over his heart as if her words had truly injured him, "such hostility when I come bearing a gift of peace." His hurt look fell away and was quickly replaced with a warm and friendly smile. "You will join me for a special supper won't you? You have my word as a Gentleman, that I shall remain so during our meal. That is if you can find it in your heart to be civil and act more like a lady."

Tori just sat and looked at him, she did not really trust him and yet she would enjoy having someone to talk to during the meal. Eating alone day in and day out was getting old and this cabin seemed to be closing in on her. Maybe she could butter him up a little and get him to allow her to go up on deck for some fresh air. At least she might find out where they were headed and if he intended to take her back to New Orleans.

"I would be glad of the company but as you can see I am not really dressed for dinner, now am I?"

Jean had been observing her, why even dressed only in his shirt she was something to behold. She stirred his blood. Her long sleeves were rolled up above her elbows and the front of the shirt was unlaced, exposing the soft round curves of her breasts. The length of the shirt would be like that of a mini skirt. To

Jean who had never heard of one, it was just plain exciting. He noticed the way her damp curls hung around her shoulders framing her face. A face that held the large soft brown eyes which seemed to reach right into his soul. God, she was a beauty. But was she somehow changing? Could it be possible that her skin was lighter than he remembered? No, it had to be because she had been so ill that she looked pale. For every question there is a reasonable answer he assured himself. Still she looked far whiter than the wench he had seen living in Rose's only a few weeks before.

Tori was well aware that he was appraising her. His eyes had traveled up and down her entire body. Yet this time she decided that she had no reason to cover up or play shy. He'd seen it all already after all and it really did not matter to her. She was far from ashamed of her body, as for bashful, well a naturalist just did not know the word existed.

He finally answered her question breaking into her thoughts. "You are most enchanting the way you are and as I don't really have a supply of gowns readily available, we shall just have to imagine that your attire is other than what it is."

"Fine by me, but let me warn you, if you think that it will bother me any, you are sadly mistaken. You are not the first or shall you be the last, I am sure, to see all of me."

Jean was shocked and a little upset by this statement but decided that things were going along smooth enough without him getting irritated at her so soon. After all, she most likely did not mean what she was saying. She was just trying to get him so aggravated that he would leave, something he wouldn't allow her to do. The thought of other men seeing her nude, did unnerve him slightly. But why? That question was quickly pushed aside.

The meal was one that Tori could not imagine having on a ship of this kind, in this day and age. They could have no kitchen as such on board, so how this food was prepared truly amazed her. She could not contain herself in telling him so. "My compliments to the chef, this is wonderful. Just how do you manage to cook up something this great in the middle of nowhere?"

He cocked his head to one side perplexed. Her use of words baffled him. Her question though did not seem that out of place. "That I do not know myself. Our cook has even surprised me occasionally. He was one of the very best in New Orleans at one time." More at ease now Jean relaxed as he continued. "I was very lucky to acquire his services. He came to me looking for a position," he took a sip of his wine. "Seems the authorities wanted him for chopping up one of his clients who made a bad remark about his cooking or some such thing."

He spoke so seriously that she almost believed him, then she laughed out loud, it had to be a joke.

"You are kidding me aren't you? Chop up someone, oh Jean really."

"Madame, let me assure you, that I kid, as you say, about nothing. I tell only the facts as they are, which is far more than you do."

Tori took another bite of the fish and seeing that the conversation was headed in the wrong direction, she tried to change the subject.

"Jean do you think it would be possible for me to have a glass of wine or brandy?"

"Brandy? My, you do have strange tastes but if my lady wants brandy, then she shall have it."

Jean was very much aware of what she was doing, but asking for brandy to change the direction of the conversation was going just a little too far. After all, wine for a lady was fine, but brandy? Still he would play along. It would be interesting to watch her drink the amber liquid, and see if she could handle it.

"You keep calling me your lady. I thought we had cleared that up."

Jean saw his chance to open up the line of questions he wanted. He answered handing her the brandy. "Ah, but you are right, we did and you are not mine but Linni's no?"

Tori spluttered on her drink. Had she heard right?

"The brandy is too much for you maybe?"

"No, the brandy is very good. It's what you said. How do you know about Linni?"

"You talked a lot while you were sick Tori and I must tell you, that not much of it made sense to me. I have indeed many questions for you. I think maybe that now is as good a time as any to start talking don't you?"

"It is a long story and I'm not sure what it is you want to know."

"We have all the time and brandy we need and I am a good listener. You may not know this fact but I can also be a good friend. Tori you need a friend don't you?"

She looked at him, and into his eyes that were truly like windows to his soul. Somehow from somewhere down deep, she knew in that moment he could be trusted. Just how much had she told him in her delirium she wondered? He just sat there waiting patiently. The way he was looking at her just made her want to pour out her whole story. She had been alone for far too long and he was right, she did need a friend. Yet how could she ask this man to believe something that she had no proof of, her innocence, where she was from, who she was?

"Just what is it you want to know?" She had to stall for time to think, to put him off for a short time. She rushed on, "I would like to know some things also. Like where we are going and what do you intend to do with me? I can't stay in here the rest of my life can I?"

Jean rubbed his clean-shaven chin that rested in his hand as he leaned on the table. "Well, I will answer some of your questions if you will answer some of mine. Seems a fair trade to me. Only I get to ask first." He turned slowly away from her as he filled his glass. "It is my ship and I am the captain. Without my cooperation and help, you may never see New Orleans again."

She could see that she was at this man's mercy and had no choice for the moment, but she could limit her answers couldn't she?

"Now let us start with just who you are and what were you doing at Rose's? No, wait! Better than that, just who is Jack and Kate and what did you have to do with their deaths?"

He had struck home fast and to the point. She must have told him more than she could have guessed and now she had to tell him what happened, because she did need his help, and she needed him to believe her side of the story.

Many hours later, when she had told Jean what had happened to her, she sat tired and miserable. Tori looked as if she had just lost her last friend rather than just gained one.

"I know it is some story. Jean it is true I can swear to it. You must believe me. I did not kill anyone and I am who I say I am. You do believe me don't you?"

"It would seem that I have to believe you for now. I shall learn for myself the truth about your tale when we get back to New Orleans."

"You mean you will take me back? Oh thank you Jean. Thank you. I just know if I can find that lake, then I can go home again, I just know it."

"Slow up there. All I said was I would determine for myself the validity of your story and I will." He rubbed his puzzled brow while mumbling to himself. "You would not lie about the murders I'm sure. It is my experience that one cannot tell lies when delirious with fever." Jean turned his eyes toward Tori's and held her gaze as he continued. "What you just told me was the same as when you were ill, so I hear only the truth in that, or what you think may be true. You can dream a lot and believe the dream. I believe you are innocent with the murders and I will help you there but as for the rest, well we will talk more later! In the next few days maybe."

Tori was just so happy he believed her. He was going to help her whether or not he believed she was from the future. It really did not matter. She was going to get back to the lake and get home she just knew it.

Her face was radiant, yet the lines of fatigue were there also and Jean knew she needed her rest. What she had been through if it was all true and he had a gut feeling it was, then she was indeed in need of a long rest and a true friend. The part about time travel, well that he would put out of his mind for now. The fact that she had claimed to be white would explain the color fading from her skin. Just so much to sort out and he himself was tired, slightly drunk and needing a good night's sleep. He would deal with it all tomorrow, when the day was fresh and they could talk more.

"You had best get some rest now." His voice was soft and he sounded concerned. "Here let me help you to the bed."

Tori did not refuse him this time, in fact she was glad of the help. The brandy had gone to her head and she was still shaky on her feet. She climbed into bed and watched Jean as he went over to the lamp on the table and put it out. He was moving around doing something, but she could not quite make out what, when he suddenly sat down on the side of the bed.

"Just what are you doing Jean?"

"I am removing my boots Madam, it is more comfortable to sleep without them you know."

"Oh, will you be comfortable in the chair? I mean shouldn't you go back to the other cabin or wherever you have been sleeping? I will be fine now I'm in bed. It was just the brandy that had me shaky on my feet."

"No, I will not be comfortable in the chair and have no intention of sleeping in that chair again for a long time. As for where I have been sleeping, on deck is not my idea of comfort either. I will not put Dominique out of his cabin, which leaves two places that I can go. One, the bunks with my crew, which is out of the question, the other is my own bed."

"Your own bed? But I'm in it and Jean, I don't think that I can sleep sitting up in that chair."

"You will not have to do that either."

With that he pulled back the covers and slipped into the small bed pulling Tori to him.

"Jean! I demand you let me go and get out of this bed, you animal. I should have known that you would not be a Gentleman for long, you good for nothing pirate."

"Now just calm yourself and go to sleep. I am exhausted and just want to sleep in my bed. I can assure you that I will remain a Gentleman."

"Oh yes that's right. I quite forgot that you are the one who always falls asleep when he goes to bed thank God," she said sarcastically, "because I have to tell you, the idea of sleeping with you is beyond words." Maybe if she got him angry he would leave, she thought. She continued. "The idea of making love with you is just out of the question. Do you understand that? You just sleep and leave me alone."

Jean reached out and pulled her closer to him. Her naked legs left the side of the bed by the cabin wall and found themselves right next to his body. The fact that he was dressed did not help her anguish and try as she might to pull away, she was stuck. She had no choice in the matter. He was strong and yet gentle. He simply pulled her close and with his free hand pulled the sheet and covered them up.

She was quite a vixen all right and he must be mad to not take her right now but damn it, he would teach her and her sharp tongue. "I can assure you that I have no desire to force my intentions on you Tori. In fact, if we make love, it will be because you come to me, not I to you. So just go to sleep and fear not, unless you make the first advance, you are safe." He was quiet for a few seconds then he whispered into her ear, "You will make that move sooner or later, mark my words and I can wait."

Tori refused to allow the notion of her ever going to him as he claimed. Her whole body stiffened as she hissed her reply.

"Never! I just want your word tonight, that you won't touch me."

"You have it."

Tori did not say another thing. She just lay in his arms and listened to him breathing. Soon it was evident that he was asleep and Tori did not know why, but it made her angry that he had not tried anything. Was she upset because she had really wanted him to? No, that could not be, because if that were the truth, then he was right. She felt so confused. Softly she cried, and as if knowing her pain instinctively, Jean held her closer to him. His breath was on the back of her neck and his warmth was spreading from his body to hers. She could not help but to feel safe in this pirate's arms. Somehow she knew he would not harm her; she knew he was her friend. Tori had been so lonely, so afraid for so long. The tension left her body and she cuddled closer and relaxed against him warm and safe.

She drifted off to sleep content for the moment. Jean let a smile cross his lips. She was trusting him and she felt so right next to him. One thing was clear and he was certain about it. He would not let anyone hurt her again. With his mind made up on that subject it allowed him to look at other questions that bombarded him. Why did she effect him like this? What was going on? How could he have let her get under his skin in such a short time? He would have to be very careful. Yet knowing this he still found himself wanting her, to make love to her. He had to have her and he would, sooner or later she would come to him. She could not avoid his charms forever. He would make her desire him, if it was the last thing he did.

For the next week the two of them existed together sparring and jabbing at each other continually. Neither would give in and the quiet moments seemed long gone. Tori would answer some of his questions but most of the time she tried to cut the pirate down to size. It seemed to her, that the attitude he had about women was completely wrong. He was a true male chauvinist pig, worse yet; he was a conceited one at that.

For his part, Jean had never met such an exasperating female. She had no idea how to act. At times she seemed to be more male that not. How could she think he would let her have her way, just because she claimed that in her time it was normal behavior? One second she was every bit the lady, then boom she would do or say something to blow him right out of the water. This latest however, this slap against his ship and seamanship, that was the last straw.

It had happened all so fast. One minute they were just talking, the next she was telling him this fantastic story of a ship in her time, that made his look very small indeed.

Exasperated she yelled at him, "Jean, I tell you, I did cross the Atlantic in five days in a ship that held thousands of people. Why you could put this wooden heap on its deck, along with six or seven more. The best part about ships in my time though, they did not rock about so damn much." She calmed down a little and spoke in a normal tone as she continued to try and explain things to him. "They had gadgets. Parts built into them called stabilizers. If you did get green around the gills so to speak, a doctor would come to your cabin and give you something to take away the awful feeling. Speaking of cabin, well that was something to see. It would make your so-called cabin here, look like a broom closet."

She had made fun of the one thing that was truly dear to him and now she was standing there telling him that his cabin was a broom closet. It took all of his self-control not to throw this woman over the side. He was inwardly fuming but outwardly he showed very little emotion.

"You expect me to believe that you crossed the Atlantic in five days? Huh! And next you will tell me that those ships that go in the sky, could do it as well?"

"They sure can and in only eight hours. The one plane called the Concorde can do it in four hours. This trip we are taking right now would only have taken a few hours at most."

"You are impossible Madam and I am here to tell you, that even though I find I like listening to your wild tales, I will not have you belittling my ship, or my sailing abilities."

"What's wrong Jean, did I hurt your feelings again? When are you going to grow up and listen to what I'm saying and have the guts to believe me? Why I could tell you so much."

"Until you say something I can find I believe or give me proof, I am sorry to say that I find it hard, to take anything you tell me seriously."

"Jean, I have not lied to you. I cannot, you are my only friend and I'm learning to trust you. Can't you trust me?"

"I have had enough. I am needed up on deck I am sure, and I tell you this, it will be good to get away from you and your tall tales for a while."

"Speaking of going up on deck, could I not go up for just a short time please? It has been weeks since I have seen the sun. Tori was sorry now that she had goaded him as she had, if only she could learn to go slower with him. After all, it would be hard for anyone of this time to believe in such things as she had been telling him. Was it too late now to change how she had been acting towards him? A little begging and the sad look, that always worked on family. She just did not want to be left alone again in this stinking cabin. She had to win him over.

He turned and looked at her. God how he hated the way she looked at him sometimes. He just had to get out of there before she got her way. He turned and stormed out, locking the door as he went. Tori, mad that he could treat her this way picked up the plate on the table and heaved it at the closed door.

"You bastard, you will pay for this, just wait and see."

Jean laughed out loud. This was something he could handle, her temper. He found that he loved having the upper hand, having control over her. Control, that was a laugh. He knew he had no more control of her than the sea. Never before had any woman fought him like she had.

"You wish to come out? Then you will have to act like a lady and talk like one too."

Tori knew she had lost again. She had not intended to make him so angry at her, but he got what he deserved. The only trouble was she would now have the long day to herself with nothing to do. How much longer would this blasted journey last and worse yet, she had to face doing it all again in reverse in order to return to New Orleans. No, if she was going to survive like this, she would have to deal with him in a different way. One of them was going to have to bend a little, but why should it always be the woman?

Jean had spent his days fighting with himself. He would listen to her stories at night, and even though he said to her he did not believe them, the truth was that they fascinated him. Indeed, he found that as he went over them in his mind during the day, he believed she was telling the truth more and more. In fact he believed a great deal of what she was telling him. His temper had cooled some by the time he found Dominique on deck. He had to talk to someone about Tori and what to do about her moods, which were becoming increasingly harder to predict.

It was Dominique who told him, "anyone being kept in a small cabin all the time was bound to be moody." He threw his head back with laughter and jokingly spoke. "Add that to the fact, that she is a female. What you have trapped down there could be more explosive than the powder we carry."

"You can't expect me to bring her up here on deck in broad daylight can you? Why she is hardly dressed."

"Knowing you Jean, I'm surprised that she is wearing anything at all," he laughed slapping his leg. Dominique continued his deep throaty laugh. He was enjoying himself fully. The older man, who acted more like a father than a friend at times, had never seen Jean at such a loss for words over a woman. He had watched him the past few weeks and seen a change come over his friend. Was it possible that the wench had done what no other had before and stolen his heart?

Now that was funny, a woman had Jean on the string and not the other way around for the first time.

Dominique's eyes were well weathered and even after he pulled himself together, composing himself for his friend, the laugh lines remained. His forehead was filled with worry lines, lines that on his leather-like skin only seemed to add to the wise old man image. In spite of some powder burns to one side of his rugged face, he was rather good looking for his age. His hair was grayer than black now but his charm and personality endeared him to all. Always playing jokes and enjoying life, he was the kind of person that warmed your heart just by looking at him, pirate or not.

Jean could see his friend looking out the corner of his eyes at him.

"Well what would you do then?"

"It would seem to me Jean, that you should take some of the wind out of her sails with some fresh air this evening, when most of the crew is below. I will see to it my friend, that this end of the ship stays clear."

"Fine then. If that's what you think is best, but if it does not work out the way it should, well you will answer to me."

My how angry Jean seemed. The sad thing was, he had no idea who or what he was angry at. Dominique watched him as he walked away and he smiled to himself. It was more of a sad look that crossed his wise, weathered face. Almost as if for a second he remembered the feeling himself, that happy sad confusion that now faced his captain. Love was the hardest thing that could happen to a man and he felt sure that Jean was in for a lot worse. Never had he thought he would ever see this day. He only knew the weeks to come would be interesting, amusing even. This voyage would be far from smooth sailing regardless of the weather. A different storm was brewing on the horizon, a storm whose wind was emotions, its rain was of tears and calm would come only when love conquered all.

Tori had finished her meal when Jean showed up. He walked over to the bed and ripped off the bed sheet and then walked to the door. Tori said nothing. She just watched as he stood there, as if trying to make up his mind about something.

"Tired of sleeping with me Jean? Giving up and leaving so soon?"

She could have bit her tongue. Why did she always have to snap at him like that? But then why did he have to act like he did? What was he up to this time?

"Nothing like that I can assure you. Now if you care to take some air, you had best cover up with this and come with me."

He stood there holding the sheet and even though his face was calm and showed no emotion, his eyes were sparkling with what she thought could be amusement.

A few minutes later the two of them were standing under the stars looking out over the water. The moon was full and hung just a few inches above the horizon like a big silver ball. A soft breeze was blowing at the sails above them. The snapping of the canvas and the sound of the sea was almost musical. Standing there she told herself it was a magical moment.

"I can see why you like the sea so much. I have never seen it so calm and peaceful like this. It's just too beautiful for words."

Jean had not expected her to talk of such emotions. He had wanted to hear her saying over and over thank you for bringing her up. However he was not disappointed either. She had sensed the feeling of the moment much as he had. This lady whoever she was, was remarkable.

"Sit here for a moment and don't leave. Can I trust you to do that?"

Tori was not about to do or say anything that might cause him to take her back below. She was willing to do almost anything he asked of her, so long as she could sit here for a while, even if it meant sitting alone.

"If that's what you want. Captains orders will be obeyed." She said this with a smile on her face and a lighthearted tone in her voice. "Besides, if I did move, where would I go?"

"Overboard maybe my lady? You don't seem to have your sea legs even yet."

He smiled at her cocking his head slightly to one side, then he turned and left. She could hear him as he gave one or two orders, his voice fading until she found herself listening to the soft sound of someone playing what she thought to be a flute.

Jean was back shortly with the bottle of wine and the two of them sat for some time drinking and enjoying one of their peaceful moments. They enjoyed these times together when they happened, but neither of them would admit it to themselves. Tori talked the most, of her life, her child and her time. Jean sat and listened and wished he could take away some of the pain she was feeling.

"Tori, if it would help, I have to admit that I find I do believe you. I really like hearing about the future, but if it hurts too much maybe it would be easier not to talk of it."

She turned and faced him. Had she heard him right? "Jean, you really mean it? You believe me?"

"Yes." he said, smiling at her, "I do."

"Well then, I don't mind talking about it. In a way it helps me too. Somehow I don't feel so lost if I do. Can you understand?"

"Yes, I believe I can and you can talk to me all you want but only me. Let us keep this between us for now. Others might not take to it so seriously."

It was agreed upon then and the two headed back to the cabin. It seemed to Tori that things were going to be easier now between them. She would no longer have to watch what she said. He not only believed in her, he had stopped fighting what she told him. That was more than she had dreamed possible. She would be able to talk for hours with him, to teach and to give him a look into the future. At least now the hours would not be so empty and the days so long and lonely.

# Chapter 9

Within minutes of being back in their cabin the two of them were at each other's throats. It started out light heartily enough, but one thing led to another and before they knew it, once again they were not talking. The unspoken truce had come to a screeching halt.

Tori lay in bed on her side and Jean on his. Both of them wanted to say something, to reach out to the other, yet neither of them would give in. Finally Jean could stand the silence no more, even fighting was better than the cold shoulder he now faced.

"Tell me Tori, why should I be the one to sleep in the chair? You are always telling me that women are equal and should be treated as such." He waited for a response and when none came he continued. "Well my lady if you don't like my company, then may I suggest that you leave my bed and set yourself up in the comfort of the chair."

Tori could not believe him, she would never give in to him let alone talk to him right now. Her answer was to move an inch further away. Even doing this, the distance between them was cramped. She could feel the heat radiating from his body. His stubborn unmoving form was just waiting for her to make the next move. The intolerable situation almost made her give in. Tori could show him that she could sleep very well in the chair if she had to. If she did that however, it would be giving him exactly what he wanted and that would never do. No she thought. She could be just as stubborn as he was. Tori was not going to give him the satisfaction of seeing her in that damn chair. She wasn't even going to consider it an option.

Stubbornly she lay listening as the boat rocked back and forth. The creaking of the timbers had become second nature to her. Strangely it was only at night that she even noticed the sound anymore. And even then she was no longer afraid that they were going to sink at any moment. Sure the cabin creaked at times like it was coming apart, but she had soon found out that it was a sturdy craft. It was just the continuous movement that she couldn't get accustomed to. This was something that no matter how long she stayed aboard she just never seemed to adjust to. Jean rolled over bringing her thoughts back to their argument about the chair. But before she could make up her mind as to what she should do, she drifted off to sleep.

When morning eventually dawned, it was not the morning sun blazing through the window that woke her, rather the lack of movement. The stillness of the boat was obvious, and with it came the silence of the wooden hull.

She was definitely alone in bed. This she knew right away because of the amount of room she had. She guessed Jean had left sometime in the night, when she had finally fallen into a deep sleep, exhausted from all the fighting and the roller coaster of emotions her mind found itself going through.

It took her a few minutes further to realize what was going on and why the boat was so still. The view from the window showed very little, just sea, sky and the few birds that were flying around the boat, squawking as they dove down to the sparkling turquoise water, grabbing the unsuspecting fish. The water was flat calm. Almost like a mirror to look at, and the boat lay dead on its surface. She could tell they were not even drifting. Could they be anchored in a bay instead? Were they at journey's end at last?

The muffled sounds from above deck could only mean they had reached their destination and were unloading Jean's cargo. Swinging around from the window, hugging herself with both arms, Tori could only sing out loud. She was so happy. This would mean she could get out of this cabin and put some much-needed space between her and that miserable pirate. Not to mention a bath, wash her hair and eat. Oh yes, eat something besides fish and not be afraid of it swimming right back up again.

Immediately she went to the door to call for Jean. He would have to go shopping, to pick up something for her to wear. After all she could justify this by telling him it was his fault that she had nothing decent to wear. Anger started to flare as she prepared her argument. Stamping her foot she continued as if he was already there in front of her. "How can a lady go ashore dressed in only a man's shirt?" A thought crossed her mind then, followed by a look of determination which slid across her smirking face. Jean and herself were not what you would call on the best of terms. He might still be very upset to say the least. He might even want to punish her. If he had any intentions of keeping her on his ship by not getting her any clothing, he was in for a shock. One way or another she was leaving this God forsaken hellhole.

The door as always was locked, and calling out for Jean did not get her anywhere. Her cry for help was drowned out by the noise of the cargo being unloaded. Jean's men were working hard and shouting joyfully amongst themselves. The last thing on their minds was their woman passenger and her plight.

Tori's anger grew, and with it her temper. Just knowing that Jean had left her in there like a caged animal, without even telling her that they had docked, was bad enough. Not as bad though, as the fact that he must have known last night they were going to be docking today. Just wait until she told him what she thought of him now!

Stamping her foot again on the floor and walking over to the table to get something to eat, she continued to curse the insolent behavior of the so-called gentleman pirate. She was even going to light up one of his horrible cigar-like cigarettes and smoke it, knowing that would be sure to annoy him when she saw what was on the table. Instantly her flaring temper was doused by what she was looking at. She found not only fresh fruit but also a note from Jean. How could she have missed the bowl of tropical splendor that lay before her she wondered? She reached out and touched the tropical flowers and with them all sorts of mixed fruit. The note had been placed next to the bowl, in what should have been plain view. If only her anger had not got the better of her, clouding her vision, she would have seen it. Ashamed of herself and glad that no one else had been witness to her outburst, she picked up the note and could not help smiling briefly to herself as she did. It told her to be dressed and ready to leave when he returned, as they were going to be staying on shore with friends of his. Her eyes then caught sight of still more goodies. Sitting on the chair neatly folded was a dress and shoes along with undergarments, stockings and other accessories.

Tori grinned openly. Maybe she had misjudged him just a little she told herself. "Oh all right, maybe a lot" she whispered allowing a small grin to cross her expression. She should be more understanding and not so fast to jump to conclusions she scolded herself. Tori felt a twinge of guilt about the temper tantrum she had just had and about the way she had treated him last night. He must have had this all planned. Why didn't he just tell her? Or maybe it had been just a spur of the moment idea for him, one that materialized out of guilt. Maybe here in front of her lay proof that the man was trying to make amends. She would have to try to be more civil to him, and not let him get to her. It was just that he was so exasperating at times...

Tori washed herself as best she could with the jug of fresh water, then rinsed out her hair with what was left. It had been weeks since she had had fresh water to wash with. Jean had let her have all the salt water she could ask for but little or no fresh water, that was for drinking only. Next she dressed as best she could. She hurried, sure that Jean would return at any moment. Tori was just so happy at the chance to be getting out of the cabin and off the ship, that she forgave Jean for having picked out everything in the wrong size. The shoes were too big, the undergarments too small, and the dress; the dress was an abomination. The shoulders kept dropping down and it was way too long for her. Still, that would help hide the fact that she would have no shoes on, she thought.

The hours passed and Tori paced up and down the small area. She would sit for a while, then start her pacing again. Each time she sat down to rest she felt sure that at any moment he would come in to get her. She could not let him find her just sitting waiting for him however, for she was sure that would be how he would expect to find her. Oh no, she had to be standing facing the door! Tori knew that her patience was wearing thin but what she could not understand was what was taking him so long? It was way past lunchtime and she was starving, not to mention burning hot. The cabin was stuffy even while the window was wide open at sea. But with the boat sitting dockside in the tropics, the small compartment had turned into a sauna. And walking up and down in this clothing had only made matters worse she fumed.

Giving up at last and lying down on the bed to wait, Tori could listen to the African rhythm of the men as they unloaded the boat. She could just picture them singing as they worked. The TV shows she had watched had shown her how in the old days the slaves would use this method of singing to help them with the labor they faced. She had seen slaves working and heard similar songs on Leone's plantation. How long ago that seemed to her now. Lying there listening to the actual songs filter down from above, she found herself tapping her fingers in time with the beat, and drifting back in her memory, grasping for something.

The tune was haunting and yet somehow familiar to her. Then it became clear in her mind, the song reminded her of some of the albums she and Linni had. Linni like herself loved all types of music and often they would sit, just the two of them and listen to them for hours.

Jean had told her that he did not think that she would get back to her time. That if such travel were possible, people would be time traveling all along and it would be well known that it happened. She had argued with him about that, yet deep down she too could see the logic in what he had said. Still, people did just disappear, never to be found, just like she had. Maybe they had traveled like her but then none of them came back saying they had been to another time. Who would believe them anyway? How would she deal with never going back? Knowing she had lost her family, her friends, even her way of life? The thought was too frightening to face, and tears stung her eyes as her throat constricted. She would not give in and cry.

"I have to be able to get back to you Linni. Maybe people do it all the time, this traveling. They just don't talk about it. There has to be a way home. Please I need you my little one. Do you hear me? I need you!"

Tori cried then for sometime, partly from the loneliness of missing her daughter and partly out of frustration of the situation she was in. Oh how she hated self pity, the emotion was intolerable to her. But she was just so lost and she felt she had to blame someone, to strike out and hurt someone as much as she was hurting. The tears dried slowly, not so the emotions; they were left to fester and grow in intensity.

When the cabin door finally opened, it was to a pacing female that resembled a tiger caged and ready to fight. Had Jean known what he was about to confront, he may not have entered so boldly. As if nothing were wrong he swept into the cabin, bowing gracefully, hat in hand. He was dressed in the finest of clothes, and was once again clean-shaven. He had a positive air about him that was dashing and daring, a carefree attitude.

"Is my lady ready to depart this vessel?"

"Once and for all, I'm not your damn lady! And just where in the hell have you been anyway? All day I have waited in this oven for you, without a thing to eat or drink might I add, which is more than I can say for you. I can smell rum all the way over here, you son of a bitch."

The color rose on Jean's face. True, he had gone drinking for a while. It was his duty to see that his ship was well taken care of while in port. He sailed under so many different flags and this time was no different. He had to find out which one to use on this stay and how much to silence any questions asked. Business came first and this female was yelling at him, with language that only a common whore would use. It took every ounce of control to keep hold of his temper.

"If you are ready like I said My Lady," he emphasized the words my lady, "I will see to it that we leave immediately, before I think it best to keep you and your foul mouth in this cabin for our entire stay here. You will refrain now and in the future from using such language. Especially in the company of my friends! Is that quite clear?"

It was too late to stop Tori now. She was on a roll and had just started. Seeing that she was getting to him only spurred her on.

"And this rag you left here for me to wear is ridiculous. It's too big, not to mention stupid looking. I would have preferred to wear my old dress, if you had not disposed of it that is. That I might add, I am sure you did, just to have me naked, at your beck and call. And not to be able to leave or go up on deck decent." Her voice was growing louder as she went on. "The undergarments are just as bad." These she tossed in his face, as she yelled, "they are not only impossible to put on but even if one could do it, they are way too small. You have seen me, could you not tell that everything you got was way off? Or did you do it deliberately just to humiliate me?"

Jean had had enough. As far as he was concerned this woman had gone too far. True she was a sight to see standing there all fired up, and the way the dress kept falling off her shoulder and slipping slightly lower down each time was tantalizing to watch. How she stirred his blood, flashing her eyes the way she did. She was truly beautiful, even when she was raving mad he told himself.

"So Monsieur, just what in the hell are you going to do about it? I want to know Mr. Jean Laffite, are you going to just stand there or what?"

Jean would never know what came over him. In years to come he would think back on the moment and remember every detail clearly. Never in his life had he taken a woman that did not initiate the interlude and never again would he.

He walked toward her with the intent of shaking some calm into her. Once his hands were on her bare arms however, all reason slipped from his mind.

Too late, Tori sensed she had gone too far, but for her to back down now was out of the question; she was just too fired up.

They stood for a second staring deep into each other's eyes, hers flashing with the heat of temper, his with passion. The shoulder of the dress slipped again, only this time Tori could not reach to pull it up. Jean grinned as the top of one breast was now very visible. His next words came out none too gentle.

"If you do not care for the garment, maybe we should remove it. After all, I would not wish for you to wear something that you did not like."

With that he ripped the dress the rest of the way off, exposing her completely.

"Why you son of a bitch!"

"That my lady, is the second time you have referred to my mother as a bitch and I do not take kindly to that. It is you who is the bitch. Tormenting me day after day with your body. Laying night after night next to me, not touching me. Walking around my cabin, in my shirt. Allowing me to watch, yet not touch. Is that not the actions of a cold hearted bitch, I ask you?"

"You are drunk Jean. Let go of me! I could not help it if you would not give me anything else to wear, or if you chose to sleep next to me. It was you who said I would come to you. You, so sure of yourself. You gave me your word, your word Jean! You said you would not touch me. A word that you seem to be going back on I might add. What you said, did it backfire on the Gentleman pirate? Did I not succumb to your charms, as you had planned? I have to hand it to you, up until now, you did keep your word but why I wonder? Was it because you could not stand to lose face, or your pride before a mere woman who was stronger than you?"

His grip tightened around her arms, driven now by both passion and rage, he let go of what little self-control he had.

"I may have given my word but it was for as long as we were at sea, if I recall and no longer are we traveling. As you know we have reached the end of our voyage and our agreement. I shall therefore show you my lady, that I am right, that you do want me and I will show you now!"

With that Jean picked her up and carried the struggling Tori to his bed. Tori was really afraid of what he would do next. Surely he would not carry on with what he obviously intended. She had to stop him.

"You will not do this Jean. Let me go now do you hear? I will call for help."

"Call all you like, no one will hear as the ship is empty. All the men are ashore having fun, which is what I am about to do."

Tori hit at his back with her closed fists, but it was useless. His body was in such great physical shape that he seemed not to feel the blows. He was trying to bring his mouth down on hers, as she moved her head from side to side. This could not be happening; he would not rape her, not now surely? Deep down, she knew that the truth was, he indeed was about to take her, no matter what she did or said, for this time she had pushed him too far.

She had to try and reason with him, talk to him somehow. Turning her face towards his to talk only resulted in his lips crushing down on hers. Fight him as she might, the burning of his lips against her mouth, seemed to somehow be weakening her. Their touch was draining her strength and her will to fight him. Feelings she had not expected rushed over her in waves.

His lips left hers and traveled down her neck, leaving her skin tingling where they touched. His hand brought her face back to his as once again he placed his lips softly to hers. His hands caressing her, stroking the side of her face. His tongue entered her mouth searching and yet not finding the response it was looking for. It was he who was kissing her, not she him but Jean could feel the fight going out of her. He would not give up yet. She wanted him he had to believe that. He wanted her to desire him, more than he had ever wanted a woman to desire him before. This was far more than just wanting to make love to her; he wanted her to make love to him. To give of herself fully and freely. He was determined to arouse that sleeping desire in her.

Tori felt his every touch, she was trying not to give into him but it was only her mind that was holding her back now, for her body was betraying her. It was responding to him and she found herself weakening more and more each second. Her hands that had been hitting his back, were now doing so softer and a lot slower, until they no longer left his back. His caresses were assaulting her, like bombardments they worked on her senses. She was drowning in the mixture of feelings that he had awakened. All at once she knew only that she wanted this man. That she needed to be close to him, right or wrong, she no longer cared. All she knew was that she had hopelessly lost. He had won and she was for the moment glad he had.

Her tongue reached out for his, the passion with which she kissed him, gave Jean the answer he had been waiting for. She would not fight him any further. She was giving herself to him at last and he would not wait for her to change her mind.

The remains of her dress were easily stripped from her body and within seconds she lay before him naked. Once again he had before him the goddess he had seen so many nights ago at Rose's. Only this time, she was reaching out to him, wanting him to take her, as he had dreamed of doing so many times. Jean continued to kiss and caress her as he removed his clothes, then the two of them lay side by side touching, kissing and holding each other. He had waited far too long to possess this woman, and could wait no longer. Covering her mouth with his he took her.

It was over and finished before either of them had time to think what was happening. One minute Jean was on top of her, his hot body burning into hers, seeming to melt with her and become one and the next he rolled off to her side, lying there sweating and breathing heavily.

Shame overcame Tori instantly. She had betrayed herself and her vow to not get involved with him. How could she have let this happen? How could she have given in so quickly? She had wanted him that she knew, but why? Turning her head from him now, she felt far lonelier than while she had waited by herself for him all those hours.

Jean lay waiting for her to say something, anything, after all he had been right! She had given in. She had wanted him like he knew she would. Sitting up on one arm and reaching out to her he turned her face to his but the look he found there was not one of afterglow, it was of hurt. Her eyes no longer flashed with a fiery spirit; instead they were filled with tears. How could this be, he had not hurt her physically surely? What had he done?

"Was I not right my lady? You wanted me, no? You cannot deny how you responded, how we just made love, N'est pas?"

"You don't know the meaning of the word love. What you just did was no more than rape. You took advantage of me. Even if my body responded to you, my heart did not. Sex without love is lust, and what just happened was pure sex, pure lust. You, in your blind arrogance of proving your so-called manhood, took what was not yours to take. You call it what you want; I'll call it rape. Now leave me alone, get out of here."

Jean was shocked beyond all bounds of feeling. The words leaving Tori's mouth found their mark sobering him. How could he have done this to her, been so blind? It just had not occurred to him that she would not want him as much as he wanted her. If what she was saying was true, then he had indeed raped her and he was going to have to live with that knowledge for the rest of his life. Looking at her now, he wished he could take the hurt away from her eyes but most of all he wished he could erase the guilty feelings he had. She had to be lying to hurt him because he had won. She had responded to him but how could he really be sure? He had to get out of there to think, but he could not leave her, the ship was empty, there was no one to watch her. She would have to come with him; she had no choice and neither did he.

"You had best get dressed. We will leave for my friend's house as soon as we can. I will see to it that you are taken care of and have all you need while we stay here. Then if you still want, I will take you back to New Orleans. Fear not, I shall never allow this to happen again, especially as you found me so repulsive. I would never put you or any woman in such a situation. The art of making love should be enjoyed always, even after, in our memories. Will your memory of today always be so horrible I wonder?" Jean could not talk any further he just dressed himself and sat in the chair by his desk not looking at her while she attempted to put the gown on.

What he just said caused her hands to shake and her mind to reel. Would she remember making love to Jean as something dirty and degrading? Or would she regret pushing him away, when she knew that it had been so good? Had she really wanted him all along like he said? Did she still? She could not allow herself that thought ever. He was wrong, damn him, and damn the stupid dress he had ripped. How in the hell was she supposed to wear it out in public? "I cannot leave this cabin in this rag," she threw it at him, "there's no way. It was bad enough before when it was too big but now it is torn and I can't do a damn thing with it. I'm not sure I even want to go with you to your friends anyway. I think I would prefer to remain here, if you don't mind?"

"I do mind. We are expected and when I tell someone I will be there, I keep my word. You will cover up as best you can Madam and escort me off this ship either by walking, or over my shoulder, the choice is yours?"

"Well then, if you put it that way I shall walk. After all, it is not I who will have to explain to my friends about the condition of these clothes." She bent down and picked them up off the floor. Tori then pulled the torn dress on and walked out of the cabin.

Jean followed behind her, with a silent grin on his face. She was strong willed and had more courage than any other woman he knew, that was evident.

Tori did not give a damn what he thought. She would show him she told herself. He might own her body for now but he could not control her mind. She did not care what his friends would think when she met them or how she looked. Jean would answer for what he had done and she would see to it.

Once on land and in the fresh air, her temper quickly subsided. The ride in the carriage was so exhilarating. Tori was so glad to be outside and off the ship, that she pushed from her mind all that had happened between them.

It was not hard to do with so much to look at and take in. The land had a crimson glow about it caused by a large setting sun, which dipped low on the horizon. It was just touching the water and as it did so, it seemed to turn the very sea into liquid fire. The sky was filled with deep pinks and purples, mixed in with gold tipped clouds. Streaks of blue in shades from light to dark spread across the entire sky. In some places, it was hard to tell where the water began and the sky ended. With the setting of the sun, came the evening sea breeze, softly carrying sounds and sweet scents of this tropical paradise.

As they traveled away from the port, she could see that the town was well populated. All races of people walked the streets, from the blackest of black, to the palest of whites. Some dressed in the tradition of the Caribbean, others in the best European fashions. Even though she knew she looked a mess, the people did not pay much attention to the carriage and its occupants as they went by. Still, feeling ashamed, she slipped a little lower down in her seat.

The smells in the air of food and spices only served to remind her how hungry she was. The colors that swarmed all around her, the flowers and the brightly dressed natives only reinforced how drab she must look. The happiness she so briefly had felt at the first sight of this paradise slipped away. It could have been wonderful, all of it, except for the man who sat silently next to her, driving along as if he had not a care in the world.

"This friend of yours, I hope he is expecting us for dinner? After all, you have not given me anything but fruit to eat all day. Another cruel twist no doubt to what you had planned for me."

"There will be plenty of food, and I can assure you, that had I known you would be so long on the ship today, I would have seen to it that food would have been provided. However, I had not planned as you say, for things to go as they did. Even if for a short time we did enjoy ourselves, oui?"

Tori flashed him a look that could kill. "Speak for yourself." She growled.

The rest of the journey was taken in silence. Tori neither looked at him nor acknowledged any remark he made. In the end Jean gave up trying to make conversation and just sat watching her out of the corner of his eye. She was the most frustrating female he had ever come across, and yet he knew deep down, that he had acted like the barbarian she thought he was. Why did this woman affect him this way? He was bound and determined to not let her get to him ever again. He would however find a way to make everything up to her. He really had not meant for things to occur the way they had. Jean convinced himself that he was not all to blame. She had to take some of that herself. What he needed the most right then was a drink, no, he needed a bottle. He just did not know what he had let himself in for with her, or what to do about it. He could feel his temper starting to take over. At least he understood that feeling.

The carriage pulled to a stop at last in front of a lovely home. The house itself was set back from the road and surrounded by the most beautiful flowers. Torches had been lit and in their golden glow she could make out quite clearly the surrounding area. The garden looked as if it should be in a home and garden magazine. Surely this could not be where they were to stay Tori thought. She had expected a hole in the wall. A pirate's den, some place where they could hide away, but not this.

The home had a sign hanging out front which read Doctor Paul Linder esq. The name sounded very English. That she reasoned, could explain the landscaping of the grounds. Yes, that was it, a tropical English garden.

"So your friend is a doctor, and English I presume? Well I hope you can explain why I look the way I do, because I will not disclose what has happened, that is up to you?"

"You have no worry Tori. I will not embarrass you by mentioning our little tryst. No explanations will be necessary, as you will soon see. Now come on we are already late."

Tori could not believe him. He was acting as if nothing had happened and in fact seemed to be putting it out of his mind. Well, she had no intention of doing any such thing. She might very well ask this doctor friend of his to take a look at her and tell him why.

The two of them reached the door and were about to knock when the entrance was thrown open. The person who greeted them or more like greeted Jean, was not the doctor but instead a very attractive auburn-haired lady, who by the way she wrapped herself around Jean, must know him very well indeed. The intimacy of the moment did not go unnoticed by Tori, nor did the fact that Jean was obviously enjoying his reunion with this female, whoever she was.

Finally Jean held her at arms length, appraising the vision before him. "Red, it's good to see you. Why, Madam, I do believe you get lovelier all the time. Maybe I should not have let you slip through my fingers, but then life must be agreeing with you, oui? It shows on your face. I doubt that I could have made you this happy."

The woman just smiled at him and then for the first time brought her gaze toward Tori. "And this must be the passenger you spoke of. It's Tori I believe is that right?"

All eyes turned towards her. Red seemed not to notice her dress or how uncomfortable she felt standing there. Jean had an almost but not quite, grin about him, as if he were waiting for her to make a complete fool of herself in some way. She had to say something that was clear. Red just put her hands on her hips and seemed to ask with her expression, well?

"Yes, that's right. You will please have to excuse the way I look, Monsieur did not seem to think it would be a problem." She shot him another of her dagger looks. How could he have brought her here looking like she was, knowing that Red would greet them? How degrading to meet another woman for the first time, especially one so attractive looking. Tori felt that she must look like one of the homeless tramps they had seen dockside. Still she had her pride and simply held her head high as she continued. "He said no explanations would be necessary."

Red watched in amusement as Tori once again flashed her eyes at Jean. This time he caught the look and held her captivated with an ice cold stare in return.

He was not happy with his companion, in fact he looked as if he wanted nothing more than to get away from the woman. The tension between the two was very visible. Red knew she had to do or say something quickly, to ease the friction. Or the storm she could see brewing would surely break.

"Tori, let me be a introducing myself to you. As Jean here seems to have forgotten how to act like a proper Gentleman. I am known to all my friends as Red. I guess it will be a coming from this Irish hair of mine. My real name, praise the saints, is not one that I take kindly to. My dear mother, God rest her soul, thought it to be a fine choice. Now I tell you, what kind of a name is Molly O'Donnel? I should be introducing myself to you as Mrs. Molly Lender now though, shouldn't I?"

Tori noticed how Red was looking towards Jean when she said this last name. Could it be she was letting Jean know that she was married? If so why? Something was going on here that was very clear to see. Part of her felt as if it was really none of her business, but then something inside said she would like to find out what was going on. The way Red looked at Jean, it was clear the woman was very fond of him. If Tori did not know better, she would say that Red was in love with the man. What was it Jean had said? Not make her as happy, slip through his fingers indeed. It was going to be quite a story, that was for sure.

Jean had had enough of the two females. One was looking at him as if she hated the sight of him, the other as if she longed to be in his arms. He had to get out of there and into the company of another male. At least he always knew how to handle men. They were never this complicated.

"Is Paul in the front room?"

"No, he just got called out, and like always he said he would not be long. He should be back for dinner. You best be a going on in and make yourself a drink. Heaven knows you look like you need it. I'll be a taking this lass up to her room and see if I can't be a finding her a better choice of clothing. Really Jean, I would have bet my soul that you had better taste than this. What were you thinking of? Better still, what have you two been up to? This gown she's wearing is almost ripped in two."

Jean stalked away mumbling something to himself in French and Red just smiled at a very embarrassed Tori, taking her by the arm and leading her into the house.

"Saints above, I have never seen him in that state. Sure'n you've quite upset him. And I for one will be a wanting to know all about it. We will have a lot to talk about while you stay here. You'll be having to let me know what you did to get our Mr. Laffite so all riled up." She was laughing as she led Tori upstairs to her room. The woman kept up a one-sided conversation all the way, telling Tori this and that as if the scene downstairs was for now quite forgotten. She was explaining to her, where everything was and how they would find her some clothes, but Tori was not really listening. She was thinking to herself that this woman was quite something and in fact Tori found that she liked her right off. Still she had to remember that Red was a friend of Jean's and she would have to go carefully until she found out who her loyalties lay with. The women of the world or that damned pirate? She wondered also if Red even knew what Jean was, that he was nothing more than a professional pirate and not the suave Gentleman he professed to be?

The room Tori was shown was light and airy, simply furnished and filled with bowls of highly scented flowers. She could see how Red had spent a lot of time decorating, adding soft touches here and there, such as hand-embroidered pillows and small nick-knacks. This along with the flowers, succeeded in making it a warm and friendly place.

Red herself was easy to like for she was open and seemed genuine enough. She asked Tori no questions, just seemed to accept her house guest as if she had known her for a long time.

"I know you have a lot of questions to ask me Red and I thank you for not asking them right now. It's just I don't think I really want to talk about anything tonight. You do understand don't you?"

"Look lass, I've seen a lot of things in my day and I learned one important thing, that is when someone is ready to trust you and become your friend, then they open up on their own." She turned away from Tori to turn the lamp light up. "Like my pappy used to say, if the man is dead set on going to hell, no amount of trying will stop it." She looked at Tori knowingly. It was if she already guessed what had happened. "I have no need to be a asking questions. What you're a wanting me to know, you'll be a telling me when you're ready like. What you don't, well it's none of my business now is it? As a friend of Jean's, you are a friend of mine and are very welcome in my home. I hope you will become my friend Tori, and feel you can trust in me. "Saints above," she rolled her eyes. "We women need each other, especially where that man's involved. I won't be a pushing you into anything, just thought you should know that's all." Her hands went on her hips again. "I can see that something is going on between the two of you. A person would have to be blind not to see that. When you are ready Lass, I'm here. I'll be telling you for sure anyone who gets involved with Jean, is going to need a female friend to confide in. Sure'n I know it to be true enough, if only I had had one, things might have been easier." She shook her head as if to shake some unwanted memories away. "Enough of that then. Let's get you settled, and when Paul gets back, we'll have him take a look at you professional-like. Jean told us how ill you have been and was concerned." She saw Tori's look of surprise. "Aye that he did. He insisted that Paul see you himself today. I must be agreeing with him there. You do look a little peaked. How would you be feeling about staying up here the rest of the evening taking it easy like? And when my dear husband comes in, I'll pop him right up then?"

Tori readily agreed, as the thought of facing Jean did not appeal to her at all. She just wanted some time to herself and sort out in her mind all that had happened and the emotions that were overwhelming her.

So it was, that the first night Tori spent in the house, she stayed in her room. Paul, after looking at her, decided she needed rest and prescribed some good tonics. The journey, along with her illness, must have been really hard on her he decided and she needed to recuperate slowly, so as to gain back her strength fully. If he had any other questions, to do with her personally, he did not ask. His only concern was that of a doctor, getting his patient healthy.

Tori had liked the look of Paul. His bedside manners only confirmed her first impression that he was doctor first and friend second. He was older than his wife by quite a few years. The gray around his temples had a distinguishing effect; it also gave him a fatherly image. His attitude was light hearted but serious and when he gave orders, they were not to be taken lightly. You either followed the doctor's orders, or put up with the consequences, and word of mouth told that it was better to do as you were told Red explained.

The next week was spent with Tori getting to know Red and Paul, and as she did so, she found she liked them both very much. She and Red rapidly became best of friends and slowly the two began to open up to each other, with feelings that only another woman could understand. Under Red's loving care, with Paul's tonics Tori found herself fast returning to normal.

Very little was seen of Jean. She knew he was staying in the house but he was not there during the day and at night when the meals were served, he hardly talked to her at all, which suited her just fine. Besides it was fun listening to them talk in French and pretending not to understand a word of what was being said. It was a way of getting back at Jean, without him knowing and she enjoyed it tremendously. Once in a while she would hear Jean ask Paul how she was doing, or if she needed anything.

Upon hearing this, Tori would inwardly fume. How insensitive, not to mention rude, to ask his friend and not have the guts to ask her himself. It took all her willpower to maintain an outward calm, and not show any reaction at any time. She would catch him looking at her sometimes and it would put her stomach in knots. The man had such an affect on her, and not only when she was around him. Her nights were filled with dreams of Jean and of making love to him. These brought such terrible feelings of guilt, that sleeping was becoming hard for her. She dreaded going to bed, for fear that her dreams would be of him and not of her old life and Linni. After about a week of sleepless nights and out of desperation, she confided some of this to Red.

In return her friend opened up and told Tori that she and Jean had for several years been lovers. Of how Red really cared for him but in the end had given up waiting for what she knew would never happen. For him to give up the sea and settle down for any woman, it would never occur. She had known Jean cared for her but did not love her the way she loved him. So fearing she would end up alone in life she had married Paul. She knew Paul loved her and she only wanted to make him happy.

"I will always be carrying a spot in my heart for Jean. But my life is with Paul now and he does loves me so. I'll be loving him in my own way but there is something about Jean that gets into your blood and stays. Sure'n you'll be knowing that now, don't you?"

So it was, the two women were able to trust and understand the other's feelings. For Red's part she wanted only the best for her two closest friends and that is what she considered Jean and Tori. After a few weeks she became convinced that Jean had met his match, that he was in love with Tori, even if he himself did not realize it. Just how the two had met, she was not sure. Jean had told them that Tori was being framed for a murder in New Orleans that she did not commit and had run for her life, hiding on his ship. Just what had happened on board, she could only put together a little at a time. The two had made love. It was no secret for Tori had told her herself in one of their talks. But why her friend was fighting guilty feelings, when she was obviously so attracted to the man, puzzled her. It was as if Tori was fighting a ghost and her true feelings, not allowing herself to fall in love with him. The two of them belonged together there was no doubt in her mind. So it was, that she came to the only solution she could find. If she could not have Jean, who better than Tori. Jean's friendship was all she asked to keep now, and what better way to guarantee she would always have it. If Jean were to end up with Tori, she would not take him out of her life like some stranger could. No, she was going to try her best to make them see how much they cared for each other. Once they did, the outcome would be as plain as the nose on her face.

Red was a true romantic at heart and she knew that she had to do something to get her friends together before it was too late and they made the same mistake that she had. His love for the sea and his freedom had always been the most important things to him. That was until now. She had seen the way he looked at Tori, never had he looked at her that way. She knew that he had at last given his heart away. The sad thing was, that he did not realize it for himself.

Therein lay her biggest problem. How would she get the two of them to admit what they felt? She knew it was going to be a difficult thing to do. Red was going to need the help of her husband to succeed. She did have a plan and it just might work, but it could only work if Paul would go along with her.

Paul knew how his wife felt about Jean. He had married her fully knowing that she was not in love with him, not the way she was with Jean. He cared for her so much though, that it did not matter to him. Paul hoped in time that she could come to love him as deeply as he did her. If not, what did it matter? She was his to love and take care of. So when his wife talked to him about her plan, it was the happiest day of his life and it was with a very happy heart that he agreed to help her in any way possible.

"You are truly an Irish Rose, one which I think can bloom fully now, don't you see? You have put behind you, your love for Jean. Dare I hope that we have a chance at love? Can it be that my prayers have been answered, that you love me?"

As her eyes filled with tears, Red realized that her dear Paul had never been fooled, that he had known all along of her true feelings and still loved her enough to wait for her to return his feelings.

"Oh Paul, my dear husband I do love you. Sure'n I can truly say I love you. I really am happy and glad that you married me. Ah, that you loved me enough to wait, to not give up. God only knows how could I have been so blind? I have put you through so much pain. You'll be a forgiving me I hope?"

Paul took her into his arms and the two of them held on to each other as if they were afraid to let go, afraid that they may be dreaming. Red knew at last that she was where she wanted to be, that it was as Paul said, her feelings for Jean had been put to rest.

"I realize now Paul, that Jean and I could never have been this happy. It never would have worked and you knew that didn't you? I only hope you can understand me when I say, I only want him to be a finding the happiness that we have. I want him to wake up before it's too late like. Before he loses the one lass that he will ever love. He is not like you. He won't be a waiting for her like you did me. Oh Paul, will you help me in this? We have to get Tori and Jean together."

So he had not been the only one to realize that Jean and Tori were in love. Red confirmed what he had been thinking for the past few days. His dear stubborn friend had at last found himself a woman, a very beautiful one at that. If the fact of their feelings was plain to both he and his wife, then what was keeping the young lovers from realizing it also?

"Red my dear wife, of course I understand. He is my friend too you know. I think that you are dead right, but it has to be their wish to be together my darling, not ours. They cannot be forced you understand. Jean is the type of man, that if he thought for one moment we were arranging his life, well, he would forever fight us and his feelings towards his lady. We can only hope they get together with a little prodding in the right direction." He grinned and winked at her. "We can't force them to admit their feelings, no matter how much we would like it but we might be able to help them along."

"I'll be a knowing that for sure. We can help can't we? I mean, just a wee bit. If you talk to Jean and I talk to Tori, well then they can get a wee push from us in the right direction. It won't be a hurting nothing at all. Sweet Mary Mother of God, it is for the right reason, love! It's not like we are meddling or committing some large sin now is it?"

"My little matchmaker, you may think that all you have to do is talk to them, but don't you see, that is the one thing we cannot do. They are both stubborn and I'm afraid they would not like us meddling in their lives. No, we have to be far more subtle, devious if you want. What we need is a plan of action, my dear."

"Oh praise the Lord, it just so happens that I was hoping you would be a saying something like that. You see I do have a few plans in mind. If you will follow me to the bedroom, I think I might be able to persuade you to help me carry out one or two of them."

The look in Red's eyes told him that she had far more on her mind than just talking out plans. How could he ever say no to this woman he had married? As far as this match making, well he did want his friend to be happy, however it would have to wait until later for his attention. He had far more important matters on hand to deal with...

Tori slipped deeper and deeper into depression. She felt miserable and nothing Red said or did seemed to help. She liked her green-eyed Irish friend but no matter how she pleaded with Tori to tell her what was wrong, there was just no way she could give her the answer. Tori could not stand the thought of those green eyes turning on her. How could she tell Red that she was held hostage in her feelings because of her family and daughter, and not tell her why or where they were. Red would want to know the whole story and it was a story that she knew she could not tell anyone again. Each time she had told it, things only seemed to get worse, either for her or whom she told. So it was that she carried the guilt and confusion around with her day in and day out.

To add to everything, she felt used. Jean hardly ever spoke to her and avoided her as much as he could. Now he had bedded her he did not care she thought. She had become just another conquest to him, another notch in his belt. Red had told her that he was married to the sea and loved his freedom too much to ever settle down, that no woman could hold him long. How he used women as playthings and though he never meant to hurt them, he always did. She was told also that many broken hearts lay between here and New Orleans. Tori knew beyond anything else he was nothing but a pirate in every sense of the word, with a woman in every port. Had she known the true reason he avoided her was entirely different, she would have been shocked.

Jean was feeling none too proud of himself these days and every time he saw her he witnessed the sadness in her eyes. Why he should care so much about how she felt was beyond him. He just knew that he could not look at her or be around her for fear of taking her in his arms and trying to take the pain away. Pain that he had put into her life.

She did not look well this evening sitting across from him. Sure she was dressed in the loveliest of gowns. He had ordered a whole wardrobe of clothes made up for her trying to make up in a small way for the wrong he had done. But instead of bringing out her beauty it only seemed to enhance the frailty of her. Turning to the doctor he spoke in French once again so Tori could not understand the conversation.

"She does not look well, are you sure there is no illness you have overlooked my friend? What is wrong with her, it's been many weeks now and she seems to have grown worse, she hardly eats, look at her."

"I know Jean and I can tell you that the lady's problem is not with her health. She is not sick in any way that I can assist her. I do have an idea that might help. She needs to get out of the house, to see the surrounding countryside maybe? You should take her out and go on a ride, rather than leave her here all day. Perhaps a picnic?"

"Why me? You know that I don't wish to be around her." He looked briefly her way, "and she does not want to be near me. I can assure you. Why can't you or Red show her around the island, she enjoys your company, oui?"

"You might be right, but I cannot take the time away from my patients right now."

"I cannot either Jean. I am sorry. I promised Paul I would a helping him tomorrow didn't I darling? So it looks as if you are the only one left my friend."

Red was smiling and Jean had a feeling that he was being set up but what was he to do and besides a day out with her could be fun. He had missed talking to her. She had so much to tell of her time and he enjoyed hearing about it. Looking at her now picking at her food, he though it was just what she needed, a change of scenery.

Switching to English, he asked her if she would like to see some of the countryside with him tomorrow. Jean even came up with what he thought was a clever excuse. He told her he was going to take a look around for some property, he was thinking of buying some land while he was here. She might like the change of scene; after all she had not been out in weeks. Jean steadied himself for her answer of no, his hand gripping the wineglass firmly.

How he can lie she thought, why in the hell doesn't he just come out with the truth for once? It was on the tip of her tongue to let him know but then he would find out she understood all that had been discussed at the table, that she understood French and that was no good. No, she wanted to keep that knowledge to herself just a little longer.

"If that's what you want. If I won't be any trouble to you, it might be nice."

No excitement, no thank you Jean, nothing. She didn't even look at him when she mumbled her agreement. She had a way of getting him mad but he would be damned if he would let her know it this time. Yet he had to ask himself was it anger at the disappointment in her reaction, or something else? Hell, he needed a drink. "That's done he said," and emptied his glass.

The next morning when Tori came down for breakfast, the house was quiet and the table out on the patio had been set for two. Tori walked out to the table, at the same time that Jean came into the area from the garden. The two of them looked at each other and then without talking just sat down to have their meal. It was Jean who broke the silence.

"How about a truce of sorts? We really have to learn to get along somehow; we have yet to spend so much time together. I mean if I'm to take you back to New Orleans and help you once you get there. Don't you think you should put behind you what happened and accept my sincere apology and go on from there?"

"I don't know if I can do that but I will try. You will just have to give me time that's all. Speaking of which, how much longer will we stay here?"

"That I do not know, I await a boat and her cargo, along with some important paperwork. I await letters of Marquee. As soon as I have those I will sail under the flag of Carthagena. A privateer my lady, not just a pirate as you so delight in calling me. It is then we will sail for home."

So that's how he became a privateer she mused, but he would always sail under many flags according to history. Interesting though, to think she had sailed in the year 1810, the year he had sent his ship to Carthagena, a province of Columbia for the one purpose of making him a Gentleman pirate. She smiled to herself. He did not seem to notice as he buttered his roll and kept on talking. "Until then I think that Red is right, you and I could spend some time seeing the sights together."

"I had not known it was Red's idea that we spend some time together."

"Well mark my words it is and I know that lady and how she is. Unless we start spending some time speaking to each other, I think we will make her ill, n'est pas?"

He was laughing now and Tori could not help but smile back at him. She also could see the funny side of what he was saying. Red could very well be playing matchmaker. This was something she would have to discuss with her later and put a stop to at once.

The way he sat there in the morning sun, his shirt so white and his skin so tanned! He was relaxed and happy, how long had it been since she had seen him like this? It had been weeks ago, on one of their times on deck at night. Yes, that was when he had seemed the happiest to her, when he was at sea. She pushed that thought from her mind.

"I suppose you are right, a truce then for now. But just because Red is my friend and I don't want her sick, not because I have forgiven you, is that understood?"

"Clearly my lady. Now if you will hurry. I have a carriage awaiting us for our first outing."

Nothing was going to upset him today. She could say and do whatever she pleased; he did not care. The fact was he had missed her and their times together.

In the coming weeks Tori and Jean took many outings together. It became an everyday event. Some days they would be gone until dusk, other days the outing would last only for a few hours. But no matter how much time they spent together in any one day, it left them wanting more and looking forward to the following morning.

They still had their spats and Tori still became frustrated by Jean and the way he acted at times, so sure of himself and his appeal to her. Not that he had tried to do anything, just that he seemed to be watching her so closely. It was as if he knew that she was struggling with her feelings about him.

It was on one such outing that Tori was feeling like putting him in his place once and for all. She was just not sure how to accomplish her goal, when the idea hit out of the clear blue.

They had taken two horses for a ride and had traveled well beyond any populated area, when they came upon a deserted cove. The beach had warm white sand and the water looked as if it was just waiting for someone to enter it, to splash and play in it's aquamarine depths. Tori rode on ahead of Jean and down to the cove, where she got off the horse and tied it to a piece of drift wood.

The tranquility of the place reminded her of one of the small bays she had seen long ago in the South Pacific when she was a student. That had been the time of free love and hippies, and experiencing all that life had to offer. She and some friends had done just that and for a short time, had lived in a bay very much like this one.

"Tired of riding?" Jean looked around as if noticing for the first time the beauty of the place. "You might be right. This looks like a good spot to rest. I forget sometimes I am riding with a lady and that you would tire before I do, forgive me. It is just that when I talk to you and we look at the splendor of this land together, time slips away."

"There is nothing to forgive. I am far from tired, in fact I stopped because I thought a swim would be great, how about it? Would you like to join me?"

"You mean here and now?"

"Well of course, you can swim can't you?" Tori was laughing, the look on his face was classic, she wished he could see himself, the male chauvinist put in his place. Why did he think only men were allowed to swim and that ladies should stay on dry land? Maybe he had never seen a woman who could swim before. She would not be surprised if women of the day dared not to go near water, let alone swim. After all, what would they wear; no swimsuits in this day and age, and to do what she was doing now, never! Tori was stripping her garments off one by one.

"Here make yourself useful and help me get these boots off will you? I can't swim in them. Come on, don't just stand there."

Jean was amused by this latest development. Could it be she intended to really swim or was she playing some kind of a game with him? He would just wait and see. If she thought he was going to demand that she stop and get dressed, she was very wrong. He was going to enjoy calling her bluff.

Her boots came off easily and then he sat back and lit up one of his small cigars, admiring her. Inhaling deeply and slowly blowing out the soft scented smoke, he watched Tori strip.

"Just how much clothing do you intend to remove, may I ask?"

"You may and the answer is all of it. That is if my being naked is not going to upset you? It's not like you haven't seen me naked before now is it?"

Jean only smiled; he found this an intriguing game indeed. Just what was she up to? The last few weeks had been great, talking and exploring with her but he had missed the fun of her high spirits, of her willful ways. She had been too quiet and too good, the proper lady, enjoyable but predictable. Now she seemed to be once again the cunning high-spirited vixen he knew she could be. No, he would not put a stop to this indeed he planned to see what she would do next.

The next thing that did happen, really shocked him though, totally naked and not seeming to care, Tori sauntered towards him and reaching out, she simply took his cigar from him.

"You don't mind do you? Now we are alone and I won't shock anyone, it's just that I am having a nicotine fit."

Tori just stood there in front of him and took several deep inhales, the last of which she blew back in his face. Jean jumped to his feet but before he could catch her, she had dropped the cigar and was running for the water. He had no intention of getting his clothes wet chasing after her, something she must have gambled on, but if she thought he would not come after her at all, that she was safe, she was mistaken.

"So you think you are safe in there do you? Well we will see about that, smoking is not for a lady and you should be ashamed of yourself," he called out as he started to unbutton his shirt.

"I should be ashamed of being naked in front of you?" She was taunting him and teasing, splashing at the water trying to get him wet. Jean stood for a second more and then he sat and removed his boots, and he started to strip. She was watching him closely he could see that.

Pretending to be serious he called back at her. "Well it's not like you haven't seen me before now is it? Will it bother you any, or may I remove the remainder of my clothes and join you?"

He would see now, just how far she was willing to go with this game. His bet was that she would ask him to stay where he was and go no further. He just knew he had called her bluff.

"No, by all means go ahead. I would love the company, that is if you are not too embarrassed."

Now she had gone and done it; she had called his bluff and won. He had no intention of stopping. He quickly removed the remainder of his clothes and started towards the water and Tori.

Tori was in waste deep water and watched as he walked with ease towards her. Jean's body reminded her of a Greek god, or better still a Tarzan figure. His face had a look of determination on it and a look of success mixed in with a touch of mischief. He had to be thinking that he had won, wasn't he in for a surprise.

Tori was going to let him think he had her caught and then she intended to dive under and towards him, not away from him as he would suspect. She would come up and out of the water, run and dress and sit on the beach laughing at him. At least that was what she had planned. It seemed like such a great idea. He would never think she would swim towards him to escape.

Jean had other ideas as he walked slowly towards her, watching her closely all the time. She did not seem to look too worried, yet, she was inching back into deeper water but his instincts told him she was up to something.

"I do hope you know what you are doing, the water could drop off at any moment and the depth would be too deep for you. You can swim can't you?"

"I'll let you be the judge of that, come on and find out Mr. Macho."

Jean could see the mischievous smile on her lips and the way the water rippled around her body; it was making it harder and harder for him to control his excitement, the anticipation of catching her in his arms, it was enough to drive anyone crazy.

"Lady, if I catch you now, you might very well be sorry. I will not be responsible for my actions."

"I understand very clearly Jean, but first you have to catch me and I don't think you can."

Jean made a dive and started swimming for her and in an instant she was gone from sight. She could swim, damn it, that became quickly all to clear to him, now all he had to do was out swim her and catch her before she got away.

Tori's plan had been a good one, but she had not counted on the clarity of the water or the power of his swimming. Jean simply dove under and he could see what she was up to right away. She was swimming towards him, not away from him, why she was trying to backtrack, a trick he had used himself many times to escape an unwanted boarding by a few ships.

He surfaced and pretended not to see her swimming below him. Instead he kept up his pace heading towards where she had disappeared.

Tori was so pleased with herself. She had finally outsmarted the pirate and put him in his place. She would show him that she could be equal to him, not some weak female that had to be taken care of.

Her smile left her face as she broke the surface. Expecting to see Jean way behind her, searching the water for some sign of her, she turned her head. What she found was the big smiling face of that damned pirate right next to her.

Immediately she tried to back away from him, then realized it was too late. Jean's arms came around her and she had no way to escape. She had not succeeded in outsmarting the man at all instead he had outsmarted her.

"That's not fair you cheated Jean. You did not give me a chance."

"Me give you a chance. Why my lady I am truly hurt. It was you who gave me little chance. I did not know you could swim, in fact I don't know any ladies who can, come to think of it. Your plan was a good one. I must commend you. Still a good plan should be worked out slowly and every weakness found. The water was too clear for your plan to succeed. Always you should think of how a plan can fail before you carry it out. Be ready to have anything go wrong, then you can have other ways to try and make it work. And if it should fail, then be ready for the consequences, to pay the price."

With that Jean pulled her to him and kissed her softly. Tori did not fight him and she realized that her plan had not failed like he thought. She had wanted him to catch her; she had really wanted him to do just what he was doing right then and there. Too many nights she had held him in her dreams and too many nights she had woken up alone. Tori was tired of being alone and she was terrified that if she could not get back to her time, that she would be stranded, lost and completely by herself. No, she would use Jean to fill in that loneliness. She would survive her ordeal in this time. She would however keep her heart for her own time. Only her body and her guarded emotions would be Jean's, at least for now.

Jean could not believe it; she was kissing him with all the passion of a lover. They sank under the waves still in each other's arms, letting her go he watched as she swam before him like a mermaid, around and around him she went. Each time he got a little closer she would back off. She slipped beneath the surface and he followed her, swimming alongside her until in the end, his lungs screaming for oxygen forced him to leave her for the surface.

The two of them came up for air at the same time and laughing Tori screamed at him, splashing water into his face with her feet as she inched away again.

"See if you can catch me this time."

In a flash she turned and stood up, running through the water towards the beach as fast as she could. Jean's reaction was instantaneous, as he made his way after her closing the gap rapidly.

The water quickly became shallow and as it did Tori's speed increased. Instead of heading up the beach however, she chose to run in its shallow depths, spraying water behind her as she went. The water was running off her body leaving her skin shining in the sun as it did so. Her hair hung in wet curls, gleaming with the same golden highlights that sparkled in her eyes.

He was so close to her he could hear her breathing and see the muscles in her shoulders flex as she worked her arms back and forth to give her that added push. He lunged forward reaching out for her waist and then as contact was made, the two fell in the water rolling about and splashing.

This time Jean was not about to let her go and even as she slipped from his grip he caught her by the ankle and pulled her back towards him.

The sand was in her hair and on one side of her face. The white powdery grains stuck to her skin. Tori was laughing like Jean had never seen her before and she seemed truly happy. They rolled along the beach together in and out of the water several times until Jean ended up on top of her where they just stopped...

The silence between them was complete; each was looking to the other for some sort of a sign.

"Tori you have to know, I want you, but my lady I will not take you like I did the last time. Tell me now do you want me? Do you wish me to make love to you? Will you make love back to me? Because that is the only way I can ever have you. I never want to see the hurt in your eyes again after we have made love. I want only to make you happy, to bring to you the full enjoyment that I know I can if you will allow me."

Jean took her chin in his hand and turned her face towards his. He had to see the answer in her eyes as well as from her lips. He had to be sure this time; the truth was what he needed. She had to want him, as much as he did her and with no regrets.

"Jean, I do want you. It is only fair though that I tell you it's not because I love you, just because I need you. Does that make any sense to you? Can you possibly understand that and still want me?"

Jean could very well identify with her, when he himself was not sure what he felt for her. He knew only one thing; no woman had or would ever tie him down. That did not stop him from wanting to make love to them, to her, so it could be the same for her could it not?

Slowly now he reached down and put his lips to hers, parting them softly and kissing her deeply, tasting the salt from the ocean and the sweetness of her mouth. This time he would not hurry. This time he would take her slowly, he would take her to the top of her pleasure and keep her there as long as he could.

As his hands slipped up and down her wet body, he felt her responding to his touch. There was no need for words, each was speaking through actions, their bodies talking to one another in small movements, their hands stroking and conveying the language that only lovers understand.

Jean was surprised that his motions and reactions were being matched. She was making love to him just as tenderly and caring. Amazingly it was if they had been lovers for a long time. They seemed to instinctively know each other's pleasures, wants and needs.

Each sensed they had begun something that neither would ever forget. What they did not know at the time was they would seal their love for each other, changing not only their fate but also that of many others in New Orleans and history.

The rest of their stay on the island was like something out of a love novel. Red and Paul could see that the Jean and his lady were falling deeper and deeper in love, even if the two of them would not openly admit it. So when the time finally came for Jean to set sail, it was a very confident Red who spoke to Tori on the last night.

"I know you'll be a sitting there and telling me that you don't love him but Tori lass, it's a written all over your face. Why, whenever he enters a room, your face just lights up. No matter, I'll not be a trying to get you to admit anything tonight. You'll be a finding out for yourself that what I'm telling you is the God's truth."

Tori smiled at Red and then frowning she felt she had to explain to her. "Even if I did care Red, which I'm not saying I do mind you, Jean has not once said that he returns any love. We both have an understanding Red. One that suits us just fine. I don't want to hurt you by telling you this but I just can't give Jean what you think he wants." She added softly, "Anymore than he can me. I know that you had hoped before we sailed that we would be, shall I dare say it married maybe?"

"Aye, well tis true. I won't be a denying that. I would have praised the saints if that had happened for sure. You both are so dear to me. To have Jean settle with you, knowing that you and not some cold bitch would be the one to catch him."

"I give you my word Red, that I will see to it, that no cold bitch as you put it, gets near him. I care about what happens to him as much as you do. That is all I can promise you at this time. All I can do is stay by him and anyway if like you say, he sees no other woman, what do we have to worry about?"

"Tori you are so trusting. 'Tis a good thing to be so but not in the matters of Jean. There are a many women back in New Orleans that await his return. And mark my word, they will not take kindly to him a spending so much time with the likes of you. So take care of yourself and do be careful."

She had tears in her eyes and her voice had grown husky. So she just hugged Tori unable to talk further. Jean and Paul walked into the room and Red made a big show of how much she was going to miss them and how she hated good-byes. Tori could not talk to her anymore on the subject they had been discussing and found herself wondering just what it was that Red had really been trying to tell her...

The physical good-byes lasted only a short time, then Red and Paul waved to the carriage as it passed out of sight. And Tori felt a sadness as she watched the small house and her friends disappear from view. She knew somehow that it would be the last time that she would ever see either of them again. She had to put them out of her mind for now or start to cry and she had told herself she would not do that.

"You know Jean, the whole time we have been here it has been so special, I will always cherish it. Jean put his arm around Tori as they drove on towards the ship; he had become very protective of her these past few days. She had a strange feeling that his mysterious actions had more to do with the cargo that he was going to be transporting back to New Orleans.

"Jean does this over protection attitude of yours have anything to do with the cargo we will be carrying. I mean you are a pirate aren't you and well, are we going to be shipping something we should not?"

"There is that word again, how many times do I have to explain to you that I am not to be called anything other than privateer. As such I am doing only that which is legal by the papers I carry. Now my lady, you ask too many questions, you need not bother yourself with what it is I ship or don't. All you have to do is be by my side on this trip home. If ever for any reason we should run up against, let's see how do you say it? Ah yes, the law, then you do not know me or what I am doing. You will be fine that way and I will not worry about you so much."

He would have gone on explaining to her but they had reached the ship and Jean wanted Tori on board and below as fast as possible, the less of his men that saw her the better. Hurrying her down the stairway towards the cabin, they ran into Dominique You who was grinning from ear to ear. He spoke in French.

"So it's as I said it would be. She returns with us? You must have lost your head Jean, this is no trip for a woman."

"You let me worry about her and just see to it that we are ready to sail with the tide, and Dominique, the less said about our passenger the better."

Dominique walked away shaking his head; this woman must have some hold on Jean. He had never considered bringing anybody along before that was not crew. Maybe Jean was in love, and if so, they were all in for a rough trip home. A man in love has nothing but love on his mind and Jean needed a clear head, not one full of fanciful thoughts. Yes, it was going to be a very long trip indeed; he was not only going to have to do his work but that of wet nurse for Jean.

Tori entered the cabin and the first thing she saw was that Jean had a larger bed put in along with her trunks of clothes. The large chair was gone, as well as the case with the books and maps. These had to go in order to make room for Tori's belongings. Fresh flowers were on the table along with a large box.

"What's all this Jean, and is that for me?"

"I see no other person in my cabin do you?"

"Oh, you are something. May I open it?" She did not wait for an answer and took the top off the box like an excited child on Christmas morning. Inside the box lay a shirt, like the kind Jean wore, only smaller and a pair of breeches along with a pair of boots. Tori looked at Jean with a puzzled look. "What does this mean?"

"Well, you are always telling me how you miss your blue jeans yes? They are not blue jeans, but they are breeches and if you give me your word that you will only wear them in here, they are yours. It's to make you feel more comfortable. I mean if the trip here was an indicator of how ill you can get, then you might as well be comfortable and green is that not what you say." He laughed at her. "The thought of turning green with sailing is amusing if not close to how you looked. Speaking of which, here." Jean held out a small long velvet box, his expression told her that whatever it contained, he was sure she was going to love it.

She took it from him and slowly opened it to reveal a necklace that almost took her breath away. It was a necklace of emeralds and diamonds. Seven emeralds in all each surrounded by small white diamonds. It was a necklace that looked too large to be real, yet Tori knew that what she held in her hands was genuine.

"I can't take this Jean, it's too expensive and anyway I would have no occasion to wear such a lovely piece."

"You are right. You can't just take it. The deal is, if you get as green as those stones then they remain mine, if you can stay halfway like those diamonds, then the necklace is yours to do with whatever you like. It seems safe to say that I will remain the owner of the necklace, don't you think?"

"Since you put it like that, you're on. You will learn not to challenge me. I'll have it, you'll see."

The two of them laughed and Tori who had been dreading the trip home, now found that it was most likely going to be a lot more fun that she had anticipated. She did after all have her secret weapon that Jean knew nothing of. Red had given her a supply of ginger. Paul had told her, that some ginger along with the herb tea he gave her would help her sickness until she got her sea legs. Jean had also been dreading the voyage home, he knew he had given his word to help Tori find the way back to the lake and her time.

What had he been thinking of? How could he let her go? Each day of the trip would take them closer to the day he would have to run the risk of losing the lady before him and he now knew more than ever, that he could not ever do that. He loved her and had to convince her to stay somehow. He had to find a way to get her to fall in love with him and want to stay, to forget about trying to return to her time.

# Chapter 10

As determined as Tori was to earn the necklace, she just could not get used to the constant movement of the ship. The only time she seemed to be free of the sickening motion, was when she was asleep or making love with Jean. The trip going back had started out smooth enough but now the waves seemed to be getting larger and more determined to turn Tori permanently green. She soon found that sleeping all day to escape the hellish feeling was not the answer either. That just left her wide-awake at night, living in the quiet darkness of the rolling cabin with nothing to take her mind off her condition. It was always worse at night, until Jean came but lately he did not even come to the cabin at all.

Tori knew that Jean was worried about being caught with the cargo, whatever it was and she knew also that the men did not like the fact that he had brought her once again on board. Jean had told her how he had over heard their grumbling. They were sure she would bring them bad luck he had told her. As silly as their superstitions were, she could read through his forced laughter and see that he was upset. Was it because he believed in the superstition or was he worried about his men and their behavior she wondered? She did not know and did not dare ask.

The nights that Jean did not make it to bed, were always the worst. She would sit in the semi darkness, listening to the creaking of the wooden timbers, mixed in with the sloshing of the ever-growing swells, as they smashed against the hull. At least in the beginning she had been allowed a lamp at night. That had been bad enough, casting shadows that swayed back and forth, setting her very nerves on edge. But for the past few nights, she had not even been allowed to light a lamp, unless the wooden shutter was down over the window. She had tried that once for a few hours and found it to be a living hell, hot, stuffy and smelling. In the end she had gladly put out the lamp and opened up the small window. Oil lamps she had learned put out horrible fumes that needed ventilation or one would quickly receive the worst of headaches. Besides after the first few trials it became clear that it did not matter if the shutter was up or down, if it was light or dark, the results were the same. She was just not meant to be a sailor on the high seas! Tori blamed the stuffy and claustrophobic conditions, and the loneliness, along with the hours of boredom. She had tried to read and even to write down her thoughts but in the end even that had become too much of a task. Even the preparation of the concoction or tea as Paul had referred to it, was beyond her.
The very smell of the ginger that he had given her would bring on more waves of nausea than not. They would sneak up on her making her wish she were dead.

Jean had told her that in a few days the temperature would cool off but for Tori that did not solve the problem of what to do this night.

"Do I stew or do I sit in the dark, that is the question?" She was talking to herself again and knew it was because of nerves. That and the total silence that blanketed the ship. It was if she were on a ghost ship she told herself.

Earlier in the evening, Tori had been sitting talking with Jean, when someone had called down. A ship had been sighted off the port bow. This did not seem to worry Jean too much; he gave orders for them to keep out of sight. This was followed by a frantic response that another ship was behind them on the horizon, closing fast. Jean sprang to his feet cursing and had left her with orders to stay below and in the cabin until he got back.

That had been hours ago. At first there had been much activity on deck, from what she could hear. The noise of men coming and going, of Jean's voice as he called out his orders. But that had been what seemed like such a long time ago and sense then nothing else had happened. The minutes ticked slowly by, as she sat wondering what she should do?

The knock on the cabin door, followed by the voice of the young cabin boy, finally broke the eerie silence that had fallen upon the boat.

"Yes, come on in." He was barely inside when she bombarded him with questions. "What is it? Do you have any news? What's going on? How come you have a candle? I thought the orders were no lanterns, or light?"

"No Mam. Yes, Mam. I mean the Captain thought it would be better if we had a bit of light. As for the rest of your questions, well…" He stood scratching his head with his free hand as if trying to decide what and how to answer. "That is I can't say what's going on and all. But the Captain has sent me down here, to stay with you and see to it that you stay in here, until it's over like."

"Till what's over? What in the hell is going on? You had best tell me or I will go and see for myself and I'll tell you right now, you are no match for me."

The young boy was very uncomfortable in this situation. He had his orders, but to carry them out he might have to physically hold this lady and that he was not sure he wanted to do. Her being a lady and the Captain's at that. There again, what lady used language like she had? If he did tell her what was about to happen, it just might frighten her enough that she would want to stay below. Anyway he saw no real harm in explaining their situation. The captain had not told him that he must not say anything, just that he was not to alarm her with the news. Looking at her now, in the soft candlelight, he knew he had no choice.

"Well, the ship we saw earlier tonight, you know the one that was not far off at sunset? It was too far off for the captain to see whose flag she sailed under and, well, they could have seen us and be coming after us. We were lucky that it was nearly dark like, cause we can sail with no lights and they will have a hell of, excuse me Mam, of a time finding us."

"If that's so, why did you say, what's about to happen? If they can't find us, then surely nothing is about to happen right?"

"No Mam. I mean yes Mam something is about to happen. You see, we turned about two hours ago and now we are behind her, the other ship, Mam. We are coming up on her from behind. Captain Laffite is going to take her by surprise, before she has a chance to take us. See why you have to stay below? It's going to get nasty up there. Could be some fighting. You'll be a lot better off down here. Just wish the Captain had let me stay and fight."

So he had used the old turn and swim towards him trick! She smiled as the picture of that day on the beach flashed before her. But he had known her trick, she had failed, what if this other ship had guessed what Jean was doing?

Tori did not know what to think at this point, the realization that she was on a pirate ship, began to sink in. This was no game. It was very real. They were about to take another ship, but what if they lost?

"What if we fight and lose? What am I supposed to do then, did your Captain say?"

"No Mam. I would not worry about that too much if I was you. The Captain, he ain't lost one fight yet Mam."

This was not much help to her, she had to do something to prepare, and she could not just sit and wait helplessly. Tori took action; she had the cabin boy stand outside the door while she changed. She put on her breeches and boots, the shirt she left out instead of tucking it in, so she could slip one of Jean's knives in her belt, where it would be safely hidden in case she, heaven help her, needed it. With this done, and the cabin plunged once again into darkness, she opened the window to look out.

The night was not very dark; the moon was bright enough to light up the tops of each and every wave. This was madness she thought. How could Jean think he could sneak up on another vessel and not be seen? Was he stupid she wondered?

Tori called the cabin boy, who because of the lack of light in the cabin, did not see what Tori had on. He merely assumed that she had wanted a moment to compose herself and to put the cabin into darkness for safety reasons, something he totally agreed with. She seemed calm enough and even talked to him. He answered some of her questions which was better than just sitting there in the cabin with nothing to do but wait for what was to come. It even helped to pass the time and ease some of the tension. He told her that Jean knew what he was doing. Even if the moon was slipping in and out from behind clouds, they had no choice but to attack. What they needed now, was to pray for some good luck. "Something Mam, that everyone seems to think, cause you are here, we don't have with us. No offense Mam, but you seem to have brought us bad luck! At least that's what I heard most of the men saying. As for me, I don't believe in bad luck, and the Captain he said it was just an old superstition, that's all."

Tori crossed her fingers and hoped that Jean was right. Then in a fleeting moment of doubt her worries turned to far more grave concerns. She hoped that Jean would not be hurt. "How much longer do you think we will have to wait?"

"I don't know Mam. We were closing in on the other ship fast, when I came down here. You had best sit down now, cause when we get alongside her things get kind of bumpy like and I was told to keep you safe. That means not hurt in any way. Mam, do you hear me? You can just sit, please."

Tori sat down on the bed and for the first time on this trip she felt afraid, really afraid. If anything went wrong, anything at all, it could ruin her chances of reaching the lake and home for ever.

So far, the waiting for what was about to happen, had been hard, just sitting there doing nothing was unbearable. It was as if they were on a trip to death's door and on a ship hell bent on getting there. Be careful what you wish for she thought, or you just might get it! What was it that Red had told her, something about a you couldn't stop a man hell bent on going to... "Oh forget it," she whispered.

The cabin boy looked at her but said nothing. He had not heard clearly what she had said and assumed that she was praying. No one should ever interrupt someone praying. He remembered his mother had told him that when he was small. Funny he should recall that now he thought.

They just waited in total silence. There was not a sound, no voices or footsteps could be heard, only the ship herself moaned as she rode swiftly over the waves. Tori's nerves were about to snap each creak and groan that sounded out of place would make her heart skip a beat. She had to find out what was going on. She just had to!

Jumping to her feet to get out of the cabin brought a quick response from the cabin boy, who stepped immediately in front of the door to block her way. "Now you don't want to try and leave do you? After all I got my orders, and Mam, I plan to carry them out."

Before Tori could answer him, a soft call came down to them, from one of the men somewhere out in the night. "Get ready! Any minute now, we are about to board her. Captain says to hang on."

"You best do as we been told," said the boy. "It's going to get rough, like I told you, when we pull alongside of the other ship, we bump around a bit at first."

Tori did not know just what to expect but she did know one thing and that was, she would not stay down in the cabin for long. As soon as her first chance came, she was going up on deck. At least there she could see for herself what was happening. She would not sit and await her fate in the dark.

It was less than a minute later, when the silence of the night was broken by a gnarling sound with a sudden thump, followed by a loud grating sound. Not once or twice but for what seemed to be an eternity the ships heaved and ground against each other. The force was tremendous. Tori could hear things in the cabin being tossed to the floor as she herself clung desperately to the bed. Surely at this rate, one of the ships would be damaged beyond repair and sink! She thought. The shouting of the men up on deck and the crashing objects falling in the cabin panicked her. If they were going to go down, she was sure as hell not going to drown below decks. Tori was on her way to the door before the cabin boy knew what was happening. He would have stopped her, if the boat had not chosen to at that very moment, make its final large bump into the other vessel. The crash was like thunder, twisting the timbers that seemed to be screaming out in agony against such a force. The cabin door burst open, as the table slid across the floor towards her, stopping only inches from crushing her. The boy was thrown off his feet, flying through the air like a rag doll. Luckily for him, his fall was softened as he landed on the bed. Finally the last big roll of the ship, as if it were sighing and giving up, helped propel Tori out into the passageway.

She slammed up against the wall and fell forward catching herself just in time, before she hit the stairway. Waiting a second to see if the ship was going to calm down, she started crawling up the stairs towards the open door above. Reaching this, she stood up to get a better view of what was happening. Nothing much came to sight at first, just a lot of dark shadows and shouting men. She could see the ship was right alongside the other, and she could hear Jean calling out orders from somewhere, to secure the two boats. The yelling and shrieking of the fight that was now in full swing soon drowned his voice out however.

Suddenly she was pushed from behind and went face first down onto the deck. Rolling over quickly to see who it was that had pushed her, she was relieved to find the shocked face of the cabin boy only inches from her own. He had not realized it was Tori dressed in breeches, thinking only that it was one of the men from the other ship standing there. He wasted no time in dragging her off to one side and putting her between the door and a large oak water barrel. He knew there would not be enough time to get her below. He had to keep her out of sight, but hiding up on deck was not an easy task, especially if she would not stay put. At least from their vantage point, securely behind the barrel, they could both watch the battle that raged before them.

It was just a mass of sounds and shadows at first. Nothing made any rhyme or reason to her. Then, as if the lights had come on in a theater, the moon slid out from behind the clouds and lit up the whole area. From nowhere, it seemed a few lanterns had come down from above. They were hanging there, swinging back and forth on each swell of the sea, casting shadows one-minute and lighting the deck the next.

Tori was to learn later, that this was an old trick of Jean's. He would have some of his men up in the rigging with covered lanterns and as soon as they boarded the unsuspecting ship, they would remove the covers and lower them to help aid his men in seeing in the dark. It was also done to help confuse the other ship's crew, who unlike his men were not accustomed to fighting with such distractions. Something else aided his men that the boy pointed out to her. All of Jean's men had on bandannas, either around their necks or on their heads. They were all of the same bright yellow and could easily be seen. In this way in the dark each man could tell if it was friend or foe he faced.

Tori watched now in horror, as the real life drama unfolded before her eyes. This was nothing like she had ever thought a fight at sea would be like. This was a hundred times worse, for this was life and death.

The light from the lanterns reflected here and there off the blade of a cutlass as it swung between men. Every now and then there was the sound of a pistol shot. The orange flash of fire as it exploded, would briefly light up the face of the man who pulled the trigger. Sometimes this would be followed by the scream of a man as the bullet found its mark.

Nowhere could she see Jean and this frightened her. He just had to be all right! But every time she tried to see a little further around the barrel the boy would pull her back.

"Who's winning? I can't tell. Where did all these men come from?" She frantically asked. Tori had to scream at the top of her voice to be heard and the terror of what was happening all around her was plainly written on her face.

"It's just the light Mam, and if I had to bet, I would say we is winning. See it's starting to come to an end now."

Tori could not see, in fact all she could tell was that bodies seemed to be lying still all around the ship's deck. She had seen one person go overboard and now before her eyes, she watched as the man she knew as Dominique You, began fencing with a man twice his size.

Dominique's sword was thin and long and he was swift in his every action, as was his opponent. His movements were as agile as those of a man much younger than he was. Yet, the one he was fighting had the power of youth on his side, and he was behind a much larger and heavier piece of steel. It would be only a matter of time before the fight would end and not for the good of Dominique, of this Tori was certain.

The blow from the big man's sword, came down so fast and hard that Tori was sure it had taken Dominique's arm off but the quickness of his movement and years of training, had given him just enough edge to back off at the very last second.

His arm had been slashed open right through his shirt. Blood streamed out just as fast as the scream of agony and anger left Dominique's mouth. His sword had been knocked clean out of his hand and he would have met his death then, if the adversary's weapon had not bedded itself deep in the wood of the main mast.

Tori watched as the big man tried to get his weapon free and she could see that Dominique who was down on his knees, had little or no chance of survival.

Without realizing what she was doing, Tori reached up under her shirt and found the knife still safely tucked in its hiding place. Standing up, she reached into her belt and withdrew it from its sheath. The blade slipped out smoothly as she started forward. All she knew was she had to help.

A hand reached over hers and without a word the knife was taken from her as easily as if she had willingly handed it over. Seeing that it was the cabin boy who had relieved her of it, she made no protest, just watched as he aimed and threw.

It found it's mark and the big man stumbled forward two steps before dropping to his own knees with the weapon sticking out of his back. Slowly he turned his head, wanting to see the face of the man who had taken his life before he died. He looked back toward the direction of Tori and the boy. The last thing he ever saw was the look of triumph on the young boy's face and that of shock on his companion, a woman! But that was impossible; no woman would be here on this ship, it was known to be bad luck he told himself.

Tori did not hesitate; she went straight to the stricken Dominique, calling to the boy to follow her. In seconds she reached his side. He was losing blood fast and by the way it was running down his arm, she knew that she had to apply pressure to stem the flow. Taking his yellow bandanna off his neck, she pulled it around his arm directly over the wound.

He made no protest, just stared at this woman who had appeared from nowhere and dressed in breeches no less.

"We need to get this man taken care of, take him down to my cabin. I'll find Jean and see if he can find someone to help."

The cabin boy looked at her, his eyes wide and mouth open, as if she had just given the worst order ever. He had already disobeyed his Captain's orders by allowing her up here and now she wanted to find Jean herself!

"That won't do Mam. The Captain will kill me if I let you go around here by yourself. How about you take him down and I will find help?"

Tori did not want to go. She wanted to find out if Jean was safe but she really did not want to stay on this bloody deck either. It had not been anything like she had expected with so much gore and so many killed. She was only too glad of an excuse to get out of there, for the time being.

"Can you walk Monsieur? You can lean on me a little and I will try to support you as best I can."

"To go with such a brave little angel, would be my pleasure Mademoiselle. Now may I suggest let us both get below, where we will be out of harms way, n'est pas?"

The two of them made their way below slowly, as there was no real reason to hurry. To both of them it was very apparent that most of the fighting seemed to be over. There seem to be just a few diehards here and there. Still she would feel better when they were safely in her cabin. Once there, she felt around in the dark. Damn she wished she had a lighter or matches; she needed a light. Instead of the lamp she found the deep set shelf with the decanter of brandy still intact.

"Monsieur, I think we both could use a drink and if you don't mind drinking after a woman from the bottle, then I don't mind sharing it with you?"

Dominique's laugh was low, even in pain he found this female a delight. No wonder Jean was so taken with her. She was not only beautiful; she was spirited and strong. Most females he knew of would have swooned on this very bed, rather than come up on deck and as for the sight of blood.

"I would like it very much if I could share that drink with you. I would toast you for saving an old man's life and offer you my services for as long as I live, which may not be that long, however," he said dramatically.

"Don't you talk like that! Jean will be here in a minute and he will know what to do, you wait and see."

Such trust she had in Jean. He would not tell her that Jean would have no idea as to what should be done. No, he would just drink this brandy and wait for what he knew would be the loss of his arm, followed by the loss of his life's blood and a slow death.

The darkness was broken at last by the cabin boy with a lantern. He was excited about how everything was finishing and the last place he wanted to be right now was down here. He might have a chance to go aboard the other ship, something that he really hoped for.

"Captain said he was glad you are fine and that he will get here as soon as he can. We have taken the other ship but it will be a while before he can see you. Now I have got to go and help."

"Wait, are there any other men hurt bad?"

"No Mam, just a few bumps and bruises, a few small cuts, that sort of thing, why?"

"Well, bring anyone who is hurt and needs help down here to me. I'll do what I can to help them."

"You sure Mam? Down here in the Captain's cabin and all?"

"You heard me boy, now move or I will tell your Captain you disobeyed me and he won't like that will he Monsieur You?"

Dominique was as shocked as the boy but he backed Tori up laughing to himself; this was going to be interesting. To see Jean's face when he returned to his cabin for his lady and his brandy. One gone, that being his brandy, and his lady in the company of the injured. Yes, this was going to be almost worth dying for. At least he was going to be amused, laughing and good and drunk!

"One more thing. Did we lose many men? Did many die?"

"We lost men Mam. I don't know how many but I think maybe it will be quite a few, the other ship put up a good fight."

With that he was gone and the cabin fell silent as the news of so many lost sank in. Gentleman pirate indeed! There was no such thing. What had just happened was something she would never forget and something that could have been avoided. Still they did this for a living she supposed, these pirates. Who was she to tell them any different? She didn't have to agree with it but she could try to help mend the wrong by helping the survivors, starting with Dominique You.

"Now let's take a look at that arm of yours. First we have to get the shirt off, can you help me?"

Dominique did as she asked and Tori took her first close look at the nasty gash. The flow of blood had all but stopped, it was just a trickle, and she released the bandanna to allow the blood to flow for a second and then quickly tied it back in place. There was no doctor but it didn't take one to know that the cut was very deep. The blood had not squirted or pumped, as it would have if a main artery had been cut. That was the only good sign. It had to be stitched up that was for sure but they had no doctor and no medical supplies.

She knew it would be weeks before they made port and if infection set in, which she had no doubt would happen, he would lose his arm, or, worse yet, die. Tori decided she was not going to allow that, she would do what she could. First, she got another bottle of brandy from Jean's chest and handed it to him.

"You had best get good and drunk my friend and drinking the Captain's best brandy should do the job, wouldn't you say?" She was smiling at him with a sort of teasing glitter in her eyes, that made him laugh.

"I am in your command Mademoiselle. Besides, I would be an old fool to turn down such an offer as to drink the Captain's finest, would I not?"

While Dominique drank, Tori saw to the other injured men who had a few minor cuts. A bandage here and a drink of brandy there was all it took. Each one sat silent as she worked on them but they were not blind nor did they lack emotions. She patched up not only their wounds but sent them back up on deck swearing she was an angel in disguise. She was not bad luck they told each other and all who would listen. Far from it, she was just the opposite.

Word spread, the healing she did was wonderful they said and she was even going to help old Dominique. Not that there was anything short of a miracle that could save him. Even if she did, he was surely going to lose his arm. The loss of his arm they all knew would be far worse than death to him, it was after all his fencing arm and next to the sea, his whole life was his joy of fencing.

Tori looked at what she had available to her. Silk thread from her sewing kit that Jean had supplied. A needle that she had held in the flame and then soaked in brandy. Clean cloth taken from one of her linen petticoats and torn into long soft white strips. Now all that was left to do, was the sewing up.

"Have you saved any of that brandy for me?" she asked Dominique.

"Just a little bit in the bottom but drinking won't stop me from bleeding or from losing this arm when we get to port, if I make it that long," he slurred.

"Well I don't think you will have to lose the arm, if we can close the wound and stop any infection from setting in. The bleeding will stop once we sew you up. That's why I wanted you drunk, so the pain would not be too bad for you. You see I have not done this before."

As what she was telling him began to sink in, he raised his eyebrows and rolled his tongue around inside of his cheeks.

"I have seen it done and I think, God willing, I can do it but you are going to have to be still. I'm going to have to have your help on this." She sounded so confident; not a glimmer of the fear that gripped her showed. He had to believe she knew what she was doing.

Dominique could only nod his head, what did he have to lose? He did in fact he told himself, have a lot to gain and she seemed to know what she was talking about but then he was drunk, so what would he know anyway?

Tori took the bottle of brandy from his hand and took a long swig, then before he knew what she had done, she poured the remaining amount on his arm. The searing pain shot through him like a lightening bolt. He wanted to scream, to tear the cabin apart in his agonizing pain, and heaven help him, never had he come so close to striking a woman.

A scream was building inside his head, one that he would have let loose had he been alone, instead he let out only a low sound somewhere between a growl and a moan. Pride and raw guts kept him still, as the beauty before him started working on the gash.

"Sorry about that, but I had to sterilize the wound and that's the only way I know how to. Now the hard part. Let's see what you're really made of, shall we?"

Slowly and painstakingly she stitched his arm. She talked out loud as she worked, to help calm herself and to give him something to listen to.

"We will have to keep you away from all dirt until this has closed and healed. It's so important. If we can keep the infection away we can save the arm."

It had always looked easy in the hospitals or dentist's offices but she soon found it was not that simple. The stitches were uneven and each time she pulled the thread through she knew he was in pain. But not once did he move or call out, and this gave her the courage to go on. Pulling the wound together and closing it was no easy task but it would have been a lot harder if the gash had been jagged instead of a clean straight slash. Once the wound was closed, the bleeding had all but stopped. She took a brandy soaked cloth and wrapped it around the long line of ugly stitches, then put another dry cloth around that one and sat back at last finished. She had done all she could; now it was up to luck and time to heal.

Dominique looked at this remarkable woman and reached out weakly, with his good arm taking her hand in his. He raised it to his lips and placed a gentle kiss on the back of her hand, before dropping it to his lap.

"Merci Mademoiselle. I shall owe you my life, you can always count on me being your friend and if you ever need anything, you come to me." He closed his eyes then and passed out.

Tori wiped the perspiration from his brow and lay his head back against the pillow. "Sleep well my new friend, because come morning you are going to have one hell of a hangover, not to mention a sore arm."

"But he will have his life no? Thanks to my lady. It seems my lady that action agrees with you. You are no longer the same shade of the stones; you have color in your face!"

"Jean! I did not know you were there, how long have you been watching me?"

"Long enough to know that you are truly the bravest and most beautiful woman I have ever known. The more I learn about you, the more I come to love you."

There he had said it. He had said it out loud, what he knew in his heart. He, Jean Laffite did truly love her. She had not only shown him what kind of a woman she was but she was exactly what he wanted in his life, what he had hoped for, not really believing that anyone like her existed. Now that he had found what he had always been looking for, how could he ever let her go?

Tori stood for a moment contemplating what he had just told her, it was not so much that he had said those words of love but how he had said them. There was no doubt that Jean was indeed very much in love with her. Her poor Jean, how could she make him understand that she did not belong here, that he should not love her. More that that, she could never allow herself to love him in return.

She would never give up trying to find the lake and once she did, she just knew she would be leaving for her own time and for her family. How could she make him understand that what she felt, all that she would ever feel, was deep and abiding friendship but not love, not the way he wanted and deserved, not now or ever.

Jean looked at her and wanted to stay but he had just come down to see how she was and to see how Dominique was doing. Now that he knew they were both safe he had to get back to his duties. After all, there was a matter of a captured ship to handle.

"I will not be gone long. You stay and rest as I have to take care of a few things."

"No, I don't want to stay put, I want to come up on deck. I need the air, you know it's hot down here. Just what happens now anyway? What do you intend to do with the other ship?"

Jean did not want to argue with her; she had been through so much, done so much good with such bravery. Besides, he knew her moods and looks well enough to know that she would not take no for an answer. He allowed her to accompany him up top, telling her as they went that the ship they had taken was a British vessel.

She was a slave ship on its way to deliver what was left of its cargo of blacks. Not a full cargo because they had stopped off once and sold half of the blacks in Santo Domingo. But as there had been an embargo placed on slaves in the America's, the British captain had seen a chance to make a larger profit by selling them illegally in the South.

Jean already had on board his ship the gold from the first sale, along with the other goods she carried in her hull. Now he was debating what to do with the slaves and the boat that was left. "Can't you take it back to the island and let the blacks go? Slavery is wrong Jean, please don't let them go on to New Orleans or anywhere in the South for that matter."

"Tori I know well how you feel about slavery. You have told me many times about how wrong it is. Let me relieve some of your fears about those poor souls and explain my actions. If I send them back to the islands, they are doomed to a life, a short life in the cane fields. If I sell them they will go to good planters, men who I trust to treat them well. They will have a far better chance at life by going with us." His voice was deep and serious; its tone was also one that Tori recognized as his firm and final, decision.

Orders were given that the British ship would be taken with them as it now belonged to Jean and his men. Those that wished to join them were more than welcome. If not, they would be let off at the next island they passed.

Many hours later, Jean held a sleeping Tori in his arms as he sat on deck thinking. How things had changed since Tori had come into his life. What would happen next he wondered? It was sure to be far from calm sailing for he had that little matter of her framed murder to clear up. He looked at her sleeping face, so calm and serene in the early dawn's light. She had changed so much in the past months, he doubted that she would be recognized at all by anyone who had known her at Rose's. Still they would have to be careful. She had made some powerful enemies in her short stay in the city, and he would have to tread cautiously.

Even with all that murder matter cleared up and put out of the way, he still had to do the hardest of all tasks and keep his word, and that was to take her to the lake. He would not let himself believe that she had any chance of returning to her own time. If she had to be hurt finding out there was no way back, then so be it. He would be there to help ease her pain and in time she would learn to love him as he did her. He hugged her gently to him; she would forget her old life for he would give her a new one and a new family. She belonged here with him now, in this time. He would help her to adjust to this time and all that it involved. He would do anything for her, anything at all.

The rest of the trip went smoothly enough, especially after a few things had changed. One of them being, that Tori had the run of the ship, she could go anywhere she wanted and at any time, unescorted. The whole ship's crew thought of her as some sort of saint. She had earned not only their respect but their loyalty as well. Not a man or boy among them, would harm her or allow her to be harmed. She had become a hero to them. Tori had saved their beloved Dominique from certain death, not to mention his arm.

As for Dominique, he had taken a liking to this woman of Jean's, and he made himself a promise that he would personally take it upon himself to tear Jean apart, if he treated her wrong, friend or not.

Tori found herself spending quite a lot of time with Dominique. There was something about the older man that somehow seemed wise and calming to her. She enjoyed talking to him about so many different things. He was, she found, a very educated man and very interested in debating any subject that she brought up. The two formed a strong bond, rather like that of a doting grandfather and his granddaughter. Tori had been worried at first that her stitching would not work and that the undying trust he had placed in her would be for nothing. For if somehow the arm failed to heal, she would lose him. Everyday she would look at it and tend to it as best she could, even though he would huff and gruff. She knew that he really did not mind, in fact she sensed that he was just as worried about his arm, as she was. The days passed by and with each new dawn came the realization that the wound was healing. It became slowly clear to both of them that they had succeeded in doing the impossible. This was the cement to their friendship, and in the closeness of this bond, each filled a lonely gap in their lives and found comfort in the depth of their association. It was a kind of relationship that asked nothing but gave so very much in return and each knew in a special way, that it would last a lifetime.

Days passed and each grew to learn much about the other, about their personalities. Dominique learned that she was no woman to just set aside, all pretty-like. This was a new breed of woman who he talked with, feminine and strong in a masculine way. He loved the very spirit of her, the way she stood up for herself. Tori found that Dominique loved to put on a show of huff and anger, it was just that though, all bark and no bite. It seemed funny; that he should be the only one that did not know everyone else could see through his rough exterior. Maybe that is why he was so well loved. He would do anything and stand up for any man. He would even fight to the death if he found the cause justifiable. She learned also that he let no one near him emotionally since he left France many years ago. The closest to showing any real emotion as far as she could see, was his brotherly love towards his Captain.

Jean found his old friend's attachment to Tori amusing. That the tough old Dominique had let Tori win his heart like she had, was nothing short of a miracle. It was truly comical to see Dominique falling all over himself and doting on Tori the way he was. Still it did not bother him any, as he knew deep down where Tori's heart lay. He trusted her like he had no other woman and he would always feel that way, he would bet his life on it.

The day before they reached port, Tori took out Dominique's stitches and even though the scar left behind would be long and ugly, to Dominique it was a symbol of something far greater than a mere fight. The scar was a symbol of a miracle to him and he would always show it with great pride and love.

"You see my young Jean, how your lady has taken such care of this old fool but I tell you now my friend, that you had best take equal care of her or answer to me, n'est pas?"

"Why Dominique, do I understand you? That you would actually call me out over a woman?"

"Not over any woman, just the best damn woman that has touched your, no, our lives. One that I know your father would have given his blessing to, had he lived long enough to see this day, God rest his soul."

Jean smiled and looked at Dominique, who for many years had in many ways become his father.

"You can be assured that my intentions are honorable where this lady is concerned. I plan to have Tori as my wife one day and that day can't come quick enough for me. Just give us your blessing you old sea dog and then keep your mouth shut. It would do neither of us any good if the men found out we both had gone soft in the head over a mere woman, now would it?"

"Like they have not?" he laughed.

The two of them stood and laughed; they hugged each other and were truly in a joyous mood. It was then that they looked over to where Tori stood smiling at them. She had not heard all that they had said; just enough to know that the men might think Jean and Dominique were soft in the head over some woman, surely not her? Damn the sound of the wind she thought, if it had not blown so in her ears, she could have heard all of their conversation.

"You must excuse us my lady, we will try to make it a point to speak English in front of you from now on, won't we Dominique?"

"Ah, oui. We will do just that. Why I might even try to teach Tori some French."

At this all three just laughed. Tori the hardest, teach her some French indeed. One day she would enjoy watching their faces as she rattled off in their language and see who laughed then.

# Chapter 11

Tori had been told that they were not sailing into the port of New Orleans. In fact, she had amazed Jean when she had asked him outright if they would be going to the area called Barataria and his home port of Grand Terre.

"You know of Grand Terre?"

"You might say a little. I have not told you this before and I don't know why come to think of it? Guess it never entered my mind. Anyway, I do know a little bit about you, not much mind you, just what I picked up while on my visits to New Orleans and what I read about here and there. You are in some books you know? Anyway, I'm a bit of a sightseer whenever I travel and Linni and I just love local legends. So I kind of paid attention to what was said about you. Just wish I had paid more." Tori laughed a little at that and then continued to hide her embarrassment. "You see in my time you were known to camp out there and sell your illegal goods. They also said you were a major slave trader, a rich and powerful man, the Gentleman Pirate is how they referred to you? Tell me, were they right?"

Jean looked at her. He was somewhat flattered that the people in the future knew so much about him. What bothered him, was, that these people of her time, seemed to think of him as the pirate, why? Hiding his irritation he answered her.

"You might say that some of what you said is true, if not all. I do bring slaves, but only when I acquire them as I did on this trip. Now as for rich and powerful, hmm... That's something I had not considered."

He was lying to her, she could tell by the look on his face he knew only too well that he was doing very nicely. Once again Tori could see the sparkle of mischief in his dark eyes and the laughter behind them. The few creases deepened and added to his roguish look that seemed to draw her to him. She could feel her heart pick up its pace and her stomach tighten. This man had a way of making her want him even without trying. She reached up with her hand and placed it on the back of his neck, pulling playfully at his hair.

"You? Not knowing that you are powerful, is like me not understanding French."

The statement hit him full force, was she inferring that she understood French, or that he was stupid and did not understand that he was powerful?

"What my lady do you mean by that statement?"

Tori realized at once that she had let the cat out of the bag. But she was not ready to reveal this information and had to cover her tracks quickly.

"Just that you could not know that you are powerful, just like I do not know French, how could you? There is no way you could know history, not like I do, or about what you are, or should I say whom you become. It's all so tangled up isn't it?"

He looked at her long and hard, her face said she spoke the truth, her explanation was one that he could believe but he had learned in the past not to underestimate her. He would have to be more careful around her; at least until he knew for sure that she had no understanding of his native language. The possibility of her speaking French had not crossed his mind at all, that was until now. He would have to find out for sure, just for his own peace of mind and he knew only one way he would try, as soon as possible.

The moment was broken by the call of "Boss, land ahead," from a sailor up in the crow's nest. Tori looked hard, holding her hand over her brown to block out some of the sun's glare. She wanted to see once again the coastline of home. Land was still some way off, but it was just visible to the naked eye as a thin dark line on the horizon. A few hours later she saw that the thin dark line was not one solid shoreline as she had expected but broken pieces of land, with many small islands and inlets. Mesmerized, she stood excitedly by Jean's side watching as he guided his ship homeward.

It was afternoon when Tori sailed into the home port of the pirates located just as history had told, in the famous Barataria Bay area. His base was where two large islands lay close together. One called Grand Terre the other Grand Isle. The home of Laffite was located amongst a network of bayous on Grand Terre; across the narrow straight on Grand Isle were scattered small settlements where the bulk of the pirates lived.

As far as the eye could see the swamps and the islands seemed to blend together, only the waterways, which were many, broke up the land. Spanish moss hung from the trees dipping down to trail in the marshland and water. The shadows amongst the trees and undergrowth were deep, long and dark. Somehow it did not look like the romantic hideout of the pirates that she had imagined and the mosquitoes were big, black and hungry.

As they sailed slowly in towards where they would anchor, the shore came precariously close, with shallow depths visible below the crystal clear water. To one side of a small bayou, Tori thought she caught a glimpse of an alligator but told herself that could not be; it had to be a log or something! All of a sudden the ship rounded a bend taking her mind off the creature and to Tori's utter amazement, a line of buildings appeared. Jean explained that they were the warehouses that held in them everything one could imagine. She could very well imagine in her mind what a pirate horde would look like, but it did not change the fact that all of it was contraband, spoils taken from many different ships whose fate only a few knew. Like a dark shadow passing over her excitement, that thought temporally tempered her excitement. Her attention was brought back to what Jean was saying when he slipped his arm around her waist and proudly explained further about his business. She quickly learned that at this very moment the warehouses were full and awaiting only the command of those in charge to be emptied. This was done by holding an auction in a location known as The Temple. The contents would be sold to the high society of New Orleans and the surrounding countryside. Auctions were held regularly, and the people would come to sample and buy what was up for grabs. They would arrive by boat, carriage, and horseback or by any means they could. The afternoon would be an entertaining time of illegal shopping, that all enjoyed. It had become an acceptable illegal set up. Even regular merchants stopped frequently to unload smuggled cargoes, so they could avoid the customs tax in New Orleans. In this way Grand Terre had been born and became home to Jean and his men.

Dominique had joined them at this point and laughed as he watched Tori's expression. He could see she was impressed and wanting to help his Captain, he added his own bit of information. He told her proudly how Jean had gained his power and his wealth. It was by taking a band of unorganized men and becoming their leader, known as Boss, that he had turned a small smuggling band into what it was today. But she need not worry, her Jean was not considered anything like his men. He was accepted in New Orleans and treated as a rich Gentleman of the South. The ladies of society would have it no other way he laughed. Why the chance to claim Jean Laffite as a guest at a party, was considered a coup.

At this outburst, Jean shot Dominique a filthy look, one that cut short his belly laugh and sent him hurrying off. Tori who always loved Dominique's sense of humor, jabbed Jean in the ribs with her elbow. "Now why on earth did you do that? It is no secret even in my own time that you were quite a ladies man. Really Jean, you should be ashamed of yourself."

Jean did not know how to react to this bit of news, or to her having caught him glaring at Dominique. His only defense was to try and change the subject. "Ah my lady, you and I could stand here and discuss this matter for hours I think. However that is about how long it will take for me to settle my ship and its men. You might take that time to go below and rest, then I will take you ashore."

"I don't care what you want at this time," she grinned playfully. I think I will join Dominique and his hurt feelings while you do whatever it is you do. Now go on with you." She pushed him toward the front of the ship. As tired as Tori was, she did not feel ready to rest and give in. Twice Jean had asked her to wait below decks, until the ship had anchored and the unloading completed. But stubborn as ever and with her new ally Dominique, Jean lost that argument and she remained on deck watching for herself the whole operation.

Like he had explained, it was several hours before Jean was ready to escort his lady to the house. But before he would even consider doing that, he insisted that her breeches had to go. A dress was more befitting a lady and would be worn or she was doomed to stay aboard she learned. Jean won the argument easily but not without a payback from Dominique.

"So the pup has to use blackmail to have his way." He laughed heartedly as he walked away. "For me she does anything. For you tis different, no?" He did not stay to listen to Jean's answer. Rather he joined a few of the last men on board, who overhearing his exchange with the boss, were laughing. "Don't worry, we will leave you and your lady the pirogue to come ashore. We'll see you later." And with that last statement they all quickly departed, knowing a final joke was on Jean. He had never rowed himself ashore, let alone even considered it!

The camp itself was well set up looking very much like a small town. The houses were small, shack-like in appearance, yet neat and clean. Some were constructed of groundup oystershell and plaster while others were simply lean-tos. Most small cottages came with small gardens and some had flowers and fresh coats of paint. There were numerous small children of both black and white backgrounds; still many more of mixed bloodlines were happily playing together.

As they walked past, many waved or yelled hello to Jean. "Most of my men have families or just keep their women here if they choose. They know that they are safe here and it suits both them and myself. If they are happy, then they work better, keeping me and the operation sailing smoothly so to speak. But don't let them fool you Tori, they are a rough group of men and unlike my crew, would love to have their way with you if they could. Word I'm sure is out that you are my lady but that would not stop some of them from taking you. Even if it means risking ending up on the end of my sword if caught."

Jean was speaking very sternly and Tori knew he meant it when he asked her to promise him she would remain in the house and if she had to go out, to be escorted by either himself or someone he assigned.

"It's for your own safety, not to mention my sanity. If I catch you not doing as I have asked, I will take it upon myself to lock you in, and I mean it Tori. This is not a safe place, though it should be somewhat more stabilized than it used to be. As if he knew she would want to hear the story of how that had happened he went on to explain. "Things around here were getting out of hand. Too many leaders and not enough leadership. Each one working for another Captain or for themselves. I was challenged one night in front of two very powerful and dangerous men. I have no doubt you will meet them soon yourself. Both Italian, and proud of it. One called Gambi. The other Chighizola. You'll know him when you see him." He grinned as he put his finger to his nose. "He has the name of Nez Coupe'... lost part of his nose in a fight and he's none too friendly."

Tori was horrified yet fascinated. He was telling her about historical characters, people that she would no doubt be meeting.

"Those two you have to watch out for. Though I think after I shot and killed a troublemaker in front of them, they will think twice to go up against me?"

"You shot and killed a man?" She couldn't believe her Jean could just kill in cold blood.

"Ah do not look at me so, for it had to be done. This rabble of men needed a leader and with Beluche backing me, along with a few others, I only had those two Italian rebels to bring into line. I formed a council and put Gambi and old Nez Coupe on it, along with Beluche, Dominique and myself. This place should run a lot smoother and if what you have said history says, with me as the boss, we will profit, no?"

Tori had been so involved in listening to Jean that she had not really paid much attention to where they were walking. When Jean stopped suddenly and pointed off to one side, she could only stare and smile at what she saw. True, the house was not a grand plantation style home but she had not expected to see anything quite like she was now looking at. It was of moderate size, sturdy to look at, with a verandah looking out towards the Gulf. The windows had wrought iron bars covering them in fancy designs and the red brickwork gave it a European appearance.

"I take it that the lady approves of the living quarters?"

"The lady does indeed. It looks quite comfortable. I would have to say Jean, that you never cease to amaze me. Who would have though that you would have such a place in the middle of nowhere?

They walked towards the door, which was thrown open before they got too close and a large Spanish looking lady stood there, all smiles and laughter. She reminded Tori of a grinning cat. Yes she told herself. She did look like the cat that swallowed the canary.

"So the Senor brings home at last the Senora?" She laughed. "You have taken my advice and made yourself happy, si?"

Jean just laughed and escorted Tori over the threshold and into the cool interior of the house. He simply answered her with a nod and a wink of his eye. He whispered a response in Spanish in her ear saying, "Something like that."

The inside complimented the outside appearance for it was decorated with only the best furniture and artwork. Its warmth and beauty stunned Tori. Here was a side to Jean that told how different he was from the pirate she had grown to know at sea. This home told of a caring man who liked his home to be just that, a home, both warm and friendly. Her thoughts were interrupted as his voice broke her silent appraisal.

"Your room awaits you upstairs, along with a small something." He held his finger to his lips to silence her questions. Then he continued quickly. I have to leave for now but Carlotta will see to it that you have all you need until dinner. I did not tell you before but we will be joined this evening by a guest. So do look ravishing for me."

Jean smacked her lightly on her behind and then seeing the look on Tori's face and knowing that she did not like being told what to do, he quickly pulled her into his arms and softly placed his lips to hers. The spark was instantaneous and the passion, with which she returned his kiss, caused him to feel himself arousing.

"My lady, if you detain me now, I will be late this evening and that would not do. One thing I am known for, is promptness."

Tori smiled and simply turned and headed up the stairs, swaying her hips slowly and moving in the most seductive way she knew how. The response she got was not what she had expected. Female laughter echoed through the hall as Carlotta spoke.

"It's not going to do you any good Senora. The Senor, he already slipped out but I can see why he chose you. You are one to stir the blood, like the Spanish. Ah the passion."

Tori turned and saw that he was indeed gone and she was disappointed. But a sly smile crossed her face, as she thought to herself how she would tease him that night at dinner. She would drive him crazy wanting her and yet he would have to play host. After all the gentleman could not just leave and have his way. Yes, tonight was going to be fun.

"Carlotta I think maybe you and I had better get to know one another." She smiled her face full of mischief. "Then you and I will have some fun this evening, shake things up a little." The two woman talked and after a few hours the plan had been set. She left Carlotta loving the idea of serving her dinner like the famous cook Tori had told her of.

Toward the end of the hall, at the top of the stairs, a door stood ajar. "It is the door that is open Senora," said Carlotta, "the other rooms are for the occasional guests that stay the night."

The room was large, open and airy. A huge bed sat between two open French doors. A slight breeze blew at the curtains and the color of the room with its pale blues and grays gave it a cooling effect. Her gaze fell upon a bathtub full of hot rose-scented water. On a small table next to the tub were bottles of oils, soaps, and perfumes. He had known she would want this more than anything else and lying on the chair waiting for her was a new silk gown. Its hue caught in the sunlight that streamed across the room. It was not yellow and yet it was not golden. So subtle was the color, that she found words could not describe what she was looking at. So this then was his surprise, his little something that he had mentioned.

Smiling to herself and closing the door, Tori stripped and climbed into the water, sinking down into its luxurious silky touch. She just lay there and let her body relax and her mind wander. Closing her eyes, she put her head back and then as if a hammer hit her very soul, the painful memory of her child shot before her.

Overpowering guilt swelled up around her, consuming the happiness and filling her with such sadness and despair. How could she be enjoying herself like this, when somewhere her family must be worried sick? She did miss them; heaven knows how many nights she lay thinking of them all and crying out in the dark for her daughter. She longed to see the smile on her round face, full of love. A look that had no demands. A love that felt safe, in the arms of the one person who would always be there for her, her mother.

Tori sat up, opening her tear-filled eyes and once again like so often since her crossover, she pushed these feelings deep inside. The pain was so raw, so real, that it would consume her if she allowed it. The thought that she would never see her time again was so unacceptable to her, that her only way to deal with it was to not think about any part of it. She would find a way to return to the lake one day, to see for herself if that the way back was closed. But until that time, she had to hang on, she had to be strong. Jean would help her.

Thinking now of Jean, she started to examine her feelings in depth. What was it she felt for him? Could it be love? Or was this emotion she held for him purely a physical attraction...? She did not know. Either way, she had to stop thinking, analyzing her needs and desires. She had to control her feelings and be fair to both of them. After all it was just a matter of days now, before she returned to the lake and home. Home and out of this nightmare. Only this was no longer a nightmare; it was becoming more like a daydream, a wonderful daydream.

Tori raised her hands to her ears, as if by covering them she would block out the sound of her very thoughts. Voices that shouted one thing one second and then seemed to scream another the next. Nothing made any sense and nothing could stop the pain or the joy. She was being torn apart and nothing and no one could make the voices stop.

At first she did not hear the light knock on the door and the small voice that asked if she could be of any help. "The Boss, he said I could work for you as long as you be staying here and I could help you an all. If you need some help with washing your hair, I be glad to do it."

Tori froze; she could hear her own heart beating in her chest, as she slowly turned to look at the girl whose voice she recognized. Tori turned her head to face the young girl who was standing in the doorway. She knew before she saw her, that it would be Lacy.

"Well of all the damnedest things, of all the people to meet out here, Lacy it's me, don't you recognize me?"

Lacy looked closely now, she knew the voice and then she realized who it was but she looked so much different than she remembered. Still all in all it was the same person who had escaped the Madam Rose's clutches on the same day she had. She had learned that such a fuss had been put up over Tori's disappearance, that they had not realized for a whole day, that she herself was missing, making her escape not only easier but also a total success.

Lacy moved quickly across the room, her joy shining on her face. The young girl dropped to her knees at Tori's bath side and threw her arms around her, not caring that in so doing, she was getting soaked.

"I know'd you had got away. Never heard nothing about you been found and all. But how'd you do it? What you be a doing here?" She looked around the room as she spoke, as if meaning in that room.

Lacy was staring at Tori with a true puzzled look that broke into a grin of recognition. It was if a light had gone on as realization hit her. "That's stupid of me ain't it? You be the one they calling Laffite's Lady, the one they say has stolen his heart."

Tori smiled at this. It had a nice ring to it, Laffite's Lady. What else were they saying she wondered?

"Slow up Lacy and let go of me. You are getting yourself soaking in case you haven't noticed." Pushing her away gently, she continued. "There is so much to tell and I have a lot of questions myself."

The two caught up on the past few months, while Lacy helped Tori to dress for the evening. The long hot hours slipped away, and before they realized it, the time for dinner was upon them.

"Lord you best go down, we been talking too much and if there is one thing I knows he hates, that is being late."

"You don't have to worry about that Lacy. I'm sure he will understand when I tell him about you, but do me a favor."

"Anything, all you have to do is ask. You need me here when you come up? I'd be glad to wait."

"No, not that, you have your son to take care of. No, I only want you to give me your word. You don't tell anyone about me, or about Rose's. It's very important that no one find out who I am. Can you understand that? I must not let anyone know."

"You can trust me. Ain't a going to say nothing to no one, not even my man. Don't you fret none. You ain't got to worry like. Look, everyone here is dis place be a hiding from something or someone. It don't make much difference like, but you'll see that when you been here a while. I ain't going to say a word. I owe you something. I be free here, with my man because of you and your help. Well sort of. So I ain't going to say nothing to no one, no way." The two hugged each other and then Lacy held Tori back for a last look at her, before she went down to dinner.

"You sure look a lot different than when we's were together last. Your lighter. Yes, you are, and it ain't pale from sick like neither. You ain't a fancy like Rose said are you? Black don't fade. You be a white lady and your hair, it's not only longer, which I know'd how that happens but it be a lot straighter now." She ran her fingers through her own curly mop as she laughed. "You going to have to tell me one day, how you do that. Oh stop your laughing. I ain't a said nothing stupid, it be the truth. One thing bothers me some." She frowned at her. "You not stupid either. But to me it seems pretty stupid to want to pass yourself off as a black and go and get's mixed up with that Aunt Salle, the bitch."

Tori stopped laughing, she looked at Lacy and realized that the girl was right, that she did have a point and she would want answers to her questions, questions she did not want to cover.

"Maybe one day you and I can talk but for now please let's just leave it as it is." Then changing the subject she turned around, her arms in the air, "you sure I look all right. Lordy be, you sure my hair is a going to stay put this way?"

Lacy just laughed at her mimicking her way of speech and assured her that everything was fine. She was perfect in her opinion. Even her face with its hint of rouge was stunning. She had learned how to apply some of the makeup they had used in such a different way from what she was accustomed to. She knew of one other in New Orleans who did it very similar; she herself had learned how to fix hair from her but never the art or applying makeup. Maybe that's where Tori got her knowledge of makeup she told herself.

"I think maybe you could teach me things like, but lord you go downstairs talking like me and I be sure to be sent out and told not to come back. I'll have to watch how I talk around you and do my best not to slip back to the old way. I do know the right way and all, it just be hard like."

Tori smiled at her friend and took her hands in hers, holding them tight, as she spoke softly. "You can talk any way that you want. When we are alone I want us to be close, and not have to worry about such things. You are my friend and I hope you will let me become yours. Friends can joke around. I was not making fun of you, just fooling around."

Were those tears filling Lacy's eyes as she turned away and walked towards the long mirror? Tori guessed it was and let the girl compose herself rather than push further. Slowly she walked over to the long framed glass and as Lacy stepped away the image that filled the frame was hardly recognizable.

Once again the twentieth century woman was gone. Before her stood a woman of this time, dressed for a dinner, and looking every bit the Southern Belle. Lacy stood for a few seconds really studying her. Here standing in front of her was truly a beautiful and bewitching female. No wonder she had the pirate's heart. Lacy said thanks to Tori then, for letting her go back to her place and gave her one last hug before she left. Tori felt strange and a little frightened, that a slip of a girl could hold her future in her hands and yet she trusted her not to tell anyone. She knew Lacy most likely had never been trusted like this before in her whole life. Combine that with the fact that they were friends, with a past in common and well Tori just knew that she was safe for now.

One last look in the mirror and feeling rather awkward in the full gown, she made her way down to the front room, where she could hear Dominique and Jean talking. They were discussing something to do with the sale of the cargo off one of the ships. The very sight of her caught him off guard. He had forgotten what she could look like in a silk gown, and with her hair pulled to one side as it was, she was a sight to behold standing in the doorway. It was like a frame surrounding a perfect picture. She was bathed in the soft golden glow of the oil lamps. A glow that seemed to set her eyes ablaze, as the color of the gown reflected in them. Jean could not move for he knew this vision of her he would hold in his memory forever, every line, and every detail.

It was Dominique who walked forward to escort Tori into the room, scolding Jean on his lack of manners and chuckling to himself. Jean was acting more and more like a lovesick puppy, but then he had to admit to himself, that if he were younger, he might very well be doing the same thing. Instead, he had his role of friend and confidant to play out with this ravishing creature. A role that held dignity, with none of the foolishness or pains that accompanies young love.

"Is there something I may get for you before our guest arrives, something light to drink maybe?"

"Why Dominique, such a Gentleman as always. Yes, that would be nice, a glass of wine and something to smoke."

Jean choked on his drink and Dominique laughed out loud rocking back and forth as he did so. For balance his short legs were spread slightly apart, his hands were on his hips and still he looked as if he would tumble right over, so hard was he laughing.

"The drink I will be obliged to fetch for you, as for the smoke. Well now, if I was to comply with that request Madam, Jean would run me through, or drown on his drink!" He slapped his hand down on the tabletop and turned his head towards Jean as he continued lightheartedly. "It would be amusing, however, to see the look on our guest's face as he walked in and found you, sitting like an angel and acting like the devil was in you."

Jean coughed the remainder of what he had swallowed the wrong way, and huskily commanded, "stop encouraging her, she might just do it." He coughed again, only with a laugh this time. "Stop this, both of you."

Everyone was laughing now and the three of them turned towards the door as Carlotta announced the arrival of their guest. What greeted Tori's eyes as he entered was a rather tall, well-dressed Creole gentleman. He had the blackest eyes that she could ever remember seeing and the fact that they were small and weasel like, only helped to make his nose seem too large and out of place on his pale face.

Jean and the man bowed slightly, when greeting each other, as did Dominique. Then this stranger turned towards her and his full attention fell on Tori. It was in that second that Tori felt an instant dislike for this so-called Gentleman. Her unease continued but known only to her, outwardly she was unchanged. The guest was making his way over to where she stood and as he did so her opinion of him was sealed. He was nothing more than an overdressed rake if she had ever seen one. His beady little eyes ran up and down he. It was as if he were undressing her in his mind and his walk towards her was just a little too fast for her liking.

"Madame, it is truly my pleasure to meet such a beauty in such a wild setting. I had no idea that I was to be in the company of such a vision. I look forward to getting more acquainted this evening." All this was spoken in French and Tori would have liked to tell him where to go but then she was not supposed to understand him was she? Then there was his disgusting greeting. His lips, that brushed the back of her hand, were far too wet for her liking, and she felt like ramming her fist into his pompous, little rat-like face.

"You will have to excuse Victoria Monsieur. She does not understand our language I am afraid. We will have to speak English."

"Ah, pardon me, I did not know. You will forgive me, yes, and let me introduce myself to you. I am Bernard Louis Toutant but please, you must call me Bernard."

Tori withdrew her now very wet hand and smiling at the man as sweetly as she could she answered him.

"I am charmed I'm sure. Jean the glass of wine you so kindly offered me, is it available?"

The intended obvious snub to Bernard seemed to go right over his head. He was not about to give up and lose his chance at getting to know this woman.

"Please allow me Madame. It would be my pleasure I am sure. But first you must reveal what lovely name you go by, I am certain it will be just as lovely as the lady?"

This man was impossible and Tori could see over his shoulder Dominique shaking his head, rolling his eyes and smiling to himself. In fact he was doing much more than that, he was trying hard not to burst out loud with laughter.

Jean's face however was blank and his eyes piercing, his lips were straight and thin, and he obviously did not like this Bernard or his attentions towards her any more than she did. It was a cold controlled voice that spoke out. In French he addressed his guest in a calm tone, a tone that Tori had never heard him use before, it had such a threatening sound about it.

"Monsieur, the lady's name is Victoria and she is to be treated as a lady who is unattainable to both yourself and all others. She is my lady and I will not stand for any man trying to ah, shall we say, place certain advances towards her. I would take any such actions as a personal insult and would have to call that Gentleman out, do I make myself clear?"

Bernard was angered by Jean's words but like Tori he hid his emotions well. It would serve him no purpose to make this pirate angry with him now. It was, however, only because Jean had spoken in French, thereby saving face, that he could let it be. He wanted to see this arrogant Laffite dressed down and squirm a little. "Indeed you make yourself perfectly clear. Forgive me I meant no harm. I had no idea that she was your, your…just what is she?"

"She, is none of your business. Now let us speak in English and have dinner before we discuss why you came here tonight."

With that Jean walked pass Bernard and took hold of Tori by placing his arm around her waist in a protective possessive manner. In this way he guided her towards the dining room.

"Forgive us Victoria we will speak in English for the rest of the evening I assure you. Now let us go and eat, you may find the wine that I have chosen for dinner more to your liking."

So my name is to be Victoria is it? She thought. He was quick, her Jean. She may not have told this Bernard anything about her past, but he looked the type that would visit that awful house and keep up with all the gossip. If she had been introduced as Tori…the thought caused her to shiver and to inwardly thank God for letting such a careful guardian as Jean come into her life.

Carlotta's dinner was wonderful; a mixture of Spanish and Creole with just a touch of what Tori fun lovingly referred to as happy happy, and kicked up a notch Emeril's style. She even had Carlotta saying bam! when adding her hot spices to the various dishes. She did it with such a flair and so seriously that Jean had to hide his amusement behind his napkin. Her antics obviously encouraged by Tori had his guest in quite a dither. Bernard he guessed, found Carlotta's actions thoroughly improper, and the strange conversation perplexing. Not to mention that both she and Jean cleverly avoided answering any of his personal questions about her. Time and time again he would sway the conversation in her direction and Tori found that she was not so upset by this, as she was by his constant and very obvious attentions. Attentions that had the two of them been left alone, she had no doubt would have been less than honorable.

The evening ended with Jean announcing the Gentlemen would retire to discuss the business at hand. Business that would surely only bore her and as she must be tired from the trip, she might prefer to retire for the night. Normally she would have not given into his suggestion but she was only too glad to leave and get away from the glaring stares of Bernard. Stares that not only made her feel uncomfortable but were truly beginning to anger his host. She feared that if she did not depart soon, Jean might lose his patience, business deal or not.

Tori stood slowly and leaving her chair walked to Jean's side where she leaned forward. She bent down from the waist so as to give Jean a clear view, which she was sure in the low cut dress must have been quite revealing. She kissed his cheek lightly and then as if she was quite unaware of her actions, she spoke like a truly genteel Southern bred lady.

"Thank you for a lovely evening Jean and you are right. I am feeling a little tired. Your suggestion of an early night is just what I need." She turned then to face the other two, "Gentlemen if you will excuse me?"

Bernard, who was sitting on the opposite side of the table, realized if he did not move fast, he would miss the opportunity to say his farewells. To hold once again her hand, to squeeze it suggestively, thereby letting only her know... His chair fell backwards and hit the floor, and in his haste he quite forgot himself.

Tori had to smile to herself, as Jean and a very embarrassed Bernard assured each other that everything was fine. Then acting as if she had not even noticed the incident, she made her way to a very amused Dominique. She placed a light kiss on his unsuspecting face and spoke loud enough for the others to hear.

"Good night, Dominique, my dear friend. May you sleep well." With that she walked out of the room. She turned slowly in the doorway and as she closed the two doors she thought she would burst out laughing at the dumbfounded look on Bernard's face. Now that was a much-needed improvement over the face she had seen all night.

Once in her room, Tori laughed out loud. The scene she had just left had her in stitches. She could see them still; Dominique sat red in the face with embarrassment. Jean smiling to himself and that idiot Bernard, standing there with his mouth hung open. It had been such a look of disappointment that crossed his face, when he realized he would not get to physically hold her as he said his fond farewell. Then his cod-like mouth had closed rapidly, followed by the lowering of his bottom lip; this developed into a full pout. Much more Tori could not have handled. She had shut the door and made her way up the stairs fast, holding her sides, as they threatened to burst from the laughter that now filled the room.

It had been sometime before she controlled herself. She had not laughed so hard in such a long long time. The evening had left her drained, yet far from sleepy.

Carlotta had been busy since she left the room for dinner. Not only was the bed turned down, there was a nightgown and small soft slippers neatly awaiting her. The vase on the table was filled with fresh flowers, whose soft scent filled the room. The brandy decanter was full and Jean's favorite cigars filled a small beautifully hand carved box. She stroked the box with her fingers and then reached inside to touch the long thin rolls of tobacco. If only she could have a menthol cigarette and a cold beer. Funny she should think of a beer right now, when before her was one of the world's finest after dinner drinks she mused.

The evening was still young and the balcony called to her with it's evening breeze, a perfect ending to a perfect day. Tori helped herself to the brandy and one of Jean's cigars. She stood drinking the amber liquid that warmed her as it slipped smoothly down her throat. She inhaled the soft scented cigar and found that she enjoyed the relaxed feeling that was sweeping over her. The sound of the bayous came like nature's music to her ears; this she knew was the true sound of mother earth, unpolluted by the noises of the future. No radio waves, no cars or planes, nothing but the gentle call of the night. She was sure that the night air was very different also and that reason could be, that it was pure air, like the sounds, it too had not been touched as of yet, by man and his pollution.

The sound of the door softly closing behind her warned her that she was no longer alone and instinct told her who the intruder was. She did not turn as she spoke.

"I thought you had business to discuss?"

"Ah, but I did. And I must say never before have I put off business, but then the thought of you up here was more than I could stand. Dominique is capable of taking over for me tonight and besides I think if Bernard is down there, thinking of me up here with you, that we will come out ahead in the deal, nest pas?"

"You are so bad Jean, where is your sense of fairness?"

"And where, might I add, is yours? Kissing Dominique and making poor old Bernard squirm like you did?"

"Why I did nothing of the sort, now come here and show me why you say you left your meeting."

He walked toward her and taking the cigar from her hand, inhaled from it once, before throwing it over the balcony. The aromatic blue smoke slipped from his mouth as he reached for her glass. This he emptied in one long swig. Then taking her hand he led her back into the bedroom. He placed the glass down and then took her in his arms.

Slowly he kissed her pulling her closer to him, his body melting into hers. His hands found the pins holding up her hair and he removed them one by one. He pulled her hair down and then pushed it away from her face. His lips were traveling down her neck, leaving a tingling sensation. His breath was warm against her skin; his breathing was slow and deep.

She thought of her promise to herself to not allow herself to love him. She had to stop Jean, but it was only her mind that wanted him to stop, once again her body was telling her something completely different from her conscience.

Sensing some kind of a battle was going inside her, Jean made his mind up to caress her until it was she who called out for his love. No matter what, he would hold back his desire to take her now as he wanted. He would make her want him as bad as he needed her. He would wash away any doubts that she was having. Jean decided he would help her win this battle she was fighting and give her the freedom to love and live with him here and now, forever.

Slowly he slipped the gown down pass her shoulders and exposed the top half of her body. Then gently further down he pushed the garment, until it rested on her waist.

"Why Madame, you are shameless, no undergarments?"

"You know that I hate to wear those old fashioned things, besides, no one could tell or know that I omitted them this evening. No one but you that is. Who else got to take a sly gander down the top of my gown as I bent to kiss them goodnight?"

His hands slipped around to the front of her shoulders, as a knowing chuckle told her he had understood her intent only too well. He caressed her breasts tenderly, his lips traveling down to the tops of both and then back up to her shoulders. The gown he pushed now over her hips and then without warning he picked her up and carried her to the waiting bed and laid her upon it.

Slipping out of his clothes in what seemed only seconds to her, he then lay down by her side. Not touching, not talking just looking deep into her eyes with a look of compassion and understanding. He would not demand anything of her ever, if all she wanted this evening was to be held, then he would give her that. There was torment on her face but passion in her eyes. How he wished he could fight her battle for her, releasing her from her past, yet he knew she had to win this fight alone.

Tori was trying not to let the guilt of earlier that night swamp her and drag her down into the depths of despair. She found herself wondering why now? Why, after all the time she had been here and most of all, in Jean's arms, should she feel that it was so wrong? Tori turned her back on him, she could not look into his face, into those eyes, knowing that what he wanted, she might never be able to give him. She could not allow herself the pleasure of making love with him, it was wrong, and that was that.

Jean traced the outline of her body; the light touch of his hand running up and down her skin caused her to shudder. She could feel herself weakening, knowing the heights that this man could bring her to. The pleasures that he could show her. Was it because it was forbidden fruit, that she enjoyed it so much?

His mouth was on her back and traveling lower and lower, her hips burned where his kisses had passed and now he was traveling down her legs. Slowly he turned her on her back. Then pulling himself up and covering her with his body, he kissed the top of her forehead and then her neck, burying his face in her shoulder.

Now he started speaking in French to her. His voice smooth and seductive was bombarding her will. She was losing her resolve of never again and she knew it. How could she fight against something so romantic? How could she not want him to make love to her? Right or wrong only time would tell. He had won her body before, but tonight was different because tonight he had won her heart as well. There would be no more right or wrong, no more guilt.

Reaching up she put her hands on his head, her fingers in his hair and pulled him to her. Her mouth was on his, her kiss deep and probing, Tori pushed her body up towards him and every inch of her wanted this man to take her.

Jean's French continued as he entered her and moving slowly at first they molded into one. Tori was beyond clear thinking and caught up in the passion of the moment. She felt as if she were floating. Jean's lovemaking soon had her soaring to heights that she had never known, while Jean himself felt that never before had he made love to a woman so completely, or had it been so fulfilling.

They reached the climax of their union together and Tori called out his name and her joy. She answered his French in French. Tori was lost in the world of Jean's lovemaking and Jean knew finally that his suspicions had been right, he had found out not only that his lady loved him but she also fit in his world better than he had thought. She spoke French very well, perfectly in fact. He knew he should be angry at her deceit, but he could not, for he too was lost in the passion. Now was not the time to confront her, now was the time to enjoy their lovemaking...

Morning found Tori by herself; the side of the bed that Jean had been on was still warm, so he could not have been gone long. Smiling to herself remembering the previous night's events, Tori had to admit that the feeling she had for him, had to be real and far deeper than she had allowed herself to think. Jean was an adventure and a chance to live out a fantasy of sorts. Her family was real and solid, they would always be loved by her and thought of...but they were not here and never may be again.

She knew that a big part of her heart would always belong to her time, her family and her daughter. That no matter what happened to her now, she would always have them or a part of what they shared locked away deep in her soul. She knew also that part of her would forever hold a place for the romance she now shared with Jean. They were two completely different kinds of love, in two completely different times and she loved them both for different reasons. She needed them both, that fact was clear. One would most likely never know of the other, how could they? As for Jean, he would not have to know how she felt how torn she was, maybe one day, but not now.

Putting on a robe and brushing her hair, she started downstairs. There was a new light in her eyes and a New Hope in her heart. Still she had a promise to keep to herself, the lake and the way back, but now she was not going to keep panicking about it. When the time was right, Jean would find a way to take her.

The dining room was her first choice of destination, not only was she starving but her guess was that was where she would find Jean. Long before she got to the door she heard his voice; it was strange to hear him speaking to Carlotta in her native tongue. To speak Spanish was one thing, but to do so with the perfect sing song of an accent was another. His Spanish was very good, not that Tori spoke very much of the language, just that she could tell by the speed and confident way he was holding the conversation, that he had long ago mastered the art of this language along with his English.

"Good morning Jean, I hope I'm not intruding? You never told me that you could speak Spanish so well."

"Indeed my lady and you never told me that your understanding of French was, how shall we say, magnifique?"

Tori's mouth dropped open. She looked from Jean to Carlotta, who just rolled her eyes and shrugged her shoulders. No help would be forthcoming from that direction. She would just have to face Jean and see just what he meant.

"But Jean."

"No buts Madam. Last night you were not only wonderful in bed but wonderful in your art of conversation as well."

Tori remembered then and realized that he had tricked her into revealing that she spoke his native tongue. She did not know if she should be angry or laugh, and in the end she decided just to enjoy the moment and laughed. At least now it was out in the open.

"So the cat is out of the bag so to speak?" Are you very mad at me? I think that you might be, knowing you. Just remember that I have had to sit on many occasions listening to you talk about me, saying a few things, I might add, that were infuriating."

"Now how could I ever stay mad as you call it? I admit I should be but I have suspected that you might be fluent in French for sometime and in a strange way I can understand why you did what you did. But now you know that you can trust me. Well, I see no reason for any more secrets do you?"

"No. I do trust you and you have my word that I will keep nothing you need to know from you again."

Jean frowned at this. She had a way of saying one thing and meaning another. "Tell me do you speak Italian? The truth now?"

"No Jean, I do not speak Italian, or Spanish for that matter, why?"

"Just checking. In the future if I should have something that little ears should not hear, then I shall have to speak in Spanish or Italian." He was laughing at the look on her face. She had a look of thunder on it and by the way she started towards him he knew he had sparked her temper.

"Why you conceited, bombastic, overstuffed pirate." She would have continued with her verbal attack but Jean knew that she was not truly angry, it was just that her pride was a little ruffled. He silenced her with a long firm kiss; this in turn was interrupted by a cough coming from a smiling Carlotta, who was letting them know that they were no longer alone.

Dominique stood in the doorway; he was looking at them in the most perplexed way. "How do two people, who care for each other as you do, fight so much? It must be that you enjoy the making up more, oui?"

Tori blushed and broke free from Jean to greet her dear friend. "Some coffee, or would you care to join us for something to eat?"

Jean laughed, "Now you have gone and done it, Dominique never turns down good food or the company of a lovely lady. I guess we will have to put up with him for an hour or two and mind our manners."

Dominique ignored his younger counterpart. His attention was directed towards the lady who made him always feel years younger and wanted. Not that Jean did not need him, or want his friendship. No, this was different, this was the young and beautiful Tori, talking to a foolish old man and listening to what he had to say.

"I would love your company for a short time. I did, however, come to see if I might escort Tori around Grand Terre this morning," he flashed her one of his inscrutable grins, "just while you are working?"

"Oh Dominique, that would be wonderful! I was wondering what I would do today. That is all right isn't it Jean? You did say I could go out if I was escorted."

Jean nodded his approval, "yes that would be fine. The girl Lacy was by earlier and asked of she could stay home today. Her man sails on one of my ships tonight and will be gone for a while. I told her that she could. Even though you have Carlotta to help you, you would have been alone anyway. Besides, Carlotta has the house to run, not keep you out of trouble."

"Just what is that supposed to mean?"

Jean threw back his head and laughed. He knew that she understood him. It was not that she looked for trouble, it just somehow always managed to find her, and this island was full of situations that could result in far worse scenarios than she had so far experienced.

It was then that Tori remembered she must tell Jean about Lacy. He needed to know who she was and the quicker she told him the better. Excusing herself from Dominique for the moment, on the pretense that they had to sort out a misunderstanding, she went with Jean to his library. Once there, she hastily explained the problem to him.

"What do you think we should do? She knows who I am."

Jean's brow furrowed in concern. "I am not sure what we can do." He saw Tori's face fill further with worry, "let me work on it, and remember this, no problem is too big that it can't be solved. One important detail has come of this." He placed his hands on her shoulders looking lovingly into her eyes. "I am so glad you trusted me enough to confide in me and not try to handle this yourself. Don't worry, after all you told me about her, I think we will find that we can trust her not to tell a soul. Now run along and have a good day." He was now all smiles. "Tell Dominique I will see him later. And Tori, try to stay out of trouble," he chuckled.

With that he was gone. He could be very exasperating when he wanted; still she knew that he really cared. Now, as for Dominique, she had some plans for him. A sly smile crossed her lips. She knew that unlike Jean she could talk him into anything. While she changed for the day, she put her plan together. Over breakfast revealing her intentions nearly caused Dominique to have a heart attack.

"All I asked you, Dominique, was would you show me how to shoot one of your pistols and teach me how to fence, what's so wrong about that?"

"That is just it. I see nothing wrong, but my dear, Jean and society most certainly would!"

"I don't give a damn about society and Jean does not have to know now does he? It could be our little secret couldn't it? Just think how surprised he will be when I can show him some of what I have learned."

Dominique was won over before it had even started; he really loved the idea of teaching her behind Jean's back. Better still, he loved the idea of just plain teaching. Why it had been he himself who had taught both Jean and his brother Pierre the finer points of the art.

"Agreed!" He slapped his hand down upon the table's wooden surface. "That is my dear, if you give me your word, that not a breath of this is to reach Jean's ears. If I have your word on that, then I see no reason to delay the first lesson. It could be this very morning."

Dominique's enthusiasm was infectious. Tori lost her appetite, as breakfast now seemed too slow and a waste of time. She was far too excited to do anything other than start right away with her lessons. It was Dominique however, who convinced her that a short walk around Grand Terre, would be beneficial to both of them. He felt that he needed to see for himself, that Jean was indeed busy with the business of the day and that Tori should see a little of her surroundings.

"Never hurts to know the lay of the land. It's one thing to know how to fight if necessary but far better to know how to avoid it if you can, even if it means leaving, you understand?"

"I think so. What you are trying to tell me is, that if a situation occurred that called for a fight, if I know Grand Terre, I could obtain help getting myself out of danger, am I right?"

"You are going to make a fine student. It is important however, that you know I am only agreeable to teaching you the art of fencing for fun. Never is it to be for anything how shall we say? It is not for you to actually fight."

"Oh, of course it is for fun. Why Dominique, you don't think that this lady would be silly enough to pit herself against a far more experienced opponent do you?"

She did not give him a chance to speak. Not really liking the conversation, and fearing Dominique might change his mind she boldly took him by the arm and walked him out of the house.

"Now let's see the area. I want to see every square inch. After all it is rather a notorious place you have here isn't it?"

The two of them walked for several hours, Dominique proud to show off the whole compound. Why he himself had quite a hand in its smooth running he told her.

Tori found out that it had everything that a small town would have and more. The population was larger than she had first guessed. It numbered around several hundred on Grant Terre at any given time, and it was where a variety of languages could be heard at any hour. Dominique explained that on the other island still more men arrived every day to join the operation. Never could she have guessed at its size and as each hour grew her admiration for Jean as a leader and businessman expanded.

She found a café, a gambling den and even a bordello. The last, not one of Dominique's ideas to say the least, but even he had to admit that it kept the men happy and out of New Orleans.

"It's far better to keep their wagging tongues drunk in our domain, among our people and out of harm's way. Besides, Jean hates to see them waste their money. He likes to see it come back to the company so to speak," he laughed.

Tori broke into his laughter with her serious tone, "a company that seems to be doing very well indeed. I had no idea that so much cargo was shipped from here to New Orleans." Her gaze was on the quiet bayou. "That barge alone looks to be about one hundred feet long and fully loaded."

"Quite a good guess, it is in fact just under one hundred feet long. It was built from raw pieces of cypress found in this area. "It along with two others," he pointed further down the canal, "will travel, as they do most days, up and down the waterways, with goods and men. Jean likes to say we take the back door to New Orleans," he was laughing again as if the idea was comical. Then seeing that she did not share his humor, he quickly reverted to the serious Dominique. "Our canals have been widened by the men and only they know the way through this huge wetland maze," he threw his arms around in a large circle as if to emphasize the enormity of the area.

"How many men work for Jean?"

"That I'm not sure of. It changes now and then but I would estimate between one thousand and twelve hundred. Not all live here, you understand? They come and they go."

"I had no idea it was this big, in fact I am amazed that he handles it all himself."

"Well not quite by himself." He placed his hands on his hips. "There is his second in command, at your service." He bowed dramatically. Then a little embarrassed at trying to overstate his importance he quickly added, "and his brother Pierre among others, but tis true most of the decisions are now made by the Boss."

Tori walked and questioned more and more, always Dominique answered her, and he was amazed that she should be so intelligent. Once again he made a mental note to let Jean know that he would be a fool to let this woman slip away.

Finally they came to an area behind two of the large warehouses, and it was decided this would be where the two of them would meet every day, for a few hours, to have their fencing lessons.

On the walk back to the house Tori noticed an area being torn down. It seemed odd to her because everywhere else she had seen building going on.

"What's going on over there?"

"Ah, that was the barracoon, the area where the blacks were kept until the auction."

"You mean the slaves?"

"Quite. But upon landing, Jean gave orders for it to be torn down. A silly decision if you ask me, a lot of money to be made in slaves you know?"

"You mean you believe in slavery?"

"Well no, not as you think I do. Not does the Boss. He is a proud man you know, with certain values. He even has a sense of humor that escapes you at first until you get to know him. Take the name of this area, Barataria. Do you know what it means?"

"In English yes I do. It means deception. I see what you mean, there is a lot more behind the man than one first sees."

"Exactly and when you really get to know him, you will find that he in himself is quite an extraordinary individual."

"Are you playing matchmaker by chance my friend?"

Dominique looked at her; he was surprised that he had become that transparent to his new charge. He would have to be more careful in the future. Still in all, it would be of no harm to let her know that it would not hurt his feelings any, if she were to settle down with him. If settle down was the word.

Standing there as he was, his head turned to one side, a slightly embarrassed look about him, Tori thought for an instant how very much alike he and Jean looked at times. The eyes were of different color but there was something in the mannerisms that bound the two together. Not like father and son, no more like brothers. That, she thought could not be. Tori remembered there was only one brother, a Pierre. She could not think of ever reading about Dominique being a relative of Jean's. All she knew was he was only his first Lieutenant and nothing more. Still the resemblance was there. Could it be that for some unknown reason it was kept secret that he was a relative of Jean?

Dominique broke the silence. "Which one of us is looking at the other the closest I wonder? And for what reason do we just stand here looking and thinking to ourselves?"

"Oh, no reason, other than I never thought I would see the day when Dominique You would blush."

Dominique would have picked up the challenge and tried to deny that he was an old fool caught in Cupid's role but a call from Jean turned them both around.

"So here you are. I've been looking all over for the both of you. That little matter you and I talked about this morning concerning your friend? It has been solved and quite nicely if I might add. Follow me, my lady, and say your fond farewells to the lucky couple."

"Did you say farewells? Jean how can you ask them to leave, or are you forcing them? Because if you are, it's no way to solve the problem you know."

"Why? My lady," he pretended to look wounded, "would they be forced to leave and for what reason?"

Dominique was quite lost by all of this; the fact that they seemed to know what was going on did not help him any. Looking from one to the other, he could see that at least Jean seemed to understand what was happening. He was not so sure about Tori.

"Am I not understanding something here Boss? You look too smug and Tori looks as if she could kill you at any moment. It might be best to clear the air don't you think? Too much you two fight I tell you."

Jean was thoroughly enjoying himself that was very evident. His humor continued as he baited Dominique. "For whom should I clear the air Dominique? Seems to me that it is you who wants to know what's going on. Tori is not angry with me are you my love?"

"I don't know what to think at this moment but if you are thinking of sending Lacy and her child away, or worse yet getting rid of her man to force her to go, then you will have a fight on your hands." Her expression and tone of voice were making it very clear she meant what she said.

"See why I find this lady so irresistible Dominique? The fire in her. When she gets worked up over something she believes in, it is like a storm at sea. It is amazing is it not, such a gentle woman, having such a fight, n'est pas?"

Tori could see that he was having fun with her and decided that for once she would say no more and just wait and see what would turn up but an uneasy feeling was creeping up inside her.

Lacy saw them walking towards her long before Tori did, and ran towards them all smiles and laughter. She was so excited that she was talking a mile a minute in a Creole and Cajun mixture that Tori could not understand. It took Lacy some time to stop hugging Tori and stand still. Seeing that her friend could not understand her, she spoke slowly in English.

"Thank you for this chance. You are an angel as the men from the Boss's ship say. You think of others and I hope that one day it all comes back to you and that you find the happiness you deserve."

Tori stood there totally bewildered as to what was going on and looked to Jean for an explanation.

He stepped in between them and placing his arms around Tori's waist proudly spoke for all to hear. "Victoria is quite something isn't she? Here she does this for you and thinks nothing of it. Asking me to send you and your family to the islands to work for me. Free from the bonds of servitude, all because you showed her kindness, by being her friend."

Was she hearing right? Had Jean just said that? She looked up into his face and then at Lacy's nodding head. "I know that we have had very little time together miss and I won't be able to help you none anymore. One day, somehow I will find a way to thank you both."

"We both will." Added a deep masculine voice.

The tall young man, with a little boy in his arms, had joined the group. This had to be Lacy's man by the way he looked at her with love in his eyes. His gentle hold on his son gave her no doubt that he loved his family. He handed the child to Lacy and held out his hand to Tori.

"I'm not one for words Mam, best I can do is thank you. I will see to it that Lacy here and our son will be happy and you have my word on that." He looked at both Jean and Tori as he continued, "you have both made this possible, so we will work hard and you will see profits from your land soon. I always did want the chance to leave the sea and work the land again. This here will be my last voyage." He looked towards his love. "Never have to sail off and leave you again Lacy."

The two looked at each other as if they could not possibly get any happier. Jean, however, was not finished with surprises. He reached into his jacket pocket and pulled out two envelopes, which he handed over to the couple.

"The first paper is to go to the doctor and his wife when you arrive. It is instructions that a friend of mine will marry you soon after your arrival, in a small church that I know of." He frowned at them adding, "jumping over the broom, somehow doesn't seem binding enough for a family who is going to work for me." He saw the flash of concern on Lacy's face and stopped her cold by adding, "now we all know it's against the law for you to marry Tom. Let's just say this priest owes me a favor and believes that no matter what, two people should stand before God." He cleared his throat and handed the next envelope to Lacy. "This second envelope is a little something from Victoria and myself, to help you get started."

Lacy took the papers and with tears in her eyes, handed them over to her man. "Here Tom you best take these. I'm just too happy to stand still for much longer."

Tom was truly moved and as he opened and looked inside the envelope, he looked back at Jean and simply nodded his head. Then he stepped forward and hugged Tori and Jean together. Jean, all smiles now, embarrassed Tom and in the French style, kissed him on each cheek. He hugged Lacy and repeated the kissing. Then he spoke with a voice full of emotion as he commanded the two of them to get on board or miss the tide.

Tori hugged Lacy and kissed the little boy; she was crying and laughing at the same time. It was sad for her to lose this friend so soon but she was also happy at the freedom that her friend was about to gain. Tom broke the two apart, his Captain had given an order to board and he intended to obey. It was easier to do that, than stand here like a fool not knowing what to say or do. How could he ever express his thanks to any of them? It was impossible.

Taking the boy from Lacy and walking towards the ship, they boarded arm in arm. Lacy was almost skipping as she went. Laughter and pure joy were radiating from her face. Once on board she called back to Tori.

"I will never forget you, never and forever my lips will stay sealed."

Both Jean and Tori knew what she meant. A smile slid slowly across Tori's face. Her secret was safe once again, thanks to her pirate.

"Good-bye my friend, God bless you both," she called out. Overcome by emotion then she simply laid her head on Jean's shoulder and sunk into his arms. His hold on her was protective and understanding, her sadness was his, yet he knew it was a happy kind of a sad that she was feeling.

"Let's go back to the house, it will be sometime yet before they sail and I think it would be easier on all. Come on he coaxed."

Tori was glad that Jean had taken control once again. She stood tall and proud, gaining strength in knowing that he was by her side. She looked from him to Dominique, who seemed somehow not puzzled at all by what had taken place. He was just carrying on, as if this sort of thing happened every day."

You want to join us Dominique?"

"No, not right away, later maybe?" Dominique knew he was at it again, matchmaking. They did not need him around right now, no way, he had a feeling that Tori was going to thank Jean for all he had done. It had been obvious that Tori had not known a thing about what had just occurred. Yes, Tori would want to thank Jean all right and that meant he had best be on his way. Watching the two of them walk towards the house, he knew that the time was near and that Jean was ready to settle down. Just look at the crazy things he was doing and all because of this woman.

Tori was overjoyed. By the time they reached the house, Jean had told her the whole story of his plan for Lacy and Tom and how he had put it into action so fast. She lost her tears and was just overcome by the need to show this man of hers how wonderful he really was.

"We need to celebrate," she laughed.

"That was what I had in mind, you don't think I did all of that just for them do you? I had thanks in mind from you. And pray tell just how do you plan to show me how grateful you are for my stroke of genius? Not only did I solve our problem but if I might say, I did it in a way that left everyone happy, did I not?"

Tori was laughing at him and teasingly added, "Well now let's see how smart you are. If you really thought this all through, you would have known that champagne was in order and one of those cigars would not hurt any. And if you really planned ahead, well they would be upstairs waiting for us but then you really could not be that scheming, could you?"

Jean just laughed and laughed, this woman knew him better than she realized and he felt that he would always want this way of life to go on and on.

"If you are truly brave my lady, and wish to see, then may I suggest that we go. But beware if I did scheme, as you put it, then I feel it only fair to warn you, that the rest of the day may very well be spent sipping champagne and making love. That is how you plan to show me your gratitude, isn't it?"

"Oh, you are impossible. So you're calling my bluff are you? I will go see but you best know that if the champagne is not there, I will not remain."

She was running up the stairs and ahead of him. This was all like some sort of a crazy dream from a romantic book. How could this be? He had to be lying, yet when she pushed open the door to their room, it was clear from one look that he had won. How did he know her so well? Was it a lucky guess? More than that, had he done all of those things for Lacy or for her? So many questions, so many feelings, and then his arms came around her waist, his breath in her ear.

"Never underestimate me, my lady, never..." he whispered as he gently pushed her into the room, closing the doors behind him.

Carlotta was leaving as she heard the upstairs door close. She smiled for all had been done as he had asked. She now had some time for herself knowing she would not be needed until the next day.

# Chapter 12

The days had flown by so fast that before she knew it a new month had started. It had not escaped her thoughts however, that in all that time she had not once attempted to return to the lake. She had not even bothered Jean about it, seeing how very occupied he was with running the business. But knowing him as she did, she realized in due time he would keep his word. When he was ready he would escort her to the very spot she wanted.

Her days had been filled by Dominique's company and her nights had been with Jean. Most evenings they dined alone, but there were the times that Dominique had joined them, along with some merchant or business acquaintance.

These evenings she found to be enjoyable, as it gave her a chance to really brush up on her French. Always, she was introduced as Victoria and if guests wondered what her role was in the house, they never questioned. It seemed to her that the Creole gentlemen were either far too polite to ask such a question, or far too smart. It had become clear to her that no one dare upset Jean for his temper was well known.

Her fencing lessons had proceeded and she found that not only was Dominique an excellent instructor but she herself had somewhat of a natural flair for the sport. As for firing the pistols… Well once was enough for both her and Dominique. Guns were not her forte.

The lessons had been kept a secret the whole time, just as they had agreed in the beginning. A simple task really. On the days that Dominique could not make their rendezvous he would send a message to her, thereby avoiding an awkward situation, namely her being caught waiting at the arranged spot unescorted.

This had been one of those mornings. A young boy had arrived shortly after Jean's departure and waited for Tori so he could deliver his message. The note had simply stated that Dominique was sorry but he would not be available for a few days, as he had to go into New Orleans on urgent business. He regretted deeply letting her down but hoped she would understand.

The small boy had stood before her not knowing if he should leave or stay. His big round eyes looked anywhere but directly at her, and as he stood fidgeting, standing on one foot then the other, he continued to look away. Tori could see how nervous he was and how it must have taken him a great amount of courage to deliver the parchment to the Boss's woman. She smiled to herself and asked him to wait where he was until she returned.

"Carlotta," she called as she walked towards the kitchen, "do you have some of those small cakes left over from last night?"

"Si Senora, you can have as many as you want."

"No silly, they're not for me. They're for the little boy at the door; he just delivered a message from Dominique. Honestly, for the life of me I don't know why it is you want me to eat so much lately? I'm beginning to feel like a balloon."

Carlotta just smiled and shook her head. She could not believe Tori did not realize that food was not the reason she was getting like a balloon what, whatever that was? Did the Senora not want to admit that she was with child, or could it be that she truly did not realize it she pondered? Still it was not her place to ask. She left and a few minutes later returned with the cakes for Tori who was looking at her strangely.

"Is there something wrong Carlotta? You're looking at me as if I have done something to upset you?"

Carlotta smiled, shaking her head adamantly, "Nothing, no! Everything is well; you had best give the cakes to the child. He will leave soon, he is so frightened." She could see the young boy in question slowly backing up.

"Why is that do you suppose?" Tori turned to face the lad and lowering her voice asked, "I have never even seen him before so how is it that I scare him?"

"It is not so much you, as it is this house I think?" She looked towards the boy and smiled kindly. "Then maybe he is just very shy?"

Tori gave the little boy the bag of cakes, which he did not seem to realize were for him. When at last he got the message right, his whole face lit up and for the first time he looked directly at Tori without uttering a word. His expression was all the thanks she needed. Then as quickly as he had appeared, he was gone, running off down the pathway as fast as his little chubby brown legs could carry him.

Tori couldn't help but laugh, "poor little guy, probably thinks he had best leave before I change my mind and take the cakes back."

The child was running so fast that he did not see Jean and ran right into him. The result of the collision was that the bag of goodies fell to the ground and the child looked on in horror as his cakes rolled out of the sack around Jean's feet. Almost at once speaking and crying in rapid Spanish, he was declaring that he did not steal them. It was the angel at the house that had given them to him. The child was hastily picking up the small cakes from the ground and seeing Jean held one he reached out and snatched it from his hand. He was so insistent that they were rightfully his, that Jean had to admire his spunk. He gave the child a small candy from his pocket and helped him pick up the remaining few cakes.

Jean was talking to the boy softly. He had a smile of such caring upon his face that even a stranger would have known immediately of his soft spot for children. It was the smile that seemed to calm the child, as he listened to him. He was told to be more careful and watch where he was running in the future. This was followed by a playful pat to his rear, as he was sent on his way. The child was gone in a flash, too fast even for Jean to call him back and find out why he had been at the house in the first place. He hoped Tori was not making friends with the children. It would only be harder for her to leave for the townhouse in the city. How was she going to take to moving into the city he wondered? Whether she liked it or not it was inevitable. The time had come for him to leave, and no way would he allow her to remain here without him.

Tori's reaction was nothing like he expected. She was elated and excited about the move. She asked all sorts of questions, with an expression on her face showing the enthusiasm she felt. Then as the implications of what was about to happen sank in, a worried look clouded her radiant face, and panic took hold. "Jean, if I go with you, then the people, all of your friends, they will meet me. What if one of them should recognize who I am? What if I should run into that son of a bitch Edward and he should realize who I am? He could make all kinds of trouble."

"That my lady, is part of the reason that we have to leave now. I have had some of my contacts asking questions around New Orleans, to find out where you stand. I think it's time that you found out don't you? Anyway, looking as you do now, no one will see you as Tori the runaway fancy, but instead will see you as my lady. A lady I might add, of great beauty and charm. You will be a success I am sure." His hand took her face by the chin as he tilted her head up so he could look deep into her eyes as he continued. "Let us not worry about such matters. We will handle together whatever comes our way, as it unfolds."

This statement helped calm her but now another thought presented itself to the forefront, and it was one she could not ignore.

"One other thing Jean. I have not asked you these past weeks," she hesitated then continued. "I would not bring it up now, but," she hesitated again turning her head away from his gaze as she continued, "well now that we are going into town and all, does this mean that you intend to keep your promise and take me to the lake?"

Jean froze, this thought had been far from his mind, he had almost forgotten that he had indeed agreed to take her to the damned lake. Yet he knew that he had to keep his word. To delay it once they got to the city would be impossible to do for very long, but to return her to that God forsaken place; he ran the risk of losing the one woman who had stolen his heart. Did she not know that she was his life? He loved her even knowing that as he held her in his arms at night, a part of her was not his. He understood that she wondered if there was a way back. That until she had made the attempt, she could not let go of her life in her other time. Jean realized he had no right to hold her here if she had a chance to return but how he hoped he could keep her. How he prayed that he could somehow this one time, be selfish with her and keep her in this time with him. These thoughts were all very clear and very strong but his love for her was stronger. He would give her anything, even the ultimate sacrifice of letting her go, if it made her happy.

"You have my word, that as soon as it is safe and it can be arranged, I shall see to it that you get to the lake. Now if you will excuse me, I have to make ready for the trip. We depart tomorrow early. Carlotta has already started packing your things. You had best see to it that she chooses some good traveling clothes for you, as the trip is long and far from easy."

He had turned so cold and without even a good-bye he was out the door. She stood looking at the floor shaking her head slowly from side to side, thinking about what had just transpired. How could she have been so stupid? She had hurt him that was obvious; it was the talk about the lake that had done it. Lifting her head she spoke out loud her next thoughts. "He does not want me to go to the lake, but he has to understand that I must." Tori was a complete mess as she ran to her room, tears falling freely down her agonized face. How could she have been so insensitive, how? And why couldn't he accept it? These and other such thoughts kept screaming in her mind. She flew into her room and threw herself down on the bed; there she cried and cried, not really knowing why she let herself carry on like she was doing, it just felt good to give in and sob her heart out.

The door opened and Tori looked up to see Carlotta entering with a tray of glasses and a pitcher. She watched as she poured her a glass of the cool lemon and orange mix, a drink Tori had come to love in the past few weeks.

"Here, you need a drink to feel better, no? You have needed to cry for a few days now. I have seen it coming, now you can go to New Orleans feeling better."

Tori knew she meant well, but it hadn't helped any to cry. She felt no better and didn't think she ever would again. "No I can't. I feel awful. I just don't understand him or myself. You can't understand Carlotta, but thank you for trying and for caring like you do."

"So what is there to understand I ask? True, I have never had a child of my own but I have seen many Senora's in your state and they all act so mixed up in their feelings in the beginning."

Tori looked at her curiously, "and what state would that be might I ask? What do you mean? I don't understand what it is you are trying to tell me."

Carlotta couldn't stand it any longer and with a look of understanding and compassion she stood her ground and spoke softly. "It's because of the baby that you cry. You are going to be a mother we both know that. I think the reason you cry so, is because you are not married to the Senor, but do not worry he loves you. I see that with my own eyes. He will do what is right, he will marry you, you will have a father for your child!"

Tori could not believe what Carlotta had just said, how could this be? "Just what makes you think that I am going to have a child?"

"You do not believe you are? It can be the only answer. Ask yourself. You have been here now long enough for us both to realize it. Tori you have not bled once since you have been here and you could not have without me knowing. You would have needed my help. Besides, you have the look on your face, the thickening in the middle, yes, you are going to have a baby, it is all too clear."

Tori froze, now that Carlotta had said it, she knew she could not deny it any longer herself. She had known deep down but kept trying to talk herself out of it. It was true, she had not had her period, and she knew that awful feeling in the morning was not from too much champagne the night before. You don't get hangovers from one or two glasses!

Resigned to her condition Tori admitted it, "you are right Carlotta, I am with child." Then grabbing Carlotta by the hand she pleaded with her, "please say nothing to Jean, do you hear me, nothing?"

"Si, I will say nothing, but you will have to tell him soon, the way you are growing, the whole world will know."

"Yes, I know. I need to be alone. Please leave me for now. And Carlotta, send Jean up when he gets back. I think we need to talk."

"You have nothing to fear; he loves you. He will marry you, and he will be so happy you wait and see. Carlotta she knows these things. Now you rest. I will finish up here later."

Once alone, Tori walked to the verandah and sat down to face the truth. How could she have allowed this to happen? What was she going to do now? This changed everything! She lowered her head into her hands and closed her eyes.

"Linni forgive me, what have I done? What can I do?"

The hours passed and Tori never left the verandah, she just sat trying to sort out in her own mind what was to become of this situation. Worse yet, she would have to try and explain it all to the father of this child.

The sky was turning dark, the sun had gone down behind the cypress trees and the sounds of the evening had once again begun its nightly symphony. This was the only sound that Jean could hear as he entered the front foyer. The lamps had been lit and the smell of the evening meal filled the air. Dinner, however, was the last thing on his mind as he looked around half hoping to see Tori's forgiving face.

Jean had come home after finishing what he had called his rightful duty, and that was to spend some time in the canteen with some of his men, trying to drown his feelings. Instead of feeling better and freeing himself of guilt, he had just drank and felt worse. There was no hiding in a bottle this time for him or his thoughts. He had acted like a fool; she had every right to want to try to get to her time, and he knew that she never meant to hurt him. But damn it, he loved her so much. She had to understand how he was feeling too!

Carlotta broke into his train of thoughts as she greeted him. It was however the look of concern on her face that alerted him to the fact that all was not well.

"She has not been out of her room all afternoon. I tell you now Senor; you had best go and see her. She asked me to send you up as soon as you arrived. That was hours ago!" She shot him a filthy look of disapproval.

This news worried him. But it was Carlotta's glare and tone of voice that told him she knew more than she was letting on. "Are you not telling me everything? She is all right is she not?"

Carlotta did not answer him; in fact she acted as if she had not heard a word he said. She was walking away mumbling to herself, something about men and drinking. She was not going to be of any help that was for sure. Carlotta could be very stubborn when she wanted. She also knew when to stay well out of the way and this seemed to be one of those times. Jean was left alone to make his way upstairs. He was going to have to face Tori and apologize.

The first thing he realized upon entering the room was that it was nearly dark. No lamps had been lit, an indication that Carlotta had not exaggerated when telling him that Tori had been left totally undisturbed. He could not see her at first and then he looked towards the verandah and her favorite chair. She was sitting so still, just watching him as he walked towards her. Jean found himself hoping she would say something first and make it easier for him. The moon had been up for quite a while; it's full silver rays adding an eerie luminescence to her sad face. The first thing that hit him was that she was crying and this tore at his heart. He could never hurt her and if staying in this time with him was going to cause her this much pain, then he would not hold her here. He would not ask her to stay. Kneeling down by her, talking gently, he brushed the tears from her cheeks as he spoke.

"Tori my lady, please forgive the actions of a fool. I was wrong this afternoon. It was selfish of me to act so. You have my word, that next week we will find this lake of yours and you will have your chance to go back to your time. If you do manage to find your way home, you have my word I will let you go. I will settle for the memories we have made together." His voice was trembling with emotion and sounded somehow false even to his own ears. He would have to do better than this if he were to convince her that he meant what he said. "I know you have a family who I am sure loves and misses you. And a child, a little girl who you must need and miss so very much. I do understand believe me, far better than you know."

This was about all she could stand. The very mention of her child brought a new flood of tears and she fell into Jean's arms. They stayed like this for a while until she was all cried out and then from somewhere deep down inside of herself, she drew on a strength that she seldom called upon. Pulling herself up and sitting straight, she looked into the eyes of the man she knew loved her enough to understand what she was about to tell him.

"Could you light a lamp and get me a glass of wine?"

Jean looked at her and saw that he had best give her a few minutes to herself while he did as she asked. By the time this simple request was complete, a composed Tori had come in and sat down on the bed. She took the glass from him and then taking a sip put it down on the side table.

"Jean, I think you had best sit down, I have something that you need to know. It's not going to be easy for you to hear but you have the right..."

Jean did not like the tone of her voice, of the way her hands started to tremble as she spoke. He knew that what she was about to tell him, was that she could get back to her time and this was farewell.

"I do not want to go to the lake next week, or the week after that. I'm not sure if I will be able to go to the lake at all."

Was he hearing right? Dare he hope that she loved him enough to stay? He could hear his own heart pounding in his chest, his very soul was shouting let it be true. His exterior stayed calm and the look on his face was guarded.

"Please don't get me wrong. I think the time will come one day when I will have to see for myself, if my return can occur. It's just that things have changed and I don't know what or how to handle it all."

Tori stood up, and paced back and forth. Something was really bothering her and he sensed that she was struggling hard to find a way to tell him, or ask him.

Jean had to talk; he had to help her somehow, to reassure her of how he felt. "If you want to know if I want you to stay, you have to know the answer is yes. I love you more than I could ever love again. You have become my life. I love you enough to let you go if that is what you wish, just tell me, which shall it be?"

"It's not that I don't know how you feel, Jean. I do know only too well. A part of me loves you also. We both know how we feel, of how much love we share. I don't know how or why? God help me for saying this but it seems that I am in love with you, almost as much as I love my own family. I'm caught in two times and in two different ways. I'm not making any sense am I?" She looked at him knowing that she could delay no longer what she had to tell him. "I better just come out with it hadn't I? Oh, how do you put it? You say you love me and you want me to stay but would you still feel this way if I were carrying your child? If I were pregnant?"

The words hit him like a slap to the face. Could he believe what he was hearing? Jean was so quiet at first that Tori was afraid to look at him. She took his silence to mean that his response was going to be negative. Her mind screamed at him to say something, anything.

"Are you telling me that you are going to have a child, our child?"

"Yes Jean, that is exactly what I am saying. I am carrying your child."

Still no reaction. She could not bring herself to look at him. His silence seemed to be answering for him.

"I know I will be an embarrassment to you and if you don't want me around, well maybe you could find me a place to stay. Maybe I could stay here until the baby is born. I will stay out of your way. I will move into the other room." His continued silence was causing her to panic; she rambled on trying to explain it all to him. "It's just that I don't know what it would do to the child, if I tried to cross back to my time. It might hurt the baby and I can't do that. So if I could stay here…?"

The sound of the door banging closed stopped her mid sentence. She stared at the empty room. She had her answer.

Carlotta had been wrong and in a way Tori was glad. She would not have to deal with the love part of him any more but would he let her stay? Tori worriedly looked around the room. God help her she had nowhere else to go. Maybe Dominique would help, that was the answer, he was always saying how he owed her. He would help. But hell she needed Jean, how could he walk out on her like that, why if he loved her as he claimed, would he treat her so? Had he lied all along? Her temper was growing, how dare he! She was about to go and see where he was and have it out with him, when the door flew open and he burst into the room picking her up in his arms and swinging her around and around.

"You silly beautiful little fool. How could you think that I would not be anything but thrilled by this news? A father!" he shouted, "I am to become a father! You are wonderful but we must set things right. Straight away and with no delay, we must marry. No son of mine will be a bastard!"

"Jean! Put me down and slow please. Let me get this right you mean you are happy? You want this child? I can stay?"

"Of course I want you and the child, I could not want anything more." He was holding her so close and so tightly afraid that if he let her go he would wake only to find it all a dream.

Relief and happiness sounded in her voice as she softly answered him. "Oh Jean, that's more than I hoped for. I was so sure when you left that you did not want this. But now I know how you feel." Suddenly she stopped and pulled away from him, "I have to say some things. The first is I won't marry you. I can't. If I was to do that it would, might, change history. Don't you see, I must not do anything to disturb the time line." She could see the look of puzzlement on his face. He did not understand or want to. She had to make it perfectly clear and now. "I have thought it out and that's that!"

Jean knew only too well the stubborn streak of hers, but this time she had to listen to reason. "Tori be reasonable, the people will call you such names and my child will be labeled for life. I can't have that. Surely you can't do that to our child? In your time it may be fine to have a child born out of wedlock, I don't know, but in this time, I can assure you, it is not so. You will marry me as soon as we get to New Orleans. That is why I left you when you gave me the news. I have already taken the liberty to send a message ahead to a priest that I know and trust." He took hold of her and took her gently in his arm, talking softer now but still very sternly. "It will all be done very fast and secret, so no one will ever have to know that it was necessary."

"I will not and you can't make me! Anyway I have thought about this all afternoon and I do have a way around the problem, one that you will have to agree to, because Jean get this in your thick stubborn head, I won't marry you!" His face clouded over, he was fighting hard to control his temper she could see that, she had to defuse the situation before he exploded. "Besides who's to say we weren't married in the islands and I am already your wife. Carlotta calls me Senora, so why can't we pretend and then we both can have our way." Jean was quiet, he needed time to agree to her demands she realized that, but he had to understand there was no other way around it all. In time she knew he would come around to seeing it her way. So when he finally spoke it was a shock to hear his demand.

"If I agree to this, then you must tell me now, give me your word, that the child is mine to keep. When you try to go back to your time, and you will try won't you? You will do it alone, you will leave the baby."

"I don't know if I can do that. I know that I must try one day, whether I succeed or not, one way or the other, yes I have to try. My family has a right to know what happened to me Jean. My daughter deserves to have her mother..."

"That might be so, but I have the right to keep my child, if you feel that you have to go. He will be a child of this time not yours will he not? His place will be here with me."

The two of them stared at each other and Tori could see that Jean meant this, he would have his child no matter what and maybe it would be the right thing. How could she turn up at home and say, "well here I am and by the way this is my child. How could she take Jean's child away from him and leave him nothing?

Sadly she agreed. "You are right, if I do try to go back and if it works, you have my word I will go alone. This baby is of this time, not mine like you say. It will need you as much as you will need it."

Jean looked into her eyes holding her captive so she could not look away. Somehow he had to make her understand. "If, however, you do not try to return, you fall in love with us enough to stay and I give you my solemn oath that I will do everything in my power to make that happen. Then you have to promise me, that you will become my wife. Until then, we will pretend, as you say. Do we have an agreement, my lady?

"We do, Sir, but Jean I will have to try as soon as I can after the baby is born." Tears filled her eyes. This was the hardest thing she had ever had to say to anyone, even herself. "I have another promise to keep, you see I promised myself that I would get back to the lake and like you I intend to keep my word. I promised Linni on the day she was born, that I would never leave her like her father had. He wanted no part of her, but she became my life and I always told her that. I told the child that we would have each other until death parted us. I don't know how this time travel thing works. God only knows I could be dead to Linni in my time. Maybe this is how life works?" She turned from him, angrily wiping her face with the back of her hands. In the silence that followed she was thinking, all I know is that I have no choice but to try, yet the longer I stay here, the less chance of crossing back I have.

Jean broke the silence, "until then, for both our sakes and the child's, can we put all this time travel in the back of our minds? He will need you to be strong and happy if all is to go right over the next few months."

"Ha! What if this he," she put her hand over stomach, "turns out to be a girl?" She forced a laugh.

"That my lady would be fine, because she would always remind me of you."

His lips came softly down on hers and the two of them felt the strength of the other. They would take one day at a time and the baby would have to be first in their thoughts and actions. This child was very much wanted and that they both knew.

Jean delayed the trip to the city. His main concern was making sure Tori was both physically and mentally strong. So over the next few weeks he became even more attentive and sensitive to her needs and emotions. Christmas was kept a small celebration mixed with bittersweet memories for each of them. This was followed by a small New Years Eve party and the beginning of 1811.

The trip to New Orleans went smoothly. Jean saw to it that the utmost care was taken to make it an easy trip for Tori. The good-byes at the house had been tearful. Carlotta making Jean promise that once the baby came, she would be allowed to visit them. Tori had wanted her to come along but Carlotta had told her that she had to stay and look after the house. No one else it seemed to her could do it as well as she. The final farewells had almost made her change her mind for she had grown very fond of Tori, even if she was hard to understand sometimes. Like the news they told her right before leaving. She had been puzzled over that. They had explained to her that they were really man and wife, already married. The reason they gave for keeping it a secret, was that Jean wanted to tell his brother Pierre himself. He wanted it that way, because to hear it from a stranger or friend, was not right after all. At first it had made sense, but the more she thought about it, the more she knew that was not the only reason they had kept the marriage a secret. She would bet her life it had something to do with that married woman he had been seeing. Oh yes she knew about that rumor everyone around her knew. Well, that little rumor would quickly stop, stop as fast as his love affair with her had. Jean belonged to Tori now, there was not a doubt in her mind, but a woman scorned is one to fear and there was going to be trouble, she could smell it coming. If she knew it, then Jean would surely know what he was up against. Yes, she was right on this one. Jean had kept the marriage quiet until he could calm the waters ahead. If only she had known how wrong she was; it was the last thing on Jean's mind.

The bayous were cold in the early morning as they traveled on one of the barges, slowly making their way through the complicated maze of waterways.

"We will go some of the way on the water and then travel by coach the rest of the way. Madame Jean Laffite must enter the city in style." He laughed at this statement. It sounded so right, Madame Jean Laffite. "Look at it this way, no one will ever dare say you are Tori now, how could they? You are more than safe as my wife."

Tori smiled at him for she knew she really had nothing to fear. He would always look after her, but then he did not know that Edward. She shivered a little just thinking of him and hoped they would never have to cross paths. Maybe they never would, after all the city of New Orleans was a big place, wasn't it? Tori decided to stop worrying about it and just enjoy the trip and the surrounding view.

The waterways were well organized. Jean's men knew each turn and current, each canal they navigated seemed to fit the barge as if it had been custom made. One such canal had been built with barges in mind but not really for Jean's private use. It had simply just worked out that way he told her with a sly smile.

After many hours of travel the barge pulled close to shore, where Tori was able to see a carriage waiting, along with a couple of blacks.

"Is that for us?"

"That it is, and I must say, that had I known the weather was to be this cold, I would have had a larger, closed in carriage awaiting you."

"Oh don't be so silly, I'm not ill you know and anyway it will give me the chance to see the countryside and New Orleans far better.

"And a chance for New Orleans to get a glance at you, n'est pas?"

"Why sir, you flatter me."

They both laughed as she mimicked a Southern lady. She held her fan and batted her eyes, while coyly smiling all proud and proper. Jean found himself thanking God he had not fallen for such a belle. That his woman was as far from a Southern lady as she could be.

The day was crisp and clear, the sky a blue that seemed to border on silver. Tori could not remember ever seeing such colors. Maybe she thought it was because she had never really taken the time to look before. The wanting to see now, every detail, every shade, was due to the fact that she wanted to etch it into her memory for all eternity as clearly as possible. It might happen that one day it would be all she would have of this time and her stay with Jean. She wanted to remember always her stay in this time if she made it back to 1995.

Jean had been watching her as they headed to the grass-covered bank. He could see how she was taking everything in, and he loved how her face would light up over the simplest of things. He himself was a lover of nature and to have found someone else that took joy in just looking, well it was an overwhelming feeling,

The transfer to the carriage only took a few minutes. All the baggage would continue on with the barge to be delivered later. The two of them watched as the large raft slipped slowly and effortlessly back out into the canal. The men were pushing hard on the long wooded poles, to ease the barge over to where a slow strong current ran. As they entered the spot she could see how the craft picked up speed. It was a simpler time, but so much harder in many ways. Those men had to really work at moving the large craft. "You must remind me to tell you about outboard motors sometime," she told Jean.

Jean looked at her with a quizzical sort of smile.

"Out board what?"

"Oh nothing, just a little something that would sure make things simple for your men, that's all."

Jean knew he could not carry on with that line of conversation with the servants around. They were trusted, but why talk of things that they no doubt would find outrageous and be sure to spread among themselves. Word would soon travel and questions would be asked. That would not do, so he made a mental note to talk about this another time. They would have to be careful and he would have to remind Tori to watch what she said and to whom. Look how Dominique had picked up on some of the things Tori talked about. Till in the end they had had no choice but to bring him in on the secret or have him think her crazy. Jean smiled now as he thought back to how Dominique had taken the story. He had taken it a lot better than he himself had. Maybe it was because he had such a soft spot for this lady of his. Or maybe because he already had known deep down that she was different and special, not of this world. Still it was good to have his Dominique know. He knew this secret was safe with him. He would die before letting anything slip to do with family. Dominique was very good at holding such secrets, and not just because of friendship, it went way beyond that. No one knew except them, that he was a lot more than first in command and trusted friend. Beside himself only his brother Pierre knew that Dominique was indeed their oldest brother. A secret they would keep hidden always.

Tori could see that they were approaching the outskirts of the town; buildings and side roads were becoming far more frequent. It was like going on to a movie set, she thought. The costumes, the carriages, the very air of the place was foreign. Once again she had to remind herself that she was a part of it all and it was very real. Every now and then another carriage would pass them by and the occupants would acknowledge them. The curiosity of the men and women did not escape Tori. She could actually see them strain to get a better glimpse of her, trying to see who she was. Why even the people on the sidewalks and sitting in the cafés would wave at Jean and then stare at her, turning to talk amongst themselves as they passed.

Jean was thoroughly enjoying himself; his soft chuckle accompanied a protective embrace as he spoke proudly. "It is as if all New Orleans wants to know you. See how you've already caused a stir, my lady. Why, I bet we will have callers at the townhouse before the afternoon is finished."

"I had no idea that you were, shall we say, so well known."

"You don't know the half of it yet but at least now I have you to accompany me." He was laughing and in such good spirits that Tori felt as if he were enjoying it all too much. Knowing him he might continue to drive around and around just for the sheer fun of it.

"How much longer before we reach the house?"

Concern crossed his face. He had been so engrossed in the moment that he had forgotten about his lady's condition. "You will see it around the very next corner. You must be tired, how do you feel? Have I put you through too much?"

Exasperated at his continuing concern and insinuating that somehow she had become frail when she became pregnant she became exasperated. Tori realized that she had to set him straight once and for all. That or suffer the consequences of being treated like a weaker sex, which she despised.

"Jean if you don't stop treating me like I might break, I will be forced to do something, to show you that I am not fragile. I only asked when we would arrive, because the thought of a glass of something to drink and the chance to get out of this ridiculous outfit and into something a little more to my liking..."

Jean broke into rambling, "I'm afraid my dear, you will have to become accustomed to dressing like a true Southern lady now that you are in town. As my wife, it will be expected." He raised that one eyebrow in a questioning manner. "Do I have your word, that you will save your favorite outfit for when we are alone?"

Tori could see that he was trying to be very serious and thought she could see more than a little concern written on his face. He had to know she would do nothing to embarrass him in front of society. "You have nothing to worry about Jean. I will be the perfect lady but get me alone, and I promise it will not be a lady you will have."

Jean put back his head and roared with laughter. "I shall hold you to that bargain my lady."

The carriage pulled into a small courtyard, very beautifully landscaped. Before they came to a complete stop, a black man was at their side opening the carriage door. Jean caught her look and smiled.

"You will find that I have a small staff here. I keep a cook, two girls to help maintain the place and three men who keep the horses, gardens, and help out, as they are needed. Before you ask I will tell you yes they are slaves. Well treated I may add and trusted. They like their work and their home and have been with me for sometime. That is the way it is, and knowing how you feel about the situation, I will now remind you, that this is how it is and will be. You had better understand now, that it is only when we are alone together, that you may comment against it. You have to learn to keep your feelings on the situation to yourself, if you are to be accepted in New Orleans." He took her hand and more kindly and lovingly added, "that is the way it will have to be." Tori just nodded, she knew he was right but that did not mean she had to like it, just that she had to mask her true feelings.

The door into the townhouse was open and once inside its warmer interior she could see she was going to love the place. Jean guided her through the hall to the right and into a large formal room, whose doors opened out into a small but lovely sun-drenched garden. This area was completely enclosed from the outside world by a high brick wall and three sides of the house. Once again she found herself thinking of a movie set. Outside was a small table and some very comfortable chairs. Jean had called out that some wine be brought out to them, as he guided her into the garden.

"This is one of my favorite spots. The peaceful feeling one gets here seems to make one forget that they are in the city. Even on a day like today the sun warms it and the wind is held at bay."

"It's beautiful Jean, it really is and I think it will become one of my favorite spots too." She was looking around unbelieving "it is like a dream."

The two of them were like young children, one delighting in the discovery of a new place, the other in showing off his very own secret hideaway.

The wine was brought to out to them by a young girl who Jean introduced to Tori as Leona. Her real African name was not to his liking and hard to pronounce, so he had named her after one of his early acquaintances, a young

French girl that he had known a long time ago. A girl who had taken his boyhood innocence and shown him a whole new world.

Leona was told that Tori was Jean's wife and to inform the others that they would meet her later. As for now, they wanted to rest after the long journey. Rest could only mean one thing as far as Tori knew and she guessed that at any moment Jean would volunteer to show her around the rest of the house, ending up in the bedroom.

Leone had left them with a big smile on her face. She had been the first in the house to meet his wife. That was something indeed, and she felt as if she was all but bursting with the news. Why all of New Orleans would be shocked, not to mention a few ladies that came to mind.

Jean and Tori sat down for the moment to enjoy a glass of wine and Tori pulling off her shoes, started to remove the hat that she had had on her head all day. The two of them were so involved with each other, that they did not see someone was staring at them from the doorway. It was only when Jean leaned over taking Tori's hat, kissing her lightly, saying to her, "I think that my wife feels at home," that the man in the doorway broke the moment.

"So the mystery lady is none other than your wife."

Jean turned to look into the face of his older brother Pierre. The two of them stared at each other both with broad grins crossing their faces and then they turned towards Tori.

"Pierre, may I present to you my wife. Tori, my brother."

Pierre walked towards Tori as he spoke. "A brother who is just a little upset at not being told of this situation before now. But then all can see why Jean would want to keep you a secret and to himself for as long as he could. Such a find my brother, she is a true beauty."

He reached Tori and placing a hand on each shoulder he raised her gently and welcomed her into the family with a kiss to each cheek. Tori felt such warmth towards this man, who in many mannerisms was a mirror image of his brother.

"You are not too upset with Jean are you? After all everything happened so fast, that we really did not have time to tell everyone of the marriage."

"Upset with him, no. I learned a long time ago that my younger brother will do as he pleases. I am only happy to see that he has finally settled down. But however, I must warn you Madame, that in so doing, he will have broken more than one heart in this fair city."

Jean and Pierre laughed at this and Tori sat back down looking at them. It had not occurred to her that Jean would have had anyone else. Yet that was silly wasn't it? He must have had quite a few ladies. A slight smile crossed her lips as she looked towards Jean now, her handsome rogue of a pirate. She would have to talk to him later about his other ladies. Right now she wanted to get to know his brother.

There was something very familiar about him; she did not know quite what it was yet. He reminded her of someone, yes that was it, but whom?

Tori had such an exciting day that by the time she found her head on the pillow it took no time at all for her to fall into a deep sleep. She had talked with Jean and Pierre for hours. The three of them had even dined together and it seemed to Tori that she had known them for years. Pierre had accepted her into the family immediately. He was a lot like Jean and yet once again Tori found herself reminded of someone else. In the end she gave up trying to figure it out and just enjoyed his company. Things went along smoothly and it was not until after dinner when Pierre started asking questions of her, that she could not answer, that the situation became difficult.

It was then that Jean made the decision that his brother was going to have to know the truth also. It was not an easy thing to get Pierre to listen to what he called a fantastic tale, but seeing that the two of them believed in what they were saying, he had to take it a little more seriously. When all was said and done, he stood shaking his head from side to side with the inscrutable Laffite grin. He told them that their secret was safe, even if he had his doubts about the whole idea. The two of them must have their reason for wanting to believe in this time travel.

Seeing how tired Tori was, Jean had suggested she go on up to bed, he still had some things to talk over with his brother and then he would join her. Leona appeared from nowhere, to show Tori the way. It was right after she left the two brothers alone that Jean faced Pierre.

"There is something else that I must tell you about Tori and on this matter I must have your help." Pierre started to interrupt. Jean simply silenced him with a look and continued.

"No, wait until I finish and then we will talk. From here on out she will be known as Victoria, the reason for this is simple enough as you will soon understand."

Sometime later after hearing how Jean had come to meet her and of how she was wanted for murder, Pierre stood and walked across the room to stand with his back to his brother.

"You are sure of all of these facts brother? You have had this lady, your wife, ah how shall we say, investigated? She is somewhat of a mystery is she not? Could it be she is lying?"

"No Pierre! She is what she says she is, of this I am sure. So I might add is Dominique, he is the only other one who knows her story. She is not black, brother, that you can see for yourself. Your eyes can see it can they not? And the facts that she tells me, of what the future brings, well it could be stories but I think not. To imagine things that she has told me, so many different and wonderful inventions, no, she could not make up so much and keep it all straight in her head. It's impossible.

So will you help me? Ask around; find out all you can on this so-called dandy, Edward Duval, this despicable bastard who set her up at Rose's! Will you do it for me? I ask only this of you, for if I were to do it, I feel that I would not control myself and should I be the one to find him, I would call him out the minute I set eyes on him. I had tried a few months ago to learn some facts but nothing much came of it. Seems this Duval is not always an easy person to find." Jean's mood had darkened and his eyes flashed as he spoke the next thoughts on his mind. "I think if I were to call him out, I would gladly end his miserable life and enjoy every moment of it."

"To do that, would be stupid and completely out of character for you. There would be questions, far too many questions I feel. No, you had best stay clear. I will learn all I can. Fear not dear brother, if there is anything that needs to be known, then I will find it out." Pierre decided a change of subject was needed to lighten the atmosphere.

The two of them talked of Pierre's wife and his mistress, a young woman from Santo Domingo, who lived in their dwelling at the corner of Saint Philip and Bourbon streets. Tori would recognize the establishment as soon as she saw it, for it was known in the future as Laffite's Blacksmith Shop.

"You know my dear brother, you are not the only one that has surprises this evening," chuckled Pierre. "My Adelaide, she has given me a daughter while you were away. We have named her Marie Josephe Laffite."

Jean embraced his brother. "Why you should have told us right away, forgive me for not asking. I simply quite forgot that she was with child. Tori will be thrilled for the both of you and tell me, does Francoise know?"

"She does. I told her myself. If she was unhappy with the news, she did not let on. She is resigned to the fact that she is my wife and Adelaide will always be a part of my life. As long as I am discreet in the matter, it is acceptable."

Jean rolled his eyes and jokingly spoke as he handed a glass of brandy to his brother. "You are fortunate to have such a wife. Something tells me that my Tori would not be so understanding. A toast to the baby then."

The conversation switched to the business and the upcoming social season. This time of the year would bring the dinners that they would undoubtedly be invited to, and it became clear to both of them that Tori had best be ready to answer questions on who she was and from where she came. It was going to be harder to present her to society as his wife than he thought. A situation that was already unavoidable, as invitations had been delivered to the house, invitations that could not be turned down…

"Are you sure I have to go? I mean couldn't you make some sort of excuse for me, blame my condition? I'm sure they would understand," Tori pleaded.

"Come now Madam, where is your sense of adventure? We have been all over this. You can do it. Tori my love, you can hide in this house if you choose but if you do not come out, they will take the liberty to come in and pay you a call."

"It's just that someone could recognize me and I could get you into trouble. Besides, I am what I am, what do I know of being a Southern belle?"

"You are right, you are no Southern belle," he said jokingly. "That is why we are telling everyone you come from Europe." He could see the doubt in her eyes. "You can do it. You don't have to be anything else except the beautiful thing you are and anyway I will be right by your side to help you all the time. Not that you need it. Now hurry up or we will be late and I am not known to be late. Besides, I look forward to seeing an old close friend. You will like him and his family I am sure of it."

Tori took one last minute to look in the mirror. The image looking back at her was a stranger. She marveled at herself. The necklace that hung around her throat sparkled in the lamplight, the earrings hanging there twinkling like stars. Two inches of small brilliant diamonds cascading down, swinging as she moved her head from side to side, catching a soft curl every now and then as they did so. And to think that her hair had been fixed by none other that Marie Laveau.

Imagine as she might, she could not think of anything that had excited her as much since coming to this time, as when she had met the young girl, who she knew was destined to become the most famous voodoo queen of New Orleans. She had known that the girl had been a hairdresser in her time, but never had she imagined that the quality of her work was so refined. Looking at herself, Tori began to remember all she had read or heard about this mysterious girl.

Marie she knew, was a free mulatto, who started out her career by working with prominent families, such as she had just done with Tori. She also remembered that Marie gained a deep understanding of these families and their lives by picking up inside information on the job. In this way she knew who was alcoholic or impotent, who was feeble-minded or crazy. Most important though, was her knowledge of who was cheating on whom. She was a practical sorceress, who mixed black magic with blackmail. Her network of black spies and servant slaves to the city's prominent families enabled her to gather even further information in greater detail. This allowed her to successfully practice her black art for years. Tori knew she would be followed and respected by all, both black and white, rich or poor, it did not matter. Even in modern times. Many people still paid a visit to her grave, performing a ritual of knocks on her vault, followed by the verse they would repeat, all in the hopes of gaining voodoo power.

Tori studied her appearance. Her hair was gathered up in soft swirls and the young girl had pinned in some extra hair pieces that fell loosely down her back, giving her the allusion of having longer and straighter hair than she did. The weaving in of some delicately placed flowers, and strands of seed pearls, added to the creation. Still not happy with what she had created, Marie extended her work. The finishing touches had been expertly applied makeup. Tori noticed that Marie did not use the techniques of the day, rather she used her own style and even had her own powders.

The two had talked during the time spent together but Marie liked to listen more than talk, Tori soon found out. Tori had to be very careful with what she revealed to her. Marie was very good at drawing you into a conversation, getting you to spill the goods so to speak. If she had not been aware of Marie's little game, she was sure she herself would have fallen prey to her charms. Just how did a girl of around sixteen, become so good at what she did? Tori did not know but one thing was certain, she did not come by it without a teacher, someone in this city was helping and guiding her. In the end they had spoken very little and it seemed to Tori that this relieved even Marie.

Then with the job completed, Marie had just smiled and told her that she was a very beautiful woman, one who had caught the biggest catch in the city. This statement had ended in a hearty high-pitched laugh.

Tori was smiling as she turned toward Marie and saw Jean standing in the doorway. He did not acknowledge overhearing the last statement; in fact he did not utter a word. He simply extended his arm, holding out his hand towards her, inclining his head slightly. He had come to escort her to the waiting carriage and to satisfy his curiosity. He just had to see if his lady was going to look as beautiful as he imagined. He stood like someone in a trance, mesmerized by what he beheld. So deep in thought was he, that he did not even notice Marie Laveau, as she quietly slipped pass him, leaving the two alone. His lady was a vision of beauty in a gown that he had commissioned especially for her.

He found that he could not talk, all he could manage for the moment, was to stand and wait as she slowly walked towards him to take his hand. How was it he wondered that she could render him so speechless?

The evening was colder than it had been up until now. It was evident that the crisp winter air had finally arrived. The wrap he placed around her helped ward off some of its chilling touch but still Tori was glad when at last they had arrived and would be going inside.

Immediately Tori's stomach tightened into a knot and her palms began to sweat. She hated being nervous and calmed herself somewhat by the knowledge she held within. She knew deep down she could carry off this charade. More important she knew she had no choice at this point. Here goes, she thought. It's now or never.

Then, just like that, they were inside the grand home, entering a large overcrowded formal room. As everyone turned to look, a silence fell over the place and had it not been for Jean holding onto her, she was sure she would have turned and run. Just don't start talking to yourself she thought. Then, rather than look at anyone in the room, she looked up into Jean's proud face for support.

A friendly male voice broke the silence as its owner warmly welcomed them as he walked quickly up to them. He slapped Jean on his back and then hugged him in the French tradition of greeting as he spoke. "So, we finally get a chance to meet the woman who has stolen your heart and broken many others I am sure."

Tori wished people would stop saying that, even if it sounded good. It made her feel uncomfortable.

"Jean, you old rogue, you should not have kept this beautiful vision all to yourself for so long."

"You are right my dear friend and please forgive me my bad manners, but as you will soon see, I had my reasons for doing so."

Before he could go on however with his announcement, a female voice from across the room was to break into this conversation and cause Jean to visibly stiffen.

"Why, you must tell us Jean darling. I am sure we are all dying to hear the reason. Could it be, that you wished to keep the woman from the almost assured advances from other possible suitors?" Laughter filled the room only to stop as she continued. "Why, shame on you. I'm sure that the Gentlemen would love to meet your new friend, wouldn't you Gentlemen?"

There was more good-hearted laughter around the room, as a few of the men actually stepped forward, eager to be introduced to the lady in question. Tori felt, rather than saw Jean's reaction to all of this. She looked at him closely to confirm her assessment, only to see his lip twitch ever so slightly, an indication of his anger. Then she watched as he let a smile slip across his face to camouflage his true feelings.

Jean forced himself to relax; he had to gain control. In all their preparations for this evening, he had never anticipated this woman being here and yet he should have known she would be. She was always at these dinners, that was how they had first met.

Tori knew that something was wrong; she could sense the uncomfortable feeling that this woman had placed on him. The woman in question looked beautiful, whoever she was, standing there fanning herself, even though there was no need as far as she could tell, other than effect.

Her long jet-black hair, the white porcelain complexion, so perfect. She had long dark eyelashes framing the most exotic green eyes she had ever seen; eyes that bore into her. They reminded Tori of snake eyes, sly, cold and calculating.

The elegant clothes and the way she conducted herself were demanding the attention of all. She stood surrounded by both young and older good-looking admirers, who seemed to hang on her every word and action. All of this led Tori to quickly surmise that she was looking at the spoiled belle of the ball. But why this should upset Jean so, was at the moment beyond her.

It was Jean who was talking now, sounding calm and in command as if he were on board his ship. Yet no one could see what she could feel, the way he was holding her around the waist, in a tight protective sort of way. Then all pandemonium broke loose as quite a few Gentlemen pushed forward to be among the first to make this ladies acquaintance.

"Gentlemen, Gentlemen please do not be in such a hurry, you will all be introduced to my wife in due time, I assure you!"

The look on the woman's face was quickly hidden from view by her fan, as she herself was obliterated from Tori's sight by the sudden crush of well wishes. The congratulations from all around started as the up-until-now unbelievable rumor had finally been confirmed.

The throng of people, who came now to meet her and wish the two of them happiness, overwhelmed Tori. It was the host's wife who came to her rescue and took Tori off for a few minutes to freshen up.

Mrs. Drestrehan was so happy for her, that she did not seem to notice at first that Tori was in a state of panic, but when she did, she took pity on the girl and simply took over, as it was her nature. She ushered everyone from the small sitting room they were in and promptly mothered her way into Tori's heart.

She fussed and "pooh poohed" the crowd and their actions in the other room, telling Tori not to worry. She clucked on and on like a mother hen in the barnyard, protecting her young chicks. In the short time that followed, they became instant friends. Tori knew that she had nothing to fear from her, unlike that other woman in the main room, the one whose looks could kill. Instinctively she knew that the woman was her enemy. It became obvious that Jean knew her and her husband very well. For once back in the middle of the mayhem, he had made it a point to go over and introduce her to them. He had seemed determined and yet cautious as he spoke.

"Madame Simone Claudette La Combe, I would like to present to you, my lovely wife Victoria."

Oh, she had greeted her gracefully enough, even introduced her husband. "Ah pleasure I'm sure. As well I might add, as somewhat of a shock. There are those of us who would have bet that Jean here," she patted his arm, "would never settle down with just one woman. Especially in matrimony, isn't that so my dear?" She looked lovingly at her husband, then turned back to Tori, "Why I do declare, where are my manners? May I present to you my darling and devoted husband, Monsieur Adrian Philippe Le Combe? And please do call me Simone."

They had talked briefly; mostly the conversation had been between Jean and Adrian, while Simone fussed continually over her aging husband. Had it not been for the way she would turn and stare at Tori, sizing her up with dagger stares, Tori might very well have fallen for her stupid act. Thank goodness Mrs. Destrehan had come and whisked her away, or she might have told that Simone whatever her name was, where to go.

Mrs. Destrehan made Tori feel at home, she insisted that she be called by her first name Marie and before the next half-hour had passed, Tori learned more about this remarkable lady and her family. She discovered that they were very good friends of Jean's. That they considered him family of sorts and as such included him in on most of the goings on that they had.

"You must come and spend some time with us. We would love to have you join us for our winter ball. Why, I just won't take no for an answer. There is more than enough room out at the plantation. I will talk to Jean and my husband Jean. My, we have a slight problem don't we, what with his name being Jean also you know? Of course you do. But we often call him Noel. That's his second name and the one he likes better." She was babbling on and happily planning. "Anyway I will see to it that you come to us, for it will give me a chance to formally introduce you as Jean's wife at the ball. You and Jean will be our honored guests of course. That will ruffle someone's feathers for sure." She giggled like a schoolgirl planning a dirty trick on someone. "Oh, my yes, it's going to be wonderful and such fun. Now I must get you back to your husband, I am sure he wants to be with you, to show you off." As she guided Tori towards Jean, she kept up the conversation hardly giving Tori a chance to get a word in edgeways. "You really must tell me more about yourself and your family my dear. Still we will have plenty of time to chat in the days ahead. Come on now, or Jean will not be too pleased with me."

Tori loved the way she seemed to go on and on about so little and the way she took control of everything and everyone around her. Not bossy, just in control.

Jean saw them enter the room. He had not worried about her while she was with Marie, but now she might need his support, so excusing himself from Adrian and Simone, he made his way quickly to her side. He had told her he would be with her every step of the way, to help her get out of tight situations about who she was and where they met and so on, but by the looks of how things were going, he could only smile to himself.

She was not only beautiful; she had talent to go with her looks. There she was, winning everyone's hearts just as she had his. She was talking and laughing as if she had done this a thousand times before, making friends of everyone, all except Simone that was.

Simone had always laid claim to being the young attractive belle of the ball, that was until now. She had always been the one who was the center of the evening, flirting and laughing her way around the room. Tonight, however, she had not had a chance. Tori had taken the spotlight and Simone's green eyes, were a deeper shade it seemed.

Jean knew she was going to be trouble. How much he was not sure but then you could never predict what she would do or say. That was one of the things he had liked about her, that and the fact that she was a vixen in bed. Married to a man old enough to be her grandfather, she had been without sexual encounters until their affair, or so she had told him.

It had suited him well enough, their times together, and there had been many. The meetings were always discreet and carefully arranged. Her love of her husband's fortune kept her so. Never would she run the risk of losing that. Whenever her husband was present, she was totally devoted to him, the poor fool. He had no idea that his money was her only attraction to him. She had often told Jean that when he died and that could not be very far away, she would be a very wealthy widow. One who would be free at last to see him in public?

Jean could see now that she had had more in mind that just continuing the way that they had been. It had become clear to him that she had wanted to become Madame Laffite. He knew also that she was far more disappointed than she let on. Watching her across the room, as she stared at his lady, he could not help feeling somewhat sorry for her. She would have to accept his marriage he told himself. After all there was little else she could do and in time he had no doubt that she would find herself another lover to console her loss.

Tori saw Jean making his way towards her, but before he reached her side, she was surrounded by strangers anxious to invite the new couple to their homes for dinner and parties. Each vying to be among the first to have them as their guests, thereby to be envied by all. Mrs. Drestrehan, however, made all the excuses for her and Jean and let it be known that the couple had accepted their invitation to spend time with them. Tori was amazed, as she watched the speed of the woman as they flocked anew towards Marie, each to offer their help in any way for the preparation of the up-coming event. Why, some actually pushed their husbands to the side in their haste to make their voices heard. They would do anything it seemed, to obtain an invite to the ball.

It was sure to be the event of the season, common knowledge that had somehow spread like wildfire. Tori found herself forgotten for the moment, which was a relief. Looking around for Jean, she caught his eyes and smiled as he mouthed the words "meet you outside." She nodded and stepped quickly to the French doors and slipped outside into the cool evening air.

It felt good to be out of the stuffy house. All the people in there had made it quite warm and the verandah she found herself on was peaceful as well. Looking briefly behind her at the interior she couldn't help but think it was such a lovely home. So beautifully kept and furnished with all those antiques. She had to smile; she was sure Marie would not appreciate her new furniture being called antiques. The sound of the door opening behind her caused her to turn, glad that Jean had joined her so quickly. Instead of Jean standing there however, it was Simone.

"Well, seems we both had the same idea. Or did Jean ask you to meet him out here as well?"

Tori could hardly believe her ears. This woman had it in for her she was very sure of that. The tone in her voice and the way she was acting made it all very clear at last, as to what her problem was. Simone walked right up to her as she continued coyly.

"Why, don't look so shocked my dear. Of course we always meet on balconies such as this one and in the gardens I might add." She fanned herself and

Tori found herself thinking how very much she would like to shove the feathers up her...

"He is such a romantic. Ah, but do forgive me. I completely forgot you are his wife now aren't you? I should have remembered that, silly me. You would not want to hear about such matters would you now?"

Tori was fuming but didn't want to give the bitch the pleasure of knowing she had gotten to her. So in a calm and casual voice as if she didn't have a care in the world, she set out to cut her down to size. "It does not bother me one way or another what he used to do and with whom. As for him asking you to meet him out here, I think you are gravely mistaken. Why, Jean only has eyes for me, or can't you tell?"

Simone had not expected such a reaction; a shocked look of horror maybe, or running back inside crying, but never this! Tori was supposed to feel anger towards her newly acquired husband, or be devastated and fall to pieces. But never was she supposed to be filled with self-confidence. It had thrown her completely off her guard. This Victoria was so sure of Jean's love, a love that the bitch had stolen. Love that by all rights was hers alone. He would be meeting her out here if it were not for this conniving hussy, making plans to meet later, to make love to her. It was more than she could take.

"You must be very sure of his love for you but as a friend and someone that knows him far better, I feel it only right that I warn you sugar, he won't stay yours for long. I know far better than you can imagine what will happen in the days to come. I know what he likes and what he needs." She was almost spitting her words at Tori. "Why my dear, for now marriage might seem right, but it will bore him soon enough. Then you will bore him. I can assure you that I can wait. I will never bore him, nor would I have been so stupid as to marry him. To try to tie him to you as you are trying to do, will never work."

Tori could not believe the audacity of this woman, to talk to her as she was and so brazen too. She was acting like some of the so-called popular girls from her high school days, when faced with losing their bigshot boyfriends. Very spoiled and very bitchy, poor losers. No, better still, she was acting like one of those bitches on the daytime soaps; the ones who were used to having things go their way! But this was no soap opera. Tori could stand it no longer. No woman was going to talk to her like that and get away with it. Sure Simone could dish it out, but could she take it?

"Poor, poor Simone, not marry him you say? Seems to me if you get any greener with jealousy, you will match that dress you have on perfectly. No, better still, you will match the emeralds around my neck that Jean gave to me as a symbol of his love. It is obvious to me now, that you do not know how to handle the loss of Jean, and the chance to snare him for yourself."

Simone was stunned for a second time, as Tori had hit close to the mark. She fired back quickly with a venom laced-voice as her ice cold eyes raked Tori's image, trying to rip it apart. She intended to shatter her with her next words.

"I do not need to stand here and listen to you. I do not need to miss my chance at snaring him as you put it. I had him many nights. Does that shock you? I know how he makes love and I will have him again in my bed. He will soon miss our nights of hot passion together. Maybe he already does. Maybe that's why he asked me out here." She saw these words did have some effect, but not quite enough as she continued her onslaught. "He had not told you of our love had he?" She laughed, enjoying the upper hand and the cruelty of the moment. "No? I did not think so. He kept it from you."

Tori simply laughed back at her; this was ridiculous, and she was ridiculous. "Oh, just shut up before you make a bigger fool of yourself. You are living in a dream world. I don't doubt that he slept with you. A man will sleep with anyone he has to satisfy his needs. That does not, however, mean he loves her. I'm sure he kept you from me, as you put it, for a very good reason. Out of respect for your husband maybe? I do feel sorry for you though, your bed will have to do without Jean, now and forever." Now it was Tori's turn to enjoy herself, and she was on a roll. "If you had really meant anything other than a quick lay, he never would have married me now would he? I suggest that you get your ass back to your husband before you are missed and I have to explain what it is we are arguing about. I'm sure, you have not told your husband about your little and I stress little affair, now have you?"

Simone's color drained and she knew that for the moment she had met her match. This bitch had won for now, but she would not have the winning hand for long. She would have continued but the sound of the doors behind her opening stopped any further retort.

Jean walked outside, his face carefully concealing his worry over finding Simone with Tori and upon stumbling into a situation that looked very close to be exploding. He looked closer at Tori who winked at him, then quickly at Simone and smiled, it was plain to see who had the upper hand.

"Everything all right ladies?"

"Everything is just fine Jean. Simone and I had to clear a little misunderstanding and I think that we have done that haven't we? As a matter of fact, Simone was just leaving; she knows how newlyweds like to be alone. Now come here and show me how much you have missed me." Tori stretched her hand out towards him.

Simone was furious. The laughter on Jean's face not only hurt her but made her all the more determined to seek revenge. She would see to it, that one day Tori paid for this humiliation. Until then, she would play this silly game. A silky smooth voice slipped from between her pouting lips, as she spoke to Jean.

"I will see you both again soon no doubt. Victoria be sure to keep an eye on him now. He does seem to roam day and night. Enjoy the evening, Jean."

With that she turned, gathering up her long gown in one hand, and left. Her laughter could be heard as she closed the doors behind her.

Jean leaned his head close to Tori's and whispered, "should I even dare ask?"

"No Jean, you should not, but next time let me know when one of your ex-lovers is going to be around, will you?"

Tori laughed at his shocked face, the roguish grin that crept across his mouth. His eyebrow went up in a playful sort of way, as he took her in his arms.

"I am amazed you are not upset. You understand?"

"Listen to me Monsieur playboy, in my time we are a little more open minded about such matters. What you did before we met, well that is your business. What you do now is up you. I have no real hold on you. Just please be discreet if you have to have an affair and not with her all right? Stop grinning," she slapped at his arm, "to have an affair, it's not all right. Oh, what I am trying to say is, if our marriage were real, then to have an affair even in my time is wrong. There again our marriage is not real, so what can I say?"

"Come here you crazy woman. I could never have another affair now that I have you. I need only you my lady. You know that. I love you. You are carrying our child," he placed his hand lovingly on her middle. "You need not fear anyone, least of all Simone. She is of my past and a big mistake I can see that now. I should have told you about her, but I just did not think it that important." He grinned as he continued, "I can tell you safely, there are no others, well none that you will meet anyway. Now how about us going home? So I can show you in more ways than words how I feel about you?"

"You are something Jean Laffite. I would love to go home with you, but let's stay just a little while longer. I need something to drink and warm me up. It's freezing out here, not to mention that if I leave now it could be misunderstood. I don't want Simone thinking she has chased me off now do I?" She winked.

# Chapter 13

In the weeks that followed, it seemed to Tori that she was either in her room being fitted for a new gown or attending some dinner given in her honor. It was always the same guest list, with maybe one or two exceptions, but never the same location. In this way she experienced, what she fun lovingly referred to as the life of the rich and famous of New Orleans.

They were the hit of society and nothing it seemed could alter their popularity. Even the fact that she revealed nothing about herself, was not interpreted as a negative quality. An issue that should have caused concern and suspicion, worked more to their advantage, than against them. The mystery that surrounded her only served to increase both interest and speculation.

Mystery and romance, the Creole's thrived on it. And Tori began to realize to a great extent, both of these influences had been half the reason the Laffite brothers had risen to such fame and glory.

Jean and his brother had arrived in New Orleans a year before her. They, like her, were surrounded by an air of romantic mystery. No one knew where they had come from. Some speculated Europe; still others asked was it South America? No, said many, impossible, for it was rumored that the French King was a personal friend of Jean Laffite himself. Some even reported that Jean had been seen with royalty on several occasions. By whom, no one bothered to ask, it was just accepted as fact. This led to the rumors, that Victoria herself had high connections to royalty. Why, the way she carried herself, her gracious actions, spoke for themselves, did they not? It was whispered from behind fluttering fans, that personal reasons connected to France, were the key to her silence and as such, should be respected. To pry would be considered nothing less than an insult.

All these speculations and goings-on helped amuse her, and Tori really enjoyed the fact that she held the spotlight. Something she did with ease, since Simone had not been at any of the subsequent parties. It was said that Simone's husband was ill. She was by his side day and night, and perceived as a dedicated and caring young wife. Little else was ever mentioned about her or her husband and soon the couple was forgotten altogether.

The day came at last, when Jean and Tori headed for the Destrehan's Plantation. Tori looked forward to meeting them again and the idea of spending time on a real plantation was intensely exciting. The ride was slow and the weather overcast, gray and damp. The countryside had taken on a wet new coat for the season, even the roads in places, were nearly impassable. They had flooded after the last heavy rains, something that rarely occurred to the river road in her time. Once they were well out of the city however, the going smoothed out and the remainder of their trip passed with ease. It was along this river road, that

Tori caught her first glimpse of Destrehan. She found herself wondering, if it would ever be one of the ante-bellum mansions that would be restored and set up as a historical place you could visit? Just seeing it from a distance, she hoped it would not fall into ruin. Something so grand deserved to be shared and admired in the generations to come. The front of the house faced the river, and like a picture frame, magnificent gardens surrounded the building. The gardens had been lined with what one day, would be magnificent old oaks.

Jean was pointing out and explaining to her that Noel had added to the original structure. Two wings on each side had been built, due to his ever-growing family. He laughed and hugged her as he playfully frowned.

"They have many children of their own you know," he patted her stomach and added jokingly "and I worry with just one on the way."

Tori laughed at him, then jabbed her elbow into his side playfully. "You're terrible you know. But speaking of children, we will have to tell everyone our secret soon. I'm afraid that I have begun to show and I just can't hide it any longer."

"Well then my lady, we had best let it be known this evening at dinner." He was beaming. "I have looked forward to announcing our news. I want to share with everyone the joy that I feel. The Destrehan's will all be thrilled. The fact that we have chosen them to be the first to hear our news will mean a great deal to them. You think I spoil you. Well look out my lady. There is nothing more they like to do, than spoil a mother-to-be. Something they do very well, after all, they have had enough practice at it."

Jean was laughing and Tori felt a warmth come over her as his happiness and pride of her condition visibly showed. She turned and looked out toward the house as it drew closer. This was the home of his best friends, people who seemed like family to him. Yes, she knew he was going to enjoy sharing their secret with them.

Jean told her Noel was presently at home, something that was a rare occurrence these days. Tori had learned that the man was quite something. He had been one of the authors of the Louisiana Constitution and was at present, President of the Legislative Council. His political connections reached all the way to the White House itself.

At the last few dinners she and Jean had attended, it had become clear that the Creoles held no love for the Americans, which they saw as barbaric in their actions and manners. Tori felt it best to leave the politics of the day to the men as most of the women did. Not out of indifference but out of fear she would not be able to keep her strong views to herself. Also was the fact, that she knew a little of New Orleans history, something that could get her into trouble if she were not careful. Like at the dinner they had been to a few nights ago. Noel had introduced her to the then much-disliked Governor of the Territory of Mississippi and Louisiana. The American's name was William Claiborne. He spoke no French and that was probably a blessing, considering what the Creoles were saying about him behind his back and even sometimes to his face. It had been Noel's acceptance of the man that amazed Tori. He was a wise man indeed, for he could see that things in New Orleans were not destined to remain as they were. She had overheard him telling Jean, that it would be far better to have Claiborne as Governor of this new state they found themselves in, rather than some other unknown American. She smiled to herself, as she knew that Noel would have his way, history bore that fact out.

Tori was brought back to the present by the sounds of shouting children, running up to greet them. They were a few of the younger Drestrehan's children, followed closely by a few young plantation slaves. The excitement of their calls only increased, as they recognized who was in the approaching carriage.

"Uncle Jean. He is here Mama. Oh, do come see. Jean is here!"

The carriage came to a halt surrounded by the children both black and white, who did not seem to notice her at all. It was their Jean that they were so glad to see. He helped Tori down, as he continued to greet each of the screaming youngsters. Tori could see that he was truly enjoying their attention as much, if not more, than they were his.

She looked away from them and concentrated on her surroundings. The small crowd had moved off to the side, leaving her view unobstructed. The house was a grand one, much larger now that she was right up to it. The eight white columns that ran along the front, shone in the little bit of sun that seemed to be creeping out to greet them. The top and lower verandahs were deep set and ran the entire length of the structure. Where the verandah stopped, at both ends, were the extensions Jean had pointed out. These reached towards the back of the house and they had no verandahs. Each had large windows and judging from the many chimneys, many cozy fireplaces.

The grounds were well kept, even for winter and Tori wondered how they cut all the grass that the children were now running across. The small crowd of children had left Jean's side at the sight of the next carriage turning into the driveway and they could be heard even at this great distance, happily screaming their greetings. Great flower beds, filled with small neat shrubs lined the driveway she had traveled up. Nothing was in bloom at this time of the year, but Tori could well picture how spectacular the place would look in the summer.

Mrs. Drestrehan was first to appear and as always took charge of the moment. Orders were given for Tori and Jean's belongings to be taken up to the large bedroom that had been put aside for just them. Unlike the other guests who were to stay over, they were to be in the main house, not the wings.

"It is so good to see you again Victoria. I have looked forward so very much to your coming. It will be so nice to have another woman to talk to. Oh yes, the girls are growing up, but they are still my daughters and talking to them is, well, like talking to my daughters."

"Marie, if you don't stop rambling on, Jean's wife will never get a word in. How are you my dear? You look as lovely as I remembered. No, lovelier in fact, doesn't she dear?"

Tori was touched by the man's warm greeting and blushed a little at his remark.

"That is very kind but before we go any further there is a small matter that I need to clear up."

"Anything my dear, please just ask."

"It's just that I know Marie here calls you Noel and that still others call you Jean. Now please tell me is it Jean or Noel? I am never sure which to call you?"

"You may call me whatever you desire I'm sure. Now go on in out of the cold, while I greet our other children that are about to arrive. They never seem to leave home for long, always dropping in for a visit with their families, isn't that so dear?"

No one paid much attention to this last remark, as Marie was hustling them in the front entrance. It was the size of the place that struck Tori first, then the furnishings and the atmosphere. It reminded her a little of Leone's plantation, different yet the same. So grand, so large, so Southern.

Marie took them into the room, where a fire was burning and the decorations were hung for the upcoming ball. The place was warm and it was filled with laughter and love. This was the dining area; a very long table sat dead center and was already loaded with food. They walked straight on through and out into an area where a curving staircase led upstairs. To Tori it looked as if they had entered the home the back way instead of the front, which she was later to learn was correct. Most carriages pulled around to this side of the house and the guests would enter into the hall where they now stood.

She and Jean followed Marie upstairs and into the front parlor as she called it. This was a real family room to Tori. She found it was warm and cozy and full of laughter and love. For an instant then, she felt a pang of loneliness. She thought of her daughter alone and wondering where she was. Strange how the memories of her would pop up in her mind for no reason, she thought. But like so often now she was able to reassure herself that her daughter was in good loving hands. Her own family would see to it that the child was well taken care of. She would have everything, everything but a mother. Quickly she pushed this thought to the back of her mind. She had to remain happy and not spoil the day. Everyone was being so nice to her and they were all just so festive. Noel entered the room and Tori took the opportunity to announce that she had decided what she would call him. So it was, that J.D. gained his new name. It had never occurred to anyone before that he should be called by his initials. It was an idea he was very fond of from the moment Tori explained how she arrived at her decision. From that day on, until he died, friends, family and all who knew him, would refer to him as J.D.

He was a big man and his graying hair gave him an air of dignity. His whole face laughed, when he did, and his children all adored him. He was the boss of the house and ran it with a firm hand but his love and kind ways made it so he very seldom had to raise his voice to be heard. This, with a house full of children, their friends and adults amazed Tori.

The evening meal was served in the large dining room, with everyone sitting around the long highly polished wooden table. Marie remarked to Tori, that she had had it made special for just such occasions. She loved for her family to all sit at one table, at the same time, for important meals. She was about to go on when Jean interrupted her. He stood up with his glass raised.

"Speaking of important, I would like to take this opportunity to make a rather special announcement." With that Jean raised his glass higher and turned to Marie and J.D. with such a grin upon his face, that Tori was sure everyone would guess before he got the words out.

"You are the closest I have to a family here in New Orleans and you have always treated me as such. So it gives me, no us," he turned and faced Tori as he continued, "great pleasure, to announce that in this year, we too will be in need of a larger table. We are to become parents. I am to be a father."

The room filled with happiness and excitement. Everyone was hugging and laughing, and congratulations came from all. Even the young ones, who did not have an understanding of the word, found themselves caught up in the moment and ran around screaming "congratulations."

Tori was quite unprepared for such a response. She had thought a few, "that's nice dear," would have been ample, but no, they were acting as if it was the most wonderful news in the world. Watching Jean hug J.D. was the last thing she could stand. Overcome with emotion she simply burst into tears.

Jean was at her side immediately wondering what to do and what could have caused his lady such grief. As one by one, the others noticed her tears, the room fell into a deadly hush.

"Is anything wrong? Are you all right?"

"I'm fine Jean. Just a little, oh I don't know. A little overwhelmed that's all."

J.D. half laughed as he spoke to Jean. "Of course she's overcome, all this noise and carrying on. Take my word for it Jean, all women seem to do is laugh too much, or cry for no reason, when they are pregnant. If that's not enough, they have you getting up at all hours of the night, for some of the silliest foods. You just wait Jean and if that's not enough..."

"Oh stop it J.D. you do go on so. All Victoria needs is some rest. It's been a long day for you and I'm sure you will feel a lot better after a warm bath and a good night's sleep. Jean you just stay here and enjoy the rest of your dinner. Victoria and I will excuse ourselves and see you later."

There was no arguing with her. Everyone knew once Marie was set on doing something, it was done. So Tori went with her upstairs, glad for the time she would have to be by herself, to gain her self-control.

"I'll just send in Mamsy to help you, silly name I know, but I gave it to her when I was very little. She's been a part of our family and helped me bring into the world each and every child. Now don't you worry none, the men will be busy and when you're ready I'll have Mamsy bring you down so they won't see you. Anyway, dressed in a robe it will be fine. You are like another daughter to us, so don't fret yourself about getting dressed. Now then, I knew that you would like a bath, so you will find it ready for you. Just say I have a mother's instinct. Besides you showing like you are, I was wondering when you were going to break the news." She was looking very pleased with herself at having been right.

Tori hugged Marie and her eyes started to mist up again. She was so grateful to her for being so understanding.

"Now, none of that. Off to the tub with you and you will feel better you will see. Lord I've been through it myself enough, I should know."

Tori entered the bathroom and her mouth dropped open. She could hardly believe what she was looking at. There up against the wall, was another marble tub, one that made Leone's seem small. Ever since leaving Leone's plantation house, Tori had had baths in all sorts of tubs; some were metal or wood and moved into a room and removed after the bath was finished. Others if you could call them a bathtub, were placed in very small rooms, but never had they been made of marble. Even in her own time, she had never seen anything quite as magnificent as this.

She was still standing looking at it and thinking how in the hell did they get it up here, the thing must weigh a ton, when her thoughts were interrupted by a knock at the door.

"I's be Mamsy and I's kin help yo now. Yo just lets ole Mamsy take care o' yo. I's dun take care ob da misses, an I's know'd how to make you's feel, like yo don't a knows yo has a babe a comin."

Mamsy was a blessing and Tori soon felt like a new woman. She was bathed like a child and massaged like she had never been. Instead of relaxing her to the point of sleep, she felt invigorated. She was a new person, ready to face the world. Then just as suddenly it occurred to her, she was hungry. No, it was more than that, for the first time in weeks she was starving.

"Mamsy, if you ever need a job, you come to me. You are a life saver."

"Oh misses, yo be teasing me some. I's be happy here an all. Dis here be my home. Sure'n will thank yo kindly for da offer."

Chuckling to herself, the old lady left Tori and went to fetch the robe that she had unpacked earlier. A few minutes later, guided by Mamsy, a well relaxed and much happier Tori entered the downstairs dining area.

Marie was waiting by the roaring fire, with a plate of cold cuts and fresh baked bread. Two large chairs faced the fireplace and she motioned for Tori to join her.

"She is a dream isn't she? I doubt that I would have had fourteen children without her. There again, maybe its because I like the way she pampered me so much. When I'm with child that is. Maybe I kept getting pregnant to get pampered. The two of them laughed and Tori knew at last she had a family in this time.

Tori and Marie talked for hours sitting by the open fire. No one came near the room to disturb them, not even Jean. It gave Tori time to ask questions and to listen as she learned about the history of the Destrehan family and the plantation that they now lived on.

"You know Victoria, as much as I adore the countryside my favorite place will always have to be New Orleans. My father had the Manor House built for my husband and I when we were married you know? He loved St. Charles parish and the city life reminded him a little of home I think. I do miss the excitement of the city. You and Jean are so lucky to be living in town. Still, I will be back in town in time for Lent."

"You truly amaze me you know? Here you sit surrounded by a wonderful family, in a wonderful home and no one knows how you long to be in town do they?"

"No one, but you my dear. Now don't get me wrong. At certain times of the year, as you will see, it is a blessing to be out here and not in that hot and airless city. We always have a breeze here you know; it comes right off the river. Then there is the running of the place; we simply can't stay away for long. Noel, I mean J.D." she giggled, "now don't I? He has built the plantation to quite an impressive size. It's nearly a thousand acres now, stretches from the Mississippi to Lake Pontchartrain. It takes so much of his time. Why, between this place and his playing politics with Jean, it's any wonder that I had one child." She laughed playfully and openly at this remark. "You know my dear, sometimes I do wish I had him all to myself, like you have your Jean. That man of yours is always surprising me; here he was, up to his neck in introducing us to all sorts of visitors from France. Then he turns up after a trip away, with you! Unlike J.D. however, who continues to work at his politics, your Jean has made you his life. Keep him at your side as long as you can Victoria, enjoy your time together..."

Marie was staring into the dying fire and for the first time that evening, seemed to be in a world of her own memories. Tori did not disturb her, for she too was thinking. How much she had learned about her pirate tonight. The mystery man was really that. Just who was he and where did he come from? They had never talked about it and somehow Tori knew they never would. If he wanted her to know, he would tell her. Until then she would have to respect his need for privacy. To think that many only saw him as a pirate, made her chuckle. He was highly educated, had friends in high places, both in America and France. If Marie had told the truth, and she did not doubt that, then some of those friends in France were of the royal connection. One thing was certain though; J.D. and Jean went back along way together. She smiled slowly; she did know one other very real fact about them, which they themselves did not know. Her dashing rouge of a pirate, one step ahead of the law and sensible upright virtuous Statesman J.D., would make history together. These two men would have a great deal to do with the future. Sure it would be in different ways that they would accomplish what they had too, but the result would be the same. They would not only effect the history of New Orleans but all of America.

Marie's voice broke her daydream. "My it is late. Forgive an old woman for keeping you up so late. You must be so tired. It has been a delight though hasn't it dear? I do hope we will have many more evenings together. Somehow I feel as if I can talk to you. I trust you and love you like a daughter."

Marie did not have to say anything else. It went without saying how each felt and they hugged briefly, before heading up the quiet stairs to bed.

Over the next few days couples began to arrive for the ball. They came two and three days before the grand event and the house took on a whole new air. If Tori thought it chaotic before, she had not known what chaos was. The plantation was now so full of people rushing here and there. Some were cooking and others were arranging where to put people, what to do with them, how to entertain and keep the peace. And through it all Marie was the expert. She was every place at once and never seemed to tire. She was in her glory and Tori could now see why she would find the regular plantation life dull, compared to the activities that now surrounded them. She seemed to glow in the challenge, to make this ball the success she knew it could be. They had little time to visit each other like the first night, but that did not seem to matter. Each of them was caught up in the excitement and preparations that had taken over everything and everyone.

Servants ran everywhere, gowns were being fitted, and hair was to be done by only the best, Marie Laveau. She had been sent for and would remain for the week, staying in a cabin in the slave quarters. The gentlemen, it seemed, put up with all this and found their own form of entertainment. Jean and J.D. spent hours talking or playing chess. Tori on the other hand, reveled in the art of nosing around. She was able to observe the kitchens in operation and the preparation of all the food that would be served in the days ahead. When she was not there, she could be found in their room with Mamsy, getting a rubdown after her long walks around the plantation grounds. So much to see and learn, so much to remember...

Finally, the big night arrived and from the bedroom window Tori watched with Jean as the carriages began to arrive one by one. The line went completely down the driveway and out onto the river road itself.

"You know of course, that they are all coming to meet my lovely wife, the one woman who has stolen my heart."

"Jean stop it! We both know that is not true, I have already met most of them, I'm sure."

"So my lady doubts me, you have hurt me deeply. I would never say anything that was not true, exaggerated maybe, but not true..."

"Oh stop teasing, and do come away from the window, what will people think?"

"I don't know what they think, but I think we should have a glass of wine before we go down. This is one time that I believe we should arrive a little late and make a grand entrance."

"You are terrible, I promised Marie that I would help and here you are asking me to stay up here and drink."

"Well, I could think of a few other things that I would ask of you, but you do look as if you would run me through, if I tried to get you out of that gown."

"You're damned right I would. It took forever to get into this thing. Never again will I think it romantic to wear so many petticoats. And really Jean, I feel as if I am going to fall out of the top of this. Look, do you see what I mean?"

"Indeed I do Madam and it will be driving me mad with wanting you all night, along with all the other male guests I'm sure. Maybe I should have your gowns made, to conceal a little more, in the future?" He was in one of his teasing moods and enjoying himself. To get him to be serious at this point would be hopeless. Besides, Tori knew that he loved the way she had her gowns made up. They were stunning and unusual for the times, and she knew, no one would dare say anything against any design she wore. They would never wish to offend her or her husband. Anyway, Tori had already noticed a few daring ladies had copied her earlier gowns. She guessed they were thinking the dresses were the latest fashion from Europe, and they wanted to be among the first to join her in showing them off. Was she influencing fashion she wondered? Once again she reminded herself that she had to be careful with what she did or said. She was not sure why she felt this way, it was just something she had a gut feeling about. She took her glass of wine from Jean and toasted him. "Here's to the one glass of the day then. I would rather enjoy it here with you now in the quiet than not."

"Tell me again why it is that you insist on only one glass a day," he grinned. "You are sure it has nothing to do with the fact that wine seems to agree with you and your passion. Which I am sure I do not have to remind you climbs higher as you drink..."

"Oh Jean stop it! I know you think I am overly passionate when I'm loaded but that has nothing to do with it and you know it. I've explained to you that one or two glasses of wine a day won't hurt the child, but more than that could. Same with coffee and smoking and do I have to go on again?"

"No, not again." He laughed. "I believe you and love you all the more for taking such care of him." He saw her look of disapproval and quickly added, "Or her. Let us not discuss the child now, let's just sit and enjoy this time alone. I am sure it will be the last for hours to come."

The two of them did wait, for about another hour, before Jean decided it was time to join the party. He was going to be quite the showman this evening and planned to make the most of their grand entrance. This would be followed by the moment he loved the most, the introducing of his wife to those who had not yet had the pleasure. He really did consider her that. He thought of her his truly wedded wife. To him it was not acting. He did not need a church to change how he felt. And as his wife she would be the hit of the night, he was sure. In the gown she wore, she still did not show her condition that much. This would be the last time he thought, that he would see her dressed in such a form-fitting gown until after the baby was born. The mother of his child looked like a temptress, not a mother-to-be. Tori would turn some heads and start some tongues wagging when their news slipped out, that was for sure, and he loved it.

Most of the guests were already in the dining room, which had been cleared of furniture to form a ballroom. The doors to the adjoining room had been opened. The effect created one large ballroom, instead of two separate rooms to accommodate the throng.

Jean and Tori started down the stairs that wound down and around the main hallway. He had hoped to get Tori to the door of the ballroom before being seen and in so doing make his grand entrance. As it was however, a few of the guests spotted the two coming down and alerted the rest, who all seemed to be pressing into the hallway, for a better view of the couple.

Tori had hoped not to be seen until downstairs, but for a very different reason. Maneuvering about in all the material that made up both the gown and petticoats was extremely difficult. The fact that the material was so fine and clinging only added to her problem, as it insisted on wrapping it's volume around her legs threatening to trip her. Going up and down stairs gracefully, with everyone watching her, was damn near impossible.

"I can't do this, if I move one more step, I'm going to land up on my ass," she whispered through her smile.

"And if you whisper any louder, everyone will hear you and your choice of colorful words. Some angel he retorted!"

"Tori continued to smile and speaking through her teeth simply said, "If that's what you want, the choice is yours, help me or by God, I swear…"

He was chuckling now, "I am well aware that you swear Madam and if we stand here any more, smiling and talking through our teeth, everyone will think us gone quite mad."

Jean took her by her hand and placing his free arm around her waist he started helping her down the winding staircase.

"My, my, my, it would seem that Victoria is not accustomed to wearing such grand garments. Or could it be that they don't have such fashions where you are from. Or is the ability to maneuver gracefully, beyond you my dear? Jean you darling, you are such a good husband. Wouldn't you say everyone? He is all but carrying her down, now that's what I call dedication."

"Now that's what I call a bitch," Tori thought. She was there! The bitch had returned to claim the spotlight. Tori had thought that she had seen the last of her. Now, once again, Simone was trying to make her look like a fool. Jean was furious and had he not had his arms full he would have marched over to Simone and escorted her outside to tell her a thing or two. He knew that he would have to put her in her place very soon to silence her.

"Simone, ah pleasure to see you. Does this mean that we also have the pleasure of Adrian's company?" Jean said as they made their way down.

"You do indeed. Adrian is awaiting the party in the parlor. He's been ill you know? It's been hard for him to get around. Maybe Victoria would like to visit with him. The two of them do seem to have the same difficulty, getting around that is."

Everyone was shocked at her behavior; the whispers by the woman could be heard in the background, this was followed by a silence, as everyone waited to see what would happen next. None of this seemed to bother Simone; she just proudly stood her ground with such a demure look upon her face.

Tori would have loved nothing better at that point, than to walk up to her and wipe that stupid expression off with a good slap. But on second thought, she realized Simone was hoping for just such a reaction. It would give her a great satisfaction to prove Tori not quite the lady she was portrayed to be. Jean was acting the calm Gentleman, so she would act also. There was more than one way to skin a cat she thought.

"Simone, you are too kind. Between Jean here, looking out for my well-being and you offering your help, I feel so fortunate. It is hard for me to walk down these stairs safely, as you have observed. Let me assure you however, that it is not because of the gown, it's just that a woman in my condition would not want to fall."

By the time Tori had finished her sentence, they were at the foot of the stairs and one of Jean's old friends stepped forward.

"Does this mean that Jean here, is going to join us in fatherhood? That the rumor is true?"

"It is indeed," he announced loudly.

"Well, congratulations and let me be among the first to offer our, that is my wife's and my help in any way."

Here they go again she thought, this Southern hospitality was more on who could out do the other or who could stay in with the most popular. Now more than before, they could be wined and dined, Tori had to smile at that. At least she was smiling; Simone's face was an emotionless mask.

Tori and Jean became the center of attention and the sulking Simone was pushed aside and soon forgotten. This was not to her liking or custom, as she was always the life of any such gathering. She stormed off to find herself a drink and try to gather her thoughts as to what to do next. Once again she had lost face and it was all that Victoria's fault. Now she had gone and got herself pregnant, no doubt in an attempt to hang on to Jean and to gather sympathy for herself with the ladies. Probably wasn't even Jean's child. Now that would be poetic justice, she thought.

As the evening progressed, things went along smoothly enough. Simone stayed clear of Tori and the entourage that followed her. The women, most of them, seemed to accept Tori as one of their own. Those who held back did so out of feelings of inadequacy or jealousy. Even these remaining few, were won over slowly as Tori was introduced to each one. She was a true diplomat, always remarking on something positive when such an introduction took place. Sensing the feelings of slight animosity she would immediately go to work. She really enjoyed doing her best to win over the person involved.

"I do hope that I can look as lovely as you do, after the baby comes. You did not mean four children, surely? But you look so, so, well. You have a figure of a woman with no children."

With positive remarks like this, the end result was that the top of society decided Victoria Laffite was a truly gracious person. One who could be admired and loved by all.

The only one who did not believe her act was Simone. She had watched from across the room half the night, ignored and totally out of the limelight. She had been drinking continually, enough to give her courage to try once again, to obtain the upper hand. She walked up to Victoria and Jean, as he was about to take his lady to the dance floor. The crowd around the two fell silent. Simone lowering her eyes and speaking softly sounded believable to all but Tori.

"I must apologize for my actions earlier. I truly did not mean any harm. It's just that I have been under such a strain of late. Really, I do not know what came over me." She forced a tear to fall from her eye. "Really I don't. Could you find it in your heart to possibly forgive me and maybe even understand?"

Her Southern drawl heavy and laced with self pity was more than Tori could stand, but she just looked at Simone and smiled.

"Of course we all understand, it must be hard for you, now if you could excuse us? Jean I think a little fresh air would do me good, can we?"

Jean and Tori left the crowd and one or two of the women who had been close by were now turning their attention to poor Simone. Simone was milking it for all it was worth. She was back in the center of attention, not the way she liked to be but it was a start.

Simone could be heard talking to those around her. "Victoria is so understanding isn't she? Why, I do declare, Jean is so lucky to have her. They were made for each other were they not? It's so hard when you don't have a husband to take care of you. I mean, I'm the one who has the burden of taking care, you understand? Not that I'm complaining, it's just so hard, and I love my husband so..."

Once outside Tori and Jean just laughed and shook their heads. To Tori it was quite something, the way she had seen Simone pour out her charms to all who would listen, knowing she was lying and her audience believing every word.

"You mean to tell me, that they believe her? How can they?"

"They will for now, but the time will come when her true colors will show. After all, she had me fooled for a while didn't she?"

Tori was standing looking out over the dark garden and shivered. The night air was cooler than she had expected and Jean seeing this, took her in his arms, slowly kissing her before leading her inside through another door, that led into a small study.

"If I don't have a few moments alone with you, I think maybe, it's very possible, that I will go crazy."

"I think you are right. Never have I seen so many people and all wanting to talk to us. It's not so much fun when you're the hot couple of the night."

"Hot, is that what they say in your time, hot? Seems strange some of the things they have done with the English of your time."

"No stranger than what they have done with French." She was teasing him and loved the puzzled look that played about his eyes. "Do we have to go back in there right away, or can we just slip upstairs and not be missed?"

"My lady what an intriguing idea, but an impossible one. If you think that we would not be missed, you are mistaken. I'm afraid we are as you say, stuck. Besides there are still people who have not yet had the pleasure of your company. They would feel insulted if they did not have the chance to greet you. Duty calls my dear."

J.D. had just hugged and kissed Tori on the cheek, when a voice from behind her, asked to be introduced to the lovely Madame Laffite, so he also could have the honor of wishing her the best. Tori's blood ran cold as she visibly paled, swaying slightly so it looked as if she were to faint. J.D. took her by the arm, concern in his voice as he spoke.

"Is something wrong my dear? Do you feel all right? Can I get you something perhaps, a cool drink, a chair?"

"No! No, I'm fine. It's just all the excitement that's all. The baby, this is a new condition for me. I'm just not used to it I suppose. Maybe I should go up and rest a little. Would you go and find Jean for me and let him know?"

The voice behind her spoke full of concern. "Very sensible idea, you go and find her husband, it would be an honor to be of assistance I'm sure. I shall stay by her side, until Monsieur Laffite is found. May I present myself Madam?"

Tori turned slowly, feeling her heart pounding in her chest, then skip a beat, as her mind raced so fast, making her head swim. Her hate for this man must not show and she had to act calm somehow. He was bowing and raising up, to look her full in the eyes.

"Monsieur Edward Duval, at your service."

Was there any recognition behind his eyes? Did he know her? She could not tell. His gaze was steady, and his smile deadly. His arm was extended towards her, then as if in slow motion, he was reaching for her. God how she wanted to scream and run, she needed Jean. She desperately needed to do something, to say something. What though?

"Sir, please excuse me, I'm afraid that I am not feeling too well." Turning now to J.D. who was looking more than concerned, she excused herself and all but ran out of the room. The stairs were a lot easier going up than down and it was only minutes before she found her room and rushed in, locking the door behind her. Edward Duval was here, at this party! How long had he been watching her? Damn him. Did he know who she was? How could he not? She had panicked and run and she knew that, but what choice had she? Any time now they could come for her, to take her away. And Jean, would he be able to prevent it?

With her back on the door, she stood there waiting, tears of terror slipping down her face, as she covered her eyes with trembling hands. She was shaking so hard, that her legs were threatening to collapse from under her. What was taking Jean so long? Why was he not with her, helping her to escape?

Simone had been sitting with her husband and some of his friends, when she saw the confrontation that had just taken place and it puzzled her too. Just who was that man and why had Victoria acted so strangely? She had seen the panic, written all too clearly on her face as she fled the room, but why? She would have to leave her husband's side and investigate; instinctively she knew this could be very important.

"You will excuse me my love? I have just seen someone who I do need to speak with. Just stay and I will be right back, my darling." Her husband smiled up into his beautiful young wife's face. He was so proud of her, how could he deny her mixing with the guests. After all, it was he that she always came back to. It was he who she was so devoted to and loved. Nodding his approval, he let her leave, knowing he would have her to himself later.

Quickly she made her way over to the punch bowl by the stranger, who was helping himself to another glass of champagne. "Excuse me kind sir, but could I possibly impose on such a fine gentleman as yourself, to come to a lady's aid?" It seems as though my glass has been misplaced and I'm in a desperate need to quench my thirst."

"The pleasure is mine I assure you. May I present myself, Edward Duval, your humble servant Madam. You will I hope call me Edward?"

"Why, certainly Edward. I would be delighted, that is if you will consent to calling me Simone?"

Simone was pouring on all the charm she could and it was working. She was using her eyes seductively and touching his hand, stroking it as she spoke. None of this attention went unnoticed by Edward, who was now glad that he had come to the party. Indeed he was very glad, it seemed the evening was going to be far from a loss that was for sure.

He had of course, come to meet the lady who all of New Orleans was talking about and calling the most beautiful. She was that, even pregnant. He had found her striking so. Ah but more than that, she was very familiar, something about her kept pulling at his mind. She looked like someone he knew, but who? Had he been sober, he was sure he would remember. What did it matter, Laffite's wife was off limits to him and here was a beautiful woman who found him attractive, and she was all but throwing herself at him. He found her very interesting and very desirable. Yes, he would think about Victoria Laffite later. Right now he had to get to know this Simone better. If he was reading this woman correctly and he was seldom wrong, he would soon know her intimately...

Jean could hear her crying and had tried several times to get her to unlock the door and let him in. He was getting more worried as time slipped by and not knowing what else to do he raised his fist and beat upon the door, demanding that she let him enter. Tori more in a daze and not really knowing what else she could do, opened the door fully expecting to find the rest of the guests standing with him, waiting to bring her to justice.

"My God! Look at you, what's wrong?" J.D. said you ran from the room and that you were not feeling well. Is it the baby? Are you ill? He put his arms around her and held her, as she collapsed into them sobbing, trying to tell him all at once what had happened. Jean could not understand much of what she was saying and knew that if he were going to, he had better calm her down first. With Tori carrying on like she was, it could not be good for her or for the child he thought. Besides acting this hysterical was not something she normally did. Whatever had upset her must be very serious and he needed to know what it was in order to help her.

"Tori now listen to me. This is not doing you or the baby any good. Now calm down please for both of your sakes. I am here and I won't let anything happen to you. But listen to me, you have to help me understand just what it is that has you so upset. You have to gain control of yourself."

Tori took in long ragged breaths and slowly she was able to stop crying. As her sobs subsided, she got back some self-control. He was with her now and he would save her. Her Jean would not let anything happen.

"Edward." That was the only word she could trust herself to say clearly.

Had he heard her right? He knew that name and what it meant but he needed to know more. She had to talk to him. He continued to hold her and waited knowing that when she was ready, she would tell him just what it was about Edward he needed to know.

"Edward Duval is downstairs and I'm sure he recognized me. Jean do you understand what I am telling you? He is here! He will tell everyone who I am and then they will have no choice but to come and get me. We have to get out of here. You have to get me away fast." She threw her arms around his neck pleading with him. "Jean I did not kill anyone, you know that. But no one else will believe me. You do believe me don't you?"

Jean was stunned by what she had just told him. The fact that this Edward character was here, let alone had gotten so close to her, frightened him. He had been so stupid not to have taken care of him long before this. Right now however, he had to keep his lady calm, and find out just what this bastard was up to. "Of course I do and let me put your mind at ease. I doubt that he knows who you are, or he would have done something by now. If he does send for you, he would have a hard time proving his story against yours tonight. You are my wife and among friends here remember. You look nothing like the Tori I found hidden on my ship. Look, I'll go downstairs and see what I can find out. You stay here and rest. Try not to worry, as I'm sure everything is fine. When I come back up, it should be with good news."

Tori only nodded her head, she had the awful feeling that the party was over and that from now on, she would have to fight for her life. She watched as he left and did not miss the worried look he too had on his face, or the fact that he had picked up a small derringer, slipping it into his coat pocket as he walked from the room.

The time seemed to drag by and nothing occurred to give her a clue as to what was happening. The only sound she could hear was of people having a grand time, laughing and carrying on as if nothing was wrong. When at last the door opened and Jean walked in, she ran to him, demanding to know every detail.

"Well nothing much to tell. I went down and looked everywhere. Seems as though our guest had left shortly after you came up here. He either did not know who you were or he left knowing and trying to decide what to do with the knowledge."

Tori was worried. "Well, I guess it's just wait and see then. What can I do other than that? Running away is one option but you won't do that will you?"

"My lady, trust me. I won't let that bastard near you again. He has taken on more than he can handle he knows that. I do have some good news to cheer you up." The twinkle in his sparkling eyes told her that it must be something she was going to like. "Seems that Simone got tired of the party and she and her husband left for home."

"Weren't they to stay over? I mean Adrian's health and the long drive back to the city?"

"Not such a long drive. Adrian has a place not far from here."

"But she seemed to have told everyone she was staying over."

"That's what I thought," he said puzzled, "it seems that the lady changed her mind. Anyway you won't have to face her sarcastic tongue in the morning."

Tori was thankful for that. Whatever Simone's reason she was glad. She also decided that as she could do nothing about Edward and worrying about him was wasted energy. She would put the whole horrible incident out of her mind for the time being.

"You know it's a hell of a way to start off our child's life isn't it? I mean, this should be a good year for you, it's 1811, the year you became a father. I'm sorry Jean, I have messed it all up for you, haven't I?"

"You have done nothing but bring me joy. Did we not have a wonderful Christmas together on Grand Terre? The first I have celebrated in years I might add. The celebration of the New Year was to me a symbol, of not only our new life together but of the joy that awaits us in the birth of our child. Now don't you worry, this will be a great year. If it will make you feel any better, I have my men already checking into this Duval character and the whole damn mess. I just did not push them hard enough. When we get back to the city, we should have some answers. Enough talk for now. You need your rest and I will go down and let Marie and J.D. know that you are fine. They will only worry if I don't."

Tori lay in bed for a while wondering what was really going to happen in the months ahead and just before she fell asleep, her last thoughts were not of Edward or Jean, they were of a lake and home and safety...

# Chapter 14

Less than a week later Tori found herself safely back in the townhouse, but afraid of running into Edward again, she had refused to go out. Jean had not forced her and had himself agree with her, that until they learned more about the situation they would remain secluded. Then one morning he broke the seclusion when he announced they had a guest, one he wanted her to meet.

"Tori, I would like you to meet a close friend of mine, even if he is an American," Jean laughed heartily. Then quickly turning serious "He is also my attorney, a small fact that very few people in this fair city are aware of." This last statement had been spoken in such a manner; Tori automatically knew it to be information that had to stay within the compounds of their home only. "He is here with some rather interesting news for us. No, mostly for you," Jean was smiling like the Cheshire Cat. The news obviously was going to be good. "John, let me introduce you to my lovely wife Victoria."

"Madame, Mr. John Grymes at your service, and I must say it is a great pleasure to finally have the chance to make your acquaintance. I'm of the understanding, that you have had a certain, ah, shall we say, misunderstanding hanging over your head?"

Tori flashed a look in Jean's direction; it was a questioning stare that he saw, one that held no surprise or fear at all.

"It's fine Tori. I trust John and so should you. He is well aware of all the details of Kate's murder and Edward's involvement."

"That I most certainly am Madame. It's a most deplorable set of circumstances, if I might be allowed to say so. It has been a very trying and difficult matter to investigate I can tell you both. That is why it has taken so long. Now, if we can just sit down, I will attempt to put the whole ugly matter to rest."

The story came out then in bits and pieces and gradually they began to piece the puzzle together, of what had happened after Kate's death. John had been able to quietly investigate the murders and what he learned was very interesting indeed. Tori was not wanted for murder, nor had she ever been.

"It seems that this Mr. Duval, that's Edward of course, kept you in the dark about the charges. We can only assume, that he had unscrupulous reasons of his own, for doing such a thing. Now this is how I see it. You may have to answer some questions as to what happened that day, and it could get a little uncomfortable shall we say? I mean it would become your word against this fellow Edward's. Especially if he chose to stay with his outrageous concoction. Therefore my dear, it is our consensus that to avoid any further incriminations, that you meet with one Leone Duval first." He mumbled the next statement to no one in particular. "Damn decent chap that Leone, known him for years, such a shame about that brother of his. Anyway, back to the point I was making. You would discuss with Leone the matter of what happened that fateful day. It should shed some light on one or two rather troubling questions. Once that is done, then, if this Edward decides to pursue the matter, one visit from me should put a stop to any inclinations he might have, say of blackmail or the like."

Tori had listened carefully without interrupting. She knew that Jean would not have chosen just anyone to defend her, he would only have the best. This man before her now, was more than just an employee of Jean's. He was a trusted friend. Jean had introduced him as a friend first, and he chose his friends carefully. Her fate lay in the hands of these two and obviously they had discussed it thoroughly. Tori just wanted to hear it from Jean before giving them the go ahead.

"Do you think it's a good idea Jean, that I meet with Leone? I mean, he could ask a lot of questions that I would have some difficulty answering, if you understand me? Do I tell him everything?"

"How do you feel about him Tori? You know him better than I do? All I know, is what John here has told me. John holds him in high standing, something that puts him in a trusted light." His top lip twitched slightly as he half-smiled. "What do we have to lose? As I see it, we have no choice, do we?"

John looked towards her, making a statement more than asking a question it seemed. "It's settled then. You will meet with him?"

"Yes John, I guess I have to, for more reasons than just trying to protect myself. I have always felt that I owed Leone an explanation. This will give me the chance to do just that. The only thing left to do now is to tell me where and when this meeting will take place."

"That is the easy part my dear. He is, at this very moment, outside this establishment. He is sitting in my carriage, waiting for me to finish up a small piece of urgent business, before we attend a luncheon together. You see my dear, Leone is also a client of mine, as well as a friend; has been for years. That is how I was able to arrange the circumstances, so that we were on our way to lunch, when I had to stop here. Rather convenient don't you think? Seemed to me that you would concur with my findings and so Madam, if you would like, we might get this meeting over with. Shall I send for him?"

Tori looked at Jean and then down at the floor. Things were going so fast. What would she say to him, and how? One thing was clear; putting off the inevitable would not make it any easier. Something that Jean and Mr. Grymes must have known she might do, why else would they have arranged it all this way? She took a deep breath. "Might as well get it over with," she said looking towards Jean. "You will stay with me won't you?"

"Now where else would I go? I intend to be right by your side so don't worry. John here seems to feel that this Leone fellow is of a decent sort, very unlike his brother. I think we will find an ally in Leone."

John broke into their conversation, standing up and walking towards the door, "my thoughts exactly." He stopped and looked back at them both, "The only way I see it, is to beat this Edward at his own game. To stay a step ahead. Take the wind out of his sails before he even gets going." He was all but laughing. "Fancy me trying to tell you how to sail a plan. I think it better if I stay with land locked terms, funny that, sails and land locked..."

He left the room in good humor and still mumbling to himself. Mr. John Grymes it seemed was obviously enjoying himself.

The room fell silent, as the two of them waited for his return. Tori was trying desperately to make up some sort of a speech, explaining to Leone what had happened.

Jean paced the floor, going over every detail in his mind and the consequences of what they were about to do. Once Leone saw Tori, then her cover of Victoria would be lost. In essence, they would be at Leone's mercy, as well as those of his brother. His only hope lay in John and Tori's judgment of character.

"Just thought it would be nice if you could step in and meet them both. Such good friends of mine, least I can do, sort of make amends for delaying our lunch so long. Here we are, Mr. Laffite, Mrs. Laffite, may I present to you both, my trusted friend Mr. Leone Duval."

Jean's pacing around the room had placed him between Leone and Tori. So it was, that Leone walked forward and took Jean's hand first. It was a firm grip that Jean felt and the man looked him directly in the eyes, a positive trait as far as he was concerned. If first impressions counted, then he knew he liked what he saw. It was Jean who led him over to where Tori was standing and as the two came face to face, his arm slipped protectively around her waist.

Leone took her hand and lightly kissed the back, all the time looking strangely at her face.

"Is something wrong?" Tori had said the words slowly and directly, she did not avoid his close scrutiny. She knew to try to avoid him now would be senseless. Leone could not be sure so he shook his head, as if to clear the images he had in his mind.

"Please forgive a foolish man his manners. I do not normally stare at someone in such a manner as to cause them embarrassment."

"Especially, when their husbands are so close at hand," added Jean. He was trying to make light of the situation, something that John picked up on. The tension was broken when he added to the conversation.

"I would say not! Especially when that husband is Jean Laffite, the notorious pirate, n'est pas?" He laughed and looked at Jean's stern face. "It is what some of the fair citizens of the city are calling you, you know?"

Everyone laughed and the room took on a whole new atmosphere, one of friendship and warmth.

"I feel I should offer an explanation for my behavior, before your husband calls me out. It is just that you remind me of someone who was once very dear to me. Madame Laffite, you look so very much like her."

The sadness in his eyes hurt her, she could not delay telling him who she was any longer; it was too cruel. But how she thought? Then without fully realizing how she was doing it, or where the words were coming from, she spoke softly to him.

"I am known as Victoria to most, but to a few I am Tori. You are right Leone. Your eyes do not deceive you, I am she."

Leone froze. The stunned look upon his face stayed as he turned towards John.

"I think John, you had best explain what's going on here. This is not just a chance meeting is it?"

Tori could hear the anger in his tone of voice. They should have told him whom he was to meet, not handle it this way. Still what was done, was done. She would have to make him realize that John was not the only one responsible for this blunder.

"Forgive me Leone. It's not how it looks. This is not a cruel joke, played for our amusement. John is our friend and we have asked for this meeting for a very good reason. Please, give us a chance. Join us for lunch and we will explain everything?"

Tori had reached out her hand to Leone and when it touched him, he thought he would die. His Tori was alive! Very much alive and nothing else mattered. His anger was quickly overshadowed by his joy.

Over the next few hours, Jean and Tori made a decision to take Leone and Jean's attorney, into their full confidence. They could see no other way around the problem, of answering all the questions that arose. In order to be protected, she had to be believed, and to do that, the truth had to come out, all of it. After many hours of discussion, the room was still. The four of them sat silently looking at one another.

"Leone, do you see now, why I had to keep the truth from you about where I came from? You're having a hard time believing me this minute. If I had told you back then, the whole story, you would never have believed me, would you?"

"Tori, you should have trusted me. I wish you had. Never would I have let anything happen to you. I do admit, that I might not have believed you at first, but you seem to have won over quite a few people with your account. You would have convinced me in time. Your physical appearance alone, the change would have accomplished that by itself. One just can't go from, forgive me my dear, black to white. Here you sit before me, with proof my eyes cannot deny. You're skin color. Your hair. These changes would have occurred anyway. I would have had no choice but to believe you. I had very strong feelings for you. You knew that. I still do. I must admit, but seeing you here with Jean, his wife. Even a blind old fool can see you are happy not to mention carrying his child. It never would have worked for us, would it?" He stood and walked towards the French doors, his back towards them. "Please forgive me for rambling? It's just been a shock seeing you again, and finally learning what occurred at the plantation. Not knowing what happened to you, that was the hardest you know? But now, finding out that my own brother had a big hand in the whole damnable mess, it is unforgivable. I shall give you any and all assistance you might ask of me. But never will I find it in my heart to forgive Edward for what he has done!"

"Can I take it then, that you believe us?" Tori's face was expressing her relief and joy, as she already knew his answer would be positive.

He turned to face them. "You already know that I believe in you, but I have to tell you, on this matter of time travel, I'm having some difficulty, it does take some getting used to. We will have so much to talk about; so much I would like to know. Ah, I have jumped ahead of myself, that is, if I am allowed to pay you and your husband visits in the future, as a friend to both of you that is."

"Of course you may, she said smiling. She knew that Jean would not mind; he had taken her hand in his and nodded his approval. "But be warned I may not answer all your questions. Some things should remain untold. I don't want to have the responsibility of having changed anything. Just coming here to your time, I have done enough of that already I fear."

"Who is to say. You may well have been destined to come here my dear. I just wish I had known. I could have helped you. I feel it's my fault that you had to suffer so. I have always felt Edward knew more than he let on about Kate's death and your disappearance. I can't say that I'm sorry, that the beast I had working for me is dead. Beast is the only way I will ever refer to that nasty piece of work, after what I learned about him and his actions." He walked over to Tori and sat next to her, looking directly into her eyes. "However, it does seem clear to me, that the only one who could have killed Kane, was Edward! He has taken another human's life and as despicable as that life was it did not give him the right. Then he tried to manipulate your life through lies and intimidation. That is the lowest! And for his actions I apologize. I give you my word, that he will harm you no more. He will pay for this!"

Leone was angry and hurt. It was clear he was far too emotional to think rationally. John had to act quickly for all their sakes. "Now the way I see it, we have to go carefully. The law would be on his side at the moment. It would be his word against Tori's and forgive me my dear, but your story would not hold up too well in a court of law. Also, there are many in town, who would see this situation as a golden opportunity, a chance to strike at Jean. That Claiborne chap for one, dying to get on the merchant's good list, he is. No, I think it best Leone, if none of us says or does anything for the moment. Just sit and wait a while. Sort of see what young Edward's going to do next. Rather like a good game of cards, wouldn't you say?"

Leone shook his head, he knew his brother too well and knew that the time to strike was now, or he might very well harm the one woman that meant all to him. Even if Tori could never be his, he would see to it that she stayed happy and free. He could always admire her from a distance and be there for her.

"No, I firmly disagree! Let me face him and as soon as possible. He must be stopped. I'm sure he knows just who you are my dear, and knowing him as I do, he will try to use the information for his own gain. This emotional blackmail has to stop and stop now! He slammed one fist into the other. "I will put the fear of God into him, along with the law," he looked at John. Then turning his attention to Jean he continued. "Not to mention Jean, your reputation is well known and feared as much as respected."

Tori smiled, as the three men nodded their heads together in agreement very pleased with themselves. Right away they started making plans, on how best to deal with Edward.

As the four of them planned, across town in another house, two figures frolicked in bed, enjoying each other and the pleasures that they found together.

Edward had indeed found his dream come true. His luck it seemed was about to change. No, it had already changed, for in his arms, was what he considered, the ultimate catch. She was going to be the answer to all his monetary problems. Simone was not too young, about his age. She was very pretty to look at and she was married to a dying old fool. A rich, far richer than Leone, dying old fool! Looking at the woman he held he knew he would tell her anything, in order to keep her. Why, he would even tell her he loved her, when he knew he did not. It was then Edward made up his mind to do whatever was necessary to win her. He didn't need to have her love he told himself. He knew what kind of female she was, a scheming manipulator, like himself. That however was just where the similarities stopped. Unlike himself, she needed to hear terms of endearment, to feel loved. Slyly he grinned to himself. He was very good at knowing what to say and sound very convincing. Edward was not about to let this new golden opportunity slip through his fingers. The way her husband was failing, she would no doubt be a very rich widow in the very near future and he, Edward Duval, would be there to console her. He would of course have to give her time to grieve, not too long though, and then he would make her Madame Duval.

That would be only the beginning. Her money would be ample to live on, to gamble and enjoy the lifestyle of the grand plantation owner. He looked at her lying beside him. Ah, to have a woman such as this to come home to every night. She was a vixen in bed as well as a woman who was respected., but one that he had no doubt he could keep in her place, unlike that Tori bitch. He frowned as he thought of her. Oh yes, he had remembered who Victoria Laffite was. There was no doubt in his mind. How she had managed to get where she was, married to Jean Laffite and loved by all New Orleans society, was beyond him. Then, there was that other puzzling matter, the color of her skin, she almost looked white? How she had accomplished that, there could only be one explanation as far as he could tell. It was said that Marie Laveau had fixed her hair, something else that had taken on a new look, longer and straighter. Marie was known as the one who could do that voodoo magic. Yes, voodoo had something to do with it. Fear of the voodoo caused him to shiver slightly. He would have to go slowly and very carefully to obtain all he wanted. Simone would help him, Simone and her money. When he thought of all the money Tori had cost him. All the gold that he had paid for her upkeep, while he waited to have her. That was something else he had lost also, his chance of bedding her. But now he could make her pay. He would have her yet.

If things got messy, well he would simply destroy her, kill her if that's what it took. The woman in his arms, would be there to take the blame, if need be. Let it look as if it were Simone, the jealous wife. Yes, then the voodoo and Laffite would not get him, Simone would hang and he would be a rich man.

Smiling at her now, he reached up and pushed back Simone's hair. She was beautiful to look at, how the fool Laffite could let her go was beyond him. Still it was his gain, and anyway Laffite already had enough power and money.

"What are you thinking about Edward? You seem to be miles away from here. Do I bore you so?" She pouted.

"How could you think such a thing my love? It's just your beauty, takes my breath away. I was thinking without you it would be the end of my life. I love you so my Simone and you were meant for me. I can bring you such joy, if you let me. Such a small price to pay for happiness."

His mouth covered hers before she could answer him and the passion, with which he now kissed her, was no act. It was true passion, driven by his lust for wealth and power.

Simone on the other hand, went through their love making, as if it were a mechanical duty. He was so wrapped up in his own pleasure Edward did not notice. True, when his mind was not elsewhere and he paid more attention to her needs instead of his own, he was a very good lover. But he was not Jean. No one could ever be Jean or take his place. The one person she wanted more than any other in her life had been stolen from her.

Victoria. What a lie! Edward had told her everything that first night, when they had been together at her husband's plantation house. While her husband slept upstairs, drugged by his medication and brandy, she had let Edward in. They had made such love that night, and in the heat of his passion, he had talked the fool. He had spilled it all before he passed out. Just how she was going to use the information she did not know yet. What she did know however, was that she would keep using this fool. Edward helped fill the lonely nights and feed her sexual hunger. But more that that, he could help her to either get Jean back or destroy him. If she could not have him, then no one would. It was very clear to her, she wanted Jean and for her own reasons, and Edward wanted that Tori bitch. If she were careful, they both might get what they wanted.

A sharp pain raced up her thigh, bringing her attention back to where she was and what she was doing. He seemed to instinctively know what she wanted and that was to feel pain. The sadistic side in her enjoyed it when it was added it to their lovemaking. No one, not even Jean had known this about her. She would miss Edward, when she had to end their relationship and she had no doubt, that she would do just that when the time suited her. As for now, she would enjoy herself and hope her husband would die soon. She was going to need more freedom to come and go, along with his money, if she was going to succeed.

"Edward if you bite me one more time, I will have to spank you and if I do that, then you will get angry at me. You will have to show me what a naughty girl I've been. Only this time Edward darling, really spank me hard."

A sadistic smile came over Edward, as he put his head down and placed his mouth once again on her thigh. This afternoon was going to be a lot more fun than he had imagined. Maybe he would not get rid of her after they were married. Maybe he would really show her who the boss was in this relationship."

Outside the door, a man stood silently listening to them, his face sad and broken, tears filling his eyes, as he turned and walked slowly and painfully back to his room. By the time he had reached his bed, Adrian was beyond hurt; he was filled with a hateful revenge. He sent immediately for his attorney and asked to be left alone until he arrived. He had been told Simone did not want to be disturbed as she was resting! Lies, all Lies he thought.

"Why, Simone? Why did you do this to me? I had thought all along that you loved me and that you were truly mine. But by God, no you were not! You lied to me and now you lay in your room, like a common whore, bedding down some young man, who no doubt thinks that once I am gone, will have you and my money. Hell no! It won't happen!" he shouted.

Adrian grabbed at his chest and sat heavily in his bedside chair. Sheer willpower would keep him alive now. He was close to death and he knew it, but not until he had made a new will would he allow himself the pleasure of dying. He knew, that Monsieur Grymes would come, as soon as he got word that he was summoned. Why had he been so stubborn and not listened to his dear friend? He had been made a fool of. His anger was causing the pain in his chest and he cared not. He would show them he was no fool. He knew what had to be done. He would get the young houseboy to find out the name of his wife's lover. And he would see to it that neither of them got a penny of his fortune...

Tori lay in bed watching Jean as he poured her a cup of black coffee, topping it off with thick rich cream. She was glad that he had invited Leone to dinner last night. She had wanted to spend some time with him, try to explain how she felt. It had been obvious to everyone involved that he was still in love with her and she had never wanted to hurt him. Jean was so good; he had realized the two of them needed to be left alone and had offered to accompany John on his ride to his office. One of John's clients had conveniently summoned him. John's houseboy had known where to find him, but all of John's papers were in his office and so it had worked out for all.

Leone and Tori spent the next hour talking and healing. For Leone it was a very special time, one he would always hold dear. He learned how Kate knew about Tommy before her death and that pleased him. He knew he was the boy's father but until now, he had not really cared. Tori did more than give him pride in his son. She gave him a part of her heart by telling him he would always be very special to her. This was something far more than he could have hoped for. She told then, of how she had very strong feelings for Jean but of the deal she had with him.

"So you see Leone, before I can allow myself to love freely here in this time, I have to know, beyond a shadow of a doubt, that I can never reach my own time again. Only then will I be able to love and live here, free of guilt."

"What guilt can there be? As I see it, you have no need to feel that way my dear?"

"Oh, but I do. My whole life is not really here. I still have a family, who must be so worried. I owe it to them and to myself to try once, to get back to them. Don't you see, I not only let myself down but them also, if I don't try?"

"So you will try, after the baby is born? You will come to the plantation and the lake?"

"Yes I will. I have to and now that you know, I hope you will help me when the time comes?"

"You only have to ask. Anything I can do for you, no matter how hard it will be for me, I will do it. You will of course be my guest at the plantation, along with Jean. I would have it no other way and if you should succeed and return to your time, then you have my word as a Gentleman and friend, that Jean and your child will become my family. I shall stand by them always."

Tori remembered this part of the conversation over and over in her mind. Jean would not be alone, should she make it back. He would have friends and he would have their child. Leone would always look after them. Jean at least would know that she had made it back and would have that comfort. If she did not make it, her Linni would never know what happened to her. She would go on suffering the rest of her life and the mystery would never be solved.

Jean was handing her the cup of coffee. It did his heart good to see her relaxed and not worrying about Edward. For weeks she had brooded over him, waiting for the Governor to send his troops to drag her away, for a crime she did not commit. Leone had been a good friend to them, and he had enjoyed his company. He did feel for him though. It was plain to see how he felt about his Tori. Could he have been so gracious, if the boot was on the other foot? He did not know. If she were to go back to her time, then he would find himself very much like Leone. She could end up with another man; he would no longer have her.

A knock at the door caught them both by surprise and they were even more shocked when they were told they had a visitor downstairs, one who urgently requested their appearance. It was a Monsieur John Grymes, and both of them knew that he must have very important news, to come calling so early.

He was sitting calmly in a chair sipping on a cup of coffee and looking extremely tired. He did not seem worried or upset in any way.

"Good morning to the both of you. I am so sorry to drop in like this but some developments have arisen, pertaining to our case. I thought you both needed to know about it right away."

Tori was far more concerned by the haggard look of her attorney, than by any news he might have. He looked as if he were about to have a stroke or something and one could not just dial 911 for help could they?

Her voice full of concern she asked him gently, "John, you look as if you have not had a moment's sleep, does this have anything to do with your client, the one that sent for you last night?"

"Oh dear, please forgive the way I look Tori. You don't mind if I call you Tori, do you? I know you won't. It's just that I have been up all night, like you said, and yes, it was with a client. He wanted his will rewritten, seems he found out that his wife was not as faithful as he had thought. He died shortly after the completion of the new document. I have full instructions to read it directly after his funeral. The problem is my client was someone we knew Jean, it was Adrian La Combe."

Jean stood there for a moment and just stared at John. Was he telling him that Adrian had found out about his affair with his wife? Had Simone told him? He had liked Adrian and it had never been his intent, to hurt the old man by having an affair with his wife. Indeed, he thought that bit of information would be safe from public knowledge, but now?

"The thing is Jean, that before he died, he learned the identity of his wife's lover and wanted to make sure, that he got not one penny of his money." John saw the shocked look upon Jean's face and quickly raised his hand as if trying to stop Jean's obvious conclusion. "It's Edward Duval," he hastily added. "You could have knocked me over with a feather. I did not even know that the two of them were acquainted. Anyway the will, and I can't really go into it with you. You do understand? The will is quite clear. I can tell you this much however, and that is Simone will be left very little." He hesitated before going on. "The only reason I'm here now is because of Edward. One of the servants, a decent Irish butler, confided in me. He had heard your name Jean, along with Tori's, several times. The servant seems to think that the two of them, Edward and Simone that is, were planning something no good, as he put it. What do you make of all this?"

Jean stood there and rubbed his chin, an act he did unconsciously when he was deep in thought, or worried. He was not sure what to think. But one thing was certain, and that was Simone had become dangerous. To be left without the fortune she thought she was getting, and to have an affair made public, would to her be intolerable. Her humiliation and resentment would get the best of her. She could very easily make her past affair with Jean public knowledge, standing to lose nothing in so doing. Then if she knew anything about Tori, that would put her in a very deadly position. If Simone had to fall, she would not go down alone. Edward on the other hand was obviously a fortune hunter. He must have set his sights on her forthcoming money. Now both of them were about to lose and that multiplied the danger. For himself he did not care, but he would not allow Edward and Simone to hurt Tori in any way. This was something he had to avert.

"Seems to me, we have until the reading of the will, to get to Edward. Time is no longer on our side. We must act and act fast. I'm involved in this now John. It won't be only Tori they will want to discredit. No, they will want more. They will want to destroy us both! Simone's involvement changes that." A puzzled look clouded Jean's face. "You don't seem shocked my friend."

John frowned. "I'm not. Forgive me. It may not be common knowledge; you're past activities that is, pertaining to a certain married lady. But I do my own investigating you know? Only I do it to help, to be ready, to protect my client's interest you understand? Especially if that client is a good friend. Once again forgive me if I overstepped my bounds but I have known for some time about you and Simone." Then realizing what he had just said in front of Jean's wife he turned to her. God help him. He had just let the cat out of the bag and had to put things right. "Tori, I assure you that Jean is dedicated to you and you alone. This unfortunate affair of his took place long before you entered his life. This I swear to you on a Gentlemen's honor."

"Calm yourself I know that John. I have also known for some time about Simone. So let's not worry about that. What I want to know is, what do we do now?"

Jean answered first. "We send for Leone and we make our move with Edward today. That my lady is what we do. Edward will be easy; the hard part will be Simone. She is going to be like a storm at sea. So calm at first, then so vicious!" He spoke this last word with such description, that it caused Tori to audibly inhale. With her gasp, he could see he had alarmed her and set out to quickly make amends. "Don't worry my lady, this old sea Captain has weathered many storms and I will never allow any storm, man-made or natural, to get the better of me."

Leone had been staying at John's townhouse and was easily summoned. It took him no time at all to arrive at Jean's and before the hour was up, the small group had told him he would have to confront his brother that very day and why...

Leone and John found themselves outside of John Davis's establishment not two hours later. Edward had rented a small set of rooms upstairs around the back of the hotel and would most likely still be there at this time of day. Just what Leone was going to say to his brother, was somewhat of a problem? He knew that for Tori's sake he had to reach him, making it quite clear that she and Jean were off limits.

"I'll go up first John. We'll do it as planned. Let's just hope that it works."

"I see no reason why it shouldn't. It has been my experience that men like your brother can be dealt with, if you handle it right." He grinned at his old friend and gave him a slap on the back, John did not like the fact that Edward had to be dealt with in this manner, but what choice did they have? Leone was their only hope of reaching the bastard.

Leone knocked at the door and waited calmly for Edward to answer. However the longer he waited, the more impatient he became and his temper was slowly rising.

After what seemed an eternity, Edward finally opened his door and was very surprised to see his older brother standing there. Leone was obviously very agitated, a sight that caused Edward's surprise to quickly evaporate and suspicion take over.

"To what do I owe the pleasure of this visit and at such a damnable hour too, if I might add?" He asked sarcastically.

"This is no time to become insolent and if you know what's best, you would allow me to enter." Leone took a step forward while continuing in a firm but controlled voice. "That is if you don't want the whole of New Orleans to hear what it is I have to say, and believe me dear brother, you don't."

Before Edward could respond, Leone simply pushed his way into the small room.

"Please, by all means enter and make yourself at home dear brother." He slurred. "I am afraid I can't offer you anything to drink, unless you would like some brandy?" The disgusted look on Leone's face made him laugh as he bitterly continued. "At this hour? I thought not. You're such an upstanding Gentleman aren't you? You don't touch the stuff before sunset, how could I forget?"

"Edward, if you don't shut up, I just might take it upon myself to beat the living daylights out of you, and believe you me, I have wanted to do just that for a very long time."

"My, my aren't we in a testy mood today? What's got you so riled up, or do I want to know? If you are here to give me another one of your so-called lectures about my conduct and the family name, you can quite simply, go to hell," he spat.

That was the final stroke. Leone was beyond holding his temper. This so-called brother of his had pushed him too far. Not only had he brought out Leone's anger but his contempt as well. Before Edward could duck out of the way, Leone had connected a full forced blow to his chin, followed by another to his midsection that sent him flying across the small room. He slammed up against the wall, hitting his head and slipping the short distance down to the floor unconscious.

Leone looked at him for a moment; all he could see was a person that he despised. How they could have come from the same womb, be raised by the same parents and turn out so very different was beyond him? He had loved his younger brother at one time, but that seemed a lifetime ago. Looking at him lying there on the floor half-naked, bleeding from the corner of his mouth, Leone could not help but feel pity at what he had become.

He looked around for some water and seeing nothing that even came close, he walked to the other room. This small enclosure served as the bedroom, and it too was such a mess that Leone was about to give up, when he spied a pitcher over on a small table by the window. It was almost hidden from view, by the dirty clothes that lay where they had been thrown at some time or another. Carefully he picked his way around the obstacle course and retrieved the half-full pitcher. He returned to the front room and then very slowly and deliberately, poured the contents onto his brother's head.

Edward's reaction was instantaneous. Swearing and spitting blood from his mouth, he regained consciousness. Painstakingly he pushed his body to a sitting position and watched Leone through half-closed eyes.

Leone walked over to the far side of the room and pulling open the curtains, he swore out loud, as he opened the windows. "God damn it. This hell hole smells like old whiskey, dirty women and low living. How can you live like a pig? To be in such dirt and still try to remain a Gentleman. I cannot for the life of me fathom how you do it? What did you do, gamble all your allowance away? I see to it that you have more than enough to live comfortably. There should be an ample amount left over after your expenses, to at least hire someone to come and clean, or do you enjoy living in such squalor?"

"If you are referring to that measly amount of money you allow me each month as enough, well I would like to see you live on it. If you don't like what you see, then may I suggest increasing the amount? Or do you enjoy forcing me, your own brother to live, how did you say, like a pig?"

"I did not come here to talk to you about your lifestyle. What you get is far more than you deserve. If you continued to push me Edward," he shot him a cold look full of warning, "I might very well stop the allowance altogether. In light of what I have learned in the past few days, it would not take much to get me to do just that. Do dear brother, I think it best if you close that sarcastic mouth of yours and pay attention to what I have to say!"

Edward could tell by the way his brother was talking that he had better stay quiet and let him have his say. He had heard it all before a thousand times, so there was no need to pay attention. Another lecture on the evils of gambling, was a small price to pay to get what he wanted. He would put up with Leone and his high and mighty ways, just so long as he could collect his allowance. He had to have it this week. He had to get himself cleaned up and get Simone to think of him as a Duval. In fact he might very well use this meeting to his advantage and win over Leone as well. If he admitted he had a problem, which he did not of course, and ask his forgiveness. Better still he could ask the one question he knew Leone had always hoped for, and that was could he come home to be a respectable Duval again? If that were to happen, it would ensure winning Simone's hand when her husband died. All that lovely money for the taking. No! He quickly rationalized. He had better stay in town; the plantation was too far away. Someone else might pay attention to her before him and he could never allow that to occur. Once he had Simone and her wealth, then he could tell Leone to take a long walk, hopefully to hell…

"So you see Edward, I have talked to Tori and I now know the whole sorry story. If you were not my brother, I would indeed turn you into the authorities myself for murdering Kane and kidnapping her."

Edward could not believe he had heard right? He had not been listening until her name came up. His face drained of all color and his breathing became short and fast, causing sharp pains in his side as he struggled to gain his composure. He had to think quickly. What had Leone said, damn it, he wished he had paid better attention and stopped daydreaming.

"You mean to tell me, that that black bitch has contacted you after all this time? She has told you a pack of lies. What does she really want? You back in her bed? More maybe, your money? It's her word against mine you know." Panic and lack of control over the situation was making him desperate. "I might be the one to go to the authorities myself. Have you thought of that? I see you have, why else would you be here? Yes, I can do that, they would believe me before her and even if they did not, her life would be ruined. I after all, have very little left to lose."

"You mean to tell me, besides everything else you are guilty of you would lower yourself to commit the act of perjury? You would deliberately try and get someone who is innocent, to take all the blame for a murder you committed?"

"Why not? I might even come out a hero if I play my cards right on this. There are many people who have wanted to get something on the Laffite's for some time and hiding an escaped black, who is wanted for murder, well..."

"How quick you forget Edward. She is not wanted for murder! Only for questioning."

"That would change rather fast, if I came forward, would it not?"

"You would do that wouldn't you?"

"Well maybe, maybe not. The way I see it, you want your precious little Tori to remain free and I need more, how do I say it? It would be nice to have a larger allowance for a short time, do we understand each other?"

"So now it's blackmail is it? On top of murder and lying, you are despicable. You are filth, worse than the dirt beneath my feet."

"Careful Leone. I don't see that you have much choice in the matter, now do you dear brother?"

"Well that is where you are very wrong. It is you who has no choice in the matter. I have not come empty-handed to this meeting. I am the one who will offer you a deal my baby brother. One that you will accept I am sure. You will not go anywhere or tell anyone of this matter. In exchange I will not report to the authorities as I would like to, that it was you who murdered Kane."

"You make me laugh Leone, do you not understand? Only you and Tori know I killed him. If you ask me, I did you a favor, the bastard deserved to die. As for Tori, the only witness. Ah well the authorities will not listen to a Nigger! If you do speak up, people will only think you want to protect your former mistress and destroy me. It's no secret in this town that our relationship borders on hate. Now once again, I ask you, who will listen to you? He laughed. "I fear you not and had best be paid well."

"No! I will not and that's final. You have hung yourself this time Edward. I told you. I did not come empty-handed to this meeting. What would you say, if I were to tell you that there was another witness to your admitted crime? To not only your blackmailing me but to your hand in murder. A witness who is not only white but highly respected? Yes, even by the authorities."

"I would call you a God damned liar!" He shouted. "You are only grabbing at straws. No one was around to see what I did. No one knows or they would have come forward long ago. You lose dear brother."

"No I don't, you do!" whispered Leone.

With that, Leone walked over to the door and opened it; you can come in now John. Let's see if we can't come to a little understanding shall we?

"John Grymes, Attorney at Law and the about-to-be-appointed U.S. District Attorney for Louisiana, at your service. I must say however, due to what I overheard just now, I am sorry to admit that I cannot represent you. I can however watch you hang!"

Edward realized he had been outmaneuvered. He was trapped and there was nothing he could do but listen to what they had to say and then abide by their wishes. He would get even with Leone for this and more. He would see to it that the bitch Tori suffered. Oh yes, they would pay for this humiliation, he would find a way...

Later that afternoon, Jean, Tori and Leone sat laughing and drinking champagne. The celebration was fully underway and Tori felt safe from Edward's clutches at last. He would not talk now or ever; he could not, for if he did, he ran the risk of paying for his crime of murder. Jean on the other hand, was not convinced they had won. True this round was theirs but unlike Leone and Tori he knew better than to let his guard down. He would have this Edward followed for a while longer and he would have to keep an eye on Simone also. After tomorrow's reading of Adrian's will, she was going to be as dangerous, if not more dangerous than Edward. She still had to be dealt with.

Upon hearing of the death of Simone's husband, Edward wasted no time in rushing to her side. He played the perfect Gentleman, trying only to comfort her, in her so-called time of need. This comfort was given in bed as the two of them lay side by side drinking and celebrating her newfound freedom.

Edward started laughing as he looked towards her. He could see that she cared not a damn about the sad news. Only that she was now very wealthy and free to do as she pleased.

"You will have to excuse me from laughing at you, it's just that you look so pleased with yourself and it somehow strikes me funny. All of New Orleans is sad and wondering how the devoted wife is holding up and here you lay, looking more ravishing than ever. In fact, I would dare say, that you are the happiest I have seen you. My, how you would shock some of those lady friends of yours. They would positively swoon at your behavior Madam."

"You had best be careful Edward. I am not all that cold hearted you know. I mean, I do kind of feel sorry for Adrian. After all, he was good to me but it goes deeper than that you know. Way deeper. I think that's why you and I understand each other. A common bond of sorts if that were what you would like to call it. My family has disinherited me. Thrown me out without a care, but never did they expect Adrian to marry me?"

"I'm sorry, I don't follow you. You did say your family disowned you? Are you exaggerating my dear? I mean, for what reason would they do such a thing? You must have been a very naughty girl," he kissed her cheek, "do tell."

Edward was rubbing her shoulders and caressing her body, paying attention to how she responded and keeping her talking. He was really interested in these new facts. It was common knowledge that her family did not seem to care what she was doing or where she was. Why hadn't it been rumored, that she was even snubbed by her own father at the last Governor's ball?

"You see Edward, I knew that father would leave all he had, the land and the title to my brother. All I would get would be married off to some idiot, who most likely would be less than desirable to my needs. So, at one of father's gatherings, I set out to find my own beau. Adrian was what I needed. He was older and very rich. Problem was he was also one of father's friends and considered me a little girl, nothing more. What was I to do? All those young fops falling all over me, when all they really wanted was my dowry and to get in good with my family...I could never allow myself to be packed off with the likes of one of them. So I seduced Adrian, making sure that we were found of course."

"Why you little minx, and by getting caught, you knew that your father would demand that Adrian marry you?"

"Well yes, that was what I had planned, but in fact it sort of went crazy. Father was so upset that he went quite out of his head. He said things to me that were quite cruel and not true, to say the least. Anyway, in the end, he had said far too much and I simply could not tolerate any of it. He threw me out literally. I was banned from anyone in the family and the house for good. It was as if and still is, that I am no daughter of theirs. Adrian must have felt that it was all his fault and we were married quietly and quickly, leaving right after the ceremony on a long honeymoon."

"It was on that honeymoon, that I realized, I had to get him to fall in love with me, to think of me as a devoted wife. I would end up very well off. I would not need my family of their money, now would I?"

Edward felt a new bond with Simone. He did know what it was like to be denied family, more so, money. Taking her in his arms he told her she would never have to be alone, that he understood and he would always be there for her.

"Now Edward, if I can only get that Tori bitch out of the picture, then Jean would be free of her and turn to me. Then you know what? I would teach him a thing or two. I would ruin him, bring him to his knees, then leave him."

She had a look of true hatred in her eyes. Her whole body had gone stiff, as she went on about getting even with the two of them and now she had the money and the power to do it.

"Simone, there is something I had best tell you first. For reasons that I shall explain to you, we have to do this a different way than we planned. You see, Tori is not wanted for murder as I had thought. Fact is, she is not wanted at all. If we go to the authorities, there is a good chance that I will be the one, through false incriminations and lies by my own brother, who you know hates me." He coughed at his next thought, it terrified him. "That yes, I would be the one to pay for the crime. It seems that my own brother wants me ruined, so the family fortune does not fall into my hands, should something happen to him. He can do it, trust me, he has Laffite's help on this."

Simone looked into his face and could see the fear and concern there. She believed he was telling the truth. Her Edward stood the chance of having to suffer like she had. Of having the humiliation of losing what is rightfully yours. And all because of that bitch and Laffite. How could she get that Nigger Tori out of Jean's life now? That alone was the one thing that would hurt him, losing his beloved. She would have to rethink it all. Simone did not want Jean or his money for herself any longer. She had all the money she wanted. No, what she wanted now was respectability and power. She wanted revenge against her family; to become something her father thought impossible. If she helped Edward, she might just end up Madame Simone Duval, mistress of one of the largest and most respected plantations along the Mississippi. The family's name was well-known and highly regarded. Edward and his family name were just the solution she needed. But how to go about it that was the question?

"Well what do you suggest we do? I want to teach Jean a lesson and you want his wench, how do we do it? We have nothing on them that we can use, or can we?"

"I'm not sure but we will find a way, let's bide our time. After all, we have all the time in the world don't we and tomorrow you will have all the money you need and me, to help you through your sorrow."

The two of them laughed at this. They were becoming much more than cold calculating lovers. They were becoming close friends who needed each other and thought they knew just where the other stood…

Edward watched as she dressed for the funeral. He had not left her side once since arriving the day before and he was not so certain that he should let her go by herself even now.

"Are you sure that you don't want me to come along, to support you, in your hour of grief?"

"I'm quite sure, let's not start people talking. If you escorted me, it would not look good you know. Let's just do this as it should be done. Some of Adrian's friends are coming by for me, the doctor also. I have asked him to accompany me, as I feel too weak and distraught to go alone. Nice touch don't you think?"

Edward smiled at her; "You are quite an actress. Tell me how will you play out your roll at the reading of his will?"

"Well, I am not going to attend and clap my hands that's for sure. It will be hard not to smile though, guess I'll have to swoon." She dramatically raised her hand to her forehead and demonstrated for him, the little scene she had in mind. "I shall say, I never knew he was so rich. After all I married him because I loved him so. Married him, against my family's wishes, giving up all claim to them, for the love of my dear husband."

"Now don't over do it, you have to be believed. I mean we don't want people getting the wrong idea. You go overboard with this and they may think that you're acting. After all, you have to stay in good graces with New Orleans society. That's the only way we will keep track of Laffite and Tori."

"Yes, yes I know all that and don't worry. I will have to decline all invitations for a while you know, out of respect and I will have a period of mourning. What a way to mourn, here in bed with you." She wrapped her arms around him. "Maybe I'll have to mourn for quite sometime."

He untangled himself from her embrace and pushed her away frowning. "You had best finish dressing or you will be late. And I will run a few errands that I need to. You can count on me being here tonight though," he winked at her. "We will celebrate together and you can tell me in detail, all that happens today."

He was enjoying this; his high spirits and confidence in Simone only served to strengthen her determination to successfully carry out her charade.

"You do know, that Jean will most likely be there at the funeral? He did know Adrian, did he not?"

"He did, why I had not thought of that. I really do have something to look forward to. If I can convince him, that I truly am in mourning, then the rest will be easy."

"My, how you do love challenges, my beautiful, wonderful lover. Such an actress, such a face," he held her face between his two hands looking at her closely. "No one would guess you to be anything other than a very sad woman. Hiding your true emotions is not easy to do, but let me be the one to inform you, you are an expert at it. Let me teach you the game of cards sometime. I feel that you would do very well." Picking her up he swung her around the room.

She playfully pushed him away and smiling coyly asked him to leave, so she might finish getting ready. He kissed her long and hard, then left, careful to use the back way, lest he be seen. Soon he would come in the front entrance and no one would care. It would be his right to do so, but for now they had to keep their affair a secret.

Simone placed white powder on her face, just enough to make her look as if she were truly ill with sorrow. Then, remembering how that girl Marie Laveau had told her, she rubbed in the darker powder, under her eyes, just enough to give the no-sleep look. She had sent for the girl yesterday and late last night while Edward slept, she had met with her. It had cost her all that she had hidden away, for both the spells and the know how of applying the right make-up. This voodoo stuff came with a high price, but worth it. What did she care anyway? She would soon have all the money she could ever need.

The drops were the hardest. The girl had told her only two for each eye. They would burn and make her eyes red, causing them to water for at least four hours. She would look as if she were crying, as if she had been crying for a long time. This was something that she required if she were to pull off this act of hers. She had not asked what the drops were, just that they were safe and would not do any permanent harm. Marie had told her, if she followed her directions, she would be fine. The drops had been such a stroke of genius; she was so clever she had thought of everything. Even if Marie were to tell anyone that her tears had been bought, it would be too late. They were going to produce the effect she needed. She doubted the girl would tell, but had thought of an excuse if she did. She would simply say that she could not cry. Try as she might she had not been able to grieve. Then fearing for her health, she had sought out Marie, in hopes of her being able to have a potion that could help her. Marie, she would tell them, had helped her and the tears they saw were real. Once she started to cry, she simply could not stop. With the drops in her eyes, she quickly became aware of how true that statement would be.

The sky was overcast and gray, a light wind blew making it unusually cold for this time of the year and the weather seemed to befit such a somber occasion as a funeral. She could not believe how everything was working her way. If she were truly lucky though, it would start to rain during the service. How positively wonderful of God to be on her side. God she thought, huh! He had nothing to do with it at all. She did not believe in God or praying. Oh no, she believed in making things happen. Adrian had believed in God, and look at him now. Where had his beliefs gotten him?

Adrian's attorney had made all the arrangements that had been Adrian's wish. Simone had not protested. She was glad that someone else had to perform the mundane task and deal with the church. The spot where his remains were to be laid to rest, was alongside the rest of his family, in a large white marble mausoleum. She made a mental note then, that it be written down somewhere, that she would have her own crypt built. No way was she going in there, with him and his family.

The Catholic Bishop held the service instead of the parish priest, not unusual for someone like Adrian, who through the years had been so good to the church. Simone sat thinking while waiting for the service to begin and did not pay any attention to what was really happening. Looking around the church she told herself she would have to remember to see to it, that the annual allowance Adrian gave, be cut back at first then stopped all together. What right did the church have to any of her money anyway?

The choir had stopped singing and the service began in earnest. So then did her act. She was for all purposes, the young grieving widow and many women of society came to her side but try as they might, they just could not seem to console her, or stop the flow of silent tears that ran down her face. Even the doctor was concerned about the way she looked. Truly in shock, he had told several people around him. He then made a point to make it clear that he would under the circumstances be the one to accompany her to the cemetery.

She knew she was good at acting and the people were unwittingly playing their part also. Why she actually found herself liking all the attention, bringing a slight smile to her lips. She might have slipped at that point but caught herself. Out of the corner of her eye, she saw Laffite watching her, and she reminded herself, that to convince him she was truly in mourning would be the final coup de Gras.

Jean had been observing her, staying clear out of her view, not wanting her to know she was under any kind of scrutiny. He knew that he would have to pay his respects to the widow before he left. He would rather not let her see him until the end and then he would make it short and sweet. The longer he delayed going and talking to her, the more time he had to scrutinize her. At first he could not believe the act she was putting on with all the people believing her to really be the grief-stricken widow. How could they be so stupid? She really did deserve credit for pulling this off he told himself. But then, as he made his way closer towards her, he could see the tears that fell freely down her ashen face. She looked terrible, as if she had been crying all night. Even through the widow's veil he could see the dark circles under her eyes. Then there was the way she stood, bent and shaken. Could it be that he was wrong about her? Could the cold-hearted Simone, really have cared about Adrian?

The graveside service was over and the rain that had held off until then began to lightly fall. The people were quickly departing, many of the women, saying how they would drop in on her and see how she was doing. Some of the older friends of Adrian's were telling her, that she was not alone in her hour of grief as they too would stop by. Jean overheard two saying, that it was a crime. No a sin, nothing less, that her own family still had not forgiven her for marrying Adrian and not even attended the funeral. They promised each other that Simone would not be alone, that they would see to it that the women of New Orleans took the place of her own family. It was the least they could do for Adrian's grieving widow.

Jean reached her at last, the doctor was telling her that it was time to leave and that he thought it best if she went home instead of to the reading of the will. He was truly concerned about her health; she was just too overwrought he told her. She simply shook her head and told him that it would not be any easier to go later. She would rather get it over with, and then be left alone for a while to grieve her loss.

Jean stood before her; she looked up into his eyes and then lowered her tear soaked lashes as she spoke. "Thank you for coming Jean. Adrian would have liked to know that you considered him your friend. He was very fond of you." She looked back at him and tried to smile through her tears that continued to fall slowly down her cheeks. The dark drape of fine lace could not hide the fact that she was still crying, or the way she looked. He was really concerned for her, reaching out Jean touched her arm.

"I am sorry Simone, for everything."

"Me too Jean. I am going to miss him so. I am going to be all alone now, but then maybe that is the price I am to pay for all my evils."

She started to cry now and instead of going to Jean she fell into the very concerned arms of the old doctor. It was he who insisted that he accompany her to the attorney's office, if that's where she was determined to go.

Jean watched them as they left and feeling really low for thinking the worst about her he headed home to tell Tori. He did feel sorry for Simone because if indeed she were that upset and he felt now that it was no act, then what she was about to find out, would hit her really hard.

Once in the carriage, Simone turned her head to face away from the doctor and she smiled. She had succeeded. Jean had bought her act. Falling into the doctor's arms, instead of Jean's had been pure inspiration! What a touch. That had been the crowning glory. Hell, she hoped her eyes would clear up soon. The burning was easing some but the watering was still causing her to have to wipe her face continually and it was becoming irritating. Now for the last act of the day, this was going to be the fun part. God, how she hoped Jean felt bad, how she hoped he went home to his Nigger wife and told her how sorry he felt for Simone. If she had been alone in the carriage at that point, she might actually have laughed out load.

The rain had started to fall heavily and the roads ran with muddy water, like little rivers. The doctor was commenting on the fact, that the Mississippi would overflow her banks again if the weather did not improve. Flooding he explained, only meant sickness and more work for him. She did not answer him and he shook his head. The weather was reflecting the somber mood of his beautiful patient, who sat so still and sad beside him. Little did he realize that her stillness and quiet, was the only way she could contain her high spirits?

She had to remain the grieving widow for just a short time longer. How she wished they could get to the office of the attorney and get the formalities over with. She felt like celebrating. Oh she could just imagine the evening that lay ahead of her and Edward.

It was if she was thinking about being at the attorney's one minute and actually there the next. Simone did not like John Grymes much, and the quicker she could get out of his office the better. It would give her great pleasure to take all her money and business somewhere else. She had a long memory where he was concerned. Sure he had been polite to her whenever they met, but she knew that he did not like her one bit. He had almost talked Adrian out of marrying her in the first place. It must be killing him now she thought. He was sitting there pretending to be so smug, knowing that in a very short while she would become the sole heir to Adrian's estate. And there was not a damn thing he could do about it. She turned her head away from him briefly and grinned with pure joy at that thought. Then taking a deep ragged breath she turned back to face the attorney.

John looked at Simone and saw a very sad young lady. But unlike Jean, he was convinced that it was an act. She made him feel physically sick. However he would go along with her little charade for a little longer. It was going to be quite something to see how she would react to the news. He was going to thoroughly enjoy this.

"The circumstances of Adrian's will, are shall we say, a little out of the ordinary. He requested a few stipulations be met before the reading. One was that a doctor be here, which I see we already have. The other, that the Mother Superior also be present. So if you would excuse me, I will just go into the outer office and escort her in."

As strange as it was, Simone still had no idea of what was about to happen. She imagined that Adrian, being a God-fearing man his whole life, had left the church some money, the fool. It was her money he was giving away, but then as long as it was not too much, it didn't really matter. Why it might help her position if she insisted that a modest sum of course, in her dearly departed husband's name, be added to the amount for the convent. It could never hurt to have the church on your side and word would spread of her good deed, winning over the doubting few. Yes, that was the perfect idea; she did feel as if everything was going very well. If only her eyes would stop this infernal watering, it really was truly beginning to infuriate her.

The doctor stood off to one side and Mother Superior sat in the chair next to Simone. The woman was short in stature but in her presence one did not notice this. The atmosphere she created could make one feel very small indeed and as if they had best confess their sins before her and God.

Simone found it a little difficult to look this woman in the eyes for fear that she would see the deception that lay hidden there.

"Now that we are all present, the time has come for me to do Adrian's bidding. Before we start, I would like to take this opportunity, to tell all of you; he was a dear friend of mine and one who will be missed. I would like to think that I was more than his attorney, that he considered me his friend." John was silent for a few seconds; he seemed to be reflecting on something, then he continued, "I think maybe he did, now down to matters. Simone, he asked me to request, if you would care to read the will yourself or if you would prefer me to do it for you? I know it is somewhat strange but he felt it might be easier for you this way."

Shaking her head no, Simone spoke softly and with a tremble in her voice. "Monsieur Grymes, my husband always tried to do what was best for me. However, I feel that in this case, if you would please read it aloud for me. I don't think that I could manage it at this time. You do understand?"

"If that is what you wish Madam, I will oblige you. It is very short; in fact it is simple and straightforward. I will start. I, Adrian Philippe La Comb…"

Simone found her stomach in a knot; this was it, what she had waited for all these years. What she had planned for from the very beginning and now here it was. It was going to be very hard not to show her satisfaction of finally winning.

"It is my wish therefore, that the following be administered to the last detail and complied with before a time period, of not more than six weeks after the reading of this my last will and testament. To Simone my wife, for everything she has done and only she knows, just what I am referring to by that. I do here by leave her the following. One, the townhouse on Royal Street with a staff of two servants, an allowance of…"

Simone wished he would just hurry up with the reading. To her he seemed to be enjoying himself, as if reading it so slowly gave him more self importance. Of course she would get the townhouse and an allowance to run it…

"She is to be allowed to furnish it with any articles from the Manor house in town. All and any personal articles, such as clothing and jewelry, are to be included. It will be up to her sole discretion as to what she wants to take. The remainder of the contents, the house, the household servants, the carriages and all other blacks and articles therein, are to be sold at public auction. My attorney John Grymes will oversee this project for me and see to it, that all the proceeds are given to Mother Superior and the Sisters of the St. Ursula Convent. The remainder of my estate, land, plantation house, slaves and all there in, are to go to my second cousin and his family, whom I contacted by letter and are at this present time, on route to assume their inheritance."

Grymes paused briefly here to look at Simone, to see if any of what he was saying was registering. He continued, "The running of such a large estate, would have been far too difficult for such a delicate woman, as my wife and I'm sure she knows why I have chosen to do what I have…"

Simone was paralyzed. If she understood what had just been said, then she was not the wealthy widow she had planned. There had to be some sort of mistake. There just had to be! Her blood was boiling and if she had not been in the presence of witnesses, she would have jumped across the table and destroyed all evidence of any such will. She had been a fool. Somehow it had all gone wrong, but now was not the time to make a scene, to do something that she might regret. No, she had to think. She had to cool off. She had to get out of there before she lost her temper!

"That is it then, like I said before, it's simple and straight forward. Are there any questions?" No one spoke and John had difficulty keeping a somber face as he observed Simone. She had gained a reddish color in her face, due to her raising temper no doubt, one that boiled inside her and was making her visibly tremble. He was watching her closely wondering what her next move would be. He had to admire her, for someone who had just lost a fortune, she was controlling her emotions very well. She stood calmly and quietly, turned and walked out of his office and into the street. How could he have done such a thing? The will had to be wrong, there had to be a later will, one leaving everything to her, like he had always told her he would. Adrian would never have humiliated her so; he had loved her! How could he have done such a cruel and bitter thing, and why?

Stamping her foot and letting her true emotions show she made up her mind right then and there. She was determined to fight it. Somehow she would get what was hers. She would not let all that wealth and money she had worked for slip away from her.

The doctor came to her side; he was really concerned for her health. The reading had been very strange. It was very clear that such a fine woman had really no way of living in the style she was accustomed to, not on such a small allowance. It hurt him to see such a devoted wife as she was cut out of so much. What had Adrian had in his mind when he wrote such a will? It made no sense to him. Why he had loved his wife and had been so proud of her, you could ask anyone.

"Doctor, I feel as if I have been hit with a bigger grief than his death. My poor husband, he must have been out of his mind when he wrote that will. Never would he have done such a thing." She grabbed his arm desperately continuing, "You must tell them he was sick, so sick he did not know what he was doing. Please, you saw him last; he was not well was he? He did not know what he was doing surely and has not done so for some time?"

"Quite the opposite Simone," John was standing there on the steps with Mother Superior. "He knew exactly what he was doing when he drew up the will. If you would step into my office, I will be happy to explain it all to you as best I can. Doctor, would you please be so kind as to escort the Mother Superior home? I will see to it that Madame La Comb gets home safely after our little chat." He took Simone by her arm and escorted her back towards the door. "Good day to you both. I will be in contact soon, now excuse us please. Madame La Comb needs to be inside, out of this weather, as do we all."

Once inside, Simone let go. She did not care what this idiot of an attorney thought of her and with no other witnesses to her temper tantrum; she just unleashed her pent-up rage. She spat out the words, while her eyes clawed at him like talons.

"You had something to do with all this, I know you did. Adrian never would have cut me off like this, never!"

John walked over to her and as he did, he looked at her with a half smile. Her rage increased, as she took his grin to be an affirmative answer to his part in what he had done.

Her lips were drawn thin across her mouth in anger and her nostrils flared with her fury as she inhaled. The flush was draining fast from her face, as her eyes seemed to glass over.

Jean's words of the night before came to his mind then; she was indeed like a storm. Simone, her emotions completely out of control reached for the closest thing that she could pick up and threw it. Seeing what she was about to do, John ducked in time to the oncoming missile and the vase smashed against the wall behind him. Looking at her, his voice deadly calm, yet laced with the contempt he felt for this woman, he simply demanded she stop the antics. A cold stare came back at him and for a few seconds there was silence.

"Why should I listen to you? You bastard. You will pay for what you have done to me. I have not started yet."

John lowered his voice as he spoke to her calmly. "I have done nothing that you should hold against me. In fact my dear Simone, this was simply all your doing. Adrian called me to his deathbed, that's right, his deathbed, to change his will. Up until he found out about your, shall we call it your little indiscretion with a certain young man, you were indeed to have all of his estate. You Simone, in your stupidity, brought this on yourself."

"Lies, all Lies, and I will fight this will, to the end. You have no proof of what he thought he knew. He was very sick, out of his mind. I loved my husband very much, anyone will tell you that. I left my own family because of my love for him. It's you; you changed his mind on the day you came to the house. You told him a pack of lies. Lies that most likely killed him!"

Breathless now with rage, Simone stood there glued to the spot and she spoke in a low cold and calculating voice. "If you do not see to it that I get all I am entitled to, I swear to you, that I will bring you down. I will see you and your career ruined. I too have friends in high places, so don't underestimate me."

His eyes bore right into her, and his next words would ring in her ears for days. "But I have seen to it, you got what you deserve my dear and I intend to see to it, that it stays as it is. You had best let me take you home, so that you can tell Edward Duval that you will be meeting him in your new place of residence in the future and not in your room, down the hall from your late husband. It is also my hope, that if you do not want any of this sordid affair to come to public attention, that you let well enough alone. New Orleans would not forgive you or would they be as generous as your husband was."

She was visibly shaken. It was true! Somehow Adrian had found out about Edward. Damn! She had been a fool; she had been so close, so very close and now she had nothing, well almost nothing. Ever the survivor, Simone started thinking. She at least had Edward and there was always New Orleans society, friends who would feel sorry for her. They would not cast her out. She could not let them find out, for if they did, he was right, that would truly be the end. With this realization she broke, the fury of seconds ago was gone, it had been knocked from her.

"What am I to tell anyone? How will I explain to them about the will, my status?"

How pitiful she looked now, she was a woman facing the harsh realities of having lost, and losing was not something that she handled well. For a fleeting second he felt sorry for her, but then he remembered his old friend who had died with a broken heart.

"I must say that I am sure that you will come up with some story that people will believe. You normally do. It was my agreement with Adrian, that as long as you do not hurt anyone, with whatever you do to explain your situation, that I was to leave well enough alone. Now I can see Adrian's wisdom. You will pay enough for your actions and I have no reason to darken his memory by revealing all."

She had had enough; it was more than she could handle. Rather than let this vile man see her sink any lower, she stormed from his office, into the rain and the waiting carriage. She started screaming at the driver to take her home.

The carriage did not move. The driver was waiting for approval from his master. He would not move without it, no matter what she yelled. Screaming at the top of her lungs for him to move or she would have him whipped, the situation was getting quite out of hand and the poor driver was ready to leave his seat and find his master when John appeared in his doorway.

Simone was beyond reasoning and John had no intention of entering the carriage with that hellion. He nodded his head in approval from where he was standing. It was not a moment too soon for the driver, who raising his eyes to the heavens as if to say heaven help me, slowly headed off down the street, with his still-screaming passenger.

That night Jean had his guilty feelings put to rest, as John felt it his duty to inform Jean and Tori about the reading of the will and Simone's outburst. Tori felt sad for her but was soon convinced by the men that a scheming woman like Simone would soon find a way to be back on top.

One fact that they all acknowledged and promised John they would remember, was that there was no longer any doubt that they all had made an enemy. And she was the most dangerous kind of enemy. A woman scorned was about the worst, especially when that woman was Simone.

# Chapter 15

In order to stay close to Tori, Jean had all but turned the running of Barataria over to Pierre and Dominique. He had an uneasy feeling about Simone and Edward. It was nothing he could put his finger on, but it was always there. He had learned a long time ago to listen to his intuition, both in business dealings and games of chance. This time however was for something far more important. It was for family. He would never let any harm come to Tori and the baby he repeatedly assured himself. Besides he enjoyed the idea of spending more time alone with her, something he had sorely missed doing, since their return from the islands.

As he predicted to Tori, it did not take Simone long to land back on her feet. Even after she moved to her new home on Royal Street, the sly actress that she was, had won the hearts and sympathy of all who heard her story. Playing the ever-grieving widow, who was bound and determined to abide by her late husbands' wishes was all part of her plan. To all who knew her she maintained a position of dignity despite the hardships that she now had to endure. "I intend to mourn my dear late husband and will refuse any help offered no matter the consequences," she told everyone. In this way Simone wormed her way higher up the social ladder. She gained the respect of the older generation and the loyalty of the younger, who thought it to be the most romantic and courageous act of love that they had ever seen.

Jean and Tori were somewhat taken back by the lies and trickery displayed by Simone, but on the advice of John they did nothing to discredit her. So it was that the months slipped quietly by, with what seemed to be an unwritten truce between them.

Edward and Simone had their own lives to worry about and it seemed that they had forgotten about Jean and herself. To Tori it looked as if Simone and Edward and all their hostilities had only been imagined.

The long hot days of summer, which should have come later in the year, suddenly appeared. June felt like August, with it's high humidity and soaring temperatures. Day and night the sweltering sticky heat continued with no escape for anyone. Tempers were short and as hot as the weather. And Tori soon came to know the truth in what Marie Destrehan had told her. There simply was no way to avoid the wet blanket of heat that had descended upon the city, if you remained in town. Those who could, were already taking trips up the river, seeking out the cooler refuges of the mighty plantation homes. Many of them would not return until their was a break in the weather or better still until the summer's end.

This seemed the perfect solution to Tori, but due to her delicate condition, as Jean called it, he insisted they had to stay until after the child was born. She was to have the best of care and her doctor practiced only in town. Going anyplace else was simply out of the question.

Even heavily pregnant, Tori radiated beauty. Charm seemed to flow from her, as naturally as breathing. The few dinners that she and Jean attended were made special it was said, by the presence of Madame Laffite.

William Claiborne himself was enticed by her looks and seductive charm, but not enough to give up his dream of catching the Laffite brothers and their gang of cutthroats. He might have let a lot slide, even turned a blind eye, given enough time. But the truth was that Edward was by his side most days, always feeding his insecurities and misgivings about his public opinion. William Claiborne knew that the Creole society of New Orleans did not like him and if he were to be elected the first Governor of Louisiana, something that he desperately wanted, he would have to win them over. On Edward's advice, he married for the third time, a woman of Spanish heritage, from Santo Domingo. Cayetana Susana Dosque y Fangui, was the daughter of a wealthy ship merchant. She did not have a chance against the smooth talking American and his allies. William had courted her continuously, declaring his undying love, in order to win her hand. While Simone had helped in her own influential way manipulating both Cayetana and her parents. Always she would praise the dashing American and his attentions toward her dear friend.

Edward on the other hand applied his talents to William exclusively. His best moment had been when he told a doubting Governor-to-be, "You don't have to really love her, just use her and her family. Besides its not like you're really deceiving her, you do have strong feelings towards her."

The wedding won Claiborne high standing in the Creole society and acceptance among the general population. Seeing Edward had been right; with his advice he listened to him more and more.

Edward made sure, that Laffite was becoming an ever-increasing thorn in Claiborne's side and a large source of embarrassment. Following Simone's advice, he never allowed his remarks to be overheard by anyone outside of Claiborne's inner circle. It was in this way, that he was able to gain the respect, trust and better still, the friendship of not only the future Governor, but of all those around him.

Simone and he did nothing that would openly make their hostilities known to the Laffite circle. They would work slow and bide their time, picking their opportunity carefully as to when to destroy those that they hated with a vengeance. It was a vengeance that had become an obsession to both of them, one that grew with each passing day.

At different functions, Tori would often catch a glimpse of one or the other, mostly Edward, who would be staring at her. He would always look away and acted as if he had not even noticed her. Yet she felt that he and Simone were only attending some of the parties and dinners, just to follow her or Jean.

"Did you see Edward at Claiborne's side last night? I don't know how he has become so close to him or what he's up to, but I'm sure it has something to do with us. You don't think he has told the man about me do you?"

Jean rolled over and took her in his arms. The cool of the morning was the only time that the two of them could lay close together, naked and in comfort. The oppressive heat of the days and nights made being close very sticky and uncomfortable. He missed holding her close for hours and of making love with her. Holding her now, feeling the empty spot in his life, that only she and their lovemaking could fill made him desire her all the more. He could feel the baby moving inside of her, and knew that as great a love as he had for his unborn child he resented it also. He needed to be with his lady. His body and soul cried out painfully. How much longer would he have to wait, he wondered? Shaking his head clear of those thoughts, he concentrated on what Tori was talking about.

"I saw them also, and I agree with you, it did seem as if the two of them were rather close. I shall have to find out what is going on." He stroked her brow gently pushing a strand of damp hair back off her face. "The past few months with you have been so wonderful, that I fear I might have become too lax in my observance of that dandy. He spells trouble I am sure of it, even if nothing has happened yet. I have not wanted to say anything to you, but I still do not trust him or Simone for that matter. Did you see her last night? Her husband's not cold in his grave and she is out on the town and getting away with it. Even the old widows, who would normally be shocked and horrified at such goings on, are condoning her actions. She should still be in mourning. It is the custom to have up to a year or longer to morn, but not her. She has rewritten what is accepted it seems." He frowned, "I overheard a couple of ladies and they actually think that it was just what Simone needed to do. To get out and about. Can you imagine? The poor child, they called her. I can tell you my lady, that when I heard that, I all but choked on my wine!"

"Well I must say, it did seem that she has changed somewhat. Simone was revolving around Edward and his friends, instead of the whole room. Jean, you don't think she's after Claiborne do you? J.D. seems to think he will be elected Governor, and like I told you, that assumption will be correct. History tells us that." Tori only wished she knew more about William Claiborne than she did. Seeing the worried look on Jean's face, she playfully added, "A Governor's wife would be right up Simone's alley!" She was teasing him, trying to lighten his mood. He seemed so tense. More somber and trying to alleviate his worries she added, "Simone did not even look our way last night at all. Maybe she has forgotten about us. Could be, don't you think? She has Edward now and a lifestyle that suits her. She could have put her jealousy aside and moved on."

"What I think, is that we had best keep our guard up. The two of them are up to something. They have not forgotten nor changed their feelings towards us. You can be assured of that fact."

He had pushed away from her as he spoke; the closeness of their bodies was causing his to respond, with a desire he knew he would have difficulties controlling.

"But don't you worry, nothing in the world will ever hurt you or our child. Speaking of which, he sure is active this morning isn't he?" he touched her midsection, caressing it gently with his caring hand.

"You truly amaze me. How many times do I have to tell you, it could be a girl? You know you just don't seem to get that through your head, do you?"

Jean smiled, and continued to stroke her swelling abdomen, his very touch driving sparks of electricity up and down her spine. It had been weeks since they had made love, all because he insisted on doing what was right. That stupid doctor had said that there was to be no loving of any physical kind, due to the heat and how far along she was. Surely they would not want to jeopardize the baby or it's mother he had asked them? A fact that Tori argued with him and lost.

Some doctor, she thought to herself. No matter what she had said or done to get Jean to change his mind and not listen to that dumb doctor on this one matter, she had been unsuccessful. He could be so stubborn and bullheaded at times, that she could scream. She had begged him just the other morning, pleading with him, telling him it was not dangerous. It was perfectly safe she had explained. After all she should know shouldn't she? This was not the first child she was going to have, and in the future they had proven lovemaking was not going to do any harm. But all her pleading had fallen on deaf ears. Thinking back to that fight she remembered it all...

That morning had ended up a disaster. He had stormed out not trusting himself to stay by her side a second longer least he give into her demands, thereby hurting the child. Tori had cried partly because of his action but mostly because he had caused her to face some painful memories. The memories of another pregnancy, another time and how that child must be missing her mother so.

Tori's face had unconsciously saddened as she lay reflecting. Jean ever vigil, stopped his attentions. He pulled his hand away as if it had been stung. He had seen the change that had taken place in her mood and also the memories of the other morning were still fresh in his mind also. He was determined not to have a repeat of that performance. The after effects had taken days to smooth over.

Looking into her eyes, their color seemed to darken with desire and draw him into her, where he felt he could drown in the ocean depth of them. He knew that she wanted him as much as he did her. But he would stand firm, he had to. Maybe if he could get her to see the funny side of their situation it would lighten her mood.

"My lady, only a son would keep his father away from what he most desired. For surely a daughter of mine, would only want her father's happiness, to have all that he wanted," he chuckled. Jean left the bed quickly avoiding her embrace. He was laughing at how he had escaped her anticipated move and stood looking down on the naked body that lay enticing him.

Jean had not heard of body language for if he had, he would have known, that what Tori was saying was not to be taken lightly. "If I stay a minute longer my love, I will have to take you. Even full with child, you are ravishing." He was dressing as he playfully talked. "It is cruel how you torture my body and mind. My need for you grows more each day. The next few weeks are going to be the longest of my life. Lying by you so close and not being able to possess you in the way I dream of." Pulling on his boots he looked at her, "Even now I find myself weakening. It is time I filled my mind with something other than making love to you. I shall contact Pierre and see to the business for the next few weeks. That might help some, but heaven help those around me. I fear for them. So foul will my mood be!"

Tori could see the longing in his eyes and the torment he was suffering. She felt for this man, and yet he was bringing it on himself. She knew in her heart that he was right. He had to leave, but oh how she wished he would stay. If only he would believe in her and listen to what she said. If he would only trust her. Did he think she would do anything to harm their baby, putting herself before its safety? Her temper was beginning to boil. If he had to go, so be it, she would not beg anymore but she would not make it easy for him either.

Pulling the sheet up over her, she smiled up at him. She was trying her best not to let her disappointment turn to anger, but anger was what she felt, along with resentment and a deep need for a revenge of sorts. He had to be made to feel guilty.

"I will try to make it easier for you, but you have to help me. It is not easy you know? Just because I lay here fat and happy, does not mean that I don't want you and need you as much as you do me. Maybe it is best if you just leave now and put work before my needs."

Jean felt the words hit him like rocks being thrown at his heart. Did she not understand that nothing could ever take her place, nothing and no one? Anger and hurt, along with his bruised pride, caused him to spit back angry words as he stormed out.

"You my lady, can be well assured, that as long as your emotions are like a rip tide, I shall steer clear. More so because you requested it."

With that statement, he left, followed by the slamming of the door. In the foul mood he was now in, what he needed was a good long hard ride and someone who could explain it all to him. Just what in the hell was happening? Women! He would never understand them, especially pregnant. His friend J.D. might be able to shed some light on the matter. After all, he'd been through this so many times.

Tori was left alone with nothing but her angry mood for company. Emotions indeed! Just what in the hell did he know about her emotions? For weeks now she had been waging a battle against herself, always managing to hold on somehow. It was not easy dealing with the guilt of loving one man in one century and having a family and a child in another. There she had said it, finally said it. But he was more than just a lover wasn't he, she told herself.

It was all she could do at times, to push down the wave of raw emotion that threatened to overtake her and drown her in a pit of despair. A cold knot seemed to fill her heart. If this was going to be Jean's attitude, blaming her for everything, then she was not about to go running after him.

The tension between the two of them had been building she knew that. Why didn't he get it? It was not her fault that she could not reach out to him and satisfy his sexual hunger like she wanted. He was the one who always pulled away. He was the one who did not accept that her condition was not an illness!

Her whole body seemed to tense at the very thought of him and his boyish way of dealing with the situation. Gone was any form of reasoning Tori might have had. She was past tolerating or understanding; she no longer cared why she felt as she did. It was just far easier to blame Jean, than admit that she was letting her guilt and her emotions run away with themselves. She flatly refused to acknowledge that she was the one who was being difficult this time.

Tori felt awful. The day was hotter than normal and the air that hung in the room was stifling. She had to get out, maybe downstairs into the cool of the courtyard. Once outside however, she found it no better. Even under the shade of the tree, she could find no relief. The air was so thick, she swore she could physically drown on each breath she took. If only the humidity would drop and her mood cool down, she might feel more comfortable, she thought. It seemed to her that even the weather was conspiring against her.

So it was a very moody and impatient Tori that stormed back inside. She angrily screamed out to the black servants, demanding that a tub of cool water be filled right away! And she insisted it be placed in the bedroom regardless of how much extra back breaking work this would be.

Never had she talked in such a hostile manner to any of the household help, and briefly she reflected on her actions. Guilt flooded over her and brought with it a sense of great embarrassment and shame. What was wrong with her, she asked herself?

"One thing is clear I'm mad as hell and I'm miserable," she shouted at the ceiling. God how she hated New Orleans, it's weather, and it's people. Most of all she hated being stuck here in this time, in this state, with a stupid man who did not want to understand or care how she felt. All this on top of being pregnant. And she had to put up with it all without the aid and comfort of a simple gadget like an air conditioner!

Upon entering her room, she stood watching impatiently while the tub was being topped off with cool water. Her whole body was crying out for relief from the infernal heat that surrounded her. If she could only find a way to cool off and relax. Maybe then she would find her spirits lifting and despite this mixture of anger and self-pity put it behind her, to become the old Tori once again?

Giving orders that she was not to be disturbed, and was going to spend the day resting, she pushed the young girls from the room and slammed the door. God it felt good to be awful even if she knew it was wrong. She knew in her heart that the girls had done nothing wrong, that she should feel bad about the way she was treating them, but she just could not. The way she felt right then was simple in her mind. If she had to feel miserable, then so did everyone else.

As she stripped down she mused again about what had come over her? It was Jean that's what it was. She knew that he and his actions were causing her to behave this way. Her whole-depressed mood was his fault. He'd ruined her day. "And to think, I even thought that I loved him!" she said with tears springing to her eyes. Angrily she wiped them away while concluding that she would show him. He was not going to get the upper hand. She would just put him out of her mind.

Slipping down into the cool rose-scented water was like opening the refrigerator door on a hot summer day. The instant relief felt so wonderful that she knew she could relish it for hours. Tori slipped down further, until only her head was above the water line. True, the tops of her toes were left sticking out at the other end, but who cared about toes being hot and sticking out all ugly? All she knew was that she had been foolish trying to stand the heat, when she could have been in here, in the tub all the damn time.

Off in the distance she heard the rumble of thunder; it had done this for several days in a row. Nothing had ever come of it; just a big show of forked lightning on the horizon for a few hours was all that occurred. Tori closed her eyes and prayed that this time it would be different, that it would rain and cool things off.

Touching her stomach she talked to the baby. "You would like that wouldn't you?" She could not feel the baby moving; and in thinking about it, she realized he had been still for hours. For a child who loved to toss and turn so much, giving her little time to rest, this was a blessing. Laying her head back, her eyes remaining closed, a very emotionally and physically drained Tori drifted off into a cool blissful sleep...

How long she slept she was not sure. Neither was she fully aware of what had caused her to wake up so suddenly from such a deep state of slumber. She yawned, taking in a deep breath of the muggy air. Disappointed, she realized nothing had changed, she could feel the hot stagnant atmosphere around her, it was as still and as heavy as ever. The room however was different; it was bathed in an eerie green light. The kind of light that appeared when a big storm rolled in back at her parents home in Texas. She remembered how she would put on the weather channel when the storm was getting close and get the storm update to see how hard they were going to be hit.

A sudden flash of lightning lit up the room, followed closely by nothing short of an explosion. This brought her sharply out of her day dream and back to reality. It's crackling blue charge burst forward and caused her to sit up and grab onto the sides of the tub, out of sheer terror.

Sitting there Tori winced in pain at her stiff neck. She knew that she must have slept for several hours in one position to cause it. Standing slowly she felt what she called a crick in her upper back and shoulders. Reaching up and rubbing her shoulders, she spoke aloud to herself, half out of anger and half out of fear of the oncoming storm and being alone. "Wonderful, now I have a stiff neck to add to my discomfort." Tori stood and listened as the next clap of thunder rolled. It seemed to just go on and on. One continuous low rumble. The main storm, she figured, must still be some distance away, but at least this time, it looked as if they would actually get some rain.

It was so still, and looking around the large room, she could not help thinking how eerie and quiet everything was when the thunder stopped. There was not a sound in the house, only the approaching storm with its bolts of lightning and crashing thunder were keeping her company. Tori knew that being alone was her own fault. She had told everyone to not disturb her hadn't she? An act she now regretted.

Not bothering to dry off, she walked over to the verandah and pulled back the thin lace curtains that hung lifeless. She had hung them in hopes of keeping out some of the mosquitoes when she first came to the house, but they had not helped much. Looking at them hanging limply, Tori was sure that the only thing they were doing at this moment was keeping the cooler air out.

Pulling hard, she tore first one and then the other down, tossing them to the side, where they fell in a heap. Then as if in answer to her angry actions, the threatening storm pushed forward with its first gust of wind. Like magic it came out of nowhere and not slowly, or gently like a caressing breeze but hard and forceful, with a gale force strength. It blew in on her almost taking her breath away, causing her to take a step backwards. Unafraid of the sudden onslaught, she stood there loving the way the wind cooled off her wet body.

Tori stepped forward to the open doorway and looked toward the darkening sky. The clouds, like great ocean waves tossing in a raging sea, came racing towards her. They were purple and black, rolling and boiling as they blew overhead. Their very power seemed to surge through her body. An almighty bolt of electricity shot across the heavens, it's fury tearing open the abyss above with an explosion of noise. The crack vibrated the floor of the balcony she had stepped onto. So large a noise and so close was it that it shook the windows and from somewhere outside she heard the scream of a terrified child.

Then the rain started, slowly one drop, then another. Large and heavy they fell towards the earth. Each drop spitting down from above, landing hard upon the parched ground, bouncing and dancing about before the thirsty soil sucked them up.

Tori watched the rain splashing upon the garden as if each drop were trying to penetrate an invincible surface. At first she thought it must be hail, the drops were so large and bouncing so high, but they fell slowly and after the first few hit, they settled on the bone-dry land and were immediately consumed. Another flash, quickly followed by a blast of thunder was so close, that she knew the storm had to be right on top.

This last clap it seemed was nature's signal and the heavens responded to its call by opening the floodgates, and letting the deluge begin. It came toward her like a sheet of solid water. The whole sky just seemed to open up and let loose. Tori stood and watched mesmerized by the sight. One second she was nearly dry, the next she was soaking wet.

She thrilled in the lovely cool shower, as if she had never seen a rainstorm in her life. Standing naked on the balcony, she had no fear of the storm and it's fury. Rather, she enjoyed letting the rain sting her body as it hit, not caring because she was really cool at last. The wind whipped around her to add to the pure thrill of finally feeling the sensation of shivering. Exhilarated and caught up in the glory of the moment nothing else mattered. Her hair, soaking wet, hung below her shoulders dripping the cool liquid down her back. Little rivers of water ran down her skin, slipping and sliding to the floor. She could feel each stream of water on her back, like ice cold fingers. They tickled her. It seemed to her that every pore on her body was responding, sensing and thrilling to the sensation. She turned slowly, slipping her hands up under her hair, as if she were in the shower, letting the onslaught bombard her. Tori let the sheets of rainfall pound upon her, and then like a child she leaned back her head, opened her mouth and tried to catch some of the cool fresh liquid.

Suddenly pain grabbed her, from nowhere, like the storm that was raging around her, powerful and hard. The first labor pain left no doubt in her mind as to what was happening. A crack of thunder drowned out her screams, as she buckled over grabbing her midsection.

With the pain came the realization that it had not been the storm that had awakened her. It had been the beginning of labor; she had just not wanted to face it. For hours she had been in the beginning stages. It was instantly clear to her then, why she had been so moody and upset. Why hadn't she admitted it to herself or to Jean?

"Because I'm scared, that's why!" she shouted. There it was, she had said it, but it was too late. There was no time left to think on it. She was about to have a baby with no modern hospital, no doctor and no help if something went wrong.

The first contraction had been hard and long. It seemed to go on and on, and all she could do was grit her teeth and groan. Her mind raced as she tried to remember back to how it had been the first time when she gave birth. To be so strong so fast, it had not been this way before, but then she had heard how second babies came faster.

Slowly she uncurled and let go of her stomach; she reached for the railing to steady herself as she prepared to walk back into the bedroom. Then like before, it hit again, and before she knew what was happening, she was down on her knees. She had no time to call out, just time enough to grab a deep breath and try to gain control over the wave of agony. She bit into her lip, trying desperately to keep from screaming. Just when she felt she couldn't stand it any longer the pain began easing.

Panic overtook her, how could this be? The baby was not due to be born for another couple of weeks, and here she was, all alone and about to give birth, in a time that had no help for her or her child if something went seriously wrong. She realized the doctor had to be sent for and fast. His medieval help was better than nothing at all.

With the storm right overhead, she knew calling out for help would be useless. The noise would simply drown out any cries for help. She had to think and act clearly she told herself. First things first she thought, I have to get inside. I can get my robe and then go and get help downstairs. One of the household servants will run and fetch the doctor, while someone will stay with me.

Once again she rose to her feet, only this time she acted fast and walked as quickly as she could into the bedroom. She grabbed her robe, slipping into it as the next contraction began to hit. Before it took hold rendering her helpless, she made her way to the door opening it, then using the door frame for support she held on, gripping the wood until her knuckles were white. All the time she kept thinking it was too fast. The contractions were coming too close together.

The hallway was dark and empty, not a sign of life. The whole house seemed to be like a tomb, dark and foreboding. The labor pain seared through her like a knife and again she found herself buckling over. Tori knew either something was very wrong or this child was about to be born a lot sooner than she wanted to admit.

It had been so easy with her daughter, she had breathed her Lamaze, and her sister had coached her. The pain had been controllable, but this was like nothing she had ever gone through. Tori was frozen in the door way afraid to move.

It was more than the pain that kept her in its grip, much more. She was terrified! Terrified of having to face the unthinkable, that she might have to deliver the baby all alone and worse, that something would go wrong. "No, I won't let that happen," she swore through clenched teeth.

As the contraction eased up and she could catch her breath, she let lose a terrified scream that echoed through the empty house. She called out for help with all the strength she could summon refusing to believe she was by herself. Tears of fear filled her eyes as she strained her ears, listening for someone, anyone. The seconds passed like hours to her and she knew that she did not have long before the next contraction would render her helpless. She was just about to give up and make her way over to the bed, when she heard the sounds of footsteps pounding up the stairs.

Then at last, she saw the shadowy shape of Bessy their cook come round the corner and just before she let herself slip to the floor, the words "Lordy be child," came to her ears.

It had completely slipped Tori's mind, that today was market day and also the day the help was allowed the afternoon off. She had insisted that if she and Jean were to have slaves, that they at least be treated the way she thought they deserved. Along with Sunday, they should have one afternoon a week to themselves she had explained. It had been a stroke of luck that the cook had decided she did not like the look of the sky and stayed home, instead of joining the others on their afternoon trip out.

It only took Bessy a few seconds to realize what was happening and she knew immediately what had to be done. Reaching down she lifted Tori to her feet, talking to her in a calm kind tone the whole time. "Come on now, you don't want dis child's ta be born on da floor, now do you? We's best git's you into dat dere bed and settled down all comfortable like. Den we's a going ta send for dat doctor. You don't a worry any, Bessy's here, and everything be fine. Da first child, dey take their time a coming and we's has lots ah time to get ourselves ready. Dat be a real good thing, us having da time. Cause it be just da two's of us here in did here house. But don't you worry none. No sur. You be just fine, ol Bessy she see's to dat. Dare be a plenty o time."

How could Tori tell this woman that she did not think that would be possible. That this was not her first child and that deep down inside, she had this sinking feeling she would have to go it alone, without the doctor. Before they got her back to the bed another contraction hit confirming her suspicions. It took her breath away but somehow having another person by her side helped. She did not lose control of this labor pain; instead she automatically started to do her Lamaze exercises.

Bessy looked at her strangely. This white woman was not only brave, but she had obviously been around someone who had given birth before. She knew how to breathe to ease the pain, something that few if any white woman practiced. Most ob dem, she'd been told, just screamed and carried on something fearsome, making the labor harder on both demselves and those present at da birth.

With the pain easing, Tori looked up into the kind black face, and saw the puzzled look and realized that her Lamaze breathing must have shocked Bessy.

"It's all right, really Bessy. I learned this breathing from someone who used to deliver a lot of babies. I have even seen it work. Don't look so worried. I assure you I'm not going to swoon or scream. I'm just going to have a baby and that's a natural thing, just hard work right?" She took hold of Bessy's large hand and squeezed it reassuringly.

The black cook broke out into a large grin. Her smile seemed to fill her face as she shook her head from side to side. Ahh huh. Dis here was a going ta be something ta tell about. It would be da talk of da household for some time. Imagine a white lady so strong and brave and not fearing da pain o' birthing. She herself would not have believed it, if'n she hadn't seen it wid her own eyes. "I best try an goes ta git help. You going to be a wanting da doctor here. What wid da baby's coming early like."

Tori weakly smiled up at the woman. Oh how she wished with all her heart that they could reach the doctor but in this storm, she doubted that. She shook her head slowly. With no one else in the house but the two of them, Bessy would have to leave to go for help and Tori did not want to be alone. The thought of that drove a flash of terror into her and made her search quickly for a solution. She had to think of something that would keep Bessy from leaving her.

Jean was sure to be worried about her in this storm, he would be here soon, and then he could go for help. She knew now, the reason she had not been thinking clearly earlier that morning, why she had been such a bitch to him, picking a fight. She had been in the first stages of labor, most likely in and out of early labor for the past few weeks. Once again she scolded herself. She had been so stubborn and foolish not admitting that the baby was on its way! Now it was too late to ponder and to try and figure out her actions. What she had to do at this moment, was the best she could and with only Bessy there to help.

"I think that I am going to need your help. You can't leave me now and go out there in this storm," Tori grabbed her arm holding her tight. "There is not going to be enough time! Bessy, have you ever seen a child born?"

These last words came out through clenched teeth as another contraction hit. She started her breathing, faster now, and held on to Bessy's hand for added support, as she concentrated on working through the pain.

"Lord child, I seen em come, yes sur. I seen em easy and I seen em hard. It ain't nothing new ta me. An I think you be right for sure. We's best git's you ready. Cause I a guessing dis little'un ain't a going ta wait's for no doctor ta git here."

She reached up and pushed the wet hair away from Tori's face and mopped at the beads of perspiration that had formed on her forehead, with her apron.

Tori struggled to breathe, as the pain seemed to reach into her and twist it's way all through her body. Her midsection rose up in a tight ball and went as hard as marble. Bessy's large black hands rested on her stomach and then she began to stroke and rub as the contraction peaked.

"It's a easing now. You kin take some slow breaths in through yo mouth. Blow out slowly and try's ta think o letting your body rest. Dat be da way."

Tori listened to her voice as she concentrated on relaxing; There had been no time for Bessy to prepare anything. For it seemed to her that as soon as she got over one contraction another would start. She was not frightened anymore as she had regained control. Bessy it had turned out, was one hell of a good coach.

Time swept by, as the two of them worked to bring the child into the world. The wind howled outside, blowing the rain inside the room, soaking everything in its path. The thunder rolled as the storm raged in its full fury. The height of the storm was upon them and neither noticed or cared. And so it was that between the violent flashes of lightning and the roar of wind driven rain and thunder, Tori pushed a new life into the loving hands of her cook.

Jean had his son; small but strong, crying out in protest at having to leave the warm sanctuary of his mother's womb. The baby boy was handed to Tori, who placed it next to her skin, in between her breasts, where he nuzzled and instantly became calm, oblivious to the cataclysmic violence, ragging around his new home.

Tori studied the child, "He's just like his father, do you see Bessy, look?"

The black woman just put her hands on her hips and laughed. "In more ways than just looks if you asks me. His papa don't have da patience ta wait for nothing either. Always got ta do things in a hurry. Yep, his son weren't a going to wait none ta be born. A huh, he like his papa." The two of them laughed together then. Relief and joy expressed in their faces. They had done it. Bessy wiped at her eyes with the back of her hand, tears of joy rolled down her round face. She was so happy. There was nothing like the successful birth of a child to make a person joyful...

A soft lullaby left Tori's lips as Bessy cut the umbilical cord, setting the child free of his mother's body, to start his own independent life. "Tommy's song," had long ago put another child to sleep; during a storm, now it would do the same for her son. Gradually the thunder and wind eased off but the rain kept on falling. Tori found herself wishing it would stop also, or at least ease up a little. It would give Jean a chance to come home to them. Looking down into the sleeping face of her son, she smiled.

"Your mother can't seem to make up her mind upon what she wants little one. First I beg for it to rain, then I want it to stop. I'm sure it's the weather that's keeping your father away. This deluge is keeping him from us, at least I hope it's just that? I was such a fool."

Tori had thought he would have been home hours ago. Surely he would not have stayed away from her this long, without good reason. He had to be worried about her. Then again, maybe he was still upset with her and her crazy moods.

Bessy came into the room and lit a few more lamps, and mopped up where the rain had washed in. With the wind all but gone, the remaining rain that fell would do so without blowing in anymore. It was safe to leave the French doors open, allowing the cool fresh air of the evening to circulate. The whole world seemed fresh and new. Praise the Lord, she thought.

Bessy left and came back with a tray of food. She was in her glory fussing about taking care of Tori and the baby. A baby she would tell everyone that she alone had helped bring safely into this world. Normally her duties kept her confined to the kitchen, but now she knew the situation would change. She was going to become important, very important indeed. She might even have a chance at being the child's nanny.

"Now it be's just a bowl of broth and some cool juice to drink. A few tasty bits to bite on. You got ta eat and git strong. Dat baby he might be small now, but da way's I see's it, he's a going ta eat a lot, ta catch up like. So's you best make a heap o'milk. A tired, underfed mama, she don't make good milk." She looked at Tori and shook her head negatively. "Still don't understand you any. You kin git a nanny ta feed him an all. I'nf I had any milk left, I be glad and proud like, ta feed him myself. Dare be no way, but like I dun told you afore, I know'd me a someone dat could."

"Oh Bessy, you're a dream for thinking about us and all your help. But I told you. I want to feed the baby myself and when he gets to wanting solid food, well I'm sure I won't mind if you help then. I understand other women might want to hand over their children to be raised by nannies, but I'm not like other women."

Bessy's face was crest fallen. She didn't have a hope of being the child's nanny. "Dat you ain't, ta be sure, she said. Then she lightened up some, "I be very proud ta know's you misses, and da master. And he's going ta be a proud of you too, when he gits here dat is. You see if'n he ain't."

Tori just nodded her head. Where in the hell was he? Why was he staying away so long she wondered? Later that night, when sleep finally overcame her, she held her son close. She had prayed that it was only the weather that kept Jean away and nothing else. Little did she know how right she was?

The river was running full and in some spots had already burst its banks in many places. In one place on the low-lying lands of Destrehan, the slaves along with the help of many whites had fought to keep the angry water at bay. The large cane fields were the reason so many worked so hard, desperately trying to shore up the levee. But after many hours of back-breaking work, in knee-deep mud and water, the river had finally won the battle and burst its banks. There was nothing left to do but leave the fields and wait until the swollen river receded.

Jean had not made it as far as Destrehan and J.D. Ever the sailor who watched the horizon, he had scanned the sky as he rode and knowing only too well the signs of stormy weather he had decided not to go on. The air was too heavy and far too still for his liking, something he had experienced so many times at sea. He knew it was the calm before the storm.

Jean's gut instinct told him that this was going to be one hell of a storm to boot. So he decided to turn around and head for home. What he had not counted on, and had seldom seen, was the speed with which this storm traveled. It blew in off the Gulf, catching him and several other travelers off guard. He had had no choice but to take shelter from its onslaught and wait it out.

A small tavern just three hours ride from home became his sanctuary, as the tempest howled outside. Hour after hour he waited for a break, his anxiety building as he sat helplessly waiting for Mother Nature to play out her drama.

He could not sleep. He wouldn't allow himself that luxury, for fear of missing his chance of making a dash for home when the break he awaited finally came. Late afternoon turned to night and as it did so, so did his chance of reaching his lady until early the next day. For to ride in the inky blackness on roads that would by now be nothing short of muddy waterways, would be insane. The long night dragged by each hour seeming like an eternity.

Then finally with dawns early light only a few hours off, and the worst of the storm gone, he could wait no longer. While most thought him crazy to depart before any light, they knew better than to try and talk him out of what he was determined to do. Jean was no crazy fool as many thought him to be, rather a realist who weighed his chances well. He knew in his heart that although the first part of the ride would be slow going he could be well on his way home by the time the sun started to rise. Jean knew these roads better than most, and judged it to be safe if he stayed alert and made his way cautiously and slowly until daybreak.

The rain came in short heavy showers for the first hour of his ride. Several times he stopped his animal, just waiting for the visibility to clear. At times like this, he could only see a few feet in front of him. The road was a quagmire in spots and lay deeply covered by flooding water in others. His ride was exhausting and very slow going, not to mention treacherous for both rider and horse but still he pushed on. At one point just as dawns gray light was filling the sky, Jean stopped and dismounted his mud-covered weary beast to rest. The rain had ceased and the sky was partially clear. He could see the gray hint of daylight; no longer was it inky black. He was so close to reaching the city, but so worn out, that he had slipped from his horse begrudgingly and sat with his head between his knees, listening to the raging waters of the Mississippi.

The swollen, swift-flowing river raced by him. The thought had occurred to Jean that if he had the strength and a boat he could be in town faster than riding. Maybe as fast as, what did Tori call them, cars? He grinned at that thought. Carriages that moved without horses. But moved by something she had called gas and horsepower! He was drifting off to sleep with that crazy thought and a grin from ear to ear, when a voice rang out, jolting him upright.

"So you just a going to sit there like that! Last thing I heard about you, was that you was no quitter."

Jean had not heard her approach, whoever she was, and turned to see where the voice came from. It had sounded like the voice of a woman, so that was what he looked for among the early morning shadows.

He saw her off to the side of the road, just on the edge of the clearing. She appeared to be black and showed no fear of him or of talking to him like she was.

His hearing had said one thing while his eyes told him another. Her voice might have the command of a woman, but her build however was that of a young girl. His confusion had to come from his exhaustion and the trick of the early light he told himself.

"May I ask who addresses me so?"

"You may but idle talk wastes precious time, when you could be home with Victoria, where you should be!"

He was shocked but did not show it. He stood and looked even harder towards this mysterious character. She stood clearly just outside the range of his vision, her face hidden in the shadows, yet he felt he knew her. Who was she?"

"I passed by your home earlier and in the sound of the wind, came the sound of a woman about to bring life into this world. The water of the river runs free of the road in this the last few miles to home. You can safely travel to her side if you leave now."

Jean was mounting his horse as she was finishing this statement, and then quickly he turned the animal towards her. He rode a few steps towards where she stood, intent on finding out more. But all he found ahead of him was an empty road. She was simply not there and he knew if he searched, it would be a waste of time. In these swamps and bayous, whoever it had been could avoid being found for hours, if not for good.

A sobering thought hit him; if what she had said about Tori was true, then his lady needed him. He no longer cared who the stranger was; something far more pressing took hold. Jean spurred his horse forward and headed for home no longer drained but filled with excitement that brought with it revitalization.

He thought he heard laughter, a sort of crazy high pitched sound, followed by words saying something about his child awaiting him. It could have been the wind and his imagination, or the stranger's last words calling his way. He was not sure. Was she trying to tell him something about the birth of his child or was his imagination playing tricks on him?

With that question echoing in his mind, he rode harder still. It had been no dream. Whoever the girl was, she had known somehow about his lady and who he was.  How this had happened he did not care, he just had to get home.  He had to make sure for himself that all was safe.

Marie Laveau smiled to herself.  Jean Laffite would not stop for anyone or anything now for she had seen to that!  The look on his face as he had ridden past her crouching only inches away had sent her into fits of laughter.

She loved the power she had.  The power of scaring the shit out of people the way she did.  He would tell his story and wonder who had called to him in the middle of nowhere, and she would see to it, that word leaked out among the black network of slaves, that it had been none other than Marie Laveau, the voodoo queen.  Everyone would say Marie always knew all!  No one would have to know the real truth, that it had all come about by sheer chance, would they?  Oh, this was so good.  She was so pleased with herself.

It was early morning when at last he approached his home.  It had taken him many hours of hard riding to reach the house.  No one met him as he rode up to the house and the interior of his home was dark and silent.  Jean rationalized as he made his way inside.  Who would be up at this hour?  Why would they be?  The quiet had to be a good sign and another thing to relieve his mind was that he could see no evidence of storm damage.  Quickly with his heart pounding and praying that everything was alright, he made his way up the stairs, and towards the back of the house.  Outside the door to their room he hesitated momentarily, listening for any sound.  His eyes had caught the sight of a faint glow coming from under the door, so he knew that the lamps were still burning.  Cautiously he pushed on the door and looked in.

Sitting by the side of the bed was their cook Bessy.  Like a good guard dog, she nodded awake; turning towards the door to see who it was that had disturbed her.  Upon recognizing Jean, she quickly put her finger to her lips to silence him.  Walking slowly towards him still holding her finger in place, with a look on her face that said she meant it, she pushed him outside into the hall.

"Now don't you go waking her up any.  She needs her sleep and dat son of yours, he's a going ta keep you both up many nights ta come."

Disbelief covered his face.  "Son? Did you say son?"

"Yes Massa.  I sure n'uff did.  And she do it all herself and all.  I just helped her some and you best be proud of her.  She be one special woman.  She didn't have no doctor nor nothing.  She just work herself birthing dat child, till she plumb worn out.  You best be real good ta her…"

Bessy lowered her eyes, as she realized that she had over-stepped her bounds and gone too far, telling the master of the house what he should do.  But Jean did not care, all he could hear was the word son.  He hugged Bessy to him thankful for what she had done, taking care of them both.  The girl in the bayous had been right after all but what would he have done if something had happened?

"How will I ever be able to thank you for what you've done?  No, he laughed joyfully, "How will I ever be able to live without you after this?"

Jean was laughing softly, his eyes alive with such happiness, he took her by the shoulders then and very seriously he spoke.

"You do not have to worry now Bessy.  I will not wake her.  You can leave and get yourself some rest.  Don't look at me like that, it's fine.  Who else do you think should have more right to sit by her side than me?"

Bessy just chuckled as she looked at this man; he was acting more like a child at Christmas who had received every toy he wanted, than a responsible adult. She knew that to try and tell the person standing before her, that he needed to sleep by the looks of him, as much as his wife, if not more, was useless. So she simply smiled and mumbled to herself, as she headed downstairs to start breakfast.

Jean stood for a few seconds outside the door. He felt as if he could shout from the rooftops. Never in his life had he felt such joy, such happiness. The woman he loved had given him a son. Slowly he entered the room, tip-toeing his way towards the bed, careful of his every step.

Tori lay there softly sleeping. Her breathing was deep and slow, her face so peaceful and calm. On her lips he thought he saw a hint of a smile? Then he saw the baby nestled close to his mother. His blue eyes were open and looking right into his father's face. Jean knelt down by the side of the bed, and held his breath as he reached out slowly to stroke his child's face.

How small he was, and how perfect. As Jean touched the little fellow's hand, his finger was surrounded by his son's own small hand. It was a firm grip and one that did not want to let go. Jean was overcome. If ever he had felt ecstatic before in his life, it came nothing close to this. The emotions he was experiencing were such that he felt he would explode.

The strong pirate's eyes were filled with tears of love, as slowly he reached forward and gently picked the baby up. How big his hands seemed in comparison, how gently he handled this small human, in fear of hurting him. The child made no sound, just looked back at the man who now held him close.

This was his son, his flesh and blood; this child was the result of his love for the woman whom he really had no claim to. Looking at Tori, Jean felt that the hardest thing he could ever do would be to lose her. Then the thought hit him. He realized that now she had something to hold her to him, maybe he had a chance at keeping her.

As if sensing someone was looking at her, Tori opened her eyes and seeing Jean by the side of the bed holding his son so lovingly, she knew she had no need for words at that moment. The two of them looked deep into each other's eyes, and spoke without a sound. Gently Jean lay the baby in his mother's arms, and then slowly he lay by her side. The child nuzzled closer to Tori and finding her nipple started to suck hungrily. Jean put his arm around them both and tried to say something but his throat was too constricted, it was as if he had this large lump blocking any sound. He just smiled and for the first time in his life he let the tears fall freely down his face.

"I take it that you are pleased it's a boy?"

"My lady, I am far more than pleased. My state of mind is beyond more than you can know. That you have given me a child, us a child, is beyond mere words. True, I am very happy it is a boy. But my lady, you have given me something that I can't seem to find the words for. Just know that I love you both beyond all reason, for now and forever."

Tori smiled, she knew that she could sleep safe and happy in the knowledge that he was finally there by her side...

## Chapter 16

One day quickly and happily followed another; the weeks flew past in a blur to both Tori and Jean. They were so involved with their newborn son and each other that they had become oblivious to the world around them. Jean's small family became the center of his life and every hour spent with them, was etched in his memory for all time.

A brilliant idea hit him out of the clear blue one morning, as Tori sat on the balcony nursing the baby. Quietly he walked to where they sat, and kneeling besides them, he tenderly stroked the cheek of his son, who seemed far too intent on his breakfast to allow anything or anyone to distract him. Without looking away from him, he spoke softly so as not to disturb him.

"You know, as much as I adore keeping you both to myself, the time has come. I wish to share my new son with the city of New Orleans. I shall show him off, with great joy and pride to the people of this town. They shall meet the newest and by far the most handsome Laffite." As if in response the child seemed to smile, finally letting his little mouth relax. Smiling himself, Jean looked into Tori's eyes as he went on to explain. "The idea has just come to me that we shall have a grand party. No! Better still, a ball, in celebration of his christening. What do you say my lady? Are you and my young son here, up to such an event?"

She could see how pleased he was with himself and how it would mean so much to him. Still she could not resist having a little fun. With a straight face and stern voice she answered. "Oh Jean, you are such an exhibitionist, but if that is what you want, then by all means go ahead," she laughed at his playful expression. "It is your right to show him off. I'll agree to this idea of yours only because he does need to be christened." She put the baby over her shoulder and began patting his back gently. "Which brings me to a very important point." The baby burped and was returned to his original position in her arms where once again he latched onto her nipple. "Something I might add that you can't put off any longer. We need to come up with his full name. And there is another thing to consider, it's the small matter of who you want for Godparents? Jean, are you listening to me or are you just going to sit and stare at him the rest of your life?" She was grinning at him, not really angry. How could she be mad? There was nothing wrong really, it was fine by her if all he wanted to do was be close to them and gaze in wonder at the bundle of joy that for now had fallen asleep in her arms. His son was still refusing to let go of her breast; his little mouth had anchored him once again firmly to her. His little hand was gripping the edge of her gown, as if he were defying anyone to separate him from his mother and breakfast. Tori smiled at her son. He was already showing some of his father's traits, one of them being his stubborn streak.

Jean's voice was filled with a mixture of disbelief and joy. "You mean, that you would not mind if I were to throw such an affair? You really do feel up to it?"

Slightly annoyed now, she reached out and pulled Jean's face up with a firm grip under his chin. If she could get him to look her in the eyes and really listen, maybe he would believe her once and for all. "Jean, how many times must I continue to tell you, I am not sick or weak. I am not a frail female, who has to be waited on all the time, nor do I want it." His face showed a trace of disappointment at this statement. She realized she had hurt his feelings and tried quickly to make it up to him. "Well some of the time is all right, but you have to get it in that thick head of yours, all I did was have a child. It is nothing new you know? Women have been accomplishing this feat for quite sometime I hear. Now, you just go ahead and plan whatever it is you have in mind. I know you too well. That expression on your face, tells me that to try and get you to do otherwise is useless, am I right?"

"Quite right but..."

"No, buts about it. There is one small request that I want in return for all this hullabaloo though. Just one little condition." She was looking at him with a coy expression on her face. "I get a new gown." Then she began laughing at the expression on his face; of course she had been teasing him. She had not meant it, but he was taking this all so seriously. Little did she realize, that he had already had a gown made for her some weeks ago, it was to go with the gift he wanted to give her.

A gift for a gift, that was how he looked at it. After all, his son was the most important gift he had received in his life. It was only right that his lady should have something special.

Together they agreed on the idea of the ball, but it was to be Jean's affair as she put it, and all the arrangements were to be made by him. Tori was just going to sit back and enjoy the baby and the precious time she had left to be with him. For always banging at the back of her mind, was the thought that eventually she would have to try to get back to her own time. Soon she would have to leave her son and his father. It was a thought that she tried to ignore whenever it arose. She knew she could not put it off forever, but lately whenever she was faced with it, she would hastily tell herself she would deal with it later. Tori did not want to face the problem and all the questions that came with it. Questions like how to find the right time and the right way to approach Jean with what she knew would hurt him deeply. No, it was far easier to put it off for just a little while yet.

The invitations that were sent out were sought after by all. The Laffite Christening was considered to be one of the events of the year, and everyone who received an invitation was held in great esteem by those who did not.

That was everyone but Edward and Simone. The two had not been invited. Not that they expected to be, but that did not stop Simone from fuming about it. After all there was nothing preventing her from attending such an event. She had come out of full mourning, telling the women of society that Adrian had requested that she not morn his death, rather that she celebrated life. She, being the ever-devoted widow to his memory and wishes, was going to follow what he would have wanted. It was whispered in the old quarter, that she did it for Adrian; why, for no other reason, would she ever have considered breaking with tradition?

Such a short time in mourning would never have been so readily accepted otherwise. But her deceitful explanation had blindly fooled them.

The women and indeed a great many of the gentlemen had not turned their backs on the now somewhat lowered-in-status Simone, regardless of whispered rumors. True, she was merely the widow of a once prominent and wealthy gentleman. And she was greatly impoverished they said, but was that her doing? And did they really care or understand why Adrian had left her so? Unfaithful some had said, that was why, but if she had been unfaithful to him in life, there had never been a scandal and she had certainly been true to him and his memory. No, many just pushed the ugly rumors away, dismissing them as just that, ugly rumors. Besides you only had to be with the grief-stricken widow to know what a truly Christian woman she was.

Then there was this matter of the young Edward Duval and how she had changed his wild and frivolous ways. It was the talk of the parlors and more so, that of John Davis's gaming establishment.

New Orleans society loved scandal and gossip, especially the Creole's who thrived on it. They held their heroes high and quickly outcast the fallen. Emotions and opinions changed rapidly and one's whole life in the city could be ruined or made, depending on the hysteria of the people.

Simone it seemed had held her status because the people had blindly allowed her to do so. In their romantic view of what had happened, they no longer concerned themselves with the question of why Adrian had chosen to do what he had. That matter was far less interesting than the fact that the beautiful Simone had taken the fallen Edward and changed him. It seemed to them all, that he was now trying very hard to gain back the respect of his brother, to live up to the good name of Duval, a name that for years he had tarnished. It was whispered behind women's fans and gentlemen's smirks that young Edward loved the young widow and would do anything to raise himself to her standards. He had become the dashing young hero, trying to gain the hand of the eligible and vulnerable young widow, who in her beauty and wisdom had managed to bring home once again, one of their own.

How people would have been shocked if they had realized the ugly truth going on right under their blind eyes. Con-artists to the hilt, together Simone and Edward were linked for the same reasons, greed and revenge.

Simone had laid down all the rules, first of which, was for his gambling to stop. She assured him it was the only way to succeed in their plans of gaining control of Leone's plantation and thereby have the power to ultimately bring down Tori and Jean. Second, his public drinking and wild nights on the town had to end. Not that he minded that too much. His nights were filled with the pleasures her body could give him and all the wine he needed, behind her closed doors.

After these first and biggest changes in Edward's behavior had taken place, it was easy through Simone's connections and the Duval name, for the two of them to wangle their way into the inner circle of Claiborne and his friends. Once accepted and trusted, the two were invited to many affairs, which included Claiborne and his new wife.

The Claiborne's were only too happy to be among the first to help the young couple establish themselves, as they liked to put it. And were proud to call them themselves close friends, not merely acquaintances. Many nights would find the four of them attending one function or another, amicably enjoying each other's company. It was at these gatherings that Simone and Edward slowly and gently began poisoning the good name of Laffite, something which was made easier as William Claiborne already had a mistrust of the Laffite brothers and their business practices.

Simone had worked hard to gain the standing she now held, and felt as upstanding citizens they would be expected to have been given an invitation to the Laffite ball. To not have an official invitation could start questions and possibly start larger problems that would ruin all they were working towards. She had not come this far to let anything go wrong now she told herself. There had to be a way to make it clear to Edward.

"It is imperative that you obtain an invitation to that event and escort me. To not show could undo all that we have fought for the past months. To show up will seal the beginning of the end for those two, can't you see that?" she shouted.

"Madame, how do you expect me to obtain one?" he spit back at her? The stupid bitch, could she not see that some things were not that simple? "Am I supposed to just walk up to Laffite and say, I would love to attend the christening of your Nigger son, how about inviting me?"

"Don't be so stupid, of course I know we can't get one by asking, or any other way for that matter."

Simone sat down as if giving up, but then the cat-like grin that he had come to know so well, slipped across her lips. She spoke in a low voice laced with contempt.

"In fact, we don't need an invitation at all. We will simply accompany the future governor and his wife to the church, then ride with them that evening to the ball. Who in their right mind would dare to ask to see our invitations? I mean, can you think of anytime, anyone has asked to see the Monsieur William Claiborne's invitation? We will walk right in with them and then once there, I'm sure that Jean will not want a scene. Of course he will have to be the Gentleman and let us remain, no?"

For a moment Edward stared at this woman who sat smugly before him. His beady little eyes were open in astonishment. Her solution was simple and so perfect.

"You are truly brilliant as well as beautiful. It will a be sheer delight to be able to pull it off. Think of it, the challenge. The look on their faces as we enter with the Claiborne's. It's marvelous! Nothing and no one can stop us! If we keep this up, very soon, we will end up with everything we have ever wanted."

The two threw evil smirks at each other. Simone's eyes flashed like a feline on the prowl about to pounce, and Edward's small and slit like eyes resembled that of a snake about to strike. She watched him warily as he walked towards her, his face handsome and determined, his desire written there clearly. There was no mistaking that look. Her body went rigid with anticipation of the thought of what he intended to do...

The Cathedral was packed to capacity; every seat taken and all the room in the aisles and back of the church filled with those not lucky enough to obtain a seat. Tori knew that most of these people had not been invited, that they were here merely to be able to say they had been present at the Laffite christening, but so many!

She was so nervous her hands were shaking. Quietly, she thanked God that it was still early enough in the morning and the church was still cool enough, that she could tolerate it. Otherwise she was sure she would have screamed for everyone to get out. Was it the claustrophobic feeling that had her so wound up, or was it the gift Jean had given her before leaving for the church that morning? She did not have time to sort out any of these thoughts or emotions as the priest began. The ceremony had started, and her full attention was now required.

She handed the baby to his Godmother Marie Destrehan, as the long ceremony began. If the fact that the child had far more Godfathers than Godmothers was visible, no one seemed to care. She had had no difficulty choosing the two women that stood by her son's side. Pierre's wife Francoise and Marie were the only two women whom she trusted and loved enough to watch over her son once she was gone. As for the Godfathers, well he was named after each of them. Something that pleased both Jean and herself.

"I christen you Christopher, Pierre, Dominique, Leone Laffite, in the name of the Father, the Son and the Holy Ghost. Amen."

Dominique turned with his Godson and smiling at Tori handed the child over to her. Tori could see how much it had meant to him, that he had been asked to be one of their child's Godfathers. It had meant more than he could express in words. When they had first asked him, the gruff old man had just nodded his approval and left, leaving Tori and Jean staring at one another. His whoop of joy once outside the house, had left them laughing.

It also had been a proud moment in Dominique's life when the name Christopher had been chosen. It had been his suggestion to Jean that the child have his own name rather than one of the uncles. He had claimed that it would be less confusing in the years to come, for Christopher.

So it was, that the child now had the names and protection of all those who loved him the most. He would be well looked after. Why, then did she have such sadness haunting her deep down inside? People were talking and congratulating her, tearing her from her thoughts. She blinked as if waking from a dream, and put a grip on her emotions. Tori would not let anything spoil the evening. She was determined to share in the joy and happiness that was all around her. There was time enough yet to face what was approaching.

Their home was filled with friends and well wishes. All afternoon people came in and presented the young Christopher with lavish gifts and compliments on what a good child he was and how perfect. Remarks like, how beautiful, how very much he looked like his father, filled the air. But it was his eyes that drew the most attention. They were pools of deep blue, like an ocean at night. The expression they held had such an effect on everyone and the little lad would win all hearts that day, even that of Simone.

If Tori was shocked when Simone and Mrs. Claiborne walked up to see the child, she did not show it. Instead a sort of sadness filled her, as she looked at Simone. How lonely she must be and how desperate, to be clinging to Edward like she was. She had heard how he was a new man, but doubted that the leopard had changed his spots. He had to be up to something, she thought. Watching Simone closely, she had the overpowering feeling that most likely both she and Edward were up to no good. But for now she would forget them and just enjoy showing off her son.

Claiborne's wife asked if she might hold the child for a moment and Tori agreed. The fact that her Christopher was getting fussy was a sure sign that it would only be for a short time indeed, there by giving her the perfect excuse to take him upstairs.

Simone casually looked over at the baby's face and her heart seemed to soften as she looked at the child. What had she expected to see, she had not been sure. Plain and dark maybe, but this child was beautiful. Small and perfect in every detail, with a mass of dark soft curly hair, framing his cherub face. Even at his tender age he was so much like his father to look at. That immediately drove deep an icy wedge of jealousy pushing her hate of the child's mother to the surface. So overpowering was the feeling that it completely smothered any tenderness, which she had been feeling. This could have been her child, should have been, if Tori had not come along when she did. She should have been the one to give Jean his son. She stared at Mrs. Claiborne who was fussing over the brat as if he were her own for God's sake. Realizing that she was beginning to lose control she bit down on her lip, tightly closing her mouth as she took hold of herself. Like a mannequin she masked her emotions as she moved even closer to look upon the child.

She had to study his features. Surely there would be proof of its tarnished heritage, but try as she might; she could not see any black in him. How was that possible? She shook her head slightly. How stupid of her, if not in him, then it would most likely come out in his children, would it not? He was pale to be sure, but that had come from Jean. What a shame he had not inherited his mother's true color, not the shade she was now. She looked at his mother's golden brown color. It was a shade helped made lighter by some sort of cream or potion, Edward had told her. He swore to her that when he had first laid eyes on the woman, there had been no mistaking her true heritage. Tori had been so much darker than she was today he had insisted and she had no reason to doubt him. Simone had heard how the women discussed her olive complexion. They all had said it was Victoria's European bloodlines, that and the fact she did not stay out of the sun that caused it. Simone smiled to herself. She knew better! Bloodlines all right, but African not European.

Tori watched as she saw Simone studying the child and she rightly guessed what Simone was hoping to find a hint of color, as a polite person would say. But then Simone was no such thing. No doubt she had hoped that the baby would look like a slave spin-off thereby confirming what Edward believed her to be, a Nigger. It made her sick to see that Simone had not changed. She was still the spiteful bitch she knew her to be. Tori felt angry at herself, to think she had felt pity for her. The woman was here in the hopes of exposing the shocking news to those around them she was sure of it. Well she was the one who would receive a shock she decided; two could play at this game.

"My, you do look well Simone. It must have been so hard for you these past months, yet you seem to have maintained yourself." She touched Simone's arm gently and spoke with concern in her voice as she proceeded. "I see sadness in your face? You do study the child so closely. Maybe it would cheer you to hold him for a while. You could carry him upstairs for me if you would like. It's time for his feeding and we would love the company, wouldn't we son?"

Simone could hardly believe she was hearing right. Oh yes, she would love to carry this brat up to his room. Once there she would be alone with his mother and would love to tell her a thing or two. She smiled at Tori who in her mind was being way too agreeable. She would have to be careful and stay on her guard. Something was not right here because she knew this woman did not trust her. Why then would she act so friendly she wondered, what was she up to?

"Why, I would be honored I am sure. That is if you really mean it?"

"Simone dear, I never say anything I don't mean, do I Mrs. Claiborne?"

Mrs. Claiborne did not have a clue as to what was going on or of the hostility that now encompassed the child's surroundings. The gesture was just such a lovely thing for Jean's wife to do. She was such a thoughtful girl. Her husband William might have reason to dislike Victoria's husband, but she would tell him that his wife was nothing but a true compassionate lady.

Tori and Simone headed up to the baby's room and once in there Tori took possession of her child. She walked calmly over to a large chair as if nothing was wrong, and positioned herself in full view of Simone's curious gaze.

"I have to sit while I nurse him. Would you like to stay? You do seem to have something on your mind." She looked Simone straight in the eye as she continued. "Is anything wrong with Christopher? You do study him so."

That was about as much as Simone could stand. Whatever she was up to, was of no importance to her anymore. She was the one that would say what she wanted, she would tell her all right. "You know why I study him. So don't pretend with me. The child may look white, but we both know that he's as black as you are, is he not? Tell me, does Jean know or have you somehow neglected to inform him that your blood is tainted?"

"Why, I don't know what it is you are talking about I'm sure. Could you just help me, I need to pull this sleeve down lower?" Tori had a plan and she could hardly wait to see the look on Simone's face, as realization hit her. The sun had been hot the past weeks and Tori had been sitting out in it. This time however, she had been more careful. This time she had made sure that parts of her stayed covered, and as she slipped her gown down to expose her breast for the baby, she was also exposing her very white flesh. Her face was tanned, her arms and neck were brown but there was no denying the fact that white was her true color. Once and for all she had shown that the color of her skin came from the sun and nothing more.

Simone saw it immediately. Her own face blanched at the realization of what it was she was looking at. How could this be? Edward had told her that the bitch was black, but here she could see for herself that he was wrong, dead wrong.

"What's wrong Simone? Have you never seen a child nurse from its mother before?"

It all fit. Her hair was long and wavy, but not kinky as Edward had told her it used to be. This was no voodoo spell she was seeing. No creams or magic, could explain away what was obviously pure fact. Edward had been truly mistaken! This woman was white and she hated her for it even more. Tossing her head and putting her nose in the air she spoke, sounding as if disgusted by the sight of Tori nursing the child. She spoke aloofly, "I am not accustomed to a lady of your stature nursing her own child, no. Why my family, any decent family of good breeding that is, always has a nanny, a black nanny to do that loathsome chore. The husbands I know, care about the mothers weakened condition, and want to help them regain their health and figures of before." She turned and faced Tori, "if that is possible that is. In some I am told, the ladies figure never seems to go back though does it?" On a role and enjoying herself, spurred on by the disappointment of learning the truth, she continued. "I must say I am shocked that Jean makes you do this bothersome task. It does not seem right, even for you?"

"On the contrary my dear Simone. It was not his idea to have me do this bothersome task as you put it. I told him that I wanted to do it. You see, I love this child and wish to do the best for him and Jean agreed with me. Besides, it is common knowledge where I come from, that if you nurse your own child, your shape returns faster."

Simone had to get out of there. She knew if she stayed, she would expose her and Edward's plans on ruining them by letting something slip. How she wanted to tell the self-assured bitch, to enjoy what little time she had left with her son and husband. How she wanted to wipe that smile from her face. Her blood pounded so hard in her temple and her breathing was now so shallow it was beginning to make her dizzy. The explosion she was fighting to keep under control was fast approaching the eruption stage. Both of her hands were gripped in vice-like fists at her side, as she slowly turned towards the door. Not looking back she seethed as she let free her last remark, hoping it would hit hard. "Well we shall see about that tonight at the ball, won't we? I do hope you have a gown that fits you my dear. I hope the eyes of Jean are for you only and that they don't stray, to shall we say, shapelier ladies."

Simone swept out of the room and left Tori laughing softly. "Oh Christopher, will she ever learn? Will she ever give up? I hope so my son, because if she does not, she will end up a lonely and bitter old woman."

Tori spent the next hour holding her son close to her and thinking about him and his future. What would it be like for him without her if she went back to her own time? What was it like for her daughter now? She had to face facts. When she finally did get to the lake she might cross back to her time. That meant taking care of Christopher's long life ahead of him now, of making sure he had all the security he would need. A stupid thought really for she knew that the people who loved him would surround him with love. And when he was old enough, unlike her daughter, he would be told what happened to his mother. But when to leave, when to try the cross over, that was the question that had to be answered. Just how was she going to pick the day to say good-bye? Her eyes misted over with tears, as she looked into the gentle sleeping face that nuzzled close to her bare skin. She could feel the moisture of his warm breath on her own body and feel the pulse of his tiny heart that beat so fast beneath his little shirt. Slowly, as she sat in silence, a plan began to form. It would be Christopher who would be the one to seal her fate, one way or the other. He would be the one who would let her go, not the other way around. She would not worry about when or rush the day, rather she would wait content, knowing the decision was out of her hands. The day her son stopped needing his mother's milk, the day he pushed her away, no longer needing that part of her, would be the day to say good-bye. Even though the decision brought with it sadness, the relief of having a solution at last, gave her the strength to carry on with a sort of new lease on life, at least for a little while.

That evening at the home of Leone Duval, people started arriving for the long anticipated ball of the season. He had insisted that he be allowed to host the event and won his case in the end by the simple fact that his home had the space and resources for such a gala.

By the time Tori and Jean arrived, the evening was well underway and everyone was eagerly awaiting the honored couple. Their late arrival and grand entrance was not a mere coincidence but rather a planned maneuver by Jean and Leone. Their entrance was spectacular, standing there, at the open doorway, as Leone proudly announced to the guests they had arrived at last.

Those who turned to greet them, let out soft oo's and ah's, whispers spread rapidly around the room, followed by a silence that hung in the air for what seemed to Tori, as forever. Then someone started clapping, and while the applause grew, the cheers washed over the room. The festive mood was flooding the couple with such pride and joy, that it radiated from them.

Jean could not ever remember feeling so overwhelmed by such a reception and at long last he had a deep feeling of being home. Of having found what he had so long been looking for. His happiness and pride set a glow about him that shone and danced from his sparkling eyes. Their flashing seemed somehow to dim the diamond pin fastened to the cravat at his throat. Like his eyes, the stone shot sparks of light reflecting from its perfect prisms. It was a diamond of blue white color, which seemed to draw its shade from his coat. His jacket was the darkest of blue; a white cravat made of the purest silk, only enhanced his already bronze tan. His boots were of the softest black leather, whose high polished surface acted like dark mirrors. His pants fit his legs snugly and were made of the whitest cotton. His shirt, whose ruffled cuffs peaked out of his sleeves, had a soft hint of blue. As his gaze fell on first one guest then another, his ebony eyes seemed to change color as they captivated each person, leaving them with a sense of awe. He was every bit the dashing new father and proud husband of the vision that was on his arm.

Tori had not believed it when she had dressed for the dance. The gown was a work of art, far surpassing all the others in her wardrobe. It was the same color as Jean's dinner jacket, but of a different material. It was made of the same soft silk that his cravat was made of. But the light on the indigo blue material made it shimmer like moonlight on the sea. Her waist was small and the garment seemed to cling and mold to her shape. The gown fit each body curve like a glove. The low cut front tastefully outlined her more than ample breasts, but it was to her neck that all eyes fell, for around it lay Jean's gift.

Flashing in the lamplight, the necklace of diamonds and sapphires lay against her soft skin, framing a picture-perfect face. The necklace had been a token of thanks to his lady for the wonderful gift of a son. To Tori it was far more; it was a bittersweet gift she knew she would not get to keep. It had filled her with such emotions; torn open the wound of her love of her new family here and that of her need to return to her family in the future. The weight of the necklace hung around her throat like a hangman's noose. Still she had accepted it and worn it to please him, and hid the true sadness it brought her. No one looking at her standing by Jean's side would have guessed she was anything but ecstatically happy.

As friends called her name from one direction or another, her beaming face turned towards each individual and with each recognition her mood lightened. For the time being she would forget her sorrow, as the atmosphere swept her up in its festivity. Jean turned from the crowd and looked at his lovely lady admiring her appearance and her choice of style. Like the stones around her neck, she was unique.

Instead of her hair placed up, as was the fashion of the day, Marie Laveau had swept it to one side and held it in place by a mother-of-pearl comb. Her hair fell in soft swirls around her shoulders and shone with hints of red, flashing as the candlelight fell upon her head. She was stunning, transformed from the morning vision of a new mother, to the evening vision of the goddess Venus. He could not have been prouder of her. He leaned over and kissed her lightly on her cheek.

Edward had openly gasped as he had seen her, a fact that did not escape Simone's ears. She watched him admire her and even if she did agree that Tori was attractive, she did not have to stand by him and allow him to drool and dream. With her nails digging into his arm like claws, she very quietly took him off to the side and through clenched teeth, jealously spit at him words that hit like bullets.

"So your Nigger grows more beautiful each day and you can't wait to have her can you? After all, she is just a Nigger, high class of course! You can hardly wait to abuse her and use her like the black whores down on the river, right? Well, what would you do if I were to tell you she is out of your reach my dear Edward? Not only out of your reach but out of your league too, now and forever."

"Just what do you mean by that? And for God's sake keep your voice down, someone might hear you." He was pushing her further into the corner of the room as he spoke, but smiling as if nothing was wrong. Only his voice sounded the annoyance he was feeling towards her.

"I mean my dear love, that you cannot abuse her without having all of New Orleans come after you. They would never stand for it."

She was making no sense whatsoever, rambling on like she was. He knew that she might feel some jealousy, but this was ridiculous.

Are you listening to me? If you were to abuse a Nigger you might have a chance but to abuse a white woman and get caught, never!" She watched her news register on his face. "Yes, that's right my dear Edward, I thought that would get your attention. You have been wrong. At first I thought you were not telling me the truth, but then you had no reason that I could find to lie to me about her. You really do think she is of mixed blood. You think she's a Nigger don't you? Well, let me tell you my dear Edward it's just not so. She is white, as white as I am, as you are. Don't you dare question me on this; I know what I am talking about, because I have seen the proof for myself. That bitch made sure of it, and Edward it was no mistake. So now what do you plan to do? How will you get your hands on her now tell me that? That is if you still want too."

Edward hated Simone at that moment, but he also loved her when she hissed like a she-cat clawing and spitting. That's what he had imagined it would be like with Tori, all hellcat. He shuddered as he acknowledged to himself, that's what turned him on. But now, hearing this news, that Tori was not of mixed blood, he would have no chance of blackmailing her to some degree of submission. Did he still want her? That thought was fleeting because he knew nothing had altered. His intentions and plans remained unchanged. When she went missing, Jean would still look for her. That had never worried him. He had plans for Laffite that would get him out of the way. As for Tori, the fact that she was a real lady, one that all of New Orleans would look for, well this just upped the stakes, didn't it? It made her all the more desirable. As for now however, he had Simone and her spiteful ways to deal with. She had enjoyed keeping the bit of information from him until it could be thrown in his face. She was jealous, that was plain to see and a jealous woman needed to be satisfied. This one also needed to be taught a lesson and kept in line.

He took hold of her face in one hand, and squeezed her jaw tightly, pinching the skin as he pulled her towards him. Once he knew he had her attention, he released his grip on her face, his fingers then dug slowly and painfully harder into her arm with each word he uttered.

"I don't know how, but I will have her. I will abuse her and by me doing that, you will get even with Jean and I with my brother. That is our purpose and goal. To have our revenge on them both need I remind you of that fact? Then my dear, when I have finished with her, she will be disposed of and we will end up with each other. We will be together, because you and I know and understand each other, that is a simple fact of life, and that's the way it will be. Now let/s leave this damned party and let me show you just how little I think of that bitch and how much more appealing you are to me."

Simone had no quarrel with his suggestion, the last thing she wanted at that moment, was to let that bitch or Laffite see her and how upset she was. If they caught her staring at Tori, as she was now, looking so radiant, that would be a victory for Jean and her. On the other hand, if they did not get to gloat and show off, and she was sure that was what they intended to do, she would have won the evening.

Inwardly she fumed. They both must have planned this whole affair, plotted together, knowing that she would be here. How could they be so cruel she asked herself? She would not give them the pleasure of seeing her squirm, not that she would ever do that. She turned her back on the crowd and smiled at Edward, licking her lips seductively and nodded her approval of his idea. Edward had aroused her and it sounded like it would be one of those special nights with him. Simone knew she had angered him and because of it the evening ahead would be long and painful, beautifully painful!

They would not leave without making the necessary excuses to Claiborne and his wife of course. Neither wished to offend their new-found allies and if presented properly they could turn the early departure to their advantage. While Simone was talking with William's wife, Edward took him off to one side apologizing to him for interrupting his campaigning. "You are already the respected Governor of Mississippi and this new Territory sir. I should therefore think you have both the experience and integrity to win in the upcoming election." He boosted the man's spirits and then skillfully steered the conversation in another direction. He explained why he and Simone were departing early. Telling him that he was sure it was no headache that was causing Simone to act so rash, rather he felt it was the fact that she was missing her dearly departed husband Adrian, and was too upset to stay. Claiborne was observing Simone as Edward talked on about how lonely she had been lately. He felt sorry for the young widow and had a certain amount of admiration for her also. He insisted that Edward bring her by in a few days for dinner. Maybe to be out and about with a few close friends would help her overcome her melancholy mood.

Not long after, Claiborne watched the two discreetly leave. Edward's arm he noted, was protectively around her, guiding her escape. A look of self satisfaction slipped across his somber face. He admired how much the young Edward cared for her and wanted to help the young couple if he could. To secure that young man's friendship was a must in his books, as Edward's help and friendship would only assure his own success. Over the past few weeks he had noticed that Edward Duval seemed to be dedicated not only to his private life, but also to his own sought-after position of first Governor of the state. He knew he came from a high standing and well respected family, with a powerful and influential brother at its head. Yes, Edward was a man of great potential. It never hurt to have someone like that in your hip pocket. He would have to include him a lot more in their social rounds in the weeks to come.

As for now, he had another matter to deal with. Where was his wife? He had to get closer to this Laffite character and learn what he could. If Edward and the rumors were right, he had more to fear from this gentleman pirate, a lot more.

Tori had a wonderful time and the evening was a great success. She had noticed Simone's departure shortly after her arrival and breathed a sigh of relief. It seemed that the woman did have a bit of diplomacy after all. Or maybe it had been out of shame, having come with no formal invitation. Whatever the reason, she was glad. She and Jean spent many hours dancing and enjoying the company of so many close friends. But the big surprise of the evening had been when the Claiborne and his wife came over to offer their best regards.

It had been on Jean's attorney's advice, that they had received an invitation. The fact that they had come was not that surprising but that the man himself would talk with Jean was. It was common knowledge that there was friction between the two. Most said that their conflicting personalities alone, was like a burning fuse to a powder keg. On this occasion however, the two gentlemen had found a common ground in being civil to one another. After their encounter, the evening continued with no further incident, and all enjoyed themselves well into the early hours of the morning. The ball became the talk of the town and those few who missed it, because they elected not to make the long trip into town due to the heat, found themselves wishing they had.

September was long and hot and Tori found herself wishing for the winter. Even the gulf breezes that usually stirred this time of year were stagnant. The oppressive heat hung over the city and its populace, slowly baking not only the land but also the tempers of all who lived there. Night and day, there was no escape from the sticky steambath. Its dampness crept and clung to everyone and everything, living or not. Clothes already damp to the touch, when put on, were soon wringing wet from perspiration. Then to make matters worse, the swarms of bugs both large and small, biting and stinging, never seemed to rest. New Orleans was well and truly in the grip of what Tori called a living hell. While to most of New Orleans, it was nothing more than a summer heat wave.

Nothing could be worse, than being foolish enough to stay in the city to endure the worst that summer could bring, not when escape was possible. Most of those who could, would leave early in the season, for the cooler temperatures of the inland plantations along the river. Going up river was something Jean had tried to get Tori and the baby to do for days now. He had reassured her, that he himself would join them, just as soon as the business would allow him to get away. Stubborn as she was, Jean could not make her budge. If he had to stay, then his family would stay with him, was the only response he could get.

        Tori so far had avoided being packed off, as she put it by one delay or another. These excuses though, after the hellish day she had just had, were beginning to look like a foolish decision. People's tempers were short; moods were quick to flare into vicious outbursts, or sobbing self-pitying fits. Friends, the few who remained in town, no longer came to visit, as the heat was just too much. It seemed to Tori that the hot humid weather had turned every task into such an effort. Every joyful activity seemed to have vanished overnight, as one just struggled to be comfortable. Even Christopher, normally a placid happy child, was crying out of misery. As much as she wanted to stay with Jean, she finally had to confess; being stubborn about leaving was not gaining her that much. She would admit defeat to Jean at the evening meal, and agree to take his advice and leave the city as soon as it could be arranged.

# Chapter 17

    The first reports of something wrong came by way of the slave grapevine. Somehow, they always seemed to know things before anyone else. The reason behind this was a simple; the slaves and household help would spread among themselves any news or gossip that came their way. Like a wild fire it would spread rapidly through their intricate network jumping from one home to another. It was whispered among the white population that nothing could happen in the city that the blacks did not know of.
    Tori had been told that a couple of sailors down on the docks, had died of the fever in the past week. She had insisted that it was not just an ugly rumor but something to sit up and take notice of. Tori had worried about this and mentioned it to a few neighbors. Their reaction was nonchalant. It was nothing to worry about they had assured her. After all if the story were true, the boat they came in on had left port, taking with it any further chance of contamination.
    It was Bessy who told her of the latest update. It was said that one of the families who had arrived on the ship had sent for the doctor. It seems their daughter, only a few years older than Christopher, was very ill, and even though they insisted it was not the same fever that had killed the sailors, their household help knew better.
    "It's a starting Miz Tori. Lord have mercy on our souls. Yes sur, it sure be a starting. You see if'n it aint. I seen it afore. It spreads so fast like, like da fire in dem cane fields. If'n you aint out of da city in time, you was as good as dead. I neber stayed afore. Da master, he always see's ta it, dat we be long gone, and I'm a telling you, it be time to git!"
    Tori looked at Bessy. She had never seen her so upset, and scared. Sure she had learned about the fever outbreaks that had hit New Orleans and of the terrible death toll, but this could not be like what she had read. First of all, she was sure she remembered the fever outbreaks took place in the middle of the summer. It was far too late in the season to seriously worry about such an occurrence. And then she seemed to remember that the big outbreaks happened later in the century. She wasn't sure. But anyway she had nothing to fear, having been vaccinated against yellow fever in her time. It would be the baby and Jean, along with their slaves and friends she would be frightened for. Right now she had to calm Bessy down, and somehow reassure her that her worries were needless.
    "Bessy, look I'm sure you are getting all worked up over nothing. If it was the fever, yellow fever, then I am sure we would have been officially informed. I can't imagine something like that could be kept quiet, and for what reason would anyone want to anyway? Look, you trust the master, and I'm sure he

would have heard something and if he did, do you think he would allow me and Christopher to stay in town. Now do you?"

Bessy could not make her understand, how could she. But Lord if she didn't make her, it could be to late, they might catch it. She had to get her to listen. Putting her hands on her hips and lowering her voice to her most serious tone, she spoke with such sincerity that Tori found herself reconsidering. "Miz Tori, you ain't going ta listen, but you must. It be right what my peoples say. Dey know da truth. Ain't got no reason ta lie, more ta tell da truth though. I ain't a caring what da white folks say or don't say. I just know dat if we stay here, den someone is going ta git sick. It might not happen." She shook her head. "I know crazy thing dis fever be like. It be da devils work for sure. Some peoples never get it, even after they be right close ta it. The doctor, he never gits it. Then dere's dem dat thinks dey be safe and don't go out. Don't get any place close ta it, and Lord next thing they knowed, dey be dead," she rolled her eyes upward. Bessy was pleading now as she continued, her eyes filled with unspent tears of frustration and fear. "I just a fearing for da little un. He and da rest o my family. You and da master are my family and I ain't got da heart ta see no one's git sick. You just aint seen it. It's be horrible, and you can't run once it git's you!"

Tori listened to her and a small voice in the back of her mind told her to think this through carefully. If this was indeed the beginning of an epidemic, she wanted no part of it. She had no desire to witness such an event and to put those she loved in danger was the last thing she wanted. And what did it matter if they left a little sooner than planned. After all she had already made her mind up to leave the city for the cooler river front home of J.D. and his family. She would ask Jean as soon as he came in about leaving first thing in the morning. They would all go. Looking at the woman's beaming face, Tori knew Bessy guessed what she was about to say, still it had to be handled in a way that left her in control.

"Bessy I want you to know, I still do not think there is any yellow fever, but the heat is so unbearable and Christopher is so miserable. I'm going to take Jean's advice and go up river until it cools off. Please see things are ready to go by morning."

Bessy was on her way out the door as Tori added, "and Bessy, we might as well close up the house until we get back. Everyone could use a break don't you think?" Instant relief flooded the round black face, she did not care what reason Miz Tori used for their leaving, the fact was they were going and that was plenty good enough for her. She would pack and work all night if necessary. She could rest once they were safe and only then.

Before Jean arrived home that evening, plans had taken another drastic change, and with no time to stop and think of the consequences of her actions, Tori found herself hurrying to Leone's townhome. She had left Christopher in Bessy's care and told everyone to keep on packing. Tori left word for Jean to be told if he got home before her, that she had been called out to Leone's and to meet her there. It was a message that would not be delivered until almost midnight, due to his late homecoming.

Tori had been busy with plans for their trip, when she had been interrupted by the doctor. Seemed he was on his way to another patient, when he received word that Leone was ill and needed his attention. Knowing it would be sometime before he would be able to stop by the Duval home and knowing that he lived alone, with only his servants to keep him company, he had worried until passing the Laffite's house. It took him only a short visit to explain his concern to Tori and ask that she send a message to the convent, for one of the sisters to stop in and see if there was anything Leone needed. The doctor never thought that it would occur to Jean's wife, to take it upon herself to see to Leone.

As she rode toward his home, Tori went over again what she had been told. What was it the doctor had said, she asked herself. Could it be true that Leone's stable boy had said, that the master had been ill for days? What was Leone thinking of, not sending for the doctor earlier? What if he had the fever? Her mind reacted violently at that thought. He was just sick, a mild something or other, that was it. Nothing to worry about at all, some chicken soup would do the trick. Her mind kept going on and on, not the fever, can't be. But she knew that it could. The doctor had confided in her, that yes, he was treating many cases of the fever and it was spreading. He had advised that she and her family leave town as soon as possible because in his opinion it was going to be quite an outbreak.

Was it her imagination or were there less people outside than normal? Passing by some of the large homes, they looked dark and empty. The normal activities one would see, such as slaves working on the beautiful gardens, children playing or adults sitting on the verandahs, were nowhere to be seen. Oh there was the odd household that showed signs of life, but still more were seen loading carriages with belongings, as they prepared for a hurried departure. Tori realized that this all meant one thing; word of the impending plague must have spread. People were staying in or packing up to leave, if they had not already done so. These realizations sank into Tori's mind and like a dreaded quicksand pulled her optimistic mood slowly down deeper and deeper.

She held out hope of finding Leone just slightly ill, after all, he had not been near the docks that she knew off. His life and dealings kept him well away from that part of town. He socialized with the same friends as Jean and her and none of them were sick. These thoughts accompanied her all the way to his driveway, where she faced the truth.

Leone's house was quiet. No one was in the garden and no one came out to meet the carriage. She stood looking up at the front of the home and knew instantly that something was really terribly wrong. All of the windows upstairs were closed and the curtains pulled shut. The verandah doors, which at this time of the day were normally wide open to let in the early evening air, were also shut tight. Had there been a mistake, could the house be locked up and Leone already gone to his plantation? Somehow she knew that was not so. He would never leave without sending word, or stopping by to say farewell.

Her hand reached for the brass knocker and as she listened to the loud thumping on the door echo inside, she began to pray softly. "Don't let it be. Please, he has to be all right." The door opened and stepping aside was a very thin and sickly looking black man, that at first she did not recognize. It was when he spoke in a whisper-like fashion, that she realized who he was. He was Leone's trusted servant and valet, that was, what was left of him.

At first too stunned to speak, Tori just stared in horror and then fear. Could this be her first contact with yellow fever? "I's sure pleased that you come by Miz Tori. I be so tired. No one else take care of the master. He tell em to stay away. Told me too." he shook his head no. "but I just can't be a doing that. He needed help. He's real sick Miz Tori. I send for the doctor when I know it's the fever. He said he didn't need him none. But this morning, I knew it was time for help, no matter what he ordered. The doctor has not been here yet, but bless you you're here now."

On these last words he seemed to be slipping to the floor, too weak to carry the conversation on or even to stand. Tori reached out and took his frail arm, guiding him to a chair in the front room, where he thankfully sat his shaking body down.

"This is not right Mizz Tori. I'm not supposed too..." he hung his head down, "the Master Leone, he is the one that needs help."

Tori pushed him back into the chair, as he struggled to get up. "I don't care what is right or wrong, you are worn out and if you don't get some rest, by the looks of you, you'll be the next sick person in this house. Now you listen to me. I'm telling you to stay here until I need you. I know my way around. I'm sure I can find Leone's room by myself. I will just go and see what he needs and be right back."

He did not fight her, the poor old man. He must have been on his last legs, for sheer exhaustion was clearly written all over his face. Who knew how many hours he had kept going in the past few days, without sleep.

Tori made her way upstairs and onto the landing. It was gloomy and stifling hot. All the doors along the hall in each direction were closed, letting no sound of life escape from within the rooms. To her right there was only one long window at the far end to light her way, which had not had its drapes drawn. She was thankful for the light as dim as it was. It would have been more than ample but the suns rays were filtered by a large magnolia tree just outside. It had been planted for shade to help keep that side of the home cooler in the summer. Now its thick foliage blocked most of the sun's rays and cast dusty beams of light, down the already gloomy hallway.

Knowing Leone's room had to be one of the doors toward that end of the house Tori started in that direction. She listened for any sound that might help guide her quickly to the right one. In the end it was not sound that did the job, but the odor of the sick room. Even with the door closed, the stench permeated the air in the hall. There was no mistaking the odor of urine and vomit but it was mixed with a vile sickening smell, one that assaulted her senses, halting her in her footsteps.

She stood outside the door fearing what she would find on the other side. She knew she had to go in and yet like a physical barrier the stench held her back. Had she come this far she wondered, only to turn and run, leaving a sick friend waiting for a doctor that might not come for hours? She knew she could not do that. She would have to enter and fight down the nausea that was threatening to overtake her.

Tori put her hand over her nose and taking a deep breath entered the room. Standing just inside the doorway, she let her eyes grow accustomed to the darkness and looked frantically for the curtains, so she could open the room up and let out some of the stink and heat. If she had thought it was hot in the hall, she had not been prepared for what hit her. This room had to be ten times worse. It was nothing short of an oven.

Rapidly she went to the first set of curtains and pulled them back, unlatching the window and throwing it open. She leaned out as far as she could, to take in a much needed breath. Her mouth filled with saliva, a sure giveaway, that she was about to throw up, but once again she fought back the feeling. Holding her breath again, she went to the next set of drapes and pulled them back. Behind these she found a set of French doors, which she opened wide and almost fell out of as she did so. Tori quickly made her way to the railing trying to breathe fresh air. This time the stench had somehow followed her, or maybe it was in her nose now and she could not get rid of it. Either way it was too much and leaning over the balcony, she heaved for all she was worth.

For several minutes she stood like that and waited for the contents of her stomach to finally quit coming up. She had never felt so awful or so afraid. She was scared of what was in the room behind her. Was it a dead Leone she had found, could that be what smelled so bad? As if in answer to her question, a moan came from within the room. It was a pitiful sound, agonizing and pleading. Leone was alive alright and he needed help.

She was horrified when she finally saw him and the condition in which the room was in. Someone had left soiled sheets and towels piled on the floor. A bucket filled with what one quick look told her was vomit, sat by the end of the bed. Flies greedily buzzed around the rim and still others hovered over the bed, landing on the excrement that surrounded Leone's lower half.

Leone was laying on top of the bed, covered in his own vomit and filth. For several days now the household help had been too scared to come near him. Their fear of the black death, of what the whites called Black John, was upon them. Only one of his slaves had tried, but this was too much for one old black man. This was almost too much for her.

The sight sickened her and also made her mad as hell. This was Leone, a human, not some animal. He did not deserve this; no one did. Tori went to the hallway and called down for help, she snapped her orders quickly, leaving no doubt that if they were not carried out, the whip would fly. Satisfied that things were rapidly moving along as she wanted, Tori could now turn her attention back to the man inside the bedroom.

It took several hours to clean up the mess. The room was emptied of anything that came close to smelling. Leone was bathed and his bed changed. A new mattress from one of the other rooms was exchanged with his and bowls of scented water were set around the room. Her anger had allowed her the power to get all this done and more. The soiled sheets she had burned and everyone who entered the room scrubbed with soap and water when they left or touched anything that was soiled. She was not sure how yellow fever spread but she knew it was highly contagious. Could a person get it from another who had contracted? For all she knew it was in the air that they breathed. One thing was certain, washing and sterilizing could not do any harm.

The windows stayed wide open. The twilight was not strong enough to hurt Leone's eyes and she kept the oil lamps low. A breeze came every now and then, helping cool off the room but not Leone. His fever raged unabated, burning into his mind, as well as his body. Time and time again Tori sponged him down, calling for fresh water after each effort. She tried to get him to take small amounts of fluid, lemon scented water, then mint flavored, nothing worked. He was too far gone to be induced into taking anything, and as the hours slipped by, he grew weaker and weaker.

Tori had to do something for him until the doctor came. She could not just allow him to slip away. If she could not break his fever, then she could keep trying to force water between his parched lips. He was severally dehydrated. You did not have to be a doctor to diagnose that. If he were in a modern hospital, an I.V. would be supplying his body with the necessary fluids and antibiotics. Here she had only one way to administer the life giving liquid and each time she attempted to get him to take it, precious little, if any slipped down his throat.

"Leone it's Tori, do you hear me? I'm here. Come on now let's try again. You have to drink. Please Leone I know what I'm talking about." She was holding his head and trying to force the rim of the cup between his lips, as she spoke. The water was once again spilling and running down his chin onto the pillow. His glazed eyes looked up into her face not really seeing but searching for the source of her voice. His face was so gray, his eyes were sunken, set in black holes that encircled them. Leone's appearance resembled that of a living skull, not the man who she called a friend. Tori hardly recognized him anymore and knew that only a miracle could save him.

Then for an brief instant, she thought that was going to happen, he seemed to know her and realize what she wanted him to do. He was going to try and drink something at long last. Gently she held his head and placed the cup to his lips, hope surging through her as she coaxed him softly. Suddenly and without warning he retched, his whole body rising up off the bed, his head rearing forward knocking the cup from her hand, as he rejected the vile contents of his stomach. He heaved with such a force, that within seconds everything in range of two feet was showered with the black scum.

Instantly Tori realized what was going on. Her brain registered the horror and she reacted without hesitation. A terrified scream escaped her, as she released his limp body and hysterically backed away. Her hands were covered with the thick black blood he had thrown up, and all over the front of her gown it began to seep in. On her neck it began to trickle down, gooey rivulets of stench, coagulating quickly as it cooled. The odor of it assaulted her nose. The knowledge that it now lay against her skin, hit her mind driving all semblance of sanity into the recesses of her soul.

From somewhere she could hear a woman screaming, over and over again, not realizing that the sound she was registering, was her own hysterics. She was frozen, paralyzed by the horror and the sight of Leone laying still upon his pillow. No matter how hard she wanted to look away, to run and keep on running, she could not. God help her she knew she was going to lose her mind.

Downstairs the doctor had just arrived and as tired as he was, he hastily made his way up to the room, pushing his weary bones and aching muscles to their limit. His ears could hear nothing of what the old black man was trying to tell him. The only sound that vibrated in his head, was that of a woman's terrified screams.

Bursting into the room, the old doctor realized at once what must have happened, followed quickly with sheer shock, when he recognized the woman standing by Leone's bedside. Where was the sister from the convent? Why was Madame Laffite here? With no time for answers, the doctor rushed to her side.

"Now calm down Madame. Do you hear me? It's not going to do you any good to carry on like this." He pulled her away, moving her to the other side of the room where he sat her down. She had stopped screaming, a good sign. But was he reaching her, he had to know? "Here let me wipe your face," his hand reached into his pocket and pulled out the last of his clean handkerchiefs. "Madame can you look at me?"

She did not move, only shook her head and softly uttered the word, "Leone."

She was in shock but he knew in time it would pass. She would be alright. His first concern was to get her cleaned up before taking any other steps.

He turned and spoke to a young wide-eyed lad, "Boy, you there. Don't just stand there gaping. Get down and fetch one of the girls. Tell her to get in here and take Madame Laffite to another bedroom, to strip her and bath her immediately. Move boy, now!"

He turned back to Tori, a look of concern on his face. She was white and still visibly shaken, yet she was also calmer, her breathing slower and more rhythmic. The doctor knew that for the moment she would be fine. After a bath and some laudanum, she would sleep. Lord she looked as if she could use it. He prayed that exhaustion and shock would be the only ailments she would have to deal with. Madame Laffite had placed herself in grave danger by coming to this man's side today. She could very well catch the fever. In the doctor's mind there was no doubt that that was what he was dealing with here. Like all of his cases so far that week, one after the other, all of them infected by the dreaded disease and all of them dying.

There was nothing else he could do at the moment for the lady, so his attention turned toward the quiet bed, where the unmoving body of Leone lay. As he approached the bedside, he knew before he reached him, that he was already gone. The lifeless eyes stared up toward nowhere. His lips pulled back in agony, frozen in a hideous sort of snarl, as the last racking painful spasm had left them. How may more eyes would he have to close with his gentle touch, before this plague ended? How long would this outbreak go on? How much longer could he stay on his feet before he himself collapsed from exhaustion he wondered?

Turning toward his living patient, he caught the anguished look in her eyes, as she accepted the knowledge of her friend's death. Suddenly the stress and sadness was just too overpowering for her. She had suffered too many shocks to her system, in too short a time. Tori could stand no more; she had to escape all this horror and grief. She wanted to forget and let the blanket of blackness cover her with its blissful oblivion. Closing her eyes, it swept over her, fainting brought a wonderful, peaceful sleep, safe and secure, where no one and no pain could touch her...

At first she thought it had been a terrible nightmare and she was glad to wake up to find herself safe and sound in her own bed. The movement off to the side caught her eye and she saw Jean walking toward her. His face wore such a worried expression, as he softly spoke.

"So you finally wake up. I have been so worried about you. It has been hours," he took her hand in his, as he sat on the side of the bed. "Do you remember anything?" He had to know, the doctor had told him that in cases where the mind had been given too much to handle, it simply would wipe all memory of the ordeal. After hearing what she had been through, it would not shock him if that were going to be Tori's case.

"Jean, was it only a nightmare? Tell me it was? Please tell me that I have been dreaming. Leone is not.. he's all right isn't he?" Tori felt his body stiffen and deep down inside she felt a fear raising up on a wave of sadness. "Jean, answer me?" God, how he wished she had not gone through it. That it had been only that, a bad dream. He took her in his arms and rocked her slowly back and forth. "It was no dream my love. Leone is at peace and will suffer no longer."

Tori let her body go limp against Jean's. She would have to face the fact that it had all been horribly real, that their friend was gone. Slowly and quietly she started talking, as if somehow it could help her make sense of the madness that ran wild in her head. Through her tears and clinging tightly to Jean, she spoke. "I'm glad I was there to help make his last hours more comfortable really I am. No one should have to die alone, especially like he did. I never want to have to see anyone die such a horrible death again, never!" A shudder shook her body as she continued. "I had read of these plagues in my time and the horrors of it all. It just never seemed real. It was just words that I read. How could I have known the real truth or imagine how terrible it was? Now I know. I will never forget it, never. Oh, I know in time it will dim, the memory of it will ease somewhat, along with the pain..." Did she really believe that? Or was she just trying to make herself believe it so the image of it all would somehow stop flashing so vividly in her mind. Then another thought pushed her sorrow to one side. "Jean we have to get out of town and away before you or the baby get sick. Promise me that we will leave, promise me." She knew she sounded desperate and far from rational but he had to be made to see. They had to get out right away.

"We can't Tori. There is nowhere we can go. You have been to close to the sickness. Already what you did today, has been talked about from one house to the next. You know how these things can't be kept quiet. Even if it could, I would not ask our friends to have to turn us away, because that is what they must do. Don't you see? In their minds, you could be bringing the fever with you. They would have no choice and I won't ask them."

"Jean you listen to me," she had pushed him away from her, "look at me. I cannot get the fever. In my time they have medication to stop you from ever getting it. I had that medicine. It is you and the baby that are in danger. You must believe me."

"My lady, I do. I believe anything you tell me. But how can any of our friends believe that you cannot get sick. They simply will not, and we cannot convince them. This sickness drives people to do desperate things. They will only think you are desperate and lying, to get away from the city."

Frantically now, she tried to make him see her point of view. There had to be a way. "Jean we cannot stay, we must go. Somewhere, somehow, there has to be a way. We could go to Barataria. Can't we go there? It is your home, we would be asking nothing of anyone."

Now it was Jean's turn to have to make her understand, and firmly he spoke, "No! We would not be safe even there. Some of my men, I do not trust under the best of conditions and we would not be welcome under these circumstances. They are good men, but desperate times call for desperate acts like I have said. These are men who have killed before for far less a reason. No, I am sorry you have to understand. We have to stay put for a while. In a few weeks we will leave. When people see you don't have it, we will be safe. Until then we will stay in the house and see no one. We will have no contact with the outside."

Tori saw there was no other way out of the situation she had got them into. She knew he was right and only hoped that for her family it was not too late. Now that was settled, her mind drifted back once again to Leone, and as it did so, a thought occurred to Tori. She almost whispered her question. "Jean, does this mean that we will have to miss Leone's funeral?" Surely he will be buried soon and if we are going to have to stay anyway, to prove that I am not contagious, well what harm could there be in going?"

"I have already made inquires and John was by earlier to let me know that he has seen to all the details. He was Leone's lawyer remember. The funeral is to be in the morning and like you said, I doubt it will make that much difference. I'm sure the gathering will be small and short." He rubbed his brow in thinking and nodding his head he spoke, "Yes, he was a good friend and we owe him our respects. We will attend if you are up to it. Now rest. I will go and see Christopher then join you. It is almost dawn, a few hours of sleep are needed, for both of us."

John Grymes arrived at the house early that morning to accompany them to the funeral. He had no desire to leave town and no fear of catching the fever. As many times as he had been exposed to the sickness in the past, if he had not caught it by now, he figured he never would.

The sadness of losing a close friend had been tempered early on that morning by his discovery, one that left him in a high state of agitation to say the least. His mood was foul, pacing the floor of the parlor, slapping the side of his leg with his cane as he did so. His face was dark and his eyes were drawn together, making narrow slits, out of which came a look that could freeze anyone or make them turn and run.

He had been greeted at the door by Bessy, who upon seeing the look of thunder instead of grief upon his face, had left him to himself. Besides she did not want to expose herself to anyone outside of the house, no matter who they were. John's face softened slightly as he saw Tori enter the room with Jean. She was pale. A condition made all the more evident by the black outfit she was wearing. A sadness hung on her face and in her voice, it showed clearly and for an instant he debated adding to her grief. But he wondered if by telling her his news, if it were to replace the burden of grief with that of anger, might it be a far better emotion to bear? Sadness could eat at your insides, leaving a hollow helpless feeling. Anger could bring life and determination. Yes, far better she be angry.

Tori did not seem to notice John's mood. She walked up to him and the two hugged without saying a word. She knew that he like herself, had lost a good friend, and she was glad that he would be with them today, and not alone.

John had grown close to her and admired her strength and spirit. To see her crushed as she was now hurt him. He had heard how Leone had spent his last few hours and of how Tori had gone into shock when he had died. He doubted that most men could have had an experience like she had and walk away unscathed.

"Here Tori, you can sit down for a while and have some coffee, maybe something light to eat? You must keep up your strength you know. Besides my dear, after I tell you my news, I think that you will need to have a lot of strength to avoid physically killing someone."

Tori looking from John to Jean, had an expression that asked what was going on now? It was obvious that Jean had no idea what he was talking about. His perplexed face was asking another question, how much more could go wrong?

Look, there is no way to tell you this except to come right out with it. I went to the office this morning to pick up Leone's papers. He had changed a few things in the last weeks, ironic if you think about it. The provisions of his will and a few other wishes he had wanted revised. I myself had helped him work out a lot of the details and was in full agreement with what he did. You have to understand, that as his acting lawyer, I could not, nor would I break the trust, by reveling anything till after his death. Even if it involved you both, which it did. Neither did I think that he would be taken from us so soon. Leone was a good man as we all know, and even a better friend than you could ever have known. You see my dear, he did not expect to die so soon but he was smart enough to know, that in case the unexpected did occur, that it was better to be prepared. He did not want his estate to fall into the hands of his so-called brother. Despicable as he is, rotten to the core and deserving nothing, he still would have received a small inheritance. What I am trying to say is this. The bulk of the estate was to have gone to Christopher on his twenty-first birthday. Jean was to oversee the running of the plantation and I was to be executor. I say was, because as of right now, I have no proof of any of this!"

"Just what are you getting at?" Jean asked the question as if he already knew the answer.

"Jean, Tori. This morning when I got to my office, I knew something was wrong, just felt it. Nothing seemed out of place at first, but the more I looked around, the more I knew someone had been there. The door was locked when I arrived, so I checked the windows. They too were secure, so why did I have an uneasy feeling? Then it hit me, papers were not where I had put them, I was sure of it. Little things were out of their normal places. Then my friends my fears were confirmed. The place that held Leone's will, all of his papers, it had been riffled. Everything was still in place, that was almost everything... his will was gone! No matter how many times I went paper by paper, thinking it had been slipped in between them somehow, it was not there. The fact of the matter is, that someone has taken it. Without that document, I'm afraid that there is nothing I or anyone of us can do. What I'm telling you is this. Christopher will not inherit what Leone had hoped. Everything as I see it right now goes to Edward, and there is not a damn thing we can do about it." His fist hit the table and the temper he had fought to keep under control, came boiling to the surface. Physically shaking, he faced the two of them and his head went from side to side, "It's all my fault. It is always the professional practice to have a copy of such an important document drawn up. I just never got around to having a copy made. Never expected anything to happen. God, how can you forgive me for making such a stupid mistake? It was my responsibility and mine alone. I not only let Leone down, but you also!"

He sat down so hard, that his breath escaped his mouth making a whistling sound. He was beyond himself at this point, never could he accept anything but perfection when it came to his law dealings and here he had not only let himself down, but his two closest friends. To John it was unforgivable.

Tori was the first to act she went to his side and kneeling down she spoke directly to him. The softness of her seemed to melt him. Her hand held onto his with such firmness, yet so lovingly it reminded him of his mother. The way she had handled him when he was a small child, caught in the act of having done something wrong, but not unforgivable.

"John, don't be so hard on yourself. In fact, it might be a good thing that it has been taken. My mother always told me that things often happen for a reason. I was with Leone in the end and that meant more to me than anything he might have left to us. He died with someone taking care of him. Now I know he might not have realized that, but I believe he would have wanted it. Don't you see, I love him for wanting to make our son his heir, but think of all the problems it would have given us. Edward would never have given up trying to take back what he would have believed his. Our son would never have been safe, no matter what you did to safeguard his well-being. I think it is far better that we just leave things alone for a while. It will work out in the end, I'm sure of it."

Jean had listened to what she had said. And yes, he did agree with her and had his own idea now as to who it was that had taken the will. He broke into the conversation adding his opinion. "It is clear that she is right on the matter of Edward, and might I add, that he, and he alone, had the most to gain from stealing Leone's will. I assure you, that if you find Edward, you will find the will."

Tori shook her head no. "I don't think you will ever see a copy of that document again. I agree it had to be Edward's doings. But think for a second, he is not going to be so stupid as to keep the incriminating evidence around. Especially when that evidence can take away all that he now has. Gentlemen, I think he has the upper hand, he and Simone. I'm sure that she is in on this with him somehow. They have won this round. At least we can let them think so."

John spoke now, intrigued by where her thoughts might be leading. "Just what do you mean by that statement?"

"Simply this. Edward and Simone I'm sure, will be so filled with what they have acquired, that they will most likely not think of me or my family at all and leave us alone once and for all. They have everything that they wanted after all. And if they leave me and my family alone, then we have what we want. We win."

"Yes, I see your point, but it is just so damn maddening. It is inexcusable as far as I am concerned, to just let him get away with it. I just don't know if I can do it. Damn it to hell Tori, that bastard has no right, none at all!"

Jean broke into the conversation once again. He also was seething, yet he had to agree with his wife. "John, look she has a point to all of this. We could make it work to our advantage for a while. If we do nothing, that will put him off guard, he will think he's won. That we don't know it is him or someone working for him, that took the will. He is going to expect that you will fight him on this, so why not do the unexpected. Then in a while, we will rethink this whole situation, and John my friend I assure you, that we will find away to make that weasel pay. Oh yes, we will take back in time, all that belongs to Christopher, not because he needs it, no. But because it was our friend Leone's wish that it be his."

Tori smiled at the men. It was not much of a smile but it was a start. "Look, already I feel that in an odd way this news has helped each of us here. I for one was dreading going to the funeral this morning. Now Leone's burial will not be as difficult for me, nor do I think for you. I have something other than sadness hanging over my shoulder. I have a spirit in me that like the two of you, is fighting mad. Edward has helped us, he has given us purpose." Tori was smiling even more as she continued. "I hate the man, and it will give me the greatest of pleasure, to know that we will take it all away from him one day. That we will hurt him when it counts, more so than if we took it today. It will be sweet revenge, a way of getting even with him once and for all. For all that he has done to me and his brother, not to mention countless others. This is going to be one battle that we will not lose if we play our cards right and we all know that Edward is a lousy card player, don't we?"

John and Jean laughed, it was good to see the color return to Tori's face again and indeed she had needed something to get her through the loss of her friend. The fact that the fighting Tori was back with them, convinced John that he had been right in his judgment. Telling her had been a positive move. But with or without his friend's help, he would see to it, that one day the child would inherit all. On this he made a silent oath.

Across town, a very happy Simone sat with a smug look on her face. In her hand she held Leone's last will and testament, and as Edward handed her a glass of champagne, she waved the papers in the air triumphantly and gloated. "I told you if you followed my directions, you would be all right and you would win." She frowned and her voice trembled as she went on. "That old fool Grymes took away what was supposed to be mine, when he had Adrian change his will. But not this time," she finished her drink in one large gulp. "I swore then, that if I had got Adrian's will and destroyed it, I would have had it all. Unfortunately I was too stupid and trusting. Grymes outsmarted me, but not you my dear, not you!" Simone walked over to the half-empty bottle and refilled her glass, talking as she did so. "I learned my lesson well, and now look at the results. We beat him to it darling. I just wish we could have seen his face as he entered his office. So sure of himself, that fat idiot. He must have gone into quite a rage to see that he had been outsmarted."

She began dancing around the room, unable to contain herself or her joy. Her glass slopping its bubbly contents as she spun around, waving the papers in the air as she did so. You have won! You, Edward Duval, are the sole owner and Master of one of the most grand and powerful plantations in all the South. And you know what? There's not a damn thing anyone can do about it."

Edward did feel proud of himself. He was as ecstatic as Simone. For once in his life, it seemed that everything was finally going his way. He would not forget though, that the outcome could have been very different, if it had not been for this ravishing creature that spun around the room before him. He knew that he would be sitting right now, with nothing more than a pittance of an income, while that bitch and Laffite had it all. It had hurt when he had read the copy of the will in Grymes's office, the fact that he was to get nothing of the plantation, his rightful home. A home that was a Duval heritage, was to have gone to that whore's son. If he had despised Tori before, he really hated her now. In his blind rage, his warped mind now blamed her for turning his brother against him. She had turned Leone against his own blood. Leone had loved him until she had meddled in their lives. He was glad he had gone to the office and seen the will, glad he now knew that Leone would not be made a fool of. His brother would have wanted him to destroy it if he had known the truth, he was sure. He had been blinded by the bitch's seductive ways. He did not blame Leone, after all, had he not also almost fallen into her trap. Hadn't he had found himself fantasizing and wanting her in the past? She was clever alright, but not clever enough. She might have expected to get it all, and now she would have to look him in the face and know she could never get her greedy little hands on one thing with the Duval name attached.

"Edward are you listening to me? I said are you sure that there was no other copy of this will? If there was one written, we could still lose you know?"

Edward came out of his happy dream world with a crash. Simone with her concerned face, had a frightening point. Could there be a chance of another document?

"I'm not sure. There was only this copy in Grymes's office. I went over the place just like you said." He rubbed his worried brow as he thought over that mornings activities carefully. "I have gone over all Leone's papers at his townhouse and there was nothing. That's why I went to Grymes's establishment. I suppose he could have sent a copy to the plantation for safekeeping. That would be the only other place he would have put it. Not to worry, after this morning's ceremony, I will ride to the plantation and see for myself, that my dear brother's papers contain nothing more than the books and deeds to the working of the land. I had planned on leaving anyway, too much fever around for my liking." He topped his glass up with the sparkling liquid and relaxed his worried look. Everything was under control.

Simone looked at him. This was a different Edward she saw before her. He was more in command of himself and his surroundings. He had gained an air of confidence that he had not had before. It would not be so easy to control him from this point on. After all, he no longer needed her. He could buy anything and anyone. Edward was truly independent for the first time in his life.

He looked up at her smiling, "If you want Simone, you may accompany me to the funeral. Leone was your friend too you know. But do as you choose. You may stay here if you wish, it should not take too long."

Was he already dismissing her? Didn't he realize he still needed her, the fool. She'd got him this far hadn't she? Simone had lost Adrian's fortune. Now it seemed she stood to lose becoming mistress of the Duval plantation and all its wealth as well. She was not about to make the same mistake twice. She had to make him want her, and it had to be now and forever. Simone walked over to him and reaching up with her hand, pushed back his hair, that carelessly hung over one eye. She traced his face longingly, then tenderly she let her hand wonder slowly down the front of his shirt where she could feel his heart thumping against his chest. Holding his attention with her misty eyes, she looked into the depths of his, while a solitary tear slipped down her cheek. When she was sure he had seen the tear she looked away, dropping her head in sorrow and dejection.

"You sound as if you no longer want or need me by your side. Now that you have what should have rightfully been yours anyway. That you no longer care for me, maybe you never did... I feel lost Edward. I have come to care about you so much," she hesitated before going on. "To love you. Was I wrong to think you felt the same way? Everything I have done, was to show you how I feel. I have helped you in every way I could. Now it seems I am to lose you."

At this point rather than breakdown and cry, making her look as if she were begging him to stay, to keep her, she turned the tables. After all, she had to make him want to keep her. She went to the door and opened it to let him out. Standing there ready to let him go, she neither looked at him or away from him. With her face clearly visible she spoke softly. "I will not keep you here. Go! Maybe in a while, you may come to think of me as a close friend at least. I will always be here."

Edward had meant nothing of the sort. To toss her aside as she was implying, had been the last thing on his mind. He had grown very fond of her, maybe even loved her, if such a thing was possible. To see and hear now how much she cared, the fact that she would just let him go like this... Edward studied her closely. He was well aware that she was just as conniving as he. That she was his match in that department was not in any doubt. But he was convinced that this was no act. He knew that she would find someone to take his place if he left now. Someone like Simone could not be on their own long. Being both beautiful and talented, she would get whoever she wanted, and he wanted that man to be him. With a woman like her and the power of his fortune and the family name, what more could a man want. In the back of his mind, a small voice seemed to echo the name Tori, but he pushed it away as he walked to the woman he knew he could control and have for his own. One who for some strange reason, he could not let go.

This was Tori's first visit inside a New Orleans graveyard, in this time. She had driven by them many times in the future, looking at the scene as it buzzed quickly by, marveling at the sight. It had really looked so foreign, with all the standing tombs and marble statues. She remembered how compact they were, with not an empty space to be found. Some had been closed to further burials simply because they were too rundown, or no space was left. She remembered how in her time they had become part of the tourist attractions. There were many who would never leave without saying they had seen the crypt of Marie Laveau. What a horrible thought, that young girl who fixed her hair would some day be brought here to her last resting place. Tori felt more out of place than ever, and hesitated in her walk.

The place was nothing like what it would become, still a long way from full and for now it was beautifully kept up. Far off and in another time were the narrow walkways, among the twisted maze of burial sites littered with trash and decaying tombs.

In the morning light, a great span opened up before her, dotted here and there by works of art. The white marble angles and saints looked down from the tops of the mausoleums. Some of these tombs were the size of small houses surrounded by their own landscaped gardens and wrought iron fences. It was very much like walking into a town for the dead, shining in the early sun, just asking to be explored. She could see the heat radiating from the white marble stones, the wavering air distorting a clear view of the far side of the cemetery. All this only added to the mystique of the place and to the dream-like quality of the day. To Tori it was as if she were walking in a bad dream, that she was not really there to say good-bye to her dear Leone.

As they walked further and further into the graveyard, she soon realized that they were not the only people that sad day, with a funeral to attend. She counted six other groups in the area they now found themselves in. All were there to bury some loved one who had died of the fever.

Jean looked over at his lovely wife, this was one place he had hoped she could have avoided for a long time. If it had been left up to him, he would have insisted that she stay home with the baby, rather than face this sad affair. Yet looking at her now, determined to survive the ordeal, he was so proud. He knew that nothing short of death itself, would have kept her from his side today, and that knowledge comforted him.

They had reached the Duval's family tomb, where already a few friends had arrived. It was going to be a small turnout, for such a fine man. Many of his friends would not know for days yet, that he had even passed away. Jean acknowledged the few people there and Tori tried bravely to smile. Those who knew her moved off to the far side and covered their mouths with hand held scented handkerchiefs, nodded their hello's but came no closer than they had to.

Tori felt hurt by this action, but how could she blame them? They had no idea that she was no threat to them, that in fact they had far more to fear from each other than her.

The small group was joined almost immediately by the priest. He had just finished a service not more than a fifty yards away. He stood looking around at the few people gathered and was sadly shaking his head. It was as if he were reluctant for one reason or another to begin. He seemed quite perplexed.

"Is something the matter Father? Can I get you anything or help in any way?" Jean had stepped forward as he spoke, worried that the old man before him might be ill and in need.

"No my son. It is that I have so many services to attend today, so many dead. Still others sick and in need of me at their side. I have to give what little comfort I can." The tired old priest rubbed his sweaty brow with a weary hand smudging dirt across his skin as he did so. He squeezed his aching eyes tight against the bright light reflecting into them. Impatiently his voice echoed as he went on. "You would think that Leone's brother would once in his life be on time. This is after all, the last of his own flesh and blood, that we bury here today. Two brothers, so very different and here I thought that he had begun to mend his ways of late. Well, we shall just have to proceed without him. Let us begin."

His words seemed far away to Tori, who still could not put from her mind the horrible death. The sudden sound of silence brought her attention back to what was going on around her. The service had stopped and everyone was looking behind her. Tori turned to see for herself what drew their attention. There off in the distance walking toward them, was Edward and Simone.

The two walked right by Jean and Tori as if they were not there. They joined the priest, standing close by his side. Edward's head dropped down as he quietly spoke to the man and Simone looked only upon the coffin. Clearing his throat, and obviously moved by whatever it was that he had been told, the priest started the service over.

As the words droned on and the morning heat intensified, they all stood listening and thinking about the friend they were saying farewell too. That was nearly all of them.

Edward's gaze would travel from his brothers coffin to Tori and back. Each time his look became colder and his stare raked her. The hatred jumped across the small space, physically making her take a step back. It was the crazed look of a demented man that held Tori's eyes paralyzed, frozen to his. She could feel the fear he placed upon her, creep down into her very bones.

Jean did not miss the looks that passed between the two of them. His squeezing of her hand, was to hopefully add some bit of comfort that she could hang on to.

Feeling his touch, she knew that she was safe. Her Jean had not missed Edward's hateful glare either. Jean's tight hold on her hand, was a reminder, that he stood between her and this twisted individual.

All too soon they were placing the coffin inside the tomb to lay next to the other family members. The end of the service was at hand, and like all those there, Jean and Tori turned to walk away.

"Just a minute Madame Laffite. I would like to say something to you if I may?"

His voice was laced with sweetness and his face a mask of sadness, as Edward joined them. Jean's arm slipped quickly around Tori's waist and pulled her closer to him, an act that did not escape Edward.

"I simply want to ask you, why you did not send for me when Leone was so close to the end? You must have known, or was it your hope to get him to leave his once mistress, more than just memories? You tried my dear to come between my dear departed brother and I for a very long time, didn't you? Even on his deathbed you did not give up, did you? But I won. Leone loved me and he left you nothing, everything we had, stays with the Duval's name. But don't be too sad, he did leave you with one small thing," his lips curled up in a cruel smile as he continued, "he left you Edward Duval to deal with. I will never forgive you or forget how you drove him from me. You turned him against me with your lies, keeping him away so we could not communicate. Even in his final hours you kept him away from me."

The few people left standing around let out a gasp. Had the grief of his brother's death made Edward insane, or was it the heat that had gone to his head? Surely he did not know what he was talking about. They might not have understood but Jean most certainly did. Before John had a chance to stop him he had released his hold on Tori and with the swift movement of a practiced athlete's body, moved between the two. The next thing people saw, was Edward laying on the ground, his face down in the dirt.

Simone was quickly by his fallen side, wiping the blood from the corner of his mouth. "How could you? How could you hit a man in his hour of grief? Is it not enough that he is suffering already? Have some compassion, some understanding. If the truth hurts, if you can't take it, then may I suggest that you take your wife and leave us alone. Go on, get out of here." She was spitting the words out, directing them right at the pair and had she not felt Edward's hand on her arm at that moment she would have said more.

Jean looked at the two of them and as if they no longer existed, he dismissed their presence. Taking Tori by her arm, he turned and walked calmly away.

Edward was not finished. He could not allow Jean to just walk off like he was. He had one last thing to say to them in front of witnesses. Shouting at them through tears, he had to fight from breaking down completely. "On my dead brother's soul, I promise you, that God will help me to seek out just revenge for all your sins. You think that you are above the law, above us all. Well your time is coming Laffite. And may I add also, that if I ever catch either you or your wife on my land, I will see to it that justice comes swift, by God I will. Do you hear me? You will pay for all you have done. Leone will be proud of me yet!" Edward could go on no more, his voice broke as he lost his composure and tears of frustration streamed down his face. He cried into Simone's arms, as the small group walked away shaking their heads in disbelief. Some of them came as close as they dare to Tori, offering their apologizes and condolences, telling her how brave she had been to be with Leone at the end, risking her very life as she did. They were sure it was guilt that made Edward carry on as he did. It should have been him not her nursing Leone they knew that. Didn't she know he had chosen to stay away out of fear, not that they could blame him. All his anger would pass in time, when this horrible plague left and things turned once again to normal. He would have to live with his actions and grief and learn not to place the blame on others.

Tori was not so sure. She knew in her heart that today Edward had declared war. He was going to try everything he could to destroy her and those she loved, the question was, could he?

Since the funeral the only people Tori and Jean had seen were his brother Pierre and Dominique, who stopped by to keep Jean up to date with the business. Pierre had left the day before to join his family up river and let them know that they would not have to be exiled much longer. It was obvious that the worst was over and soon, they, like many others could return in safety. Already the days claimed fewer and fewer casualties and as the weeks had past, Tori had stayed healthy and was now considered safe and free of the dreaded Black John.

Finally the morning had come, when at last they would head up river and leave for a much needed break in the cool countryside. Jean and Tori had talked to Bessy and found that she was only too willing to pack and be ready to leave whenever they wanted. She had prayed day and night for Mizz Tori to be safe and now that she had her prayers answered, she was taking no chances. Bessy wanted her family safe and sound, away from the city, until not a case was left of the awful sickness.

Tori had been up for sometime, Christopher had fussed most of the night and the last time she had gone to see him, she had picked him up and rocked the little lad until daybreak. Did he know as young as he was, that they were about to take a trip? Or was it his teeth that had kept the poor boy grizzling hour after hour? She was not sure but then once she had held him, he had slept contentedly in her arms.

It had seemed like such a good idea to make breakfast for Jean and take it up to him. As she stood outside the bedroom door she could imagine his face when she told him that she, not Bessy had made the whole meal. As tired as she was, the fact that she could surprise him with this, had her walking lightly up to the sleeping mass, trying to contain a giggle.

Slowly she placed the tray on the side table and slipped toward him with the intention of jumping back into bed. She got no closer than the bedside, when the baby started up with his morning "I'm hungry" cry. Knowing that if she ignored him he would simply get louder and wake Jean, she decided to take the baby to Bessy. She was determined not to let Christopher break the sexy mood she was in and ruin her little rendezvous with Jean. She tiptoed out of the room and into the nursery, where she picked up the child and carried him down to the kitchen.

"Here you go young man. I think it's more than mother's milk that has you fussing. You're ready for some real food aren't you?"

Bessy who was now up and busy in the kitchen with the mess Tori had left, started laughing. She reached out and took the baby from his mother's arms, happy at last that she would have a chance to feed the child. Christopher was going to have whatever he wanted to eat from now on, if she had anything to say about it. She had been waiting for weeks for this day. Known only to her, every morning a bowl of food had been waiting for the child, but today it would not waste. She would spoon the mash into his chubby little face.

Tori had intended to leave the two alone and return upstairs, a thought that left her mind, for thirty minutes as she watched and laughed with Bessy, as the baby spilled and slurped his way through his first solid meal. She had finally left the two, when it was clean up time.

Upon entering the bedroom Tori was surprised to find that Jean was still asleep. It was not like him to be so lazy. He had to be playing a game with her, she thought, that was more his style. Smiling to herself, she picked up a pillow from her side of the bed. Boy was she going to let him have it. A shiver of anticipation crossed her body as she had a flash of how these pillow fights of theirs often ended. Trying to cover the excitement in her voice she spoke seriously. "Jean. Oh Jean, you lazy good-for-nothing pirate. You had best protect yourself because you are about to pay the penalty for playing possum."

He did not move. Tori stood over him pillow poised and ready. Jean was definitely playing with her she told herself. Slowly he turned his head. She held her breath as he rolled toward her. This was it, her moment to strike was at hand. But his weak voice halted her action.

"Tori. Tori, my head hurts so bad, can't shake it. The light hurts. Thought I would feel better. Don't want to disappoint you, must go today."

His voice was raspy and the feel of his skin, was burning to her touch. It sent a screaming message to her brain, even as he continued to try and talk.

"Better get the doctor, too sick to go today, sorry." His apologetic look came from behind two fevered eyes, that he tried to shield from the light with his shaking hand. A weak smile left his lips, then he turned away burying his face, pulling at the sheet, to cover his shaking body.

Tori dropped the pillow and quickly ran to the door shouting for someone to go and get the doctor fast. She wanted him dragged here if they had to but they were to make it clear, that he was to come immediately, if not sooner. She did not wait for confirmation that her orders would be followed, she did not have to. The sound of the front entrance slamming shut did that. Turning she went back towards Jean's side, knowing that what she was looking at once again, was a clear case of yellow fever.

As time passed, she kept herself busy waiting for the doctor by wetting a cloth in cool water and wiping Jean's fevered brow. She refused to believe that her efforts were futile or that Jean's outcome would be that of Leone's. She would keep a positive attitude and keep Jean fighting. As for the doctor, surely he had learned something in this last outbreak, that would help Jean. After all she reasoned he had spent more time with the disease than anyone.

Jean would wake now and then, taking a sip of the water that she insisted he drink. The last time he had tried to drink, had been difficult for him. It was even harder for him to talk. He had guessed he had the fever and wanted to make one thing clear to her.

"Tori you must keep Christopher away from me, do you hear? No one else but you to come in." He struggled to continue. "It is the fever I know it is." Weakly he took hold of her hand and tried to sound reassuring as he spoke. My lady do not fear I will not leave you. I love you and the baby too much." It broke her heart to hear his weakened voice struggle through the pain and weakness that already raked his body. He was getting worse as each hour passed and she had no control, no way to help stop this devil. Twice she went to the door to call for Bessy. How come the doctor was taking so long? Didn't they understand how sick Jean was? His fever was climbing and the rising temperature outside did not help matters.

She sat looking at him, he was strong but no matter how many times she wiped him down or fanned him, it was not going to help. She had to face it, after the doctors visit, she knew that there would be nothing else they could do to help save Jean's life. It would be out of their hands.

Her thoughts swirled, mixed with both hopes and doubts. She knew in history that Jean helped fight at the battle of New Orleans, and that would mean he would live. In that knowledge she had her hope. But what if by her coming to this time she had in some way altered it all. What if she had given him this fever and he died? Therein lay her doubt. History, she thought, would be forever changed and it would all be her fault.

The facts about this fever were grim, and strong as he may be, they did give him a chance but not much of one. Panic was taking hold right alongside of her fear. She just did not know which way this could go, or what she could do.

The doctor had done nothing more than confirm what she already knew and to tell her he would be back the next day to see how he was doing and maybe bleed him. Tori knew of the old practice of bleeding and of how it did no good, it only weakened the patient more. She would never allow that. He needed all his strength and more if he were going to win the battle. What she needed was help from someone who could give him medication to fight the fever, someone who had drugs that worked! The only problem with that idea, was that what she needed was out of reach in another time.

She had to think, where and how in the world could she get drugs that could help? Both modern drugs and doctors were out of reach but maybe not everyone. Marie Laveau, that was who would have the medication he needed. Tori knew the young girl was doing not much more than fix hair and hand out the odd potion. But she also knew, in time she would have a lot of remedies for sale, some of which would cure. They would work because they had the base of many modern drugs. Marie would draw from herbs and plants the ingredients that Jean needed. Tori knew Jean would have a chance, if she could get this girl to come and help. She just prayed that Marie had already started mixing her medications, that she wasn't a few years to early.

"Bessy, tell her I'll pay whatever she wants, anything, anything at all. She just has to come and see him. It's his only chance!"

If Bessy had been surprised by Tori's request, she had not shown it. She just listened and then left to do her mistress's bidding. How could she explain to Mizz Tori, that she was plain scared to death of that Voodoo. That no matter what the church told her, she knew it to be more powerful and nothing to mess with. She would go and take the message to Marie because she dearly loved Jean and Tori. She knew also, that if he were going to get better, then it was going to have to be with the help of some mighty powerful gris gris!

It was late that night when a light knock came on the bedroom door and Tori let in the young black girl. She stood looking toward the bed in which Jean lay, not saying a word. Her gaze then fell on Tori's worried face and she could see the hope and desperation written in its worried lines. What if she tried to help this man who all of New Orleans loved? What if she failed, what then? Ah but if she were to succeed, if he were to live, then this family of power would be indebted to her for life.

Marie was not stupid, she would only take on this challenge if she thought the odds were on her side. It would not take long for her to decide what should be done, and much depended on the strength of the woman who stood before her.

Jean was burning with fever and twice he had made such a mess that Tori felt she could not handle the situation without going out of her mind. Still she had managed to keep control of her emotions and now that help had arrived, she was able to calmly tell Marie everything she could about Jean and his condition.

Marie listened, still in silence, as if she were not sure yet of what she was going to do. She stood so still, her eyes questioning and seeking the truth. It was as if she were in some kind of a trance. Could she have been wrong about her abilities Tori wondered?

Then as if in answer to her doubts, the girl pushed past her and walked toward Jean. She removed her dark wrap and placed a cloth bag she carried, on the foot of the bed. Without a word yet spoken, she started to work. There was no fear in her actions as she examined her patient. Standing watching her, Tori had the odd feeling that she was watching a modern nurse at work. The girl took his pulse, looked in his eyes, and felt the glands around his neck. She touched his forehead with the back of her hand and mumbled something close to his ear, then she put her head to his chest, listening to his heart as it raced beneath. Satisfied with what she had found, she turned toward Tori and smiled for the first time.

Marie took over and gave orders of things to be done and things that she would need in the next twenty-four hours. Carefully she lay out the small bags of herbs and powders. A cross was placed on the table and a small candle lit. Incense was burned and prayers said, as she waited for all that she had asked for to be brought into the room.

"We have a good chance of healing him. He is a strong man with a will to live. You have done well. Everything you did so far, was what I myself would have done. But now the real work begins. You will help me for a while, then you will leave. You must believe in me, in him and pray. You must do as I ask, if we are to drive the devils away, no questions, just obey." She had been deadly serious and very determined as she spoke. But then seeing that Tori was not going to oppose her, she softened and smiled toward her. Fear would not have to be used here to get her way.

Between them Jean was stripped naked with only a cloth laid across him. This Marie told Tori was so she would not have to feel embarrassed or uncomfortable.

"But he is my husband. I won't be embarrassed. Should I be? I mean if it will help him in any way to lay naked completely, then let him lay that way. He's passed the point of realizing what is going on."

"I'm sure it would not embarrass you, but how about me? I'm just a young girl, not supposed to look at any man that way." She was laughing, her face letting Tori know that it had all been said in fun. Marie had spoken to Tori in this manner to lighten the moment and help her in some sort of odd way cope with trusting her.

"You seem to be so young and yet so wise, how old are you Marie? How have you come to know and learn so much?"

"I am as old as you want me to be. Years, days, they really don't mean much do they? It's what a person is that counts, don't you think? Now let us wipe this man of yours down again, he's still getting hotter and the worst is yet to come."

Again and again the two woman worked on cooling him down. The only time Tori left his side, was to check on their son and by the second day, she was so exhausted, that Marie insisted she sleep for a few hours.

"The fever should break soon. One way or another we will have our answer today. I will call you if there is any change. You are the one that concerns me now. Please go. You need your rest. You must prepare for that which lays ahead." For a fleeting moment she looked saddened, as if she knew of some horrible fate. Tori felt her heart skip a beat, as this strange girl looked at her. Just how much of this Voodoo Queen to be was legend and how much was fact, she did not know. One thing was sure though she did seem to have a sixth sense. Afraid to stay and ask questions of what she meant, a very tired Tori welcomed the few hours of rest. After all, she knew it would be days yet, before Jean would need less attention. With her son in her arms for company, she slept deeply for the rest of the afternoon.

Marie worked with Jean. He was strong and true, he had the will to live, that would help but he needed more. Mixing together more of the herbs she had with her she forced his parched lips apart and let the vile liquid trickle slowly into his mouth. Every few minutes she would force him to sip the concoction, knowing it was his only chance to beat this fever. Jean called out often for his love. Tori's name was the only one on his lips. Over and over the man went on about his love, about her staying with him. Marie sat and listened, taking in the jumbled ravings, which at first sounded like nothing important. A few hours later, a sly smile crept over her face, as she put the pieces of his delirium into a story that made a whole lot of sense.

In the late afternoon she stood and looked contentedly down on Jean speaking to him softly. "You will live Jean Laffite, the fever has broken and the sleep you have now will be deep and silent. I have learned much from you about your Tori. Much that will come in useful in the future. Maybe for you, maybe for me. It will be a secret for the two of us to hold, until I know what to do about this knowledge you have let fall my way." She was pleased with herself. Jean Laffite would owe her his life and now she had information that could come in handy. Marie looked at her slumbering patient and let her own happiness slip away, as a grim look caused her lips to tighten. She bent down to speak to Jean, whispering in his ear, "Sleep my friend, for soon you will carry a far heavier burden. Your life is about to change once again and you will have to be far stronger than ever before."

A piercing scream let loose from the other room. It could be heard all over the house. Marie turned knowingly, looking toward the adjoining room where the scream emitted from. Behind that closed door, she could hear the wailing of a servant join in with Tori's desperate cry for help. A sadness clouded Marie's eyes, the lids closing as if wishing to deny that which she had hoped could have been delayed. The hours of no sleep and the worry that fell on her now, aged her far beyond her years.

"So it starts. I had hoped that you would have had longer to recover my friend, but it is not to be. You will rest this night, my drugs will see to that, then you must be strong. I cannot help this time, for this time I already fear the cloud of death approaches. God help this home and the people here. They will need all the help they can, to bear what comes their way."

Jean slept on blissfully unaware of the girl who stood talking at the end of his bed, unaware of the panic that had griped his house.

Marie walked toward the door as it flew open. Tori was racing toward her, holding the child in her arms. Tears fell from her and terror was written across her face, as she stood before Marie.

"He has it! You knew didn't you? That's what you meant earlier today. My son has the fever! God, Marie do something, help him please."

Marie took the child from his mother his little eyes seemed to plead with her. Marie's heart twisted in agony, as she knew that there was nothing she could do to save him. Children of this age did not last long with this devil's curse. The fever would go too high, too quick. All she could do, was try and make the child more comfortable, and that was something that Tori his mother could do far better than herself. How she hated the feeling of not being able to do anything. How would she explain to his mother, that it was hopeless?

"See to your husband. His fever has broken and he will live, but let him rest. Do not wake him this night with such sad news. He is still so weak. I will do what I can for the child." Tori walked toward Jean with a mixture of happiness and hellish worry. She was so relived he was going to be alright, but now her son, their son, was so sick and how would she tell him that when he woke up?

That night was like a living nightmare for Tori, one that seemed endless in it's horror. Jean slept and Marie worked with her child. She would go from one bedside to the other, praying that one would continue to sleep and the other would stay awake and fight. By early light, it was obvious to her, that the stronger Jean became the weaker Christopher got. Looking at Marie who had not stopped her endless work at trying to win against all odds, she dropped all hopes of his recovery. Marie did not need to tell her that which she could see for herself. Jean had lived, Christopher would die! She had to let Marie know she understood, that she did not blame her.

She touched the girl's arm letting her know she was alongside, so intent was she on trying to cool down the baby' fever. "Marie, I know he is very ill, too ill for you or anyone to help." Marie looked into her agonized face and found something she had not expected. Along with Tori's pain she found compassion and understanding. She really did know her son was dying and she did not blame her.

"If I were to tell you that I thought he would survive, I would be lying. You are right. I just did not know how to tell you, I had to try." Tori could see she was so tired, so sad. The young face that looked toward her, was like that of a lonely child. Marie raised her hands toward the ceiling and spoke in frustration to both the heavens and Tori. "You can hold him and try to keep him cool, but the little one just gets hotter and hotter. If only we had a way to break the fever, but there is not, not for him. I have done all I can! Forgive me, I can do no more?"

"Oh Marie you have done so much already don't you see? Without you, I would have lost both of them. At least I am to keep Jean. It is out of our hands. The child's life is in God's hands now." She picked her child up, and rocked him gently as she spoke to herself, "Maybe he was not meant to be. I guess I should have known, never did I read of Jean having a son."

Tori was making no sense to Bessy, who stood wringing her hands and sobbing quietly, but to Marie it was as it should be. Knowing what she did now, she had a understanding of what Tori was going on about. She had to agree with her it was as it should be. She might not be able to help the child but a few words of wisdom might help comfort the mother. Taking Tori aside and out of earshot of Bessy, she talked softly and knowingly to Tori.

"The little one will not have to grow up wondering where his mother is. I think it is as it is written. All has passed as it should and still much will happen. Have strength in the time to come Tori. Your love for this child and for Jean, will get you through." She smiled a knowing sort of smile filled with love. Once again the wisdom of years filled her face; she seemed to understand.

Tori had heard her right, but how could she know? Could it be that she really knew or was she guessing? Had Jean spoken out loud in those hours that she had left him in Marie's care, or was it that power, that ESP she had?

Marie saw the questioning look and decided to avoid any further questions that might giveaway her hand. She quickly changed the subject.

"Jean has a right to see his child I think. The time grows short. You must go to him now. I will leave, there is nothing left here for me."

Tori looked at Marie and could hardly see her for the tears that clouded her eyes, as she held her dying son. The girl Marie, and that was what she was, knew so much. She seemed to know everything. So many questions swam in Tori's head, questions that would have to wait. She was right, Jean as weak as he was had a right to see his son before the end. She could not talk further. Tori walked slowly toward Jean's room.

Marie closed the door and looking at Bessy she told the woman to leave them alone until they called for her. Then she swiftly collected her things and without a further word left.

It was not until she entered her home with her closest friend and lover, that Marie broke down and cried. Life it seemed to her, was nothing more that a cruel trick played upon all, by the devil himself.

Tori sat by Jean's side of the bed. He looked too weak. His color was not even back yet in his face. He was so pale and drawn but his breathing was strong and clear of any rasping sound. His forehead was covered by a film of glistening perspiration, a good sign. He might still have a fever but not one that was raging out of control. Jean was on the mend. He would live, but how would he ever heal from the loss of his son?

The baby was so hot. His little hands just lay wherever Tori placed them. He was already so weak and dehydrated that even crying was too much of an effort for the little lad. His little face was as if he were sleeping. If only that were the case, just sleeping instead of near death, she thought. She knew that she had to wake Jean soon, the end was coming fast. The baby's breathing was labored and his little heart raced so fast that it felt as if it would jump out of his chest.

Touching Jean's arm gently, Tori spoke his name. Twice she felt as if her voice would break, as if she were about to lose control and fall to pieces. She stopped for a second and took in a deep breath, and drawing on a strength that she did not know she had within her at that moment, she spoke to Jean.

Finally he awoke forcing open his eyes in response to her gentle coaxing. His tired face looked at her, as a weak smile acknowledged the fact that he knew he had won his battle. He mistook the look on Tori's face for one of relief.

"I told you that I would not leave you did I not? You and the baby can rest easy now. It's going to be fine. Had the damnedest dreams. Thought I saw a young black girl here with me, seen her before... the night the baby was born. She was the same one who told me about the baby coming." His speech stopped as he seemed to gather his strength to go on. He wanted so much to make her realize that he was going to be alright. "I see you have Christopher there. Let me see him."

Jean lifted his head up slowly, struggling as if this simple effort was going to be too much for him. The already pale color of his skin blanched further, as the room started to spin before his eyes. Tori waited a few seconds to give him time to adjust to the new position and then looking straight at him she heard a voice say clear and firmly, what had to be told.

"Jean, the baby... he is sick. He has the fever." How she had said those horrible words she did not know but she watched as they registered on Jean's face. Instead of sinking into despair as she had thought he would, she watched as a look of determination filled him as he pulled himself up higher in the bed. He was fighting the waves of nausea and weakness that flooded his body, nothing else mattered but what she had just said.

"We must do something. Send for the doctor. He must come at once. He saved me. He can do it again and save our son." His head fell backwards against the pillow. "What can I do?"

Tori became frightened at his strong reaction. He would kill himself trying to save the child if she let him. "Jean listen to me. The doctor has not been here for days. Marie Laveau saved your life. She was the young black girl that you saw. If it had not been for her, you would not have made it. She has looked after the baby for hours, but Jean, oh my love, he is just so small and he is so very weak now." Gently she went on, "Jean our son is dying and there is nothing we, or anyone can do."

Jean shook his head, he would not accept it, the fact that he had lived, only to lose his son! He tried to get out of bed, only to fall back too weak to go anywhere or do anything. How he hated himself, his child needed him and he could not do a damn thing. Tori watched him as he struggled, she wanted to hold him, to try to take away his pain, but all she could do was sit and look on, as she rocked the child in her arms.

It was as if Christopher knew he was needed, he opened his eyes and let out a small whimper, so weak and yet so powerful. His little cry stilled the room, and Jean leaned back looking at his son in Tori's arms.

"You are sure it's the fever? That there is no chance he will get better?" His voice was pleading and frail. It sounded hollow and dejected, yet resided to the fact that there was nothing he could do.

"I wish with all my heart I could tell you different but I can't. Even with all I know from my time I can't change this. Do you want to hold him? If you want sometime alone with him, I will leave."

He loved his lady for caring so much, even willing to let him be with their son alone, hurting as she must be. She was thinking of him, putting aside her own grief. "No, I don't need time alone with him. Let's lay him between us, let us both be with him, we need each other."

Tori put the child on the bed gently between them. His burning body lay limp. The only movement was his sunken stomach raising up and down, as his little lungs struggled to bring in the life-giving air.

"My son, my little man, your father loves you. I have always wanted a son and no child will ever take your place. You know it's your father's voice don't you? Look see how he turned his head?" Jean moved so his child might get a better look at him but the baby turned his head away and looked toward his mother. This did not upset Jean it pleased him. "See I told you we should be together, he knows we are both here. Oh Tori, how can I let him suffer. I feel so helpless, I am his father."

"And I am his mother. I can't do anything either. I should have known better. I blame myself. I should not have been around him after I exposed myself to the fever. I am to blame. Can you ever forgive me?"

"Tori don't. It is not your fault or mine. We love him, neither of us would hurt this child. He knows as we do, that all we have is love for him."

The baby's eyes closed and opened slowly, his breathing seemed to be easing somewhat, and Tori reached gently and stroked his face with her finger. His eyes were so glassy as he looked beyond them both. She started humming a lullaby. Once again Tommy's song slipped forth and she found that it came out soothingly, as Christopher closed his eyes to sleep.

Jean watched, as his heart broke into a thousand pieces. Each burning with a pain far beyond anything physical. He knew his son would not open his eyes again. As he watched his son's small face, he felt a part of himself was slowly dying along with his son. He did not fight it.

Before Tori finished the tune, the baby stopped breathing. He simply gave up his fight and peacefully slipped away. Jean and Tori stared at him for some time. Both knew he had gone, but neither moved, they needed to spend some time with their child...

Across town, in a darkened room a wind came up from nowhere and blew out a candle that stood besides a statue of the Blessed Virgin Mary. The instant the flame extinguished, one could here the crying of a young girl somewhere in the darkness. A tall man walked to the sobbing sound, to comfort and console. He said nothing, in his wisdom he allowed the grief to spill through the painful words that filled the silence.

"He is gone. The little one has passed on. If only I knew more, maybe I could have saved him. Marie Laveau knows nothing, but on that child's memory, I swear to you, that I will learn all that you can teach me. You must teach me more, all that you know."

Jean and Tori stood supporting each other, as they looked down upon a small wooden coffin. Each was silent drawn inside themselves with grief and with a painful awareness that on this day as they buried their child they would be burying a part of their lives, a part of their love.

Tori looked sideways at Jean. He stood stooped as if the love of life had been drained from his soul. The sadness that hung about him like a halo, touched all those who looked upon this grieving man. Since the child's death, he had put a grip on his emotions, and placed a mask upon his face. It was a look that was blank unless you read the agony deep in his eyes.

Nothing she had said or done, had seemed to reach him. He had loved the child far deeper than she herself had realized and now he was dealing with the loss by pushing her away. If it had not been for Dominique taking over all the arrangements, she doubted that they would be standing here today at this small funeral.

So it was that on this day in the year 1811, in a country cemetery far from the sickness and death in the city, they had come to lay to rest in peace, a much-loved child. Jean had insisted that his son not be buried in a cold place, surrounded by people he did not know, like Leone had been. He wanted his son to be placed in a surrounding that was green and peaceful, one that felt like a garden, instead of a city of the dead. He did not hear the words spoken over his son as he looked beyond the grave and out over the river. What would happen now? He had hoped that the child would have kept his life full. That he would have grown up, to share with him everything that he himself had been denied sharing, with his own father. The loss of a friend or even a parent had been hard, but this loss was beyond that. He felt that he would never be able to put behind him the emptiness that ate at his heart.

Standing next to Tori and leaning on her like he was, seemed another unfairness to him. He should be the one supporting her. She needed to lean on him, but he felt his legs growing tired and his head hurt so. His illness had left him weak, something he deplored in a man. Damn the fever, and damn New Orleans. He hated it all and if he could, he would board his ship and leave.

She knew he needed her right now. His whole body had begun to shake. She understood that it was a huge effort for him to be standing by her side, so soon after being at death's door himself. Tori's arm went around his waist and she pulled him toward her. He did not resist, rather leaned closer and looked down into her face with a look of gratitude.

Tori let herself cry. She cried for her son, for his father and most of all for herself. She needed Jean to share this with her not close her out as he had done. Her whole grief-ridden body reached out for him, as she could no longer contain the dam that held back the flood of tears. He had to see, to understand that she was hurting too, that he was not the only one in pain.

As if he had been awakened from a dream, the sight of his lady slumped in his arms, with a painful look of grief written so clearly on her face, slapped him hard. He realized that she needed him, they needed each other. Jean took her in his arms and the two of them clung unashamedly, slowly rocking back and forth, as the service ended. He looked down into her face, lifting it up with his trembling hand and gently brushed the tears from her cheeks. The long dark lashes that framed her eyes, held large tears. They clung to them like drops of dew on a morning flower.

"We will get over this together. Starting now my lady, we must share this or lose what we have. For Christopher, we will make it."

His voice was cracking, but the strength and determination behind it was as strong as ever. She was no longer alone and as he held her, it was as if the two of them were the only people in the world. Looking over to Pierre and his wife, Jean asked if everyone would leave them alone for a while. They just needed to say good-bye to their son by themselves. Without a word, the few friends and family drifted away from the graveside. J.D. and his wife deeply moved, and understanding only too well, hurried the small gathering away.

The day was still and only the birds could be heard to break the silence of the surrounding countryside. The spot was peaceful and quite beautiful, with large old oak trees shading the ground here and there. The Spanish moss, swayed in the light breeze that every now and then floated up from the slow-moving Mississippi. It was the kind of place a young boy would have loved to play at, to explore and climb the giant trees, to run in the cane fields. Dominique had chosen well, when he had found this spot for Christopher.

"I want a tree planted here so it will grow and shade this spot where the lad is to lay." Jean was talking to himself yet the two blacks that were waiting to bury the coffin, overheard him and nodded their sad faces.

"Yes sur. We's see's to it. We's be a plantin da tree right away massa."

Jean looked over to the two and seeing the shovels in their hands, knowing that they had a job to do, one he did not want to be around to witness, he took Tori by the hand and walked away from the graveside.

"We will be back soon, you can start now," he snapped. "And be quick. Get the job done."

"Oh Jean, please, let's just walk. I can't stand this, my heart is breaking," she whispered, as she pulled him still further away.

The couple walked over to the riverbank and sat on it's grassy side, watching the muddy water flow slowly by. Jean lay back and looked up at the clouds and just stared not speaking or moving. He seemed lost in thought, frozen in time. Tori dropped down to his side and lay her head on his chest. She could hear his heart beating. His breathing was heavy and slow. His hand came up and stroked her head rather like a father comforting a child.

"I can't cry any more, Jean. I feel empty and numb. He just can't be gone. We had him such a short time."

"But that's just it isn't it? We did have him and I will always have him with me. You gave me a son my lady and for that I will always thank you. We shared something that no one can ever take away from us. He will always bind us together, no matter what happens from this day on."

What more could she say; he would start to heal now she knew that, and yes she could put some of her fear for him away, his silence spoke for itself.

It was late in the afternoon that the pair walked back to the gravesite and there they stood looking at the little mound of dirt. Someone had covered it with flowers and a small tree had been planted close by. This was it then. All that remained was to have a small gravestone made and it would be finished.

"He needs a headstone, but a simple one. I shall talk to my brother and have one made up. One day people will walk by here and look down on this tiny grave and wonder who he was. Let's leave it like that, let's let him rest under his tree. You say in history, that there was no mention of me ever having a son. Well let us make sure that it stays that way. For some reason it seems right."

"I said I did not know Jean. I do not know everything about you or your life. It is possible that you will have another son or sons in the years ahead... But I can't pretend he did not exist Jean. He was our son, so how can we walk away and forget him?"

"We won't, not ever. But my son is just that, he's my son. Our child. He does not belong to history or the future. He belongs to us, and now to God and I want to keep it that way. The headstone will read only his first name, simple and full of love."

"Jean, I believe that he would have wanted it that way. Yes, it only marks his remains, his spirit is free and only our love for him, nothing else did he take with him. It's perfect." Her smile was soft and her face was filled with a calm that slowly seemed to fill the air.

The wind blew gently and off in the distance the sound of a horse coming down the road broke into the somber mood. Jean looked up and recognized the rider. It was Dominique, and as he stopped outside the graveyard, Jean knew it was time to go. Taking Tori by her arm he walked slowly away, and pulling himself up, he took in a deep breath, his old swagger coming back into his step.

"I will take his memory with me my lady. Always he will be in my heart. But I will never again come here, not until I die. One day I will lay by my son's side, that I promise you. No matter what happens, I will see to it that he will have me with him one day."

"Jean, I love you. Let's just go now, we can talk about this later," concern and doubt sounded in her voice.

"We don't need to talk about it. I have made up my mind. Now let us depart. We have a life to live and get on with. We have to heal, and my lady we will heal, together..."

Tori had been so absorbed in reliving her story that to her the reality of sitting in a hotel room with Tommy had ceased to exist. The pain of remembering the loss of her child had awakened a long buried grief, that once again had with all its raw emotions been allowed to surface. She had not uttered a word for several minutes. Instead she just sat in the still room sobbing uncontrollably, while Tom held her.

"Miss Tori ma'am," he let go of her and stood up watching her closely. "Please ma'am can you listen to me? Do you hear me?" Like a voice far away she heard him breaking through the mist of all her yesterdays, and suddenly she found herself looking into Tom's very distressed face. In the space of a few seconds she traveled in her mind back to the reality of what was happening and nodded her head.

"I'm sorry. Guess it just got to me. All the memories, all the agony of his death." She put her head down in her hands and shook it as if trying to release the vivid pictures from her mind. Tori looked up at him and trying to smile spoke in a calmer voice. "Tell you what, let me go and wash my face and pull myself together. You do us both a favor and call downstairs to room service, and order us something to eat. See if you can't get us a bottle of wine to go with that." She could see his expression lighten up some, but the boy was still very anxious that was obvious to her. "Tom, I'm alright really I am. Now go on make that call and I'll be right back."

He watched her as she left the room and once alone he moved like a man in a dream toward the phone. He could hear his own voice in his ears as he ordered two burgers and a bottle of house wine. It was as if he was functioning on automatic drive, doing one thing while his mind raced on and on thinking of another. His eyes were traveling around the room looking and yet not really seeing anything, when the voice on the other end of the phone asked if that would be all. Tom's eyes caught the empty packet of cigarettes laying on the table and a slight smile exposed itself as he added an order for a pack of cigarettes.

With that taken care of and the room to himself, he had time to think over the past few hours and all he had learned. One thing was certain, if she thought for one second that the story was finished, that she could not go on, well she was in for a fight. Having heard this much and being drawn into the tale, Tom wanted to hear the rest. It was like stopping in the middle of a good book or putting a movie on hold he reasoned. Sure he had a million questions to ask her but something inside of him told him to stay quiet and hold them until she had finished. He had to get her talking again, to continue but could he?

"You seem to be deep in thought, not that I blame you. It must seem incredible to you." Tori was standing in the doorway looking at him.

"Yes Ma'am, you could say that. I did what you wanted and put in an order for a couple of burgers and a bottle of wine and all. Added a pack of them to it for you," he pointed to the empty crumpled package on the table. "Thought you might need them and all."

She smiled then for the first time in hours and joined him, sitting down on the couch. "I really should give them up you know, but somehow I just can't quite do that yet." She looked up at him and added, "maybe after tonight I won't need them anymore."

"Tori, ma'am," he walked over to join her, sitting down only inches away. "I have to ask you..."

She held up her hand, placing her finger on his lips to silence him. "I really wish you wouldn't, not now. I know you have a million questions and just as many doubts but Tom please for now could you just wait. I know I'm asking you a lot here but you see there is still so much more I have to tell you. If you could just find it in your heart to give me a little more of your time and patience, I promise you, I will answer all your questions when I finish."

A knock at the door interrupted her. "That should be our dinner and I don't know about you, but a glass of wine sounds good to me."

Once the food was set out and the wine poured, it became evident that neither one was that hungry after all. Tori picked at the odd French fry and watched as Tom pushed a half-eaten burger away. It was not fair to keep him in suspense, sitting there brimming with questions and doubts, no matter how much she dreaded carrying on with her story. She had after all started it and now she had no choice but to finish.

"You know, as bad as those first years were I did make some good memories also." Tom looked at her, nodding his head in agreement but not uttering a word. He had hoped she would continue and now that it seemed she was ready, he was not about to interrupt her.

"I don't know if I can go on with this Tom." Her hands were shaking again and she had looked away from him. "That next year, after the baby died, is mostly a blur to me now. We both hurt so much, Jean and I. I think maybe we just went day to day trying to deal with the what had happened. Each moment was an effort for both of us you know. Then before we knew it a whole year had slipped by. Without realizing it we had begun to heal. The pain never fully leaves you. You just sort of learn to live with it, until one day it is a dull ache in the empty place in your heart. You see in the first weeks after something like that you ask yourself, how can I go on? How can I possibly survive this pain? But you do go on, you do survive and life continues..."

Tom settled back once more, realizing that Tori without knowing it had started back into the story. She was back in her memories once more reliving it all. As she talked, like before, her vivid descriptions soon had him quickly slipping back with her. He sat motionless, entranced again, listening carefully to her every word.

## Chapter 18

Fall came to the city of New Orleans and with it cooler days. The horrors of that summer and its plague slipped or rather were pushed from people's minds. To dwell on something so bleak was not the nature of these people, who seemed to Tori to be forever pursuing the art of pleasure.

September came and with it the knowledge that the year of 1812 was fast approaching it's end. Tori was so full of mixed emotions. Her life had been full of turmoil the past year leaving her confused and hurt. She had in no way expected to stay so long in the past that was for sure. And she certainly had had no intention of becoming so entangled emotionally. Not only had this caused her upset but had succeeded in delaying her attempt at crossing back to her own time.

Once again she reminded herself that no matter the outcome of the attempt, she had made herself promise she would at least try. Why then did it seem that from the very beginning of her arrival, something was always happening to keep her from that one important goal. Like the threat that Edward had made at Leone's funeral, that if he found Jean or herself on Duval land they would pay for it. The lake therefore had been put permanently off-limits. Another roadblock to add to the already growing number it seemed. She had begun to think that maybe she was not meant to go back, not meant to even have the chance to try.

The death of their son had delayed her attempt by months. She could not bring herself to mention to Jean, that she felt the time had come to make the trip. So Tori had kept herself busy by entertaining their friends and studying the art of fencing with Dominique. They had returned to Barataria for the month of November and back into town the beginning of December.

Jean had become a different man. In the last year he had spent long hours with his brother at the blacksmith shop, or in meetings with buyers of the illegal goods he now handled. His men took more British ships each month. The cargo they carried were rich in nature, the spoils were more than one could imagine. If other ships of different nationalities were taken, which Tori knew was the case, that fact was kept under wraps. Jean worked from early morning to late at night, falling into bed, where sleep allowed him a few hours of grief-free dreams. His work and his lady had become his salvation.

The two of them had slowly started to heal, and the loss of their child became a raw pain that eased with time and understanding. Each knew what the other felt and in that one clear fact, they were able to reach out and share all that had to be experienced and talked about. It had been the advice of Marie Laveau to talk about it that had helped them. She had told them that her mother often said, "like a wound to the body, a wound to the soul heals faster in the open, rather than covered and left to fester. For surely a festering wound of any kind, would in the end kill."

Marie had just left from one of her visits. She was the only person that Tori had fixing her hair for special occasions, and this night, she had been told, was to be a special night.

At first neither Jean or Tori wanted to attend the ball that was been given by the now newly-elected Governor Claiborne and his wife. But somehow Dominique of all people, had managed to acquire the necessary invitations.

There was to be an American General there, who for one reason or another had impressed Dominique so much, that he had wanted to attend. He had explained again and again to Tori, that without her and Jean accompanying him, he would never be admitted to such an grand affair. In the end feeling sorry for him and just a little intrigued, Tori had helped persuade Jean that it might not be so bad. Just who the American General was she did not know, after all the only one she could think of from her history lessons, was not due in town until the Battle of New Orleans, and that was still some time off.

This general had come into town to raise money for his men, who after waiting to fight a battle somewhere against Indians of some sort, had been told to go home. His troops it was said, were hungry and tired and camped a two-day's ride from town. The ball was in his honor. The money raised tonight would help him send his men home, fed and warm.

Dominique had met one of the General's men, and arranged a deal. It was to be from the Laffite brothers, that this man would receive a lot of the General's supplies. That was all Jean or Dominique would tell her. Jean had found it a great game teasing her; after all this would be the first American she would have talked to in years, centuries even. He did not count Grymes or Claiborne in the running.

"Let us see if your history lessons were of any substance. Maybe you could let me know if he will be back for more arms when he fights again," laughed Jean.

"You are impossible you know that? The both of you expect me to remember everything I read or learned. I do not know this date and that date, this fact and that fact! Well! let me tell you, this so-called General tonight is probably some poor bastard who slipped through the cracks of time, dying of starvation and or an Indian arrow. The only General I would like to meet is not due here for a year or two at least!" she shouted. Even if she was not really angry just a little heated, she hated being teased like they had being doing, and now they had gone and fired her up.

"You are the most lovely creature when you get angry, have I ever told you that?" Jean laughed. "But please for all our sakes, and most of all dear Dominique's, who is not used to woman with such fire, can you forgive us our teasing and calm down? And my lady, no pouting please. That does not fit well with the vision before my eyes. Come now my little minx save that fire for later, n'est pas?" His grin was inscrutable yet loving. How could she stay mad? Besides she knew that curiosity alone would force her to see just who this American General was.

"I wonder if Davey Crockett was ever a General?" she asked to no one in particular as they left for the ball. The shock on her face less than an hour later, as she was introduced to the General was obvious to all. She knew she should say something but all she could do until Jean's squeeze on her arm broke the spell, was to stand like some codfish, with its mouth hung wide open.

"My, I have met a lot of lovely women in my time Madame, but it is I who should be in awe making your acquaintance. After all, I don't think my appearance is such that it has ever dumbfounded anyone before. But please do call me Andrew; General or Mr. Jackson is just too formal a title for such a pretty little thing as yourself," he chuckled.

"General, you flatter me. I assure you that if I offended you in any way by my actions, I am truly sorry. It's just that I have not met many Americans since I have been in New Orleans and I had no idea that you were even in town." She could hardly believe it herself, she sounded like an idiot, like some dumb, star-struck, school girl meeting the president. She just wanted to die.

"No offense taken my dear, I assure you. Why, making the acquaintance of Jean Laffite's wife will no doubt be the highlight of my evening. Even us backwoods Americans have heard of your dashing husband Madame, he has himself quite a reputation!" His face had been toward Jean as he spoke but he ended looking at Tori and the humor behind his eyes told her he was enjoying himself, he even winked as he finished. "Now tell me Mr. Laffite, am I allowed the pleasure of one dance with your lovely wife this evening, mine not being here to escort me? I ask your permission sir, as I do not wish to find myself the object of a duel, something you folks down these parts seem to partake of so easily?"

Jean could see that the General was having a little bit of fun and decided to humor the man. He was sure that this American was far from worried about ending up in a duel. His reputation was one that spoke only too well of his bravery and integrity.

"Mon General, you may have any dance you choose with my wife, so long as it is not the first or the last. Also let it be only one. I am not a man who easily shares what is his." He was twisting his mustache with his fingers, an act that Tori recognized was done to hide the smile that curved around his lips. He was fooling around, but would the General know this? She was about to explain, when both men started laughing, none more heartily that Jackson himself.

With the tension between the two men released, the evening continued, and as the music once again started, Tori found herself in the arms of the man who was known in history, as old hickory. She was dancing with a President of the United States! If only she could tell him. There was so much she could tell this great man.

As they swirled around the room, she was far too involved to notice that they were under close scrutiny by the Governor and his close friends. Simone, in particular watched as the couple slipped gracefully by, admired by all. "It would seem that Laffite's wife is quite taken by the American General. She will soon learn that the uncivilized Americans can offer New Orleans and its people nothing. Louisiana may be a state now, but New Orleans will never become American. Why, that thought is absurd is it not? They are all barbaric, no class at all. They lack understanding of any proper manners let alone protocol." Seeing the general agreement around her, many had quietly spoken such. She continued. "Why, it is almost a slap in your face Governor, that he should be dancing with a pirate's wife, when it is clear to all that his duty should be for him to oblige his hostess with the honor."

Edward loved her. She was stoking the fire once again for him. The Governor's dislike of Laffite was growing. Soon he would have the man so full of hate toward his enemy, that he would be willing to do anything to get rid of him.

"I agree Simone my dear. Just how much longer are we citizens of this city going to allow Jean Laffite and his bunch of cutthroat thieves to get away with walking our streets. Their very appearance here this evening was a slap to our Governor's face, indeed to us all. We must be the very laughing stock of the Americans." The small crowd was beginning to get worked up, a little to much for Edward, who realized that the time had not presented itself yet, for Jean's demise. He had to calm the Governor. He needed to put the flame low for a while longer. It had to smolder before it could consume.

"Let us not jump and hastily make the wrong move. We are after all Southern Gentlemen are we not? The Laffite's will make a mistake soon, and when they do, we will be there to catch them. The city has many eyes Governor and you have many friends. I for one, will not rest until you have the respect you so deserve. Now let us not ruin this evening with anger. Let us show these Americans true Southern hospitality shall we?"

There was agreement all around. Edward Duval was not only a fine and true gentleman, but he had become a respected friend and a powerful citizen of their beloved city.

Edward had achieved his goal, and satisfied with himself asked Simone if she would care to dance. Snapping her fan closed she looked at the dance floor and grinned one of her sheepish smiles, suspecting an ulterior motive was at hand.

Quickly he swept her onto the floor maneuvering her into the flow of the dance and close to the General and Tori. Pulling Simone close to him he swiftly spoke his message, leaving no doubt that she should follow his lead. "Just do as I suggest and for goodness sake, no scenes please," he said firmly.

Before she had a chance to ask what he meant, they bumped right into the couple. He had accomplished the move so as to look totally innocent, and followed it with all the charm and manners that protocol required.

"Please do excuse me. It was so very clumsy of me to lead my lovely lady into you as I did. I was just overcome by her beauty, don't you agree General, is she not a true Southern Belle?" Angry at first by this intrusion, Jackson's temper quickly melted, as he was soft-hearted man when it came to the matters of love, and love was obviously what this couple was all about. "I do indeed agree sir, and your apology is duly accepted."

"Why thank you sir. And might I add, that you are a true gentleman to be so kind as to excuse such a blunder. You show us sir, that we might have misjudged you Americans. We have a lot to learn I think. If I may be so bold as to offer you the hand of my lovely lady for the remainder of this dance. I would be so honored, and feel truly vindicated." It all happened so fast that Tori did not have a chance to object. One second she was with Andrew Jackson, the next she was in Edward's arms. Simone on the other hand found the whole maneuver a delight, as she was now the center of attraction and loving it.

The General was soon under her spell and forgot completely about Tori, who at that moment, would have slapped Edward's face and walked away, if he had not reminded her quickly that to cause a scene at such a time, would indeed be in poor taste.

"Just relax and enjoy the dance. I have waited a long time to have you where you are right now and I can assure you, that this is only the beginning my dear," he said smugly.

Undaunted, Tori spit back from behind a sarcastic smile. "You can say whatever you want but I can tell you this, if Jean sees you dancing with me, then you will have to face the fact that your measly little life might very well be in danger of being challenged to a duel. Have you thought of that?"

His body stiffened slightly, then just as quickly relaxed. Edward just pulled her a little closer and whispered in her ear, "your pirate's days are numbered my dear, and then you will come running to me, for no one else in this city will have you."

"I would not come to you on my hands and knees. You disgust me, you overdressed pompous pig."

Edward's face twisted in anger. This bitch seemed unafraid or undaunted. She always seemed so sure of herself. "Let me assure you, you will pay for your harsh treatment of me. You will learn your lesson. And if you would care to observe, let us begin your first lesson shall we? Your downfall has begun my dear. As you can see for yourself, your husband watches us and does nothing. I fear he is a coward after all."

Tori's gaze towards Jean was aided as Edward swung her around so she could have an unobstructed view. She would have laughed out loud as Jean winked and gave her the thumbs up, a signal to her that he knew she could handle her situation. Winking back to him, she confidently leaned closer and hissed into Edward's ear, "No Edward, just a gentleman who knows his lady can handle swine like you. Now if you would please excuse me, the very stench of you has me in need of fresh air. May I suggest you leave and take a cold shower. You need to cool off. Even a randy dog has more manners, something you seem to lack a great deal of." With that she pushed herself free and walked over to Jean, who smiled at her, took her by the arm and walked straight past Edward, toward the open doorway.

"Whatever did you say to him my love? He looks as if he's about to explode. His face is positively the color of Simone's gown. Which by the way, she never did look good in that shade of red," he laughed, enjoying himself. His laughter could be heard clearly across the room, as the music had ended and the dance floor was clearing. The Governor's wife placed her hand on Edward's arm. She could not wait for that horrible Laffite to fall from grace she told him. She had seen how he had been left in the middle of the dance, and now they laughed at him. Poor poor Edward, to have to endure such rudeness, it was a disgrace.

Edward was so angry, that he missed completely the quick maneuvering of her lace trimmed fan, something she did in order to hide the smile and enjoyment on her face!

Later that night back at the townhouse, Tori and Jean once again reminded themselves that Edward and his hate would always be around. But they felt that his threats were only empty, a lot of hot air. He would never call Jean out, or would he do anything to disgrace himself; therefore, they told themselves they had no real worries.

Tori wanted to tell Jean about Andrew Jackson and about the fact that the new year was just around the corner, and with it the Battle of New Orleans was a year closer. She wished more than ever, that she had studied her history, and paid attention. How she had hated it in school, never dreaming that one day she would actually have any use for any of it. If only she could give Jean some dates, real dates, and times. What she did remember gave her hope. She had nothing to worry about, after all she knew the outcome. It was not as if the English were going to win, was it?

Jean had been busy with something by his desk. A small package that had been delivered while they were out. She had seen the pleased look upon his face when Bessy had told him it had arrived and now he looked far more than just pleased with himself. She conveniently pushed the problems of history and Jackson to the back of her mind. She went to see just what it was that had placed such a look on her pirate's face.

"Tori could you come here and sit with me for a moment?" His voice was soft and smooth, his eyes intense, as he looked at her. The light was shining on his hair that curled around the base of his neck. He looked as if he had a halo, a thought that tickled her funny bone. How could a rouge have a halo? His shirt was open exposing his chest, the soft linen so pale, made his tanned skin seem darker. The way the breeches molded to his thighs and the soft brown leather boots to his legs excited her. Could this man ever look bad she wondered? His very manner was a turn on. How was it possible that she should always find herself desiring his touch?

"Is something wrong Tori? You look as if your mind is elsewhere?"

"No! No nothing is wrong. What is it you want, or should I ask?" she said moistening her lips seductively. "Why my lady you shock me. Do you think that is all I have on my mind?" he answered. "Come, sit here by me. I have a gift for you. It is something that I have been waiting for. It took so much time to get it just right, but now it is ready." He held in his hand a small velvet box, and she noticed that as he held it out to her, his hands trembled. "Go on open it. It's something that you can keep with you. Something that will always be close to your heart from mine."

Tori did not speak. She took the box and sat next to him as she opened it to see its contents. Inside on the red velvet interior, lay a small intricately designed gold heart shaped locket. It was so delicate and beautiful that to her it was far more appealing than the diamonds she wore. "Open it," he had placed his hand on her shoulder and moved closer, his face next to hers as he urged her, "go on."

Carefully she held the heart shape in her hand and turned it to release the catch. It snapped easily and like a miniature book the locket folded open. Holding it toward the lamp so as to see the contents more clearly, a small gasp of surprise left her parted lips. Tori's body went limp, and her eyes brimmed with tears as she gazed upon the small lock of hair. The solitary baby soft curl, formed a tiny circle, as it lay in place under glass. Behind it was inscribed the words, "Christopher forever our son."

"Oh, Jean it's lovely, it's just beyond words," her voice was catching, tears of love and joy had begun to tumble down her face and now her hands too were shaking, as she held the necklace. Tori turned and buried her head into Jean's broad shoulder.

Crying was not what he had wanted, it was supposed to have made her happy but as he took her face in his hands and raised it to look deep into her eyes, he saw for himself that they were not all tears of sadness.

"I know it's been hard. It's been hard for me also, I miss him, but then at least I did have a son for a while, you gave me that. Now I give him a part of him back to you. You can have him with you always. Let me put it on. But first there is more, did you read the oppressive side? I had it put in Italian." He smiled. "A private joke between us. It says Love passes time. Time passes with love. So much meaning behind so few words, n'est pas?"

There was indeed she thought. Tori turned her back to him and lifted her hair to make it easier for the gold chain to be fastened. In seconds the cold locket warmed next to her skin and she felt as if it had always been with her.

Jean did not speak or move away. His fingers trailed down from the base of her neck slowly tracing an invisible line to the top of her shoulders. His lips brushed the back of her neck as she heard the words "sealed with a kiss," spoken in a deep husky voice. She let her hair cascade down around her shoulders, as shivers of delight began to arouse her passion.

Jean's body was so close, his face brushing hers as he bent to kiss the top of her bare shoulder. His hot breath against her skin sent another shiver through her body. The muscles in her stomach tightened in anticipation. The master of seduction was applying his skills, her body becoming once again his to command. "I love you my lady and I need you, now, here, this moment." Those words whispered into her ear, were more than she could take. She turned to face him, knowing what she would find. His desire burned with such passion, that it caused her heart to skip a beat in its racing rhythm. He was sitting there looking at every curve, mentally undressing her. His eyes wandering slowly up and down, stopping only to bore deep into hers with their hypnotic power.

Reaching out, she took hold of his hands and placed them on the top of her breasts, an action that caused her nipples to instantly harden under his touch. Not once did she look away from his gaze. Not once did she utter a word. Jean took hold of the material and easily slipped the gown down toward her waist. Lightly his fingers traced the valley between her breast where the locket lay. It was a gold heart shining if the fire light next to the heart of the one he would love forever. Her erect nipples caught his attention, drawing him to them like a magnet. Jean lowered his head toward her breasts, placing his mouth tenderly upon one and then the other, biting at them lightly, teasingly holding each of them firmly but gently between his lips. Each time he took hold of her in this manner, it brought forth the same soft moan of delight. And when he stopped to listen for a second to her pounding heart, cradling his head in between the soft fleshy mounds, she entangled her fingers desperately in his hair, deliberately guiding his head back for more.

Fully aroused and not willing to delay any longer the desire to have him inside of her, she passionately begged him to take her. Now it was his turn to groan, as her hands brushed against the throbbing bulge in his breeches. She was expertly and successfully unfastening the buttons of his pants, to release its prisoner from within.

Quickly he took hold of her hands. "Not so fast my little minx, I intend to enjoy you slowly like a good wine, to taste and sample at my leisure the delight of each sensation. I will savor every inch of your body, all night if I want. I will not be made to hurry." And like the fire burning hot, its embers aglow with a life of its own, so was their love making. Many times that night he took her. And each time together they rode a wave of sexual intoxication into oblivion, until in the end, sheer exhaustion sent them both into a deep and contented sleep.

It seemed to Dominique that his two favorite people in New Orleans had once again regained their former love of life. The way they looked at each other across the blacksmith shop and the way each would react, was like lovesick children. He was almost tempted to send Tori out shopping or something, just to keep Jean's mind on what was going on with the business. Love was one thing, but work was another and right now he needed Jean's full attention. His gruff attitude and looks of thunder toward Tori's direction caused her to chuckle inside. She knew only too well that his bark was far worse than his bite where she was concerned but that was where his control stopped. Winking in his direction and smiling slyly, she turned away to let them have their meeting in peace.

Tori wandered outside over toward the blacksmith and his fire. She stood watching him as he hammered out a piece of red hot iron, shaping it slowly into what she assumed would end up as part of the wrought iron grill on someone's balcony. The man known only as Thiac, was a person of few words and undying loyalty toward the Laffite brothers. He owed his freedom and way of life to them, a debt that he took as seriously as life itself.

Watching him work, his body naked from the waist up Tori could see the strength that rippled in his muscles with each swing of the hammer. The strip of metal was placed back into the inferno and hot as it was Thiac took up the bellows to urge the flames higher still. Small sparks escaped from within the closer and briefly flew up toward the sky, like fireflies they danced about, lighting their way in a glorious pattern, not unlike miniature fireworks on the Fourth of July. Undaunted, by the heat or the licking amber flames that would shoot out as if trying to follow the sparks ever upward, Thiac reached in with the tongs and removed the now white hot metal and resumed his hammering. Then he stopped to dip it in a bucket of water. A white cloud of steam rose in the air temporarily blocking her view of his sweat-covered face, that turned her way.

"Thiac, I was wondering would you be able to make something for me? I mean if I were to describe it to you, maybe even draw it out, as crazy as it might seem, can you try? It would mean a lot to me. Just an idea that I have about a new shape razor."

"Mizz Tori, I can try, but why you'd want a new shape for a razor when the old one do the job just fine?" Thiac was shaking his head slowly from side to side and scratching the top with his hand, as if the action would help him puzzle out just why it was that women folk, especially white ones, came up with the most ridiculous ideas.

"Oh, you wonderful man," she said taking his hand and shaking it as if they had a deal. "I know you won't understand. I can't think why I have not thought of this before now, but there you are that's not anything to fuss over, is it? Here, let me show you what it is I want." Tori led him over to a clear patch of dirt and squatting down she looked up into his face indicating that he should join her.

Now Thiac had seen things in his life. He knew only too well that ladies, white ladies that is, just did not act, would never deem it proper even, to carry on the way Mizz Tori was. But then, Mizz Tori was special. It was not that she was not a lady, oh no. It was just that she did not seem to see anything wrong in her actions or the way in which she treated him. Her small soft hand was holding his firmly and with no hint of disgust she was pulling him down beside her, to ask him to do her a favor. She was speaking to him and showing him what it was she wanted. All the time making him feel that he was important and needed. It was not an order, it was a request and that made him all the more determined to deliver up whatever shape or size razor her little mind could conjure up.

When at last Tori and Jean left the shop, it was obvious to all that she was pretty pleased with herself. Whatever the reason was though remained her secret. The only thing she would say to Jean when he commented that she looked a little too smug about something, was said laughingly. "Well you will have to just wait and see, but it's an idea from my time, that I miss. Your wonderful blacksmith, that big gorgeous hunk of a running back, has agreed to make it for me. This small invention I can tell you, will drive you wild."

He could hardly contain her, it was as if she were walking on air, laughing and spinning around him as they made their way slowly down the street. She was at it again. Didn't she know that just being near her like he was, watching her walk and remembering last night, was more than enough to drive him wild. Who cared that people were stopping to stare at the spectacle she was making of herself, talking about things that made no sense. He would ask her later just what a hunk running back was though. As for now, her joy was his also, and damn anyone who did not accept it. She made him happy she was Tori, his wild and uncontrollable lady.

Tori was so excited about her new invention, well not exactly her invention she told herself, but then in a way it could be. What if by her coming to this time she did manage to introduce a few odds and ends. A razor here, a hamburger there, boy was she hungry. She found herself thinking about the invention of the hamburger, when Jean's voice broke into her daydream.

"You seem miles away. Did you hear what I said?"

"No, sorry Jean I did not. It was something about tomorrow wasn't it?"

"Yes, it's that dinner, the one that I told you about. I feel as though it is something that we can't avoid. It's just that I won't be able to escort you there. Something has come up with one of our shipments and I will be a little late. You don't mind do you? I wouldn't ask you to go without me, it's just this can't be helped." He was looking at her, concern with a touch of pleading, written across his face. This was important to him, that was obvious, but to let her go unescorted?

Tori did not mind at all. She knew he would show up and join her. If she had to bet on it, he would most likely be at the gathering before her anyway. It might be fun to go alone and see what everyone would do as she arrived without him. A mischievous grin turned up the corners of her lips, as she looked sideways at the man who was scrutinizing her every move.

"Now don't you go getting yourself into trouble. You can be a little minx when you want."

"Isn't that what you like about me?" she pinched his rear as they walked, and Jean shot her his how-dare-you look. "Madam, may I remind you, that in the house I do not care how you act but out here in public, on the street you will act as a lady."

This only seemed to add flame to the fire. Tori was in a very playful mood and tossing her head she mockingly answered his reprimand, in a teasing reply of her own. "Why sir, would that be a lady of your time, or mine. I can assure you, that mine would be more to your liking. But, then, if it's a lady of today that you want, I think I can accommodate you." She battered her eyelids and within seconds had outwardly assumed the image of a southern lady. Inwardly she was cracking up with laughter and knew that she would burst any second, especially if Jean kept that dumfounded look on his face.

"All right, you win, you know what I mean. Now stop acting so, so infuriating..."

"Proper. Is that the word you are looking for?" she laughed.

This was getting him nowhere and if he kept playing this game with her, he knew that the day's work ahead of him would never be finished, let alone started.

"Madam, you are impossible to say the least. I know when it is better to retreat from a battle you cannot hope to win." He bowed before her, then took her hand to his lips and brushed them with a light kiss. "I have decided it would be better if I were to leave you now and see to the important matters at hand, concerning work my lady, so put that idea out of your mind."

"And what idea would that be?"

"You know exactly what I mean. Now if you don't have any objection, I shall be on my way." He slipped his arm around her waist and headed toward the waiting carriage. "I shall of course drop you safely on our doorstep on my way, just to keep you out of trouble." It was his turn to laugh now. "Don't look so sad. Look at it as a good opportunity to rest up for the evening ahead of us. I should be able to finish my work early if I start now, and then who knows? I might escort you myself, if you still want?" He might have said that he had lost the battle but Tori felt that the tables had been turned once again. She felt, no she knew, that it was very seldom if ever, that Jean Laffite did not get his way. Another round for the pirate she thought, but then who was counting anyway?

Tori had taken his advice and rested most of the afternoon. Now it was early evening and the time had come to dress. The gown that lay waiting for her was like nothing she had worn before, at least in this day and age. She had had it made without Jean knowing about it. The design was something that had not been seen anywhere in town, of that she was certain. The color was black. This was another thing that was never done. Black was only for mourning, color was the fashion of the day. Was this to be another something she was going to introduce to this time, the black formal? Looking at it her nerves gave a twitch. It was bound to cause a stir, still with Jean on her arm, what did she care? But there it was, the nerve-gripping reality slapping her in the face. Jean would not be on her arm, at least not right away. She knew it was a knockout dress, one that would drive Jean crazy, something she loved to do. However a small voice kept asking her, if this was going just a bit to far? It was a small voice, and as she stared at the gown it became weaker and weaker till at last it faded. Nothing was going to stop her from having some fun. What could they do anyway?

Slipping into the black silk-beaded design, that outlined her figure, clinging to her hour glass shape seductively, she felt a surge of confidence mixed with just a touch or two of rebellion. Tori felt sexy, hot and sultry not feminine and demure. The gown had been constructed with seduction in mind. The very sight of it, in this day and time, would send a message that was sure to ring loud and clear.

She turned before the long glass mirror. One last look for herself just to be sure. "Oh yes!" she shouted. The image before her was sure to drive the Gentleman pirate wild with desire. "Score another round for me," she spoke softly, smiling back at woman in the mirror.

The dress was backless, and cut low, far lower than anything she had seen. The front was simple. The top of the gown was like a choker around her slender neck. Small black beads had been stitched on, in a design that cascaded down, swirling and spraying like an open fan, down to her waist, where they turned and swirled to the side, slipping the full length from her hip to the floor. The back side of the gown hung plain and free of any design, with just enough material to give her freedom of movement, yet tight enough to show every curve. Her gloves were long and tight fitting, to her just above her elbow. Here she put a thick gold bracelet on each. The locket was all the jewelry she wore about her neck and in her ears the gold and diamond earrings that Jean had surprised her with Christmas morning.

Marie had come and fixed her hair, which was swept to one side and left down long and slightly wavy. She had sprayed it with the sweet smell of Gardenia and here and there she had strategically woven in a few thin threads of gold chain. The gold picked up the light which danced as the hair moved when she walked. All in all, the vision was exactly as Tori had planned it to be. The look of the future.

Jean had not been home, so it was going to be quite a surprise for him. Excited and impatient for him to see her, she hoped that he would not be too late. Whatever the problem was that had taken him away, was sure to be solved quickly. After all, the fact that Dominique and Pierre had gone with him assured that.

Across town, down by the river, the dock area had grown quite. At this time of the evening most of the people had either gone home or were in many of the small taverns. A few were on the streets, hurrying along, wrapping themselves against the cold wind that had picked up. Night fell early this time of the year and the dampness of the evening had caused Edward to pull his cape up closer to his face.

He had been here for nearly an hour, and his impatience was showing. He lit a long thin cigar and was about to give up when out of the dark shadows a figure approached him.

"You got my money?" the rasping voice asked, as the man came closer. He was obviously in a hurry and the way he kept close to the wall and its darkness, indicated that he did not want to be seen meeting with Edward.

"If you have any information that I can use, I assure you that you will have your money. Now, what is it that you had to drag me down here at this time of night for, and in this damn cold. Keeping me waiting for over an hour I might add, it had better be good."

"Oh, it's good all right, and I've been thinking that it's worth a bit more'n we agreed on. Me sticking my neck out like I am. If they found out it was me who told like, well I'd be dead for sure." He motioned his hand across his throat. Edward looked at the man who stood before him. He looked like a weasel to him, a dirty little weasel. The broken down, ugly wretch of a man was nothing more than a low-life, ready to sell his soul to the devil. Edward's way of looking at it was, if this scum was so hell-bent on going to purgatory, then who was he to stop him?

Red-rimmed eyes sunken in black hollows, surrounded by tallow skin spoke of heavy drinking, the reason behind his need for the money perhaps? His appearance must have been handsome once Edward thought. His younger years would have held a body of strong build and dashing good looks, now what stood before him was a broken shell of a man, a very frightened one at that. But then what did he care, so long as he got what he needed.

"Of course, of course if the information is good, I will see to it that you get more. Now come on out with it before someone sees us."

The sailor looked around and then making up his mind to go ahead, pulled Edward further into the shadows, where he revealed his secrets through a toothless grin.

Edward could hardly believe what he was hearing. At last his chance had come. Indeed this was exactly what he had been hoping for, and more, much more. Reaching into his pocket he pulled out a small leather pouch of coins and placed it into the dirty outstretched hands.

Greedily it was snatched away. Trembling fingers with broken bitten nails tore it open. The sailor looked inside as anger covered his face.

"This ain't enough. I done told you I risks my life telling you what I just did. You owes me more, you agreed." His free hand had graded Edward's shoulder and was gripping with a strength that somehow seemed too strong for such a frail individual.

"What I think is that you would sell your own mother's soul. If you think you are in danger of being found out, then my advice to you is to leave town," he shook himself free and brushed at the place that the filthy hand had been, as if removing any remaining dirt or grime that had been left behind. "Now get out of my way. You have all I intend to give you." Edward was pushing past the dirty little man when he felt his arm being grabbed and something pushing into his side. He froze as the face of the sailor came so close to his. The vile breath of stale rum and rotten food almost made him gag.

"I ain't about to leave here and I ain't about to risk my neck for this," he shook the small bag in Edward's face. "Now you best empty your pockets or say hello to my friend that's knocking at your side door, if you gets what I mean?"

Rage, not fear, surged through Edward; no one threatened him. He struggled to control his emotions. In a situation such as this brain not brawn was needed.

"Indeed I do know what you mean. Point well taken my good man," he chuckled. "And maybe I was a little hasty in asking you to leave. After all, you might have some more information for me at a later date, might you not?"

The unshaven face looked into Edward's eyes as if trying to read what was there. He squinted his bloodshot eyes almost closed and turned his head on the side, pushing closer still, toward Edward. Then as if he had answered a difficult question and come up with a satisfying solution, he grinned, baring his front teeth, missing a tooth and spoke. "Aye, that I might. I can see you're a real smart business bloke and all." He released his grip on Edward and placed his knife back in the folds of his jacket, reaching up and pulling the collar around his neck with his free hand. "How's about it then? Where's the rest of my money? Words is cheap, I need to know that our continued agreement like, is going to be worth my while."

Edward reached into his inside pocket and slowly withdrew a pouch, the sound of coins clearly jingling from within. He tossed the pouch in the air several times, catching it each time with the same one hand. It was as if he were trying to decide just how much of the contents should go and how much should stay.

The suspense and anticipation built. Clearly the sailor thought he had hit home at last. His dry lips smirked as he wiped at them with the back of his hand. Finally Edward tossed the pouch toward him and quick as lightning his hand snapped out and grabbed it.

"You take out what you think is fair, and we will call it even," Edward said leaning his body up against the wall, tucking one leg behind the other, giving him a very relaxed look.

The sailor just nodded his head stupidly, and turned his attention to the contents of the purse. So busy was he counting out the pieces of gold that he did not see Edward casually reach inside his cape and pull out a small derringer. Once he had the gun in hand, his actions were fast. He struck with a deadly intent not much unlike that of a viper. Holding the small weapon right up against the man's chest, Edward pulled the trigger. A muffled shot rang out in the still night air. Only then did the sailor stop what he was doing and raise his eyes to those of his killer. The look of horror registered as the white hot pain seared though his body, his heart quivered then raced and quivered again, fighting to keep the regular rhythm it had known for so long. Slowly he slipped down to the ground, his one hand reaching to the point of entry where the slug had tore toward its target. His hand came away covered in warm blood that steamed in the night air. Upon seeing this Edward looked away. The sight of blood had always made him feel ill.

"You filthy bastard. Damn you. I'll see you pay for this you son of a bitch," he coughed, as his mouth filled with blood. The bullet had past into his lung, nipping at his heart on its deadly journey. The realization that he was going to die, had not yet set in.

"Oh, I very much doubt that I will pay for ridding society of the likes of you," Edward spat back. He grabbed the pouch out of the man's hand and hit him hard in the face as he spoke.

Not expecting such an act, the sailor's head snapped backward and hit the wall rendering him unconscious. Edward looked at him for a few seconds as he reloaded his gun. Then very slowly he looked around to make sure that no one but the two of them were in this dark dank alley. The place was deserted, only the noise from a nearby tavern drifted down their way, breaking the night's silence with music and broken laughter.

"I don't think you will talk to anyone my friend, in fact it's far better that you don't. Can't have the likes of you linked with me in anyway, can we now?" He placed the gun for a second time close to his victim, only this time it was up against his temple. He looked away as he pulled the trigger. Funny sound, the sound of a shot to the head he thought, so dull. He also found himself thanking God it was so dark and he could not see the results of his work, for surely he would pass out if he could. Not waiting to even pursue that train of thought, Edward quickly ran form the scene of the crime and headed for the safety of his own apartment. He would have to clean up and change for already the hour was later than he had planned. Edward still had so much to do before the evening's activities. He had to stop in on the Governor with his information for one and then go and meet with a very angry Simone. Still he mused, she would not be angry with him for very long when he explained why he was late, now would she? If ever a man looked pleased with himself it was Edward at that moment. Caution however caused him to hesitate. He would not celebrate this time not until he new it was all finished as he planned.

The Governor met with Edward in his study making it very clear that he had done so, only because he had been told that it was a matter of utmost importance and trusting Edward's judgment in such matters, he felt it must be so. Curiosity was closer to point. Just why would Edward call at such an early hour of the evening, when they would have seen each other in a few hours had intrigued him. This was the time that one would normally spend attending to one's attire and preparing for the evening's festivities, not paying social calls..

Entering his study he found that Edward was pacing up and down like a caged animal. Excitement was clearly written all over his face. Whatever was going on with him, was not something deplorable that was for sure.

"Well Edward what brings you to my home I wonder? You look as though you have lost total control of your senses man." The Governor took the younger man by the shoulders and giving him a hearty slap on the back, led him to a seat and pushed him down into it. "I would have thought that you would be picking up Simone for the dinner this evening. You do realize that women tend to be a little overly sensitive in the area of promptness, that is when it is ours and not theirs." He chuckled to himself as he continued on, not letting Edward get a word in edgeways. "Woman hate to be late to these darned affairs. My wife for instance, bless her, just goes on and on about the importance of us always being prompt, that it is my job to set a fine example. Must say she seems right on that subject, what do you think?"

Edward was back on his feet, springing up so fast it would seem that the chair itself had propelled him. He was all but spluttering trying to get the words out of his mouth he was so agitated. "Yes, yes of course I agree. But I think when you hear what I have to tell you sir, you might not mind being a little late this evening." Edward walked to the sideboard and the glass decanter, then without thinking simply helped himself to the contents, an act that caused Claiborne's eyebrow to raise. He was just about to remark on the impudence of the act when Edward calmly turned and continued oblivious of his rude actions. "You see mon Governor, it has come to my fortunate attention, that a one Jean Laffite and his band of no good pirates, will this very evening be moving a large and very illegal shipment of goods. Right as we speak, this very second, I suspect that they are hard at work, confidently going about their business right under your nose. No offense intended I assure you. It is just that tonight they are in New Orleans herself, at the old warehouses. All those goods coming right into port and smuggled right past the law and no duty paid. It is an outrage!" he shouted. "A slap to all the fine citizens of this city."

Claiborne had taken a seat. If what Edward was telling him was true and he had no doubt that it wasn't, then this was the chance he had so long been waiting for. He could finally capture the so-called Gentleman and expose him for what he really was. He would use the contraband as evidence. A smile crossed his lips at the thought of Jean caught red handed. It would be enough to put the man in jail for a very long time indeed. The sudden thought of failing once again, and being the laughing stock sent a chilling sensation through him, causing him to stiffen and look sternly at the grinning Edward, who stood awaiting his response.

"Just how did you get this information and are you certain you have the facts right? I mean for both our sakes, I would hate to act hastily, only later to find out it was a mere rumor so to speak."

"I can assure you William, that the information is correct. I would place my life on it. The individual who supplied me with the facts did so at great personal risk. He told me he knew I could get the knowledge of such a transaction to the right people. I am sure he meant for you to know. It is widely known that we are friends and do frequently entertain together. He wanted the Laffite's brought to justice is how he put it to me. Before you ask me, I have to tell you, that he made me give my word of honor as a gentleman, that I would not reveal his identity and I intend to keep my word. I can tell you that he is a man of great integrity, who wants to have no part in the glory of Laffite's fall from grace. The glory of that man's dishonor and capture will be yours alone."

Edward could see the Governor's emotions starting to rise. The color in his cheeks had brightened, their redness burning against the sickly white of his fingers that rubbed his chin as he listened. The man however was not won over to act yet. He still had to be convinced that now was the time to move.

"I think, no let me restate, I know William, this is just what you have been waiting for and if I might add, to hesitate any more might let the damn pirate slip through your fingers once again. Time is critical, we do not know how long it will be before he leaves the area of activity. Should you arrive after he has gone, he will simply deny any connection with the goods. No, you must catch him in the very act and that time is now!" Edward had slammed his fist into the tabletop besides him, reaffirming his conviction in the matter.

The governor looked at him as his stomach lurched at the thought of losing his chance after being so close. He could not take that risk and Edward was plainly convinced that now was the time. It was his turn to stand abruptly, his strides were full of determination and self assured as he came toward his friend.

"All right Edward. I will trust your judgment on this. We will act immediately. This should not take us much time if all your facts come to bare. The evening does not, however, have to be spoiled. I will have my wife escort Simone. We will meet them together with what I hope will be very pleasing news. News I might add, that should get us out of the deplorable situation of arriving late." With that both of them laughed and set about to ruin once and for all, the up until now, untouchable Laffite.

Jean had finished with the first barge, the unloading had been slow tonight, hampered by the wind which had brought with it the choppy conditions. The normally stable platform had moved constantly, not ideal to their precarious situation. Under normal conditions it would be of no circumstance but these were far from normal. It was dark, with no light allowed to alert the authorities to the beehive of activity that was now well underway. If the barge moved unexpectedly heaving its mass against it moorings, the unwary man would either find himself in the murky water or worse crushed between the pier and boat.

What had been planned to take only two or three hours was now going to take far longer. The goods were numerous and easily moved once on dry land but getting them from point to point was tonight frustrating beyond belief. Standing there in his seafaring outfit, his head wrapped in a bandanna to keep his blowing hair out of his ever watchful gaze, Jean looked the part of the smuggling pirate, impatient to have his goods safely stowed.

"Hurry it along men we can't take all night. Dom, what is taking them so long with that barge? I tell you, old women could work faster than they are."

Jean's worry over the amount of time already spent in the open, caused him to bark his question at his second in command, something that hardly happened and if it did, never in front of the men. Dominique found himself wanting to box Jean's ears to bring him round. They had done this many times, and always things ran like clockwork. So they ran a little slow this evening, this was cause to speak to him no better than he would a stranger who angered him?

"Old women you say? Seems to me that the men are working as fast as they can. With one barge loading and the other already finished we are just about caught up, if not a little ahead considering the conditions. You will make your dinner in time, have no fear little pup, this old sea dog will see that you do." Dominique's laughter could be heard across the water and some of the men were heard to snicker, as they had overheard his remark to the proud Laffite. This was far better than boxing his ears, Dominique thought, this verbal bashing, the look on Jean's face alone, at being called a pup was astounding. He reminded him of a puffer fish with his cheeks all blown out and eyes bugging. It was Pierre who hushed him with a punch to his shoulder and a drop-dead look that sobered the moment.

"I tell you, for some reason I do not like it; there is no one on the docks this night, have you not noticed. My Marie Louise, she had a bad feeling about this evening and somehow I wish I had listened to her. Merd, the hairs on my neck are standing on end." He reached the back of his neck with his hand and turned to look up and down the empty black stretch of dockside. "I tell you I see no one and that is not right, n'est pas?"

"Pierre, think with reason? Would you be out in weather like this if you did not have to?" Dominique chuckled. "Why this is the type of evening that one should be inside, preferably with a good woman, a bottle and a cozy night of love making. Not taking a balmy walk, seeing the sights. Who would want to watch a bunch of pirates unload their wares anyway?" He saw his chance to have some fun with Pierre and laughingly he started. "I think you yourself would rather be in the arms of your lover Marie, or have you grown tired of this one also? Is no woman ever going to be enough for you I ask? You have a wife that you see seldom. Then you had Adelaide. But no, you take yourself a mere child woman, shipping poor Adelaide off with the children. When will you stop thinking like a pirate, and start thinking with your brain and not your..."

"I do wish you would not refer to us in that way!" Pierre snapped, "you know that I detest such a reference. We are privateers!" he insisted.

Jean had been watching his brother as Dominique teased him. He himself could not help but smile. Privateers was just another name for pirate any which way you looked at it. "It seems to me that you two have everything going along as it should. Gentlemen, if you don't mind, I shall leave you to your debate and to the remainder of the evening's endeavors. One can't keep a lady waiting, nor can one escort her dressed like I am. Why most people would claim that I was dressed like a pirate. Wouldn't you say so, Dominique?"

Dominique could hardly contain himself, as he answered with a very serious sounding voice.

"I would indeed Jean. Don't know why you can't escort her in such attire though. Seems to me she likes you like that. All the way to the island and back if I remember? Or has the lady tamed you some, turned you into a land lover after all?" Jean burst out laughing,

"You may be able to bait my younger brother with your sharp tongue, but not so with me my friend. Now off with you both, finish that last load. I for one will be on my way."

Jean was still smiling to himself, when the first shot rang out, followed closely by another. At first no one was sure what was happening, then as if in answer, the whole area seemed to explode into a hive of activity as soldiers swarmed quickly around shouting as they ran. No one had a chance of escape with all avenues of escape cut off. All to quickly it became obvious that they were so out numbered they had no choice but to surrender.

The soldiers had come out of darkness, bringing with them lanterns that had been shuttered until the last possible moment. Now in the eerie light Jean stood in horror, as the realization of what had just occurred sunk in. It was over before it began, and a very pleased-with-himself Governor sauntered up to the Laffite brothers, lighting a cigar from the lantern he carried. Though his face was a mask of his true feelings, his voice could not hide the pleasure of his success. "Seems I have caught you at last," he held his lantern higher casting a dim light to fall on the scene of a half-loaded barge and men dockside. Some were still holding the goods they had been unloading. "My, my. This should keep you and your men in prison and out of my hair for quite sometime don't you think? That is, if you don't swing for it." Jean just looked at him. "Nothing to say for yourself? No, I doubt that there is," he whispered. Then in a loud voice so all could hear he sarcastically announced "you won't be able to talk your way out of this one. You and your men are finished once and for all in New Orleans."

The Governor inhaled deeply on his cigar and turned to face Jean. He blew out a long wisp of smoke, taking his time before speaking. He was enjoying the sounds around him, the sounds of soldiers rounding up the pirates. "Oh, but before I forget myself, the gentleman that I am, I will of course do you one favor this evening. You may not concern yourself with the worry of the shock of your arrest, pertaining to your lovely wife that is. I will of course take it upon myself to inform Mrs. Laffite of your demise personally." Claiborne turned triumphantly giving no chance for Jean to reply and walked away giving orders as he went.

"See to it that they are under guard at all times, and no special treatment for the so-called gentleman. Put the scoundrel under lock and key in the same cell as his men." His voice was crisp, his stride fast, as if he had other matters to deal with now that Jean's capture was complete. Not once did he look back toward Laffite as he walked away. Claiborne's figure was rapidly lost in the shadows.

   Jean cursed himself at having being so stupid. He should have listened to Pierre. The docks had been too quiet. So quiet in fact that they had been screaming a warning. Now with his brother, his first lieutenant and himself in jail, there was little he could do. In fact he could not see any way out at all. This time it looked as if the Governor and the law had caught up with him. The evidence would way heavy, maybe too heavy. John Grimes would have his work cut out for himself, and as good as he was, Jean doubted he was a miracle worker.

# Chapter 19

Tori took a deep breath as the carriage pulled to a stop in front of her destination. Almost at once the door was opened and a foot stool put into place. All this while two small black boys pulled and tugged at the red carpet clutched in their small eager hands. Once in position, the stool was lifted quickly onto the end of the carpet to help hold it down, then the two small lads faded from sight. They slipped into the shadows so fast, that to Tori it seemed as if they had not even been there. How many times would they roll and unroll that same stretch of red rug she wondered? She could see they were always under the watchful eye of the doorman, who at that moment was nodding his approval. No wonder they seemed nervous she thought. No doubt they were terrified that their job would not be satisfactory, thereby resulting in a good swipe to their heads.

The sound of a large crowd filtered out from inside as the front door opened and closed to emit the couple who had arrived just ahead of her. Music drifted softly on the crisp night air, its swirling sounds surrounded her, as if to greet her arrival. The doorman's hand extended toward Tori, as the tone of his Irish accented voice acknowledged his recognition of her. He gladly offered his assistance. This was one guest he was truly fond of. Over the past few years she had often stopped and talked with him briefly, never treating him as if he were below her, yet maintaining her standing. He was just a servant, true, but that was no reason for people to act as they usually did. This guest was a true lady and a good human being, with a heart of gold.

"And a good evening to you Mrs. Laffite," his face smiling as he touched his cap. "By yourself this evening are you then?" He took hold of her hand, steadying her as she made her decent. Her voice, caught in her throat, rendering her speechless, so she just forced a smile and hoped he could not tell how nervous she was.

"Begging your pardon and all Mam, but if I had a misses that looked as good as you, I'd not be letting her out of my sight," he said admiring her winking his eye. "You look right wonderful. Be hitting em away with sticks you will." He had felt her trembling hand the moment he had taken it. Never would he had thought she had anything to be frightened of especially with notorious Jean Laffite as her husband. The fact that she was by herself had to be the reason she was nervous. Lord knows looking like she did this evening many of those hot-headed Creoles would act no better than a drunken sailor down by the docks sniffing after a whore. That had to be it, she was missing the protective arm of her husband.

"My husband should be joining me very soon I hope, maybe I should just wait until he arrives?" He did not know if she was asking him or herself that question but one thing was for sure, she was hesitating. Just standing there frozen to the spot, staring ahead with that silly frozen smile stuck on her lips, and her hand glued to his, just what would people think? He felt truly sorry for her, and partly to blame. His missus was always telling him he mouthed on to much, what had he been thinking about? All that blarney about her being alone and such. He had to put it right and quick like. He had to say something to boost her courage and get her moving. Another carriage had pulled up behind hers. "Still a lady like yourself and a husband like you have, maybe you won't have no trouble," he squeezed her hand and winked his old eye, tipping his head slightly. "You just go on about your evening and have a good time. I'll be telling the Mister that you're here when he arrives."

Tori started up the walkway toward the door thinking as she went. Why had she ever decided to go alone this evening? Would she ever learn? Time and time again she had put herself into compromising situations. Was it for the attention or the challenge she wondered? Sure she would know many of the guests and under normal circumstances she would not have been so nervous but then under normal circumstances, she would not be dressed in an outfit such as the one she now wore. That it would no doubt be the scandal of the evening was a sure bet, if that doorman's reaction was any indication. And he had only glimpsed the outfit under her cape. Dressing for a stir with Jean at her side was one thing, but this...

"Good evening," she said as she presented her invitation card to the stern looking gray hair'd black man who took it without even reading it. Not that he could have even if he wanted to, his job was simply to take the card and place it on the silver tray, nod his head and greet the guests with cards, admitting them. Anyone without a card, was to be denied entrance at all costs.

How simple to crash one of these affairs she thought, and a smile slipped across her grim face, as the idea of handing a card that read, "bullshit I'm coming anyway," at the next affair popped into her mind.

"I will be joined by my husband, Monsieur Laffite in a while, you do know my husband?" Tori asked.

"Yez'em," his head nodded. "Everyone done knows who he be. Don't you worry non. I know'd I got his card." The frail old body turned, as he pointed his bony old hand toward the silver dish. "It be right here safe like, where I done put it. I be a letting him in da second he gits here. Yez um, sure en I will." His stern old face was beaming with pride, and his lips she was sure were fighting a smile. But then his gaze, Tori couldn't help but notice, was wandering all about the hallway, anywhere but on her.

A young black girl had come to her side and helped her remove her cape and without a comment, curtseyed and disappeared, taking the garment with her. Tori turned back to the almost grinning black man. "Thank you," she said and seeing his face slip back into its somber mode once more she left.

The old man's eyes followed her. Now that her back was toward him, he had a chance to study her as she walked down the hallway. If that was what these white folks was going to be calling a gown, then Lord God, he was thankful his girls was all black. He had seen something's in his days. The goings on that white folks did just made him wonder sometimes, but now, a fine white lady dressing like she belonged in the dock district, or in one of them houses. Well it just didn't seem right. Nice to look at though, he had to admit that, nice to look at... A slim smile crossed the old mans lips, "Dis job might be a gitting better, ahuh, ahuh. Hours is long. Legs is old, but these Nigger eyes sure'n going to be enjoying demselves," he mumbled. "Best not let on none any though. Da maser he might go and git him a blind Nigger for da job," he shook his head. His old face grew stern as he took control of himself. "No sur, I be careful now, real careful. Come on now face, you git dat look of don't know'd nothing, and Nigger you best stop yabbing like, cause more folks is a coming your way."

It was only a matter of seconds before every face turned toward her. The ladies, some of whom raised their fans to conceal their shocked expressions and to whisper among themselves, could hardly stop talking. It was not only about the way Tori was dressed that caused such a stir but the fact that she had arrived obviously unescorted, was to many, scandalous behavior.

Tori could no more turn and flee, than she could move forward. Her very feet had become immobile, frozen to the spot. It was as if she was physically been held in place by a pair of invisible hands, hands that not only gripped her body but had somehow taken hold of her mind as well. She knew she had gotten herself into this predicament, what she was to do about it at that present moment, she had no idea.

It was her dear friend, who undaunted came to her rescue. Mrs. Destrehan arrived out of nowhere it seemed, proclaiming in a voice of authority her greeting. She did so, so all around could hear and thereby pass on what was to become Tori's lifeline. "Tori, it is so very good to see you my dear. We were not to sure you would take our advice and join us ahead of that dear husband of yours. And do tell me, about your gown, it is most unusual. I can't say that it would suit me at my age, but then, if that's the latest fashion in Paris, younger women like yourself will look simply ravishing in the coming season." She placed a motherly kiss to Tori's cheek and then taking charge, slowly moved the two of them toward her own husband.

Like being released from a nightmare, Tori was able to hide her amazement at what had just occurred. "Just how did you know about Jean?" Tori quickly whispered.

"I didn't my dear. But seeing you standing there looking as if you were about to run, or worse yet, never move at all," she giggled, "well I told myself and that husband of mine, I had to do something. I do hope I have not stepped over my bounds, it's just those silly fools carrying on like they were. Frankly dear, it got me quite angry. You do look ravishing, not quite the style from Paris I am sure? No, I thought not? But that little lie will give them all something to carry on about and less time to gossip about other matters."

She was acting like a schoolgirl and enjoying every moment of it. It was so good to see her really having fun but more than that, she was thankful her dear friend in her wisdom and lies, had given Tori what she needed to get on with the evening. She was in full control of herself and her surroundings once more.

Quickly, like a buzz of bees swarming in a flower-filled meadow, the ladies mingled spreading the latest gossip. The gown was from Paris and was it not just the most exquisite creation. Just look at the way it moved when she walked, the way it hugged her form, causing a silhouette-like vision. The more they looked, and talked, the more they increased their desire to obtain such a garment. The last thing on their minds, was to question the validity of its origin.

For had it not been deemed the latest design from France, by none other than Madam Destrehan and she would know, having strong family ties in that direction. Still others had made mental notes to find out who Tori's seamstress was. They had to have a gown like it they told each other, or something close to it. Just look at the way the men flocked to her; already she was the hit of the party. But then wasn't she always of late? It was said everything she did and said was duplicated by many trying to emulate her. Not every person felt this way however.

One such lady, green with envy, was to be overheard saying, that if Tori were to cut her hair off like a man, then most of the women of New Orleans would do so, but not her. Then with an air of haughtiness she announced she thought them all fools. While talking she sauntered across the room to join a small group who stood openly glaring, while nodding in agreement to further comments made from one in their midst.

Simone was sickened by the admiration once again so unjustly thrust upon the so-called beauty. She hated Tori with such a vengeance now, that if the hate could have physically killed, Tori would have surely dropped dead.

"I can tell you," Simone said to the Governor's wife standing by her side. "I for one would not be caught dead in such a gown. If that's what you can call it. Why, it's just not proper. Fashion or not I find it in very poor taste and this time I think she has gone too far. The very way she has our men running to her like that. It's like she was a common street... well you know? Nothing more than a lady of lesser means shall we say?" The small group, some of whom secretly would have loved the chance to be in Tori's place, looking half as good, lied in jealous agreement. Simone tired of the spectacle, turned her back and walked away, followed closely by those around her, who took comfort in the fact that Simone felt as they did. While these simpering, sniggering Belles continued to divulge ugly accusations amongst themselves, hoping to impress the prestigious Governor's wife, Simone turned her dwindling attention elsewhere.

Off to one side of the dance floor, stood a gentleman that had caught her eye. He was tall, dark, very well attired and had an air about him that intrigued her. His obvious Spanish features would have normally affected Simone in the exact opposite way than they were at the present. But something about his eyes had held her captivated. They were the kind of eyes that had a way of stripping one naked, slowly and deliberately, as they traveled the length of your body. She found herself wanting nothing more at that moment, than making this stranger's acquaintance. Visions darted about in her mind. She had flash after flash of herself in this strangers embrace with his hands traveling the length of her body. Oh yes, he was the type of man who made love with deep deep passion, and no commitment. The way his eyes raked each woman he gazed upon, as if he himself was visualizing bedding them. Oh, she knew that look well enough. Her blood was running hot so it seemed. Here before her stood a man whose passion was as raw as her own. True, Edward could satisfy her as a lover but she had become somewhat bored with him. The thrill of seducing a new lover was like no other thrill she could imagine and it was the very spark she felt she missed and required. The thought of it squeezed at her insides sending undeniable messages up and down her spine. She could run the risk of losing Edward by pursuing a relationship with whoever he was. To be found out, caught, that was impossible. Edward after all was not even here. Off gambling no doubt. That he chose such a time to ignore her made her only more determined to approach the stranger and to hell with what he would think.

"Excuse me ladies I see an old friend of Edward's that I simply should go and say hello to. It would not be polite of me to do otherwise and Edward would never forgive me if I neglected one of his associates. You do understand, do you not?" They all understood very well. It had not gone unnoticed, the open flirtations that had been passing between them. Simone had always had a reputation of being rather forward and flirtatious. Not one of the ladies for one moment had believed that the gentleman was anything but a total stranger. Obviously she had not changed her ways but then a little innocent flirting could hurt no one, and why should that Laffite woman have all the fun. The small group almost fell over themselves moving out of Simone's pathway, so she could go and greet her so-called friend.

The gentleman in question was not new to these gatherings. Rather he chose to go to only those that he felt would not bore him to death. It was all those stupid women and their silly games that infuriated him. Why they had to play so coy, he could not and did not understand. Only too often he would seduce one of the virginal beauties to find out that he was not the first to lay with them. It had become somewhat of a challenge to go to these gatherings and lead them on, then drop them cold and watch their little faces crumble as he left with someone else, or no one at all.

Standing by himself, looking the part of a rich well-dressed gentleman, he could bet all he had, that tonight would be no different. It would be only a matter of time before his sordid little game would commence and not started by himself. It never was. Sooner or later, one of the ladies would approach him. So sure of this eventuality was he, that he would try to guess which would be the first. He was seldom wrong. The manner in which they went about this often amused him and he would give them points on just how they used their minds to come up with an original idea. An original idea however, was something that as of yet seemed beyond any of them. Being original was a rare characteristic about these so-called ladies. He found nothing real about them; rather they were all like sheep to him. They all talked alike, dressed alike and God help him, acted alike. Those few he did give high scores to, were those who refused to fall victim to his charms. They were to be truly admired. Most times he would leave these ladies alone, respecting their wishes most, but not always. It was the pursuit that drove his passion, not the conquest.

His name was Senor Francisco Armando y de la Garcia de Vegas. To his close friends, he was simply Cisco. He was of definite Spanish heritage there was no doubt in this. He told most who inquired, that he came to New Orleans from Spain, in hopes of starting a new life, in the new land, that he had fallen in love with from the first time he had heard about it. Just how he made his living was not common knowledge. Some claimed that he came from a very wealthy family and did not have to support himself by any means. This was however, a simple rumor, started by himself. It was a necessity in order to obtain invitations to events like this one, by anxious mothers looking to make a good match for their eligible daughters. Still others whispered that his life was supported by gambling, as he was often seen around John Davis's house of gambling and they would have nothing to do with him. He was known to reside in a suite of rooms at the largest of hotels and his business dealings, whatever they were, kept him away days at a time.

Cisco loved to keep them all guessing and had built himself quite a reputation both as a mysterious gentleman and a well recognized honorable citizen. If ever the word dandy fit anyone though, it truly fit him. The term gigolo was more to his liking, or as he put it, a true gentleman, always available for a price. And those who paid, were always trusted to keep it to themselves.

Cisco had come here tonight to meet one woman, one he had been watching from a distance for some time. He was not disappointed. Her entrance had been spectacular. The way she dressed for the evening had everyone a buzz, ladies and gentlemen alike. Like a queen bee with all the little workers swarming around her, she was far from the sheep syndrome. She was not following the trend, she was setting it. Like himself, she seemed to enjoy shocking people but then there was something else about her that fascinated him, drawing him to her like a moth to a flame. He had become so caught up observing her every move, that he did not see Simone approach him, nor the frustration that flashed across her smiling face.

As she approached him it was not hard to see what held his attention. God damn that bitch; she even had this one panting after her like a dog in heat. This was one fire that she intended to put out, then re-ignite it herself later in the evening.

"I see sir you are shocked by the choice of gown that our dear Tori has chosen to wear this evening. It is shameful is it not?"

Cisco looked at Simone with his deep chestnut colored eyes, carefully hiding his emotions behind a cool mask of unreadable dimensions. He sensed quickly her jealousy and hatred. Emotions that she hid very well herself, behind her cold porcelain face, where her smile seemed out of place. He could have some fun here with this vixen for surely she was just that her type had it written all over them.

"Did you say shameful? Why madam, I myself find it exciting that she should dare to be the first to expose such a fabulous new fashion." Crushing jab, now bring her hopes up. "One I might add, that would I'm sure look more ravishing on you. But pray tell, do excuse me. I do not believe we have been introduced."

"Simone Claudette La Combe, monsieur, and you are?" Was that her normally cool voice that was quivering?

"I am Senor Francisco Armando y de la Garcia de Vegas, at your service." He bowed low, taking her hand in his, as his lips brushed lightly across the back of her hand. The way his name rolled off his tongue never did cease to amaze him. Nor did the obvious reaction it had on those so easily impressed by what they assumed to be the name of nobility. "Did you say that you know that ravishing creature? I should very much like to make her acquaintance, to pay my compliments of course." Just a little fuel on the fire of jealousy he thought. Let's see what you will do with that remark he thought.

Simone was seething on the inside, yet calmly, smiling sweetly. She coyly maneuvered her damning blows toward Tori. "Why of course she is a friend of mine. I would be glad to introduce you to her but I feel it only fair that I should warn such a gentleman as yourself. She is not the lady she seems to be sir."

Cisco almost burst with laughter. He was having so much fun but to laugh would only giveaway that he was merely toying with her. No, instead he spoke seriously taking a step backward and with a look of concern on his face. "You mean to tell me, that a lady of your obvious standing, has such a friend. I am truly shocked, or maybe I misunderstood you? She is a lady of standing is she not?" He could tell Simone was fuming and thoroughly confused, yet she played the game well, far better than most of her contemporaries. Her next move he imagined would be the old turn tail and run.

Simone was panicked a little but turning around and leaving was the furthermost thought from her mind. She had to say something to the insolent idiot who was smitten by Tori. She had to ruin her in his eyes without touching her own integrity. A different tactic was needed here if she were to succeed.

"You did indeed misunderstand me Monsieur. I did not mean her character is in question, it is just that the gown she wears... It was made to hide, shall we say flaws in her appearance. Tori had a child not long ago you see and it is so hard for a woman to maintain her youthful appearance once that has happened. You see before you a vain individual I fear. She has herself so tightly pulled in by her undergarments, why I declare, she can hardly walk for the very act of breathing is strenuous and she might very well burst the seams of her gown. She is nearly pushed out of it already." Simone knew she was not making any sense and was just babbling, but at least she had his attention, something that only spurred her on. "I have spoken out of turn and surely you must think me terrible talking of such things to a gentleman, but then I seem to sense that such talk does not shock you, am I right?"

She was dropping the coy look and putting on her pure sexy I'm yours and I want you approach. The way she was coming on to him was almost as if she were screaming take me to bed I want you. If Cisco had not been so involved with his one and only intention of meeting Tori, he would have taken this Simone up on such an open invite. This was after all a new approach from a lady of her standing and he gave her a high score. He would have to remember her for the future but right now he was interested in only one woman and Simone was not her.

Cisco looked openly at Simone, his eyes running slowly over her in a appreciative way. She was a beautiful vixen this one and he was sure he would be missing a great time in her bed by what he was about to say, but he could not resist it. "You mean to say Simone, that her figure is held in place by a corset pulled so tight that it gives her the allusion of a youthful appearance." He seemed to ponder what he had just said as if in doubt.

"That is so I'm afraid, she has such vanity, she cannot let herself age as a woman should." She had him now she was certain. He was doubting Tori's overall appearance. A smug smile curled the corners of her mouth ever so slightly.

"Then how is it done? I do not see. In fact I think it is you who is mistaken? Look at her gown closely my dear. If it is a corset such as you say, why it would have to be invisible. For even the finest garments such as the one you have on yourself, are visible to the well trained eye, are they not?" Simone turned to look at Tori to see what he was talking about, invisible indeed. Yet the view that hit her was speaking for itself. She could see for the first time the back of Tori's gown. What little there was left her waist clearly visible. Anyone could see that she had nothing on to support any part of her body. Simone's mouth dropped open. She could not believe it. How could that bitch do such a thing? Stomping her foot now in disgust she knew she had made a complete fool of herself. There was no graceful way out of the situation she had put herself in.

And upon seeing this, Cisco quickly moved to excuse himself from her company. "If you will excuse me, I think that I shall join her other admirers and introduce myself. I somehow feel that you are suddenly in no mood to have me meet the lady in question." With that he left Simone standing by herself. At that moment, she wanted nothing more than to march up to Tori and rip the gown from her body.

Cisco was chuckling to himself. That had been entertaining and to think he nearly passed this party up tonight for a game of cards. Why, this night was positively more fun than he had had in a long time and it was only just beginning. His enthusiasm continued as he thought about future evenings when he would have the chance to see just how smooth he could be. Winning back Simone was going to prove interesting and difficult, after what he had just done.

Tori found herself meeting and greeting old and new acquaintances. She enjoyed some and could not wait for others to leave, almost as fast as she started talking to them. She and Marie were laughing quietly together, when one of the older grand dames approached them, followed closely by two very distinguished looking gentlemen.

They were dressed to the hilt as far as she could tell and reeked manners and decorum. One of the gentlemen was tall, blond and handsome with eyes that seemed to read her thoughts as she looked at him. The older of the two was being introduced to her. Tori would have had a hard time under normal circumstances understanding the grand old lady but add to her soft spoken voice the noise around them and it was almost impossible. She caught bits and pieces of what the older woman was saying and then his name along with his friends.

"It is my great pleasure to introduce to you my dear, these two sweet boys. I had told them that you would not mind an old fool such as myself doing so?" She laughed and then not waiting for an answer, continued. The noise level raised as a group close to them all laughed about something or other, and because of this Tori only heard two words of the introduction clearly. Both part of names and both known to her from her time.

As the taller of the two gentlemen was bowing and lightly kissing the back of her hand, the names Louis and Lestat spun around inside her head. Amazement and wonder filled her mind, quickly giving way to many questions. His touch had been cool but not uncomfortable and his description did fit. But one other fact made her think twice that the man who was walking away with his companion, before she could talk, was real and not just a fictional character was clear. It had been his nails, they looked like glass! She was about to inquire further about the pair when dinner was announced and with it the end of her speculation. She soon found her meeting with them slipping into the recesses of her mind.

Dinner was served and still no Jean. The meal was wonderful and the wines delicious. Tori basked in the attention that she was receiving and yet she awaited one man only. Her eyes would drift longingly to the door during polite conversations, hoping to see him entering. She had seen the Governor and Edward arrive late and found that they looked too pleased with themselves about something. The two kept looking over at her as if she were the source of their enjoyment. Edward was talking to Simone when she burst out with laughter so loud, that the dinner party stopped briefly to look her way. She blushed politely and put her napkin to her lips, trying to hide her continued mirth behind it. In the end she had been content to sit drinking her wine and looking toward Tori with a look of triumph on her face.

Tori felt increasingly uncomfortable and the more she tried to ignore Simone, the more she looked her way, each time to find her staring at her with that all too familiar smug smile.

Dinner was drawing to a close, when she excused herself and went out onto the verandah for some air and try to sort out just what was going on inside. It was as if everyone but herself was in on some sort of a joke and one she felt was aimed at her.

The whole atmosphere of the evening had changed. Somehow it had turned ugly and it had not escaped her how both friends and enemies were watching her and whispering among themselves. That was one thing that really upset her. Could it have been her imagination, that some people whom she knew well and liked, were actually turning away from her as she looked questioningly toward them? She would have to go back in and find out but first she needed a short time to collect her thoughts.

The night air was crisp and it felt good, invigorating in its caress. The moon was shining down on her and somewhere out there Jean was on his way to join her. Damn, she hoped he would get here soon or else she would have to leave. Being here without him was just no fun.

The sound of the glass doors opening broke her thoughts. The tranquillity of the evening had been interrupted when the noise of the party from within escaped through the opening. Somewhat upset by the interruption she turned to see who the intruder might be and was met by the ice cold stare from Simone's frosty glare. The two of them just stood for what seemed forever to Tori, not moving or speaking, each trying to judge the others intent.

It was Tori who broke the icy silence. "Really Simone we had better stop meeting out on verandahs. I doubt that Jean would like it much. He might think you like me or something."

"I don't give a damn what he thinks, or you for that matter," Simone snapped back.

"My, my such language. Do you kiss your mother with that mouth? Oh of course, that's right, she doesn't even talk to you. Wonder why?"

"Bitch," Simone screamed. The word was followed quickly by a full back-handed slap across Tori's face, causing her to take a step backward. "Let me tell you something Miss high and mighty, if having your family not talk to you is bad, I can't imagine having no one in New Orleans talk to you and that's what's about to happen to you. Your Jean can't help you on this one either as it's his fault everyone will turn against you."

"Just what in the hell are you talking about? I think you have gone over the edge, someone had better take you home before you hurt yourself."

"I'll tell you what I'm talking about, no one who is anyone, will talk to the likes of you, not when the news of Jean's arrest tonight, along I might add, with his brother and his men become public knowledge. Yes, you heard right.

The whole lot of them are sitting in jail as we speak and there is not a damn thing you can do." Simone forced a laugh of sorts from her mouth, as she continued almost hysterically out of control with vengeance. "Well, you can do one thing when and if you get to see him, Jean that is. You can tell him that Edward finally got even with him. At least he's started, because I'm sure he's not finished with you yet."

The sound of music returned as the band had started to play once again. With nothing left for her to say and feeling very festive, Simone turned and walked inside closing the doors behind her. The air was stilled once again and the music that had been loud was now muted.

Tori was left alone and in shock. She had no reason not to believe what Simone had just told her. It explained everything from Jean's absence, to the way people had been acting ever since Edward and the Governor had arrived. That was why they had looked so smug and pleased with themselves. There was no doubt that they had slowly and deliberately spread the news, so as to further their pleasure and humiliate her more. It became instantly clear also that the reason behind Simone's outburst at the dinner table had been due to her learning about the arrest from Edward. That had been why she had laughed out loud and why Tori's world was collapsing around her.

Turning and looking up to the sky, her emotions all raging inside her from anger to panic, to sadness and finally to the utter loneliness of the moment, she hugged herself and shook her head from side to side. The truth of it was she could not go back inside and face what by now would be a hostile crowd. Even those who sided with her and Jean, would not do so in public, for fear of reprisals.

She looked upward to the heavens as if to gain strength from its sheer vastness. Instead the night sky so full of stars made her feel so small and helpless. The moon that just a short while ago had looked friendly, now looked as if it too were laughing at her. Suddenly a shooting star streaked across the sky falling to earth in a fireball of silent color and Tori spoke to herself in a voice of despair. "How I wish you were a 747."

A stranger's voice answered her from the shadows, making her heart skip a beat and cause her to think she had heard wrong. "I repeat myself, don't you think a DC10 would be better?" The gentleman who said that stood looking at her now with a smile of knowing on his face. He stood looking into her tormented face and wished he could help this lovely lady from his time. He had overheard all that Simone had said and knew it to be true and a cause of great pain and worry for Tori. The red mark from Simone's slap was fading but her loneliness and confusion was not. Oh, how well he understood how she was feeling at this moment. He knew even more about Tori than she could at that moment guess. But right now he had to just let her know that she was not so alone and that she had someone who really did understand her. He had to reach her, and convince her of this fact.

"Look, until just now, I had my suspicions for some time that you came from the future like myself. After all we are not the first or will we be the last to travel in time. It's just that until you mentioned the 747 I could not be sure and until I was, there was no need in coming forward. Let me help you. I can be your friend and lady by the sounds of that bitch that just left, you need one." He held out his arms and Tori fell into them.

There was something so right about him, that it made her feel safe. It was not just that he was from her time. No, it was far more than that. He was her friend she just knew it.

"Now, it seems to me you have two choices at the moment, one to leave, or two, go back in as if nothing is wrong and blow them away. I opt for back in. You can even be my partner. I just love to watch their stuck-up, pompous ass ways fall all apart when someone does something out of step. Look I think you need a good drink and I need a good dance. Let's compromise and each have one of what we need."

His smile was infectious and with it somehow things did not seem so dark. But still she felt uncertain as what to do. Was going back in a good idea or not?

"Look you can't help Jean now but we will come up with something. Let's go in and blow their assess of the dance floor, ok?"

Tori was laughing. God, it felt good to have someone to talk to. She had not remembered how much she missed her time until now. "You're on, but don't you think I should know your name sir, after all I don't dance with strangers," she drawled.

"Shit, do not, I repeat, do not talk like that. These Southern Belles, they bore me stupid. Besides dressed like you are, you look far from a Southern Belle."

"You bet your sweet ass I'm not and if you think for one second I am, you're in for a shock. Just how long have you been in this time anyway?"

"Two years and the name's Cisco to my friends, you won't believe what name I go by to everyone else, but then that's for later. Let's hit the floor. After you," he bowed low indicating with a swing of his hand toward the door.

Tori was not sure that he could help her but she did feel that he was her only friend right then. So smiling at him, she squared her shoulders and walked back into the dance. After all she wanted to show them that she was not one to be ignored or shoved aside. And if they assumed that she would have done the proper thing in quietly and shamefully leaving, well guess again folks. She had a new secret weapon, whose name was Cisco.

If Simone was shocked at the fact that her information had not devastated Tori, she did not show it. She and Edward were so overjoyed at the arrest of Laffite, that they would leave early to celebrate on their own terms. Edward had assumed that Tori had known Cisco before this night and was letting him escort her home in her hour of despair. He really did not care for there was plenty of time to get her now that Laffite was taken care of. As for the moment, he had only Simone on his mind and she had such interesting ways in which to make their night a complete success.

Tori and Cisco danced more than one dance and Tori drank far more than the one drink, in fact by the time she decided that they had better leave, she was having a slight problem walking on her own. Slipping out from the party, the two of them headed down the pathway toward her carriage. Then as so often in a case of too much alcohol mixed with a dash of fresh air, it hit hard. The whole world was spinning and as much as she wanted the pathway to stop its infernal up and down motion, it would not. Toward the end of the walkway Tori knew she was either going to throw up or pass out. And to add to that, try as she might to get into the carriage, the step was too high and she just could not get up enough strength.

Cisco, who had also drank heavily, was however in a slightly better condition than his escort but he realized that the only way he was going to make it home was to hitch a ride along with Tori. After all, she had a carriage and he did not at the moment. His decision however was to change in the next few seconds as Tori who by now had just decided to give up and not really caring what happened or who saw her in such a state, simply closed her eyes and let the blackness of passing out take over. Blissfully, she could feel the blanket of sleep sweeping her away from her problems. The last thought that crossed her mind was, God there was not going to be any aspirin to help her out, with what was sure to be one hell of a hangover.

Cisco saw her slipping from the carriage step and in his blurry state he reached out and caught his lovely charge before she could hurt herself. In his arms she lay out cold and somehow the situation sobered him up somewhat. Picking her up, he climbed into the carriage and gave the order to drive to an address on Saint Anne between Rampart and Burgundy. Slowly they made their way through the darkened streets, passing by the grand old homes of what would be called the Garden District in the future.

The horses finally stopped and when no one came to speak to the occupants of the carriage with an explanation as to why their journey home had been interrupted, Cisco slipped from between Tori and the cushioned seat, letting her lay gently down, oblivious to her surroundings.

Once outside he could see the driver clearly seated looking as if he had the world upon his shoulders. "Is there a problem?" Cisco's voice sounded loud on the quiet street. "I gave an order maybe you misunderstood me. The address is 1020 Saint Anne. You do know where Saint Anne street is don't you?"

"Yes sir. I know where the place is that you want to go. I also know whose place that be and de Master, he'd not be to happy with this here boy, that is, if'n I take his lady, the mizz Tori over there." The driver who was shaking his head from side to side now turned and looked at Cisco. He straightened up in the seat, squaring his shoulders and with more authority in the tone of his voice continued. "I may be only the driver for Monsieur Laffite but he be more'n than da boss to me, yes sir. And if you know what be good for you, taken Mizz Tori in her condition and all, over there, well da Master he goin to kill us both, and I sure'n don't want to go and die yet."

A moan came from within the carriage and Cisco stepped to the open door to check on the condition of the lady within. Not only was she beautiful, she was from his time, someone to talk to. She was a liberated female, who would understand so much, so very much. Still the driver was right, she was the woman of one of the most powerful men in New Orleans. Jean Laffite was nothing to mess around with and besides everything he had been told about their relationship, was to lead him to believe that they were very much in love. A man in love was a dangerous being and especially one with a reputation like Jean's.

He could become a friend to both of them and the best way to do that would be to help Tori, and help her get Jean out of jail. First off, he had to take care of her. Make sure she was safe, no matter the risk. Now that appealed to Cisco's sense of adventure. He could have fun while sealing his new found friendship with his comrade from the future. For the first time in what Cisco considered forever, he found that he wanted the friendship of a beautiful lady and not a relationship. Sure to make love to her would be something that only dreams are made off, such beauty and what a body but then they could never be friends after and he would do nothing to run the risk of hurting her or his chance of her friendship.

"You have nothing to worry about as far as Jean is concerned, it is his order I follow this night. He is not able to take care of his lady and has ordered me to do so. Now, if I were you, I would be far more worried about the owner of the home we are to go to. For if she were to become upset with you for any reason, well need I say more?"

The driver, who's eyes were as large as they could possibly get, nodded his head in agreement. He had been ready to question further, the right of this stranger, to his so-called orders but the mention of the anger of the other, caused him to weaken in his resolve. He would do as he was asked, what else could he do, lord he hoped this man knew what he was doing for both of their sakes.

A short time later, the carriage pulled up to the house on Saint Anne street and Cisco carried the sleeping Tori to the door. The driver upset by what he was seeing, called out to them softly, almost as if he did not want to be heard. "What you want me to do now?"

Cisco turned and looked at the servant and knowing that the man was in turmoil as to what to do, he calmed him by assuring him that he was a close friend of the Laffite's simply following orders himself. He then told the man to go back home and tell none where the mistress was, as it would ruin her reputation and surely bring down the wrath of Jean himself. Instead he was to return the following afternoon for her.

What else could the man do, here was a white man giving him orders and true it was not Jean but then he did claim he was a friend and he had said to come back the next day. Right or wrong he just wanted away from the place and the sooner the better as far as he was concerned. As for telling where he had been, well no one had to worry about that, no sir. He nodded his head and without another word, started off down the road.

Cisco watched him drive away before he kicked at the door. His kicking continued until the door was opened just wide enough for him to squeeze inside.

"I thought you would never get here and open up. Give me a hand will you, we need to get this woman to bed up in the guest room, before I drop her."

Marie looked at the bundle dressed in black and held the lamp up closer to her face. The golden light illuminated the features that she recognized immediately, as the face of Tori. Marie's eyes flashed sideways towards his face, narrow slits with their dark orbs flashing sparks of light toward him. "You do know who she is don't you? Are you crazy? Her man will kill you for this."

"Her man, as you say, is in jail and this lovely lady has simply had too much to drink and needs a friend right now. Come on Marie, help me get her up to the bedroom before I really do drop her and I will tell you the latest and greatest."

Cisco lay her down gently on the soft bed and Tori sensing that she was safe and at last in bed, turned and curled herself into a child-like sleeping position, oblivious to those who watched. Marie gazed into the face of the woman she had only up until now known as a client. Now it seemed, that she would get to know her as a friend. So much pain she had seen her go through in the past months and now to have to face her man in jail. No wonder she got herself drunk but then she was sure that Cisco had helped there. Still Tori was a strong woman and a fighter. She would fight for her man and fate had brought her to them, just as she had known it would.

"You were right Marie, this Tori is what we suspected, she is from my time. That makes three of us now in this town. I wonder how many more walk the streets?" She was laughing low, as Cisco watched puzzled by this enigma of a girl, not yet a woman in years by his standards. Eighteen was hardly old enough to qualify in that department, as far as he was concerned. He had found when he first met her that she was wiser and older in her ways, far more than many other females he had ever known and so he treated her as his equal most of their time together.

She was feared by all who knew of her and respected by those who had her acquaintance. Marie had been studying for years now. She had started her learning, way before her association with Cisco. Voodoo and the old ways of healing, had been her lessons until he had come along. Now she learned things way beyond anyone in her time could have taught her and she had been a good student. She had learned from him so fast, that it had amazed him and encouraged him to supply her with as much knowledge as she could absorb. If it had not been for Marie, her understanding and complete acceptance of how he had come to be in New Orleans, he feared he himself, would have gone mad.

She had found him shortly after he had turned up in the market streets of town, wandering drunkenly around, mumbling to himself about the insanity of his situation. The young girl had taken him in and ever since they had become close friends, each one helping the other. True, they were lovers but Marie was smart enough to know that no one woman would ever have this man's heart. She had welcomed this as she herself wanted no ties or permanent relationship. He had become her friend, her teacher, her lover and protector. Yet he did not tie her to him, or question her about her life and her ways. They were the perfect match, each needing the other, yet free to do as they wanted, safe in the relationship and bond that only the two of them would ever understand.

Marie looked at Cisco now and shaking her head walked toward the door, "you will both be in need of some pain reliever in the morning, I had best go to the kitchen and prepare one." Marie stopped her exit, stiffening at the doorway, a posture he knew only too well. She was seeing something in that inner mind of hers. "Cisco," she whispered, "you had best sleep and prepare yourself for the days ahead. I feel they will be full of plans, trickery and danger."

How she could know of such things, he was not sure but then he had come to accept her and her visions of what would be. The fact that she was seldom wrong about anything, was just a way of life for him. If Marie told him to stay home because the day held evil, he found that he would automatically do as she said, no questions asked. Had she not been right when he had found his friend last year and even after that, she had told them both that they were not the only travelers. She had laughed at them, saying soon they would meet one more. That it was their destiny to be a part of a special three. Three's to Marie were a strong number, in fact in many of her spells and formulas three's of things appeared often. Cisco had called it superstition she called it the power. One thing was for sure, he had seen things happen that defied the laws of nature and he knew that if she had been in his time, that this Marie Laveau would have been studied for her talent in ESP.

He would do as she told him. Tori would sleep until morning safe where she was. He would go down the hall to Marie's room, where, when she was ready, he knew she would join him...

The light hurt Tori's eyes and her head felt as if it would come off her shoulders at any second. Once again she tried to open her heavy lids and focus on the side table. Maybe, if she tried to get some coffee into her, she might feel better. It was one of the worse hangovers she had had in a long time. Sitting up and reaching for her cup she quickly realized to her horror that this was not her room, in fact, she was not even in her house. Just where in the hell was she? How did she get here? Questions flooded her foggy brain. "Slow up, one problem at a time," she told herself out loud, as if to reinforce her courage.

First she would have to get dressed. Funny, she had no memory of undressing and if she did not, then how did she get out of her gown and into this whatever it was. Looking down at the garment, it closely resembled a man's shirt.

Panic was starting to grip her. She could remember very little of the night before, after dancing with the man who called himself Cisco. Had she dreamed that he was from her time? Was it real or was it a drunken wish? She would have to find out, headache or not.

Slowly and painfully she climbed out of bed and made her way over to her clothes, dread was haunting her, as the memory of Simone's words came back to her. Edward was not finished with her. What if that was the answer to her predicament? What if she was once again in his evil grip? Well nothing was going to stop her from getting out of there and nothing would stop her from reaching Jean and helping him. Whoever held her was in for the fight of their life.

"Let's see if the door is locked," she asked herself as she put her gown down and took hold of the door handle, "easy does it, nice and slow now." The door opened, which was she hoped a good omen. It could mean that she was going to have an easier time of getting away undetected.

## Chapter 20

As nauseated as she felt, there was an aroma that permeated the air, causing her stomach to grumble with hunger. The smell was so very familiar. It was as if she had woken up in her favorite fast food restaurant. Tori took another long inhale, just to make sure that she was not imagining the aroma. There was no doubt in her mind, something she had not had in a long time, was cooking somewhere out there and curiosity overtook her modesty. The unmistakable smell of hamburgers and fries, convinced her to step forward and investigate.

Off in the distance she could hear voices and following their sound she made her way down to the kitchen. Peeking cautiously around the corner, she could see two people sat at the kitchen table and right before them, on that very table, was the biggest most beautiful hamburger, bun and all! The man from the night before, whose name she remembered as Cisco, was about to take a bite out of just such a creation. She threw all caution to the wind at seeing this and without thinking she reacted.

"I'll be damned. How in the hell did you manage that? Are those real French fries or am I dreaming?"

Cisco and Marie both looked toward her but neither seemed to be surprised by her entrance or questions. Cisco took a large bite of his burger and wiping the juices that ran down his chin he swallowed hungrily and spoke in a teasing tone. "Well good morning to you too and how did you sleep? You look a little bit green if you ask me, doesn't she Marie? Better not show her the ketchup just yet, even though I'm sure that she's not seen any for a long time." He laughed and turned toward Marie as he added, "Nothing like you make Marie, that's for sure."

Tori could not believe him, he was acting as if the three of them were old friends, who spent many mornings like this. He was just so darn relaxed. Tori's attention had been drawn toward Marie as he spoke to her and she recognized her immediately. She knew there were going to be a thousand questions flying out of her mouth any second, but Cisco broke in before she had a chance to start.

"Tori, I know that you two females know each other and before you say anything, might I add, that this wonderful girl has just what your headache is in need of. Pull up a chair. You will be right as rain in a few minutes and then if you want, I'll rustle you up a Cisco burger and yes, some fries. Just don't tell anyone, it's sort of a secret if you know what I mean? Besides, this world is not ready for fast food yet, if you get my drift."

Tori sat down in the chair across from Cisco. She was staring at the plate in front of him. "That is something. A sight for sore eyes. You know, as long as I've been here, it never occurred to me, to actually attempt to make a burger and fries." Looking up from the table at both of them, she was filled with curiosity. "You two are friends and you Marie? You knew about Cisco? I mean she does know, doesn't she?"

"Yes, she knows Tori and I must tell you she has known about you for some time." Shock covered Tori's face at hearing this and she turned toward Marie, who backed up Cisco's statement with a simple nod. Cisco continued slowly. "Since Jean had the fever and you lost your son. I would have come to see you then but the time was not right and I had to be sure. You can understand that surely? It's not easy is it?"

Marie put a glass of yellow looking liquid in front of Tori and smiling at her, pushed the glass toward her. "You best drink it down, all of it. I warn you, it's bitter but then it does work. Go ahead, I'm not going to poison you."

Tori looked at the glass but continued talking to Cisco. She answered his question, ignoring the drink in front of her. "Oh I know it's not easy that's for sure. It's just incredible, the two of you being friends like this and here I thought that I was all alone. You're not from another time too are you Marie?"

"Me, Lordy no! I was born here. Seems to me, that I was born in the wrong time though. Your time sounds like more fun and the foods far more interesting." She laughed. "Now quit delaying and swallow."

As soon as the liquid slipped down her throat, Tori felt as if she would lose it and in fact nearly did. Cisco laughed at her and quickly gave her a cup of black coffee, to wash down the bitter bile that kept trying to make its way up. "It's not aspirin but then it works just as well. I think a lot faster. You will be right as rain in a flash. Now how about that burger and some good old fashioned conversation.?"

"Sounds good to me but I have a question first, about last night. How in the hell did I get here and if I might add, into your shirt? I assume it's your shirt?"

He smiled. "It is and Marie here is responsible for that. As much as I would have loved to help, I can assure you that nothing happened, if that's what you're worried about. You are a lady who is safe and always will be in my home."

Marie made a jab at his side with her long wooden spoon. The look he got sent a clear message.

"Ah, that is Marie's home, that's where you are right now. If I had a home of my own you would still be safe there though." Marie giggled at him, and Tori found herself amused with Cisco.

He continued after frowning at Marie. "I want your friendship Tori, yours and Jean's. Seducing you would not be the way to gain that, now would it?"

Tori looked at him and she knew he meant what he said. She felt as if she could trust this man with anything, just exactly why, she was not yet sure. She knew nothing about him, other than they had one thing in common, time travel.

"You know, he said breaking her thought, what would the ladies of the South think of you now, sat there dressed like that? God, it is good to see a woman who has no pretense or real hang-ups about her body." Cisco bent down and looked under the table as he spoke, "great legs there lady."

Tori laughed. She had completely forgotten how she must look and come to think of it, she did not feel one bit ashamed sitting there with him like she was. She made up her mind right then that just knowing Cisco would in the days ahead be like old times. A dark cloud covered her happy thoughts for a second as she remembered just where Jean was and wondered if she could ever get him out of jail. This she pushed aside with a determined affirmative motion of her head. Of course she would get him out! Looking at the grinning Cisco she realized Jean might not understand him or accept his actions right away but he would have no choice. He had a hard enough time understanding her most days but she knew that he would grow to like him. He would have too.

Tori smiled to herself as she knew already that she was not going to give up her new found friend for anyone. It was so good to have someone to talk to like this. Jean would just have to understand that.

Thinking of Jean reminded her that she had to get going. He needed her help. She started to get up from the table as she spoke. "I have a thousand and one questions to ask and I would love to sit and talk to you both but I have to get to John Grymes. He's Jean's friend and he's an attorney. You might have heard of him? I have to see what can be done, about getting Jean out of jail."

"Way ahead of you Tori. Look I did some asking around this morning, while you slept in. It seems that no one is allowed to see Jean or any of his men. There are twenty-five of them in all stuck in that place." He took a drink of his coffee and continued. "They are going to go to trial after the New Year's celebration. Until then, they are confined with no one and I mean not even you, allowed to see them. Don't bother trying," he took a another mouthful of his burger. "It would be useless I'm afraid. Even your lawyer friend can do nothing. But don't worry I think I have an idea. First let's get to know each other over this good old fashioned junk food. How about it?" He pushed a plate her way, and took hold of her hand giving it a gentle squeeze. "You are just going to have to trust me on this, ok?"

"I don't know. I really feel as if I should be doing something. Maybe if I went to the Governor myself and asked to see Jean?"

"Look Tori, I hate to remind you of this fact but this is not the nineties with bail and due process. This is now, today in this time, not ours and you and I have to go along with their ways." Cisco saw Tori's eyes flash and thinking he had blundered, cursed out loud to himself. "Oh shit! I just assumed you were from the nineties like me. You are aren't you?" She nodded her head yes.

"Oh thank God. Thought I might have blown you away. You could have come from the seventies for Christ sake. They did have 747's then you know?" He laughed at her. "Not so sure about DC 10's though. Look, trust me Tori, we will do something but before we do, it makes sense to me, that we get to know each other. How about those questions? I know that Marie and I have some of our own, don't we babe?"

He seemed to know what he was talking about and Marie nodded her head in agreement. She walked over to Cisco, pride showing in her face. Her admiration for him was very evident. Gently but firmly she started massaging his shoulders, as she stood silently behind him. Cisco relaxed and leaned back toward her, taking her hands off his shoulders and holding them close to his chest. The two of them were obviously far more than just friends, that much was obvious.

Tori sat back in her chair and smiled. "Well, if I'm to be your friend and you mine, I had better know your name. After all, I can't very well just go around calling you Cisco, now can I?"

"You could but that would raise a few eyebrows wouldn't it?" He was chuckling to himself as he leaned forward, "you're going to love this one. Bet it puts a smile on your face each time you hear it. How about this for a handle." He pulled Marie around and sat her on his lap giving her a squeeze that made her squirm and giggle as she wriggled free of his grasp. "Marie helped me so don't put all the blame on me." He stood now looking at Tori. His voice somber, with serious written all over his face, "I am Senor Francisco Armando y de la Garcia de Vegas, at your service." He bowed low and as he came up, his expression exploded with laughter. "Do you get it? No? Well let me explain. Francisco, after a certain town where I was born. Armando? Well I needed a middle name. These people seem to have a ton of them and I just had to have something easy to remember. Next Vegas, well you can guess where that came from. Besides it has a nice ring to it don't you think?"

She was laughing, it was impossible not too. Cisco's sense of humor was infectious. Stop it she thought, she had to pull herself together here, this was important, it was not a silly game they were playing at. She asked him then, "That's what you go by here, but how about before?"

"Before is not important, before is gone and thank God." He saw her look of horror. "Don't look so shocked. I'm glad I found my way here, it sort of saved my life. Ok, I'll put it in a nut shell for you, then enough of me for a while. I was a third year medical student at Baylor in Houston. A son of a prominent, overpowering, condescending doctor. I was trying to please dad, got the picture? I could not stand the pressure, or live up to his expectations so I left. I totally rebelled, went to Las Vegas and did what I wanted. I worked backstage on one of the shows. You know make-up, hair, wardrobe that sort of thing. It gave me time for the one other love of my life." He shot Marie a knowing glance, "I also loved the game Black Jack and well one thing led to another and before I knew what was happening, I was up to my neck in debts. I borrowed and to make a long story short they wanted their money. So rather than go to my dear old dad, I left town in a hurry and tried to hide in New Orleans." He took a drink of his coffee and sat thinking for a minute, as if reliving what he saw in his mind. Marie hugged him and that action brought him back as he continued. "Thought I could win back my losses. Stupid really, that's how they traced me I'm sure. It did not take them long to find me and as I ran from them during Mardi Gras, down a dark alley, I lost them. Sure did, lost them and the nineties. One minute I was running in one time, turned a corner and bingo I was in another. Got to tell you, it was one hell of a shock. I thought I was on a movie set or something. Thank God I was in somewhat of a costume for a fancy dress or I would have stuck out like a sore thumb."

Marie laughed at that and Cisco looked at her frowning as he continued. "Marie here, found me several days later and took me in. We have been friends ever since and you see before you, a man who is having himself one hell of a good time and thankful to be here." He picked up his coffee mug and took a drink then turned his attention back toward Tori. "But something tells me that you don't want to be here am I right?"

"It's not that I don't want to be here, it's more that I don't belong. Unlike you, I was not running away and I left behind a family, a daughter..." The next few hours spent in that kitchen, were hours of discussion on what happened to them both. Tori told her tale and as she did, it became very evident to them all, that she would one day try to get back, unlike Cisco, who had no intention of doing anything like that.

Listening to Tori, he felt a deep sorrow for her because he truly believed that she would have to accept that for her, like himself, the future was dead. There could be no other way he told himself. After all, who had ever heard of anyone claiming to have traveled back and forth in time? He mentioned this to her as she rambled on desperately to both of them sounding as if she were not only trying to convince them but herself also.

"Seems to me, that if I did succeed in getting back, that I would have proof of sorts. After all, I've been gone some years now. I know that's no real proof, that is what your going to say right?" He said nothing. "Maybe I would rather not talk about it once back. People would only think me crazy... So maybe, it has happened with others and they chose to remain silent. Think about it people in history have always popped up now and then. People like Nostradamus. If he did not himself travel, then maybe he listened to someone who had. Or Leonardo da Vinci, look at him, way before his time with his inventions."

He hated to shatter her hope; she looked so helpless. It was, as if she had to have something solid to believe in, about what had happened to them. "You do have a point but then we might never know. If there is a way back and you want it, I hope you find it. I really mean that. But for me and John, well we opt to make the best of it here."

"Did you say John? You mean there is another person here like us?" Tori was on the edge of her seat. Excitement was beyond what she was feeling at this point.

"Yes and it's someone who you will be meeting, the sooner the better. I have set it up already, as I figured you would want to say hi." He was grinning from ear to ear, so pleased with himself and his little surprise. "You can't very well go in those clothes from last night though, and even if John might like to see you as you are right now, well we must be proper musn't we?" He was laughing and his face looked so full of mischief. He reminded her of her brother, when he was younger and used to tease her.

"Cisco, I would love to meet this John friend of yours but I can't, not now at least. I must find away to help Jean and his men. I have to help them. This has been nice, great really, but now is not the time for sitting around on my ass talking about old times."

He broke in with a fake hurt look on his face. "How quickly you forget. I said that we would find a way and I meant we. That is why I have made arrangements for you and I to meet with John and see what can be done. Three heads together are far better than one and if anyone can come up with an idea, it's going to be one of us, but not alone. You have information, I have some and John has some. Don't you see, we can help each other and believe you me, it will be my pleasure to help you." He grinned again then quickly added, "as I know it will be John's. Now your driver should be here soon to pick you up. I sent word for him to come and get you. How about I come by, say around eight and pick you up to go out for some dinner? We will meet with my friend then."

"What choice do I have? You are all I have and you are right three heads are better than one. I trust both you and Marie and this John whoever he is. I guess I'll have to trust him too. We will meet this friend of yours. I only hope that he can help. I will get Jean out, one way or another. With or without help, believe you me. I get what I want!"

The driver arrived for her putting an end to any further discussions. So feeling somewhat stupid dressed in the same outfit she had worn the night before Tori took her leave of Marie's house. She almost ran to the waiting carriage, hoping no one would see her as she did so. Her driver asked no questions, not that he ever would have dared. Just that he had no need to. He knew exactly why Tori had spent so much time at Marie's house. She was getting some mighty powerful "gris gris." Yes, sur. His master would be a coming home real soon. Ain't no one ever crossed Marie's "gris gris." It always worked.

Look at the last time she used it on the white man's law court. That young plantation pup, that one that done got hisself into all that mess. His daddy paid Marie. Yes, he paid her good. Asked Marie to help his son get free and all. She did her spell put that "gris gris" under his chair in that courtroom. Until she did that, that white man didn't have no hope at all. Sure that boy be guilty and everyone around town know'd it to be so, but still dat judge said it weren't so and let him go. Powerful stuff what Marie did, yes sur. And that daddy was so grateful, he done give Marie that very house on Saint Anne street. Everyone know'd how powerful that woman be and now his Mizz Tori done gone and got herself some strong help.

Tori had no idea of what was wrong with her driver, the way he rolled his eyes and clucked his tongue in his mouth, making that awful sound. She did not have time to bother with him either. All she wanted was to help her Jean. Instead of going straight home like she had planned, she swung by the blacksmith shop to talk to Pierre or see if Dominique was there. Someone of Jean's had to know something, or know what could be done. She just did not see what Cisco and his friend could do to help. After all, they needed a lot more than dreams and talk to get Jean and his men out.

It was the blacksmith himself that informed Tori just how bad things really were. She had not known that along with Jean, Dominique and Pierre had also been caught. Stunned and almost in tears, she listened as the large black man told all he knew. What frightened her the most, was what Thiac said. He had told her he doubted that anyone could do much of anything.

She looked at him, pushed her emotions down and rather than give up, she stood and thought for a minute. "If I find a way to get them out, legal or not, will you help? Can I count on help from some of the men at Barataria?"

"You can count on me, maybe a few men out dere but I'm not sure what you can do to help the boss little mizz. I don't know'd how you can do anything at all but if you be a needing me, I'll be here." He had to admire this woman who had the spirit of his fire, hot and wild like. The way she spoke with sheer determination on her face. He had seen her push back the tears and take a hold of herself. He knew she would have to fight to get to Jean, and this made him think that she might just find away. Old Thiac knew a woman fighting mad was something to be reckoned with and if she fought and no doubt she was going too, he would stand by her.

Just before she left, he handed her a small object, he hoped he had made it the way she wanted and that it would cheer her up some. Tori looked at the object in her hand and realized that she held the small home made razor, shaped like she had told him. The edge was sharp as could be and he told her it could be sharpened anytime she wanted. Not that he felt he ever would have to sharpen it that was. The straight razor that most men of the day used seemed more practical and he felt that the boss would not like this new style. It had to be some sort of a joke between them and he did not want to ask it was not his place. Seeing the smile on her face was enough for him. He knew he had done a good job and that was what counted.

Long after Tori left the shop, he chuckled to himself. He hoped that she did indeed need his help to get the boss out. He would enjoy doing anything that made her happy. He just loved to see the way she looked at him with those eyes and truly meant it when she thanked him. Not many white folk ever looked him in the eyes let alone a lady.

Tori spent the remaining hours dressing for the meeting with Cisco and his friend. She was already forming somewhat of a plan in her head. She frowned as the idea grew, the idea that she would simply have to pull a good old fashioned jailbreak.

"I wonder if that's been done yet, at least in this town?" Bessy who was used to Tori talking to herself out loud, ignored her mistress. She was wise enough to allow certain actions to go as if unnoticed, like those of the night before. Even though she had stayed awake for hours waiting for Tori, who she knew did not come home, she was smart enough to know, that this was not the time to approach her with questions as to her actions. It was not that she felt it was not her place either. No, it was for the Massa. Him wanting to always keep her safe and all. However she couldn't go asking like, not yet. Mizz Tori had enough on her mind without her interfering, what with Jean's arrest and all. Besides she knew her mistress all to well. When she was ready to confide in her, she would.

Finally Tori was ready. She went down to the study and lit up one of Jean's cigars and poured herself some brandy. The time seemed to drag by. Why was it, that when you were waiting for something, it always seem to take such a blasted long time, she wondered? Sitting down and taking another sip of her drink, she also reminded herself that she was not going to drink too much this evening, as she needed to keep a clear head at all times. Then she made herself a mental note to ask Marie for some of that liquid aspirin or whatever it was, the stuff really worked and headaches were something else she didn't need.

Her hand ran up and down her leg unconsciously as she sat in thought. It was only when she realized the smoothness of her skin that she looked down upon her bare leg with a smile. The razor had worked a dream, for the first time in ages her legs and underarms were hairless and she felt really human again. Oh sure, she learned that some woman used wax but she was not into pain and using a straight razor was to her, nothing short of lethal. Shaving, up until now had been taboo for her. How many of the women went around feeling like an ape she did not know? "Maybe it was because they had never known any other way," she mumbled. As for her, the hairy days were over. Smooth as silk and soft and scented, that was how Jean would find her.

She was sat in a chair with her legs up on the table and her skirt pulled up over her knees. A cigar was hanging from her lips and the glass of brandy in her hand rotated slowly as she daydreamed. She looked more like a lady of the night than a refined lady of the South.

This is the view that first greeted Cisco as he was shown in. He raised his eyebrow before he let out a soft whistle of admiration. Bessy on the other hand was more verbal and to the point, as she moaned out loud and grunted her disapproval. She turned sharply to leave, tossing her head in the air and almost knocking Cisco down, as she pushed by him. Bessy headed back toward the kitchen mumbling and carrying on. She could be heard clearly as she walked down the hall. "Miz Tori, must have taken the news of Master Jean so bad, that she has done gone out a her head. And that Vegas man whoever he is, he smelled o'trouble, dressed up fancy like a Christmas turkey and calling on her, knowing the master ain't home. Whistling like that, like she be from done the market way." She shook her head. Lordy be this was a going to be something she had best keep to herself she thought. The Master, he didn't need to be a knowing about it either.

Tori felt a pang of concern for Bessy and almost went after the poor woman to explain, but what could she say that would put her mind at ease. She felt it safer at this point to ignore her and pretend she had not heard her at all. She turned her attention toward her guest. "Pour yourself a drink. I'll just finish mine and this cigar before we head out, if you don't mind? I think I deserve it."

He did not move rather he spoke with a husky voice as he openly let his eyes travel the length of her form. "You know, I think you were better suited as a southern lady, keep this nineties lady thing up and it's going to be hard to keep my hands off you."

She looked up at him, was he kidding around, or did that tone in his voice say take me seriously? She lowered her legs to the floor and pulled down her gown to cover herself up. Next she reached over and extinguished the remaining cigar and then looked back at Cisco.

"I do hope that was a joke?"

"Let's just say, that you can stir a man's blood and it might be a lot easier if we kept our friendship platonic." He was looking away from her as he spoke, pouring himself a drink. She would have taken him seriously, if she had not seen that his shoulders were shaking. The man was laughing at her. He had been teasing her and she had fallen for it. Walking up behind him, she took her glass with the remaining brandy in it and poured it down his neck.

"Let's hope this cools you off." She could not help but fall back in the chair hysterically laughing. He turned with such a shocked look on his face. She had caught him off guard and in so doing had got one up on him. They were acting like kids. He loved a good joke and someone who could take as well as give. In seconds the two of them were reeling with laughter. It felt good to be able to communicate on a totally different level, one that was as foreign and strange to this time and place, as were their actions. Tori loved her new ally and knew that a special bond between them would always be there, no matter what the days ahead brought their way.

"Let's go and meet this John friend of yours. You have not told me very much about him you know and I am dying of curiosity. Who is he? Where does he come from? How did you meet him?"

"Slow up! One question at a time please. How about I tell you all about him on the way over to his place. It will give us something to talk about on the way and maybe by then I'll be dried out." He took her by her arm as they walked outside to the waiting carriage. It was one thing to carry on in private but in public they had to conform to the rules of the day. Cisco did not have to give any directions, as the driver seemed to know exactly where they were headed.

Once they were seated inside Cisco, started to tell Tori just who it was that they were off to meet. As he talked, Tori listened intently. He mind drifted off now and then as she processed the information and one thought clearly stood out in her mind. She was realizing that just maybe they had been brought back in time to meet and do something and maybe that something was to get Jean and his men out of jail. Whatever the reason, Tori found herself thinking that coincidence was just too much. This was much more like fate. She was always telling Jean everything happened for a reason and now she was telling herself the same thing.

"His name is John Davis and he came over to this time in 1807. Like you and me he got himself a name to use here. Realizing he had a chance to be happy here, using certain knowledge he brought with him of course, he has built himself quite a life as you will see. I can tell by your face that you have heard of him then?"

"Who has not? He is the owner of what some call the John Davis Hotel. It used to be the Tremoulet's Hotel before he purchased the place and renamed it the The United States Hotel. I had a laugh at that one, what a name!" Tori could hardly believe it. John was well known not only to New Orleans but to Jean and his brother as well. "Jean and I have eaten there on many occasions. I have never met the man myself but I know that Jean knows him well. He owns the gambling palace where Jean used to go all the time to play cards. Shit, Cisco, even Jean's attorney, John Grimes, lost fifty thousand dollars last year at poker and dice. Why is it, I get the feeling now, that there is more to this than just a plain gambling house. It is fair isn't it?"

"Oh John runs a good place. It's just that it's the first of it's kind so to speak and that makes it popular and profitable. Now about John himself, if you ask anyone, they will tell you that he comes from Cuba or Paris, they do not know for sure. He is a gentleman and respected by many. He plans to use most of his profits in the near future to subsidize the nation's first Opera house. He helps out with the Theater D'Orleans right now. He also plans on running the Orleans Ballroom. Did you know that the famous quadroon balls are held there? And there is more. It's not by accident that all this has come about. You see John was a dealer in Vegas. He ah, used to see me quite a lot back then and watched me lose a fortune come to think of it. Anyway's he was in New Orleans on a working vacation. He was the dealer in a big game. Claims he loved New Orleans more than any other place. Maybe that's why he intends to stay here. He knows a bit more about American history than I do. I don't know too much about this time and area myself, how about you? Ah, I see by that enterprising look, that you are just like myself!" He jabbed her in her side and laughed. "Anyway back to the main subject here, he had been in a big game in one of the hotels on Bourbon Street. After playing most of the night and ready to go to his room, he excused himself from the party and made his way to his own smaller bed and breakfast down a dark alley. Sound familiar? He took a short cut, or what he thought was a short cut. Best we can figure out, is that he walked back in time, from one time to the next, just as smooth as you like." Cisco looked at Tori and gingerly asked,

"Do you think this kind of thing happens more often than we would like to admit? I mean think of all the missing persons in our time?" Cisco fell silent, while both of them sat pondering the thought. The coach hit a bump and with it broke the spell. "Anyway back to John. He was different from you or I, because right away he saw a great opportunity. Once he realized what had happened to the twentieth century that is. He sold his gold chains and rings down the riverfront, bought some clothes and started the building of his small empire. His knowledge of casinos and gambling helped him a lot. He started by playing and gambling down at the docks until he had enough to start his own round-the-clock gambling place. He did so well at his first attempt, that it was easy for him to get investors in what is now known as the Palace. He has bought his investors out, by the way. The place is all his now. If you take a good look at it, it's just the same as a Vegas casino. Runs the same, has all the traits of one and well it should, as that's just what it is modeled after. The Palace is making him a very wealthy man. He loves music, all kinds, especially country. But that had to go, its not exactly invented yet! That was John's one big disappointment about this time I think, no C and W. Well almost, he sings some now and then when we are together. He's not too bad either come to think of it. Anyway he has replaced his country music with a new love, opera. So hence, his plans for the opera house." Cisco grinned. He could see that Tori was so far very impressed and intrigued. "Fine dining and this lifestyle are right up his alley. He has fine dining for the taking in his hotel, which is just another extension of his Las Vegas life. The food is the best in town. The rooms the most luxurious and for a reasonable price, you can have whatever you need. He can afford the food you get for nothing, while gambling, because he is making so much profit from the winnings. Did you know there is no limit to the bets? Why it's not uncommon to see a man lose twenty thousand dollars or more at one time, or at least in one game. And that Tori is a hell of an amount in this day and age. It's Las Vegas style all the way right down to his croupiers and dealers who work four-hour shifts around the clock. He has transformed the game of Brag into Poker, a smooth move, one of his best. He's even using a fifty-two-card deck. That was a stroke of genius. The fools think the Americans invented the game. A game that is still so new, they don't play it so well yet. So you see, he can run it fair and as far as I know, it is all on the up and up."

"How did the two of you meet?"

"Now that was a hell of a shock I'll tell you. Shit, I almost thought I was seeing a damn time warp or something. Thought I was going crazy or about to be flung back to the future!" He tried to look horrified at that thought, over exaggerating his expression then laughing as he went on. "I was doing all right. The ladies and I, we get along fine and with my knowledge of gambling, the money was easy enough. I was able to make a comfortable lifestyle for myself. I helped Marie out with some things. I got her going on hair you know. That's how she gets most of the knowledge about what's going on. People talk, she listens, it comes in useful if one knows how and when to use such information. I have shown her on more than one occasion how to use what she hears to her advantage. I would never exactly call what she does blackmail. It does come in handy though! Like a certain judge a while back, she got him to find a kid not guilty. She had the goods on the old man, judge or not, he had a secret like most men, but unlike most, he would die if it got out. The kid's dad thought it was Marie's voodoo, he did not care how or why, but he was so grateful the kid got off, that he gave her the house on Anne street. She caught on to how to manipulate situations real quick. I hardly have to advise her any longer. I have taught her some basic medical skills, shown her a few herbs to mix her potions with. It's with my knowledge and her uncanny ability to know things, that well between them, bingo, strong Voodoo.

But back to John. I do seem to wander somewhat don't I? Anyway, I went to gamble one night and as I had done often, I went to the Palace and as I sat at the table, who walked into the room but the owner and my friend John. One look and we recognized each other. Blew us away at first. Now we help each other out, and have had some damn good times together. We checked around for about a year and found no one else like us, so we gave up looking, that was until Marie told me about you."

He shifted in his seat and looked directly into her face. She had the strangest expression on her face. Her lower lip curled and twitched nervously as if she wanted to talk but was holding back. He realized that she had no idea how Marie had acquired the information, how could she? He rushed on to make it clear, "Jean talked in his delirium and Marie understood more than you could have imagined. After all, I had been talking to her about the future for some time. At first we thought it might be Jean that was the traveler but it soon became apparent it was you. Enough for now. We are here and the hotel and a meal of a lifetime awaits you. Let's go on in and enjoy ourselves. I for one can't wait until we three get together and see what the outcome of all this is going to be."

The hotel was one of a kind for its day. It was first class all the way from the furnishings to the food. The atmosphere was one of wealth and prominence. On any given night, it was common to find the plantation owners, alongside the high rollers. Many young ladies of society often dined here, under the watchful eye of their chaperones.

From the moment Tori entered the dining room, she felt the eyes of quite a few of its patrons upon her. It was common knowledge now around town, of the Laffite's arrest. The gossip mongers were having a heyday and now with Tori out on the town with Cisco, well they just could not believe it. It was more fuel for the flames of tall tales and innuendoes.

The light from the chandeliers was soft and the music that played was soothing and romantic. Tori however felt far from calm, let alone romantic as she let Cisco escort her to their reserved table. The thought kept crossing her mind, that she should be doing more to help Jean, not chasing down this John Davis in hopes of him being able to do something. She was here only because Cisco had been so insistent. She just had to believe in him and trust that fate was playing a larger role than they knew. It was meant to be. Everything happens for a reason she kept telling herself.

They had just received a glass of wine each, complements of the house when Tori's attention was drawn across the room. "To our success," said Cisco raising his glass bringing her eyes back to the table. The waiter placed the bottle on the table and left. Cisco never paid for anything in Davis's establishments. This was an arrangement between he and John, that had long ago being worked out. Tori noticed little things such as this, her regard for detail was becoming very acute and maybe that's why she had spotted the older woman who was staring at them both and none to kindly.

"Cisco, can I ask you something personal?"

"You may but I may not choose to answer. Depends on how personal you get."

There it was again, his sense of humor. The whole world and everything in it was a game, filled with fun for him. He was sitting there looking as if butter would not melt in his mouth and that nothing he would do or say, would be anything but innocent. His face with his dark eyes was straight, too straight. The corner of his mouth was twisting mischievously, while his whole body seemed ready to spring up like a Jack in the Box. "Cisco, I'm serious."

"And so am I. What makes you think that I'm not?"

"It's just that lady over there, is looking our way and none to happy if I might add. Have you any reason to be the object of her anger? It can't be me." He flashed a quick look in the general direction. "At least I don't think so. I have never met the woman before?"

Cisco slowly turned in his seat, to take a closer look. It was on his lips to ask which woman did she mean, when his eyes locked with the hostile stare of the only person looking their way.

Tori thought that the lady whoever she was, would leave her seat and head toward him. She looked as if she could actually kill him, if she could get her hands on him that was. Then to her surprise, she watched as she saw the face soften and her glare turn to a slight blush, rather like that of a schoolgirl. He was flirting with her and mouthing something to her. She would have loved to understand what it was he was saying but damn him he was speaking in Spanish. Just what it was he was up to she wondered.

"Might I add, that her husband has already killed three on the field of honor and if you value your life, you had best desist at once my old friend." John Davis had joined them unnoticed and for the first time Tori looked at him with interest. She had seen him on many occasions before, when she and Jean would eat here but never had they met. The man had always kept his distance. She had always assumed that Jean liked to keep his business and pleasure separate, and Mr. Davis had been nothing more than that, a business acquaintance. Now he stood before her, a true showman in his glory. His gray hair was well groomed and styled she was sure, by Cisco. This along with his manner of dress set off his gentlemanly good looks. He was dressed immaculately, right down to the gold chain that was hanging from his pocket watch, shining in the light. John was tall and distinguished looking, his debonair appearance and smooth-talking char, only added to his masculinity. He had the friendliest blue eyes, that sparkled as he gazed knowingly upon her. To think that this man, who fit so well into these times and with the people around him, was nothing more than a impostor. This thought left her with a strange excited feeling. She would never have guessed that he was from the nineties, not a trace of the modern man could be seen.

"So we meet at last Tori and on a far different level than I had ever thought that we would." As was his custom, he took Tori in his embrace and kissed her lightly on both cheeks, then lowering his voice, he whispered, "I think it best before we carry on any further conversation, that we leave for a more private location?" Then in a voice that could be over heard by those close by he added,

"Let me escort you both to my office. You are here to pay a debt that you owe are you not Francisco my friend? And it would be my pleasure if you accompanied us Madame Laffite." He offered his arm and she took hold as they followed Cisco toward his office on the upper floor.

If anyone saw them leave, they would think nothing of it. Many paid their debts in private it was not unusual at all. Once inside the large room, that looked more like a sitting room than an office, John turned and while he filled crystal glasses with fine wine, he spoke softly. "Your husband has been a good customer over the last few years and might I add, a good friend. It's because of his ability to get, ah, certain furnishings for me, at a very reasonable prices, that I was able to build what you see around you now."

Tori had not realized that Jean's business dealings with John had been on such a large scale. "You mean that you bought all this from Jean?"

"This and much more. His ability to always have what I have needed and on a scale that is economical to us both, has been very beneficial to both Jean and myself. I always told him if I could ever do anything in return to help him out, that all he had to do was ask. Seems to me that the time has come at last."

Tori sat there and took a sip of her wine. She smiled over the rim of her glass and nodded her head. "I believe it has. This is going to shock the shit out of him you know. The fact that the two of you, are who you are and helping me. It's going to be quite something, to see his face when he finds out that you and Cisco here, are.. well you know."

"When and if the time comes, that we tell him." John's smile had left his face and a grave look of concern had replaced it, sending a shiver of doubt around Tori.

"What do you mean, if?"

"Just that. I am not to sure that I want anyone else to know of our little secret. I will help you get him out of jail, on one condition and that is, that if I decide to let anyone else know about me, then it will be my decision and I will do the talking. You have to give me your word on that." He held his hand up to stop her protest. "Hear me out please. I have my reasons. It's not that I don't trust him I do. We understand each other very well. It is just that the more people who know, then bigger the chance of it all coming undone. I'm happy here with what I have built and I would like to keep it that way. Look around you, not only here but the whole street. Everything you see is mine and I built it. Granted the idea is not exactly new, but this is here and now. Call it ego or whatever you want." He grinned. "I wish to go down in history as the creator of all this." He raised his hands above his head, and made a grand arch slowly, encompassing the whole area as he continued. "The man who had the vision to put this together. Way before Las Vegas or Atlantic City or any other place. I want history to say they copied me, not the other way around. I have gone to great lengths to assure that I get full credit." He took a sip of his wine, and smiled slightly as he continued. "You see, in the nineties I was no one. Here I am the biggest and the best. Me, John Davis. I've pulled the greatest con. I will have the last laugh at all of those that put me down and they will never know." He grabbed the air with his fist, as if snatching something invisible, "I took it from them!" He looked at her. "Did you know, that I won't even have a portrait of myself done, not even a sketch, if I can help it? Can't have my face popping up in the future now can I? So you see, if anyone else is to know who I am, it has to be my decision, you understand?" The man was totally obsessed that was for sure, she even thought he might be somewhat eccentric. He was however a very talented individual, to have built so much from nothing in such a sort amount of time. Talent, skill and cunning were things she felt she needed a lot of if she were to succeed in the days ahead. If he wanted to stay John Davis of this time, then that was his choice. She had no problem with that.

"Yes I can understand how you feel and why. If however you do tell Jean, I can assure you that your secret will be safe. He has after all known about me for years. I have told him so much, explained and described as much as I can. His understanding has been great. He is not the only one either that has kept quiet. His first lieutenant Dominique, Pierre and his attorney Grymes they all know. It has been kept a safe secret among us."

"That's just my point don't you see! First Jean, his brother, then this Dominique, and who's next? No, I have to have your word that you will not reveal what you know to anyone! That is the only way I can get involved and help you."

Tori looked at him. He meant what he said and she knew that he would indeed walk away from this meeting and her, if she did not give her word. "You have it. I may not agree with you but then I need all the help I can get and I see no real harm in keeping your secret. So yes, you can rest easy, I will not tell Jean or anyone else."

The relief that spread across his face was evident. The lines on his brow seemed to vanish, as the muscles around his neck relaxed. He breathed an audible sigh of relief and then as if they had never had the conversation, he broke into an idea he and Cisco had, on how to go about getting Jean and his men out of jail.

Over dinner, Tori learned that her new friends had been very busy. They had done their homework well. After exhausting all other options and avenues open to them, they were left with only one line of operation. It was going to have to be a good old fashioned jailbreak, just like she had thought, but with a bit more added, that she would never have come up with. The stealing back of all the evidence being held. Evidence that John was only too proud to say was rightfully his, as he had already paid for it. "The goods were being unloaded and headed for my establishment, when that nosy good for nothing Governor got his sticky fingers involved," he grumbled.

"Cisco broke in excitedly explaining how he saw it. "No evidence, no crime. No crime, no charges. All we need is a plan and some extra men who can be trusted and bingo your Jean is free and everyone gets what they want. You get him back. I get to be friends with you both, not to mention the adventure of a lifetime, Indiana Jones style. And John here," he slapped his friends back, "gets to pay out his debt, one that he feels he owes Jean, for all his past help."

Cisco was enjoying every moment of the evening and it showed on his face, unlike John, who was the calm hard-to-read poker player. He was the one who would do all the worrying, while his friend seemed to not have a care in the world.

"Look, until we do a lot more research into the problem of getting them out, we can't do anything. I hate to be the one to burst any bubbles here but we can't go rushing into anything. Unlike you Cisco, I don't make a move, until I feel the odds are in my favor. This is not a game! This is very real. I do not have the luxury of a fantasy, of believing I'm Rambo and can just rush in and win. That kind of attitude will get us nowhere but caught and thrown in jail right next to Jean and his men."

"Well, I know that," snapped Cisco. "I'm not stupid you know but it seems to me, that the element of surprise is going to have to play a big part in this and we do need help. The three of us can't do it alone, that's for sure. Any ideas, anyone?"

"Gentlemen, maybe I can be of help in that area. First of all, I do have some extra help. How many, I'm not sure but if I were to go to Grand Terre with Jean's blacksmith Thiac, I could rustle up a few good men so to speak."

"You mean go into the heart of the pirate's den? You by yourself, that's crazy? I hear tell that Gambi and others would love to run the place their way. They did for a while you know, before Jean took over as boss." He was genuinely worried but ever the optimist he quickly brightened and leaned forward seizing the opportunity of a lifetime. "No it's just too crazy for you to go alone. You will need someone to go with you and I would love to accompany you. In fact, I insist." Cisco sat bolt upright at the mention of Grand Terre. So eager was he, that John and Tori looked at each other and laughed.

John poured Cisco another drink as he spoke to him in a firm but joking tone. "I think I had best keep an eye on you, you crazy fool. This is going to be one hell of a jail break. Keeping you out of trouble and succeeding all at once is going to be one hell of a job. What have I let myself in for?"

Tori grinned, "John what have we started, look at him, you would think he is actually enjoying all this." Tori was trying hard not to laugh any more, as she looked toward them both. "Cisco this is nothing to take lightly. In fact I don't know if I can take you with me. You are after all an outsider. I don't even know if it's safe for me to go without Jean, his men or not?"

"Exactly, and you will need a man along and I intend to be him. Now if you don't mind, I would like to talk of other things for a while. We will finish with all this espionage stuff later. Much more talk like this and I will start to introduce myself to the beautiful ladies around here as Bond, James Bond!" They all had to laugh at that, and for the first time that night, they felt as if they could relax. Cisco downed his glass of wine and handed it to a stunned John to refill, as he spoke. "I would just like to enjoy each other's company for now. It's been a long time since I've had anyone to really talk to and have some fun with. Old stuck-in-the-mud here, never lets go, what do you say Tori?"

He was impossible and he was so lovable at the same time. With nothing left for them to do that night and realizing deep down that the next few days could very well change their lives and history, they did what Cisco advised, they just let go, and enjoyed the rest of evening.

# Chapter 21

It had all been arranged that night long before she went to sleep. Tori had sent word to Thiac to expect her and a friend around dawn. It had been decided that Cisco would meet Tori at Laffite's blacksmith shop, just after sunrise. From there with the help of Thiac, they planned to go on to Grand Terre and hopefully persuade some of Jean's men to join them in their plans.

Her carriage pulled to a stop on the side of the building, out of sight of any prying eyes. The next few days outcome depended solely on the elements of secrecy and surprise. One set of eyes however, had been waiting and watching anxiously and as the coach pulled into the small side area, his large strides covered the distance between them rapidly. Thiac was beside her before her feet hit the ground, his large hand taking hers, as he helped her down from the carriage.

"There's someone here Mizz Tori. Says he's waiting for you. You want me to be rid of him?" he asked in a whisper. "I ain't never seen him around before and thought maybe he be a lying or causing you trouble like."

"No Thiac, it's fine he's telling the truth. In fact, I would like you to meet him and hear what we have to say. Can you close up the shop for a while?" "Anything you want Mizz Tori, all you a have to do is ask." He reached over and pulled the large doors shut behind them, as they entered the confines of the small establishment.

Inside, a fire gave off the only light to illuminate their surroundings. The orange glow lit up Cisco's face but did little else. It was a soft light, of deep reds and golden yellow that lay silent, until Thiac with his powerful arms took up the bellows. Then the sound of large amounts of air, blowing under the fire filled the silent room, sending white hot flames leaping into the air. Sparks flew high and flames danced upward as if trying to reclaim them. The wood crackled and snapped as the fire came to life.

An instant blast of heat shot out, with a wave of amber light, cloaking the room. It traveled fast washing across the open space between them and the fire, taking with it the darkness and the chill of the early morning. Thiac took an old oil lamp and lit the small wick, which he raised until the light was bright enough for his liking. He placed the lamp on the small wooden table and stood back waiting for whatever it was that these two had to say. He could almost bet it had something to do with the boss, but where that dandy fit in, he was not so sure. He would keep a close watch on that one he told himself. Heaven help him if he tried anything, anything at all toward his Mizz Tori. One wrong move and he would snap him in two like a stick, the scrawny runt. "Down temper," he mumbled to himself, "No needs to get all worked up over nothing."

Thiac was a very large and powerfully built individual. He towered over all that came into the shop, standing a good seven feet or more. His body rippled with muscles and his voice rumbled deep when he spoke. His skin was the darkest of ebony and a large protruding brow shadowed his deep set shifting eyes. His large head seemed to sit right on top of his shoulders, his thick neck being so large and short, that it did not seem to exist. The overall appearance of the man, was enough to frighten even the bravest of souls. Many said, that he was nothing short of a savage beast, that could never be trusted and surely untamable. It was said that such an animal belonged in the cane fields. His strength and build told anyone who saw him, that much.

In truth, the man was a big old teddy bear, most of the time. He hated violence of any kind and had such a gentle manner about him, that it was totally out of character for the image he presented. There was never any denying that he was very good at his job. In his large hands pieces of wrought iron would twist and bend easily at his will, into designs that were so intricate, they truly were works of art. Out of this blacksmith shop, came a great percentage of the grills that surrounded the balconies overlooking the streets. It was the perfect front for Jean's main source of income, the selling of his contraband.

Even those who feared the black, would step into the shop to place their orders, knowing no other could supply such quality work. There had been times however, when Thiac could not control himself emotionally and once he was driven past the point of reason. He had become that uncontrollable beast many thought him to be. Wiser now, he let no one see his fits of temper. Rather he would go out back and let off steam unobserved. He had come too close only once before and learned his lesson well.

Last time he had lost control, it had almost cost him his life, and had it not been for Jean stepping in and purchasing him when he did, Thiac knew that he would have suffered greatly. It had happened quite a few years back before he had come to New Orleans. He had lost his temper and done the unthinkable and hit a white man. In the islands as far as slave owners were concerned, this offense, was often met with swift and deadly justice. Thiac however had been lucky. His size and ability to carry large workloads had made him a valuable slave and one that his owner hated to see destroyed. He had instead given the order for a public whipping. Lashes were to be administered until he stopped them. Loathed as he was to damage and scar this beast, for his value would decline sharply after such a whipping, he simply had no choice. It did not matter that the black had been fully justified in his actions. The fact was clear he had accosted a white.

Jean had saved Thiac. He had bought him outright for a very large amount, a deal that the former owner was only to glad to take. To be rid of the problem and make a profit at the same time was very agreeable indeed. By the time Jean and Thiac arrived in New Orleans, he was a free man of color. He had worked here in this shop giving both his loyalty and service to Jean, out of gratitude and friendship.

He stood there wringing his large black hands, keeping in check the temper that he had sworn he would never lose again. No white man was worth a beating or death he had told himself. He was no longer a slave but that had not changed the law. He was still black and therefore had few rights as a man. But

Mizz Tori and her safety, her honor, that was another matter. For her he would not hesitate to break the law if need be.

"Thiac, yesterday when I came in here, you told me that you would help Jean and I any way you could. I told you then, that I intended to get Jean and his men out of jail. Well, I need your help and if you are still willing, then Cisco and I would be very grateful."

"Yes em, I meant it, that's for sure. You just tell old Thiac what you need and I'll find a way to get it done."

"Great, I knew you would help us. First thing, is that we need more men, to put our plan into action. To get them I have to go to Grand Terre with Cisco here. If you could come along, it would be a big help to us, as you might know which men we could trust. You did work and live down there for a while didn't you?" It was more of a statement than a question. Giving him no time to answer she went right on with her speech, as she warmed her hands by the fire. "Can you close up shop here, without causing too many questions? The last thing we need, is to raise any suspicions that something is amiss here."

"I can at that. Just have to close up. The fire will die by itself left unattended. The boss, he close up the place all the time. People's, they don't ask no questions. But Mizz Tori, I be thinking, should you go to Grand Terre by yourself without the boss? I know'd it's his house down there and all, but it be so close to trouble. I mean, you being a genteel lady and all. The roads this time of the year they be a hard traveling, and once there..." He rubbed his forehead as if trying to erase his wrinkled brow, worry was written clear across his face. "I know'd you been there afore. You know'd it's not safe for you that be sure. Old Thiac here be glad to go for you. I could bring back da mens."

"No, I thank you for your concern but I have to go along. We have to be so careful. We can't let anyone see us head out." She looked toward the closed door. "Once there, if all goes well, Cisco here, will be able to explain the plan to the men, far better than myself. Knowing their type as I do, they would never listen to you. No offense Thiac, it's just the truth. I also realize that they would never listen to a woman, even if that woman is Jean's lady. No it has to come from forgive me, a white man, with me backing him. You do understand don't you?" He nodded his head, accompanied by a grunting sound. "Once that is done, Cisco also will need to meet with our contact from here in town. He will have to gather the rest of the information that is crucial to our success. We have so much to do and such a little time in which to do it. Everything has to be ready to go in the next three or four days."

The room fell silent. It was as if she had spoken so rapidly, spilling her emotions with her words, that she had exhausted herself. Looking into their faces and taking a deep breath, she quietly asked, "So my friends, if you are ready, let's go?" Thiac looked at Cisco and nodded his head, "Can you saddle a horse? Seem's Mizz Tori is in a hurry, and ain't about to change her minds."

Cisco looked toward Tori with a worried expression on his face, as he answered Thiac and also asking Tori what seemed like a reasonable question. "That I can do. I can saddle a horse but if we are to ride, don't you think that you had best find a more suitable riding garment madam? I mean riding in a dress such as you are wearing, may present somewhat of a problem, wouldn't you say?"

"I'm on my way. I left my outfit in the coach, so if you two gentlemen will excuse me, I'll be right back. Just get the animals ready to go, will you?" Cisco rubbed his chin in amusement. This should be interesting to see what she came up with now. That look on her face, it was a dead giveaway that something was up. After all, Levies for ladies were not available. Just what she intended to wear, could be worth a great deal of laughter. Pantaloons no doubt, trimmed in lace, with small pink ribbons. This vision was causing him to chuckle, as he walked to the back of the shop to help Thiac.

The blacksmith, was looking very upset and worried, as he faced Cisco. "I don't have no riding saddle for Mizz Tori, how she going to ride?"

"Just like us old man, just like us and I assure you she would have it no other way. So wipe that worried look of your face and let's get to work."

Tori picked her package up from the seat and then gave her message and instructions to her driver. He was to go directly to John Davis, who would be expecting him, and repeat only, that it was all go. "Nothing else mind you, just all go, you understand?" The driver assured he did and left on his errand, thinking to himself that something strange was going on, but what did he care. He had just been given the next few days off and that was far more important.

Tori came back inside the shop and hurriedly moved to a darkened corner, not far from the warm fire. She hung a blanket over the stacked wrought iron, making a changing room of sorts and stepped behind it.

"If you two don't mind, I will trust you, to keep your backs turned while I change."

"Yes Mizz Tori, we will and I's see to it, that his here dandy, keeps his face and eyes a pointing the right way." Thiac placed his big hand on the back of Cisco's head and physically turned it away from Tori.

"Ah, you ruin all the fun Thiac my man, and will you please call me Cisco if we are to be friends and stop referring to me as a dandy, you will wreck my image."

The big black face just grinned, as he cocked his head to one side. "Well now, I might enjoy calling you by your given name. Ain't never had no white man offer that before." He scratched his head puzzling over this latest predicament. "You and this here Mizz Tori, you don't seem to see the color of my skin. It be real black you know? But still you treat me as a man and I like that. Yes sur, I like that a whole lot. So's Cisco, we be friends. That is, when it's only us and ain't no one's else around. But you just keep your eyes forward like, all da same." He made a sound halfway between a grunt and a laugh as he propelled Cisco forward. "You just come on out back with me and help wid dem horses. Da saddles ain't a going to put dem selves on."

Tori smiled to herself. She felt a wave of confidence and safety flood over her. She was no longer fearing going to Barataria as she secretly had been. Yes, she knew that she was far safer than she could ever have hoped to be. By the time the horses were ready, Tori was dressed and ready to ride. When she walked outside, what they saw before them, was nothing short of a miracle transformation. Where before a lady had stood, was now standing what could pass for a young man.

Her hair was pushed up under a bandanna and her white blouse, that was open from just below her bust line to the top of her neck, was slowly being laced closed by long strips of thin leather. She smiled, satisfied with the results, as she finished tying them together. The shirt was baggy enough to conceal the woman that lay beneath it. That and the fact, that she had bound herself tightly around the bust, partly for support, and partly to help conceal the curves that would give her away as a woman. Her pants fit tightly and long black leather boots rode high, stopping just below her knees. A matching soft leather belt tied around her waist was supposed to hold the pants up, but to Cisco's trained eye it looked totally unnecessary.

She added the last two articles to her get up, while walking toward the horses. First a large brown jacket that hung calf length and buttoned closed, the other a soft felt brown hat, that she pulled down low on her forehead. If anyone was not looking for a lady and no one would be, all they would see would be a young boy.

Thiac was shocked and started to laugh, slapping his sides with his hands. This was truly a woman of courage, to dress like this and go out in public. Cisco's mind, was more on the female body he was looking at, aware that her pants outlined her rear end very well, he had to remind himself, that she was to be left alone but then he had to admit, that was one hell of an ass that filled those pants.

"Very impressive, could not have done better myself but what did you do with your boobs? They seem to have vanished into thin air, more is the pity." This, he had whispered into her ear, in a roguish type of voice that reminded her somewhat of Jean.

Laughing she jabbed her elbow into his ribs. "That my friend, is my secret. One for me to know and not one for you to worry over."

Pretending that her jab had hurt him, his face grimacing in pain he playfully continued. "Ow! that hurt. I was just asking, in case you need help in the future." His eyes were full of mischief and his voice was on the verge of laughter as he spoke. "To conceal any part of your feminine charms would be my pleasure I can assure you. I would love to come to your aid."

"I bet you would you dirty old man. Now enough of this, we had best get going. I would like to be out of town before too many people are about. Disguise or no disguise, no one must see me leave. As far as this city is concerned, I am indisposed at home. I want no visitors, as I am distraught over the arrest of my husband, and that's the cover that has to stay intact. So let's get going, now!"

The three of them mounted up and headed out of town, using all the back alleys and empty roads that they could find. Once on the outskirts of town, the slow pace of the horses ended and they spurred their mounts into a full gallop.

Thiac had noticed right away, that Tori was seating a horse like a man would and had felt ill at ease, never having seen a woman handle an animal in this fashion. In his mind, he could never even recall a woman handling a horse of this size and power at all. Seeing her now however, riding like the wind with ease and no sign of fear, he concluded that this lady seemed to be able to do anything she put her mind to.

The ride to Grand Terre was a long one. They had to stop and rest the animals, as well as themselves several times. The little food and drink that they had brought with them was soon consumed and stopping for more, was out of the question. Not only was there no place along their route but even if there had been, Tori could not have run the risk of being discovered.

There were times that they slowed the pace and walked the horses side by side. Tori and Cisco would talk, as Thiac rode close behind and mostly listened quietly but more often, lost himself deep in his own thoughts.

These two people with him were very different in many ways. At times he did not even understand them. It was as if they were talking a strange and new language. They used terms and sayings that he had never heard before but he told himself that was as it should be. He was nothing but a dumb Nigger boy, at least that's what he had been told enough times. He knew he was not stupid but he sure was dumb about a lot of things. Trouble was most white folk just thought the two to be the same thing he reckoned. Thiac did know one thing, he knew he was seldom wrong about folks. The good one's was as clear to him as the bad and he knew that Cisco and Tori, well they were in the good group. Yes sur, he knew that to be as true as he was a riding his horse.

As the day wore on, not only was this fact becoming more true but he found that he was considering both Cisco and Tori, as his very own personal friends. This was something that caused him deep emotional feelings, feelings he had never experienced before. His shying away from talking to them as friends was also wearing off, with each passing mile they covered. Sure, his boss was his friend, he was the man who had given him his freedom and he could never forget that. These two on the other hand, just liked him. They had no real reason to treat him the way they did and he would never forget them for it either. Maybe someday all the people of New Orleans would be this way he thought. Maybe there was a chance for them to all live equal and help one another...

Long before they arrived close to the Barataria stronghold, the pirates were aware of their presence. Word had gone on ahead of them, that they might be headed for the village. Not much happened on this route, that the men who lived and worked here, did not know about. They did nothing to stop the three, as one was well known to them as the boss's blacksmith. As long as the other two stayed in his company, they could wait to see who they were and what they wanted.

The sun had set many hours, before the three of them finally made their destination. Exhausted, Tori knocked on the door of their old home and waited rather than just walk in. After all, it had been so long since she and Jean had lived here, it felt wrong just to barge in.

Cisco watched, as the Spanish woman who recognized Tori immediately, took her into her arms. She acted like a mother welcoming home her own child.

Tori shook free her hair as they entered the hall and headed for the sitting room. Cisco and Thiac followed and seeing the look of uncertainly on Thiac's face Tori asked him to please come on in and have a drink with them. Thiac however, felt this was more than he could handle at the moment and turning to the Spanish woman, who did not show any sign that anything was amiss, asked to be shown where he was to stay.

He hoped that it was not going to be in this house. That would be too much. It seemed to him the whole world had gone mad, and right now all he wanted was to get outside to sort things out in his mind. This day had been one he would long think about. Him equal, or at least treated as such, and now asked to drink with them. It just did not seem possible.

Seeing his troubled face, Tori realized that she had not thought one bit about how uncomfortable he must be. She had forgotten and overstepped the relationship between them. Jean had tried again and again to warn her against such actions. Stupid was not the word for how she felt at that moment. Still, what was done was done, they would live with it. Thiac just needed time; they all did, to get comfortable with their new relationship. Tori knew very well that if they were not careful, their new found relationship could be misunderstood and land Thiac in a heap of trouble. Here and now he was safe, and when they were alone it would be fine but from now on she would have to watch her step more carefully. Without waiting further, she instructed Carlotta to place Thiac out back. Then she explained to him, what that meant.

"You shall stay in the little house as we call it. It's not much more than a small cabin, but you will have everything you need." She walked over to him and wanting to hug him but daring not to she simply smiled into the large brown eyes and spoke softly. "Night Thiac and thank you. We will see you in the morning right after breakfast."

Carlotta, as always took over. She hustled him from the room but not before leaving instructions to a young boy to start the fire for the Senora and her guest. A light dinner, she told them, would soon be set up and yes, she would see to it that Thiac had something also.

"Just leave everything to me. You sit and rest."

Tori and Cisco did just that, along with some of Jean's excellent brandy. Not much time seemed to pass, when as promised, they had both a warm fire and fine food, most of which was consumed slowly as they talked.

"You still miss the nineties Tori? After all, it seems to me that you have it made here. I mean look around you girl. This for instance, is quite a cabin in the woods. Your lifestyle must be something."

Tori sat back for a moment and considered what he had said. True, she did have it made, nicer than in her own time even. Yet deep down she did not feel a part of any of it and she doubted that she ever would completely. "Cisco, can I ask you a hypothetical question?"

"Sure, what about?"

"Well, say you had a girl back in Las Vegas and she had a child who you cared about. One day the girlfriend vanished and then some years later, just turned up with a tale of time travel. Let's say you believed her but then she went on and told you everything that had happened, even knowing it would hurt you. Do you think, that she would have been better off staying in the past? Or do you think that she did right, by going back and telling all?"

"I would say that this question is about you and if I might add, what makes you think that there is a way back at all? You seem so certain that there is."

"Well it's Tom, that young black boy I told you about. If he made it that way, to the future I mean, then the way back must happen every so often."

"True, but when and for how long is the doorway open? You could spend the rest of your life waiting for it to happen. Then who knows what. You could turn up in another time, you know? It could be before you were born, or even after you should have died. Have you thought of that? And if you did make it back, well who would believe you? After all, it would sound sort of like, forgive me here, well like you were on something, or crazy. Look, no matter how much your boyfriend and child loved you and no matter how much they wanted to believe you, without proof beyond a shadow of any doubt, they would always wonder. Even if you could prove it, don't you think telling your boyfriend that you lived and loved another man, had his child and all, well don't you think that would be asking a little too much?"

"Well first off I don't have any boyfriend back there, just family and Linni." Her voice broke up with emotion and she fell silent. Tori was still and as she sat there, she could feel her eyes cloud over with tears. He was right. She knew he was, yet she just could not let go. Why was that she wondered? If John and Cisco could just accept what had happened to them, then why couldn't she? Could it have something to do with the fact, that they themselves did not leave anyone behind who would always wonder what happened to them?

"Well maybe if I did go back and I could prove what happened, maybe I would not have to tell everything that occurred in my life here?"

"Maybe, but what if you did get back and found your daughter had moved on with her life. Grown up and fallen in love with someone? What if you found that you did not fit in any more? What if you found that you belonged here with Jean, in this time and you wanted back to him? Think about it Tori. What you are doing now, trying to get Jean out of jail, risking so much. Doesn't that tell you something? Like how much you love the man? I would have to ask myself, how much he really meant to me, before I tried to leave. It might be only a one round trip ticket and if you made the wrong move, you might not be able to forgive yourself. You could live the rest of your life in the wrong time and with the wrong people and really be alone!"

Tori stared at him, she had never thought of it like that, but then what if she never tried and this was the wrong time that she got stuck in? Did she really think that she could ever sit back here in this time and not always have a pull to the future? It was just too much to deal with. Her head was spinning. So as she often did when she felt like this, she found herself pushing the problem to the back of her mind.

"Those are questions that I will have to think on later right? At the moment we have bigger problems to think about. Jean and his men have to come first and foremost. Tomorrow we have to get some good men to help us and then head back into the city. I wonder if John has had any luck getting the information we need?"

"Knowing him as I do you can count on it. Let's just do our part and let him do his. It will all come together, you'll see."

"Well right now, all I want is a bath and some sleep. I feel as if every muscle in my body has locked up and if I sit here any longer, I won't be able to move for a year." She got up slowly and headed toward the door.

Cisco stood and looked at her smiling. He knew that she was still deeply troubled about her life here and he wished he could help her. That however was something she was going to have to sort out herself. He could try and ease her mind a little though before she went to bed. "I take it that I'm to sleep in the house somewhere? I hope on a bed and not here on the couch or am I to go out back?"

"Picky, picky, what if I told you, that it was the couch or outside?"

"I would have to say your kidding, you are aren't you?" His face looked like a crushed schoolboy, one who was lost. If he could have seen the expression on his face for himself, he would have known he had it just right. When he was small, he used to practice that very look in front of the mirror for hours. It always won him sympathy from his teacher!

The corner of his mouth was twitching again and Tori wondered how he ever played poker and won. It was very obvious to her that he was on the verge of laughing. He had the worst poker face of anyone she had ever met.

"Of course I'm kidding and you know it," she laughed. "You can stay in the guest room. I'm sure Carlotta has a hot bath waiting for you by now and if you need anything else just ask and you'll have it."

"Really? How about a blond about this big," he gestured with his hands, a large breasted woman, "and maybe she could have a friend so that the evening could be fun?"

"This is not a whore house where the guest can expect a bed warmer or any such things and if you think for one moment, that you can have your way with any of my help, think again my friend."

Cisco burst out laughing. My it was easy to get a rise out of her and she did look so wonderful when she sparked and spit like a hell cat.

"Madam," he bowed, "I only jest. Why such a hot reaction. Tut, tut." He was laughing and making faces of pain again. "Maybe you are far more uncomfortable than I thought, all bound up like you are. Must have made you touchy, touchy, touchy!" He was grabbing himself in all the places that she was indeed feeling uncomfortable, and over exaggerated the motions to put it lightly. The comical sight he was portraying soon had her in stitches.

Tori found herself laughing, in spite of the fact that she was dead tired and really in no mood to horse around. All she wanted was to go to her room, have a hot bath and then sleep. She walked up to Cisco and quite unexpected to him, put her arms around him and gave him a hug and a sisterly kiss on his cheek. "Thank you my friend for being so understanding and for listening to me. You really have to forgive me. Sometimes I don't know what comes over me, really."

He didn't say anything, just drew her into his arms and gave her a hug. His hand was stroking the back of her head, a action that his mother had done to him as a child. He had always found it soothing and somehow reassuring.

"Cisco, please don't ever take your friendship away. I need you. You have become very important to me you know." He could feel her heart beating against his chest as she clung to him, her head resting on his shoulder.

Were those tears he could feel on his neck. He was sure it was? They just stood there, letting her emotions drain, while he himself sorted out just what it was that he was feeling toward this very vulnerable individual.

For the first time in his life, what he was feeling for this woman was something deeper and stranger than he had ever felt for any other. For one thing, here he stood, Cisco the self-centered carefree gigolo, worrying about another human before himself. It hit him then. It was different alright this emotion that filled him. It was one of protector, friend and more. He felt this overpowering brotherly love. That was it, in an instant it became very clear to him. To take this woman to bed was unthinkable. It had nothing to do with Jean or his fear of what the man would do to him if he did. It had nothing to do with his sex drive either, no way. Somehow, somewhere along the way in the past few days, he had grown to think of her as a sister. How that had happened he was not sure but there it was loud and clear. He loved her as his sister. He held her very close and then pushed her back so he could look her in the eye.

"Tori, I want you to know now and forever that I am and always will be your friend. You mean so much to me also. Wait do not say anything, let me finish." He stopped for a moment, cleared his throat and went on. "My feelings go deeper than just friendship, if you can bring yourself to think of me as a brother I would really like that. You would feel I think so much better knowing that our bond is that strong. Listen to me, I'm not making any sense to you am I?"

"Oh yes you are and yes I will think of you as a brother. You just got yourself one little sister," she sobbed. "Just what the doctor ordered I think. Now I have to go to bed I am so very tired, physically and emotionally drained but I do feel happy. Thanks Cisco. Sleep well."

"Good night sis. Sleep well yourself. If you don't mind I'll stay here for one more drink before I go up. I'll find my way, don't worry."

Morning had come all too soon. The light outside told him that but something else had woken him. That something else had set his stomach to growling loudly as the different aromas hit his nostrils. He could smell it long before he found the dining room. The fresh coffee alone filled the air with it's aromatic sent. Someone had been frying up something like ham he just knew it, and that was one dish that could pull him from the grip of death itself.

The dining room was set for two and on the table was a fresh pot of coffee. The plates on the sideboard were full of fruit and fresh baked breads. On the far end of the table, Carlotta had a platter of ham, eggs and what looked like the fluffiest fullest omelet he had ever seen. Now this was living. Hell, he very seldom ate so much for breakfast let alone one of such variety.

"Good morning my friend, I trust you slept well? Go ahead take what you want, I'm going to eat until I can't move. Might as well I can hardly move as it is, damn horses." Tori over emphasized the spread of her legs and the stiff walk as she entered the room.

Cisco laughed at her sense of humor and rushed forward to help her to her chair. "Oh allow me please," he said pulling the chair out for her. "Your rear must be so sore. You think maybe a cushion for the chair is needed? Or maybe I can give it a rubdown, your rear, not the chair that is?" He patted her rear playfully and Tori hit at him laughing.

She did look good today. The shirt was one of Jean's, that was obvious. It fit her like those tops woman had in their time, the kind that one would wear with leggings. Instead of hanging loose though, she had it belted with a soft brown leather belt. It gathered the white linen about her slim waist and the tunic effect suited her better than she could have guessed. The rest of her outfit was hand made to fit her, not borrowed from someone else's wardrobe. The soft blue material of the pants went very well with the brown boots, which were far shorter than the pair she wore the day before. Her hair was pulled back and fastened with a piece of blue ribbon. She had not managed to catch all the hair though for some had fallen free around her face, curling slightly as it was not yet fully dry.

She had washed it earlier in Gardenia-scented water, hoping it would not take too long to dry. It was always so hard for her to try and fashion it in any style of the day. And try as she might more often than not, she would simply pull it back as it was now.

"I see that you have not bound yourself in this morning." He said grinning from ear to ear. "I would say you fill that shirt a damn sight better than Jean does. His men no doubt will think the same. Don't you think it wiser to go about dressed like a lady?"

"The men as you were saying, have seen me this way before. Granted, I was always with Jean or Dominique but maybe if I dressed as a lady, it would cause us more trouble, who knows? Let's just eat and then go and see shall we? Besides with you and Thiac at my side, I think that I will be in safe hands. That is if you can keep them to yourself?" she scolded kiddingly.

Thiac on the other hand shook his head and had his doubts when he saw her come out of the house with Cisco. He almost felt as if his heart would stop completely. How could she dress so? It just was not right and yet the most confusing thing was she still looked every part the lady. How could that be he wondered?

Tori decided to ignore the puzzled look on his face and press on. "Morning Thiac, how about we take a walk around and see what we can find out. I have a few places in mind to rustle up some support and don't look so worried. After all, these are Jean's men, or most of them, anyway. They know better than to mess with me."

Damn he hoped she was right. His eyes rolled upward to the heavens. Cause Lord it was far to pretty a day to fight, even if it was for the lady's honor. He hated fighting but then his temper always got the better of him when a lady was involved. God he hoped he could keep it under control today, because if he didn't, well heaven help the poor man that stepped out of line he thought.

By mid-morning word had spread like wildfire that Laffite's lady was in the small village at Grand Terre, looking for some men to help her get him out of jail. Most shook their heads and laughed. What could she hope to do, except get more men arrested? Hell, she was a crazy wench. Others admired her and her spirit, yet they were not about to come forward and offer help, for fear of being laughed at. Anyway, some were already saying that it was useless to do anything, because the Governor had it in for all of them, not just Jean. If they wanted to stay free, maybe it was time to lay low for a while. Besides with the boss and Dominique in jail and Gambi and Nes Coupe` away, that left no one in charge telling them what to do.

Tori met with strange looks, shaking heads and low mumbles of sorry can't help. She found her temper rising as she talked to these men. These were men who Jean had treated fairly and often gone out of his way to help. It seemed to her way of thinking they owed him something for that. Yet every time she tried, she got the same cold shoulder, along with a good many lusty looks. If it had not been for the fearsome cold stare that came at them from both Cisco and Thiac's eyes, Tori would have found herself the object of far more than dirty looks she was sure.

In the end, after several hours of talking and walking all over the area she just exploded. "What in the hell is wrong with these dumb sons of bitches!" she shouted. "You would think they would jump at a chance to help Jean but all we get is a bunch of chicken shit's. Shit! I am so damn mad. I wish I could kick some sense into their thick heads and make them see what idiots they are. They need Jean. Cisco, why won't they help?"

"Hell I don't know but then maybe we have been going about this all wrong. Follow me and stay close. Keep an eye out Thiac my old friend this could backfire and we might have to run like hell."

Before either of them could ask any questions Cisco had pulled Tori by the hand into a small tavern that they were standing in front of. This just so happened to be the very place that Jean had never allowed her near. He had told her once, that this tavern was even unsafe for him at times. The moods of a drunken cutthroat can never be trusted he had explained, and thereby best avoided at all costs. That or be ready to fight!

The interior was dank and dark. Even in the middle of the day the place had a unearthly gloom about it. Looking quickly around as they entered, one could see it held a good size crowd all of whom had fallen silent when they entered. A few burly types and the odd female who had been standing around outside when they went in, now stood crowding the doorway watching and listening. It went without question they wanted to see just what would happen next. Any form of entertainment helped with the boredom and humdrum of the day. This however would go way beyond the average bar brawl. This was top rate.

Cisco marched up to the little bar and demanded in a sharp tone for three rums and to make sure the lady's went into a clean tankard. He then turned around slowly, eyeing each and every person he could see. He was looking into the grimy faces of some of the roughest sea going men he had ever seen.

The stillness that hung in the room was almost deafening in its silence. The only sound heard, came from the pouring of their rum, splashing and gurgling from one container to another.

"Before I talk to you lot, the three of us here," he waved his hand toward Thiac and Tori, "need to quench our thirst and wash down the bitter taste of chicken shit. Seems we came here to find men and found ourselves a pack of boys instead. Boys who can't seem to get up of their fat asses and help out the fine lady here," he pointed toward Tori without taking his eyes off the crowd, "with her fight to get you yellow bellies back their friend and leader."

It was as if a bomb had exploded. Two men rose to their feet so fast their chairs fell over. Another shouted out in Spanish words that Tori just knew would make whatever Cisco had just said pale in comparison. Still more joined in and the whole room now shouted and yelled, hurling all sorts of obscenities their way. One rather besotted ruffian, intent on doing far more than just shouting, pushed forward angrily. The look of thunder on his face said it all. He had every intention of smashing Cisco and anyone else who got in his way.

Thiac quickly stepped between the oncoming thug and his intended victim and slamming his fist down onto a table in front of him, crushed it with one blow. It smashed into splinters as if it had been made of match sticks, the legs spinning out in all directions, with pieces of wood showering over those closest.

It was such a loud roar of anger that escaped Thiac's mouth as he hit the table, that it dwarfed the rioting noise. There were those, who years later, would swear that the earth shaking sound from that black beast, had destroyed the table, not his fist.

Once again the room came to a complete and utter standstill. No one dared to move or speak, for fear that the black giant would not hesitate to do to them, what he had just done to that table.

Cisco picked right up from where he had been interrupted, as if nothing had happened and in a firm but calm voice he addressed the throng. "The lady has not had her drink yet, or her say, and until then I suggest that you all stay where you are or Thiac here might have to break a few skulls," Cisco kicked at the broken table top, pushing it apart with his foot, "and for those of you who think you can stop him, then think again."

Tori did not know where or when it appeared, almost from nowhere it seemed, but Cisco was brandishing a pistol for all to see. She had not even realized that he even carried such a weapon.

"Now it might be small but gentleman it does kill and I don't think that any of you is foolish enough to die, just because he wouldn't listen to the Lady."

Tori, who had been watching all this with a somewhat stunned look, quickly pulled herself together and for anyone observing her, she seemed in no way upset or unnerved about the situation they were in. She was still so damn mad that what had happened so far, had only fired her up more. She reached for her rum and downed it in several long gulps, feeling it burn all the way down her throat as she swallowed. Her eyes began to water and her breath felt as if it had all been sucked out of her in one big rush, but to falter now would be a big mistake. What she needed was time. Time to catch her breath and get her voice back, which she was sure had been burned clean away. Tori turned her back on the crowd and started to pour herself another rum, slowly and very clearly, so all those close by could see what she was doing. It was a great stalling tactic, one that was causing a great amount of anticipation along with it. She could stall only so long that she knew, and time was running short.

She spun around and faced the crowd not daring to look at either Cisco or Thiac who she knew must be wondering what in the world she was up to? Tori slowly and deliberately raised the glass to her lips and stopped.

"On second thought I had better say my piece before I get drunk." Thank you God she thought, at least her voice had not come out a squeak, even if it was a little shaky. "Yes, I did say drunk, and why? Because you all disgust me. I thought of you as fighting men." She looked around the room slowly." "Not men who would give up a chance at a good old fashioned fight. Why Jean had always told me, only the toughest and the best came here to be with him. What I have found is a bunch of cowards willing to let me go in alone to get him out of jail."

One man started to move forward angrily. He did not like what he was hearing. Thiac simply moved himself slightly, growling low and Cisco shook his head no, while motioning the same with his pistol. It did the trick. The man stopped dead in his tracks.

Tori had not faltered but ignored the little drama and kept on talking, as if the slight commotion did not even faze her. "Now I could be wrong, maybe you are smart and just needed to know that I do have a plan, one that I know will work. I have spies, working for me right now as I speak, finding out the last of the information needed to put my plan together." She sipped on her drink and let what she had said so far, sink in. "Let me end with this thought. You all know Jean. Do you think he would just sit around if you had ended up in jail? Hell no! he would find a way to get you out. I would bet my life on it. Now, I intend to get him out. I need a few good men to help me. But I'm telling you, with or without you, I will give it a try."

"Pretty talk lady, seeing how it would not be your neck you be risking but ours. And I for one say, we lay low, until it blows over. Jean will get out. He's got himself money to buy lawyers, which is more'n a lot of us has, if we gets caught." There was murmuring of agreement all around.

Then someone else shouted out, "Why risk our necks, just so she can have her man to fuck sooner. I bet that's what she's missing, a good man between her legs." The laughter was loud, mixed in with whoops and whistles. Someone in the back yelled out that he would volunteer to take Jean's place, for a while.

Tori fumed as she walked up to a man who was laughing at her and licking his lips rudely. Cisco tried to grab her arm and drag her back but she shook him away angrily. She watched as the scoundrel continued his taunting. He rubbed his crotch openly with his hands and made the gesture that he was more than ready for her. Tori moved forward until she stood right before him. Then, before he knew what had happened she slapped his face with all her might with one hand and tossed her rum over him, with the other. The room went wild. Laughter filled the air. Even the two who held their rum-soaked mate back were laughing.

Tori held up her hand for silence. "It seems to me," she told the sailor, "that it is you who has his brains between his legs, not me. Now for the rest of you and especially you, you little shit, I will say right now that I have no intention of sitting at home while the rest of you risk your necks to get Jean. Hell, I would not ask you to do anything that I would not do myself. Is that not what Jean says? That he would never ask anyone to do anything that he himself would not do? Well, I am the same. Now, are there any men here? Or am I the only one who has the right to wear breeches? Maybe the rest of you should be in gowns!"

Those who were still snickering over their friends dowsing in rum stopped, as they waited to see what would happen next. In their opinion she was just asking for trouble. Who did she think she was, talking to them like that? The room was buzzing with low growls and whispers. What happened next, was a surprise even to Tori. The rum soaked sailor spoke up.

"I ain't no lady and I ain't no chicken shit either but I ain't no fool. It can't be done I tell you. No one ain't ever got out of where they are keeping the boss, no one! So just how in the hell do you intend to do it?" Tell us that why don't you."

"Has anyone ever tried to break anyone out before? No, they have not and I am not just going to get Jean, no way. It's all of them that I want. All of Jean's men and on top of that I intend to get all the goods back too. No proof of any crime without the merchandise, can't you see? Think of it, the Governor will be empty handed and he will not be able to do a damn thing about it."

One of the men by the door whooped and shouted, "she's got a bloody good point men. Just think of the look on Claiborne's face, as he sits eating his fancy breakfast." The man sauntered into the bar acting out his speech, every eye in the place on him. "Governor sir, Jean Laffite's gone and so's his bloody booty. What we going to do sir?" This time the whole building rocked with laughter. They loved it. This was something that they could all relate to. Even the rum soaked sailor had forgotten his anger. He stood by Tori and with a wink and a smile, picked her up and placed her on top of one of the tables. Thiac stepped forward to protect her but Cisco shouted at him to wait, he was a gambling man and right now he was willing to gamble that Tori had just won.

"I say, that we follow this little lady of the boss's. She just might pull it off. Hell she's right and I for one, am tired of sitting around here with nothing to do, sept dry off." More laughter filled the air. "If nothing else, it sure looks like it's going to be one hell of a lot of fun."

"My sentiment exactly," Cisco murmured under his breath. They had done it; they would have their men and their chance at making the jail break. Just how he was going to get Tori to stay home he was not sure. He doubted he should even try, as the men would be looking for her. Damn it to hell he would just have to see to it that she stayed out of the thick of things.

Cisco put away his pistol and Thiac walked over to Tori. She smiled triumphantly at him, while he was lifting her off the table. It was so easy for him he simply picked her up as if she were a child. Once safely in his arms he carried her to the doorway.

"I will get word to you all when I need you," she shouted back into the tavern over Thiac's shoulder.

The men quieted down to listen to her, many jabbing others and telling them to shush.

"I promise you it will be soon, so get ready."

"Hell lady, we are ready. We could leave now if you want?"

"No, not until I send for you. Cisco here, will be back to go over the plan of attack, when it is finalized. Until then just be ready to go and not drunk. Anyone drunk stays behind."

"Bloody hell, who's ever sober?" cried one of the men. The response of which was a rousing applause.

Cisco left with Tori at this point. They left Thiac behind to keep an eye on things. The way the men were all worked up, some could change their minds and try something on their own and they did not need that. If it did look as if something was up it would be up to Thiac to try and stop it. And stop it he would, they had no doubt.

Tori knew that they would have to act fast now, keeping something like this under wraps was going to be hard. The sooner they put their plan into action the better. What they needed now was the information from John and they needed it fast. As they reached the house Tori approached Cisco with an idea.

"Cisco I have been thinking. I will stay here at the house. You had better leave now, alone. It's better than taking the men with us into the outskirts. We're not ready yet, and the chance of so many being seen would blow it. You have to bring John back with you. He will tell us what he has found out, then we all leave from here, totally prepared, not going off half-cocked, don't you see?" She looked at him and his doubting expression. "We need him and his information as soon as possible. It's the only way."

Cisco had to agree with her and even though he hated to leave her, he knew he must. Before the hour was up, he was riding for New Orleans with one of Jean's men who knew the fastest and safest way. As they headed out, Cisco started thinking more and more about what was about to occur. Shit, this was going to be great. He couldn't wait to see how some of those guards reacted to Karate. His blackbelt had been wasted up until now, but soon he would be put to the test. He would find out just how good he still was.

## Chapter 22

In the two days that followed Cisco's departure, Tori and Thiac kept a watchful eye on Jean's men and spent many hours explaining that the waiting would not be much longer. Indeed the wait ended sooner than Tori herself had thought possible.

John had been able to gather the needed information long before Cisco's arrival. He had been thankful for the extra time this had given him, allowing him to place his affairs in order for a few days absence. An urgent business matter out of town had just come up. It had to be personally attended to he had told those around him. It was not far from the truth but what would they have thought, he wondered, if they had realized, just what was really going on. A fleeting smile crossed his worried face. With the facts he had to give Tori and a touch of lady luck, the raid had better than even odds of being a success. Within hours of Cisco arriving at the hotel, John was packed and ready for the trip to Grand Terre and his meeting...

John had spent the past two days at Grand Terre, going over each detail methodically, a meticulous person such as himself could see no other way. Nothing was going to be left to chance. Time however was running out, not only for himself, but for all those who anxiously awaited the word from Tori. He himself could not afford to be away from the hotel much longer without raising questions and going over the plan again seemed futile. If they were not prepared now they never would be. Only one question remained in John's mind at this point, when?

His worried frown seemed somehow to creep into his voice, giving it an anxious edge, as he spoke. "You know the longer we delay, the harder it's going to be to keep this matter under wraps. You need to act on this as soon as you can." Cisco nodded in full agreement. If he had his way, they would have left right then and there. Like John, he himself could see no need to delay the mission any longer.

All eyes were on her. Each person in the room now looked directly toward Tori waiting for the go ahead. She could see that what John said was right but on the other hand, as far as she could tell, they would only have one chance at pulling the plan off. Her mind was racing, chasing one thought after another at random. One in particular seemed now to overshadow everything else. To go now, in a hurry and bumble the operation, would end all hope of Jean and his men being rescued. She had to be sure that every angle had been taken care of. Tori found herself reflecting on the hours of conversation they had in the past few days. She and Cisco had asked John what he knew of the history of this time and what if anything did he know that could help them. His answer had been simple he knew nothing more than they did. His fascination had been with the Battle of New Orleans and all of them knew that Jean and his men had a big hand in that. The battle was still some time off and his knowledge about that was not much better either. He had just begun his research into it when his crossover had taken place. This fact only served to raise more questions than answers, all of which could not be cleared up, as they had no way of knowing how much their crossover in time had altered things. Were they making or changing history, or were they a part of history all along? Tori shook her head physically as if trying to shake out the riddle.

"I agree John we have done our part here. What we need to do is clear. The only thing delaying us going into action at this point, is you. How much time do you feel you will need to hold up your end of the plan? Without you playing your part, we could still go ahead and attempt it but I would feel a lot safer if I knew the Governor and a few of his supporters were out of harms way and detained so to speak."

"You have my word they will be so busy and having such a grand time, they will not even realize they are being held out of harms way as you so put it. Besides, it will be fun to see their faces when they get the news. Think of it. I will be the only one of us here that has that pleasure and it will be worth every bit of money that I allow them to win."

"Are you sure that's the only way to handle this? It could cost you quite a lot you know. You have to keep them there until word reaches you that Jean is long gone. Can you do that?"

"Tori we have been over and over this. I can assure you that I know just how to keep them hanging on. It will be a challenge of sorts to let them think they are winning at the table." His face went grim, then he spun around for each to see the laughter in his eyes as he continued "Yet I can't let them know or guess the game is fixed. I told you they are like everyone else. If they think their luck is holding and they are winning they will want more and more. In fact I could most likely keep them all damn night if I wanted. Now don't you worry your pretty little head. You just be sure to hold up your end. I'll have the easy job." His voice lowered as he sat down, whispering to himself as he continued, "the hard part will be getting them there, not keeping them."

Tori was wringing her hands, so much had to go right. If one bit of timing was off, or one person was out of place it could all come down like a house of cards.

"It's Edward who is your best bet, he could never turn down a good game," Cisco offered. "He seems so buddy buddy with Claiborne to boot. Maybe you could use him as the bait. Use him to get to the others."

John's sly smile and narrowed eyes was a poker face look that Cisco had seen only too often at the table and knew it to be one that told of a winning hand. "Way ahead of you there Cisco my man. Now how about the both of you just relaxing and leave the fun to me."

"Done, but you still have not answered the question, how much time will it take you to arrange this little game? When can we make our move?" asked Cisco excitedly.

John sat so still and in such deep thought that Tori found she had to leave her seat and walk around, while he pondered the question. Cisco on the other hand, looked toward John and seeing that he needed a little prodding on the matter, leaned over to his friend and jabbed him playfully in the ribs with his elbow as he spoke.

"How about a little wager on this one? I'll bet you that you can't pull it off two nights from now. If you win I'll work for you for one year." Cisco rolled his eyes towards the heavens with a look of mock agony on his face. Then he looked toward John with just a hint of despair in his voice as he added, "Just room and board, that's all the pay I will take. If however I win, then one year free go of the Palace is mine, no holes barred." The whole room had fallen silent as this new drama developed. "How about it old friend, is it a bet?"

John could see just what Cisco was up to and his first reaction was not to give into this childish blackmail. Still at the same time he thought it would be great to take some of the wind out of Cisco's sails. A large grin followed with a deep chuckle of pleasure escaped from the somber gambler. It did not quite match the seriously deep voice that answered. To John any wager that he undertook was never to be taken lightly no matter the circumstances, and this was no different. "You're on."

The two of them sat there shaking hands, sealing the bet and looking as if they were really enjoying themselves. Relief spread around the room. It was a go; everyone seemed pleased, everyone except their leader. Tori could not believe them, they were acting like children. How could they possibly put all that was riding on this plan in jeopardy with something as trivial as a stupid bet.

"Stop it the two of you. I'm not about to let you, either one of you, jeopardize the outcome of this whole ordeal simply because you want to win a stupid personal bet. How could you Cisco? And you John, I would have thought you knew better."

The two of them looked up at the angry woman that stood glaring at them and for just a second Cisco actually felt like a child being scolded by his mother. His spirit quickly bounced in the opposite direction as he told himself that all would be forgiven and forgotten as soon as he smoothed her ruffled feathers. Guilt ran off Cisco like water off a duck's back.

"Look Tori our bet has nothing to do with you and we are risking just as much, maybe more on the outcome of this. Don't you think you should give us credit for wanting to make it work also. I for one happen to know that John here works better if he's under a little pressure. And I just gave it to him, that little added pressure that is. Now I say we act and act fast. What better time than two nights from now. After all we are ready, right? There is nothing left to stop us is there?"

She nodded her head, what else could she do. Besides Thiac who this whole time had been silently standing over in the corner of the room caught her eye and nodded his agreement. He was ready and to him it seemed like the sooner the better was the way to go. It was this gentle giant's nod that pushed Tori into agreement and once agreed upon, the plan sprang into action almost with a life of its own.

It was as if the plan was now a living breathing entity that simply could no longer be detained. Once it started to move it would be impossible to kill. The death of this plan would be its outcome and God help them all. She prayed that she had given birth to an angel and not a monster ready to devour them alive.

Several hours later, even if she had wanted to, it was too late to call back the troops. John was riding hard for New Orleans and his part to play. Jean's men had the news of the go ahead. Monster or angel, she could no longer control it. Tori could only hope that she had the power to guide it and step by step make it somehow turn out the way it was planned. How was it she thought that time could go by so fast when you did not want it to and drag by when you were waiting for something you desperately wanted. It seemed to her she was asking that sort of question to do with time more and more lately.

Sleep had been hard for her and the morning had been hell. The two groups had set out to get into position by nightfall and Tori only hoped that they would get the signal from John that the coast was clear so to speak. She knew that the point of turning back had long since vanished and that the men would go ahead and try the break with or without the aid of John's little game. They were all so wound up and ready that nothing was going to stop them from releasing their friends and boss.

It was dusk when they arrived at the designated point, still well out in the bayous. The first part of the trip had gone without a hitch. The trip had even been somewhat of an mini adventure temporarily allowing her mind an escape of all the worries and pressures that pressed upon it. They had traveled by barge and pirogues, small and often swift-moving boats, through the waterways. Many of the routes taken were known only by Laffite's men, who used the narrow channels like modern day highways. Tori had sat for hours in one of the smaller craft and simply watched as the world floated by her. It was one of speckled shadows and dancing lights, of calling birds and insects, of splashing sounds made by jumping fish, and plopping turtles who slid from their Cyprus logs into the murky depths of the bayou.

Now and then the whispers of men's voices would drift on the wind, pick up and die just as fast. Each person seemed to be trapped, not only by the beauty that surrounded them but by the thoughts that danced in their own minds. The long journey held them silent for the time being and their ever-increasing excitement in check. These were men of action not of taking pleasure cruises. They were men who led rough and often violent lives. Lives governed by the law of doing what they wanted and when. The only person who had ever had any control over this fact was Jean. These were not lives used to taking orders from any woman. Oh yes, they were silent and thinking as they closed the gap between themselves and New Orleans.

Once on shore the two groups waited for the time that they would get their message and proceed. Some slept and others sat in small groups talking amongst themselves. The anticipation of what they were about to attempt hung in the air as tangible as the very breeze that moved amongst them. Every so often a group would laugh softly and all heads would be looking at Tori or turn to do so. She felt uncomfortable under such scrutiny and could only imagine what they were talking about under their breath.

Cisco had found it a wonderful opportunity to brush up on his game of chance and line his pockets with a little extra cash. Always careful to lose just enough when the situation seemed to called for it, such as when an angry suspicious brute was about to call him out for cheating. Not that Cisco ever looked at it quite like cheating. No, he liked to call it creative card counting with player beware. Most of the time he was good enough that they never knew what was going on.

Thiac could see that Tori was impatient to be on her way. He also knew that she needed a little comfort and a friendly face to talk to. Sitting there looking more like a man than a woman, her face was frozen into a stern angry glare. Her eyes were dulled but able to drill right through those who dared stare at her too long. She was a formidable woman to reckon with that was for sure. Yet he knew all the make up and acting in the world could never hide the vulnerable caring individual that she was, at least not from those who knew and loved her.

She had smeared some dirt on her face to help hide her soft tender complexion and true color of her skin tone. The hat that was to hide her hair sat on the ground next to her and tucked into her belt was Cisco's small pistol that he had insisted she might need.

Thiac approached her cautiously. Standing behind her, he cleared his throat to let her know that he was there.

"Sorry Thiac. I didn't hear you. I was thinking you know, about everything that is about to happen. Did you say something?"

"Well, sort of. I ain't good with words like you or other white folks but I can use my head and it seems to me that you should not be going with us tonight and all. It ain't no place for a fine lady such as yourself. I knows that the boss, he's not going to be none too happy when he finds out that you come along."

"You let me worry about Jean and about it being no place for a lady. I can tell you, that I can take care of myself when I have to. And that part of me is about as far away from a lady as you are from being white." She laughed, trying to cover her own doubts and lighten poor old Thiac's mood. "I promise that I will be very careful and Cisco will be with me each step of the way as will the other men."

"Yes Mizz Tori I knows that. It's just if something should go wrong. Well, the others might not be a worrying about you any. They all will be a trying to save their own skins. If Cisco gets parted from you, well you would be all by yourself. Maybe I should come along with you?"

"Now Thiac we have you in the other group because you are needed there. You are the only one I can trust to see that the shipment arrives at the warehouses and you know that the men will depend on your sheer strength at times, to get them through. You have to go with them as much as I have to go with Cisco."

"That's what I was afraid you'd say. So well here, this is for you."

He brought his hand around from his back and held out a small but beautifully crafted sword. The blade so polished that it caught the smallest beam of light and reflected it a thousand times brighter. The hilt was engraved with such intricate designs that one could sit for hours picking out shapes and images from within the pattern.

"I was walking around with nothing else to do a few days past, and I met up with a man who said that Dominique had him making this for you. I thought it must be right because of the size of the top here. See, my hand don't fit in here, to hold the sword right and I don't think there is a man here whose hand could fit in the way yours could. You having such small hands like. Anyway, this man said that he's seen you and Dominique and that he thought maybe you should have it now." As he handed her the sword with one hand his other was scratching his head. His face had a look of disbelief and questioning about it. "He also told me that you know'd how to use it and real good."

Tori stood up taking the sword in hand slipping her fingers through the golden loop that made up the hilt. Once in her hand she could feel that indeed it had been made for her and her alone. The balance was wonderful. Moving it through the air it cut smoothly and without effort. Her fingers fit so precisely that only a fraction of an inch was between her flesh and the cool smooth metal. Once in her hand, gripping the weapon it became an extension of her arm, of her very soul. It had been fashioned in such a way as to not only protect her hand but to become almost impossible to dislodge. Every detail had been mastered and carefully crafted into this gift and she loved Dominique for caring so much. He had designed it for her with her protection in mind. He had built into it every advantage he could. It was so like him.

The gift had lifted her spirits and joy radiated from her; gone was the scornful face replaced by one of excitement. "Indeed I could use this, it's wonderful. Why, I will feel a lot better having this by my side. Now don't look so worried Thiac. I will only use it if I have to and my teacher was, is one of the best."

Cisco saw what had happened and came over with a look of horror on his face. "What in the hell is going on here and just what do you think you're going to do with that thing might I add?"

"You might. I am going to wear it in my belt and if I have to, I will use it. Not you nor anybody else is going to take it away from me."

"Are you crazy? Do you know how dangerous those things are? With that tucked in your belt you might very well get hurt. By simply falling down, you could seriously cut yourself, let alone trying to use the damn thing. No, I can't allow that, you just hand it over to me right now." He just stood there with his hand out expecting to be obeyed.

It infuriated her, how dare he. The arrogance of him to just assume that she could not handle such a sword simply because she was a mere woman. "I damn well will not do any such thing and you can't make me. As for not knowing what I'm doing, well I'll prove you wrong Mr." Tori looked quickly around her and called out to one of the men. Before Cisco knew what was happening, the two of them stood apart a few feet facing each other swords raised, about to put on a demonstration. Her sharp voice rang clear on the evening air. "On guard!"

Then it began, slowly at first, with only the occasional clash of blades, as each one felt out the others skill. If she had shocked Cisco with her skill she could not tell. She had most certainly shocked her opponent though, as recognition of her talent registered on his face. Right away he realized she did indeed know just what she was doing. He found that she was very good and he could maneuver and try all he might but she was always there ready and thrusting keeping up with his every move.

"Stop. Alright, you've made your point and there is no need to go on with this display. Did you hear me? Stop!" The young man backed up several quick steps and lowered his sword.

Tori stepped forward slowly and let her sword drop to her side wiping her brow with her free hand, tucking back a stray strand of hair that had fallen down over one eye. She thanked the young lad for his help and turned to face Cisco.

"You forget my friend, all too soon, that I am not the Southern Belle but one of the liberated ladies. Now I think it's time to get ready to move. Looks like you might have won your bet after all. No news from John and we can't afford to wait much longer. With or without his help we will have to try tonight."

Cisco's face fell as did Thiac's.

"Oh Thiac, don't look so down. You have just given me one of the best gifts I have ever received. Dominique will be so please that I have it." She patted the hilt of her sword and smiled softly. "Don't you worry we will all be together tomorrow celebrating."

"You know I think you are right and I ain't a going to worry none about you no more. I's sure be worried about the man who is a going to come up against you. He is a going to be in mighty big trouble. Yes sur, mighty big. Cause he ain't a thinking a little bitty thing like you is match at all. No sur, no trouble." He was roaring his head off just laughing so loud they all joined in. Most of the men standing around were whooping and hollering their support and praise toward their leader and her new found talent.

It was into this rambunctious crowd that a lone messenger came, bringing with him a new hushed silence as they waited for the news he had brought. This was it, what they had all been waiting for.

"Monsieur Vegas I have a message for you. Monsieur Davis he told me to tell you that you now work for him and he wants to congratulate you himself on your first day of employment on this coming Monday."

Tori broke up and Thiac even found himself laughing again. How much more could his sides take he wondered. They were already sore from the last load of laughter now this. Only one person amongst this happy crowd had a sad looking face. Cisco who on the one hand had wanted to lose the bet so things would go well for them, now realized that he might not like the end result of his little wager. But then he was a man of his word and he would honor it. Ever the opportunist, an idea quickly gave him hope, a way of escape from his upcoming doom. After all he had not said that he would not try to get fired, thus ending his working days. His look of gloom turned to a sneaky look, one of knowing something secret.

He smiled toward Tori who seeing that look upon his face, knew that he had something up his sleeve. Just what it was, or what he was up to, could be anything. It was just a shame that time did not let her pursue the reason of his sudden lightness of mood. It would have to wait until later...

The night was just perfect for what they needed. The moon was full and shone down brightly, lighting the rest of their way through the swamps. There were just enough clouds every so often that one would slip across the bright orb giving them cover and conceal their movements.

Tori wished she had a watch to go by. How long they had been traveling toward the place where Jean was held she did not know. It seemed to her as if they had been going forever. The two groups had split up sometime ago, as each had a different destination and task to go with it. Right now the other group were most likely starting their task of removing the stolen goods from the dockside warehouses and loading the barges for the long trip back. She was so deep in her vision of all those men running back and forth with arms loaded that she did not at first realize that they themselves had reached their destination.

It was Cisco who got her attention as he softly whispered into her ear. "There it is. All looks quiet does it not?" He spoke low but the tone of his voice, however subdued, was full of excitement. Tori knew that each of them was more than ready for the task that lay ahead. Speaking slightly louder so all could hear her she stated. "We might as well get it going. You all know what to do. Good luck to you all," she hesitated and with a slight crack in her voice added, "and thank you." She saw the nods of some of the men and heard a few soft aye's. There were smiles from a few and the odd slap on her back from one or two. One of the larger of the men stepped forward and stood before her dwarfing her in his presence.

"Before we go, well the men and I, we want you to know that we ain't doing this for the boss. Well we was in the beginning like but now, well we be a busting him out of there on a count of you. You are one hell of a lady, begging your pardon mam, but that's how we feel and we want you to know that."

Tori did not know what to say, she could feel the tears springing to the corners of her eyes and thanked God it was dark enough so no one could see she was about to cry, or for that matter how very frightened she was at that moment, just seconds away from who knew what. She hid her embarrassment and fear by pulling down the hat on her head. She pulled it so low that the view of her face was all but obscured. She turned and facing the Cabildos said as firmly as she could the one order that would start action.

"Let's stop talking; let's do it." All at once the men went into action. It was as if they had done this all before many times, so precise were they. The first four were over the low wall before she could look down the way and see if the time was right. They had to go over when the guards could not see them but were close. She need not have worried. When two of the guards on the outside came around, they were quickly knocked unconscious.

Cisco ran forward with her at his side, the two of them covering the open span quickly. They pasted the fallen guards whose uniforms were being removed as they were dragged out of sight. Tori helped Cisco remove his coat and started dressing him in guard's clothing. The transformation happened in minutes and when completed, he stood up for her inspection chuckling to himself.

"Do me a favor and don't tell Jean that you stripped me and dressed me." He winked at her. "He might get the wrong idea. I quite enjoyed the process though, could we do it again, slower this time perhaps?"

"Oh you are incorrigible, you rogue. Now come on and quit clowning around we have to get into that gate. Hurry up before they open up."

Cisco and one of the other men now dressed in the other uniform, marched up to the gate. There they stood as if they were the original guards on duty. It was time for the guards to change and the large solid wooden doors began to open. They had just made it.

Tori stood in the shadows as she watched the new guards come out and Cisco and the sailor walk by them. It was great to see Cisco turn and in a swift karate move take the two of them out before they knew what had hit them. The other sailor stood for a second with his mouth open, his fists up ready to fight, with nothing left to do. He was supposed to have taken out one and Cisco the other.

"Just a little trick I learned my man," winked Cisco.

"One that you shall have to teach me. I have never seen anything like it. Hell not even close. Never saw a man fight with his legs like his arms."

Tori could not believe her ears. Here they were again, dilly-dallying around. Hell the last time they almost didn't get to the gate on time, now this.

"Will you two stop your talking and feeling so proud of yourselves and get those two out of sight," she whispered. "Quickly, we have to close the gates. Let's just hope that John's information is correct and that the place is not heavily guarded." They were hurriedly joined by the remaining men and all of them were inside the gates and out of sight as Cisco and his new admirer pushed the wooden doors closed. For better or worse they were in.

The men who had gone over the wall now met up with them. They had done their job well. The moment the gates had opened and the two guards passed through, they had sprung into action. Swiftly and without making a noise, they had rendered the guards on the inside unconscious.

Tori looked around nervously. "What have you done with the guards that were on the inside of the gate? I don't see any sign of them."

One of the pirates gave her a large toothless grin. He turned and spit a mouthful of dark fluid before he spoke. "Well now, that's because you ain't looking in the right place Mam. If you look over by the wall there, over that way, in that shadow," he pointed drawing her eyes down, "you will just about see what you be looking after."

Indeed she did. Some laying out on the ground, others sitting up, their backs against the wall, their heads hanging down upon their chests.

"Just like you wanted not one of them hurt bad. Just sort of taking a nap like. Nothing like a little bump on the noggin to send you off to dreamland I always says. Sides my mother, God rest her soul, used to tell me when I was a wee one, the little folk was about when you slept. You know, like the ones that brings you something for being brave when you lost a tooth. And I bloody well went and lost me last tooth! One of them buggers knocked it clean out. Least I could do was knock his out. See if them wee folk leave him anything but a bloody headache."

Now she understood. The spit had been blood, not even chewing tobacco. Her stomach turned over slowly. She was about to ask him if he was alright, when she realized that he was having the time of his life. He really didn't care one damn bit about his pain if he was in any. Instead, he was chuckling away to himself.

"How many men would you say are taking a nap?" she asked.

"Eight to be exact, not one more or less. Just like you said and right you were. You said they would be there. Hell it was so damn easy. Just thump and dump is what we did. Had that one spot of trouble with that bastard that took me tooth. Lucky shot if you ask's me. Lucky for him and there again unlucky. He got far worse than just a bump and dump." Again the sailor was chuckling, his wheezy chest gave sort of a squeak or whistle with each exhale.

So far all of John's information had been correct. The times and the number of guards exact. From here on in though it would be tricky. He had not been too sure of how many remaining guards would be on duty and at all costs they had to remain silent. To wake up the garrison would be suicide.

Quickly now, they went about with what they had to do next. Some of the men had to go and keep watch, while others had to barricade the garrison's quarters, so that anyone inside would be delayed getting out if aroused for some reason. Two others had to make their way over to the armory to secure all the weapons. It was imperative that all this would be accomplished silently and undetected. If they were discovered at anytime, that individual was to be silenced but no one was to be killed. Tori had tried to make that fact abundantly clear to Jean's men.

It had been hard to convince them but Cisco had succeeded where Tori could not. He had reasoned with them, explaining that to leave the jail with Jean and his men, leave it as if there had been no big fight would be to their advantage. Easy in and out is how they had to make it appear. This he told them would embarrass and humiliate the soldiers and Governor far more. Besides if the silenced individuals were left with a few cuts, bumps and bruises to accompany their slight headache so to speak, well people could laugh at that. But to kill someone could make things difficult. That would mean that they would be wanted for murder. Murder was a far more serious crime and one that would not go unnoticed. The men had listened to Cisco and his reasoning and in the end had agreed that they would do it all without causing any deaths. At least they would try and as for now it looked to Tori as if they intended to keep to the bargain.

An all clear signal whistled out softly in the night air. The way was now clear for them to enter the Cabildo courtyard and find the cells that held Jean and his men.

Tori moved ahead walking directly toward the small passageway that led in two directions around the area containing the small darkened cells. It would take up far too much precious time to go in the wrong direction at this point and Tori knew it. She hesitated looking first one way and then the other. A mistake now could ruin all their plans. Her legs suddenly felt weak and one began to tremble nervously as she pivoted first one way and then the other.

Seeing her dilemma Cisco pushed in front of her and quickly appraised the situation. Before him lay only one choice as far as he was concerned. Down one way the passage was pitch black and silent, the other way was dimly lit and voices could be heard mumbling and occasionally laughing. This was the way to go he reasoned and putting his finger to his lips he signaled for the small group to follow him.

Where the passage came to an intersection they halted and slowly Cisco peered around the corner in the direction of the men's voices. He took in the surroundings carefully. This did not look good to him, he knew things were going too easy and this proved it. He motioned for them to move back down the passage, away from the guards where he could tell Tori what they were up against.

"There are just two of them sitting at a small table playing cards," he whispered. "And you do know how I like a game of cards don't you?" The famous Cisco grin which Tori felt sure was on his face seemed to seep into his voice. She was about to ask him what he had up his sleeve this time, when to her horror he was gone. He had turned and boldly walked around the corner right in plain view, and none too quietly either.

The two men engrossed in their game had jumped at the sound of footsteps grabbing their weapons and reaching to hide the evidence of their gambling. Caught in such an activity while on guard duty was a serious offense, one with severe consequences. They were totally off guard and very rattled just the way Cisco needed them. They were also very angry and on the defensive. Two dangerous emotions he would have to deal with rapidly if he were to defuse the situation and win them over.

A red-faced, furious individual barked at Cisco, "It is not time for a guard change. Just who are you and what are you doing here?" Spit flew along with his words he was so exasperated. It was as if in an afterthought that he added, "You are not supposed to be in here."

"And you are not supposed to be playing at a game of chance I might add. Look I'm bored. I have to go on duty in another hour outside. I was looking for something to do and I think I've found it. How about letting me play until I have to go. Come on it can't hurt can it?"

The two looked at each other and one shrugged his shoulders. "Don't see why not, come on then sit down." He kicked a small stool Cisco's direction. He looked as though he were about to add more to the conversation when a look of recognition crossed the man's face. He was pointing toward Cisco's shoes, not military issue, and a dead giveaway. "What the hell? You're no guard. Who are you?"

Realizing he had only seconds to act Cisco went into action. His movements were swift and silent. Only his exhaling breath with a whistling sound accompanied each blow. A leg kick in one direction and swivel with an arm in the other direction both connecting. Result, two guards down but not out. As one came at him from behind the other started up off the floor. Hearing the commotion Tori and the small group burst into the room to help him. Right away it was clear to Tori that Cisco knew what he was doing but she also saw that the soldier on the floor was going for his gun. To have that go off would be like an alarm that would wake up the whole place. Cisco was way ahead of her, and before she could move, his foot lashed out and rendered the man unconscious before he even knew what had happened. Turning fast he caught a blow on the chin from the man who now aimed his other fist for Cisco's middle. It connected and the pain was instant and he buckled over as the guard came forward to hit him again. It looked as if the soldier had the better of the fight but then he had never heard of self-defense or the martial arts. In a sudden blur of action and a twist of the body Cisco turned, bringing his leg above his head and let it hit its mark full force. The soldier fell to the ground and did not move.

Tori ran forward flinging her arms around Cisco's neck. "Are you alright?" She looked into his face, concern for him clearly visible in her eyes. "You're bleeding, here let me see." He shook his head free of her hand. His adrenaline was still high from the fight and he found it hard to just stand still. It was action that he needed.

"Look, we don't have time to worry about a split lip do we. That was too close. Let's get the keys and get into those cells and do what we came here to do, O.K."

She nodded her head and as Cisco bent down to retrieve the keys from the man's belt. She touched his shoulder pointing at the man asking, "Is he alright, I mean he's not dead is he?"

"Hell no, he's not dead but he's going to have one big headache in the morning not to mention whiplash." He handed her a large round metal ring which had hanging from it what looked like twenty or more keys. She took them and headed toward the hallway leading to a small courtyard-like enclosure. What she saw before her made her heart fall. Doors one after another all the same. A long line of wooden doors with locks on, and small openings at the top like a little window. Then looking upward she saw still more cells.

"How are we going to get them out? Which doors do we open? There are so many and time is running out?" Tori looked to Cisco as if he had the answer but he did not. It was one of the other men who stepped forward and took the ring that held the keys. He pulled on it until it opened and the keys came off one by one. No one waited they just took several and started trying them door by door. A few doors had matched right off and were opened. Some of the released men were now helping. They had taken a key each and were trying the unopened cells. All the time Tori could hear her men whispering for those they freed to be quiet, that they would have them out in a minute.

The place was damp and smelled of human waste and rotted food. Looking down inside one of the open cells she could see the remains of what had been someone's meal slopped on the floor. Trying again she turned one of her keys, this time it finally fit in a lock and Tori opened her first door. A man who she did not recognize pushed past her, "Thanks lad, God never thought I'd get out of that one. Here give me a key." He took one and moved off to help. Tori smiled to herself as did Cisco across the way. The man had thought she was a boy. Oh well, that's what she wanted wasn't it?

Several doors were open now but still no Jean. Handing her keys out amongst the men she started going door to door. She would stop and call in the small opening for the one voice she so desperately wanted to hear. It was Jean's voice that she wanted to hear calling back at her, it was his cell she wanted opened. The second small window she called in found a face she knew only too well. It was her dear friend Dominique who stared back at her. He stepped forward and for a brief second could not trust what he saw, then shaking his head he spoke as a father would to a child he loved but had to reprimand.

"Ah, Ma Cherie, why does it not surprise me that it is you, n'est pas? But you are taking such a risk, no?" He was grumbling and had a gruff sound in his tone of voice, yet the man's beaming smile told another story. "I for one, could think of no one I would rather have here to let me out of this stinking hole." Dominique was in a splendid mood, one that showed his love of always finding the humor in any given situation, no matter how grim. He continued teasingly in French, "Pardon, mademoiselle. Avez-vous un guide de Cabildo?" For the first time that night Tori found herself laughing softly as she replied, "Oui monsieur. J'ai un bon guide de Cabildo. And you are going to get the hell out of here as soon as we get this damn door open."

It was then she heard Jean's voice. He was out, standing at the end of the now crowded courtyard. Once again the leader he was giving orders and helping open the few remaining doors. Someone pushed Tori aside as they tried another key on Dominique's cell and hearing the key turn, knowing he was free, Tori made her way toward the one man she had come to be with.

It was Cisco who reached Jean first and taking hold of his arm turning him face to face caught the man's full attention. "Monsieur, you and I have not met, still that does not matter at this time. What does matter is that I must inform you, that up until now the plan to free you has worked because it is just that, a plan. We will get to know one another soon but until then trust me and let me be the one to give the orders and get us all to safety. Oui?"

Jean looked at this man who stood before him in a soldier's uniform. Disdain filled his expression, "I do not trust traitors Monsieur? Even those who are helping me."

Cisco laughed at him. "No Monsieur neither do I. I am not what it seems. Take a look around and ask some of your own men if you do not believe me. I'm no soldier." He took off his coat and threw it to the floor. "Now we have no time left to argue the point. You will just have to do as you're told."

Jean could not believe the audacity of this man. Just who did he think he was to order him around taking command like that. His aggravation not only showed clearly on his scowling face but was heard in his vocal growl, as the thought crossed his mind. That this fool should assume he were not capable of escaping without his help was preposterous. He was about to hit Cisco when one of his own men broke in between them.

"The changing of the guards. It'll be soon and we have to be gone before that happens. Remember we all gave our word we would try to get away without a fight. And if that's what we has to do let's do it."

Cisco nodded his agreement. "Look there is no more time left we have to leave now. Everyone for themselves once we get outside. The gates should be opened and all you have to do is head for the river. Just be damn quiet that's all." Quickly now the jail emptied. Men ran down the hall past the fallen guards and out into the night air. They ran for the cover of the shadows and the exit.

Jean had waited with Cisco to see all his men out of the cell area, and still not fully trusting this stranger, to keep an eye on him just in case. It was then his eye caught sight of a young lad just standing at the far end of the courtyard seemingly reluctant to move, or most likely too scared too. He headed to get the lad.

Cisco called softly to them both to hurry. Quickly he surmised the situation; a love reunion was not advisable at this point and unless he acted that is just what was going to occur. He pushed past the fearsome looking pirate and took hold of Tori's hand. With no hesitation he shoved her past Jean before either of them had a chance to speak let alone get a good look at each other. The three of them ran out into the night and immediately knew they were not going to be so lucky as to escape without a fight. From down the darkened side of the wall, three soldiers appeared. Somehow these unlucky threesome had escaped being locked in with the rest of their platoon. How that had happened Cisco could not imagine.

He realized it was to late to run. Immediate fear gripped his guts as a flash of everything coming undone took hold. If not silenced in just seconds the three would alert the rest of the camp. He turned without thinking and ran with all his speed, jumping full force on top of one of the soldiers, followed closely by Jean who took on the second soldier just as he reached for his sword.

Tori had no time to hesitate. She pulled her sword from her belt and met the first blows from the third soldier, who with his own sword drawn had rushed at her. Horror and terror hit home as Tori found herself in the midst of her first real fight. Unlike her spars with Dominique this was for real and her opponent fully intended to wound, and or kill her, whichever came first. He was just doing his duty fighting to overcome her and to win. She was fighting just to survive, terrified of making a fatal mistake. This last realization hit home, as it slowly occurred to her she seemed to be holding her own and if she could just hang on Jean or Cisco would come to her rescue.

It was as if she knew just what to do. She could hear her teacher's words in her ears talking her through, even though he was not really there. Her confidence in her ability grew. She was doing so good that she found herself almost enjoying the fight and would have continued to do so if the soldier would just lay his sword down and tell her she had won. This man she knew was not going to do that. He was fighting to the death and Tori realized she was not. Why was it taking Jean or Cisco so long she wondered. Tori could hear them still fighting but dared not look. To take her eyes away from her battle would be suicide. Every second counted now and this had truly become her fight and her's alone.

Tori realized there might not be time enough left for help to reach her. She had no choice but to take a different approach to the situation or run the risk of losing. She had never dreamed that she might actually have to run her blade into anyone, and now that reality hit hard. She knew that it was run him through or she herself might suffer a mortal blow and die. Her arms were getting heavy and as she tired her opponent sensed that he was gaining the upper hand. He swung his blade fast and hard leaving her only a split second to react. Jumping out of the way of his thrust, her hat that held up her hair, fell free and down came the long chestnut curls. The soldier faltered shock registering on his face. This was no lad he was fighting it was a woman.

Taking advantage of the moment, Tori struck out. She aimed at his arm and slashed through his shirt to lay a gash that immediately turned his white sleeve blood red. Instant rage flooded him blocking any pain. The blow had humiliated him and raised his anger, blinding him of all reason and sanity. To think that a mere woman had beat him so far was incomprehensible, humiliating and totally unacceptable.

Spitting at her through clenched teeth, he hissed, "You bitch, you'll pay for that." Then he came at her with fury. Heavy hard swings, one after another. They hit Tori's sword with such intensity that she would only have enough time to block the next blow. At this pace she would not last long, no one could. She knew that if she were to win it would have to be now.

The man was not thinking; anger was clouding his judgment. Again down came his sword connecting hard with hers. The clash vibrated up her arm, hurting her shoulder. It was then that panic forced her move. With no time left, her strength failing fast she made her move. Instead of raising her sword to block his next blow, she raised it only halfway and moved forward instead of back. In a swift movement, thrusting up and forward, she had the point of her blade at the man's throat. He had not seen it coming and by the time he realized what she was about to do, it was over.

"Drop your weapon you bastard or so help me I will have to press the point home if you understand me. So do it now!" The tone of her voice, though shaking was hard and cold. The man could see that she meant what she said, but to lose to a woman, he would be the laughing stock of the whole platoon. How could he just give in? His eyes narrowed in a dark frenzy as he calculated his next deadly move.

A voice broke the silence. "I believe she means what she says. You had best drop the weapon Monsieur because if you don't then I shall have to aid the lady in relieving you of it and you don't want that now do you?"

The man looked from Tori over to the voice and seeing that it was Jean himself who stood there with a menacing look that turned his blood cold, he dropped his weapon and fell to his knees begging for mercy. Jean walked up to the man and looking at him he could see nothing but a filthy lowlife that would have run his sword into Tori if he had had the chance. His temper was hot and he had to vent it somehow. Hitting the man was one way to get even and hit him he did over and over until the man's face was bloody and no sound came from him. He picked up the soldiers head and listened close for sound of his breathing. Satisfied that he had not killed him, he let his head fall back. Sleep well you son of a bitch. Jean stood facing his lady and their eyes met and locked.

Any anger he would have felt toward her at that point simply evaporated. She was alive and that was all that mattered. "You are the most stubborn, stupid lovely creature I know but then that's why I love you." Looking at her now standing there holding her sword in her hand he found himself admiring the courage and talent of his lady. The spirit with which she had fought and the skill with which she had done it had truly amazed him. The fire that blazed in her eyes, the way her hair hung wild about her face, made her look every part a lady pirate. She looked ravishing and he was not sure at that moment in time, which Tori he found more appealing, the lady or the pirate. He was so overcome by what he had just seen, that if it had been under different circumstances he might have very well taken her in his arms and shown her what emotions she had stirred in him. Instead stepping forward he wrapped his arm around her waist and ran with her for freedom and safety.

Tori and Jean ran, followed closely by some of his men and from nowhere Cisco was at their side. "Now Jean if you would follow me, the rest of the escape awaits you as your lovely lady has planned." Within no time at all the crew was on a barge being pushed out into the current of the river and headed for safety. They talked and laughed amongst themselves each assuring the other that no one, not one soldier had been killed. They had done it and had every right to be proud.

Tori sat trying to catch her breath while Jean looked at her and leaned closer. "It seems that I owe you my life, as well as my men. Did I hear right, your plan?" Tori laughed and looked at her pirate. "Well not exactly all my plan. You will have to meet my new friends and the rest will be explained to you. We will talk later." Her expression softened as she continued, "If you don't mind, there is something I have been missing and I intend to collect." With that she leaned over and kissed him. Her kiss was not a gentle kiss but one that was full of passion. It was hungry and hot as she thrust her tongue deep inside his mouth. The message of the kiss burned into him. She pulled away slowly and looking at him through half-closed eyes she whispered softly, "You can count on more of where that came from as soon as we reach Grand Terre and you know what?" He shook his head as if say no I don't. She giggled. "I for one can hardly wait."

She snuggled into the safety of his arms and watched as the dark sky slipped by. The sounds of the men pushing and guiding the barge to safety soon faded into the background as she drifted off into a deep exhausted sleep at last.

While she slept and they traveled closer and closer to the safety of home, Jean talked quietly with the man called Cisco. He learned about what had happened since they had caught him and of how Tori and he, along with John Davis, had come up with this plan. The more Cisco talked, the more he loved the lady that slept in his arms and a friendship between Jean and Cisco blossomed and grew deep roots that would last a lifetime. Cisco did not, however, tell Jean about one fact. That, he was going to leave for Tori to do. Besides, now was not the time to spring on him that he and Tori had a lot in common. How was Jean going to react when he learned they were of the same time.

As they neared the home base a voice rang out in the early morning hours. It was the voice of Thiac, who had started to head back after waiting so long to see if everything was safe and well with the rest of the men. He pulled his little pirogue swiftly alongside the barge to see for himself that his main concern was indeed unharmed. Jean motioned for him and smiling down into the peaceful sleeping face of his lady, assured Thiac that she was unharmed, just sleeping.

"That's good, the little lady she needs rest. Don't know how she been going about boss. She hardly slept for days. Sure glad you back boss, now maybe she going to rest and be a lady again with you telling her what to do. This new Mizz Tori is awful hard on the heart and the mind."

"Thiac this lady has never done what I told her to do and you know what, I'm damn glad. Now before we do or say anything else, there is something I want to do. I want to tell you that for what you have done I am truly grateful."

Thiac grinned, his white teeth gleaming in the early morning light. He was happy and Tori and Jean were safe. "You don't need to thank me none. I just did what I was told and all."

## Chapter 23

John had handled his role expertly and even though he was worrying most of the night, as to what was going on across town, no one suspected anything. It was late into the evening when at last word reached the party. Two soldiers from the Cabildo's garrison arrived, with the news John had been waiting for. News that would tell him if all his efforts and plans had paid off.

Arranging the game and enticing the players had been hectic but simple enough. As luck would have it one of the large plantation owners was in town and John told him that he could arrange a private game of chance. It would be of course he assured him, only players of his own standing and talent, all very discreet.

Word of the upcoming game was then sent out via the coffee shop, where Edward was known to be that morning. Making sure that the so-called private conversation was overheard, Edward soon learned that Mr. John Davis was looking for Mr. John Grymes. An invitation to a private affair, to be held that evening, had to be delivered. Edward seizing the opportunity wasted no time. His appetite for gambling never ceased, and the chance to be in on a private game, one with high stakes no doubt, was irresistible. He left at once for John Davis's hotel, confident that one way or another he would acquire an invitation.

From the moment Edward approached John at the hotel, with the excuse of finding out his credit standing, it became obvious to him that he had overheard the conversation and taken the bait. John enjoyed listening to him, as he tried to ply information about the evening's events, without looking too obvious about it. After letting him rattle on for a while, John spoke to him as if he had no idea that Edward was trying desperately to get himself invited. Acting distracted, as if he were a man with a lot on his mind, John played his hand. Looking at his gold pocketwatch, with a concerned look on his face, he made it seem as if he were really not paying any attention to Edward at all. Then he let his expression change, as if an idea had just come to him.

"Monsieur Duval, may I ask you a big favor? I would normally use other discreet channels to gain such knowledge but time right now has become the issue. I feel as if I can trust such a fine upstanding gentleman as yourself, to, ah, assist me." "You may indeed Monsieur and please, I feel as if we have known each other long enough for you to call me Edward." John just smiled and nodded his head slightly in agreement, thinking this was rather like fishing, first you hook him, then you reel him in.

Edward, thinking he was now on a first name basis and about to help Davis out, was feeling very sure of himself. If he helped John out, that would mean a favor done was a favor owed. He turned on the charm as his words seemed to ooze from between his lips. "It would be my honor to assist you. And you have my word that whatever the matter, it shall be handled in the most honorable way."

"Edward my friend," John placed his arm around the dandy's shoulder, walking him over to a more private corner of the room. "It has come to my attention that you and our Governor are very close acquaintances. Indeed, I have heard it said that he holds you and your lovely lady in high regards. It is Monsieur Claiborne that I need to get this invitation to." He reached into his inside jacket pocket taking out the invitation. Turning it over and over as if mulling what to say, he slowly went on, "I was wondering if it would be possible for you to reach him for me. I have had no such luck in the matter. He is not to be found at home or at any other location that my contact tried. I'm afraid that I have no time personally to locate him at such a late date and he would be so disappointed if he missed this evening's affair."

"Oh, please do not think anything of it. It would be my pleasure to locate him for you and I personally will pass on the invitation." Edward took the envelope from John's hand and was placing it in his jacket pocket as he continued, "I will take care of the matter right away, there is one..." John cut him off mid sentence, "That is very kind of you. These games don't happen often and when they do it seems that it's always spur of the moment. You know yourself when lady luck comes a calling she is telling you, that you not only feel lucky, you are! You just know she will be at your side and my how you want a chance to play. One just knows it's right to do so. That is how my client was this morning insisting on a large high-stakes game. I have to please my clientele don't I? After all that is what I have a reputation for doing," he laughed.

"Indeed you do," Edward agreed. He hesitated momentarily; then not being able to contain himself any longer, he all but burst out his next remark. "May I be so bold as to ask you if this game would be open to a gentleman such as myself? Of course I would understand if there is no room at such a late request."

It was almost laughable, he had played right into John's hands and ever the proficient actor John looked truly horrified at having overlooked the obvious. "My dear Edward, please do forgive me. I should have known that you would want to join us. How very stupid of me. I said earlier your credit is in fine standing. I understand your plantation is doing very well this year." John started walking toward the entrance of the hotel, his arm still firmly around the younger man's shoulder. "It will be no problem at all to include you in on this evening's action. Consider yourself my personal guest. We will meet in my private suite at around eight this evening."

Edward could not have been happier. Not only did he get himself an invitation for the night's activities, he seemed to have gained the owner of this fine establishment as a personal friend, something that up until then had seemed highly unlikely.

"Until this evening then. I will deliver your invitation to the Governor." He patted his coat pocket, and curtly nodded his head. "Good day to you." With that he swiftly departed.

So it was that Edward had been conned into thinking he had weaseled himself in. Under normal circumstances, John knew Edward would have had his guard up. A dog like that always sniffed a con job out, but greed had blinded him and pushed his guards down. Just like the commander of the dragoons, a certain Revenue Officer by the name of Walker Gilbert and a Captain Andrew Holmes. Both of whom hated Jean and were responsible for the tight security at the Cabildo. They were also responsible for placing Jean and his men in there in the beginning. It had seemed only justified to include them in on the ruse. Greed had played its hand there also.

John knew with those two out of the way their men would relax more, making Tori's job easier. They were regulars at the tables, both always the officer and gentleman but far from rich enough to join such a game, or so they would have thought. It had been simply a matter of John explaining to them both that he would pay them up front, a sizable amount of money. All they had to do was join the group for security reasons of course.

A soldier's pay was not high and an officer's not much better so he knew they would jump at the chance to earn what he offered them. That was the bait. The hook came when John had gone on to explain he did not want it obvious to his guests that he had taken such security precautions. "Therefore, it would be most beneficial for all involved," he told them, "if they were to be allowed to join in the game that evening." He had gone on to explain the Governor would be told of course so they had no need to worry. In fact the Governor himself would look kindly on the arrangement he was sure. John had simply reeled in his unsuspecting fish.

Only one guest had declined the invitation causing no problems really, just amazement that he should choose not to show. Grymes had sent a note just before six that evening. It had been brief and to the point. It simply stated a certain young lady had required his services for the evening and that they would talk soon. Who this mystery lady was he did not let on, and John made a mental note to find out. She had to be very important for Grymes to miss this night. John knew that having personal information about his top clients was the best way to keep them returning to gamble.

The evening proceeded as planned. It had its ups and downs but always the game went on. The house kept losing just enough to feed each and everyone with winnings that kept them playing. The game was expertly executed and manipulated by his dealer. So much so that John made himself another mental note, to keep an eye on him in the future.

Edward had not had such a streak of luck in such a long time. Sure he had lost a few big hands but all in all he was ahead. The Governor and plantation owner sat looking very pleased with themselves also. The officers, though not doing quite as well, had more than they could have dreamed about, with money, wine, good food and Davis's ladies; ladies to keep the evening running smoothly. Everyone was having what they declared to be a splendid game. That was until a knock came at the door followed by the entrance of two very nervous looking soldiers.

They quietly asked John if they might have a word with their Commander, which of course John quickly obliged. The whispering over in the corner of the room between the small group was like music to his ears. They looked too upset and nervous for it to be anything but bad news and that meant things must have gone as planned. John understood only too well that he had to be very careful at this point. After all, he could never be connected in any way to this mishap.

"Governor." It was Captain Holmes who spoke. "Could I please have a word with you in private about a very grave matter that has just come to my, ah, to our attention." He flashed Gilbert a filthy look. The bastard had pulled rank on him making him the bearer of bad tidings. He knew Gilbert was trying to distance himself and the blame, not to mention whatever the adverse reaction from the Governor was going to be.

Claiborne looked up angrily from his hand, laying the cards flat on the table. "You may not. Can't you see that I am in the middle of a damn good hand and whatever you need can surely wait." With no response he angrily snapped, "Well soldier can it, or can it not wait?"

The look of agitation on Holmes's face as he shifted from one foot to the other spoke for him. Seeing this, Claiborne impatiently snarled at him. "Oh very well if you must. You may continue. Quickly sir!"

The Captain looked around the table. He was not sure, but then maybe if he broke the news with witnesses it would go easier for him. After all it was not his fault now was it? He had not been there at the jail. Some other fool's head would fall for this, not his. He found himself silently thanking God for this small favor, and feeling a bit safer, squared his shoulders and pulled himself to his full height.

"Sir, it is my duty to inform you, that I have received bad news,"

The Governor was on the point of exploding with exasperation, "I can see that, you fool, now get on with it."

"Yes sir. To the point then," he spluttered. "There has been an incident over at the jail. Seems that Monsieur Jean Laffite has escaped."

Edward choked on his drink spilling the wine down the front of his silk shirt. The blood red stain grew slowly across his chest, a stark difference from the rest of his pallor. As the color drained from Edward's face, it did the opposite on the Governor's. John watched in horror as Claiborne's neck, which seemed to be bulging out of his collar, turned a deep purple. This plum color of rage rapidly crept upward filling his whole face. Surely John thought the man was close to having a stroke or heart attack. It looked to him as if Claiborne's head might explode at any moment.

With a burst of air and spittle, the Governor let go of his breath roaring with rage. His fist slammed down so hard as to make the table shake. He rapidly pushed back his chair and stood facing the Captain. "What did you say?" he screamed at the now-terrified man. Then trying hard to gain control of himself he clenched his teeth, grinding them so hard, that in the silent room the sound was painfully audible. His eyes narrowed to slits as the muscles in his neck contorted and flexed with each breath. Like a Cobra, he hissed the next question, only his head moved toward the Captain bringing his face within inches of touching the other's. "How in God's name could you let something like that happen?" He then stepped forward leaving no room between them, his chest pushing the Captain back as he cried out, "Just how did it happen? I want to know now? I demand some answers."

Captain Holmes, truly shaken by the outburst and fearing for his own well-being, called on one of the guards who had brought the news to step forward and explain what he knew.

The young lad obeying his superior, stood at attention looking straight ahead, as he repeated his tale. "There had been not a sound or a warning," he told them. "It was as if Jean had just walked out sir. I might add sir, in the men's defense, that it is true all the guards had been overpowered. Many still lay unconscious when I had been dispatched with the news, but none of them hurt beyond a large headache and a few broken bones. No one had yet been reported missing and no one killed, sir!"

Claiborne did not give a damn about this last fact, overpowered indeed. His temper, none the less calmer, seemed only to swell to new heights as he burst with indignation. "And just where in the hell were all the other men at this time might I ask? We do have a full platoon there, do we not?" Are you standing there audaciously telling me that they were all knocked out?"

The young soldier's eyes moved to look directly at the Governor standing before him. He tried to clear his throat before answering but still his words came out as a whisper. "Sleeping sir. They were all in their quarters for the night." Somehow he found his voice then and spoke louder as if to confirm his next explanation. "Even if they had been aroused they could not have helped. They were locked in sir, and the armory had been barricaded as well. There was nothing they could do." He stepped back, fearing the Governor's next move.

Resigned to the fact that Jean Laffite had managed to escape, he quietly and fearfully asked his next question. His voice trembled as he spoke, "how many escaped?"

"Not one of the cells was left unopened. They all got out sir."

Claiborne once again lost control. He was beyond reason and stood yelling at the top of his voice. "Heads will roll for this." In a flash he had his hands around the poor man's neck and was shaking him violently. Like a puppet on a string he dangled, his body hanging a few inches off the ground, as he was hoisted by the raving man's sheer strength. Holmes and Gilbert just stood there watching as the other young guard took cover behind two of the ladies. It was John and Edward who moved quickly fearing for the soldier's life. They pulled the Governor off the man pushing William back, all the while trying to reason with him and bring him back to his senses.

It was Edward's voice of reason that finally brought calm back to the room, and reaching the Governor, rationalization took hold. William slumped into his chair physically and emotional drained.

Edward poured them both a drink and sat next to Claiborne as he spoke. "Monsieur Governor. William, it is not as bad as it seems." Always the opportunist, he grabbed at the chance to gain favor with the man, while also aiding to what he hoped would be Jean's demise. "If I might add, it seems Jean and his men will be caught. Only with another charge to add to that of smuggling. This last folly of his will no doubt be of great help to you. Why the masses will no doubt surely be swayed in your direction. Your conviction that he is no Gentleman sir. That he is nothing more than just a hooligan pirate will be recognized once and for all. One can come to no other conclusions after his actions of tonight. After all, innocent men don't flee now do they?" He took a long slow sip of his drink and let what he said sink in. Seeing that the Governor was not fully convinced he went on smoothly and deliberately. "These new charges and there will be many won't there Captain?" He looked toward the man who simply nodded in agreement. "They will surely help in getting them all each and every one of them convicted. The Laffite's are finished. After all," he smirked, "you still have all the proof you need in the warehouse. Now Jean and his men can be brought in every last one of them. Those who were not involved with the smuggling charge can now be assured to be charged with aiding in his escape." Dramatically he took a big swig of his drink obviously reveling in the idea. "It will be quite enough to put the whole damn lot away don't you agree?"

A smile slid across the Governor's face and relief filled his voice. "You might have something there." Then with more conviction he added, "Jean might think he has won this round but he has only hung himself and the rest of his crew."

"Er hmm..." A sound of a throat being cleared in such a way as to draw attention caused everyone to look toward the Revenue Officer. "Ah, to beg your pardon, Governor sir, but there is more I'm afraid." The small voice had squeaked out from Gilbert. He knew that sooner or later the man would have to be told about the contraband and he being the Revenue Officer would have that unholy duty. Better to get it over with he reasoned under the safety of those present. "You had best brace yourself because the news only gets worse I fear."

"What else could possibly be worse? If you have more to tell, out with it. Blast it!"

"It's about the warehouse and the contraband inside. I have been informed that there has been a robbery. The merchandise is all gone. Sometime this evening, the place was raided and well the building is empty. Not a sign of anything. Not even a break in the door or lock to show forced entry. It is as if nothing was ever in the buildings to begin with."

This was more than he could stand. If what he had been told was the truth and he had no doubt, he would be the laughingstock of the city. "No! I won't allow that Hooligan Pirate to get away with this." Jumping to his feet and once again slamming both his fists down on the table he looked around the room at each and everyone there. "Not a word of what has been said here tonight is to be repeated. Am I quite clear gentlemen? John I assume I can count on you for the silence of the ladies?"

"You may and as always you have my discretion and my confidence. I am sure Governor I speak not only for myself but for each and every one of us here tonight. You have our word does he not?" John looked around the room to heads all nodding in agreement with a few yes sir's thrown in. "This is just a shocking situation, shocking indeed."

The Governor sat heavily down in his chair, his hand shaking so violently, that when he picked up his glass the liquid inside threatened to spill. His head was swirling with turbulent thoughts one after the other. One however surfaced above all others to become his main concern. The events of this evening needed to be turned around somehow. That bastard had to pay.

"Edward, find me the States Attorney. Grymes has to be reached. Tell him it is of the utmost importance that he meet me right away. I shall be waiting for him at my residence." Edward was furious with Jean. Not only had he once again slipped through their fingers, he had ruined the best card night he had had in a long time. Blast the man, he was like a cat with nine lives. Nine lives or not though he reasoned, even cats died eventually. Their luck runs dry and so shall his.

"I shall leave at once. I will have Monsieur Grymes at your residence before the hour is out. Monsieur Davis if you would be so kind as to take care of my winnings. I shall call for them tomorrow." With that he swiftly departed.

The evening had come to an abrupt end. John looking truly shocked and genuinely concerned, escorted the Governor to the door. "If I can be of any assistance please let me know?"

"I will most certainly. Gentlemen, ladies, excuse me please. I have important matters at hand to attend to." With that he was gone, accompanied by his Officers and the guards from the jail.

The evening was at last over, the room cleared and silent. John closed the door, a happier man he could not have been. Slowly he poured a glass of his finest Champagne and toasted his friend's success. Then he laughed to himself, as he went over the whole evening in his mind. What got him the most was that no one including Claiborne knew of Grymes's connection with the Laffite brothers. Sobering a little he hoped that Grymes knew what he was doing and again that evening he wondered just where he was and who he had been with?

It took Edward hours to locate the States Attorney, doing so by accident in the end. He had tried the man's residence twice, each time to find it empty. On his last visit though, as he was departing, he ran into the man returning home. At first Grymes had been in a splendid mood. His greeting all smiles, but upon hearing his presence was required immediately by the Governor, a foul change came over the man. He became even more disgusted when Edward would not divulge the reason as to why he was been called...

For most of the morning the Governor and the States Attorney were unavailable to anyone. Rumor had it, that the Governor and he had been in his study putting together some sort of legal document concerning the Laffite's. By the time the day ended, it was all over New Orleans that Jean and his men were free once again. Late that same day, it was announced that the Laffite's and twenty-five of their men were released on bond awaiting trial. Grymes had come up with a stroke of genius as far as the Governor was concerned, no matter what Edward had thought. The attorney had simply explained that without the contraband as proof of the smuggling they had nothing. No doubt the goods would be sold at auction long before they could do anything anyway. Nor could they go to the auction to arrest Jean and his men. This would be a highly unfavorable move. Most of the respectable citizens of the state bought from Laffite's auctions. Would they not have to arrest them also? It was well known most of the homes of New Orleans, including his own, had merchandise purchased this way. His hands were tied it seemed. Even knowing that Jean's barges traveled the waterways loaded with stolen goods, day in and day out without proof what was he to do? He seethed. It was common knowledge that Laffite often sailed into the very port of the city. He had even heard it was said that Laffite held the key to the back door of New Orleans. Oh, there were going to be merchants in the city who were not going to be happy with him, when they found out that Jean was out of jail. Escaped was the hellish word that held the Governor in its grip. Too many would be demanding that something be done about this situation. They were already telling him if Jean kept his illegal business growing much longer, he would monopolize the city's import trade. Laffite might as well own them all!

God forbid if he did not do something soon about this situation, if word or proof got out that Jean was allowed to escape, his own job would be in serious jeopardy. Claiborne had no choice but to take Grymes's advice. It made sense after all. It allowed him a way to cover the embarrassing breakout and appease the merchants, thus saving face.

Grymes had smoothed the Governor's feathers and bought his client and friend some time, but it was now clear things would have to radically change. The Laffite brothers could not keep going on the way they had. He would have to talk to Jean as soon as possible...

By the time Edward returned home to Simone, his sadistic temper was soaring. All day he had stewed. Try as he might to get that fool Claiborne to go after that bastard Jean, the meddling Grymes had stepped in. He had had him damn it, and now Jean was as good as free once again.

Simone had heard him storming up the stairs. By the time he entered the bedroom it was very evident that his mood was raging dangerously. He seemed to be on the verge of exploding. He slammed the door behind him and stood clenching his teeth, his features frozen in a thunderous expression. He spat his words out contemptuously,

"It seems my dear that your lover, that bastard pirate, damn his soul to hell, has once again slipped through our hands."

A sudden chill hung in the air, as his words sunk in. Gasping she whispered, "What in the hell are you talking about?"

"I will tell you my dear. He escaped as simple as that. He is out and walking the streets of this fine city a free man yet. Walking around as if nothing happened. Oh wait it gets worse. Our dear Governor, to conceal his humiliation at not being able to keep that rogue under lock and key, had Grymes draw up a document saying that the Laffite's are out on bond. Can you believe it out on bond! What a laugh. Simply released, not escaped and hunted as he should be." His face was a glowering mask of fury.

Simone's lips thinned with scorn, shock yielding quickly to anger. The insolence in her tone of voice was ill-concealed. "And you let him be smooth talked into agreeing with this bond deal. You stupid idiot. I can see I have given you far too much credit in the past. Credit for your so-called control and manipulation over our dear William. Seems without me right there at your side to guide you, to tell you what to do, you are useless. You imbecile," she sputtered. She was so furious she could not go on.

The sudden silence that hung between them seemed somehow to shatter any remaining control Edward had. Transfixed, she coldly stared at Edward, watching in horror as his whole demeanor grow in severity. His eyes narrowed, pulling the skin around them tightly, forming deep angry furrows. They were not the normal laugh lines that creased when he smiled. Hatred and rage converted her lover's face to that of a demon. He was just standing there transforming slowly, as he clenched and unclenched his fists that hung rigidly by his side.

Her anger was rapidly obliterated by a growing alarm. It rippled through her body freezing her to the spot. As he started toward her, a wave of apprehension swept over her. She realized what she had done. Too late to take back her words, sheer terror finally took hold.

Without warning he flew at her, his hands quickly seizing her upper arms. His face so close to hers, she could feel his hot breath escaping his nostrils in rapid bursts like a bull about to charge. She shut her eyes against the horrible image before her.

For one last split second he tried desperately to control his emotions. "You bitch," he said. Two small words was all it took to unleash the fragile control he had held. All his pent up frustrations and rage had finally found an outlet.

Her stomach lurched and she stiffened under his grip, knowing only too well what was coming. Edward hit her then, over and over he beat her. First her face, splitting her lip. Then a full blow to the side of her face, knocking her back flat on the bed. He continued to thump and beat at her body as she tried in vain to curl into a ball, to protect herself from his blind rage. He ripped at her dress, tearing it away from her skin, exposing her bare flesh to his fists.

Simone gulped hard, hot tears rolling down her face, mixing with her own warm, sticky blood. Her only hope was to reach him somehow with words, because her strength was not enough to physically ward him off. Choking out a screaming plea, begging him to stop, fell on deaf ears. He was enjoying her pleas it seemed, and with each one, his blows came swiftly and more violent.

She knew that she would have to change tactics if she were ever going to get him to stop his onslaught and so from a strength and cunning that she alone understood, she completely reversed her actions. It was her tortured sob, her declaration of love for him, her apology, begging for forgiveness over and over, that finally stopped the beating.

They stared at each other across the icy silence. Her lower lip trembled, as she fought back her emotions of self-pity and struggled to keep from letting anger take hold. He had used his fists on her before but never to this extent, and never without warning. She found herself thinking it should have been he who deserved to be on the receiving end of such treatment, staying out all night, coming home when half the day was over.

Then like clouds parting, letting light sweep away the hell of only moments before, another thought entered. His clothes reeked of cheap perfume, could it be possible she wondered that he had been unfaithful? Had guilt triggered his rage? Or could it be that he no longer found her attractive, that he no longer needed her at all? Suddenly she was frightened of losing him. Maybe he was tiring at times and brutal beyond belief but she needed him. She could not let him slip away. Simone would not let that happen. She had to get him to marry her, to become Madame Duval. Oh she had worked so hard for so long to gain respectability, something that she quickly realized she would never have with Jean. Sure he would be good for the odd rendezvous like the old days, but it was with Edward that she stood to gain everything.

Edward saw the confusion of emotions on her face, a face that was swelling and turning a nasty shade of purple on one side. His voice was full of anguish as with his trembling hands he reached gently down, stroking tenderly at the blood-stained tears. "Forgive me, I was out of my mind." Realization of what had just occurred was sinking in. He had just severely beaten the one person that was really on his side and so much like himself. She was the one person in the world that truly understood him. How could he have done this? He asked himself. The corner of his mouth twisted with exasperation. She had asked for it he told himself. He was not the guilty one here was he? She had pushed him too far, and yet looking at her now he was torn between hate, and God help him, lust.

Edward lowered his head, brushing her lips lightly with his. The bloody metallic taste mixed with the salt of her tears, but instead of being repulsed it acted like a aphrodisiac. She recognized the change in him immediately. Her rigid body relaxed her arms reaching for his jacket. Slowly she removed one article of clothing then another, all the while kissing and caressing him. She would show him that she was the only woman who could give him what he needed. He would never know of the malevolence that she held for him at that moment. How was it she wondered, that one could hate him and want him at the same time? Could it be that on some level she cared for him? The passion in his eyes that raked her body, stirred a far stronger emotion causing her to further question what it was she was experiencing at that moment. This feeling was more than just care. She convinced herself it was love. Yes! She told herself she hated and loved at the same time. Simone knew then beyond any doubt that she wanted him now and always. With this revelation came a renewed determination. One thing was for certain, he was going to be hers and no one would ever again take away what was rightfully Simone's.

Edward had passed feeling remorse for his actions. He did not even pity her. She had the sexual magnetism that made him feel more a man than any other woman ever had. Her very nearness kindled feelings of excitement and desire that made her undeniable, even now. He entered her hard and fast taking her as he would have a common whore. He did not even care as she dragged her nails, digging them deep into his back, tearing at his skin leaving angry bloody lines.

Intentionally she had struck out to inflict pain to hurt him as he had her. Instead she had aroused his sick animal instincts of pleasure. To admit that he really cared for her was unthinkable. It would give her control. No, he would use her and continue to use her whatever way he wished. He satisfied himself as his body gave a sudden shudder. Finished and exhausted he rolled off her and lay on his back breathing heavily. She lay still looking at him as he turned his head her way. Their eyes locked as each recognized the inevitable. Words were not necessary, it was in their eyes, their souls, there was some tangible bond that drew them together. It did not matter if it was called love or hate. They were caught in its web and would always be so. In total silence and content for the time being, the two of them would pull close and in each other's arms sleep together long into the night. The blood from their wounds drying on their skin and the bedsheets, the bruises on their battered bodies, not half as bad as the wounds each had inflicted upon the other's inner being. Neither would trust the other ever again, in the way they had. And as Simone drifted off to sleep, she swore that soon, very soon, one way or another, she would be his wife. He owed her that much and more for all she did for him. Then once she had what she wanted she would make him pay. Then she would live as a rich planter's wife should...

Back on Grand Terre, Jean and Tori along with Cisco sat on the verandah of Jean's home, watching the sun slowly sink on the horizon. The soft sounds of the coast line, were awash with the resounding clamor of the wild and frenzied jubilation coming from the collection of huts where most of Jean's men resided. It was plainly obvious to those listening they were all well into their victory celebration, a celebration that could go on for an indefinite amount of time. Jean had learned that nothing and no one would stop their drunken antics until they themselves dropped from the sheer exhaustion of it all or until the rum ran out. He had declared all the rum from the whorehouse be distributed amongst his well deserving comrades. While he himself would not join in their celebration, he wanted to supply them with all they needed, to have as he had declared, one glorious revelry.

If what Tori had told him was true, it would be the last time such a celebration would ever be held at Barataria and Grand Terre. His way of life here was doomed to end soon. History was about to be made and his role was one of major importance. That was if he got it right and everything happened as it was supposed to. His lady, while knowing certain facts about the months ahead, was unclear about far more than he would have liked.

Cisco could see that Jean was a million miles away. Maybe he should leave Tori and he alone. It was a good excuse to go and join in the wild bash taking place he told himself. A chance to unwind and let loose before his working days that loomed ahead, tied him down with all those unwanted responsibilities.

Jean broke their silence. "It is best if I hold an auction soon I think. Something to do and to look forward to. They are going to need to keep themselves busy after this. Much of what is stored belongs to them anyway. They can't make use of the finery but most will welcome the gold that it brings. January is always a good time to make certain merchandise available at the Temple."

Tori had read once that the area the Laffite's held their auctions at, was known as the Temple. She had not been allowed to attend such a sale as of yet but felt that this time she just might. Cisco on the other hand was completely in the dark and did not have a clue just what this so-called Temple thing was about. He really didn't care either at this point as his mind was on partying and gambling.

"Well then, you two will have much to discuss and I'm sure that you don't need the likes of me getting in the way. If you would be so kind as to excuse me folks. The rollicking sound that drifts this way is calling me and my talents. I think maybe I will join in and let you two enjoy the rest of this evening alone."

Cisco shook Jean's hand and without thinking, he leaned over and kissed Tori. He hugged her and held her close for a few seconds longer than seemed right to Jean. Then winking at her and saluting, he left.

Jean had been watching this display closely and found their familiarity just a little stronger than he would have liked. The two seemed to have formed a very close bond in such a short amount of time. Just how close he dared not allow himself imagine. "You like him don't you? I have seen the way you look at him" It slipped out before he had time to think what he was doing.

"Yes I do Jean. He helped us when I didn't know what else to do, or where else to go." She was puzzled by his sudden change in attitude and tone of voice. "You do like him don't you?"

"It's not that I do or don't. I have not had the chance to get to know him, to really know him and what he is up too. He is quite a character you have to admit that." He wished he could just drop it but he had to know just what was going on here because his instincts told him something definitely was happening. "It's just the way you two look at each other, as if you are not telling me everything. I get the feeling that you are hiding something."

Tori looked away from Jean. She knew that she had best tell him now but how would he take it? "You are right you know? I am keeping something from you. We both are. It's just that I don't know how you will take it. Cisco wanted to tell you himself but he felt it would be easier coming from me."

Jean could feel his heart beating faster inside his chest. Had she fallen in love with the dashing young man? Impossible he thought quickly. But what other reason could there be for their closeness. Could it be possible that they had been physically involved? Had Cisco taken advantage of her and her loneliness? Anger flashed through him at that possibility. He told himself to stay calm. Something easier said than done. His grip on the glass was turning his fingers white. He did not say a word for fear of exploding. He had to let her talk first. He had to know, but God if it was what he feared, he would sail on the next tide. He could not bear to think of losing her to another man and he owed that man his life!"

Tori turned to face him as she spoke, excitement in her voice as she hurried on. "This is sort of hard for me to explain because I find it hard to think you will believe me. Oh! you will just have to, that's all and anyway after you get to know him better and talk to us both, well you will see it's the truth. Jean, Cisco is like me. What I mean to say is, he is from my time, from the future!"

Jean did not know whether to jump for joy or be jealous that this man had something in common with her that he did not? This meant that Cisco would have a special relationship with his lady, one that he could not partake in. Yet this bond they shared was something he could learn to deal and live with. The relief on his handsome drawn face was very evident and Tori saw only too clearly that he had thought something far worse. To think that she might have been hiding what his actions had implied made her both angry and want to laugh. "You fool, you thought that I and, you thought that we had slept together didn't you?"

"Call me the fool but what else was I to think. Never would I have guessed, that what you were keeping from me was so innocent. From your time you say? Now I have two of you to contend with, and Madame it will be my pleasure to be sure." He tried to sound sincere and keep the laughter out of his voice. Then in his sexiest low, husky-sort-of whisper he added, "Now come here, I can't stand it a moment longer. I want to hold you."

How could she stay angry at him? He was so devilish in his ways. He had the most charm of anyone she had ever met, and that added to the physical attraction was like a magnet. Still to think she and Cisco, that she would have fallen into the arms of another man? It rubbed her the wrong way and she wanted to teach him a lesson.

"Hold me you say. No way," she pushed him back. "If you want to hold me, it will cost you and I'm expensive."

"Name your price my lady and I'll gladly pay." His face was full of rakish grins and smirks. "My world is at your feet. Just don't deprive me of what I so desperately need."

"Oh really Jean you are quite something you know that? One minute you accuse me of sleeping with another and the next you want me to fall into your arms. Well I have some news for you. If you want me then you'll have to take me." She had tried to sound hurt and angry and tease him at the same time, just to teach the rouge a lesson but she knew he had seen through her little act. She was laughing at him now and could not help herself.

He could see the light in her eyes, the fun in her spirit. He knew she wanted him as much as he did her and by God he would have her. Before she could escape, in three quick strides he was at her side. In the next smooth move, he swept her up into his arms and maneuvered her body over his shoulder, holding her captive like a sack of grain. With one swift turn he marched into the house and as he did so, he called out, "Carlotta, you and everyone else should go and join the party. Enjoy yourselves." He chuckled to himself, "I know I will." By this time they had reached the stairs and he had started up with his wriggling cargo firmly in his grip.

Tori was acting the part. She called for him to let her go, something she knew he would never do and was glad of it. She beat playfully at his large broad back with her fists. Instead of screaming to be put down however she found herself laughing so hard that she felt she would not be able to take her next breath. "Put me down you big bully... Jean I'm telling you I can't breathe and this is no way to..." she tried to grab a breath, the pain in her side made her call out, "Stop it!"

Jean paid no attention to her pleas or to the pounding his back was taking. He simply carried his bundle down the hallway determined to make it to their bedroom. Upon reaching a closed door he was faced momentarily with the problem of entering. He could not let her go to reach for the door handle, nor would he put her down, that would be giving in and end all the dramatics. Tori had stilled herself, realizing his situation and giggling, asked him in a mocking voice, "Now what you going to do?"

He shrugged his shoulders and answered, "Only one thing to do." He faced the door and kicked it open with one hard determined blow with his boot, then once inside with his foot reaching backwards, he slammed it shut. Satisfied that it would stay closed he marched toward the bed. Once there grinning from ear to ear, he unceremoniously heaved her over his shoulder dropping her in the middle where she bounced twice, squealing with peels of laughter as she did so. She lay there looking up at him. Her face was so full of mischief and yet so beautiful.

Finally exhausted from her mock fight, Tori half closed her eyes, and tried to relax her body and catch her breath. Her thick soft lashes hid her eyes and the way she was watching his every move as he undressed, standing at the side of the bed. Jean could see only that her breathing came in deep heavy gulps. It was as if she had just run a great distance, causing her chest to raise and fall, pushing her bustline precariously close to popping out of her gown. His gaze was mesmerized by the site and the memory of how her breasts felt beneath his hands, how her nipples would stand erect within seconds of his touch. Any second he fully anticipated her breasts exploding over the edge of the material, his eyes were wide with expectations. His lustful stares and the cause for them had not slipped by her undetected. Tori reached for the top of her gown and holding it up she rolled over teasingly.

It was like pulling down the blind on a peeping Tom. His fun had been taken abruptly away. "Why Madame, I had thought you were paying me no heed. My little vixen is sly, no?" Jean had jumped onto the bed and forcibly rolled her back over pinning her arms above her head. Bringing his head down on the pillow he whispered closely to her ear, "You shall have to pay the penalty for spying, a serious crime in this house. That dictates immediate action on my behalf."

Tori turned to face him as she answered his accusations. "I plead guilty to all charges, to both sly and spying, guilty as charged. Do with me as you will," she giggled.

His head inched closer until his lips were brushing against her cheek as he spoke. "I intend to my lady." Then without any hesitation he released his hold on her arms and gently but firmly placed them underneath her waist. "Your punishment begins; but do not think that you are going to get away so easily. For your deceit, I will demand that you look at me." He raised her body up off the bed a few inches as he spoke, "You will look into my eyes and until I tell you otherwise, you will remain doing so, n'est pas?"

As if mesmerized and with the laughter leaving her face, she answered him willingly, "Oui," slipping her arms around his neck as she did so.

Satisfied and locking her eyes to his he gently lowered her once again onto the soft bed, and continued to remove his shirt, the last article of clothing he had on.

Tori could feel the heat of her blushing cheeks under such close scrutiny. Jean was watching her every reaction and would it seemed continue to do so. She was embarrassed by it and growing even more so, not to mention feeling totally vulnerable. Her body knew what she wanted, but did her mind? "Trust him," a small voice echoed in the recesses of her mind. And so without taking her eyes off his, barely audible, she spoke the last words either would hear until their passion was spent, "Je t'aime."

Never in her life had she made love with her eyes open let alone fixed on the eyes of her lover. Part of her wanted to look away, for it was as if by locking their eyes in this manner, he was taking more of her than she had ever allowed anyone before.

His large and dark fathomless eyes were piercing her heart and soul as he tenderly and slowly awakened her emotionally and physically. Each time her gaze would waver or if she would try to close her eyes, his hand would hold her chin firmly and bring her gaze back to his. Not a word did he have to utter, he spoke through his expression and she listened. In the end after many attempts, Tori found it simply impossible to tear herself free of his hypnotic hold. Held captive as she was, Tori knew for the first time in making love to him, he owned her completely. Her body had always been Jean's to control and play like a fine instrument, but this time the music that they made together was complete.

Jean observed the raw emotions flashing from behind her glazed eyes. He read their message as clear as if it were spoken. He saw her pupils dilate and the color deepen as he brought her closer and closer to ecstasy. And still he waited, stroking and touching her body with both his hands and his mouth, taking her finally when her eyes pleaded with him and told him she was at last his, body and soul.

Tori drowned in his love and in the depth of his gaze. She had heard it said that the eyes were the gateway to the soul, and could see now for herself that it was so true. She felt that as he looked deep and longingly into her, he was diving deep into her and claiming her body and soul once and for all for himself. Tori could see her reflection in his ebony stare. She could see herself clearly as if looking into a mirror, but that was where any similarity to a mirror ended. So large and dark were his pupils that she could not see where the outer deep color of his eyes started or ended. The two joined and melted together giving his eyes the illusion of being made up of one deep colored orb. So dark were they that she noticed for the first time, his whites, which seemed somehow light blue in contrast. No, she thought his eyes may reflect like mirrors but they were being used like weapons in a war she had long fought. Up until this moment she had had full control of her mind and her inner soul. Now however looking into his eyes, she knew she had lost herself completely in her pirate. He had taken her to heights that were beyond anything she had ever experienced or anything she could define. And with it came the realization that never again could she feel the same about him or herself. He now had a part of her that she could never reclaim. Just as sure as she now owned a part of him that she would never be able to evict. So when at last he allowed her to close her eyes and silently drift towards sleep, she wondered to herself, did he realize just how high a toll his penalty had been for both of them?

As concerned as she was about going back into New Orleans, she knew that she would not be able to change his mind on the matter. After all he had explained it to her making it quite clear he was not a wanted man, rather one out on bond. This fact had amused him greatly. To him it was nothing more than a slight inconvenience, one to be ignored. The trip was taken by both boat and horse allowing long hours of isolation in which the three of them could talk. Cisco was only too happy to oblige, and enjoyed watching Jean's surprised expressions as he discussed many subjects about the future. He was always careful about what he divulged, as like Tori, a deep-rooted fear about changing the future hung on. But what harm could come from explaining of things to come that Jean could not in any way have anything to do with? After many hours of talking however, Jean brought the conversation back around to the one subject that bothered him the most and try as he might he found that Cisco knew no more than his lady.

"Are you two sure that this so-called Battle of New Orleans is fought with my help?" he was frowning as he spoke. "It seems to me that before I go offering my services to defend this America that I should have more, much more information. Don't you think?"

Tori knew he was just trying to pry deeper. He knew deep down all she and Cisco had told him was true and yet a part of him, the practical side, found it hard to listen and really believe. She had to reach him with this, and reach the stubborn man she would. It was time to get Cisco to talk to John, to get him to open up and reveal himself also. Between the three of them maybe just maybe they could come up with some hard facts and decide just what should be done at this point in time.

On the last leg into town as they were parting ways, Tori took Cisco aside and quickly explained to him how important it had become to convince Mr. John Davis to meet with Jean. They had no choice it seemed to her, and Cisco who had been thinking along those lines himself, hugged her good-bye with his assurance that she would see him and John very soon.

Within hours of Jean being back in town, they had visitors. Word spread rapidly and once again they were receiving invites to dinner. No longer shunned but in big demand. This kind of two-faced falsehood upset Tori and made her rage inside as she remembered only too clearly how many of their so-called friends had turned their backs on her.

John Grymes turned up at the house just after dark, for a quick meeting with Jean and filled him in on what was happening. He warned Jean again and again that to hold a sale of his goods at this time could very well put him and Pierre back in irons. Jean had listened but seeing that stubborn look on his face, Tori knew that he would have his sale as planned.

John had just left and they were about to sit down to a fine evening meal, when the sound of Bessy talking and fussing something awful, interrupted Jean. He was explaining to Tori that there was no need for her concern about his upcoming decisions.

"Master Jean, there be that young man's who was here before when you be in jail. He said dat he got to see you and dat you would be happy to meet his friend. I ain't got his name but he look like a fine man's to me. It's dat young pup dat I ain't to sure about. You want me to tell him to leave cause, I will be real glad to if you want?" Bessy was rolling her eyes and clearly agitated. She thought it best to keep that dandy far away from Jean. He was the same fool who had been with the Mistress behind the Master's back and now he had returned. It smelled like trouble to her. Yes sur, big trouble.

Tori knew who Cisco's friend was, it could only be John and if that was true, then she knew that Cisco had reached him and he was ready to reveal his true identity to Jean. "Oh, I completely forgot Bessy. It's my fault. I asked the gentleman to call/ There is a matter we have to discuss. Please bring them back and Bessy don't you worry any," she smiled at the woman. "The young man in question is a friend of us both and Jean knows the other fine gentleman. Now go alone, hurry, we must not keep our guests waiting." She turned to Jean who had a perplexed look on his face.

"I don't know about you, but I for one was rather looking forward to our evening and to this," his hand pointed toward the evening meal.

Tori smiled at him. "Now don't you worry yourself, I'm sure that you can eat while we talk, but something tells me that you will want a good stiff drink first." Cisco entered followed closely by a somber John Davis who looked anything but glad to be there. He watched as Jean looked toward him and then turned to his Tori. His face a blank mask hiding his emotions. His voice the only giveaway at his surprise of seeing him. "I think my lady you are right, a good stiff drink as you put it is in order. Bessy, you can leave. We will take care of ourselves the rest of the evening. In fact make sure the house is empty. I don't want anyone here to disturb us. Gentlemen you will join me in a drink won't you?"

As Bessy left, she was relived to see that indeed her mistress had been right, there would be no trouble there. Sure was strange though, him asking for her to leave and the house to be empty. Ah huh, it was strange but then white folks be that way.

Jean handed out the drinks, including one for Tori who was standing smiling at John. Only Cisco seemed unfazed as he helped himself to tasting the cold meats and other delicacies.

It was Jean who started the evening's conversation, "John I think somehow that you are about to become far more than just a business acquaintance, am I correct?"

"I think you are. Cisco here has spent the whole afternoon convincing me that I am needed here and that Tori and you are to be trusted. Before I go on I must have your word as a friend and a gentleman, that what I tell you, that our friendship, all of it, remain a secret. Your discretion in this, your guarantee, it is the only way that I will remain here this evening."

Jean cocked his head to one side and sensing the gravity of what he was about to say hesitated only momentarily before giving his affirmative answer. "You have it," he walked up to him and offered his hand.

"You know how I feel about this John," added Tori. "I will always respect your wishes," she handed him a glass of wine and laughing softly she whispered, "You will always remain the invisible partner in crime."

John took a long gulp of his wine and then placing the glass down he looked at Jean. "I will be up front and to the point then. It is as simple as this. I have known Cisco here for a very long time. You might say we came to New Orleans from the same place, as did your Tori. I am one of them you see and between us we hope to be able to put our heads together and keep history as it should be. On track so to speak. I am here to offer my support and my help in anyway it counts for so long as you need it."

All eyes in the room were on Jean's face, watching to see what his reaction to this new piece of news was going to be. What they observed was an outwardly calm man whose only giveaway that he was inwardly excited was the twitch of his lower lip.

"I am no longer shocked; surprised maybe, but shocked, No!" Jean was smiling, "It is my guess that you helped in a far larger way in the escapade that acquired my freedom?"

"You have it right in that department, but only a few of us know of my involvement and I intend it to stay that way." Jean raised his eyebrow considering what John had just said and looked toward Cisco who sat beaming like he had just won the best poker hand of his life.

"I owe you my heartfelt thanks then my friend, and I'm indebted to you. A debt that I will pay. Name your price mon ami, you shall have anything you want."

"You can do only one thing for me Jean, and that is to listen and learn from us." He pointed toward his cohorts. "It is my hope to keep the outcome of history as it should be. I think maybe your wife had it right, when she said that the three of us are here together as destiny not coincidence."

"Jean," Tori broke in, "are you ready to listen? Can we try and sort it all out?"

"Lady, it looks as though I have no choice in the matter. We have all night, and we have a fine meal that we can share. Let's put the two together and start, shall we?"

The small unlikely group moved toward the table and sitting down started talking and bonding. First the talk was on how and where John had fit into the picture and from there they found themselves embroiled in a long night of drinking and sharing with Jean all that they could. He was like a sponge, just sat and soaked up all that he heard, breaking in only to ask further questions, wanting always explanations and descriptions. For hours they talked, even covering the one subject most on their minds. What to do about the upcoming Battle.

Try as they might, neither John, Cisco or Tori could agree on the exact date of the Battle of New Orleans. Jean had sat silently listening to them as they all discussed what they knew and to him it seemed it was what they didn't know, that was most important.

After hours of discussions it was very evident to John that all they really had was the outcome of the battle as it was written in their time, and that Jean played a very strategic role. But how would they ensure that it remained that way?

Cisco was getting frustrated at John and his ever pessimistic mood. He was about to really let him have it when Tori broke into the conversation. Up until now she had not had much to say. She spoke with an edge to her voice that forced even Cisco to listen.

"Look you two, I've been thinking about this a lot and well it just does not make sense one way or another. Seems to me we have two choices. One is to sit back and do nothing and see if it turns out the way it should. The other is to get involved. Organize what we know is going to happen and use it to see that the outcome is what history wrote. The thing is which is it? If we sit still and the outcome is different because we did not help, we are in trouble. If we help and screw it up we could be changing history. The fact is we are damned if we do and damned if we don't."

The three men looked at her and Cisco for once was silent, the normal smile on his face hidden by a scowl. John exasperated and fed up at going around in circles with the problem spoke up. "We don't seem to know too damn much if you ask me. Therefore how can we get involved at any point if we don't know what we are doing. I vote leave it alone."

Cisco was not about to stand for that plan of action and immediately reiterated what he felt was right. "Always the cautious one John. Had it occurred to you that like Tori here said earlier, that we three might have come back in time for just this purpose. To help so to speak, and if we don't, well we could very well change the outcome of so much, including our own existence for one?"

Angry now, John snapped quickly back at him, "And did it occur to you that the opposite could be true?"

"Guys, guys, please let's not fight amongst ourselves. This is not going to help Jean or us. What we have to do is approach this systematically and then decide what to do."

Somewhat put down but still agitated, John could not let the subject drop. "And just how do you go about that may I ask?"

"Indeed you may John. Way I see it, we make a list of all we know about this time and what is going to happen. Writing things down sometimes helps. But sitting around waiting for the outcome one way or the other just won't prove shit. Look, we all agree that Jean had the supplies that Andrew Jackson needed, along with men. That's a start!" She looked toward Jean who had been quiet for some time. He could see clearly what they themselves failed to acknowledge.

"My friends, this discussion is going nowhere except around in circles. It is rather like a dog chasing its tail; in the end he succeeds in catching it. We will no doubt become clearer on this subject as events lead up to it. From what we know and that seems to be far more than we thought, we will be very aware when the time is close at hand. So until such a time I agree with John, let's just keep a vigil and act accordingly." Jean looked at a very frustrated Tori and placed his arm around her waist, drawing her closer to him. "My lady do not look so forlorn. We will, I have no doubt, have enough signs in the time ahead to alert us and guide us. Don't you agree gentlemen?"

John feeling much calmer now he had the level-headed Jean taking his view on the matter, had gone over to sit at the piano and tinker with the keys. Cisco may not have liked what Jean had just said but he smiled and nodded his full agreement. Though nothing had really been solved, he was pleased with the way things had gone and looked forward to many such evenings into the future.

"I may not agree Jean, but majority rules. Besides, until such events start to guide us, we can meet and have get-togethers such as this. Isn't that right John?" "No, I totally disagree there. We can't afford to be known as friends now or ever. Too many questions and unwanted inquires would arise."

"For who? For you I think. You and your wanting to keep everything secret," Cisco slurred. His drinking of the evening was finally catching up to him, clouding his judgment and making him careless.

Tori could see another confrontation building and acted quickly to defuse it. "I agree with John, things need to appear the same. Or nearly the same. We can explain away your friendship Cisco. But to have such a high profile friend such as John here all of a sudden, well it is dangerous. Don't you agree Jean?"

"Most certainly and I did give my word at the beginning of the evening, that John's identity and connection would be kept amongst us. My word is my word Cisco," he added sternly.

Suddenly John was playing a piece of music that drew Cisco's and Tori's attention away from the subject at hand and brought instant relief to the strained atmosphere. The soft notes floated across the room the familiar tune recognized immediately by everyone but Jean.

Cisco laughed out loud "Now that's what I call appropriate. If ever there was a song for you two," he said as he looked toward Jean and Tori, "it's that one. Don't you agree Tori?"

She did indeed and laughed with him. "I had never thought of it, but yes you are right."

Jean however felt he was being left out of the joke.

John could see the perplexed look upon Jean's face and as he slowly played the beginning of the tune he spoke toward Jean. "I have not known you and your lady long. Oh sure I have known of you, but until this evening, I had not seen for myself what is whispered around town. She is truly the love of your life, your lady. Please allow me to play for you, a song from our time that Jean, I know you will approve of." With that he started to play in earnest and softly the words escaped his lips as he easily sang the melody.

Tori pulled Jean to his feet and putting her arms around him started to sway to the tune, her head down on his shoulder, as she listened closely to the words John sang. She knew the Kenny Rogers song all right. At least she had heard it many times before but listening to it now brought tears to her eyes.

"Lady, I'm your knight in shining armor..." They held each other listening to the words of the song and as they did, it was as if no one else was in the room. Jean would squeeze her close to him every now and then, as if to confirm the words with how he felt.

Cisco was even moved. He sat mesmerized by the pair and the dance that played out before him. Most of all by the love that radiated between his two friends. John, carried away by singing one of his favorite country songs, found that it now had meaning to him. He put his whole heart and soul behind the emotions the tune brought. He did not look at the couple dancing to the melody until his last words of the song were leaving his lips. "You're the love of my life, you're my lady..." It was the sight of Jean's tear-filled eyes, followed by Tori's look of wonder, that caused him to act on impulse. Putting his finger to his lips to silence Cisco who was about to clap when he finished, he stood. Walking toward the door he motioned toward Cisco to join him and together they slipped from the soft candle lit room unnoticed.

Jean and Tori stood in each others arms for what seemed to both of them as an eternity. Each was caught up in the haunting melody and it's meaning. Jean bent his head down close to her ear and whispered softly, "That my lady is exactly how I feel." He turned to thank John and ask him about the lyrics only to find an empty room. Smiling he looked into his lady's face. "I think we have very wise friends my love. Now let us not waste these precious moments alone. Let us take full advantage of how I, we feel. Come with me my lady." He reached gently and kissed her lips lightly guiding her toward the upstairs. "I think maybe whoever wrote those words, did so just for me so I could give them to you."

Tori did not talk. She walked with him, the song playing again and again in her mind. It was their song, would be from now until she died. She smiled to herself. Then suddenly a sad feeling swept over her briefly. She thought of another era and another song, but that melody was not so clear now and belonged in another time far away...

# Chapter 24

In the coming months life went on as it had before Jean's arrest. Nothing had changed as far as he was concerned and the business grew day by day. Jean and his men had held one of their infamous auctions in the bayous, its total success spurring him on. Both he and Pierre walked the streets of New Orleans with a confidence and air about them that demanded respect. To many of the merchants, who were demanding justice, it seemed that the Laffite brothers thought themselves above the law.

Grymes had tried to persuade Jean to lay low, but had failed to do so. He worried day and night about his client's blatant flagrancy, as his continued warnings fell on deaf ears, rendering him powerless to do much else. True, Claiborne seemed helpless and had his hands tied but for how much longer he wondered. The man would be pushed too far one day and then Jean and his whole operation, would be in dire straits.

Edward and Simone had their hands full at the moment and had temporally put aside their goal of Jean's demise. Edward had proposed to Simone and she only too willingly accepted. Not wanting to wait and afraid he would change his mind, Simone had started planning the day immediately. She had certain guidelines given to her by Edward but other than that she had free reign. He had explained to her that he wanted a small but well-attended wedding, nothing big but elegant and befitting his standing in society. Simone would have married him in a back alley if she had to. True she loved him in a sort of sick way, but she was far more in love with becoming Madame Duval than any other reason. Her wedding should be the social event of the month she told herself, and if she had her way, and she knew she would, then that is exactly what would happen.

As a wedding gift to his bride, Edward had purchased a new home for them and arranged to reside at John Davis's hotel until Simone had decorated it as she wanted. Leone's townhouse their place of residence, was to be sold along with Simone's smaller establishment. They would keep most of the grand pieces of furniture from Leone's but Simone insisted that the entire contents of her place be liquidated. She wanted nothing to remind her of her disastrous former life. Even the idea of making the United States hotel home for a short time, didn't bother her as long as she could continue to live in the style she was accustomed to. Had she realized how convenient this arrangement was to her sworn enemies she would have died.

John Grymes liked the arrangement very much as did Jean and Tori. They could keep a closer eye on the pair, and with luck keep abreast of their scheming plans. As prearranged, John Davis's friendship with Tori and Jean was kept under wraps. Cisco's open relationship with him at his hotel could continue.

It was in this way that any worthy news could be passed on to the Laffites without causing any undue suspicion.

Simone was a radiant bride. She looked as if nothing in the world could be wrong. She smiled and laughed with the guests all of whom had no idea that the beautiful woman was far from happy on this her wedding day. She was furious with Edward's lack of progress with the Governor on putting Jean back in jail.

This had started out as the dream wedding and ended up a nightmare. All she had heard in conversations at their reception, had been talk of Laffite this and Laffite that. She was sick of it and it had ruined her day.

Edward knew his wife very well and seeing that something had greatly upset her set out to find the cause. Taking her aside, he asked in a concerned voice. "Are you sad that you married me? Or could it be that your wedding was not as grand as you would have wished? Or my sweet Simone is it that you can't wait for this gathering to finish. Have you far more important affairs on that lovely mind of yours?" Edward had run his hand down around her waistline and once on her rear-end had squeezed a hand full of flesh, kneading it suggestively in his palm.

She shot him a smug smile, then let it just as quickly slip away. "Oh no Edward my dear. Besides this night's upcoming duties as your new bride," she turned her salutary smoldering eyes up into his, "I want you to know I was thinking about our wedding," she lied. "It was wonderful. You were right to keep it small and elegant. I am the envy of many I am sure being married in the Governor's home and attended by only the highest in society. No bride could have asked for more. As for changing my mind you silly man. I am the happiest woman. I am Madame Duval and very proud of it. I'm your wife and as such will see to it that the Duval name is one to be reckoned with."

Now she thought is the time to tell you what's really on my mind you fool. "There is however one dark cloud the reason behind my gloom. Have you not noticed the talk? Always it is about Laffite. It sickens me." Edward had indeed been fully aware of the discussions that floated amongst his guests. Damn that man and his ability to overshadow what should have been the happiest of days.

"Edward dear," Simone was using her sexiest voice, the one that pleaded and could not be easily ignored. "You know how grateful I am to you for such a wonderful wedding gift. The house is going to be the talk of the town when it is finished. But my dear, if you want to make me, us truly happy, then you have to find a way to put Jean back where he belongs. If ever you could give me a wedding present that I would love it would be that." She continued for quite a while, simpering and smoothly explaining to him that they could never really be happy together until Jean had been brought down.

Edward had to agree with her. They had delayed long enough. It was time to get back to work and destroy those that always found a way to interfere with their happiness. So it was that during the reception dinner Edward once again went to work on the unsuspecting Governor and the small group of guests. He took his line of thinking still further when the men retired to the library for cigars. Knowing that Edward was plotting and planning again Simone relaxed and began once again to enjoy all the attention. While her husband was isolated with the men, the ladies helped get Simone ready for her wedding night, a night that she eagerly anticipated.

The Governor had been increasingly agitated by the fact that Jean was able to carry on as he pleased. It further infuriated him that a large portion of the local population and most of the Creole merchants seemed to be on the outlaw's side, while the new and growing American side of town was screaming for something to be done. Many of them threatening his re-election if it wasn't.

Edward had stated to the group that it would not surprise him if they were to find Jean had the State Legislature in his hip pocket. Why they most likely were profiting by the pirate's activities themselves he hinted. "Why else do they turn a blind eye I ask you? Once again I must reiterate, something must be done soon about this intolerable situation, or else we will all become the laughing stock of this fair city. And you my dear Governor will be without a job."

The Governor shook his head in denial. "That my dear Edward I can assure you will not be the case. All morning I was myself plagued with a dilemma. What to do about a certain matter pertaining to that hooligan pirate. You see gentlemen," he now addressed the whole room, "Laffite's bond has been forfeited and as such I was forced into taking action. Therefore I had the States Attorney draw up a proclamation which by now has been posted." A rumble of voices, each expressing their own view on this piece of news echoed about the room.

"This day will go down in history, not only is March 15th 1813, the beginning of your married life Edward, it is the beginning of the fall of Laffite and his Banditti."

"But what was said in this proclamation sir?" a voice asked from across the room.

"In short," he continued, turning to face the gentleman who had asked the question, "It has made my standing on this Laffite matter very clear. He is an outlaw, engaged in unlawful activities, that I or this fine state, will stand for no longer. I have also made it clear that the citizens of this here fine city, had best desist in any such subversive practices with him." He smiled as he looked toward two of the most prominent merchants. "They had best stop purchasing from the Laffites or suffer the severest punishment."

William looked back at Edward whose stunned face was mistaken as one who was very concerned. "So you see my dear fellow I have taken it upon myself and my duty as Governor of this here fine State, to see to the end of the illegal trafficking on Lake Barataria and thereby put an end to the whole banditti activities. Jean Laffite's cruising of the high seas, plundering for his own gain, is about to be, how do you say, fini!"

Edward had had no idea that any such proclamation had been handed out, but now that he knew he would of course let his Simone believe it to be one of his ideas, a small wedding surprise. Oh this was going to be a fine beginning to his marriage and a joyful beginning to Laffite's end...

Jean and Tori wasted no time. Within the hour of John Grymes meeting, they were headed back toward Grand Terre and the safety there in. The only thing utmost in Jean's mind was he had been publicly declared an outlaw. America had turned on him, while he himself did all he could to make it his ally. Spain and England were his enemies and now it looked as though the very country he was supposed to help save, had declared him, Jean Laffite, a foe.

This was something that even Tori and her friends had not known about. Could it be possible he wondered, that they were wrong about other such facts? One thing was very evident that to stay in town would be suicidal. True the proclamation had not outright named him but the implication had been made quite clear. He had been declared no better than a banditti! On top of this slur he was now a wanted man. His so-called bond had been forfeited and he could be arrested at any time! Before departing, they had sent word of their new predicament to his brother and hoped he too would leave town, out of reach of Claiborne's clutches.

Pierre however had a mind of his own and had insisted that he would stay in town. He was not about to turn tail and run from any man let alone the Governor. Besides it was not he that the Governor wanted.

Cisco dropped by once he got word of the proclamation only to find the Laffite's had left town. Bessy handed him two letters that Tori had left for him and asked that he deliver the second envelope to his friend. With no name on it she assumed he would understand just which friend. He read Tori's short message explaining the predicament they now found themselves in. She went on to say that once they were settled in Grand Terre, she would contact him. Cisco smiled as he read the last line. He would always be welcome anytime. He frowned at the short letter and shook his head. He would miss them both. His time spent with them was cherished. He especially enjoyed it when the three of them got together, something that he felt was not about to happen again for a very long time.

Spring came and the days grew once again warmer and longer. Slipping comfortably by, one blending into the other broken only by the odd visit or new boatload of contraband. Jean was a changed man. He was withdrawn and quick to anger. Instead of laying low and cutting back on the activities he was accused of he increased them and called his men to take more risks and bring in more goods. They would, he declared to his men, sell more to make more. He would become what he had been accused of being!

Down by the French market, a free woman of color was rearranging three pieces of furniture she had acquired at a sale only the day before. It had been sheer luck that the pieces had become available to her and at such a reasonable price. All her life she had dreamed of owning a small nicely furnished home, and after long hours of back-breaking work, her dream was at last realized. For two years she had been buying one piece at a time, mostly from the sales that the Laffite's held, but since hearing the Governor's proclamation, she had thought it best to look elsewhere. It had not been easy. The few odds and ends that she had seen, were well out of her price range and not always just what she wanted. Then while delivering two gowns that she had made, she overheard talk about a sale of a home and all the contents therein. It had taken her great courage to step forward and do what she had, but it had paid off.

"Yes, praise the Lord she murmured. "For five gowns and the promise of a quick delivery I got myself some fine looking furniture." She stroked the large chest of drawers lovingly. Then taking a cloth with a small amount of bees wax she began to polish the wood to a high shine.

"That Mizz Liza, she be real good to me, buying you for me and letting me work off my debt. But now you be mine and I am sooo proud." She hugged herself briefly and then went back to work on cleaning while she continued to talk to herself. "Lord, them white folks, they don't know what they has most the time. I ain't never a going to sell such a fine piece, no sur, never."

She hummed a tune as she carefully and lovingly cleaned and worked, erasing any touch of white folks on her prize possession. Each drawer she took out was wiped both inside and out, followed by a close inspection and waxing of the inside of the chest. It was during her close inspection that much to her surprise a document was discovered. If she had not been so thorough in her cleaning, she thought, surely the document would have gone undiscovered and lay wedged for eternity at the back of the dresser. Fascinated, she took the large sheet of paper in her hands and unfolded it carefully. It was torn in one place, where the drawer at one point or another had caught it, but other than that it seemed to be intact. Just what it was she could not tell or would she dare ask. Something told her this was trouble she held in her hands, but just what she should do about it she did not know. Thoughts such as taking it to Mizz Liza or the church raced in her mind. No that would not do, "I could just put it back and forget it, but that be like lying, and that be a sin. Oh, Lord what's I going to do about this here paper." She raised it up above her head as if showing it to the heavens. Slowly she lowered her hands and placed the paper on her lap looking at it closely. If she had her way, she would have learned how to read and write, just like the white folk. Oh, she was smart enough she knew that. But it was not allowed was it? She shook her head sadly. Then a sly smile crossed her young face. For years she had been learning herself hadn't she? Not easy to do, but not impossible either.

"Maybe I could, like see if I knowd any of these here words? If'n I knows some of them written down here, that could help me some. Yes, that's it. I'll just take me a look and see." She held the document in her shaking hands and carefully looked at the words placed neatly down in dark ink. Whoever had written those words sure did a purty job she thought. An idea fleetingly crossed the woman's ever curious mind. "Maybe I can git me some paper and try to do me some purty lettering?" She was talking to herself and looking nervously about, half out of fear of being caught trying to read, and half because she wanted to convince herself to do just that, read. A few words she recognized small easy words scrawled in a penmanship that was as foreign to her as the language was. She knew a few English words but most of her self-taught reading dealt with French. Well she had her first clue she told herself, it belonged to someone who spoke English. What else did she know? The house where the drawers and document had come from, was not in the new garden district, no way. It had come from a small townhouse in the French district. So why was it written in English and better still why had it been hidden at the back of her drawers? She looked up at the chest and then back at the paper.

"Maybe it fell out of the drawer and got pushed back there. Maybe it just got lost like not hidden." She examined the article still closer. It looked very important to her, a love letter maybe? Whatever it was, she just knew in her heart that it was important. She had a puzzle on her hand for sure, but if she reasoned carefully maybe she could work it out. If it had been lost, she told herself someone would have looked for it and most likely found it. This conclusion freighted her. "No you was hidden, and you be trouble just like I told myself." She was about to place the paper down as if it were going to bite her hand, when her eyes registered a name that she recognized. Looking closely, she found the name at the very top and then again it appeared at the bottom of the paper, as if jumping out to her. It was one English name that she knew but just to make sure she would go out right this second and walk over to where it could be compared with the sign just to be safe.

"If it be the same and I knowd it already in my heart Lord, it is the same. Well then you done showed me the way. I just return it to this here person whose name I see. Yes, that be the right thing for me to do." She left her chest and her polishing hurrying downstairs to her small shop. Quickly she put on her cape and stuffed the paper in the a large pocket out of sight. She had to hurry, the day was already growing late and she did not want to spend one more night with this in her house. It was going to take her some time walking to the building where she had seen the name. She only hoped it was time enough.

As she hurried to leave, she found herself thinking how white folk were lucky to have their names on their shops. She stepped outside and closed and locked her door. What would her name look like written down above her door she wondered? Looking up at her sign that hung above it, she grinned. She had made it herself and been very proud of it. It was not her name but it was what she did. A needle and thread she had painted and surrounded it with a design of fine lace. No, it was not her name but it had worked just the same.

She turned away and started walking briskly toward the American section of the city. How was it she wondered for the first time, that with only a name hung outside the shop that white folks knew what the shop was for without going inside to look? It hit her then and became clear for the first time. "That's what the other letters be about, they are telling what the peoples needs to know." Then with pride at having solved another of life's small mysteries behind her, she surmised her sign was better by far. "Cause if'n you can't read, you still knowd what I selling." Her spirits soared. "Yes I be smarter than most folk think I am." Determined that she was doing the right thing, she hurried on her way, passing the United States Hotel and unknowingly the document's former owner.

Edward had thought that Simone had destroyed the will. Instead she had hidden it away at the back of her drawer. Ever scheming, she had done so as sort of an insurance policy of her own. Should Edward ever choose to leave her, well she would of course be forced to use it against him wouldn't she? In the past few months, the document which she had told herself, once she was Edward's wife, she would burn, had slipped her mind. The townhouse and its contents had been sold at her request, so when next she would remember it, she had no way of tracking it down. To her horror without raising unwanted questions she realized there was no way she could ask for any help, from anyone, in finding its whereabouts. For weeks she had worried and been a wreck, taking to her bed sick with a headache. If it were discovered and fell into the wrong hands all would be lost. Life had once again dealt her a raw hand. How could she have been so stupid as to forget about the blasted will? All she could do was wait, wait and see if the new owner of the chest of drawers discovered its hidden secret. As the time slipped by and still it did not surface, she convinced herself that it was safely and securely hidden and would never be discovered. Her headaches vanished and life progressed happily once again.

John Grymes had been working late and was about to leave, when a knock came upon his door. Normally one of the junior lawyers would take care of answering the call but he had let everyone go early, something he always did when he was working on Jean's behalf. Thinking it was going to be nothing more than someone delivering a message, he answered the door while putting on his coat.

Upon arriving at the building where she was sure she had seen the name written on the paper, she hesitated. Her hands trembled as she took out the paper to compare the letters. She had to be very careful at this point and not let anyone see her. Looking around she found that if she acted quickly she just might have a chance, as not too many people were walking by and those few that were, paid her no attention. She looked quickly at the name, then at the one on the sign. Sure enough they were the same. She had been right! She often passed here on her way to visit her friend and then again many times on her way to different client's homes for fittings. She always tried to learn new words and teach herself from those she figured out. This writing before her though had never been of any help to her, as she could never figure out any of the longer words. Sure she knew the word AT, that was simple but the rest remained a jumble. They had meant nothing to her until now. She had the right place and the right name she was sure of it. There was nothing left to do but knock.

She was standing there waiting, a woman of mixed color, not at all unattractive but not what he would have called pretty either. She was dressed in an outfit that while denoting her class, was clean and well made. Her face young in years was somehow older in expression. Her posture was upright and her gaze somewhat uncomfortably forthright.

"May I be of some assistance?" His voice came out sounding rather surprised and unsteady even to his own ears. She didn't seem to notice however, as she nodded her head in the affirmative.

"I'm sorry to be here so late and seeing you about to leave and all. I won't be a keeping you long. I have to see the man whose name is written right there," she pointed to his name printed on the small plaque. Will he still be here?"

He did not recognize this woman and the fact that she asked for him, caught him off guard. "May I ask why you wish to see him?"

"That's between him and me. You may tell him that I think I have something he has lost and I would very much like to return it to him personal like."

John looked closely at her, quickly trying to size her up. She was obviously determined to reach him and seemed to be telling the truth. Just what could it be that she had of his he wondered? The woman certainly had courage standing there demanding not to see anyone but himself. He knew that many in the city would take her demeanor as an act of insolence and treat her in accordance with what they thought proper. She was a proud individual and despite her obvious fear, was standing her ground. He smiled kindly toward her, trying to ease her discomfort. She was intriguing; a true enigma. The young lady had spoken in English, laced with a thick French Creole accent. This told him she was obviously from the other side of town. His guess was she was a free woman of color and an intelligent one at that. But why point to his name and not just ask for him outright? Just what her connection to him could be he could not imagine. His curiosity was peaked and he knew that he would have to find out just what was going on here.

"Please come in," he stood back and let her pass through the entrance, before closing the door. "I think maybe I had best introduce myself to you. I am the gentleman in question, the one on the wall outside. Mr. John Grymes at your service."

Her mouth dropped open then just as quickly she recovered her emotions and openly stared at him. John saw her disbelief so he nodded his head as if to confirm she had heard him right and taking her by the arm escorted her into his office. "How can I be of assistance? You say you have something I lost? That seems highly unlikely as I am not currently aware of any article missing. And may I add, I do not think we have ever met, so what makes you think this article you have belongs to me?"

The woman looked at him, suspicion on her face. "Yes that's right enough. I don't know you. Know who John Grymes is though. Just cause I'm black and uneducated don't mean I'm stupid. I've been around this here town some and in many fine homes. Peoples talk and I listen. Just never met you before or seen you. How'd I know you be this here Monsieur Grymes, the States Attorney?" she asked.

"You don't but you seem to be an intelligent woman. Look around you, this is a private office, my office and here on the desk is my name." He pointed to the small brass name plate. "I am who I said," he smiled once again toward her, "you have my word on that." John softened his tone and talked to her, in what he liked to call, his parent tone. "I could not be anyone else now could I?" Giving her some time to think about that, he walked around his desk and pulled out his chair seating himself comfortably. He then reached and opened a drawer taking out a pen and ink, along with some paper on which to write.

She had watched him and seeing he knew just where things were kept, she made up her mind he was telling her the truth. Besides she wanted to get rid of the document and be on her way home as soon as possible. "I found this in my chest of drawers," she held up the paper, "stuck way in the back. I was cleaning you see and I think maybe you owned the drawers before I bought them." He raised his eyebrow at this. Drawers, he had sold no furniture now or since moving here. She was obviously confused. Easy to do if you can't read he figured.

She saw the look on his face clearly he did not believe her. "I did buy them. Mizz Liza, she got them for me and I paid her for them." She pushed the paper across the desk toward him quickly withdrawing her hand.

It was on the tip of his tongue, to tell her that he had not sold any chest of drawers and just what made her think the papers belonged to him, when his mouth slammed shut. He recognized his hand writing immediately and still further to his astonishment and sheer elation he saw the paper for what it was. "You found this at the back of your drawers?"

"Yes sur. Like I done told you. It must have got stuck there and I got it and I see'd your name right there on the top and the bottom. Then I told myself, that I had best bring it to you and all. I hope I did right? It is yours, isn't it?"

"My dear lady you did far more than right. Yes, it's mine and yes I did misplace it quite a while ago. So long ago in fact, that I completely forgot about it." He looked again just to be sure he was not dreaming and then back at the woman. "Madame I did not get your name, you are?"

"Why'd you need my name now? I'm in trouble aren't I? You think I took it? I didn't! I swear it! Oh Lord, I know'd that it be trouble when I first laid my eyes on the thing." She was backing up toward the door as if getting ready to run. Her hands were twisting on themselves and she was all but crying, tears of fear filling her eyes.

"No, no! You are not in any trouble I promise you. I just wanted to thank you by name that's all. It was very good of you to return this to me and might I add, very clever of you to figure out it belonged to me. If you wish to keep your name to yourself then that is up to you." He was using that parent tone again, as if he were reassuring a child. "If it makes you feel any better, then by all means please do so. I do think that you should be rewarded for your honesty and integrity."

"I know'd about honesty but that other, I ain't a knowing about. I don't need nothing just want to go home and forget about it, that's' all."

John reached into his jacket and took out some coins. "Look I would not feel right if you didn't take something for your trouble and then we can say good-bye and forget about it, yes?" Seeing him counting out the money and knowing it was a comfortable sum she reasoned with herself that it was only fair to take his reward. "I will be thanking you then," she held out her hand.

John dropped the coins into her hand and would have gladly paid her much more for the document but felt it more prudent to make light of the matter. Better she forget about the paper and be on her way. He wanted no one to know he had it back safely where it belonged.

She took the money smiling at the amount and happy to be finished with the ordeal she turned to leave. Then thinking that she really could trust this man and maybe someday might need a favor from him, she turned and spoke. "Je suis Mademoiselle Musette DuPree." She was smiling now. "I own a small dress shop at the end of Toulouse close by the corner of Dauphine. It is a shop, outside of which hangs my sign. It ain't fancy words like you have, just drew me a picture showing what I does."

"That Mademoiselle DuPree is very clever of you. I can truly say it is my honor and pleasure to make your acquaintance." John was beaming and meant each and every word. He was so very glad he had let this woman come in instead of turning her away. "And now if you would please excuse me, I do have an urgent matter at hand. I was on my way out if you remember? Let me however assure you, that your meeting here with me this evening will always be remembered. I seldom forget those whose character is upstanding and as forthright as yours. Should you ever need my assistance... Well it goes without saying does it not? Now however I must insist that our meeting come to an end."

"Merci Monsieur Grymes, and please don't bother yourself. I have kept you too long for that I am sorry. I am glad to have been of some help to you. I will let myself out. I'm in a hurry also wanting to get back and all. Maybe we will meet again some day, oui? Maybe your wife she would like a gown? I would be honored to make her one. Until then, au revoir." It was obvious to Musette, that she was no longer wanted. She knew also that she had done nothing wrong to warrant his eager dismissal of her, but was wise enough to know, when to take the hint and depart. Before any further conversation could take place, or before she got herself into some kind of trouble with this important man, Musette knew to get while the getting was good.

John watched as she turned and hastily departed. The sound of the outer door closing, let him know that he was once again alone in his office. He felt a tinge of guilt for the way he had hurried her out, but his excitement over what he now had in his possession had warranted her quick dismissal. He had not wanted her to see, how very glad he was to receive what she had given him.

"Leone my friend," he spoke softly, "God smiles on you this night. I would have bet my last coin that never would I have again seen your will. Now sat here in my office, I hold in my hands, once again the proof necessary to oust that bastard and his wife. Jean and Tori's son was to have had Leone's estate. We both know that can't happen now. But by God, Jean and Tori can inherit what is rightfully theirs and I can at last keep my word to you! Do you hear me Leone," he shouted, "I can keep my word!"

Instantly John set to work writing an urgent message to Jean, one explaining that he had some very important news for him when next he was in town. If Jean could see fit to contact him at his earliest convenience, he was certain he would not be disappointed. Smiling he finished the letter and headed for the blacksmith shop, where he would pass the note to Thiac who in return would see it delivered safely to Laffite.

Within a few days Jean got Grymes message and read it out loud to Tori. "What do you make of it?"

"I'm not sure. It seems to me that the information he has could be nothing but good news though. Jean, do you intend to go into the city anytime soon?" Concern filled her voice. "It is still dangerous for you. I'm afraid you will be taken into custody again."

"No, my lady. I intend to stay right here for the time being. You may relieve yourself of any worry you have in that direction. I am not so stupid as to place myself into the Governor's hands so easily. Maybe we will go later in the summer, when things have calmed down."

"And how do you think they will do that may I ask? You are causing far more trouble these days for yourself. Why only yesterday I saw another of your ships sail in loaded down with the contents taken from another. Jean are you listening to me?"

"It is of no concern for you." he snapped. "I have given you my word that no American ships will be taken have I not? That is what you're asking isn't it? Well my lady for your information it was a British ship that was taken." His temper was rising as he continued sarcastically. "The Americans will soon forgive and forget or I will earn back my dignity. That is how it is done is it not? I fight this war for them and all is forgiven."

"You are impossible!"

"And you my lady are unreachable. I shall leave you before we disagree further."

"Jean you come back here," she called to his back, "I'm not finished."

"Well I am!" he turned toward her his face a clouded mask hiding his mixed emotions. "I have to attend to the day's work. We will talk more over dinner, oui?"

She knew they would not. They talked less and less these days about his operation here at Grand Terre. Jean had put up a wall and he was for better or worse securely hidden behind it. She knew he was having trouble with Gambi again. The men were upset that he would not allow any American vessel to be taken. If he blamed her for his troubles, why didn't he just out with it instead of these small, for no reason, blow ups. And if it was not that that was bothering him then what. If only he would talk to her or Dominique about what was really upsetting him she thought. Watching him walking away down toward the docked ship, a sad lonely look replaced the angry one. She could not help him and she could not reach him, but she could be patient.

June was upon them and with it the heat of the summer. For hours in the hottest part of the afternoon Tori would lay in the hammock that was strung under the front verandah. She would lay there trying to catch the sea breeze and fan herself desperately trying to cool off. The afternoons were the quietist and calmest part of the day. Mostly because it was to damn uncomfortable to do much else.

The bay waters sparkled and danced as the small waves rolled into shore. The deep green and blue hues of the gulf shimmered through the heat waves raising up off the land, making it look more like a mirage than a real sea. At this time of day, even the birds that normally danced about the water's edge, were gone. Nothing it seemed, had enough energy to disturb the tranquil picture that lay before her.

Tori dozed on and off, as she stared out to sea debating whether or not to go for a swim. The hot humid air was so thick and heavy that it was an effort to even breath. The damned heat was so oppressive and caused her to sweat like a pig, she angrily thought. She could see no use in wasting what little energy she had and for what? She was drenched anyway. Rivulets of perspiration trickled down her face. All of her body was covered in a light wet film of moisture. There was no getting away from it, or her damp blouse along with the rest of her garments, which were glued to her. Tori pulled at the cotton top lifting it away from her skin. As she did this, it seemed to her that a waft of even hotter air escaped her body. Maybe the idea of a swim was not so bad after all?

She had been watching the two ships get closer and closer to shore, without really thinking about them. It was not until the activity down by the small village, with its sounds of agitated men shouting, that she sat up to take notice. Something was wrong. Men were running about yelling to each other, while still others were pointing in the direction of the ships.

Tori fully awake looked again. They were still too far off to tell who they belonged to. But one thing was sure they could not be Jean's or belong at Grand Terre. Never had she seen the village react to any of their incoming vessels in this frantic manner. It was very clear an alarm had been sounded.

She knew not a ship could come or go that Jean was not told of. His network of spies covered many square miles of territory and each could signal another, relaying the identity of any given ship sighted. This was how Jean knew quickly that the vessels approaching them were trouble and that they were British. He had sounded the alarm.

After months of attacks and great losses, the British had been pushed too far. It was deemed necessary that Barataria be destroyed and that the pirate stronghold taken, in order to protect their interests.

Jean and Gambi set sail each taking the best men they could get for their ships on such short notice. It was plain that a fight was about to take place and Tori could do nothing but sit on the verandah and watch.

The British were under orders and as such sailed in on the afternoon breeze, their sails full pushing them rapidly toward Grand Terre. Jean and Gambi met the intruders just past Last Island coming into view at the last moment. The surprise forced the British into attacking at once and they fought to win.

For what seemed like years to her Tori watched knowing only too well the carnage that was taking place on the decks of all the ships involved. After much firing from both sides and just as the sun was setting, letting the land breeze blow out to sea, the battle ended. Silence at last invaded the heavens. The booms of cannons that had echoed across the water ceased. The British could see that the fight was a losing battle and after suffering heavy damage and lots of casualties, they hoisted sail and taking advantage of the evening breeze quickly departed. Their attempt to dislodge the Baratarians had failed. It would be impossible to dislodge them they would later tell their superiors, who in return would consider other methods of neutralizing the stronghold.

That night Jean and Tori talked for many hours. The British had made the first move, something else that the three travelers had not known of. Never the less it stirred Jean and made him restless. He hated this cat and mouse game of waiting, and waiting for what he thought. "We shall go to town tomorrow. I need to talk to Grymes and maybe we could both talk to Cisco and Davis again. This waiting for something to happen is driving me crazy. I need to be doing something."

"I agree with you, and who knows maybe it will improve your mood to be with friends and away from here for a while." She tried to smile at him to let him know he could open up, instead he turned from her and softly spoke.

"You had best rest my lady tomorrow will be long and hot." He talked no more and shortly his breathing became regular and deep. He had fallen asleep exhausted from the fight with the British. She soon slipped into a fitful sleep laced with dreams of battles at sea, a sea that was as red as the blood that flowed from the ship's decks. Jean who had only pretended to sleep, lay awake wondering if today had been the first sign they had been waiting for. And if so, then from now on out things would never be the same.

"I got your message that you were in town and came as soon as I could. You know of course that Claiborne and his wife have joined Edward and Simone at the plantation. With them out of town you are relatively safe."

"I had been told that by Thiac. This is the reason Tori and I are here at the house and not hiding in the blacksmith shop, no?" Jean was glad to see his attorney and was anxious to hear the long awaited news that he had to tell them. "Now tell us before we go any further, just what is this news that is so important. I know," he laughed, "the Governor has forgiven all and I am no longer wanted." He was laughing, making a joke and yet hoping at the same time.

"No such luck I'm afraid. Now don't go getting all worked up," he could see Jean's mouth tighten and knew only too well how his moods had been swinging back and forth. Tori had kept him up-to-date bless her. She had sent him regular letters which Thiac himself had delivered.

"Look you two, I will come right to the point and believe me you are not going to believe it, so here look at this for yourselves as I explain how it came into my possession." He handed the will over to Jean, who shared it with Tori. As recognition crossed his friend's faces he started the tale of just how it had all come about.

"And that is how she left me, sat in my office with that paper in my hands. I tell you I got good and drunk that night but not before securing the will in a very safe place where it has been until this evening. You do realize that we can go to court as soon as you want and take back what is rightfully yours. You should be able to take possession of the plantation and the townhouse as soon as the document is verified by the judge. Then my friend, the Gentleman pirate can settle down and become an honest citizen, a fine plantation owner!"

Jean laughed and Tori could hardly believe what she was hearing. She could never picture Jean Laffite as a plantation owner no matter what Grymes was telling her; she knew better.

It was Jean who spoke to Grymes. "John, you know you make it sound so easy, so simple that it tempts me my friend. But how am I to go to court and fight for this when I'm a wanted man. And how may I add, would it look if the States Attorney was to suddenly be standing at my side as my attorney. No, I'm afraid that this matter will have to wait for the time being. You shall have to place this back safely and we will handle one problem at a time."

Grymes looked shocked and dismayed. Of course he had known that it was almost impossible to act right away, but anything could be worked out and he had his word to keep. "Jean are you certain? I can leave the States Attorney's office and represent you. We can fight this and win. I can take on a friend of mine, another attorney. My associate and I would become your official representatives. He's very clever. Far more gifted than myself in many areas. With his talents and mine, we could get the charges dropped. There are ways you know."

"I thank you for your offer. Might need to take you up on that offer one day but for now I have my reasons to ask you to stay in your position. In so doing you will better serve me and this city. You'll have to trust me on this." Grymes nodded his head. "I still would have loved serving Edward and Simone the eviction papers. Did you know that they would be out on the streets with no damn place to go and no money except the small allowance left to Edward. Simone forfeited her income when she remarried and she sold the townhome as you know. It would have been such sweet justice to see that pair get what's coming to them."

"And you will." Tori said, "I for one want to be there also when you tell them. But Jean is right. We have to wait a while on this. We have our hands tied for now, and to tip them off that we have Leone's will, it just might spoil any chance of winning in the future." She frowned at John and then turned her attention toward Jean. "I agree with Jean we have no choice but to wait. Too many battles at one time tends to weaken one, right?"

"Well I may not understand what you are talking about or what you are doing but then just knowing that you will act one day shall have to be enough for me. I will see to it that the will is placed safely away and should something happen to me, then it will be returned to you. And now if you will excuse me, I do have other matters to take care of. I hope to see you both soon, maybe dinner one night?"

Jean walked John to the door and Tori sat thinking. The plantation was theirs and with it the lake had once again become within reach. Had Jean thought of that. Was that the real reason he did not want to fight for their rightful ownership?

Nothing could have been further from Jean's mind. It never occurred to him once for he had far more pressing worries to deal with. The evening was now clear and safe for Cisco and John Davis to join them. He needed to talk to both of them and once again see if he could extract any further details that could enlighten him on the events ahead. Then he had that problem as to how to get his brother Pierre to come back to Grand Terre with them, so much to do and so little time.

Nothing was solved in the short visit one that would have been extended had it not been for the return of Edward and his party. They had come back to town early and thus once again unknowingly caused Jean to head back to his home base. Once there, his frustration built and his need for work grew. Like his brother who had refused to join him in at Grand Terre, he became ever more aggressive and daring. It seemed to Tori that he was pushing his luck too far and one day early in October his luck it seemed ran out.

Jean had felt the need to be at sea and Tori not relishing the idea had elected to stay at the house. It was to be a simple shipment of goods taken up the waterways toward New Orleans. Everything had progressed like always and in the cool of the clear sunny autumn day Jean relaxed. The first part of the trip went uneventful and now after transferring the contraband to a smaller boat they slowly pushed their way through the marshes.

Without warning, a shot rang out and before anything could be done, Jean found himself fighting a platoon of dragoons headed by the Revenue Officer Walker Gilbert himself. The surprise attack had caught him and his men off guard and quickly they lost control of the boat and its contents. Jean was not about to allow any skirmish to be lost, especially where there was merchandise involved. He and his men fought back this time ready and more than able to take on the platoon. The fight was short and bloody, and when at last Jean had the boat back in his possession, one of Gilbert's men lay severely wounded on the shore. Jean fearing that his men, who were thoroughly worked up and blood thirsty, would do more, ordered them to push off. He left Walker Gilbert and his men in the swamps empty-handed to fend for themselves and never looked back.

When word reached the Governor of the skirmish, he was once again furious, and petitioned the State Legislature for help in destroying the pirate stronghold. Then he waited for a reply, one that he was sure would be in his favor. October turned into November and still no answer came. To him it was obvious, it was time to enlist the Mayor's help and anyone else he could think of.

So it was on the 23rd of November 1813, Edward and the Mayor and a few major merchants along with their wives, gathered for dinner. As always the subject of Laffite surfaced and Claiborne talked to them about his number one nemesis.

"Ah, but Girod my friend, as Mayor you do not have the problem on your shoulders as I do. You can always pass the problems, no matter what they be, on to the Governor's office." He laughed.

Everyone watched as the translator interpreted for him. When he finished, the mayor spluttered at the Governor's remark and was not above taking offense. He was however a intelligent man, one who knew if he was to be re-elected in the fall of next year, was going to need this American Governor on his side. He let Claiborne's remark slide but not to be forgotten.

Mayor Girod my friend, the Governor is just so upset by the news that comes his way." Edward felt sorry for the Mayor and besides he and Girod were the only Creoles present, and as such he felt obligated to stand by the man. "Each day it seems, news of Laffite's activities pour into his office."

The two of them were talking in French and as the Governor could not understand a word of what was been said, he turned to Simone for conversation.

"I myself do not know how you cope William, really I don't." Simone was coyly simpering into the Governor's face. She was setting him up for Edward, as well as plying information. "Pray tell me whatever became of your request to the State Legislature for money and men to destroy the settlement at Grand Terre?"

"They did nothing my dear, nothing. But don't you fear, I unlike others," he flashed a look the Mayor's way, "shall not sit idle, while that damned man makes a fool of me. Did you know it has been told to me this very day my dear, that that man is actually in town? Yes, I was surprised myself to hear such information. In town and no one is lifting a hand to help apprehend him."

"Maybe I can be of some assistance there," said Edward. "It seems to me that you can now with witnesses to this last skirmish name the man outright. You could even offer a reward for his capture. That would I'm sure entice someone to take action. Even one of his own men, maybe. None of them have any scruples you know." He dabbed his napkin to his lips. Then looking around the table at the other guests he remarked, "Very good food this evening, but I for one have lost my appetite. Laffite has soured my stomach and I do agree with the Governor that something has to be done. A reward is the next best step." The group talked about this idea and in the end was convinced that it was the only thing to do Claiborne agreed.

"I will have the posters made up tomorrow and spread around town as soon as they are printed. With luck Edward, we may finally snare that sly fox."

"Why Governor, I think you give the man too much credit myself," laughed Simone. "You are the sly fox outwitting that horrible snake in the grass."

Everyone laughed and even the Mayor joined in after what had transpired had been explained to him. He was thinking that if Laffite were caught he could use the occasion to help his re-election. If anything went amiss, well it would be the fool of a Governor's blunder. Oh, he liked that better and he laughed even more at the very thought.

Jean had been at the blacksmith shop since arriving in town. Thiac and he had completed the selling of some merchandise and were sat sipping some wine in the afternoon sun. He had made plans to leave the next day and head back to Grand Terre.

Cisco had been on his way home, when he spied a crowd around the coffee house. It was way too late in the day for such a gathering and being nosy he made his way over to see what the fuss was all about. At first he caught only snatches of conversation and then the name Laffite and someone saying something about him being in for it. He pushed his way to the front of the crowd and found what it was they were all so worked up about. Posted on the wall of the front of the popular restaurant, was the notice from the Governor. It was dated November 24th which meant it had just been put up. He read it and then quickly turned and headed for the blacksmith Thiac to get word to Jean and Pierre.

Jean and Thiac were starting the second bottle of wine together, when the sound of someone knocking at the front came to their ears. The shop had been closed for two days now. Thiac it was said was putting in a large balcony iron grill, over in the American side. This had explained away any questions, as it was nothing for the shop to open and close at odd times. "I'll be seeing who it is. You best stay out of sight boss," he whispered.

Jean sipped his wine and smiled, "bet it's my brother. Have him join me out in the side yard."

"Yes boss, if it's him I sure will."

Cisco was about to give up, when the large wooden door gave a groan and creaked as it opened. Upon seeing Thiac's friendly face he pushed on in and spoke quickly. "Shut the door. I need to talk to you. I need to get a message to Jean and fast can you do it?"

"Well now," said a grinning face, "pends on how fast you be wanting it to reach the boss. If you like and it be real important like, well you could take it to him yourself."

"Don't be stupid man, I can't just take off and head down to Grand Terre but this is important, very..."

"Well then you had best do as old Thiac said and deliver it yourself." Jean was standing in the doorway to the side yard. He was relaxed, tanned and smiling as if nothing could bother him.

Cisco walked over to him and the two embraced. "What are you doing in town? I could have sworn you told me that you and Tori would not be back until it was safe for you? Nothing has changed in that department you know. That's why I'm here. Look, I think we are both going to need a drink on this one. May I join you?"

"Go right ahead," Jean pointed outside to a couple of chairs sat in the small garden area. On a table was a bottle and as they headed outside, Jean looked back at Thiac. "One more glass is needed, we have been joined, our party grows." His humor was in such high spirits that Cisco almost hated to dash it so soon.

Once outside he and Jean sat down. "So do tell me, what is so damned important for me to know. If it's about the skirmish my men had with Gilbert a few weeks back I already know. I was there." He was laughing, had a bit of fun there, hard time getting the men to leave though. I take it from the look on your face it is not. Well what is it?"

"You have a price on your head. The Governor has named you and put a reward out to anyone turning you in. The posters are all over town and still more are going up each hour. It said you grievously wounded one of Walker's men." Cisco took a long drink of his wine and Jean slowly refilled the glass listening closely as Cisco went on. "It went on to say, that anyone helping you, is as guilty and then it said, get this, five hundred dollars would be given to anyone delivering you to the Sheriff of the Parish of New Orleans.

"Thiac go out and retrieve one of these posters Cisco is talking about. I want to read this for myself." He was no longer laughing, a thunderous look had clouded his eyes, which seemed to darken as the storm inside grew. "Cisco my friend, I think the time has come for us to pay a social call on John Davis and his fine establishment. Thiac forget going out. I will read this so-called reward poster for myself. If he thinks for one minute that I'm going to run and hide any longer, he is gravely mistaken." Jean was past reasoning and even though Cisco worried about what he would do if someone tried to make good on the Governor's offer, he could think of no way to prevent Jean from marching out the door.

Once outside and walking toward the United States Hotel the two instantly became aware of the looks and stares from many of the Creoles that saw them. Jean Laffite it appeared was not impressed or afraid of the Governor's reward. He was openly strolling the streets of New Orleans and many would tell of how he even stopped to read the reward proclamation himself.

"Jean my man I really don't think this is very wise of you. Standing here as if nothing was wrong, reading your own warrant for capture." Cisco reached up and took down the paper and folded it up neatly handing it to him. "May I suggest that you read it when we arrive at John's. Besides, I have an idea that you will no doubt find amusing," he pointed at the reward sheet now held in Jean's hand. "Put that in a safe place, we will need it before the night is through." He was all but dancing with joy. "I tell you Jean I would love to say that what I'm about to suggest was my idea but then I'm not sure. It's just so damned confusing. Come on man, don't just stand there we have work to do and boy are you going to enjoy yourself." He slapped Jean on the back and smiled one of his infectious grins.

Jean had seen his enthusiasm before but never accompanied by such uncontrollable excitement. He found his foul mood lifting and his curiosity peaked.

They continued their stroll to John's and many more fine citizens of the city crossed paths with the pair. It became only too clear to them both that many were admiring his indifference to danger. They openly laughed and talked among themselves about his nonchalance and even a few called his way, smiling and offering their support. No one tried to take the Governor up on his offer. The reward might as well have not been posted as far as all the effect it was having.

John was told right away that Jean and Cisco had arrived and rather than greet them himself sent word to Cisco that they join him in his suite. He had read the proclamation earlier and he too had an idea as to what should be done about it.

"John can you believe it? Have you heard? Jean give him the copy. Come on man let him see it." Cisco could hardly contain himself.

John laughed at him. "Steady on there. I take it you are referring to the Governor's latest and greatest. There is no need to show it to me. I have already read it. The point is Jean, what are you going to do about it?"

"You can't be serious?" Cisco laughed. "I know just what in the hell he has to do. What he did do, if you get what I mean? You do know don't you? Hell John, don't tell me I finally know something about our Jean here that you don't?"

John smiled at Cisco. "Oh, I doubt that very much, I see from your face that you know about the counter offer?" John was laughing as well as Cisco now and Jean found the whole situation just a little more than irritating.

"If you two would find the time to let me in on your little plan, I would be ever so happy to sit and listen." He tried to sound stern but seeing the two friends all but celebrating the poster, he found himself being caught up in their enthusiasm.

"You might well indeed sit and listen." Cisco pushed him down in a chair. "Jean my friend you are not going to believe this one, but we do know exactly what it is you are about to do. You are going to have this here reward rewritten. You are going to post them all over town." He was laughing so hard now that he found it hard to go on talking.

"What Cisco here is trying to tell you Jean, is this," John broke in. "In our time the story is told of how you posted a reward, this time with William Claiborne being the one wanted. You offered fifteen hundred dollars for his delivery to you at Grand Terre." He too was laughing hard now. Cisco holding his sides added, "You sighed your name to each one of the posters and it drove the man up the wall."

Jean loved it. He found the humor in the situation to be just what he wanted. He could see the Governor's face all red and bloated as he was told he was a wanted man. Yes, let him feel for a while what it was like. "You say that I did this?" his face was full of mischief.

"Indeed you did and the people of this city enjoyed the joke as much as you. If I remember correctly it defused the whole situation and soon the reward for you was forgotten." Cisco looked toward John for confirmation on this.

"I can't tell you much other than that," John added. "I do know that no one was able to collect either reward because as far as I know, nothing was ever done. I can tell you this," he had stopped laughing and spoke in a much more serious tone, "one of those signs we were waiting for, telling us that we must start to think about what is ahead of us all. Well my friends, this is one. History it seems is playing its hand as it should. The cards have been dealt and we are all playing the game now."

Cisco stood dead still for the first time in an hour and looked gravely at both his friends. "I did think of that. I mean is it our idea to put the other reward out or was it just because of history and such? It does get fucking confusing at times."

"I don't think it much matters. The point is, if you follow our suggestion Jean, then history goes on as it was written. If you chose not to, then it is rewritten. What you do from now on out is very much going to affect far more than just this." He held up the poster.

"Jean could see what John was getting at and knew the gravity of the situation. He also knew that what they had suggested, was something that he very well might have come up with on his own. It was just too damn good to resist. If history said he did this then let it be so. After all who was he to rewrite what was already done? He smiled broadly at them both. "You two are far too serious for such a prank. I for one think that it is too good to resist. Now just how do you propose we go about getting this done?" He was laughing and really enjoying himself.

"Pay backs are a bitch," laughed Cisco seeing that Jean had agreed to go ahead.

"You should know Cisco," added John. "Well, it will be a long night and much to do. Let's not sit around, let's get rolling."

Two days later the City of New Orleans rocked with laughter and the people just like John and Cisco had predicted had taken the two posters as nothing more than a joke. What else could they do? Each day they would hear about the

Laffite brothers walking the streets openly with no one attempting to stop them. The Governor on the other hand was not to be seen. He had become the laughing stock of the whole affair. Jean had a sense of humor and an open defiance that the Creoles could admire. Their so-called Governor and his proclamation were nothing!

Claiborne was far from amused when he got the news of Jean's counter-offer but before he could let the incident really rile him, other pressing matters came to his attention. The dispatches from Washington were not good. It was becoming ever more clear that the British would attack New Orleans but the Federal Government had its own hands full. They would not be sending help to the far off Louisiana. Claiborne was left to deal with the worry of how to protect his city and state, along with dealing with Laffite. The pirates were one problem the British and their possible invasion were another. Separate enemies for now but what if Jean and his men were to join forces with the British, he wondered? What then?

## Chapter 25

Jean and Tori had decided to spend Christmas with friends and family instead of by themselves at Grand Terre. The small gathering Christmas eve, included Pierre and his quadroon mistress Marie Louise Villars, Dominique You, Cisco and Marie and a small assortment of young children, most of whom called Pierre papa.

Tori and Jean enjoyed the laughter and excited squeals of joy, as each of the children was given a gift and sweets. Dominique doted on them all in turn, showing a softer side, that not many people would ever be aware he had. Always a favorite of the children, he was at times, almost smothered by the tiny giggling admirers. One young man however, had always stood above them all in his affection and tonight was no different.

Young Pierre Junior who was the spitting image of his papa, sat with the older Dominique for most of the evening. His face filled with admiration. His eyes spoke of a trust he felt toward his Uncle. The child was handsome, with features so much like his father, that no trace of his interracial background showed to Tori's eyes. It seemed a shame she thought, that such an adorable child, was doomed to live under the shadow of his black heritage. As if that was not enough, he had to add to that, the fact that his papa had chosen to leave his mother and take another woman. And then there was the small factor of Laffite, a name both loved and hated, it all seemed somehow too cruel.

Tori watching the younger Pierre, felt her heart close tight, as she thought of her own son and what could have been. Dominique would have had two very big admirers, instead of one, sat on his lap this evening.

Laughter from across the room drew her attention away. Pierre and his mistress sat on the floor playing with the youngest child, a chubby, happy rollicking toddler. The two of them were helping the baby walk and laughed as each step amounted to an even greater distance covered without falling. It was very evident to anyone watching them, how very much the two were in love and seeing that so clearly for herself, she understood how it was that Pierre had chosen to do what he had.

Unlike her Jean, his life was far more complicated than she could have ever dealt with. He was a married man with children, a family he very seldom saw, but took care of. Leaving them to live in a fine home with his father-in-law, to him had seemed the only workable solution. Then there had been his first mistress, who was responsible for the two young children that sat with Dominique. Tori frowned. Pierre tried to see as much of these children as he could, but they were being slowly pushed aside to make way for his new life. Young Pierre's father had left him, his mother and sister to live in the care of friends. And now in love, maybe for the first time, he had started yet another family with Marie. Just a shame so many lives had to be disrupted and hurt, for him to reach where he was today. It amazed her still, how no one complained and how it was all just accepted as normal. Nothing to anyone seemed wrong or out of place. Not his wife, nor his father-in-law made a fuss. His first mistress did not like what had happened but would never complain and his new love worshipped him. Jean only laughed about his brother and his lifestyle, saying it is his life not mine, and Dominique never commented one way or the other. After all, this sort of thing was commonplace, so why should he? Tori looked away. Some people never learn she told herself. She just hoped that Pierre had finally settled down.

The young Pierre and his baby sister Marie, who was nearly four, were the first to leave. Adelaide arrived at the door but refused to enter, choosing instead to wait outside for her two children. Tori wondered if her decision was out of pride or hurt, possibly both. Pierre had been sensitive to her choice and not pushed the issue. Instead, he sent a Christmas package along with the children and when they had gone, turned back his attentions to the love of his life. Once the older children had left, the evening started to quickly wind down and within the hour the house was left to five very grateful adults.

Dominique and Cisco swore to each other, that children were only enjoyable, when you knew they could be given back to their parents. Jean had laughed at this remark and reminded Dom how he had tried so hard, only a short time ago, to convince the young Pierre to remain longer.

A sly smile left the older man's eyes and a grin slipped across his face. "So it seems that you have caught an old fool in his true feelings toward one and I might add, only one child." His tone had changed mid sentence, taking on a more defensive air. Marie wondered if she was the only one to see beyond the man's facade. He always tried to laugh off the lonely shard of ice that held his heart. On the outside to many he was a happy old rogue, nothing more. On the inside, he was a tortured soul. Marie watched and felt his anguish, as his pain passed like a shadow of a cloud, been blown by a cruel wind. Dominique was so easy for her to read it almost felt like intruding, almost but not quite. She let herself feel and see his deepest thoughts. Thoughts, that he was fighting very hard at that moment, to hide from those around him.

He knew only too well that he himself would never have the joy of being a father. His heart would always have that agonizing void. It was an empty space, that always felt smaller by the company of Pierre's son. He felt Jean and the others observing him but had a feeling that someone was far closer that just looking. A feeling of which he could not quite put his finger on, but one that ran cold chills up and down his spine. Careful he told himself, taking a sip of brandy. He looked toward the fire pulling himself together hiding his secret ache. He would have to conceal his emotions more carefully he thought. After all they needed him and his strength not his weakness of self-pity.

Maire's eyes had filled with tears, as she closed her mind to Dominique's. His thoughts would remain his. The knowledge of his pain had been shared briefly. His anguish would never again be touched by her. Marie sat down by the fire and sipped her wine sadly, wondering what else the night would bring forth. The echo of children's laughter was growing fainter. The room had an air of expectancy about it. Cisco and Tori had been talking quietly, when Dominique realized that they were both looking toward the door every few minutes, as if expecting company. Even Jean seemed somewhat on edge and now come to think of it Dominique was sure that they were up to something. The old twinkle of amusement slowly crept back into the old sea dog's face. Dominique's longing for a life he would never know and no one guessed at, was safely put away for the time being in anticipation of just what was going on around him.

The room had just been cleared, the fire had new logs to burn and the wine re-stocked, when a loud knock at the front door sounded through the house.

Cisco looked up at Tori. Smiling to her and squeezing her hand, spoke none to softly "This is it then, here goes nothing." Dominique could only raise his eyebrow in a questioning action, as he knew better than to verbalize at this point. Whatever was going on he would no doubt find out in the next few seconds.

Jean stood, his back to the fire, facing the open doorway as the two men entered. Both friends together, in his home for the first time. They were all here now and he winked at Tori who smiled knowingly back into his face.

"Gentlemen, please come in and join our little gathering. It is about time that we all got to know one and other, as the friends we are. John for the sake of sanity," he spoke to Grymes while handing John Davis a glass of wine, "I think we shall have to call you Grymes. John here," he looked toward the other, "would be appalled, if I tried to call him Davis." Jean was ever the diplomat and had known only too well, which one should be referred to by his last name and not be offended by it. "Now as to why Tori and I have gathered you all here, I shall start at the beginning and explain. Dominique, for what you are about to hear and become a part of, I know you will hold it in your care as you would my life. I chose you over Pierre for reasons that will remain with myself." He held up his hand to silence him. "You have the wisdom and the courage my friend, to hear and become a part of all this." Jean turned and pointing his hand he gestured all around the room. "John, I gave you my word on a certain matter and it will remain so. You know you are as much a part of this by your involvement and knowledge as you are for any other reason. That is why you are here." His serious face broke into a slight smile. "And to add your musical touch which Tori and I do so enjoy." His voice light but sincere had eased the worried frown from John's forehead.

"Grymes my friend, you of course, have no idea as to what is going on here. At least if we have been careful enough you don't. I see by the look on your face, that is true? Well you are about to be changed for life and believe me, the role you are going to be asked to take on, will cost you." Jean's face had taken on a more distressing look. "We have talked about you and your upcoming role and it was decided that you have to be told all and brought into our confidence." Jean faced his friend who had the most perplexed look about him. He and Tori had told Grymes with Leone about her time travel but not mentioned it since. Now they would try again. "I am sounding like a fool here, aren't I? And you and Dominique need to be filled in, before we can progress. Gentlemen may I suggest you sit and listen and till all is said try to keep an open mind."

It was quiet in the room for the first time in nearly two hours. Grymes looked around the room at the people he called friends and saw that they truly believed in what they had told him. Even Dominique seemed to accept it.

Dominique having heard this tale before knew there was more to come, so he remained silent. This was getting interesting and he hated to spoil all the fun.

They were educated and intelligent all of them but time travel and history! "Look," Grymes's voice sounded strange even to himself, "I wish that I could just believe all you have told me. Jean, Tori, how can I put this? As incredible as it seems to me, it's not that I don't want to believe, understand me..."

Tori was worried; she had thought that Grymes would have accepted their tale and been ready to join forces with them without any reservation. He was however on the verge of sheer panic. If they lost his support because he thought them all crazy, it would not be impossible to go on but far more difficult. She looked toward Jean for help and found he was looking at John Davis.

Up until now Jean had kept his word and would continue to do so. They had not revealed his time travel, just told that he knew and believed in Tori and Cisco and had played a big role in getting Jean and his men out of jail. With so much else being told to Grymes and Dominique they had not even guessed at his real identity. Yes, his secret was secure but they needed his help in gaining Grymes as a major player. But to do that he would have to step forward.

It was that question in Jean's eyes that John could see. Was he going to step forward and risk his identity or hold back and risk his history? He had no real choice and he knew it. A small voice whispered in his head I told you so. "Tell one person and soon there is another and another. Grymes!" he snapped. "I think maybe you had better listen to them. And to me for what it's worth. I know what they are telling you is the truth." He stood and walked toward the attorney, standing inches away from him as he continued. "I know because I'm one of them. Not just a good friend. I'm a traveler in time. I'm not crazy or am I a fool but what I do have besides the truth is knowledge about you. I think maybe you and I had better take a walk and have a talk."

Grymes shook his head, "A walk won't be necessary, if you have to say anything, I think it best you say it here." He looked around the room and a grim smile came to his lips as he forced the next words out. "We are among friends." Within the half hour Grymes had been won over. He had many questions but after the initial inquiries the room fell silent once again.

It was Tori who stepped forward and raised her glass. "Friends, may I suggest that we get to the real reason why we are all here. It is nearly 1814 and due to certain events that have occurred and the knowledge we three have," she looked toward Cisco and John, "we can all be assured that this is the year that we must start to prepare for the British and the Battle of New Orleans."

John Davis raised his hand in protest. "I think maybe we should still tread slowly. I do agree that we all can start to prepare but none of us are really sure this is the year, are we? No, see what I mean. We have to go slow."

Cisco broke in at this point. "But the reward and the counter reward proves that history is going as it should. That is to say with our help. If I had not suggested the reward for the Governor, well it could have all been changed right then, history I mean. I say we move ahead, start to get things in place."

Jean raised his hand and looking around he spoke firmly. "I am not about to go around in circles again. We have gone over all of this before and we agreed that we would take things slowly. First things first. Grymes, you have been added to the group because not only are you one of my trusted friends but it seems that you have a big part to play in the upcoming events." Grymes looked puzzled yet willing to listen to what Jean had to say.

"You have told me this Jean. What I would like to know is just what is it I'm supposed to be doing. Or more important what is it you think I'm going to do?" Jean smiled at this question. He had been waiting all night to drop his bombshell and now seemed the appropriate moment.

"You yourself suggested what John. Cisco and Tori already knew you would. Let me explain before you say anything and you will understand. Not long ago you came to this very house and offered to become my attorney. You were willing to resign from the States position and represent Tori and I in the fight to clear my name and gain back a certain piece of property. If you remember I asked you to wait, that you would be of more help where you were. Nothing has changed yet in that department. However you will be glad to know that in history according to these three, you will become my attorney. However that is all we know at this time. Just what it is you did for me, for us, is still a mystery."

Grymes's face was stunned. He looked toward John Davis who simply nodded the affirmative and Cisco who was smiling like the devil himself. Tori was the only one who seemed to mask whatever feelings she might have on the matter and something told him that she was not revealing everything. He would talk with her himself at a later date and in greater detail, that was certain.

"So what is it you want me to do?"

"Keep your eyes and ears open and stay close to Claiborne and his cohorts. Nothing that you have not always done. Also, see if we can't get at least one more gentleman from the legislature on our payroll. The longer they stall the Governor and his requests to demolish Grand Terre the better. We need time right now." He turned toward Dominique who had sat listening with little or no comment. "Dom my friend, now for your role. I need you to start to move flints and powder. You have to place as much as you can in safe places in the back waters. Make sure that each stash is hidden and known only to myself, you and maybe one or two others of your choice."

Dominique smiled at this, "like the old days in France n'est pas? It will be my pleasure to play at your game, but Boss to hide as much as I think you would want me too, well I will need some distraction for the men. Something to keep them busy and the minds off what it is crazy Dominique is up to."

"I have thought of that. I shall have a large sale. The largest that we have ever dared to have to date. The posters are being printed as we sit. I have set the date for January 20. That should give you some time to ready yourself. All of the slaves that we have and any that come our way are to be sold. No more shall we take or sell." At this statement he caught his lady's eye and saw clearly the pleased smile upon her lips. He knew only too well how she felt about the selling and moving of slaves. That she should think he was doing this to please her suited him and he would say nothing to change her opinion. The real truth being, that if Grand Terre was in danger of the British or the Americans, then he wanted only his able-bodied men at the ready. He did not want to worry about the welfare of the blacks or of the chance of having loose slaves running about causing havoc. Then there was the plain monetary value to be gained by selling now. That money, he told himself, was needed to aid in the lean days ahead.

"So it is agreed that we proceed carefully and all keep our ears and eyes open and I might add," he looked toward Dominique when he spoke, "and our mouth's shut."

Dom shot him a hurt look, very over-exaggerated as he moaned and placed his hand over his heart. "Ah, Boss, you hurt me here. I would not. Never would I reveal not even to my lover on the pillow talk of love, what has been told here tonight. May the saints hear my oath now. Not even under the drink will I talk." He rolled his eyes toward the heavens, as if the angels themselves were listening to him. Then looking toward Jean he spoke in a tone so soft as to hardly be heard. "I can carry a secret as well you know!" Standing he walked toward the fire and bent to light his cigar from the embers. "Besides," he inhaled deeply blowing the blue smoke out into the room toward Cisco and John. "Who if I were to tell such a wild tale to would believe the raving of an old fool. I ask you all, who in the hell would even listen?"

Marie broke the laughter of the room as she walked up to Dominique and looking into his eyes hissed. "The devil himself would listen if he thought to gain by the information. I suggest if you don't wish him to come a calling, that the cat holds your tongue."

Dominique blanched at her mention of the devil and like a child scolded by his mother obediently nodded to her that he understood. There was something uncomfortable about her that he could not quite put his finger on but she did have the gift of sight that was sure. He knew only too well that not all her so-called powers came by the way of trickery and he intended to listen well to her advice. No devil was going to show his face anyplace close to him or what he knew.

Edward have you seen these posters? They're all over the town and everyone is talking and planning to attend. Edward where are you? Do you hear me? Simone was screaming from room to empty room looking for her husband. He had said he would be here to meet her and discuss the furniture she wanted to buy for the place. Where was he she wondered?

Edward sat in what would be the front parlor. He had heard her call for him and knew only too well what she was yelling about. It was that damned Laffite again and his sale. The brazen bastard was going to have the largest sale of exotic goods and most everyone he knew was planning to attend and buy. They thought of it in only one way, to gain cheaply what they wanted and to hell with how Laffite had acquired the merchandise. Not that that mattered right now. He had to deal with his wife and what he knew she was going to suggest.

"There you are. Didn't you hear me calling? Here look at this," she held out a sheet of paper toward him. He raised the same paper off his lap showing her he already was more than aware of its contents. "So I see you have one also. It is kind of hard not to pick one up isn't it? They are the talk of the town. The city seems to think it fair game." He was talking yet not looking at her. He was instead reading the list she had given him earlier in the day. "You have here," he pointed his finger to the list, "quite a number of items that will if ordered in the regular and rightful manner take months to obtain."

Simone's eyes narrowed as she looked at him, just what was he getting at she wondered?

"Are you implying something?"

"Simply that Laffite will have some, if not all the items that you require to furnish this place in the style you want. It could be outfitted in a matter of weeks not months that's all." He looked at her knowingly.

"You mean to tell me, that you're willing to line that man's pockets with gold? Just because you can't wait to have the place furnished. I thought you wanted him destroyed as much as I do. You actually want to tell me you wish to support him and this sale," she was waving the paper in the air angrily. "How could you?"

"Now don't go getting yourself all upset until you hear me out. And don't go acting the upright citizen with me. I know you better than you know yourself. You can't stand there and tell me that you had not planned to suggest we go ourselves to purchase a few things now can you?" He looked her straight in the face and watched as the guilty color rose across her cheeks. She spluttered to say something, but knowing that she had been seen through and would make even a bigger fool of herself, she simply shut her mouth.

"I thought not. Now if you don't mind, I will tell you what I have come up with. I think you will find it mutually beneficial to our needs. We will end up with merchandise and Laffite will end up hanging himself." His sadistic look of joy was spilling forth as he hatched yet another of his evil plans.

The day of the auction started early. Dawn's light found many camped waiting for the bidding to begin and still others by foot, by horse, by any means they could were arriving steadily.

Tori had been allowed to come to her first ever auction and was amazed to see such a mix of people. Plantation owners from Mobile and still further away had come to purchase slaves and merchandise. While many of the finer citizens of New Orleans came to buy luxury items like silks and furniture.

That Jean had so much and such a variety amazed her, not to mention the way in which it was sold. Many items sold right before her eyes, gold changing hands even before the auction started. Jean's men were everywhere and even though it seemed to her that items could be simply stolen, she took comfort in the knowledge that Dominique assured her it never happened that way. Who after all would have the courage to take from the boss, he had asked laughing?

The surroundings reminded her of a day at the fair. Food was being sold and drink was readily available. Children ran and played among the largest objects of furniture, while their parents inspected the items. Still others played at games while some of the adults who dared would try their luck at the odd game of chance.

Dressed like a boy and with her hat pulled down low, she was able to walk amongst the crowd unnoticed and unbothered. It amused her to listen to the ladies in particular, many of whom openly spoke of the handsome Laffite and how charming he was. She was smiling to herself, after overhearing just such a comment when she recognized the voice coming from behind her. She stood still pretending to look at a item and listened even more carefully to what Simone was saying.

"Are you sure all the items we want are safely on the way home? After all we don't want them to be confiscated as evidence now do we? Edward are you listening to me or not and just where are the Governor's men anyway? I thought they would be here by now."

That was all she needed to hear. Quickly she made her way over to where she had last seen Jean. He had to be warned and the sale stopped before it was too late. Damn that Edward and Simone, would they ever leave them alone she wondered?

Jean saw his lady pushing her way frantically toward him. The look on her face told him something was very wrong and he excused himself from the small group of ladies. They had been haggling over the price of an English silver tea service and continued to do so even after he left them with one of his men.

"Jean," she was very upset and panicky as she grabbed his sleeve. "Simone and Edward, here, and I heard them talking and" she had to stop to gain her breath. "You have to call off the sale and get out of here now. Save some of this quick." She pointed at the merchandise all around them. "Edward's purchase is safe on its way. He will get to keep his stuff but you will lose yours. The Governor has his men on the way." Was he smiling at her? He was damn him. Did he not understand what she was trying to tell him?

"My lady come over here and let me explain something to you." He pulled her away from the crowd to a secluded spot. "My you do look ravishing when you are all worked up even dressed as you are."

Tori stomped her foot and hit him on the chest hard. She was about to hit again, when he caught her hand in mid-flight and pulled her close to him laughing as he did so. "I think you had better calm yourself down, or you are going to giveaway your disguise and such a nice disguise it is I might add." He had patted her rear with his hand and looked around her shoulder admiring the view in breeches.

"Jean there is no time for foolishness," she slapped at his hand, "we, you have to get out of here before you are caught."

"And what makes you think that I will be caught, huh? You think that I would hold such a sale without having precautions?"

"Well no, I thought you would have some. But Simone told Edward that the..."

He kissed her hard on the lips quick and pulled back smiling. "Did you know I love you more when you have that angry flare about you. It makes my blood run hot and my mind crazy with wanting you?" He saw her flush a deeper red, then tears of frustration pricked her eyes. He would have to tell her it was cruel to keep her worrying unnecessarily.

"My love, you have no need to worry your little head or your large heart about my safekeeping. I will not stop the auction as there is no need to. I will however send some of my men to take back the shipment that those two think is safely on its way. Call it a lesson for all the trouble they caused me this morning."

Her eyes narrowed. "What trouble is that?" she asked not too sure she really wanted to know.

"I had a run in with a few of the Governor's men early in the morning. My men knew of their whereabouts long before they were within reach of here. I personally met them to persuade them to give up on their mission." His face went grim as he continued. "One of the fools did not want to listen and one of my men acted too hastily. He shot and killed the man." The look of horror on her face as his word sunk in scared him. He was no cold blooded murder and would have done anything to change the event. "If I could have stopped it, believe me I would have." His hand took her face and held it looking at him as he went on. "Two other men were shot but not killed before I got everyone under control."

"Jean this is not good. Let go of me," she pulled his hand away. "You know this will mean that you are wanted for murder. He will stop at nothing now to get you. Damn you Jean. You might have given Claiborne and Edward the ammunition they need to really come after you full force!"

Quick relief filled his soul as he saw that she was more worried about his safety than angry at what had happened. "You need not worry about that either. Without proof of what really happened they can do nothing. None of his men there this morning, will talk against me or my men. It was just an accident and that is what will be reported."

He smiled so gently that she was not sure if she had seen his lips curl up in a grin or not. Then she looked at his eyes that seemed so serious, she could see the deep lines that ran out at the corners deepen as he frowned.

"Neither will they be coming here." Now she really did look horrified. Had he killed them all to silence them?

Confused at first by the look upon her face at this last statement, he laughed out loud as he realized what she was thinking. "It is nothing like what your face tells me you are thinking. I simply sent them back home to New Orleans with their pockets filled with trinkets for their loved ones. They are very happy and contented men believe me." He hugged her to him, and could feel her body shaking as he held her close. "Nothing is going to happen to me. After all I have a battle to win, n'est pas? You seem to keep forgetting that fact and I keep reminding you." He held her for a few more seconds, then pushed her away. "I have a sale to finish and you have some shopping to do. Now smile, think about Edward's and Simone's faces when they know they have been outwitted once again."

She laughed and cried at the same time. "I think I've had enough excitement for one day. Thinking about those two right now is too much. I do admit though, I think they got exactly what they deserved. She is going to have a fit you know? Poor poor Simone!" she giggled. "That picture is better than any shopping. I'll just enjoy it and wait for you down by the boats." She looked deep into his eyes and in her soft sexy voice the one that seduced him with images of what she was really implying, she asked. "I take it we are still going back to Grand Terre tonight?"

"That we are my lady, maybe sooner than you know." He flashed his dark eyes. They spoke volumes as he gazed at her. It had been months since he had put his emotional needs before business but not today, today he was going to put his lady and his love for her first. His men could just as easily finish up the sale for him. He had more important things to attend to.

Edward sat sipping his strong coffee listening to the conversations that were going on around him. He was in no mood for company and especially that of his wife. More than once that morning he had thanked God silently, for the brief stay in giving her the news about their shipment. When she realized that all the merchandise they had bought would not be delivered, instead it was back with that filthy swine, she would be impossible to calm down. He shook his head at that thought and gave a slight shudder at the next. Simone would sleep for a few more hours yet and by the time she was up and about Edward hoped to be well out of her reach and wrath. He had taken the easy way out he knew that. Writing her a message had been the simplest way around a difficult situation. It was not that he was a coward he told himself, far from it, but damn it to hell he was just in no mood to hear again, how much she wanted that man's head!

Edward sipped his coffee au lait and sneered as he listened to the conversation at the next table. They spoke of Laffite in almost endearing terms. A man that even now, after killing and wounding the Governor's men, was considered a fair and caring individual. It made him sick to his stomach to listen to the fools stating how generous Laffite had been. They went on and on about how he had loaded the soldiers with gifts instead of killing them, and had sent them home safely. No one spoke of the injured or the one that was killed. Edward wanted to scream at the top of his lungs, to shout out that Laffite was not a hero. He wanted to make them see the truth, that he was nothing more than a cutthroat who had bought the soldiers off. That was all he had done! And he had gotten away with it. He stood up and left disgusted. He would pay a much needed visit with his so-called friend. Claiborne had once again failed to stop Laffite and Edward was growing very tired of the stupidity of the man and his office. What kind of a Governor was he anyway, he asked himself? He would have to apply more pressure and get him to act now. Surely in the wake of what had just occurred, he mused, while it was still fresh on everyone's minds, the Governor should petition again the States Legislature asking for the funds to form a militia. They needed a military to oust the thieves and murders from their stronghold. Surely the statesmen would have to agree to that now? How many more letters from the Governor could they ignore, he wondered and why was it that all requests made involving the Laffite's fell on deaf ears? Was it their way at getting back at the American Governor? Would it have been different if he were one of them? No, he doubted that. Well they would have to listen now, this time they had no choice but to act. As for himself he would never give up on the Governor he just would not.

Edward had come very close to the reason why the American Governor got nowhere with his petitions. Claiborne's continued pleas fell on a uncooperative group. Again and again they promised to listen and to come up with a solution, only to turn around and do the opposite. The American Governor was treated as if he were a man to be simply tolerated and no more. He had no power and little or no control of what was going on around him. Without their support his hands were tied and they liked it that way. He was their puppet and they pulled the strings of running the city any way they thought would benefit them. It felt good to have some kind of control over the Americans and their stupid interference where it was not wanted. Most of all Jean who was one of them, kept the Americans in their place. He was to them a true symbol of defiance, always done in such a honorable manner of course. Knowing he was driving the Americans and the Governor wild, only added to their joy.

The Laffite's continued to ship their goods into the city. Most of the time under armed guard and at night. Yet many knew that he and his men could just as easily move anything they wanted day or night and not be stopped. The waterways and the purse strings of the city belonged to Jean and everyone knew it. Many besides the Laffite's were profiting from the enterprising deals but still many more mostly the Americans were not. Claiborne was caught in the cross-fire. The State Senate was openly hostile toward him. The citizens of the city called him a tyrant and a fool. The American merchants were demanding something be done and Edward was always around adding fuel to the fire.

In the spring of 1814, Congress repealed the embargo and non-importation laws but New Orleans had her financial hands tied behind her back. The city banks under the strain, suspended payment and about this time, word came that the French Emperor had fallen from power. England was now free to turn its forces toward the United States and wanted Louisiana back for her ally Spain. The Creoles, who held no loyalty to the Americans had begun to talk about becoming independent. The whole city was openly laughing at the Governor and his continued failings at apprehending Laffite. Pushed to his limits Claiborne set out to choose a friendly Grand Jury, chosen from American merchants and bankers. Held in secret, they called witness after witness who all swore to acts of piracy by Jean Laffite and his men. Claiborne finally got what he wanted as indictments were drawn up against both the brothers and two of his lieutenants.

These pieces of paper," he shook them toward Edward, "will be the end of that damned man and my humiliation. Now we will see who will dare laugh at me!"

"William before you do anything, may I add a small suggestion, one that might be prudent." Edward was going to be cautious and very sure that they had the edge on things. "Before we, excuse me, you, send out word of what is written there," he pointed at the papers in William's grasp. "Well why not act first and then tell the citizens of this city what the Laffite's have been charged with. We don't want those two to slip out of town and into hiding now do we? Believe me that is exactly what they will do if they get one sniff of this."

"Point well taken my man, and I'm in full agreement with you. I will have a platoon of my finest leave immediately to apprehend those bastards once and for all. And this time they will be held and not be given any chance at bond or escape. We finally have them I tell you. Tonight they will be caged up and we will celebrate!"

Jean and Tori were home relaxing, when the news of Pierre's arrest reached them. Dropping everything they both fled into hiding slipping from one safe house to another, until they reached the attic at the blacksmith shop. Thiac had closed shop after a platoon of dragoons had searched it from top to bottom, but worried that they would return any time.

"Boss, Mizz Tori, it ain't safe here now for you two. I ain't one to tell you what to do, but I think it best if'n you's head out of town as soon as I can get me two horses ready for you." He did not wait for an affirmative answer but turned and left to see to the animals.

"He's right Jean you know he is. This is one of the places that they will keep searching until they get you. Look, there is nothing we can do for your brother at this point but we can prevent you from getting yourself thrown into that hell hole with him."

"I agree with you, but neither can we just ride out of here in broad daylight. Claiborne is no fool he would not have arrested Pierre if he was not confident about catching us both. The roads will be heavenly patrolled, as well as the river I'm sure. We have to wait until dark at the earliest, but waiting here is no better." He was pacing up and down, already he felt confined, the place was a trap and he knew it.

Tori tried to soothe his agitation and asked him softly the one question on both their minds. "We have to find a new place to hide then, but where won't they look?"

No sooner was the question off her lips than realization flooded Jean's face. "On Rampart! We will go at once to Marie Villars. My brother's mistress will take us in and be only to glad to do so." He grabbed her hand and pulled her to the stairs. "Thiac leave the horses," he called out, "we are walking."

"How you be doing that?" A very puzzled male voice called back.

"On two feet just like anyone else you fool," laughed Jean.

Thiac met them at the bottom of the stairs looking very perturbed. "I knows how you walk boss. What I mean is how you going to escape to the camp when you on foot?"

"We will take the horses later. I'll send word after dark where you are to bring them. Now my lady are you ready? We best move and move fast and pray to God that we are not seen."

Marie had got word about her beloved Pierre and was besides herself. Her younger sister had tried to tell her to stay calm and that she was sure the Jean would have his brother out of jail very quickly. But Marie pregnant with their second child and due any time was not so sure and could do nothing but sit and stare out the window or pace frantically back and forth. She saw Jean and Tori long before they got to the house and rushed to the door to let them in.

"Jean do you know anything about what they have done with my Pierre? I'm so worried. But thank God you and Mizz Tori are safe."

"Marie thank you for letting us in. Jean thought that it would be the best place for us to hide for a while. We will leave out the back if he see's anyone coming for us." Tori turned her head to look back at Jean who was watching out the window. She had deep lines that ran across her forehead, lines of worry that would stay with her for many months to come.

"Don't you fret yourself none Mizz Tori. Jean is a fine and good man. He wouldn't do nothing to hurt me or the children." She smiled at the little one playing quietly and stroked her large round abdomen as she talked. "Pierre would want to know I took care of you both and I know that Jean will take care of him too. He won't be in that jail long I know he won't."

That night when Jean felt safe enough, he sent for Grymes and after a short talk between the two, it was decided that he and Tori would stay put for a day or so. It was very unlikely that they would be found at Marie's and more likely to be caught if they tried to escape. That the so-called Grand Jury had found them guilty of crimes of piracy was the last worry to Jean. His first was obtaining his brother's freedom.

Two days later the news came. "It is of no use for you to risk getting caught while we try to get him out. Bond has been denied and they are holding him in the top cell chained I might add, and with full guard. So there is no chance of breaking him out either. This could take some time to fix and I think after talking with Livingston that it can be arranged if we both work on it for you. What

I'm saying Jean is this, I plan to resign my position this time and take you on as my client. Is it agreed?" Grymes had been straight to the point and the point had been sharp.

"Jean," she whispered. "It is history and I think this time he is right. You have no choice if we are to get your brother out and you know that. John did not know about this Grand Jury, which can mean only one thing. He is suspected of a connection to you already. His spying days are over for you."

"Jean only nodded his head. He stood and clasped his friend in a bear hug and then kissed him on both cheeks. "It is done then. You are sure my friend? To become my ally at such a time it will not be easy, no?"

"You leave that to me. As for Livingston he is with us full force on this and he can be trusted to work hard. A better partner I could not have asked for. He is experienced and his knowledge of the law is outstanding. He is highly regarded as you know and his reputation speaks for itself. We have talked long and hard about you and your circumstances and he feels as I do. You are no pirate and the charges should be dropped. We will fight this case and win, you wait and see." He sounded so sure that for a second Tori felt as if it would be so. But then she had an uneasy feeling that anything could happen and not necessarily the way she thought it would.

"As for my spying days well let's just say I still have an ace up my sleeve." He smiled and then he walked toward Tori. "It is time you took this man of yours out of here to safekeeping. I'm sure the roads will be patrolled but you only have to ride a short way until the river and freedom." He kissed her on the cheek. "Keep safe and I will get word to you as soon as I can." He spoke to her then in a very gentle tone. "Don't worry, we will have Pierre out soon and this too will pass." Somehow his words sounded hollow to her ears and looking at Jean she could see he felt the same way.

News of the States Attorney's resignation and his new position representing the Laffite brothers spread as fast as a wildfire. Edward only laughed at the foolish American. He could do nothing this time. The pirate's days were numbered and with one out of the way the other would soon follow he was sure. Claiborne had gained some of his former status back among a few but still had a long way to go.

The court room was packed. Pierre was there standing between Edward Livingston and John Grymes looking very sure of himself and his legal representatives. Whispers had filled the air when he had first entered and the people had seen for themselves, what up until then had only been rumored. He was indeed shackled, the leg irons had jangled as he walked, or more like shuffled to his chair. He had been held for six weeks now and prison life was beginning to show on his face and take its toll on his overall physical appearance.

The new District Attorney did not let that stop his onslaught explaining that he and his brother had slipped bond only the year before and he was a high risk prisoner. Doctors had examined Pierre at the prosecutor's insistence and found that Pierre was weakened but in no great danger of becoming gravely ill. He was to remain in his cell with one small change in routine. He would be allowed to walk free of his chains once a day. For the second time since his arrest, bond had been denied and the judge had the trial date set. The prisoner was to be escorted immediately back to his cell where he would remain until his day in court. The judge's gavel sounded, putting an end to the day's proceedings. The room filled with a buzz of disbelief and shock. He was being treated like a common criminal or worse still. Imagine a Laffite especially a gentleman like Pierre, having to endure such harsh conditions and he being in such poor health.

The general mood of the court was turning against the new States Attorney and it deeply angered the man. Looking over toward Grymes and Livingston his face flushed with rage as someone called from the back of the room, "American pigs." There was silence as the caller went on explaining to all that to treat Laffite with such disdain was nothing short of abuse.

"It is a perversion of justice I tell you, handled by a stupid ignorant baboon." Some laughed while others angrily supported this last statement.

The States Attorney had had enough. He turned his attention to John. Playing to a packed crowd, he openly charged Grymes of having been bought off with pirate's gold and having chosen to take that path, lost all honor in so doing. A smug satisfied look covered his face. Let them take that and think on it he thought happily.

Grymes had visibly been shaken and still another hush fell over the people, as all waited to see what would happen next. John's integrity was something that he held dear along with his reputation as a honest lawyer. Money had never been the issue nor would it ever play into his practice of the law. To stand accused of such an outrage was unthinkable. With cold calculating eyes and a voice that was laced with contempt he faced his accuser. "You sir have gone too far in your opinions of my character. To do so in private would have cost you a blow to your foul mouth. To stand there and accuse me in front of these fine and upstanding citizens, many of whom are not only clients but friends, well you will have to pay. I will not stand for such a slanderous attack on my integrity, both as an attorney or as a man." He walked toward the man in slow long strides, his steps sounding as they crossed the polished wooden floors. "I demand satisfaction sir. You will have until this afternoon to think upon what you have done." His eyes were cold and calculating as he stared at his now opponent. "We will duel in the style of true gentlemen. Gentlemen like my client, who will I am sure, be only too happy to make me a loan of his dueling pistols." He could see the man's face drain of color and thought for sure that he was about to offer him his apology for his outburst. "I will expect you at sunset. My man will deliver the directions as to where we will meet." With that he turned and walked through the people who parted in silence as he left.

Grymes may have been an American but in that one act of dignity he had become one of them. The whole Creole population would for the next few hours hold its breath and await the outcome.

Cisco quickly followed John outside the courtroom and was at his side before he left the building. By the time the duel took place he had become John's second and witnessed the whole ordeal. Never having seen a duel before, he found the whole procedure intoxicating. Later he would explain to Tori how the whole event was surrealistic to him.

As the sun slowly set over the field and the huge moss covered trees, Cisco had called out the paces for the duel. His excitement far outweighed his concern for his friend at that moment and it was not until the true abhorrence of the pistols firing at each other that rationalization took hold. He held his breath as in slow motion he saw John lower his hand and drop the gun to the ground. John's face was like stone as he stood staring at his opponent.

Cisco followed his gaze and saw two men standing over the man. He was moving and crying out in what could have been a mixture of pain and anger but at least he was alive. The duel was over in seconds, and satisfied that his honor and reputation was restored, John joined Cisco and they headed for Davis's establishment.

Word of the duel and its outcome even reached Pierre in his cell. He smiled weakly, as he was told that Grymes had wounded his opponent, who would carry the bullet and the pain with him for the rest of his days. Justice he thought, was maybe not so blind after all. A small glimmer of hope accompanied this thought. With the man severely injured, he would not be able to meet the trial date. That could be good for him, for it would allow more time for his defense and maybe even his release from the hell hole he was in. He knew his health was suffering, regardless of what those doctors had said and with it his mental state was sliding. No matter how he tried depression was taking hold, as sure as the chains around his ankles. The long hot summer months were intolerable to many unlucky enough to be held in the Calaboose but to Pierre who was ill and embittered it was like a death sentence. He did not know how much longer he could hold on under such conditions.

Grymes and Cisco decided that they had to meet with Jean. Livingston was working day and night on their case but to no avail leaving Grymes no alternative but to turn to Jean and his connections. It had become obvious to all involved that Claiborne was not going to be reasonable in this case. Pierre had weakened over the summer months and now came news that the British and Americans were well and truly at war. Fighting had broken out up north and as the days slipped by, to Cisco and John Davis it became apparent that they now knew the date of the Battle of New Orleans.

"It is settled then we ride for Grand Terre and decide with Jean and Tori what to do. One thing is clear we have to get Pierre out of that place and soon." Grymes looked very concerned.

"You worry too much don't you? I'm not too worried about Pierre he will be fine. If Jean wants him out then he will just damn well go and get him mark my words. More legal work for you." He slapped his leg hard laughing at the glare that hit him from Grymes. "Look we need to meet with Jean and Tori and discuss many things. So let's just do it. Besides I love it down there. Anything is better than this place right now anyway."

Jean and Tori had kept to themselves safe in the confines of Grand Terre. It was a waiting game that they played these days. Wait and see what would happen with Pierre. Wait and see what that idiot Claiborne would do. Wait and see when the British would make their move, and through all this keep a close eye on the business.

Dominique had succeeded in his mission undetected and known only to a chosen few. He had hidden a large amount of both powder and flints. With that job finally finished he found himself with time on his hands and nothing left to do. His answer to his idle hours was to sail off on a voyage that he swore would be profitable.

With Dominique gone and the days long and hot, Tori found herself growing even more restless. She knew about the news that had been delivered to the State Legislative telling how the Capitol house in Washington had been burned. The President and his wife had barely escaped capture. It was only a matter of time now before the British would come to make their offer to Jean and this was what worried her. She knew that in history Jean fought with the Americans but would he choose to do so now?

Jean had become very hostile toward Claiborne as result of the treatment of his brother, not to mention the disbelief of how he was looked upon by many. Accused of being a bloodthirsty pirate and forced into hiding out like one, was humiliating and it infuriated him. He was an educated privateer, successful and soon to be in great demand. If it had not been for his lady and her so-called history lessons he was not so sure that he would side with those who did nothing but scorn him.

Grymes's and Cisco's stay with Jean and Tori was full of long discussions both of the British and of Pierre and his predicament. Jean had decided long before the end of the first meeting, just how to handle the problem with his brother. As to the British and their arrival, it was back to the waiting game. For just under one week the four friends enjoyed Grand Terre and all that it had to offer. Each night's meal was elaborately set before them served with the finest wines. The china, crystal and silver shone in the soft candlelight.

Never had Grymes expected or guessed at the wealth of his client. The so-called pirate's hideout was so luxurious that it rivaled many of the finer plantations along the river outdoing most of them by far in its furnishings alone. He would remember and talk about his visit with Jean for the rest of his life. Always saying that the man was a true gentleman who knew how to appreciate the best life had to offer.

Jean had been seen discussing with Cisco in earnest, something that he would only refer to as a small problem. "It is nothing to worry your head over and I assure you my love. You and Grymes have no need to concern yourselves." With that statement and knowing how stubborn he could be the matter seemed closed. The worried look on both their faces made him weaken slightly as he hugged Tori closer to him. "Look I will tell you this. It is just a small surprise for Pierre's Marie. She needs some cheering up, what with the new baby's arrival and her love kept in chains. I will explain it better as soon as I'm sure it can be obtained." He smiled at Cisco who had that same look of mischief Tori had come to beware of. However, before she could delve deeper into whatever was being cooked up, Jean changed the subject by producing two small heavy wooden boxes.

"And now Grymes to the matter at hand. You will no doubt be wanting some of the money that I owe you. Fees due and a small amount to aid you in all your upcoming hours of assistance." Jean lifted both lids revealing the contents therein.

Both Cisco and Tori inhaled audibly as the gold and silver coins within caught the light. John sat down looking stunned and then laughed out loud demanding a drink.

"Yo, ho ho ho, it's a pirate's life for me!" Sang out Cisco who immediately shut up when he saw the look of thunder on Jean's face.

"Your twentieth-century humor leaves a lot to be desired. I suggest you think of a better song or remain silent." Jean was not kidding. He pushed the boxes toward John and snapped, "I think that should cover things for a while. It amounts to around twenty thousand apiece for you and Livingston," he shot another meaningful look Cisco's way. "You and Cisco can leave in the morning for home. I will make arrangements for you both to travel up the river by boat. It will be safer. Longer way around but I don't think you are in any big hurry to return are you?"

"John put his hand in one box and lifted some of the gold coins. "No not at all, no hurry here. In fact, I had hoped to stop along the way back. Have to check in on a few clients you know what I mean?"

He had asked the question but not directed it at anyone in particular. It was Cisco who answered. "Yes I know exactly what you mean, and I can't agree more." He reached to touch the other box and the coins only to have the lid slammed shut by Jean. "I bet you do. Now don't you go getting any ideas."

"Who me? Cisco tried to look shocked but there it was again, that look that spelled trouble.

"Oh don't you two worry he's with me you know and I'll see to it that he keeps out of harms way and out of my cash." John dropped the other lid, winking at Cisco as he did so.

Later that night in bed as she was drifting off to sleep, Tori spoke to Jean. "I tell you those two are up to something. You saw it as plain as I did. What do you suppose it could be? Then there is that little matter between you and Cisco. I swear are all the men in my life keeping something from me. I ask you are they?"

"Seems that way," he teased. "If however you come closer here I have something I would never keep from you."

"Honestly Jean, I don't know if you are just the horniest man I have ever known, or if you are just trying to change the subject on me once again."

"A little bit of both I think my lady, now come here..."

"You mean to sit there and tell me that the two of you left Grand Terre just over two weeks ago? That you had yourselves a gambling spree all along the Mississippi until you lost how much?" John Davis's face was a cross between frustration and pure amusement but the look he now shot Cisco's way told of another emotion, anger.

"Actually it was the entire sum Jean paid him all twenty thousand. You have to admit when you come to think about it, its totally outrageous. Ah but what a time we had. I'm telling you if I died right now I would be happy." Cisco looked as if he had been on the binge of his life and by the sound of it to John Davis, he had done just that.

Cisco he could understand but John Grymes, never. He had thought that man quite levelheaded that was until now.

"Oh for God's sake shut up Cisco, if you don't I might very well help you damn well die. Believe me right now it would not take much to oblige."

Cisco shut his mouth and looked at his friend. Hell, he had not lost the money why was Davis so mad at him?

"Look you two, while you were both having the time of your life the rest of us have been trying to hold down the fort so to speak. All hell is about to let loose around these parts and if that's not bad enough, I got to see Pierre last week and I fear if we don't find a way to get him out of that place soon, we might as well kiss his ass good-bye."

Grymes straightened up at this bit of news and looked at Cisco as he asked Davis cautiously to explain. "Just what do you mean by that?"

"I mean that the man is going to die. If you can't get him out right now, at least find a way to get the chains off him. I'm telling you that we have to find a way to deal with this and other matters just as serious. It has come to my attention that the Governor is not giving up on Jean and he is gaining support in his quarter."

"I bet, let me guess who, Edward for one." Grymes almost spit out the name.

"As always, but more, I have not had any means to really find out what it is they plan next. I have really needed the two of you here and now you sit and laugh at the wonderful time you had at Grand Terre and the trip home." He stood and marched across the room and spun around facing the two men. He had no need for words. His situation, their situation had become only too clear to everyone.

Grymes shook his head and stood up looking at the two. "Gentlemen, I think we all know what we have done and not done. That is irrelevant now." He started to chuckle as he continued. "I must say that I for one will never forget the days past. I hope that one day soon I will get to tell you the whole tale. All in all," he stopped to clear his throat, "there is work to be done and the time to play is over. I will leave at once to see Livingston and see what else I can learn from a few trusted friends in Claiborne's camp. I'll come back this evening at which time we can all put our heads together." He walked to Davis and reached out his hand, "Till later then." Davis took his hand and firmly shook it.

"Glad to have you back. Till later then?"

Cisco was relived to see the two of them make amends. It would take him longer he knew to get Davis to forgive his involvement in the grand escapade...

Two weeks had passed by and Grymes had worked relentlessly on Pierre's case. Both he and Livingston had built what they thought to be a strong case in their favor. It should have been clear cut. The chains should have been removed; they were not. The date was now August 10th 1814 and after much discussion, it was decided that Jean should be sent for. It had become clear that if they were to ever get Pierre out of the Calaboose, it would have to be done other than through the law.

All of them knew that it was very dangerous for Jean to even think about coming to town and to add to their problems they also realized that they could not run the risk of meeting with him themselves. The problem had seemed one that could not be solved so easily and so it was that Grymes found himself revealing his long kept secret.

"I do have a solution to just how we may get all that we need. We have to get word safely to Jean and he to us, right? Look what I mean is this, what I'm about to reveal to you three must stay with you." Grymes looked at the men who sat with baited breath and then looked toward Marie Laveau. She was another story, he had the strangest feeling that she already knew what he was about to reveal. He watched her face as he continued. "You all know that for some time I have had my source within the Governor's compound, that I have always had my ear to the door so to speak. Well, it is more than just knowing someone and it is that someone that I will now have to reveal to you. She has agreed to this so I am not breaking any confidence at all." Marie's face was still not showing any emotion but her eyes flashed and she barely nodded her head toward him. She did know, that was for sure, but she would never have told. "I have been involved with a certain lady. She has been in my life and is my life. There is no easy way to put this and you may be shocked but please do not judge her to harshly. She loves me and is willing to aid us in our cause." He held up his hand toward Davis. "She does not know everything. To put it simply I have told her only that we are trying to help America and need Jean for that. Look the lady is married and that is why I have kept our affair secret."

"Oh shit! it can't be." Cisco began to see the light. "Damn me, that's who has kept you busy all these years how many has it been two?" Davis was grinning.

"Now wait a second both of you. I have not told you her name as of yet."

"There really is no need to is there?" Laughed Marie. "It seems quite clear to us all that the lady in question is none other than the William Claiborne's wife herself. Is it not?"

The look on Grymes's face confirmed it. The lovely Cayetana was the woman he was involved with. It was true and he just beamed as he could share this fact with his dear friends at last.

"My God man, you are either stupid or very brave." Cisco was slapping him on the back. "You sly old fox you, and right under the bastard's nose too. I thought I was good but this takes the cake."

"Cake or not and quite an odd way to express the situation, a saying from your time no doubt? But the fact is she is going to be our go between. I have arranged for her to visit an old friend down south of town, far enough out to be safe for Jean. The family are also good friends of Jean's but will not be told of the connection between their guests. I have to protect my love and my client. It will be up to them, or I should say to Cayetana to make contact and relay all. I know she is capable, after all look what we have accomplished all this time under everyone's nose," he laughed.

"Brilliant, it's so fucking brilliant. Are you sure I didn't think of this myself?" Cisco was overjoyed and it showed in the way he bounced around the room. "You have outdone yourself and I can't wait to meet this lady and tell her a word or two myself..."

"You shall have a long wait my friend, on that I can assure you," laughed Marie.

"By this time three days from now if all has gone as planned we should have word about how to proceed. Jean will be well informed as to what is going on with us and with Claiborne and his scheming," said Grymes.

They all raised their glasses and toasted the new couple. "To John and his lady," Cisco laughed.

"Here, here. To the happy couple and may they one day truly be together," added Davis.

No one heard Marie as she whispered in Grymes ear "they will..."

"You mean to tell me it worked. Oh do give I'm dying to hear." Cisco loved it. They had been called to John's office supposedly on hotel matters but now sat listening as Grymes told them the news.

"She said that it was late afternoon when Jean arrived and shocked her hosts with his unexpected visit."

"What happened did they try to get him to leave?"

"If you will remain silent I will tell you. Now where was I? Oh yes. Cayetana said she almost burst into fits of laughter as she watched them quickly cover his identity. Jean thank God, was traveling in disguise and she pretended to not recognize him. They were left alone after dinner and it was then she was able to tell him who she was. Not just the Governor's wife you understand? She was able to convince Jean that she was telling the truth and that we had arranged the meeting. Don't ask me how she did that I'm still not clear on that myself. Anyway, the point here is we got our message to Jean and he got his to us. They parted ways the next morning. Much to the relief of their hostess I'm sure. No one even suspected them and just to be sure Cayetana has told a few of her close friends, in strictest confidence you know, that she is, after much thought, convinced that she met the Pirate Jean Laffite. Oh my, how she tells them in great detail, what a true gentlemen he is and how handsome!" They were all laughing.

"Cisco, you and I have some business to attend to. I suggest that we all pay close attention from here on out. According to Jean's letter, and Davis agrees with it whole heartily, things are about to begin. We already know Claiborne has been receiving letters as well as writing them. Letters pertaining not only to Jean and his situation, but letters telling about the British and so forth. We all agree that the time is very close now. No, it is upon us." He looked gravely toward each of them. "We must keep our wits about us. It is imperative that any and all communications between the British and Jean, and Claiborne and whoever be intercepted and put in the right hands. From here on out we are at war! What each one of us does in the next few months will affect the outcome of not only Jean's pardon, Pierre's release but," he looked at Cisco, "our history and the way it has to go."

No one spoke. They sat looking at Grymes, each deep in their own thoughts. It was no longer a game for it was now a matter of grave consequences, of which there could be no mistakes. One slip-up on their part would be devastating.

# Chapter 26

September had been unusually warm and quiet. The summer storms had ended in the first few weeks of August and with them the humidity. Days felt more like spring, followed by cooler evenings and gentle sea breezes washing in off the tranquil gulf.

Ever since Jean's trip up river and his meeting with Cayetana, Jean had stayed close to home. Any further news from the city came by way of Jean's elaborate network of men, which he had doubled all up and down the bayous and coastline. Daily reports came in from all sources, most trivial enough to be ignored, some significant enough to be questioned.

Jean and Tori were well aware that three British ships had been spotted days ago off the coast of Pensacola and that rumors ran rampant among the populous, that the British planned to invade. Day and night the horizon was kept under close scrutiny until they had the news they knew was inevitable.

Both had been awake for hours, enjoying the splendor of the magnificent dawn. The first warm rays of the sun chased away the crisp morning air, and the need to stay tucked beneath the bed covers was wonderful. Like new young lovers, Jean and Tori had renewed their lovemaking with such a passion, that it had left them drained and contentedly basking in the afterglow when word finally came. Standing by the open bedroom door, Tori had listened to the message given to Jean and to his chilled response. Before he returned with the news, Tori was preparing herself for the meeting with the British.

"I see my lady has been listening at the door again. Nasty habit that." His face was anything but worried, how he could stand there and joke at a time like this was beyond her.

"And just what are you doing may I dare to ask?" he added.

"I have had a change in mind. I think it's best if I attend this meeting with you." She saw his eyes darken and his lips tighten, forming that stubborn stiff glare.

"Now before you say anything, hear me out. I know we thought that I should stay out of the way, but Jean can't you see, I'm needed. Besides if you plan to entertain these so-called officers of His Majesty's Service men who are expecting to meet with nothing more than a heathen pirate. Well wouldn't it be to our advantage to upset the apple cart? Think about it for a second. We know you entertain them lavishly and shock them with how refined a gentleman you are but add a hostess, more than a just a hostess, your wife!"

"No! he snapped sharply, silencing her speech and halting her idea. "I know that you mean well and that your idea has some merit." The sharp edge to his tone had softened as he took her in his arms continuing with his explanation.

"We discussed this meeting at length did we not? All of us went over what little you know about it. The fact that it is about to take place only goes to strengthen your case and show me that we have to play it out as close to how you remember it was written. Look my lady, was there any reference to a beautiful lady at this meeting, let alone my wife?" He looked at her tilting his head slightly, "You understand now? We can't afford to change history, to add or subtract in any one place. If we did, it could I'm afraid, alter the outcome. If I allow that to happen, time and history could sweep you from my arms." He held her close and could feel the slight shiver of her body as his implications hit her.

"But Jean, how do we know for sure I was not with you? Just because history did not mention me or should I say, just because we could not recollect me being there."

He squeezed her arms so tight in his grip as he pushed her back from him, that she actually winced. Still he did not let his vice grip release its pressure. She had to be made to understand and time was running out.

"I'm not going to change my mind on this and deep down you know it's right. In everything I have ever done in life I have always found it best to go with my first instinct and my lady my instincts in this matter are quite clear." He released his grip and walked over to his wardrobe. "I have very little time to dress for my guests. Will you assist me or not?"

She was beaten and she knew it. To try and sway him once his mind was made up, was like trying to change the path of an on-coming storm. His reasons had held some merit and she knew that they had all agreed on just how things should play out. At least most things.

"Tori my love," his eyes watched her as he pulled on one of his best shirts. "I love you more than life itself but you have to trust me in this. I will need a clear head to play the game that is about to begin and having you there would only distract me." His grin filled his face, "You are always a distraction you know?"

"Oh stop it. Your point is well taken and I give you my word I will stay hidden if you give me yours." She placed her hands on her hips, a sign to all who knew her that she was very serious in her attentions. "You are to come up here immediately. I mean the moment they leave. You give me your word!"

"You have it and more. Should I feel at anytime that I need your advice or counsel I will seek it." He had finished dressing and stood before her. "Well Madame do I look like the rogue you think I am, or do I present the image I require of the Gentleman Pirate?" He was laughing and obviously did not need a verbal answer for it was written clearly on her face. The sound of approaching voices below halted any further conversation. Jean simply raised his eyebrows in acknowledgment of his guest's arrival and quickly drew Tori in his arms for one last kiss. His lips pressed firmly against hers, his arms wrapped briefly around her and then he was gone.

Tori sat down on the bed resigned to the fact that for the next few hours, she was going to have to try and entertain herself or go crazy wondering what was happening downstairs.

Jean received his four guests in his study raising from behind his desk as they were shown in. Clearly he had them at a disadvantage. Not one of them could contain the surprise of their surroundings or of the image of their host. He chuckled inwardly as he surmised what they must have expected, compared to what they now encountered.

"Gentlemen. Monsieur Jean Laffite at your service." His face was calm, his voice friendly but his dark eyes, black as onyx, spoke volumes. Standing before them was a man who was to be reckoned with and judging by his surroundings, no uneducated buccaneer like they had been led to believe.

The officer in command stepped forward extending his hand. "Captain Lockyer, of His Majesty's Navy and may I present to you Captain McWilliams of the Army." This man quickly stepped up and shook Jean's hand, curtly nodding his head, "My pleasure sir." Jean greeted the two warmly. His grip was firm and his gaze was direct. At least he now knew who the two senior officers were in this game he now played. The two other lieutenants were introduced and greeted just as warmly but to Jean no longer holding any importance. They would be tolerated but of no real consequence to what was obviously about to take place. Jean decided that he was not about to aid his visitors in any manner as to why they were in his home. Rather he offered each a seat and returned behind his desk seating himself comfortably before looking toward Captain Lockyer.

The officer was carrying a pouch of some sort that obviously contained the letters that he had been instructed to deliver along with the British offer. Just how they would feel if they realized that Jean was well aware of the reason behind their visit and the contents of the package amused him greatly. He was so deep in these musings that it was the clearing of Lockyer's throat that brought is attention back to the meeting at hand.

"As I was saying Mr. Laffite. We are here to deliver to you an offer that I am certain you will find to your advantage sir." He patted the pouch on his lap and then placed it on top of Jean's desk.

Knowing full well what the contents of the pouch contained, Jean found that he was in no hurry to dispense with the business of discussing the letters or the British terms about to be offered to him. It would however be not only to his advantage but to all those involved for him to glean any other information his guests might pass on. He could over drinks and a meal coerce his present unsuspecting company, into divulging information that would no doubt be useful.

"Gentlemen, I do not know what the customs are where you are from," he lied. "But here on Grand Terre it is the custom to dine first and do business second. You would honor me if you would join me in my midday meal. Let me show you some true southern hospitality." He watched carefully the reactions on the two senior officer's faces. It was obvious that they were not adverse to the idea, nor were they tempted. Duty it seemed was to be their first priority. What they needed at this point was a slight push in the right direction. "In fact I will not take no for an answer." He laughed lightheartedly. Then with a far more threatening glare added, "To do so would truly offend me."

"In that case sir, not wishing to seem rude, we gladly accept your invitation to dine. I am sure many an alliance has been achieved over just such occasions and a bottle or two." The British Captain laughed and was joined by his fellow officers.

"Very well put." The glare had been replaced by his supposedly good humor. To look at Jean, one would have thought him to be thoroughly enjoying the conversation and company. His guests at least thought so.

Jean led them to the dining room, which had been set and ready for days. Tori had added each elegant touch to the room and table herself wanting to achieve the desired effect of opulence, without been imprudent. Had she been there to see the British reactions she would have known she had succeeded. To say they were stunned would have put it mildly Jean would later tell her.

Every detail from the table settings, to the food itself had been thought out carefully. The wines and brandies to be served were only the finest. The service of both, over the next three hours, would have rivaled the best homes and restaurants in the world.

Jean proved in conversation, to be not only a gentleman of high standing but one that was world-traveled and educated. It became clear to the Captain and his lieutenants that they had been greatly misled in the reports of the leader of this stronghold. They had found themselves a charming host instead of the blood thirsty pirate they had expected. Talk varied from the discussion of the artwork on the walls to the food and wine at the table. For at least half an hour Jean had guided the conversation learning about each of the men and their service to the crown. When the politics of the day had been reached Jean wisely guided the men from the dining room to sitting room. No matter which room they entered, the men were greeted with still further signs that they were dealing with a man nothing short of an aristocrat. They no longer talked at him or down to him. They found themselves addressing him as they would have a superior or man of a well-to-do family with connections. In short he had become respected and held in the highest esteem.

The hours ticked by for Tori upstairs. She had given up trying to stay busy by sorting her closet or tidying her room. It was a useless task and totally unnecessary. In the end she had decided to take a long bath and dress for Jean's return. With that now accomplished she sat in her chair on the verandah and waited, sipping her wine. The late afternoon was peaceful enough and the day's end would soon be on hand. Her most favorite part of the day, sunset, was only an hour away at most. One of the many song birds was sat in the large tree opposite, singing away, when it took off for what seemed at first no good reason. Then she heard the angry voices and the screams of protest. A strong English accent was demanding to be released, when still another just as loud Creole accent was calling for the spy to be hung, or turned over to the Americans.

Tori jumped to her feet. Just what had gone wrong she did not know, but she was damn well going to find out. Turning to head downstairs, she bumped right into Jean and his grinning face. Without even an explanation or one word he took her in his arms and kissed her long and hard.

Tori's mind was a swirl with questions, her impatience was growing rapidly, when just as suddenly Jean released her from his grasp and quite simply asked her for a glass of wine.

"Wine, you said? Jean have you gone quite mad or what? From what I just heard going on out there you had better explain to me fast what went wrong?"

"Nothing went wrong. It all happened just as you said it would. I have in my possession four letters all asking me to join the British against the Americans. For the last hour and a half I have been badgered, bribed and in the end threatened. It was all as you said and more. But one thing we did not count on was the need to buy time with these bastards and to how to get them to leave without suspecting they had been how do you put it? Ah, yes been snookered." He laughed at the word. "I must say I like the sound of that one. Well anyway my lady I decided that if I were to excuse myself for a short time and arrange for my men to drag them off and lock them up that would get them out of my house, don't you see?"

"No I don't see. How in the hell is that going to make them think you are considering their offer may I ask you that?"

"You may," he smirked. "God you're beautiful when you're angry."

"Just shut up and explain to me, or so help me God I will show you just what in the hell angry is."

"In that case I guess I have no choice. It will be like this. In about a half hour, long enough to scare the hell out of those four, I shall arrive and demand they be turned free. You see they came expecting to find pirates and did not. Now they have! I think they needed to see I was really the boss here. But they also need to think that I have to convince my men to join with me on the side of the British. If I had just agreed well they are not stupid. I will tell them I need two weeks to round up all my men and then I will get back with them. They will think they got out of here with there lives by the grace of God, luck and my help. They will not suspect a thing other than that. We will have our time to get the letters to Claiborne and he in turn will have time to do whatever is necessary to protect New Orleans."

"You amaze me you know that? You came up with all that just off the top of your head." She threw her arms around his neck. "Have I told you lately how much I love you?"

"Not lately, no. You may however be ready to show me when I return from saving four very scared by now, British officers." He slapped her lightly on her rear end and finishing off his glass of wine in one gulp, departed.

Tori decided it best to await Jean's return in the sitting room rather than upstairs. She wanted to read the letters for herself and discuss their next move. Her wait was not long and judging by the look on Jean's face all had gone as planned.

"I take it that your little charade has worked?"

"That is an understatement. Never have I seen four more grateful men row out in their gig, nor so fast. I tell you the size of the wake they left behind could have rocked my own ship the Misere."

"Oh Jean really, stop," she laughed. "You're making my sides split."

"Now why in the Lord's name would I wish to do that? Some of your sayings really are beyond me." He looked so perplexed that it sent another wave of laughter over her. Jean not grasping what she found so damned funny, turned and left for his study. Women he would never understand them he told himself.

Tori pulled herself together and taking two glasses of wine went to explain to Jean what had made her laugh so. When she entered the study she found him reading one of the British letters, while the others lay open on top of his desk. Picking one up she asked, "may I?" Without even looking up Jean nodded his head. Tori sat down and looked over the first document. It was nothing short of an appeal to the Louisianians to join the English against the Americans. She had a hard time understanding and following the rambling letter but could see how it would not be of much help in their getting Claiborne to listen to Jean. It had been hand written by a Edward Nicholls and signed on the 29th August. The second letter was also written by Nicholls, this one on August 31st. This one called on Jean and his brave men to enter into the service of Great Britain. It asked that they stop all hostilities against Spain or the allies of Great Britain. Jean was offered the rank of Captain and the promise of lands equal to his rank. All his ships and vessels would be placed under the orders of the commanding officer of Pensacola headquarters. It went on to explain how Captain McWilliams would answer any and all questions Jean might have and that Captain Lockyer of the Sophia would also be of any and all assistance he could.

Tori looked up at Jean who was still going over one of the letters, his face a mask of his emotions. To think he had read these letters in front of the British and maintained his composure only gave her a deeper admiration of him. Stop hostilities against Spain his sworn enemy. That must have made him want to laugh out loud. And to think of all the British ships that Jean and his men had taken over the past few years, and now they think just because they ask, he will stop!

Tori took a drink of her wine and picked up the third letter, this one written by the Hon. William Henry Percy, Captain of His Majesty's ship Hermes. He was by the looks of things the senior officer in the Gulf. The letter was to Lockyer and in short was an order for him to come to Grand Terre and talk with Jean. To persuade him to join with them and then to report back.

Jean had finished reading the last and forth letter and handed it to Tori, who took it without a word and read it. It had been written on September 1st and by Captain Percy. This last letter was the one that upset her the most. Captain Percy made it quite clear that if Jean and his men decided not to join forces with the British that all Jean's ships along with Barataria and Grand Terre should be destroyed. The total destruction of all around her was the price of saying no. The letter went on to explain that should they choose to say yes, the already-mentioned land and ranks, payment and full pardons awaited them. The problem became only too clear at once to Tori, that Jean was caught between a rock and a hard place. If they could not get Claiborne to listen, to believe the threat real and Jean's help genuine, then they would be left alone to face the British or worse yet join them.

She slowly looked up into Jean's face. His eyes so dark that she had no need to ask how he felt. Yet what he was thinking or planning did not show at all.

"You know my lady the fools actually believe that my men would follow me if I chose to join them. Now that is something that they are gravely mistaken over. More than half my men hate the British and no matter what they are promised, would take great delight in fighting them. The problem being, I am not sure as to just how many they will be taking on. I know you and John and Cisco say a couple of thousand but nothing other than a slight hint that a sizable force is on its way could I get out of them or these letters. I sat and politely drank and ate and fished for information and learned not much more than you yourself now know. I have bought us time for now and I am sure Captain McWilliams left here certain I would consider and join them. Time. Time is something I need more of and don't have." He sat back in his chair, rubbing his chin. "We have to move on this," he waved one of the letters. The time has come for me to write my own and to have them hand delivered to the right people. I'll start with one to John Blangue, a trusted friend, who just also happens to sit on the States Legislature. The other of course will be to William Claiborne himself, and the last will be to our new friends." He chuckled as he spoke. "The British. I have to make sure I can delay them as long as possible. The letters along with these," he waved the British documents, "will leave tonight and then my love, we wait, wait and pray that history repeats itself and the Governor listens.

Edward sat quietly watching and listening to the discussion at hand. It had become only too clear to him in the past half hour that he and Simone had been right all along. Laffite had paid off certain members of the States Legislature and by the looks of it he now knew the name of one at least.

John Blanque had received the correspondence early that morning and immediately taken it to the Governor's office. In the pouch had been four letters supposedly from the British, along with two from Laffite himself. Edward had no doubt that the documents that William now held in his hand were genuine and that Laffite was sincere in his offer to aid in the defense of the city. This however was not going to happen if he had anything to do with it and he could do quite a lot.

The committee that sat around Williams' office was one that Edward knew he could manipulate. It consisted of military advisers from both the Navy and Army, along with the Mayor and a few of the States Legislators. To sway the Governor against Laffite proposed no great problem, doing it in a manner that did not arouse suspicion was another.

"Gentlemen," the Governor's voice silenced the room, "as you all have now had a chance to read the letters and look them over carefully, I have a couple of questions before I make any decisions. First and foremost, are these letters before us genuine? And if they are is it proper that the head of this here fine State, should correspond with Laffite or any of his associates?" He shot Blanque a dark look as he asked this question. "Your input and opinion would at this time be gratefully received."

The room exploded, each man trying to make his own statement and thoughts on the matter known. To Edward who still remained silent and observing, it seemed that only two of the committee were siding with Laffite. The mayor, who in his opinion was a fool and sorely afraid of the so-called invasion and the Major-General Jacques Villere. Villere was adamant in his belief that the letters and Laffite were exactly what they seemed to be and that yes, the Governor should at this time consider corresponding with Laffite. He had William listening to his advice, while the other fools sat silent.

"William, Governor sir. If I may be so bold as to suggest a solution to this dilemma we have here." Edward had calmly walked to the center of the room drawing everyone's attention. "You have here a fine and upstanding committee. Representatives of the highest and most moral standing." He smiled toward each, including Blanque, who shifted uneasily in his chair. "No one here wants anything but the very best for our fine city and its citizens just as you yourself. It would seem to me that a majority vote could not be ignored, nor wrong in its advice. I therefore propose that a vote on the matter would put to rest any doubts one way or the other."

Villere was immediate in his response to Edward. He could see only too clearly the direction this meeting was taking. "It is my belief sir, that the letters are genuine and that Laffite and his men are very much needed. Should the British choose to invade us at this time we have little or no defenses available."

"That sir is just my point." Edward spoke softly, but firmly. "We have no real proof that the British do intend to invade now do we? All that we have is the word of a mere pirate and a few letters that could have been drawn up by the man himself. We even have a reason why he would concoct just such a ruse do we not? His beloved brother sits in chains as we speak, awaiting trial for crimes that could cost him his life."

"So true Edward, but surely we have to consider the fact that the man is telling us the truth. We have had warnings of the British and we are at war, or has that small fact slipped your mind?"

Edward remained calm, but his voice betrayed the anger he held carefully in check. "I have not let anything slip my mind sir. If you would hear me out I shall offer another thought on the matter. If these so-called letters are the real correspondence then they can only show us that Laffite is a spy. I suggest to you Governor that the man is playing you for a fool, while he aids our enemies. His stronghold, would if in the wrong hands, be of great military use. He is strategically placed and well situated. As you yourself know his camp is all but impenetrable. No, Laffite is not to be trusted and furthermore I think that he and his men need to be neutralized."

Villere was outvoted in a matter of seconds and the seed of doubt grew against Laffite rapidly. In everyone's mind it was not inconceivable that the pirate was capable of double-dealing and in league with the enemy. Patterson and Ross both of whom were anxious to attack Laffite's stronghold at Barataria insisted the Army was more than ready to do so at once. Was the Navy behind them they questioned?

Outvoted Villere had no choice but to nod his head in agreement. John Blanque and the Mayor could only look at each other in despair, while Edward smiled to himself. Things were finally going his way and he was certain they would continue to do so.

No one noticed the door to the Governor's office slowly close. Nor was it unusual for anyone on the outside to see Cayetana depart the building. Had they followed her, her destination might have raised a few eyebrows, but none did.

Under the pretense of a business matter to do with her husband, Cayetana was shown into Grymes's office. Once alone she was able to divulge all she knew.

"You are certain of this there can be no mistake?" Grymes face was filled with concern, for what she had just told him. If true, it meant he and Livingston had just run out of time.

"John my dear, I would never have risked coming here like this if I was not certain of what I had overheard. It is just so lucky that I decided to pay my dear husband a visit and that the door to his office had been left ajar, is it not?"

"That my dear is an understatement. What you have just told me is going to change many people's lives. There is something that I now have to set in motion. You my love must leave here right now before someone questions the validity of your visit. I suggest that just in case any questions do arise, that let us say your meeting here today was for a friend of yours. After all, you would never break a friend's confidence and I am obliged to remain quiet." He smiled into her face and saw only loving eyes looking back at him. How she trusted him and cared for him, it tore at his heart. "You would not exactly be lying in the matter.

Therefore I feel it the best explanation. I would never ask you to lie for me, or do anything that would be detrimental to yourself."

"My darling, you should not ever worry about such things. What I do or choose not to do will be up to me, and because of my deep and abiding love for you," she touched his cheek softly with her hand and stroked the side of his face, "I will always hold you and your happiness close to my heart. Please take care in whatever it is you are about to do and know that I will continue to aid you however I can." She stood up on tiptoe and placed a kiss on his forehead, then lowering herself down she gently kissed him on his lips. "I had best depart while I have my wits about me. I declare you do such things to my mind and soul as to drive me wild in my thoughts."

"Cayetana, my love." Grymes kissed her quickly on her mouth and pushed her from himself. "What you do to me is beyond words."

"Not beyond physical though," she laughed, her eyes dropping down to his erection.

"Why Madame, I have no control where my body and you are concerned. Now before we completely lose our heads you must depart." He walked behind his desk and sat down. "I love you and always will." His eyes spoke of this love as he called his assistant in the outer office to come and escort Mrs. Claiborne out. Then he set to work on the next order of the day, one he had hoped to avoid and now found impossible.

Cisco had been with John Davis when the message arrived that Mr. Grymes required an urgent meeting. Within an hour of Cayetana's visit, the two men had placed Jean's wishes in regards to his brother into action. It was a plan that had been hatched months ago and set into motion on that evening long ago at Grand Terre.

"Cisco are you listening to me? We have to get this payoff to the right men and now. We already have them in our pockets, now all they need is our gold in theirs."

"Just seems such a shame to have to turn this all over to the greedy son's of bitches when you and I could have had so much fun with it all."

"Ah, but we did. Don't you remember all the gambling on the trip home?" He laughed. "Such a tale we told and I for one shall tell it till my dying day. To have gambled away twenty thousand dollars on such a spree. Ah that my man is what dreams are made off." Grymes had a far-away look in his eyes and seemed to be relishing the tale that he had told so many.

Cisco found himself looking at his friend and realized that Grymes had told the story so often, that a part of him had actually come to believe his own lie. It had been a brilliant idea of Jean and totally untraceable. The people involved had been well covered and would never be found out. All that was left for him to do was pay them off. He stood and took the leather pouches in hand. Three of them, each filled with enough cash as to be quite heavy.

"I shall leave now before I get tempted." He tossed one pouch in the air. "I tell you it's not easy giving this to those bastards, and the only reason I'm doing it is for Jean. You will have the horses ready as planned?"

"That I will if all goes as it should, we will meet in just over two hours from now." Grymes reached out his hand and took Cisco's shaking it firmly. "Good luck and be careful."

"You be careful. You have to be seen in public, with high visibility for the next two hours."

"I will be seen, don't you worry. Now go, time is running short."

Simone had slept so deep and peaceful not to mention content. The smile that filled her face had not left her lips from the moment Edward had returned home the day before. He had been brilliant in his handling of the committee. Soon, very soon Jean would be joining his brother in chains but worse off as a spy. My how the grand fall, she thought. Edward was still sleeping next to her, his breathing deep and rhythmic. Half of her wanted to wake him the other wanted to just enjoy the feelings she was having all to herself.

Slipping from bed she decided to get their cook to make them a very special breakfast and then she intended to dress and do some shopping. Her home could have been fully furnished if it had not been for that damn man taking back what she had bought. Her temper started to rise at that thought. But then if he had not, she would not have had the delight in all the shopping she had been doing as of late. And she did so enjoy shopping. The drawing room was already furnished. She had seen to it that some of the pieces had been brought down from Leone's plantation house. Her plantation house she reminded herself. It was the kind of room she had always dreamed of having and enjoyed sitting in it for hours on end. This morning would be no exception, that was why she would have the cook set up breakfast in there. She did not care that it would be a problem to do so, just so long as they did it, so what!

Her coffee was already waiting for her and after she had explained what she wanted done next, she sent the small kitchen maid out for the daily paper. Edward did so like to read it while he had his coffee and she intended to spoil him today, a reward of sorts. She started making notes in her daily planner as to who she would see and who she would invite to dinner that coming weekend. Her mind kept slipping from her task at hand to that of what was sure to be the day's headlines. Laffite declared a spy! Her daydream grew and grew in its splendor as she sipped her coffee and grinned a wicked sort of smirk.

When the young girl returned with the paper in hand, she could hardly contain herself from snatching it up. On the stairs she could hear Edward making his way down to join her. He was whistling a tune and commenting to someone that breakfast smelled wonderful.

Simone took the paper and dismissed the child who took her leave as fast as she could. Even though she could not read, word was around town of the headlines and she did not want to be around when her mistress read what she already knew.

The paper was folded in half, the front page clearly visible as was the bold top line. One thousand dollars reward. Her hand shook slightly as she continued to read unable to tear her eyes away from the page.

Edward saw his wife standing in the drawing room reading the paper she held. She stood so still and was so intent that he was sure she did not even notice that he had entered. Looking at her the way she stood glaring at the article she was reading told him something was wrong.

Simone looked up slowly toward her husband and simply handed him the paper. Words could not leave her, it was as if she was going to be choked to death on what she had read and nothing was going to help. She could not even catch her breath and God help her the room had started to spin.

Edward fearing his wife was about to faint took her by the arm and led her to the couch, where he physically forced her to sit down. He then took the paper and read what it was that had so obviously upset her. Within seconds he was sitting next to her his mouth hanging open, his head shaking no.

"You can sit there and deny it all you want but you had better believe it," her voice was almost a whisper.

"If I believe this to be true, I tell you I will personally kill whoever is responsible for letting him out."

"Edward I wish that to be true. However you know as well as I, once again the Laffite's have got away. His money and his power have to be destroyed, if he is ever to be brought down. Don't you see that? You won't find out who he paid off, but mark my words that's how the bastard got his brother out. And you won't find him so easy to put back either. If we are ever to see Jean fall and I mean fall, he has to be rendered defenseless first. Take away his men, his money, his power and then his woman. I hate him do you hear me? I hate that he always seems to get what he wants. Well no more!" she screamed, her voice getting louder. "Not again. Not now, not ever!" She screamed the last words as she threw herself into her husband's arms.

He could feel her shake as she cried the tears of hate and frustration. Soothing her and making her happy was second to what he most wanted and that was just what she needed, Jean's destruction. "Simone, listen to me. I will dress and leave at once and see what is going on. Simone, please my love, listen." The sobbing started to slow as she struggled to listen to his words. "He is nearly ours, it is so close I tell you. I will work day and night from now on. Jean is already suspected to be in league with the enemy. Time is running out for him and soon your tears and my anger will have revenge. I swear to you it will happen."

In the coming days, Edward kept his word and stayed close to the Governor and his advisors. He was there when two days after Pierre's escape, John Blanque delivered yet still more letters. One had been intercepted by Pierre himself on his ride to Grand Terre. It was a British correspondence. The other was written by Pierre himself in which he too, like his brother offered his services. Then again three days later, dated September 10th another letter from Pierre at Grand Terre. This one asking for a reply as to whether or not the Governor would accept the Laffite's offer.

The letters fell right into Edward's plans. He continued to claim the brothers nothing more than spies. To Colonel Ross and Commodore Patterson his warnings about Barataria and the treasure it held, besides its strategic placement hastened their desire to attack the stronghold. Slowly Edward worked on the committee, who had decided to listen to him, to hold no correspondence with Jean Laffite or his associates. What Edward and now others were saying made far more sense to the Governor pushing him into the only decision he could see.

On September eleventh, before the light of day, three loaded barges, filled with soldiers and ammunition left New Orleans to join with six gunboats and the Navy. The destination was Grand Terre. The mission, capture Laffite and take possession of the stronghold before it fell into enemy hands.

Jean was up and dressing before Tori fully realized why. Panic hit her as he shouted at her to do the same. The air was filled with noise that made no sense at first. She could hear screaming and yelling but could not distinguish what was being said. She looked toward Jean, who in just a matter of minutes had fully dressed and was now frantically pulling on his long leather boots.

"Jean, what is it? What's going on?" Her voice betrayed her emotions. Her face was filled with dread.

"An alarm has been raised. It would seem that we have unwelcome visitors. In short my love, we are about to be under attack, if we are not already." His last boot slipped on his foot and he walked quickly toward the far side of the room where he always kept his weapons. Fastening his sword belt he looked anxiously toward her. "How long before you are ready?"

"Ready for what?"

"To get the hell out of here if need be." He snapped. Then seeing the flash of terror cross her face he softened his tone and added. "Sorry. It's just that until we get down there, we don't know who or what is going on. Something tells me our British friends have grown weary of waiting for my answer, and have decided to take matters into their own hands. If that be the case, then I have to get you to safety and try to keep this place from falling into the wrong hands. Now come on, and bring your sword just in case," he tossed her weapon toward her as he spoke. She caught it easily and headed toward the door, following Jean.

Before they got halfway to the shore, it had become clear that it was not the British that now threatened his home but the Americans. How could this be. He was stunned and for the first time in his life Jean was at a loss as to what to do. He turned to Tori who like himself stood looking at the force headed their way. Dominique appeared from nowhere, his emotions written clearly in his demeanor. He was furious at the pigs that now threatened him and his home. It hurt his dignity to think that they were insulting him in such a manner. Jean cared not how his first in command was looking at the situation, what he wanted from his lady was an explanation.

"You did not know of this" he asked her angrily?

"I did not. Do you think that I would have kept it from you if I had? Jean you know me better than that," she replied just as angry.

Dominique looked from one to the other and then stepped between them. "It does not matter now who knew what or not. The point here is being made very clear. The American pigs are about to take from us all that we have. Are we not going to fight to protect our homes, our men? Are you going to just stand and gape like a young fool? They have betrayed us, no? Look for yourself, look." He physically turned Jean's body so he could look back at the small span of water, and the flotilla that grew closer and closer. Six gun boats sat off shore all guns pointed at them. Safely behind them sat a schooner that Jean recognized as the Carolina.

Look close at the words on the white flag she flies. Do my eyes deceive me or does it say, Pardon to Deserters." He spit to the side? "I tell you now, we must fight, the men await only your command. Already we have ships armed and moving out but most are not manned and sit ripe for the picking." At that moment gunfire came from one of the small boatloads of soldiers headed for shore, quickly followed by a loud boom of cannon fire. Behind them, the front porch of Laffite's house exploded into bits and pieces.

Jean drew his sword, raising it in defiance. His face filled with rage, his voice exploding his order of "fight!" With the boom of yet another cannon, it was clear to him that the Americans were not there to talk but to destroy.

Tori grabbed at his arm, desperately dragging him back a few paces, screaming above the havoc for him to listen to her. "Jean please, you have to leave. Look I don't know what is going on here." He shot her a dark look that seemed to ask are you stupid? "Oh stop that. Of course I know what's happening, I just don't know why. I do know that you can't run the risk of being captured or worse yet killed. Jean are you listening to me? Do you understand what I'm saying? This was not in our plans. Something has either gone very wrong, or it was just not known to us. One thing is certain. You have to leave either way." A bullet whizzed by their heads making Jean pull her down low, out of the line of fire. Anger and pure rage at seeing how helpless the situation was filled his mind. He did not want to listen to her anymore about history and what he was supposed to do. Hell, it was his home that was under attack, his men who now fought and stood a good chance of being killed or captured.

Another part of his house exploded as it took a direct hit. The explosion threw Tori into his arms shaking and crying out. It brought home one very real fact. Her life was in jeopardy now. To see something happen to her, or to see her in chains if caught would destroy him.

"Jean there is not much time," she begged. Dominique who had listened to her plea, marched up to them both. "I will stay and fight, I must. You have to listen to her. She is right boss. You have to leave, you have no choice. If we win, then you will be back. If not, then you will be safe. Listen to me, I know it is hard to run, but sometimes you have to do that which you do not wish to do."

Another bullet whizzed by followed by a cannon blast that landed not far from their position, spraying sand and dirt all over them. His decision had been made for him. Without a word to either of them, Jean stood and took hold of Tori's hand, pulling her back toward the house. Dominique turned to face the invasion, putting the safety of his two dearest friends out of his mind. They would be long gone should they lose the fight and something in his guts told him that is exactly what was about to happen.

Tori hardly knew what happened. The past two days had become a blur to her. They had been lucky to escape capture unharmed and still luckier to have made it all the way to the blacksmith shop undetected. Now they found themselves hiding and hoping for news, with each passing hour the agony grew. Jean had sent his brother to hide with his mistress, and was able to relax safe in the knowledge that for at least a short time he would be taken care of. Tori and Jean kept themselves hidden in the small secret room above the shop, while Thiac kept up his work as usual. If they were found out, the chance of escape would be slim. However, after discussing their options, both agreed it was the safest place and the last place anyone would look. News was slow in coming. For days they sat waiting and wondering. As the time passed, Jean knew it could not have gone well for his men, he only prayed that those he cared about had not been lost to him forever.

Just about the time he could stand the waiting no longer, Thiac came up to bring them news that Cisco and friends would arrive that night to talk. They had told him only that Grand Terre was no more. Jean's face showed no recognition to this sad news his only reaction was to take Tori in his arms and hold her close. Thiac knew the pain he now carried but realized that as long as Jean had breath in his body he had fight in his soul.

Late that night in the dim lit room, the small group met. They would talk for hours and Jean would finally learn the truth about his home. All had been taken or destroyed! His own ships the Misere and General Bolivar, were among the vessels taken and now sailed under the American flag. Grand Terre had been completely destroyed; not a building was left standing. His own home lay in a pile of rubble nothing of value left in its charred remains. Of his men, he learned many had been taken prisoner but still more had escaped fleeing into the sanctuary of the swamps and backwaters.

He sat still and deep in thought, while the others sat and spoke in lowered voices. He had only asked to be told the truth about what had happened after they left and now that he knew, the shock of it had hit him hard. All he had worked for was gone, taken by those he was supposed to help. Just how he was going to be able to do that, without his men and ships, he had no idea. Even if he could get back his ships and weapons, it did not guarantee his men would fight beside him for the very men who had turned them from their homes.

Grymes looked at his friend and hated to add to his burden but knew that to delay the rest of his news would not make it any easier. "Jean there is one other piece of news that you should know."

Jean looked up, dreading what else he would learn.

Grymes wanted to give him some sort of hope, even if he felt at that moment that the possibility was bleak. "It's about Dominique. He is I'm afraid, one of those captured and brought into jail."

Jean chuckled and then broke into an all-out laugh he just could not help himself. He had been so sure that Grymes was about to tell him that Dominique had been killed, that to hear he was in jail, seemed a blessing and a huge relief. "Is that all? That my friend I can fix. Those walls have not done a good job of holding me or my men in the past."

"That might be. In the past is just that, the past. This time your men and Dominique will either swing on a rope or rot in a stinking hole, of that you may be assured. You have been lucky and had the financial backing to obtain freedom, to buy what you needed. That has changed. I hate to remind you of one fact, you have at this time nothing. You are broke!" He shook his head as he quickly added, "now don't go giving up, no sir. We have some plans Edward Livingston and I. I assure you, we believe that we can fight all this in the courts and in due process get most of what you have lost back. That along with a full pardon as you are guilty of nothing. At least nothing that they have charged you with. The same goes for Dominique, a privateer and pirate are two different entities completely."

"Grymes, I am sure you and Livingston have every good intention of helping me here but the problem is, as I see it, all of what you intend takes time and time my friend is something we just don't have. Cisco, John, I need you two to put your heads together along with my lady here and try to figure this mess out.

Just what are we supposed to do now? I know what I want to do but that and what must be done have to match, or much will be lost."

John spoke up first, his deep voice sounding calm and very much in control. "I know that we did not call the raid on Grand Terre. Let us look at that first. Just because we did not know of it, does not mean it did not occur. I believe we are still on track here. You will fight at the battle and Dominique will be at your side along with your men. Now that takes care of that problem. What we have to do is use all our heads and not panic. Grymes can keep an eye on the Governor and I can still keep my ears and eyes open as will Cisco and Marie. You two have to lay low and wait for our next move."

"You expect me to sit here and do nothing?"

"Just that. You have to get ready to meet with General Jackson, who should be coming to town some time shortly. Until then, we can only make plans one day at a time. We will do our part, don't you blow yours."

Jean hated the idea but could see that to act without knowing exactly where he stood would be foolish. He could, he thought keep writing his letters, and yes he did have to prepare just how to approach Jackson and what to say to the man. Everything would hinge on that meeting, a meeting that still had to be arranged. He knew that in itself would be a difficult task. He had so many problems yet to solve and many plans to make. "I agree with you. We will stay put, Tori and I have much to work out here and this quiet time may be just what we need in which to work."

Grymes breathed easier, as did Davis. Cisco looked at Marie, who through slit eyes, was watching each of them in turn. She felt great passion here in the room but no danger, nothing yet to indicate disaster.

September's warm days passed into October's gray and cold ones. The weeks had been filled with setting up a network of communication between Laffite and his lawyers and friends. In turn, Livingston had set up a way to get word to Dominique and the rest of Jean's men in jail.

Through the ears and eyes of Cayetana, they kept a close tab on the Governor and Edward. It had become clear to all that Edward was a driving force behind Claiborne's hate of the Laffite's. Not only that, slyly he stirred the Creoles and their high emotions and fierce loyalties, in a direction away from the Americans, every chance he got. To counter these destructive activities, Livingston held gatherings of citizens, urging their allegiance to the United States. Grymes formed a committee whose job it was to help the military authorities in suggesting means of defense. He could not sit on the committee himself but was able to place along with other well respected citizens, two close allies of Jean's. Edward Livingston and John Blanque, one American and one Creole. No one suspected a thing.

Meetings were held late at night at the blacksmith shop to update and keep Jean well informed. He was in contact with his men who had escaped and made their way to a place known as Isle Derniere, and they like those in jail had sworn, if needed to they would fight alongside their boss.

Cayetana had carefully and slowly started to work on her husband and his thoughts toward Laffite and the Baratarians. Undermining Edward was no easy task and slow going. Still she persisted with patience and cunning. She also now had her hair fixed on a regular basis by Marie.

It was via the Cayetana, Marie network that in the middle of November, Jean received two pieces of information. The first that the Governor had been informed by General Jackson that fifteen to twenty thousand British had set sail from Ireland early in September. Their intended destination was Louisiana. The second piece and far more important news, was that General Jackson was himself on his way to New Orleans and that she would let them know as soon as possible when he arrived.

Two more weeks passed before that message came and when at last it arrived, Jean and Tori were more than ready. Caution though was the caller of their movements. Jean knew Jackson had to learn first, of what a desperate situation faced him before he could approach the man with his offer. Once again, he found himself sitting and waiting for the right time. He trusted his contact and laughed. Just what would the General think, if he realized that his military secretary, Edward Livingston was in fact working for him. Nothing the General did, went unreported to Jean and Tori. His first meeting with the Governor and Mayor was described in great detail within an hour of its completion. The Mayor Girod, who spoke nothing but French had to be told through an interpreter, all that Jackson said. And Girod, so grateful to the American General for coming to New Orleans, had insisted he stay at a residence on Royal Street, a home hand picked by Jean and Davis. So it was, that the General's headquarters was set up in a most convenient location.

Jean was acting more and more like a caged lion, pacing continuously up and down the small space. "I take it that waiting is not one of your stronger points," Tori laughed, trying to lighten his spirit. All she achieved from what she had thought a witty remark, was a dark scowl. "Jean if you don't sit down and stop your pacing I swear to you, I'll sit on top of you and hold you in one spot." Her voice and face were exasperated. She really did mean what she said.

Jean stopped and looking at her he almost wanted to laugh. "Am I that much of a bear? I assure you that my frustration is in no way directed at you. It's just that I feel so inadequate and out of control here."

"Jean for God's sake stop it. You are far from out of control and as for inadequate, well I would say that is the understatement of the century. You have everything running just as you please, even hiding up here. You really do amaze me you know?"

His lips finally curled upward and his face was relaxing. He was smiling and feeling somewhat self-satisfied. He really did have things under control and she had, like always lifted his spirits. No one had ever being able to do that, to reach him and understand him. He was about to go to her and show his gratitude, when Thiac called up to them they had a visitor.

Cisco entered the dimly lit room and smiled at his close friends. "I hope you both know that I am having the time of my life playing 007. Do you have any idea what it took to get me here tonight, with what I have to tell you? God this is great, and I believe it's about to get even better. Got a drink around here?" He was grinning from ear to ear and looking around for the bottle of wine he knew they would have. "Not one word of what I have to tell will you get out of these parched lips," he joked.

Jean looked toward Tori. Now he was the one with the exasperated expression. Not only that, knowing him as she did, Tori realized that he was about to throttle Cisco if he did not stop his antics. She moved quickly between the two men and taking Cisco by the arm led him to the small table and chairs. "Cisco, you idiot, you had best just sit here and start talking or I'm afraid your Bond days are in jeopardy of becoming extinct. You might say that right now, you are on the endangered list." Her eyebrow raised inquisitively as she gazed at her friend. Her warning did not go unheeded. Looking toward Jean and his thunderous glare, his smile faded.

"Sorry man, sometimes I forget how difficult it must be for you just sitting up here waiting for news." He tried to look sincere and pointing to the empty seat across from him he added "Will you join me?"

Jean inhaled deeply and without speaking walked to the chair. "You know if I were you, I would find myself enjoying these arrangements," Cisco smiled toward Tori. "Really Jean, you and your lady have the perfect opportunity to..." He got no further. Jean's temper snapped. His arm reached out and grabbed Cisco's shirt front, pulling him across the table. Tori's reaction was to act without thinking and jump full body between the two men. It was over in seconds. As soon as her weight hit the table it gave way and before she realized what had happened, she had two men laying on top of her.

"Now why'd you go and do a stupid thing like that," Cisco's voice asked?

"Jean's answer was hissed back, "Just who are you asking that stupid question of, me for wanting to wring your neck, or my lady here?"

With that a very indignant scream came at them both. "Get the fuck off me now! I can't breathe with either of you assholes laying on top of me like this!" Both men moved, they rolled in different directions and stared at her like they had never heard a woman use such language before in their lives.

It was Cisco who laughed first. "I would say Jean my man, that she is well and truly pissed off."

"I am more than pissed off. You two simpletons are acting more like immature boys than men."

"Pissed off?" Jean's voice asked. Now there is an expression that has quite a ring to it. I take it you mean she is furious with us?" He too was now in a jovial mood. She had to laugh, what else could she do? Cisco sat up and reached for her hand, pulling her to a sitting position. "Are you all right? No bones broken?" "No bones broken, but I think my stunt woman days are short lived, if you get what I mean?"

Jean always had difficulty following their conversations when the two of them started like they were now. It might be considered English but to his ears it was a jumble of words that had no meaning.

"Look you two, I came here tonight with information. Hand me that bottle will you Jean? The one that rolled over there behind you. We don't need glasses, just open the son of a bitch and I'll start. I really am parched you know." Jean gave up, he knew that if he was going to get the news, it was going to have to be Cisco's way and Cisco loved the dramatic.

"Now as I was saying before your swan dive."

"Damn it Cisco, if you're going to talk, do so in English. And for another, swans don't dive!"

"Oh, sorry there man, I'll try harder to make it plane English. Well, as you know already, Livingston and his wife had Jackson to their home for dinner last night. The Governor and Cayetana were there, as were quite a few others. No Edward or Simone though. She must have been royally pissed." He looked at Jean. "Whoops sorry, I mean angry."

"I got the meaning, now go on."

"Well today, Livingston had to write a letter for Jackson. It is on its way to Washington as we speak. As soon as Livingston could, he went to Grymes with the details of the letter and a message for you. Grymes came to Davis, who in turn told me and here I am. See I told you. It's like a Bond movie." He took the bottle from Jean and put it to his lips taking a long, slow drink.

"If you don't give me the message and stop hanging us out to dry, so help me Cisco I myself will thrash the daylights out of you." Tori had lost her patience with him and snatched the bottle out of his hands.

"Ok, ok keep your pants on." He looked quickly at Jean and added. "Nothing personal I assure you."

"I hope not but what does keeping her pants on have to do with Livingston's message?"

"Nothing." Cisco and Tori were laughing now. "Look I'll cut to the chase."

"To the what? There is going to be a chase?"

"Oh God Jean just shut up and let him talk. Cisco please will you just give us the God damn message."

"That is what I am trying to do. Its simple. The letter is asking for weapons and such. It is explaining how desperate the situation is here and how the General fears the worst. Livingston knows that the man's back is to the wall and that if the British were to arrive any time, well shit would hit the fan."

"I take it that what you are telling me is that Jackson is in need of my services?"

"That's about the guts of it. Just like we told you. You Jean Laffite are about to save the day and supply all the man needs."

Jean stood up and walked to the far side of the room. He was thinking in silence. Cisco snatched back the wine bottle and took another long gulp. The gurgle sound was loud enough to make Jean turn back to face them.

"I suggest you go easy there. We have to make arrangements on just how to go about this next step. You both know that in your time it is said I meet with Jackson and make the arrangements. That may be well and true but this is now and we have to find a way for me to get to the man and that won't be easy."

"Sorry to disappoint you my friend. It's already been arranged. You meet him tonight." Jean's look went blank as what Cisco had just said sank in. "Look it's like this. Livingston had known Jackson for years. They knew each other up in Washington. Jackson trusts him and listens to him, if you get my drift?"

"Another quaint term, but yes I understand."

"He talked to Jackson after the letter was sent. Both men know that by the time it gets to Washington, it will be too late. Livingston talked with him and the end result is that you and he will meet alone to talk. Now Jackson is not a fool. He knows that if meeting with hellish banditti will get his men what they need, then that's what he will do. Jean, the man does not hold you in any endearing light. He hates your guts to put it mildly, thanks to our dear Governor and his everlasting letter writing campaign." Cisco had gone very serious and stopped looking at Jean long and hard before continuing. "Two conditions stand for this meeting to come about. One you had best present yourself as a Gentleman. I suggest you change your clothes and two, Tori is to go with you."

Jean's face had gone from a smirk at the mention of his attire, to horror at the mention of Tori joining him. "Under no circumstances is that going to happen."

"Which one," asked Cisco trying to sound concerned? "The part about you changing or Tori here accompanying you?"

"You know just what the hell I'm referring to." His tone was deadly, matching his deadly glare.

"You can threaten and storm all you want on this Jean. But I'm here to tell you, that this is one time it is out of your hands. Tori will be going with you. The General is expecting you both." Cisco could see the look of thunder cover Jean's face completely and fearing his wrath quickly placed the blame elsewhere. "Look it was Davis's idea. Though we all agreed she is needed as our insurance policy so to speak. Grymes felt that one of us, who is fully aware of history, needs to be at this meeting with you. Besides, she will be an added insurance policy for Jackson. He is just not going to go off into the backwaters with you, on your word alone. How can he believe that you have all the flints and powder he needs? You could be using that as a ploy to take him hostage, or worse yet to the British."

Jean could see the picture clearly now. The way Cisco was describing it all, it made sense. The dark shadow started to lift, his face breaking into a softer, friendlier one. "You seem to have thought this all through. But just how in the hell does Tori fit in here. Just how can she be his insurance policy, I ask you?"

"It's simple, he will go if the one thing you love most is left behind with his men. It's insurance that nothing will happen to him." Cisco looked toward Tori and knowing he had her on his side, no fight in that quarter, he looked back at Jean, who still had a questioning glare about him. "Jean look, I don't know all the details about this. Davis and Grymes called all the shots and with Livingston's help, arranged it all. There is no time to change anything, just go along with this all right?"

"Looks as if I have no choice in the matter does it? I may not like it but I do have enough wits about me to trust in the judgment of those who I call my friends." He turned toward Tori and smiled. "Are you ready to do this?"

"Not right this second but give me an hour to change and fix myself up a bit and yes, I'm willing." She had tried to sound lighthearted about what was ahead of them. She avoided looking at him when answering his question, for fear of letting him see the truth behind her eyes. She was excited and scared all at once. So much was riding on the outcome of the meeting that lay only a short time away.

The hour was late when they arrived at the house the General now called his headquarters. No light shone in any of the windows and all looked as if the occupants had retired for the night. As Cisco had explained, the gate to the courtyard would be open and the back door to the house would be left ajar, if the meeting was to proceed. Once inside they were to make their way to the room that had a light showing, they could not mistake it. Jackson would be waiting inside.

It had been months since Tori had last met the man and that had been under far better circumstances. Her stomach was in a turmoil and her nerves visibly on edge, as they made their way down the small hallway toward the lit room. As always Jean seemed completely in control of himself and did not even attempt to walk quietly, his long heavy strides sounding on the floor, echoing loudly. Tori thought she had heard voices when they first made their way inside. Whoever had been talking though had stopped at the sound of their arrival. They were waiting in the room ahead and were well aware of their arrival. She only hoped that the greeting would be a friendly one and not a trap.

He knocked once on the door and pushed it open, allowing Tori to enter ahead of himself. At first she was amazed by this bold act of his, but then Jean never did anything without a reason. She knew that he would never put her life ahead of his and must have known that this small declaration of trust was necessary.

The room was dimly lit. The few candles that burned cast shadows that moved as the wicks swayed in the breeze from the open door. A small but intense fire burned in the hearth, radiating heat, giving the atmosphere a cozy sort of glow. All seemed friendly enough, no trap here that she could see.

Jean's eyes and ears had told him pretty much the same his raw instincts had told him that for now they were safe. The odds were even, two of them against Jackson and his man. If Jackson had thoughts of arresting him though, he would find a none too-willing participant, and a lady who could and would fight.

"Ah, Mr. and Mrs. Laffite, please do come on in." Jackson's voice sounded friendly enough but the actions around them warned them they were on shaky ground. From out of the shadows two more large, what seemed to Tori, to be mountain men, stepped forward threateningly. One had a pistol aimed at Jean and the other held a long ugly knife at his side. Behind them came the sound of still more individuals, their footsteps sounding as they approached the room. A head popped in through the door, "All secure here General sir. They came alone."

"Very good," Jackson shot his reply, "Man your post and keep a sharp eye out."

"Yes, sir. Will do." He shot Laffite a warning kind of glare and nodded affirmatively at his companions in the room. The door closed, but no sound of footsteps echoed in the hall. He had remained just outside.

Could she have been wrong? Did they make an error in judgment? John, Cisco and she had been so sure that this meeting took place and that Jean had won the General's support. Right now though, it felt more like a trap. Had they just been taken into custody?

"You must forgive my men sir," his voice was calm and sounded sincere. "On the other hand, I would not be much of a soldier if I did not take precautions, now would I? Your reputation precedes you, and even if I have been informed that you are on the same side as this uniform of mine, until I am certain of your loyalties, your ties with the enemy cannot go unsuspected."

"You have not done anything that I did not already suspect you would do. I do suggest that the poor boy up that large magnolia outside be let down though, especially on such a cold and damp night as this. No one will be following us and if they did, your men along the street would be the first to know."

Tori looked at him, astonishment clearly written on her face. She had not seen anyone watching them as they had made their way here, let alone a boy up a tree.

Jackson smiled at Jean and nodded his head at the man closest to the door. "See to it, we don't need the boy getting sick." He coughed slow and deep. "We are going to need every able-bodied man in the days ahead."

Tori was horrified at the man who she knew to be Jackson, so much had he changed. She watched as he struggled to his feet, visibly trying to gain control over the wave of nausea and weakness that threatened to engulf him. She did not need a doctor to explain the man was gravely ill, that he was nothing more than skin and bones. Neither did it surprise her to see he still remained strong in character and very much in control.

"I had begun to believe that you were not going to arrive." His eyes had been riveted on Jean but then shifted to his lady. "Forgive an old fool his manners, will you not my dear." He indicated a chair with his hand, "Please do come and join me, I have always found that under circumstances such as these, it's best to try and act civil." He smiled his eyes weary from lack of sleep but shining bright and genuine in their stare. "Mr. Laffite, let us get directly to the point sir. I am not one to beat around the bush, nor will I. It has come to my attention that you may have certain information that you think is vital to my campaign here in New Orleans. Before you speak on the matter, I would like to warn you sir, that it is against my better judgment to meet with the likes of you and only because of the insistence of close acquaintances and the dire situation that I now find myself in, did I agree to have you come here."

Jean nodded his head and escorted Tori toward the chair. He turned and faced the General looking directly into the man's face as he spoke. "Monsieur Jackson, General sir. We have much to talk about you and I but time is not about to allow us that liberty. I am sure that by dawn's light you will have a far different view of both myself and your seemingly grave situation. Monsieur Livingston has spoken to you about our short trip, oui?"

"He has sir." Jackson picked up a glass on the table nearest to him and sipped at the liquid. His hand visible shook as he raised the glass to his lips, still he stood his ground. "Though at this time I have to inform you that unless you have reason or reasons stronger than me changing my view about you, I will have to decline such a trip."

Jean could see for himself the state the General was in and silently cursed Cisco and the others for not informing him of the man's poor health. It was clear to him that the man was not in any condition to ride off in the dead of night let alone a hard ride into the backwaters.

"I see your point. Just how much have you been told may I ask? You yourself would never have agreed to a meeting with me and my wife, unless you had more information than you are letting on, or unless this is a rue, and I am now captured and no longer a wanted man?"

Jackson looked angry for a second, then quickly washed his feeling clear of his face and spoke firmly. "I had given my word that you would be able to meet me and we would discuss whatever it is that you think pertinent. That and only that, no tricks. I have been informed that you are as much a man of his word as I. It would seem Mr. Laffite that you trust me about as much as I trust you. At least we have that much in common." Jackson coughed deep and longer this time. A slight film of perspiration covered his forehead and though he was putting up a great front for their benefit, Tori could not let the man continue.

"General Jackson, may I be so bold as to suggest that you accompany me here by the fire. Please sir, take a seat and Jean, you could sit there," she pointed to the empty chair. "I don't think either of you will be taking any trip this evening. I see no point in it anyway. You can just as easily tell the General what you have come to offer and he can verify it by sending one of his officers instead." She could see Jackson's shoulders slump slightly. Maybe it was in relief from her suggestion or maybe in an ever-growing weakness that was taking over his body.

Jean walked to the chair and indicated the place beside his wife to Jackson. "I have learned never to argue with my wife when her mind is made up. Surely you understand such matters?"

Jackson chuckled, "Indeed I do Mr. Laffite, indeed I do." He took the seat next to Tori and Jean sat down opposite. "Some refreshments are in order. Mr. Sims bring us some of that fine brandy that we had earlier and then I think you and the others can leave us."

He had not spoken the words as an order but they were followed as such. Tori watched as the Mr. Sims and the other two men reluctantly did as he asked and then left their leader in the hands of what they assumed to be, little more than a pirate and a possible traitor at that.

Jackson had seen her watching his men and touched her hand lightly. "Do not let them concern you my dear. They are at times out of place, such as now, with their concern toward my safety but then they are also the finest fighting men one could ask for."

"I'm sure you are right and please forgive me, I do understand, believe you me but they have no need to fear our reasons for being here this evening."

"And just why are you here? What exactly is it that I should know about?" He looked from one to the other.

"Jean I think you had best tell the man before he begins to think us a waste of time. He looks as if some good news would at this point be most welcome, don't you agree?" She was beaming, almost laughing, her smile so full.

"I think you are all but bursting with the information yourself my dear," Jackson chuckled. "Yes indeed these old bones could use some good news. Please do go ahead sir."

"Oh yes, go ahead and make his day," she laughed. Jean flashed her a dark warning this was serious business not some silly fancy. The next few hours held not only their fate in its hands but the fate of America.

Andrew Jackson sat and listened as Jean made his proposal, never did his expression alter or give any hint as to what he was feeling. His gaze never left Jean's only movement was to shift forward in his seat at the mention of the powder and flints. When the room finally fell silent, Tori looked at each man in turn and watched as each summed up the conversation and its implications.

Jackson spoke first. "If what you have just told me holds to be true, then I give you my word that as soon as it is verified, you will have my gratitude and my full support. I give you my word that I will endeavor to see your side of the bargain met." Jackson reached out his hand, "I give you my hand on it."

Jean stood and took the General's hand and they shook.

"Sims," Jackson's voice rang out. The door flew open and two not one man flew in guns raised. "For God's sake man, put that weapon down. Mr. Laffite here is not the enemy, far from it. It turns out he is our savior. You will accompany him and return with a report to me as fast as you can. I mean to hear from your lips what I already know to be true." He smiled at Tori. "You will explain to the man on the way Captain Laffite."

Sims eyes shot open at the reference to Captain. He looked at the pirate and then back to his General. "We will depart right now sir." He moved toward the door, "Are you ready or not?" he asked sarcastically of Jean.

"I have been ready and waiting for weeks Mr. Sims. Let's not keep the General waiting any longer than he has too. Tori, you keep the General company. I won't be gone long." Then he spun around and marched out of the room, causing Sims to have to run after him.

Tori looked toward Jackson and the look of amusement on his face. It faded as the room slipped once again into silence. He was bone weary and though glad not to have to make the trip himself, would not rest until he had verification of what Laffite offered.

"General sir?" Tori asked "May I send for a friend of mine. She is a healer of sorts and I am sure she can help you. Please sir, you need help and I can't just sit here and not do something. In fact I won't."

He smiled at her and her concern. "I appreciate your offer but it's nothing a good night's sleep won't cure."

"Begging your pardon sir, but I'm not stupid nor am I about to give in. You are ill and you do need my friend's help. Please just let me get word to her. I won't rest until you see her and you know it."

"If that is how you feel, and you do feel very strongly on this don't you? I will get your message to your friend and for you my dear, only for you, I will see her." He sat back down, the fight leaving him. He was resigned to waiting for Jean and to letting Tori have her way. These Laffite's, both of them were strong willed and stubborn. Very much like himself he thought.

"Jefferson," he called out, the man's head popping in the doorway immediately. "See to it that Mrs. Laffite's message is delivered and anything else she wants. I will just take a short nap here if that is all right Madame?" He was joking, but the smile on his lips was forced and Tori knew it.

"Jefferson, if one of your men could just go to Mr. Livingston and inform him that I want Marie to attend the General, he will understand. Oh and when she gets here, could you please see to it that she comes right in."

Jefferson nodded his head and closed the door. For a while the house would sit in waiting, silent and anxious. Tori watched as the General slept in the chair and she hugged herself Before her was a man who would be president if history let him be. So much could go wrong yet. So much was riding on a fine thread of what Cisco, John and she knew. She could only pray they were doing it all right.

# Chapter 27

The gray light of dawn slipped in between a crack in the curtains. Tori had sat up all night opposite the General, watching him sleep restlessly. His fever was definitely up and his respiration was labored. It was as if he were fighting with each breath to fill his hungry lungs with air. Tori had thought that with such exertion of energy the man would be flushed instead of the bluish gray hue his skin reflected. The last time she had seen someone with that look had been Leone. This thought terrified her. It was not possible for the man to be that close to death she told herself. She would never allow herself to believe such a thing. Anxiously she kept listening for the sound of Marie's quick step, announcing her arrival and her help. But hour after long hour, the house remained still. She remained ever vigilant, her eyes shifting from Jackson to the door and back. If help did not come soon, she would have to do something herself. The next time Jefferson looked in on them she would inform him of her decision. Then as if he had read her mind, she heard the door slowly creaking open, followed by whispered voices.

"I have no time to argue with you about my identity, the matter of fact is this. I was sent for and I'm here. Plain enough for you? Now I highly suggest you move your carcass and let me by."

Tori recognized her voice even in the hushed tones and seeing Jefferson's determined face, she had to admit that Marie had a lot of guts to stand up for herself like she was doing.

"Jefferson, let the poor woman pass before she brains you one," growled Jackson, his face not matching his tone. He was grinning at Tori and actually winked at her.

Marie pushed past the man in the doorway and taking the initiative, pushed him back outside the door and closed it. "Now you stay put, afore you make me real mad like," she hissed. Then she turned and walked to Tori. The two hugged and then together turned their attentions toward Jackson.

"I can see with my own eyes why you sent for me. Thought I would have been sent for days ago though. Lordy, your head must feel ready to explode and as for them bones that ache something fierce, well I just say you be one stubborn man to put up with it that's all."

Andrew Jackson had seen some sights in his time but looking at this slip of a girl who stood before him, telling him how he felt and calling him stubborn, raised color to his deathly white pallor.

"Now don't you go a getting yourself all riled up. Mizz Tori here, sent for me and by the looks of you, none to soon." She shook her head. "I'll be needing some things, that Jefferson better be a doing as I ask, or things is going to get real loud around here and that ain't a going to please the General none," she laughed walking back toward the door.

Tori went to Jackson and knelt down by the side of his chair. "General sir, please excuse Marie, she means well enough. I sent for her late last night, you said I could." She watched as recognition registered in the man's eyes before hastily going on. "She is real good with herbs and tonics. I would trust her with my life, have done just that in fact. She will have you feeling much better in no time, if you will listen and do as she says. Please Mr. Jackson, General sir, you have to get well and fast. This is the only chance you have." She had grabbed a hold of his hand and was squeezing it.

He looked down at his hand and then back up at her. His instincts told him that she meant well enough and that just maybe if he listened to this Marie, all would be as it should. "Mrs. Laffite, first of all I would like to thank you for your concern and second of all, I believe that we know each other well enough to drop the formalities. Please do me the honor and call me Andrew. We are, after all, friends aren't we?"

"That we are, Andrew, and it would be far more of an honor than you can guess." God, how she wished she could just talk to this man and tell him what she knew and who she really was.

"You two finished with your visit, cause I got to get this here medicine down his throat. Ain't got no time to fuss about, time is not what we got." She shot Tori a knowing look. "Excuse me Andrew, I had better let Marie here do her job. Just trust her and you'll see, everything will turn out." Tori watched as Marie gave Jackson three different drinks, each by the look on his face tasting worse than the other. Still he put up no fight and after the last glass was empty, Marie put his head back on the chair telling him to sleep for a while.

"We will be right here Andrew," added Tori across the room. "Please try and rest."

Marie took the tray with the empty glasses on it and walked to the table by the window signaling Tori to join her. "We won't be needing any light for a while, so leave these here curtains drawn over. Don't need no light to talk by and that's what you are wanting to do now isn't it."

"I suppose it is. But what I really want to know is will he be all right? What's wrong with him Marie? He looks just dreadful and I'm sure he feels worse than he looks."

"That be about the truth of it for sure. I know'd some of the reason he is the way he is, sick and all. But even with Cisco's help, we can't be for sure in all the reasons." Marie saw Tori's puzzled look and smiled gently at her. "He going to be just fine if you ask me. Just takes some time and that's what's worrying me and all. I asked that man of mine I says Cisco how much time d'we have to get this here General ready for the battle and he go and tell me he don't know. His best guess not long. Not long he say's and how I supposed to cure a man with not long to do it in, I ask you?" She rolled her eyes up into her head and then closed the lids. "I just know he won't be fully well in time but he be well on his way."

"I believe you my friend, but you still did not answer my question, what's wrong with him?"

"Oh that. Well he has a case of the fever you call malaria, we calls it swamp fever. Same thing though. Cisco says you have a medicine called quin, quinin?" She was trying to remember the name but it just wouldn't come to her.

"You mean quinine. Yes we have that, I have taken it myself when I went to Africa on a trip. But do you have it here in this time?"

"Reckons we do. Ain't sure it be this here quinine but the tea comes form a bark of a tree. The tree ain't found here, no sur. It come from South America way. Good thing the bark keeps for long time, it be real hard to get some years." She was lost in a daydream for a few seconds as if remembering just such a time. Then she shook her head and continued. Cisco says the medicine he would have used comes from a plant and so it could be the same thing. Anyway we used it. If the General has the swamp fever, this here tea will cure that. His head and his pains be taken care of the second drink. You know'd about that one yourself."

Tori knew well enough and grimaced at the thought of the taste of the vile form of aspirin. Still she knew it would work and felt a slight sense of relief for him.

"The third be my own making and I know that the man be needing it real bad. He ain't been eating or sleeping for weeks and if he a going to have to fight, he will be needing his strength. You call it what you want, I ain't a going to tell you what's in it but know this, he about to have himself a real good lift of energy." She slapped her leg and laughed putting her head close to Tori's. "I give it to Cisco once. Once be all I could take. That man was on me day and night, like I was a dog in heat. Lord, he almost killed me. It was fun at first but then he came to wanting way too much, so I had to send him away till it wear off."

Tori could not help herself. She found the story hilarious and found it hard to stifle her laugh. "Oh stop it Marie. You are just impossible you know. Besides we can't wake Andrew. Look at him I think that he is resting more comfortably don't you?" Marie looked over at the man and nodded her head.

"Yes, he be resting real well. Now what we going to do for you? You look as if you need some of my powders."

"Oh no you don't. Don't you dare try and give me any of that energy boosting shit. I know Jean would love you if it had the same effect on me as it did Cisco." She was laughing again. Just the thought of it sent her reeling. "Shit Marie, stop this before I bust something." Tori was choking and trying desperately to stifle her coughing. Marie pushed her glass of water toward her and Tori downed the cool liquid extinguishing the fit. Gratefully she smiled at her friend, while wiping the tears from her eyes. "God, Marie, I didn't think you could choke to death on spit?" She sipped again from her glass and sat back satisfied that the coughing had ceased. "All I need is some sleep and I just might be able to take a nap if you will be quiet." She was trying to sound firm but her smiling lips told she did not mean it.

"You just listen to me, reason you all but choked on your own spit as you put it, is plain as can be. Your body be telling you its just plum tired out. You need the sleep as much as that man there. Now you lay down on the sofa and I'll stay and watch over you both. Go on, listen to me, I knowd what I be talking about." Her face told Tori she did mean it and the thought of sleep, if only for a short while sounded wonderful.

"Thank you Marie, I think I will take a nap. You'll wake me won't you? I mean if anything happens."

"Yes em, I'll wake you. But won't be necessary. You will wake yourself when you are needed, you'll see." Tori lay down and before she could think about all that was happening around her, she fell into a deep dreamless sleep.

"Marie picked up Tori's glass and put it on the tray with the others. "And the forth potion put him to rest for sure, just like you." She chuckled softly. Cisco was right, you did need the rest and all you needed was a little help, that's all. Just a little help for a few hours of sanctuary. Sleep is the only place you have worry free, both of you." She looked from one to the other, saddened suddenly. "I ain't a going to be able to help you none in that department again." She headed to the door carrying the tray of glasses and softly called, "Jefferson, you be there?"

Edward stormed into the Governor's office, his face sneering as if he had a bad smell up his nose. The day had been going just fine as every plan had been well thought out and executed to perfection. Why was it then that just when all seemed to be in hand and under control, that it had it fallen apart? There was no doubt as to the authenticity of the news. Dominique You, along with the rest of Laffite's men, had been released. Not only released, but given high ranks in Jackson's army. He had seen with his own eyes all the activity on Royal Street at the so-called Headquarters for the Americans. Had the whole city gone mad he wondered? Just what was going on here and why? Two questions he needed answered and would not leave until he had them.

Claiborne was surrounded by a small group of men most of whom he recognized; some he did not want to even acknowledge. Those being the so-called Kentuckians, men who seemed more savage than the few Indians with them. Not only did they look evil but they smelled rank.

Claiborne saw him enter and smiled at his friend. "So you have heard? Who would have ever thought it, Laffite has saved the day. That is at least he has given us the means to give it a hell of a good effort." Claiborne saw that Edward had no idea as to what he was talking about and left the group of men to explain to his trusted friend just what had happened.

"Laffite has saved the day?" Edward spit the words as if they were dirt in his mouth. "Just what does Laffite have to do with the release of his slime?"

"Please stop before you go any further," he held his hand up to silence Edward. "It is only your unfamiliarity with the facts that has your judgment clouded. Here walk with me, I could use some air." The two of them left the room and strolled into the courtyard. "I tell you I would never have believed it myself but these are the facts. General Andrew Jackson himself has verified it and it was his orders to release Laffite's men." He looked at the stunned Edward and put his hand on the younger man's shoulder guiding him toward the stone bench. "Here sit with me and I will explain it further. You were well aware that our forces, small as they are, had an even graver problem than size. The problem of flints and powder was desperate as you know."

Edward had a sinking feeling as to where this conversation was leading yet he still clung to the thread of hope he had not guessed right. "Did I hear you correctly, you said was a problem? Just what are you saying?" He was on the edge of his seat, his face with such a pleading look about it.

"Just calm down here my friend and I will explain. I did indeed say was. That's because thanks to Jean Laffite, we no longer have a need for either flints or powder, not to mention men willing to fight. At least Laffite has been on top of the situation. He has even bought Jackson time by having his men stall the British. They refuse to show them the way through the bayous. We have been fools not to have listened to him or respond to his correspondence, such fools."

"I can't believe what you are saying. You are sitting there telling me that this pirate, this traitor, has bought you off with the offer of his supplying flint, powder and men. William are you so blind? Has it not crossed yours or anyone else's mind that the man could be in league with the British."

"I am not blind nor stupid. I am grateful for your concern Edward but like I have already told you, Jackson has verified the supply of flints and powder. He has Laffite's pledge of loyalty along with those of his men. And the very fact that his men have not shown the British through the waterways, only goes to prove that Laffite is not in league with them, does it not?" The look on Edward's face was crestfallen. He was highly agitated and thinking that his actions were out of concern, Claiborne tried to calm his doubts. "The man is no fool Edward. I'm sure that if for one second he suspected Laffite to be anything but what he seems, he would never have acted as he has done. Jackson's reputation both as a fine leader and fair judge of men proceed him and give credence to his actions. I myself have met with Laffite only a few hours ago and have to admit that even though I still find the man and his piracy deplorable, he is forthcoming in his desire to fight and protect this city from the enemy. I wish I could divulge more." He looked as if he was about to add more on the topic but then quickly changed his mind. "You will just have to trust me on this one." He stood up and looked toward his office while speaking, "there is much to do yet, and I'm sure you will excuse me. I can only hope that with men such as Laffite and yourself, we will have a chance at pushing the British from our shores should it come to that." The Governor never even looked back at Edward as he left him. He simply called out as he walked toward his office, "We will talk later. Stop by this evening with Simone. Cayetana would love to see you both." With that he was gone.

Edward sat still on the bench, his head spinning and a sharp pain in his chest. That fool had actually had the audacity to compare him with the likes of Laffite. No, worse yet, with Laffite. Once again that pirate had pulled himself free of his demise. He had the whole city believing his story of loyalty, not to mention he would now be heralded as a hero for his supply of arms, damn the man. Edward put his hand to his now-throbbing head and squeezed his eyes shut. Simone would help him figure a way out of this mess. If anyone could help him, it would be his wife. She had never failed him and he doubted she would now. She was at her best when things seemed at their worst. A sinister snarl curled his lips. "I'm not done with you yet Laffite," he mumbled.

Jean and Tori were often seen coming and going from Jackson's headquarters. That and the fact that the French Quarter was now filled with Jean's men from Barataria, was accepted by the people without question. Tori had met with Dominique and Beluche only briefly before they departed on what they called important duty. Both were given the rank of Captain and as skilled artillerymen they were being treated with great respect. Dominique had hugged Tori as he would have a daughter and then laughing out loud had proclaimed that he Dominique You, would be a force to reckon with.

Jackson and his officers along with Laffite spent hours planning and plotting each move. Even with the added number of volunteers to Jackson's force, they knew they would be greatly outnumbered. Not only that bothered Jackson but worse still was the knowledge that they would be up against the world's strongest fighting force. All of the British military were seasoned veterans. All he had, was a handful of men who had ever seen action backed by a load of greenhorns. The worry aged him daily. It haunted his dreams and every waking hour. The thought that he might be sending young men to their certain death in a few weeks or even days weighed heavily on him.

Marie had continued to pay the General a daily visit and with her she always brought the powders. To most who saw the man he did little to show improvement, to Marie he was growing better each hour. Whether he himself felt any difference was not known. He would smile and gratefully take what was given him and then simply proceed with whatever he had been doing. Tori watched and prayed that the British would wait a few more weeks before arriving. Andrew Jackson needed time. Time to build up his strength and time for the tonics or whatever Marie was giving him to work. Time however was not on his side.

With Christmas approaching, Tori like the rest of the town felt that they had to do something. Could they though plan any celebration knowing what was coming? Tori and John Davis had met and decided to have a small gathering of friends for Christmas dinner and not worry about what the rest of the city planned.

"It's December 23rd already. I don't suppose even the enemy would want to fight on Christmas day do you?" Tori had half jokingly asked John, who stood looking out the balcony window.

"I suppose not. But one thing I have learned in my life Tori is never to underestimate your opponent." He was watching something with great interest and then he turned toward her, "Cisco is coming, and by the way he was running up the street, I should say he has something of great importance to tell us." Tori looked at John letting the pen in her hand drop to the desk. All thoughts of writing out the dinner invitations had fled her mind. Before Cisco entered the room she knew, time had just run out for all of them.

The door burst open and Cisco flew in. He stood looking from one to the other and then he spoke. "The British have been spotted and get this, they are only nine miles south of here. Seems we can't stall them any longer." Tori grabbed the side of the table gasping. "Nine miles? That's too damn close. Oh my God!" She spun facing John who gravely uttered.

"Like I said, never underestimate your opponent."

"Jackson just got word and I came as soon as I heard. Seems they are not on the move but have encamped on the Villere plantation. All hell is breaking loose down there at Jackson's I mean. I thought you should know. I've got to get back. You coming John?"

"Need you ask?" He was grabbing his coat and took a pistol out of his desk drawer. Tori who had stood frozen not really wanting to believe what was happening, made up her mind to act.

"I'm coming too." Seeing the instant horror register on both men's faces she added, "only to see if I can wish Jean luck. We all know where I have to go and what I have to do. Don't worry I'm not stupid. I'll do my part. Let's go shall we?" She grabbed her cape and took Cisco by the arm. "This is it, let's make history."

Royal Street was as active as a beehive in summer. Swarms of men were coming and going all rushing in different directions determined to carry out whatever orders they were following. Tori had seen a few women here and there waving good-byes to their loved ones. While still others stood on the verandahs overlooking the street openly crying. Chaos seemed to reign around them the closer they got to Andrew Jackson's headquarters. Several times Cisco or John had had to pull Tori out of harm's way. By the time they actually reached the front of the house Tori had been pushed and pulled so much, that she was not even paying close attention to those around her anymore. Her one thought was to reach Jean before he had to leave to defend the city, so one more man bumping into her didn't surprise her. It was Cisco's added grip on her arm that caused her to look up into her assailant's face.

"Edward!" Her voice was more shocked than fearful. "What are you doing here?"

"Tori. Gentlemen." He bowed slightly. "I could ask you the same but then I think I know why you are here. He's already gone you know? You're too late. Headed out with his men on orders from Jackson."

Something inside her churned as she struggled to keep control of her emotions. Still her eyes filled with tears at the thought of having missed Jean.

"I wouldn't worry if I were you. Seems your pirate always gets himself out of difficult situations. Still there is the chance that this escapade may be the one to undo him? Tell me my dear have you considered what you will do when the British win? I have no doubt they will prevail, and your Jean will be a prisoner or worse yet dead. Oh dear I see you have not. Well let me assure you, I will be waiting."

Cisco's punch came out of nowhere, landing squarely on Edward's jaw, knocking him backward with such a force that he lost his balance and fell flat on his back.

"That you slimy little bastard is not only for the lady here, but for Jean as well. I have to tell you I have been waiting for some time to have the opportunity to get my hands on you." John Davis's hand held Cisco back and Tori who did not want any further confrontation at this time spoke up.

"Don't bother yourself with this scum Cisco. You have put him where he will no doubt end up, in the gutter. We are needed right now, let him grovel his way around amongst the muck. Shit begets shit does it not?" She pulled Cisco and walked past Edward deliberately kicking at the mud as she went.

"You think you have won?" Edward screamed. "Just you wait and see who grovels next." Seeing some people staring at him, he pulled himself up and while brushing some dirt from his sleeve, declared in a loud voice, "This whole town has gone quite mad, quite mad indeed." With that he headed home.

Once they were inside the house, Livingston met the three of them and ushered them to the back room where the General was preparing to leave. "He had hoped you would come by and asked to speak with you if you did. Hurry this way. You just missed Marie you know?" Tori entered the room and two things hit her at once. First off Edward had lied her Jean was still there. He was talking with Jackson and putting a piece of paper into his coat pocket. Second, was Jackson himself. Seeing him standing next to the robust Jean, only emphasized his sickly form. She stood transfixed as she watched him down the last of what Marie left for him to take. His face pulled into a look that showed how vile the contents of the glass had been. Then she stared as he turned toward her, straightening himself and sloughing off any sign of his weak condition. His eyes were clearer than they had been and he did have some color in his cheeks, but Tori knew that this man was living on pure willpower and a inner strength that she realized came from his knowledge that he was needed.

"Tori my dear lady. I am so very glad you have come. Please come over and join us." He held out his hand and she took it. "I just wanted to thank you for all your care and concern. My wife God bless her, could not have done more. I have to confess that you were right about your friend Marie. Her potions or whatever they are have helped me tremendously. But remind me never to try her cooking." He laughed his eyes sparkling. "The medicines taste like, well it goes without saying that if food follows her potions," he rolled his eyes and made another face.

Tori found herself laughing with him. "Andrew, I can tell you, that I will remind you..." Before she could finish talking they were interrupted by one of Jackson's men. "General Sir. It's time sir. Your mount is ready and the men are waiting."

He looked at his officer, "I'll be right with you. Now Tori my dear, you take care of yourself and keep the homefront safe. Jean has told me that you will be staying in town with some of the fine ladies. I think maybe your job will be far harder than mine." He took her chin with his shaking hand, "permit me?" He leaned forward and kissed her lightly on her cheek. "You do your job and I will do mine. With God's help we will be together soon." Then to her amazement he seemed to suck into his body all the strength and vitality he needed. He strode from the room with an aura about him that gave him the charisma he was well known for. He was General Andrew Jackson to most but to his men he was old hickory and it fit. His last words sounded from the hallway as he left. "Don't take long Laffite. I'm counting on you." Jean turned and looked at his love. If all went as it should they would be together and he would not only be forgiven of past crimes but an American citizen as well. If that happened he swore he would be a different man. He would settle down and raise a family with the love of his life

"Something on your mind?" she asked.

"Only you as always. I have to go now you know? You stay safe and try not to worry." He took her into his arms and pulled her close to him. "I will have you with me, here in my mind and my soul. I will make history, just the way you want it and then together we will decide what to do." He kissed her long and hard, tasting her, holding her close.

Cisco called into the room, "Jean, come on man, we have to go."

Jean let her go and putting his finger to her lips he silenced her. "Don't say anything. I'll return as soon as I can you can count on that." He backed out of the room slowly, just taking her into his mind and holding her there. For a few short seconds he stood in the doorway, with the roguish smile she had grown to love so much and then he was gone. Never had she felt so helpless as she did at that moment knowing what was about to happen, and realizing all she could do was wait. That thought reminded her of her next move. She was due to arrive at Madame Poree's house, just down the street. She and quite a few ladies had all arranged to wait together. It had been Marie Destrehan's suggestion and having agreed to join them Tori found no way around it. Besides she told herself, Marie had been such a good friend to her she felt it was the least she could do. She would comfort her friend and pray J.D. would not be one of the few to be hurt...

Jean made his way to the edge of town where he met up with a small group of his men. Thiac was there, as were a few other free men of color. Some Jean knew some he did not.

"I have my orders and yours," he announced as he rode up. "You are to go with Cisco here and report to the main group south of town. I will not be joining you right away, as the General has other plans for me. Let's show them what we are capable of shall we?" he cheered.

The men all shouted their support and rallied around Cisco. All but Thiac, who stood separate with a look of worry. "I ain't going to let you go off by yourself," Thiac called out to Jean.

"You have no choice, you and I have to follow orders. You have to follow Cisco. There's nothing else you can do." Jean rode his horse right up to Thiac's side.

Thiac grabbed hold of the bridle. "That is where you are wrong boss. If I can't go with you, then young David here will." He pulled a tall lanky coffee colored young man to his side. "If you won't let me, then you have David. If you won't take David you won't go."

Jean had seen this side of Thiac before and knew that the man was as stubborn as a mule at times. When he got a notion into his head that was it. He looked again at David and seeing no fear in the lad's eyes, asked him straight out.

"Why should I take you boy?"

David stepped forward, looking him straight in the face. "Because you need me. Someone has to watch your back."

"I think maybe I have been able to watch my own back over the years don't you?"

"It be true enough, but I also growed up in dem backwaters. Been going up and down dem on your barges all my's life. I know'd these here parts better'n you and yous need a guide. Thiac said yous need me." Bolstered by Thiac, he put his hands on his hips in a defiant act as he continued, "Should be's enough for yous." Jean wanted to say no, but the truth of the matter was that he did need a guide and the boy who stood before him now claimed to have been working for him, giving him knowledge of the area.

"Thiac, do I know this boy?"

"No boss, can't says you do. You do own him though and he be the best working boy on the river you has. More'n that, he can be trusted if you gets what I mean." Jean knew he had been ambushed into taking Thiac's advice and taking David with him. He didn't like it, but he also could see that he could benefit.

"Fine, fine. But David if you slow me up or get in my way, I'll leave you for gator food, got me?"

David's face lit up, "Yes em boss. I won't be slowing yous down none and I wills do as you says."

Thiac added to David's outburst. "Anything but leave the boss's side. You done know'd what I said and boy I meant each and every word." Thiac's growl hit home as the boy looked toward him.

"I knowd what yous done told me."

Jean had had enough. He turned in his saddle and called to Cisco. "Let's move on out of here. We can keep each other company some of the way. Thiac, when we get to the parting of the way you will have my horse. Where David and I have to go, well, we have to go on foot."

Cisco moved his horse up next to Jean's and the two led the small group off. Cisco started to hum a tune and then looking at Jean, he broke into part of the song. "Ran so fast that the hounds couldn't catch them, down the Mississippi to the Gulf of Mexico."

Jean listened to the bits and pieces of the song and then laughing, leaned closer to Cisco so as not to be overheard. "Suppose that's a song from your time."

"Yep, sure is."

"Don't suppose I'm in there anywhere am I?"

"Nope, not that I can remember."

"Thought so, nice tune though," he was openly laughing, "Damn good words too. Shame you can't remember them all." He pulled his horse to a stop. "Maybe John will know them. Well Cisco my friend we part company here." He dismounted and was immediately joined by David. "You take care of yourself and old Thiac here," he added.

Cisco nodded his head. "You can count on it. If I were a betting man, I would say we will all be back together real soon." Jean grinned at him, "Just the same, take care. You ready David?" He did not look back or wait for an answer. He moved off into the dense scrub and was quickly out of sight.

Cisco turned toward Thiac, "Guess you had better mount up. We better get a move on, still got two miles to go until we reach the Rodriguez Canal. I hear tell that Jackson has told old General Humbert that he wants to make the first strike tonight."

Thiac's eyes widened at this but no emotion showed in his voice as he spoke.

"No sur, ain't got two miles if you follow me. I say we have more like just under a mile. Not easy going but still faster and we ain't a likely to run up gainst no enemy neither. We be there long before night that for sure..."

As Cisco joined Jackson and prepared to fight, Tori joined the ladies at Madame Poree's townhouse. Tori looked around the parlor at the small group of ladies. She knew most of them and was welcomed openly, many thanking her as if it had been her flints and powder instead of Jean's, that had saved the day. Marie Destrehan called from the top of the stairs and waved, motioning for her to stay put, until she came down.

"I have put the small one's down for the night. J.D. wanted me to leave them at the plantation, but lord how could I? Men, I ask you? They just don't understand us do they." She was moving about the room, smiling and greeting a few of the ladies. "Of course I left the older children but then I don't think we have that much to really worry over do we?" To Tori's ears it sounded as though she was trying to convince not only herself about having nothing to worry over but the ladies who listened to her every word.

"I beg to differ with you on that matter. I for one, feel we all have a lot to worry over," sounded Simone's cold voice. Tori turned to face the one woman she had not counted on being there. Before them stood the vision of a beautiful woman, elegant, almost regal in her appearance. Yet Tori knew behind those large tear-filled eyes lay nothing short of a venomous bitch.

"I have spoken with the Governor himself and my darling Edward, may God protect him, has confided in me. Are you aware of the enemy and its size. It is reported to be greater than twelve thousand."

One of the women gasped and promptly fainted, while still another started to openly pray, falling to her knees, her rosary in hand.

Simone went on seemingly untouched by the panic she was causing. "Edward was informed that our forces amount to just over two thousand. He has prepared me for the worse." She dabbed at her eyes with a silk hanky. "I know I should keep these things to myself but I simply cannot. My dear Edward, all our dear husbands, brothers and sons, have gone to fight a battle they surely can't win."

Someone behind Tori whimpered a response.

"But we have that fine Andrew Jackson and he knows what to do." One of the ladies spoke up.

Simone smirked and then sarcastically retorted. "Many of our men and boys have never seen war, let alone had to carry arms against another man. While on the other hand, the British are nothing short, of how do you say it?" She inhaled loudly and on the exhale spat out, "Of well-trained, blood-thirsty murderers." Another woman moaned and fainted and still more started to cry. Simone was truly in her glory and no doubt enjoying putting the fear of God into those gathered there. She was about to confront her, when as if on cue, the sound of distant cannon fire reverberated in the heavens.

Tori, like many of the women looked away from Simone and toward the open French doors, with fear and horror etched on their faces. Madame Poree was the first to act. She walked over to the doors and pulled them shut.

"Enough of that, we don't want to upset the little ones and besides, it's just too chilly this time of year. Don't know why they were open anyway? We shall pray. Yes, that's what we will do. For those of you who want to join me in my vigilance, come this way." She led a few of the ladies from the room, across the hall to another parlor.

Simone had not been amongst them, choosing instead to stay and sit facing Tori. She fully intended to make the wait a living hell for her. Then, when the British marched into town, to turn the bitch over as Laffite's spying wench. Oh, she would enjoy that very much. It was going to be a good Christmas with a lot to celebrate she told herself. Until then though, Simone intended to make Tori suffer. She would tell the bitch, that her darling Jean would most likely be killed or caught and tried as a traitor. Not that for one second did she believe he would be hurt or caught, he was too lucky. As for her Edward, she could smile safely in the knowledge that he was far from harm's way. He was at their plantation making arrangements to entertain the victorious British. He would not be subject to their wrath, rather their praise for not bearing arms against them. A perfect plan.

Edward had even come up with a backup version, should the British somehow lose. He could slip back into town, claiming he fought hard and bravely. Who could prove him wrong in all the chaos? Who would even think to ask?

"You seem to have something on your mind Simone? Correct me if I assume it has nothing to do with your little display just now." Tori's words slipped softly across the room unnoticed by the few women left there.

Simone stared at her and put on a sad and pitiful look. "Why, Tori my dear, you are so perceptive. I declare it's as if you could read my mind. I do have so much to think about, as you yourself. You must be so worried about your precious Jean. If he is not injured, he still could fall into enemy hands could he not? The very thought of that sends chills up my spine. Do you suppose they hang or shoot spies? Oh, but don't let me upset you." She dropped her head down, as if really regretful. Then looking at Tori through the slits of her snake-like eyes, she all but hissed, as she spit out her next barb. "Jean can take care of himself, I'm sure. He knows the waterways so very well. Escape seems to be that man's second name. You, however, are so brave to remain here in town. Why, I declare, if I were you, I would have never had the courage to remain here. I wonder what the British will do with the likes of you?"

Tori had had it. She stood and walked right up to Simone and calmly put both hands on her shoulders. Very kindly and softly she spoke. "Why Simone, how nice of you to be so concerned about my well-being. You are such a dear." She then pulled the woman close, as if hugging her and whispered into her ear. "You won't understand this but listen closely." She led her from the room to the hallway and out of hearing range of anyone else. To Tori, Simone seemed far too smug and she intended to wipe that feeling away. "I'm not the least bit worried about Jean, nor am I worried about the outcome of the battle. We will be victorious, you can trust me on that. We will all live to see our men march home. From which direction will Edward come I wonder?" Tori saw her stiffen. Strike one she told herself. "You can try to upset me all you want. That I can live with, but if you so much as try to upset these poor women again, I swear to you, that you will ruin the day. I will personally shut your lying mouth and don't think I can't do it. I have learned well while living with pirates." She slammed one closed fist into her other open hand dramatically making her point. "Just don't push me bitch, got it." Tori pushed her back and smiled into the shocked face before her. "If you will excuse me, I think I had best go and help Marie calm the little ones. You look like you could use a drink." On her way upstairs, she breathed deeply and prayed that she had scared Simone into behaving herself. It was not going to be easy, living in the house with her. But it would be even harder if she had to put up with twenty or more frenzied ladies. How could she explain to them, that the battle they now heard in the distance, was not the battle that would bring them victory. It was the first of many to come she knew that much. The date was only December 23rd and the decisive battle would not be fought straight off. What she wanted to hear, was an early morning boom, that would be the signal that the Battle of New Orleans had begun...

Cisco sat cold and exhausted but relieved that the first skirmish had left him intact. They had fought long and hard, surprising the British forces and pushing them back. Jackson's strategy had worked. They had caught the British completely off guard. He had seen John Davis only briefly during the fight and then lost track of him. Like many around him, sleep was impossible. They had withdrawn behind the Rodriguez Canal and were hard at work building and digging what would soon become the line of defense. He could only hope John was alright and that in the days ahead they would both be safe. Odds were in their favor. He knew that, but still he found a deep fear climbing inside of him.

He now knew first hand the meaning of cold dread. He looked out into the darkness beyond and envisioned the British disembarking like a swarm of ants. By the thousands they would come, marching toward the small but determined few. For the first time in his life, Cisco bowed his head and prayed. He prayed for history to turn out as it was written and then he cried and prayed for all those that he knew would die. And for the first time he hated being a time traveler...

Jean and David had been crawling around the swamps and backwaters for seventeen days. Many times coming precariously close to the enemy but always able to outmaneuver them and get word sent back to the front line. A few of Jean's men formed a network of spies who were able to relay his information on most of the British movements. With the river now under constant surveillance and the British closely monitored, their job had been accomplished.

Jean reached a fork in one of the small bayous and there met up with an old acquaintance of his, General Humbert. The two spoke together briefly trading information.

Humbert had told him they had won the first fight. That had happened on the night of December 23rd at Rodriguez Canal. They had not lost one man but many of the British had been taken down. "Around one thousand fell to our boys, is what I was told," gloated Humbert. "They just didn't suspect Jackson to appear like he did. They was so unprepared. Never saw anything like it, and these old eyes have seen a lot in their time." He looked at Jean and frowned. "You know the only reason we have a chance at saving New Orleans, was because we hit them first. Took the wind right out of their sails. Since then however, they have been like a stirred hornet's nest and the whole area has become a very dangerous place to go wandering around in.

Jean understood only too well for he had been doing exactly that. Suddenly Cisco's strange saying jumped into his mind. He laughed as he hit Humbert on the back and repeated it, "I would say that they are well and truly pissed off!" Humbert may not have understood Jean's statement but he did get the jest in it and found himself laughing, along with the rest of the men.

He looked at Jean trying to calm down but still chuckling to himself he added, "I would say you have about summed it up. They tried real hard eleven days ago to get at Jackson, then they brought in the artillery fire seven days ago. Suspect you heard that racket. Dominique You gave them hell that day. Damn good shot you know. He was loving it, talking to his canon like it was a lady." He threw back his head and laughed at his statement.

Jean could only grin at the mention of Dominique and his antics. "It would take a hell of a lot more than a few British cannons to get Dominique You dislodged from behind Jackson's ditch I'll tell you that. Once that old fool gets his mind made up on something, well you know him as well as I do."

"That be true enough. I talked to the stubborn fool myself not long after the red-coats tried to breach Jackson's earthworks. He was hopping mad that the cowards broke and ran once he started firing his cannon."

Jean grinned, "I heard about that myself. Seems they were smart though, not cowards. Would you have done any less my friend, seeing your own men being so easily picked off? David and I had a damnable time after that trying to learn their next move, I'll tell you." David nodded his head in agreement but let Jean do all the talking. "We were able to get word to Jackson that the British were planning to blow them out with heavy artillery fire. Got that straight out of the horses mouth. Caught ourselves a real talker. So sure of himself and the outcome too, guess they never heard of our Dominique and his talent, huh? I thought then that was going to be the big attempt, the big battle but since then we have been seeing for ourselves that it was not. I have spent so many days spying on them and harassing them, trying always to stay a jump ahead of them." Jean's smile had gone from his face and he fell silent, lost in his own thoughts.

Humbert took hold of himself in the break in the conversation and gave orders to prepare to move out. "I do know one thing and that's the British are not going to take it much longer. They have lost face too many times and the longer they wait, the less confidant they become. Jackson figures they will make their move real soon. And I think he's got it right there."

"Then I had better get to Jackson and you had better follow your orders and prepare my friend." Jean slapped Humbert on the back as the two nodded in agreement. Nothing else was said as each man simply turned and headed out in different directions.

Jean walked, thinking things over in his mind, trying to put it all into perspective. Over the seventeen days since December 23rd, they had fought small but intense skirmishes and played the game of cat and mouse, hit and run, but now it had become clear. The British were going to advance against Andrew Jackson and his line of defense. Jean had accomplished all he had been asked to, but this one last message he wanted to deliver himself. He only hoped he could get to Jackson in time and not get caught trying to do so.

True to his word, David was able to get Jean and himself into Jackson's camp undetected, under the cover of darkness. Very few men were aware of their arrival. Nor were they seen leaving very shortly thereafter, in the wee hours of a cold and damp January morning...

Jean's meeting with General Jackson had been intense and informative. His praise and admiration of Jean's men was one of the first matters he discussed. "You had not told me sir that your Captain Dominique was such an artilleryman. His handling of the cannon has put the British to shame. Never, sir, will I forget how he entered the camp here, riding on his cannon as if it were a horse." Jackson's weary grin, briefly erased the deep etched worry lines and put a light of mischief in his eyes. "He came in sounding like the boom of his weapon, shouting his orders and if I might add, causing quite a welcome relief to the tension amongst my men." Jackson's face went stern as he turned and walked toward a small wooden table and chair. "Here Mr. Laffite, please come and join me. There is a very grave matter of which we must discuss." His walk seemed a little slow but other than sitting down heavily, sighing as he did so, no other external sign was visible of just how tired the man was.

Jean's admiration for this American could only build as he looked and listened to him. He knew only too well how sick he was, of how little sleep if any he had had in the past week and yet he still continued to do his job and be the General his men expected.

"The tension is high Mr. Laffite. You only have to breathe the air to realize that we are on the very brink of the fight of our lives. I agree with you that the enemy is ready to strike. It is my belief that the British will with this very dawn's light advance upon our position." He rubbed at his eyes with his long boney fingers, as if trying to wipe away a vision he was seeing. "We have received reinforcements and our standing is far larger than I had dared hope for but still we are spread thin. We have to make our stand and pray to God that we can endure. Look here," he pointed to a map laid out on the makeshift desk. "My line is here, just about five miles from the city itself. We have sir, a rude defense at best that has been thrown up and reinforced. This parapet," he ran his finger along the line, "is all that lays between us and the enemy's fire. In some places I estimate it to be a good twenty feet thick and five feet high but that's only in a few places I'm afraid." He shook his head sadly. "The parapet extends from the bank of the Mississippi swamp to here," his hand hit the spot on the map and stayed. "It is nearly a mile long and all along that distance are my forces. So you see for yourself we are spread thin. It is my worry that the British will take full advantage of this fact and use it against us." Jackson then pulled a letter from within his jacket pocket and placed it on the table in full view, pushing it slightly toward Jean. "I have already deployed a General Humbert and his men to where I believe a breech could occur. I do not though, have any knowledge if he and his company have reached their destination, or made the information available to Brigadier General Morgan."

"Begging your pardon sir, I may be of some help there. I saw Humbert on my way here. We talked briefly and he headed out right after. I'm sure that he has indeed reached his destination by now."

"That is good news but it is of the upmost importance, that this message," he tapped the letter hard with his index finger, "reach our forces. They are situated on the right bank of the river, the far side from here." He softened his look briefly, his lip almost curling up in a slight grin. "You sir, are the person I have chosen to deliver it. You and your lad there, will depart immediately." He stood up and extended his hand.

Jean rose up and with one hand took the document off the table and with his other he shook the General's. The grip was a firm one and genuine in its friendship. Jackson's words matched the gesture. "Good luck to you, and God speed."

Jean said nothing. He just turned and called to David over his shoulder as he made his way out of the camp. While still on safe ground, he explained their mission briefly to the boy as he moved rapidly toward the river. David understood the importance of following out the General's orders but one thing bothered him and he just had to ask before they started traveling in silence.

"Boss, how'd you plan on crossing the river once we git dere?" David's whisper sounded a little horse, his voice coming and going in sharp shallow breaths.

"That boy, is the least of my worries right now. If the General's information is correct, a small flat boat with some of his men, are hidden on this side. I have a pass here from the man himself should we be questioned. It's getting across right under the British noses that worries me." Jean put his hand in his pocket once again, checking to make sure that Jackson's message for Brigadier General Morgan was still safe. He had wanted to stay with Jackson and his men and face the British. The man was right he just knew it. They would try to make their advance with daybreak. He thought to himself, how ironic not to be there after all this planning and waiting. He shook his head at the thought and the disappointment. The General's trust in him however, had reached deep inside, making him both proud and humble before the American. He had found, like so many of Jackson's men, that it was easy to follow the man's orders, even if it was not something you really wanted to carry out.

His mind was wandering with such thoughts, as he pushed on toward the river. The going became slower as they approached the riverbank and seeing their way by moonlight was almost impossible. They had to travel as silently and as quickly as possible and this took a tremendous amount of concentration. It was something that Jean was at that moment not doing. He would later realize that it was David's actions and alertness that saved not only the mission but their lives as well.

"Boss, stop!" The words hissed close to his ear as David grabbed his arm and pointed off to the distance where silhouetted against the early morning sky a small garrison of British soldiers moved their way.

Laffite reacted without hesitation, pulling the young David with him. In seconds they lay flat on their stomachs, inching deeper into the dense underbrush. Dirt filled Jean's mouth, as his face dragged along the ground, his head barely clearing the scrub above him. Still he pushed deeper into the tangle of trees and undergrowth praying that David was close behind him. Then as fast as he had moved, he stopped.

David did not have to be told to stay perfectly still and silent he knew that. What he did hear softly spoken from Jean lips, was a simple statement. "This is going to be close." Close or not, David found himself ready to follow Thiac's last words. "You take care of the Boss and see he gets back." Slowly his hand reached down to his waist, where under his shirt lay the knife he would use, if need be. His eyes were on Jean, as his ears listened to the sound of the British patrol as they got closer and closer. He watched as Jean's hand took the letter from his coat and carefully hid it under some dirt and palm roots. This was not a good sign to him. His boss, he realized, really feared they would be caught. David's fear filled his expression. Jean looked at him and winked, telling him with his eyes that he felt it would be alright, relieving some of the boy's tension. Then he placed his head down sideways, keeping eye contact with David. There was no place to go and nothing left for them to do. Both of them held their breath and waited.

From what they had initially heard in the bits of broken conversations, the British were not really sure what they had seen. Or were they sure of the exact location. Both facts that played on Jean's side. The soldiers had for a brief time ventured a short distance into the brush but soon determined that a search would prove most difficult if not impossible. They had listened as the order to cease and head out had been given. An order that Jean did not believe. They had given up too easily something the British did not do...

The time seemed to be dragging by to David and still Jean did not move. The British had headed out at least ten minutes ago and not a sound of another man could he hear. The call of a large bird answered by its mate indicated that morning had arrived. The riverbank was waking up. Then the sound of muffled canon fire, off in the distance, rumbled across the bayous like thunder. Jean remembered only too clearly, when a few hours ago, Jackson had told him, that he thought the British would attack with the dawn and by the sound of it, he had been right. Still they lay there, listening to the far off rumble, while no other close noise of the enemy assaulted their ears.

David felt it was surely safe enough now, to come out of hiding? Twice he had started to ask Jean and twice the man's flash from his eyes, had silenced him. So he continued to remain still and wait.

Jean was not about to leave the cover in which they hid. Not until he was certain that they had not been detected. One hour in his mind, would prove him right or wrong. Patience was on his side, not the enemies. If the British suspected they were there, they would wait, hoping to catch them as they emerged. But they would not wait long, with the sound of the battle rolling across the heavens. If after a good amount of time, nothing or no one emerged, then they would hasten on.

Time crept slowly by, till in the end, having no indication otherwise, Jean was sure it was all clear. He had made his mind up on this and was just about to make his move, when the sound of men, not nature, reached his ears. It was undeniably the sound of men moving about and reforming their marching column. The shuffle of feet and grumbling of voices filled the air. Then the words, "move out," floating on the morning breeze.

He had been right! Not all of the bastards had left right away. His gaze fell on David's face, as the boy looked knowingly back. Sweat covered Jean's brow. David had watched, as it broke out, running rivulets of salt stinging water, into the man's eyes. It was not from heat but from knowing how close they had truly come to being apprehended, that had caused it to form. He realized that he had come within a few seconds of moving, a move that would have proved a fatal one. If the British had waited for a few more seconds, they would have had them dead in their tracks. If David had not seen them coming and warned him... Jean squeezed his eyes closed and then slowly reached up with his hand and wiped away some of the discomfort. He smiled and winked at David, who grinned back.

"David," Jean 's voice was almost so low, that the boy was not sure he had even spoken. "We will stay here a little longer, just to be sure." Jean then closed his eyes and seemed to be resting. David could only hope that he would not sleep long. Thirty minutes later, much to his surprise, it was he who Jean was waking up.

Jean had not slept, with the sound of battle reaching his ears as he lay safely hidden. He knew the sound came from the battle he was supposed to have fought, The Battle of New Orleans. It could be no other. He prayed he was wrong, but his gut told him otherwise. Was it turning out as Tori, John and Cisco had predicted it would? He could only hope so.

By midday they had safely delivered Jackson's message and after a quick meal, headed back to what Jean knew was going to be the victorious front lines. He had tried to get David to remain securely behind but the boy had insisted he accompany him and no amount of threats or orders could sway him. The date was now January 8th and by the time Laffite and David arrived back at Jackson's the famous battle was history.

The sudden silence brought a new terror to the house of Madame Poree and its occupants. For days and nights Tori had listened to most of the women cry and pray. On the first day there had been twenty ladies to deal with, now she estimated around one hundred of New Orleans' feminine society had gathered behind the closed and bolted doors. The only light in the place was a few candles, that they kept burning all night. The days were long but the nights were longer, that was, when you had nothing to stop your mind from thinking about what was really happening. Then there were the dreams, the horrible nightmares that filled what little sleep she could catch. One such a dream had awakened her. Not that it was so bad. She really could not remember much, only Marie Laveau's voice trying to tell her something.

The fire had burned low and the room had a chill about it. Looking around the parlor, she could tell most had fallen asleep. Those that were still awake sat in silence with their own demons. The sudden sound of cannon fire, ripped at the tranquillity within the house and tore it to shreds. News yesterday from the front lines, had pre-warned them, that a major decisive battle would soon be fought. Hearing the continued boom off in the distance at such an early hour, could mean only one thing. The Battle of New Orleans had begun at daybreak. Tori knew that at last her wait was over. One way or the other history was being made that morning and all the praying and crying going on around her, was not going to change a thing. For the next two hours the sound of cannons continued unabated. Then it became sporadic and was suddenly over. During this time she had tried to calm down the most hysterical and comfort the truly distraught, who upon hearing the sudden silence took it to mean the worst. Like a summer storm that had passed, all was now calm, the heavens were at rest.

Simone who had behaved herself, after her encounter with Tori, now seemed to come alive, certain of the outcome that faced them all. "It is surely over, why else should the cannon stop?" She clasped her hands together and looked truly worried as she addressed the room full of women., but then to be up against such a force. They must have been overwhelmed and surrendered. Ladies, I think we had best prepare to welcome the British and their rule."

Madame Poree gasped at this, followed by Marie Destrehan's declaration of "Never!"

"Come, come ladies. It is the only possible way we can help our husbands, our gallant but foolish followers of that stupid American General Jackson," gloated Simone.

Tori could hardly believe she was at it again, more so, that she actually believed what she was saying. "I would be wary of what you are saying Simone. We have no indication one way or another of what our situation is. Let alone that of the fine and brave men at the front." She was about to soothe the ladies' fears by asking them to have patience and not think the worst, when the sound of cheering people outside filled the room.

Tori ran to the French doors and flung them open knowing already what the sound meant and calling to the ladies she beckoned them to come and see.

What was plain as day, was the sound of joy that rang in the air. Women standing on balconies all up and down the street, waving to each other and hugging and laughing. The word victory was been called from one person to another, passing the news quickly throughout the town.

Tori turned triumphantly and laughing at the top of her lungs, stepped back into the room and into the open arms of Marie. "I told you did I not? It has happened, Jackson has saved the town, it is over. We have won!" She could not help but cry tears of joy, as she danced around the room with her friend.

Dizzy from the spinning and excitement she stopped and sat down in a chair facing the doorway. What she then saw made her laugh even louder. Simone had a look so stricken that she actually looked comical. She watched as the very embarrassed and infuriated Simone quickly made her exit.

"Good riddance is what I say," Tori giggled. Nothing was going to ruin this moment for her. They had worked so hard for so long, to reach this glorious goal.

"Ladies, ladies please may I have your attention for a second?" It was Madame Poree and Marie standing together looking very serious. "We all know how happy we are but Marie here and myself, we can't help wonder about the condition of our dearly beloved and brave men. It would seem that their jobs may be finished and ours just begun. Ladies, Marie and I propose to aid not only our wounded but to help those of the defeated also. It is the only Christian and most charitable action to take, is it not?"

Tori had never, up until that moment, thought about the carnage that would result from the battle. Being forced to face that horrible fact, was as sobering to her elated mood, as if a bucket of ice cold water had been dumped on her head. "I do most certainly agree with you both," she announced. "I am truly ashamed to have to admit that the thought of doing such a kind and selfless act, never entered my mind." She crossed the room and stood before the two woman, taking their hands in hers. "Of course I will join you both and now seems as good a time as any. Shall we begin?"

By the time the sun was setting across the battle field, the women of New Orleans had come by the wagonloads. Makeshift hospitals had been set up for those hurt too badly to be moved far. Those lucky enough to have sustained injuries considered not so critical, were loaded into wagons and taken into the city to the Ursuline Convent, which had been converted into a hospital. When that was filled, the homes of the very citizens, who only hours before had been the enemy, opened their doors.

Tori's eyes had filled with tears again and again, at the bloody sight that met her gaze. Walking in some spots was dangerous, for the blood of so many covering the ground made it as slick as ice. The stench of death, hung in the air so thick as to make it hard for her to breathe. At first she had found it more deplorable than she thought she could bear, but the painful and pitiful calls for help, forced her to cope. Alongside Cayetana Claiborne, Madame Poree, Mrs. Livingston, Marie Destrehan and many others, she bandaged and cleaned wounds on both the conscious and unconscious. Those that could talk, thanked her over and over again for her kindness.

It never stopped amazing her, the sheer number of injured and their ages. Most were nothing more than young boys it seemed to her but she realized also, that age was not the issue that bothered her the most. It was knowing that the battle had been fought when peace had already been declared. News that would reach here too late and she had known it. She told herself over and over she had no way of getting that news to the right people to stop the massacre. It was foolish to think otherwise.

The injured kept coming, way after dark by torch light they kept arriving for help. All those that could. Still many more lay just over the embankment beyond help. To have died so far from home, English, Scottish, Irish and Welsh. Never to see again their loved ones and homeland. And she had known! The words reverberated in her mind. Suddenly it became unbearable she had to get away from there.

Tori did not remember walking out of the hospital area, of stepping over the injured and dead. She only knew that all of a sudden she was alone in the dark and crying. Her head down in her lap, she sat and cried for all she was worth. Had she tried to tell them, she asked herself, could she have got the information to those that could have stopped the slaughter? Or was she guilty of allowing it to happen? Such was the state of her mind, when a hand touched her lightly.

"Mam, you all right?" asked a young male voice.

Tori looked up into a young Kentuckian's face. The manner of his dress told her this much without asking. His buckskin coat and tall leather boots, the long rifle at his side in one hand, his lantern in the other, its soft light reflecting off the blade of his long bone handled knife that still rested in place, held by his leather belt. He looked to be not much older than sixteen or seventeen at most. It was hard to tell in the dark, with only the light from his lantern to go by. She stared at his face, at the blood-stained bandage around his head, and shook her head no.

He looked at her. She was so upset and to his way of thinking she had every right to be. The surrounding area was no place for a lady to be it just didn't seem right. He was amazed at how so many of the woman had come to help and managed the hell around them so bravely. Instead of breaking down and crying, they had rolled up their sleeves and bandaged and taken care of so many maimed and bloodied bodies. Maybe he had not seen them cry because like the lady before him, they did it in private he thought. He put his lantern down by her side and spoke gently as he would to his own mother.

"Mind if I sit a while with you Mam? I think we both need some company and maybe a shoulder to cry on?"

She smiled, he was trying to be so brave and be the man his body was not yet grown into. Yet after today, Tori had no doubt that he had earned the status of adult for himself. She nodded her head and he sat next to her, letting her lean up against him.

From all around them came the sound of men calling to each other. Torch lights flames flickering in the wind would stop moving as another body was found to be alive. They were still searching for those that cried out and those who needed it but could not utter a word. She had not realized that she had wandered so far into what was referred to as the death zone.

Tori had stopped crying and found that her young companion was sitting patiently waiting for her to speak. His hand had somehow taken hold of hers and was stroking her fingers. Then before she could react, he started to cry himself and the roles reversed she became the one to comfort.

Through his ragged sobs, his story unraveled, "I didn't think it would be anything like it was. I can still see them redcoats coming at us, wave after wave. They just kept coming and we just kept shooting." He shuddered, "I saw them blown to bits by cannon fire and still they marched, right over their dead companions. I shall never forget it, not the rest of my days. It was hell, just pure hell."

He sobbed taking in big gulps of air, no longer caring or talking. She just held him not saying a word, he had to get it out of his system, let go or go mad. After a few minutes of hard wrenching tears he was wrung out. The tears stopped and through hiccups he started to talk again. He looked into Tori's face and admitting to her and himself for the first time, something he found shameful. "I was so scared. I'm still scared. I got hit see," he gingerly touched his head, "doc said I was lucky the bullet bounced off me." He cocked his head to one side and continued, "I woke up after it was ended. The battle was over and some man was carrying me to the doctor. That's all I remember clear." Fear covered his face as he grabbed Tori's arms, pleading with her. "Tell me I'm alive Mam, please tell me I'm alright?"

She drew him into her arms again and rocked him, whispering over and over as she stroked his back, that he would be just fine. "Look at me," she demanded, when he had quieted down. "I think you and I had best introduce ourselves, friends need names you know? My name is Tori, and yours is?" He wiped his nose on the back of his sleeve, "Robert, Mam. I mean, my name is Robert Taylor."

"Well Robert, I'm here to tell you, that you are not only alive but going to recover fully from your wound. You will be home safe in no time and a hero at that." He looked at her and sort of half-heartedly laughed. "My mother will be happy about that, and my Jenny too I suspect."

"I'm sure they will be. Today was one that will go down in history you know? You and all Jackson's men fought a very brave battle and against all odds you won. You can be very proud of yourself. I myself am honored to have made your acquaintance." She smiled fully at him. "You have made me feel a whole lot better, I hope I have helped you?"

"Yes Mam, you have. I'm not so sure that you should feel so honored though, me crying like a baby and all."

She laughed lightly, "Now don't you go and worry about that. I know many fine brave men who have cried." He looked doubtingly at her. "Really I have. Do you know who Jean Laffite is?" Robert nodded his head, his eyes growing large at the pirates name. "Well Robert, if you give me your word you won't tell, I'll let you in on a little known fact about that man." Once again he nodded affirmatively. "Well, I have seen him cry. We were at sea and his dear friend got hurt bad in a fight and when the fight was over, Jean cried."

"How do you know that?" he quizzed, "you're just making it up to make me feel better."

"No I'm not. And I know it to be true because I was there. You see, Jean Laffite is my husband." Robert was dumbfounded. His mouth hung open and he held his breath, afraid that if he moved he would wake up from this fantastic dream.

"Oh, Robert I wouldn't lie at a time like this and not to you. Trust me in what I'm telling you, will you?"

Somehow he knew what she was telling him to be gospel and he did trust her. "Thank you Mam, that means a lot to me an all. I best be trying to find my uncle now, him or my friends. I know they must be looking for me and I would hate for them to worry."

"Soon as you find them, you will be headed home I guess, am I right?"

"Yes, Mam I sure hope so. Nothing to keep us down here any longer, as far as I know anyway." He stood to go.

"Robert, where is home for you?"

"That be up Kentucky way Mam."

Another thought crossed her mind as she stood up next to the young man.

"You don't happen to know a Davey Crockett do you?"

"Yes Mam," his face lit up.

"Well that, is don't rightly know him personal like. Know folk who do though. He a friend of yours?" He was looking at her strangely.

"Oh goodness gracious me, no. I've just heard about him." She fell silent thinking if she should do what she wanted or not. Then without further doubts she knew. The boy before her deserved to have a long and happy life and she could try to ensure he did.

"Robert I'm about to ask you to do something for me. Something that might sound strange and not make a lick of sense." She was trembling. "Do you trust me?"

"Yes Mam, I reckon I do."

"Well I want you to promise me something and know that what I am about to ask you to do, is very important." He looked at her, almost fearing what it was she was about to say.

"Robert, should Mr. Crockett ever ask you to join him on a trip to Texas I want you to promise me you won't go. I know this sounds strange, but I think God put us together tonight so I could give you this message. No more battles for you, alright?"

"Mam, I would be only too happy to agree to the no more battles." He actually smiled, then he reached up with his hand and scratched the side of his head. "You really think old Davey is going to go to this here Texas place, to fight another battle?"

"I know he will Robert and I'm asking you not to go." Standing in his lamp light, pleading her case she looked so beautiful. Her face was almost like that of an angels he told himself. That was it! His mother had a picture of one in her bible at home and looking at this woman now, he could tell himself she was one, it had to be.

Tori wanted to say something, but watching his face and the strange emotions he was going through, she decided to keep still and let him be the one to talk. He looked like he was going to run from her, and who could blame him? He most likely thinks I'm crazy she reasoned.

He had been raised to be a God-fearing man and once his word was given it would be kept. A man's word was his word after all. To break it would be a sin. He would never know why he agreed and gave his word that night. But years later he would bless her for asking him for it. "Yes Mam, you have my word if it means that much to you."

"It does. I get to finally change something for the right." Her eyes glazed with unsprung tears. "God go with you Robert, and be happy." She hugged him quickly and walked away, back to the hospital and those that needed help. She felt stronger and in a strange way healed.

He watched her disappear and felt that he had been healed and helped. He could not explain it, but he knew she had been sent by God. She was no wife of Laffite. He had sat and been touched by a true angel. If not a real one, then as close as one could come. He turned and headed toward town, where he knew his uncle and friends would be. His fighting days were over. He was ready to go home and settle down. No more adventures for him, he had all he wanted waiting for him at home. Her name was Jenny.

# Chapter 28

Tori and two other ladies headed back into the city with a wagonload of the injured soldiers. Too exhausted to talk and stunned by all they had seen, the three women had traveled in silence. Tori had been amazed at how well the ladies of society had taken control of themselves amongst the bloody mayhem when earlier like so many others they had been hysterical shrieking and fainting. Never would she have guessed those very same ladies, would have been capable of such bravery and unselfish acts of heroism.

Mrs. Livingston felt Tori's scrutiny and raised her head, looking curiously at her. She was almost too tired to speak but weakly smiled as she did so. "I am sure he is alright Madame Laffite. I had heard some of the men talk of him earlier and of how they had seen him with the General. I did not hear any mention of any injury."

"That is so kind of you. Really it is. I have to admit though I was not wondering about Jean. Rather, I was sat here thinking of the miracle I had witnessed today. You will have to admit, that to see so many of the ladies there, amongst the blood and pain, after such a display of helplessness this morning." Tori took in a deep breath while shaking her head, "well it was just so amazing, was it not?"

"I believe Tori, I can call you Tori can't I?"

"I would be happier if you did." Mrs. Livingston nodded her head and continued.

"Well like I was saying, I believe that under circumstances such as we have been in for the past hours, we were able to carry out our duties because we were in control don't you see? It's the not knowing that tends to make one edgy."

"I think I do understand," a tired smile crossed her lips. I have learned so much today with all I have seen and I have to tell you, my respect and admiration for the Southern Lady has grown immensely."

Mrs. Livingston just nodded her head and smiled. The sway of the wagon was rocking her body back and forth as if on a boat at sea. She seemed lost in her own thoughts, when she looked across at the third companion, who was deep in sleep. "I have to agree with you. My own opinion has taken just such a shift. Who would have ever thought it?" Tori and her laughed softly as they recognized each had been feeling and thinking the same thoughts. "You are not a Yankee are you." Her question came out as more of an expression.

"No I'm not. I'm just an American. A very tired and happy-to-be-alive, good old-fashioned American-as-apple-pie girl." If Mrs. Livingston was going to pursue the line of conversation or question Tori's strange remark, she did not have the chance. A voice rang clear on the crisp night air. It was a most welcome sound to Tori's ears and seeing her reaction Mrs. Livingston smiled all the more. The wagon driver pulled his team to a halt, as the mounted rider approached.

As tired as he was Jean could not rest until he had his lady at his side. For hours he had searched and questioned her whereabouts, finally learning that she was most likely amongst the last of the ladies to leave the battlefield. He had been on his way to collect her, when he spotted the wagon making its way slowly up the road. Her laughter had carried on the air, like welcome music to his ears, confirming her presence aboard.

"Jean?" She stood up turning to face him. He did not speak, just pulled his horse close to the wagon's side and reached out his hand to her. She took hold of his outstretched hand and let him pull her up onto the animal, sitting her in front of him, where they both hugged each other.

Jean looked over at the puzzled wagon driver, "I have what I came for, I suggest you continue and get these other two ladies to their husbands and these men to the hospital. Ladies if you will excuse us, we have to leave your company for now. Good evening to you." With that he turned the horse and spurred it off, holding his lady close to him.

"Was that Jean Laffite? I mean, really the man himself?" asked the shocked woman across from Mrs. Livingston.

"It most certainly was. Dashing isn't he?"

"Why Mrs. Livingston, I declare you are making me blush. Such thoughts for a married lady indeed. Still all in all, one would have to agree with you," she giggled.

For the first time in what seemed like forever, they were able to return to the townhouse. There they were welcomed and fussed over, by a very emotional and happy Bessy. She insisted on feeding them, while hot water was taken upstairs to fill the bath.

"Now I's won't be taking no for no answer. You both just listen to me and know'd that I be taking care of you. You just be to tired to think clear and I know'd what you be needing and all." Her hands were placed on her hips as her head swayed from side to side. She could be a most powerfully persuasive person when she put her mind to it and no amount of argument was going to alter her course of action, not when one of her stubborn moods hit.

Jean and Tori let her have her way knowing that she was probably right. Neither wanted to talk about what they had seen or been through, yet slowly as the hours ticked by, they talked and learned what had occurred since they were last together. When at last they found themselves in each others arms in bed, the talking stopped. It was early morning as they finally drifted off into a deep and peaceful sleep.

Voices from downstairs broke into her barely awakened state, one that she longed to stay in. Pulling the covers up over her head, she struggled to remain in that blissful place, warm and cozy next to her man. The only problem being, that as she reached across the bed, the space that should have held a warm body, lay vacant. Her eyes opened to search visibly for the man her touch had not found and quickly she discovered herself alone. Tori sat up and listened intently to the now distant voices below, trying to determine who had come calling at such an early hour but was unable to clearly distinguish who it was.

Downstairs, Jean and Cisco sat drinking coffee and talking about the past few days and what was occurring even as they sat across from each other.

"Jackson will remain at the battle site until the British withdraw completely. It is an uneasy truce that has taken over down there but it will hold." Cisco was trying to put it all into perspective. "You don't have to worry as far as Davis and I can recollect both sides will avoid any further confrontation. Besides the British have so many dead to deal with. The count is in you know at least on our side. We have thirteen confirmed killed. Thirty-nine wounded and nineteen missing. Jackson estimates the British losses to be nearly three thousand, an estimate that will be damn close when all is said and done." Cisco took a long sip of his coffee, watching Laffite as he continued. "You know in my time we have a saying it's shell-shocked. Our men who saw real bad action in war would sometimes suffer from this condition. Anyway this morning as I left Jackson's men, I looked across at the Redcoats and I would say that in my opinion many are suffering shell-shock. They are so stunned at having lost and Jackson's men are just as stunned at having won but no one down there is acting any way but shell-shocked. Can you understand what I'm trying to explain here?"

Jean had a very good idea of what it was Cisco was trying to tell him. He himself, even knowing the outcome of the fight, had been shocked when it had finally ended.

Tori entered the room hurriedly, wanting to know what was happening. Upon seeing Cisco sitting with Jean, she broke into a huge smile and extended her arms. "Come here you crazy fool, I have been so worried about you. Is there any news about the others how is John?"

"They are all fine as far as I know. Davis is at his hotel helping supply some of the food for the hospital and Livingston and Grymes were still with Jackson when I left early this morning. We have done it Tori. We have kept history intact but at a price."

She looked at him and could see the sadness in his eyes. He had been there, seen the battle, the killing and all the ugliness of war. Her happy-go-lucky Cisco would be changed forever.

"Davis and I talked late into the night and I have to let you know what we decided. Whether or not you join us is up to you but we intend to keep our promises to ourselves." He sounded so somber.

"I think you had better sit down and tell me, it sounds pretty serious. Jean could you fix me a cup of coffee please?"

"You know I would be delighted to do so and if you two need to talk alone..."

Cisco looked away from Tori and faced Jean, "No, please stay and listen to what I have to say."

"If you want. But before you start, I have a question for you both. It's something that has been on my mind for sometime but until now, I have not wanted to ask. If I may be as bold to at this time come forward and put this question to you?"

They both took a seat and having no idea as to what was on Jean's mind, they spoke in unison. "Yes, of course." Tori took Cisco's hand and the two of them laughed at each other.

"You may not laugh when I ask my question but I have to ask. Now that this great Battle of New Orleans is over and all has happened as it has, well now what? What do you know about what happens next to me? Or dare I ask?" Tori looked at Jean's face and could clearly see the complex emotions behind his eyes. He wanted to know and yet was afraid of the answer at the same time. She wished she could put to ease his pain and suffering but like everyone else, he would not find his answer coming from her.

"Jean; Cisco, John and I have spoken about this and well each of us only knew about the battle. John did know a bit more didn't he?" She looked at Cisco.

"Yes, just a bit. That's part of the problem, always has been hasn't it? We only know bits and pieces. Some dates or approximate dates. We know about events in history that will yet happen but like everything that has happened, we don't know any real information to help. We got lucky here, just lucky that's all." His face was so serious. "We can tell you this Jean, you will become the hero of the day. It's like we told you, in the history books and certainly in New Orleans, you will be known as The Gentleman pirate who saved the day. You, will along with your men, receive a full pardon from the president and that's about it. Sorry man, we just don't know further than that. We did not study about you in history. Our history lessons did not contain the information that you are seeking. What I do know for now and forever is that you are a fine friend and a true American."

Tori watched Jean's eyes. She saw the shadow of disappointment and then the all-over-happiness that washed it away. Ever the optimist, he laughed at them both. "Well maybe it's for the best. From here on out I can make my own destiny and the outcome will be as it should no doubt."

"I'm sure of it." Cisco stood and gripped Jean in a hug, slapping him on the back. "I'm glad that you feel as you do because it has a lot to do with what I wanted to tell you both. John and I have made a pact with ourselves, to keep all our knowledge within our minds. In other words, from here on out, what we know about the future, will remain within. We have had quite enough with this history making business and from now on, we intend to let the cards fall as they may." He looked back at Tori. "I don't know where you stand on this. It's something you have to deal with yourself. But from now on the future is the past for us, even with you. You will always remain our dear friend, nothing can change that, but we will not discuss or talk of that which is beyond the now."

He had changed. Her Cisco was talking to her and meaning it. She had no doubt that he spoke the truth for both he and John. That to them, the future was finished. From now on for herself, any talk about the things to come, would have to be between her and who? Panic flickered inside her as the implications took hold.

Cisco could see the pain in her face and wanted to try to make her understand why they felt as they did. "Look Tori, it's just that we feel that we have done quite enough and we just want to settle down. We want to live the remaining years of our lives without complications if you know what I mean?"

"I do." she spoke softly. "I don't blame you or John. It's just going to be hard not talking about so much." She had tears filling her eyes. "Look, if that is what you want, then I will have to live with it, that's all. I may not agree with you but then I can't live your lives can I? As to what or how I will deal with what I know, I can't say right now."

Jean admired Cisco's and John's decision, knowing that it was not going to be an easy promise for either to keep. As for his lady though, he found himself hoping. He did not always understand or like some of the things she had told him but how he loved hearing about the good and grand inventions. He wanted to hear more of the inventions and wondrous times and hoped that she would continue, on quiet days alone together, to tell him her stories.

"Look you two, I have got to go. Davis is waiting for me to get back and now that I have relayed all that I came to tell. Well you understand? Take care of yourselves and stop over soon. John would love to see you both." He hugged Tori and smiled his old Cisco smile. Then he was gone, leaving the room silent.

Jean sat down next to her and slipped his arm around her waist. "You know you are not alone and never will be? No matter what you decide, whether you talk to me or not, I will abide by your choice. But if it helps you any, I for one adore listening to you and about your time but only if you feel you want to." She kissed him gently and nodded her head, "I think I shall always want to tell someone, there is just so much."

Bessy entered the room making as much fuss as she could, just so the two of them would know that she was there. Tori grinned at her, knowing that she was always trying not to bother them when they were alone, unless necessary. "What's up Bessy?"

"Nothing important Mizz Tori. Just ain't a knowing what to do with that there David. He be a standing around out back, fidgeting about like a dog with fleas. He done asked me to ask the Master what he supposed to be doing now?" Jean had quiet forgotten the boy and now that the matter had been brought to his attention, he knew he had work in that area to be taken care of. "You just tell that lad to stay put and rest up for a while. I'll come for him when I'm ready."

"Yes sur, I'll be telling him right away. I sur'n will." She left happy at having solved one more household problem.

"Now my love, as much as I would like to stay here with you, I do have a few loose ends to tie up. I'll explain when I return. You on the other hand, have just about enough time to dress for a nice evening dinner. Grymes has invited us to join him and I'm glad now, as I have some papers for him to draw up for me. Don't ask me about it now. I'll explain when it's all taken care of." Like always, when his mind was set on something there was no stopping him and she was glad when he quickly departed leaving her alone with her thoughts. She did need some time to sort out a few matters of her own. One kept niggling at the back of her mind, refusing to go away. Instead it was demanding to be faced once and for all. It was the question of her promise to return to the lake.

David walked with Jean for the first time in many days. The streets of New Orleans were preparing for Jackson's victorious return and every person they passed, either seemed consumed with that or the shaking of Jean's hand. All of the city seemed to want Jean and his lovely lady to join them for dinner. A far' cry from only a few weeks ago when he was a wanted and hunted banditti.

The progress had been slow and after the last stop, David realized that it was going to take them quite a bit longer before reaching the blacksmith shop.

"I had best be getting to the shop. Thiac, he's a going to be a needing my help and all."

"That he will lad, more and more orders come into the shop each day." Jean looked sideways with his eyes only, as he watched the boy walking a few steps behind him. David you did a great job when you and I were together, you know that don't you? You are to be proud of what you did, saving my life and the mission like you did. I will never forget that."

"Boss, it's I whos will never forget. You's saved my life it seems to me. Keeping me still and all. It be me who will not forget. You's saved me sur'n you's did. I owe's you, not d'other ways. Yes sur, one day, one day David Jackson, he's going to find away to pay you a back. I swear's on my own soul, you will be paid back."

"So it's David Jackson now is it?" Jean put his head back and laughed, temporarily standing still. He continued his walking when he realized that people were staring at him. "I assume that the choice in name had something to do with the General?"

"Yes boss. It be his name and all but he done won da battle and kept dem redcoats out of dis here city. So I's thought, that I'd be a taking his name and do good by it and all. Sort of thanking him and reminding myself of him everyday and such."

"I'm sure the General would be honored but then we can't have a slave with his name now can we?" David's bright young face fell. "No, boss, I guessen we's can't." His young head hung down. Once again he was reminded of his position. What would he be needing two names for? He was stupid. He should have known better.

Jean softened toward the boy, who had no way of knowing he was teasing him. He just couldn't drag this out any longer. "You had best go on ahead and tell Thiac that I think he had better consider hiring you. I want you to work for me there Mr. Jackson." David looked up at Jean, his face full of wonder and questions. Had he heard his boss right? "Well go on, jobs are not easy to find and you had best take advantage of my offer before I change my mind." David spun on his heels, ready to take off for Thiac's when he was stopped by Jean's voice. "Wait just a second there don't be running off till I'm finished. What I have not explained to you is simple enough. You will find that Thiac has your freedom papers waiting for you. I saw to it that you would have them, that is, if it's what you want," he asked jokingly.

David did not wait a second. With his face serious and stunned he looked at Jean, the man he owed his life to and now his freedom. A huge grin filled his young face. "Yes boss, it be just what I be wanting. I'm a going right now. I's will make you's proud. You's see that I will."

"I have no doubt of that. You are already quite a man. Now if you don't mind a lady awaits me." Jean turned and walked away. He couldn't wait to give Tori this piece of news. She just loved it when a slave got his papers and freedom. Said it made her feel good and he guessed she was right after all. He felt just fine, more than fine, he felt happy!

David ran off down the street, free. He was free, and he would see to it, that one day he paid all he owed back. But how do you pay back for something like your life and your freedom he wondered?

Word reached the city on January 19th, that the British had sailed. Jackson, ever the cautious man, was going to remain at his post with his men a few more days, just to be certain they had truly departed. The city was in full readiness, when finally on the day of January 23, 1915, General Andrew Jackson and his men triumphantly rode into New Orleans and into the biggest victory celebration anyone had ever seen.

On the steps of the Cathedral situated in an area of what would later become known as Jackson Square, Mrs. Livingston standing next to her husband, greeted their old friend. Filled with enthusiasm and caught up in the moment, she placed a laurel crown upon his head.

The large crowd roared it's approval and Jackson although thoroughly embarrassed by such an act, had a good sense of humor and joined in the laughter of all those surrounding him. He waved to all and standing there like he was, proud and yet humble Tori knew he would make a good president.

The grand ball had been announced to all and anyone could attend. For the first time in the city's history, all cultures would come together under one roof, for one joyous occasion. The American victory at Chalmette, was supposed to have been the reason, but once Laffite and his men appeared, it quickly took on another tone. Now the city had the real heroes of the battle to thank, and thank them they did. With welcome arms they accepted them. Jean and Pierre were no longer to be avoided. Indeed, many tried to be among the first to invite or be invited to future dinners and gatherings with the pair. Laffite's men, who would have stood no chance at ever walking the streets of New Orleans again now called it home, and its citizens friends.

It did not go unnoticed by anyone, that even the Governor and his wife, had sought out the company of Jean and his lady. They stood with Jackson and Jean, joking openly about the tricks played on each other especially the wanted posters. To all those present, it would seem that all had been forgiven and that Jean Laffite and William Claiborne had let bygones be bygones.

Lost in the uproar and rabble-rousing, were two very disgruntled people. Edward and Simone hid their hostilities well, smiling and joining in on the celebration. They avoided any contact with the Laffite's choosing to bide their time as to what should be done. Well before the long night was over, they had slipped away to plot and plan their next depraved move.

"Let them have their moment of glory. The higher they climb the harder they fall." Simone had told Edward. "I don't think it has crossed anyone's mind my dear husband that Jean and his men are still wanted pirates. We shall have to remind the Governor of his duty once the General departs, which I hear is soon. All is not lost yet my love."

Edward who had been feeling defeated, found himself snickering and feeling decisively better. Once again his darling Simone had boosted his moral and he had no doubt that this time with careful planning, Laffite would see the end to his so-called hero status.

"Yes, my darling Simone," he cooed into her ear, brushing the hair from her neck. "You are right once again all is not lost. Let us forget about the fools and have our own celebration. I've been thinking how would you like to be married to the next Governor?" His question caused her to giggle.

"Once we get what we want I feel that fool William should lose his position for taking such a damnable long time to accomplish such a simple task. The fall of Laffite and his wench, should have happened long ago, if he had not been such a fool. Don't you agree my dear?"

His breath was hot on her neck, his lips wet and warm. "That I do my love. And what a glorious idea. Governor? Why didn't I think of that I wonder?"

They both laughed and continued the rest of the night to dream and plot, something that they were both only too good at.

The invitation dated February 10th, requested the presence of Mr. and Mrs. Jean Laffite, to the farewell dinner for Andrew Jackson. It was to be held at the Governor's house and would by all indications be well attended. This last statement had been added by Cayetana. Just what she had been trying to say was not clear but then they would soon find out. The dinner was only two days away.

Tori had wanted to see Andrew Jackson just one more time before he rode off into history and out of their lives. She had promised herself, that under no circumstances would she allow herself to reveal to him any knowledge that she had about his future, no matter how tempted she was. He would find his own pathway to being president with or without her help she was certain of that.

Jean had listened to her talk for hours, over the past few weeks, about history and the future but as the days slipped by, she talked less and less, even changing the subject when he asked her about one detail or another pertaining to what lie ahead. This had puzzled him, as she had always been only too willing and excited to explain about all the inventions and miraculous medicines. One after another she had rattled off, laughing and joking about each, knowing how ridiculous some of them had sounded to him. It was when she spoke of events that her moods would darken. Some had been wondrous and exciting, such as space travel and ships that sailed under the waves. Man standing on the North and South poles and then climbing to the top of the tallest mountains. All of these and more had taken his breath away. Then she had slipped and mentioned something about a Civil War and the fall of the Confederate South.

After that, to Jean's perspective, it was as if a curtain had come down on all that she knew and nothing he could do or say would allow it to be raised again. Some inner instinct, or fear, had forced her to finally agree with Cisco's and John's decision to remain silent about what was to be and no amount of probing on his part had changed her mind.

Jean had worried at first. The Tori he loved and knew so well had buried a large part of herself by denying the ability to discuss her lifetime. And in doing so, she had become more somber, seeking time alone, to sit and contemplate whatever it was that she was struggling with. He often caught her in a daydream world of her own thoughts, her mind miles, if not years away from him and his love. She seemed to be growing evermore distant but when caught off guard, she would bury whatever it was she had been thinking about and act as if nothing was wrong. Jean knew she was only fooling herself when she claimed everything to be all right. Behind her eyes, he would catch a glimpse of a hellish turmoil and knew a storm was brewing in her. When or if it would break, would be entirely up to her and like a sailor at sea, all he could do was prepare for whatever it held in store for him.

The Governor's dinner party could not have come at a better time as far as he was concerned. His lady had seemed to come alive with the news and whatever had been plaguing her, had for the time being died down. Marie had helped her prepare for the gala and seeing her descend the stairs, all smiles and laughter, he dared to allow himself the luxury of relaxing. They departed for the dinner, laughing and happy in each other's company.

Compared to the chill of the February evening, the house was warm and inviting. Cayetana had gone all out for the affair and was rewarded repeatedly, by many positive compliments, as to how splendid everything looked. Nothing had gone unattended, from the smallest detail of flowers placed in strategic positions, to the choice of music played. The guest list had been hers to attend to, a matter that her husband normally had more control over. This time however, he had not cared so much as to who or why certain persons had been included, trusting instead in his wife's knowledge and ability to host the perfect sendoff for the General.

Tori and Jean beamed as they realized that more than one or two of their own close friends were in attendance. What had seemed like a long boring evening ahead, now looked as if it would be filled with long hours of friendship and welcome conversation. Tori tugged at Jean's sleeve as they entered the large parlor, whispering in his ear giggling as she did so. "Seems that Dominique has the General's ear already. Just look at the two of them. One would think they had been comrade in arms for years not just weeks. Do you suppose Mr. Jackson needs a break?" They both nodded their heads in unison and laughing lightly, marched up to the pair.

The relief on Jackson's face, told Tori that she had been right. The poor man had been cornered by the well-meaning Dominique, who insisted on telling once again his tale of the battle.

"Andrew, it is so good to see you again." She extended her hand toward him only to see it snatched up in Dominique's grasp.

"Tori, mon cherie. You are as always the belle of the ball and make this old man's heart flutter like the wings of a butterfly." He kissed the back of her hand and then leaned over and placed a light kiss on her cheek, causing her to blush. "Ah, mon General, she is like the daughter to me, as Jean is like a brother. To see these two together, is like the meeting of the ocean and the sky on a tranquil horizon. They become one, n'est pas?" He was beaming and obviously enjoying the moment.

Jackson smiled toward the Laffite's, he had looked forward to this evening all day and to the news that he would reveal to all in his farewell speech. Lives were going to change this night and people were going to be very happy. If there was one indulgence he truly enjoyed, it was the bringing of happiness to those he cared about.

Laughter and a carefree spirit filled the atmosphere. Men and women mingled and talked freely, enjoying the company and the new acquaintances being made. Many of the ladies did not know in which direction to go first. They were just so excited at having the chance to actually meet men like the famous

American General or the pirate Jean Laffite. Not to mention the handsome bachelor John Davis who was accompanied by the dashing young man of Spanish heritage.

Cisco was in his glory at Davis's side. Why the women, both single and married were almost falling over themselves to get to meet them and possibly have the delight of being asked to dance. Oh, life was good and getting better by the hour.

Edward Livingston and his wife had joined the Governor and the Laffite's, leaving Edward's law partner John Grymes, to escort the Governor's wife onto the dance floor where the two seemed to enjoy themselves and the music unnoticed. Grymes was a happy man and would have forgotten the circumstances under which he held the woman of his attentions, if it had not been for the arrival of Edward and Simone.

Nothing or no one else could have distracted him as fast as that pair. Just seeing them enter the room made him nervous. He stepped on Cayetana's foot, causing her to stumble. "Please forgive me my dear? It seems that I am a little out of practice. Maybe we should sit the remainder of this dance out?" He did not wait for her answer, rather guided her to a side chair, where he seated the limping but smiling lady. "I shall get you a cool drink right this second and maybe something to prop your foot up on?"

"Oh really Mr. Grymes that is totally unnecessary. The prop I mean. A cool beverage on the other hand would be most welcome," she laughed.

Grymes was off at once but not toward the direction of the table containing the punch bowl. Cayetana frowned at this but then Simone's laughter crossed the room announcing her arrival. She watched as Grymes slipped up to Jean taking him aside to hastily inform him of the latest guests.

Jean did not even turn to acknowledge the couple. Instead he drew closer to his lady and placed a protective arm around her waist, joining back in on the conversation at hand. Grymes took two glasses of champagne from one of the silver trays, being carried around by the Claiborne's servants and returned to Cayetana.

"I assume sir by your round about manner in obtaining my beverage, that you had an ulterior motive?" she grinned. "Need I guess? Or better yet, let me say. Does the name Simone, or possibly Edward have you scurrying across the room I wonder?"

"You can wonder all you want Madame and not be any closer to guessing the truth of the matter than you already have." He scowled in the direction of the small gathering at the far end of the room. "I had no idea that those two had been invited to this affair?"

"Believe you me John it was on no account of mine. I had every intention of omitting them from the guest list, knowing the history between the Laffite's and Edward, not to mention of your own animosity toward them both. You have to believe me," she touched his arm gently bringing his attention back to her. "I tried to let them slip through the cracks but William would have none of it, so convinced is he that Edward is a true and dear friend."

Looking into her face, seeing the plea written there, so clearly etched alongside of her love for him, he had no reason to disbelieve her. "I would never consider to think otherwise my dear. Put your fears to rest." He patted her arm and raised his drink in a toast. "Here's to hopefully a calm and uneventful evening?" He smiled briefly and then looked back toward the two most despicable people he knew. He would keep a close eye on those two for the rest of the evening. "If you would please excuse me for the moment my dear? I think I had better alert the rest of the troops as to the location of the enemy." He was chuckling but the undertone in his voice told her he meant every word. She nodded her head in agreement.

"I shall endeavor to do my part after all, those two still think of me as a dear friend and confidant." She laughed softly and leaned close lowering her voice. "If you will excuse me, I shall go and greet my guests and see what the enemy is up to. I am sure my glass will need refilling shortly." She gave him a meaningful look and winked playfully.

Grymes watched as she made her way toward Edward and Simone. Just what those two scheming individuals would think about their hostess if they knew what she was up to made him smile to himself. Fill up her glass indeed, how appropriate for the lady to contrive a way for him to approach her again, without raising suspicion. He would play the gentleman and she would play the spy, telling him just what was going on. Till then, he would have time to alert Cisco and Davis. That was going to prove harder to do than he thought, as both were surrounded by the fairer sex and continually on the dance floor.

Edward and Simone had received their invitation to the dinner and had accepted immediately. Neither had guessed that the Governor had invited the Laffite's. They knew that the Livingston's would be there and his partner Grymes, who they both despised but thought nothing of it. Grymes was nothing more than a minor thorn. They were there to see the American General off and then to start in on the Governor about Jean and his men. They had agreed to start their new plan of action that very evening by dropping sly hints, small reminders of the crimes committed by the pirate. Crimes he had been charged with and yet not paid for.

As always, if Simone could not be the first to arrive, she was the last. Staging a grand entrance, sweeping into the room simpering and flirting, posing at every turn, demanding by her very actions to be the center of attention. She had the act down so well, that many, if not most, did not even realize what she was up to. Simone was splendid in her attire and manners. She was a beautiful, self-assured young woman on the arm of her dashing rich husband. She had everything she could want at that moment. The compliments were flowing like water down a stream smooth and constant. Each gentleman was trying to outdo the other in his description of what a vision she presented and how lucky Edward was to have such a wife. The ladies, though slightly jealous, vied for her attention and company. Agreeing with their men folk, they swarmed around her, as if she were a queen bee. They moved away begrudgingly only when Cayetana's greeting penetrated the general buzz of activity.

"Simone my dear friend, welcome. I had begun to think that something serious had detained you. But no matter, you and dear Edward have arrived." She reached over and placed a light kiss on Edward's cheek, something she had never done before. "I do hope you know that William and I consider you both almost like family. We have been through so much these past few months together, have we not?" Edward recovered his surprise at Cayetana's outpouring and was truly happy that she felt as she did. He would be able to manipulate her toward their goal a lot easier.

Simone was overjoyed herself at Cayetana's public declaration. To be know to have such a close relationship with her, could only enhance her own standing. She smiled slyly looking at those around her, who envied her position even more than a few seconds ago. Fools she thought, they meant nothing to her. She intended to use them all, to get her Edward elected as the next Governor. Her fantasy was rapidly progressing when the name Laffite smashed it to smithereens.

"Simone dear, I don't think you quite understood me my dear. I said that Jean Laffite himself and his wife are with the General and my dear husband at this moment but I shall be honored to escort you over to the General himself when he is available." Cayetana almost burst out laughing at the look on Simone's face and felt she would have if Simone hadn't turned away to look for Jean and Tori. "He is quite the hero isn't he? So dashing if you ask me?"

A few of the ladies agreed, as all eyes looked across the room at the Laffite's and the small gathering around them. "Did you know that earlier this evening, Jean and my husband William were actually joking with each other? They were telling the General, about those silly posters they put up a few months ago. You remember surely? The rewards they both offered for each other. William finds the whole matter quite amusing now, as did the General. Hard to think of Monsieur Laffite as a pirate looking at him now don't you agree? Why he looks more like a gentleman..."

Cayetana please," broke in Simone, "you can't possibly be serious? Gentleman indeed. Why, have you forgotten that the man was charged, is charged with many crimes. Both he and his brother and his worthless cutthroat friends are outlaws and nothing more." She had let her voice raise and get carried away. "Forgive me. I am truly sorry for my outburst. It's just that so many of our fine men like my Edward here, fought with the General and deserve just as much praise. I am just so passionate about my feelings. I do apologize." She looked back at the gathering around her calculating her next move. "I ask your forgiveness and understanding."

"Nothing to forgive my dear." Cayetana patted her hand. "Now if you will excuse me I have other guests arriving. I'll hurry and then we can go and talk to the General. I do so want him to meet my dear and closest friend."

Cisco had walked over to join Tori and warn her about Simone's arrival. He had left Davis and Grymes to handle the ladies, who insisted they could not possibly be left unattended. The men were in a deep conversation about the fine performance Dominique and his men had shown with their cannons. No one even noticed his arrival. He slipped alongside Tori and spoke low. "You look great. I find myself wishing you were available because lady, I would love to show you what I could to do to you." He was chuckling and had anyone else over heard his conversation they would have been shocked and he knew it.

Tori loved his sense of humor and looking at him now, she knew that he would remain dear to her no matter what he said or did. They moved slightly away from the men, not that anyone really noticed except Jean, who seeing she was with Cisco let her go.

"You don't look bad yourself for a dandy. Why, if I'm not mistaken, that young Southern belle, the one in the yellow taffeta by the window, is flirting with you. She has been trying for some time to gain your attention you know?"

He put on his sad face as he quickly replied, "Tori, what I need is a woman, not some simpering girl who would faint at the very thought of the things I would do to her body."

Tori could not help but laugh out loud and Jean who had been talking to the General looked over toward her. Admiration filled his face, as loved filled his eyes.

The General could not help but comment. "You have a beautiful woman there Jean. Makes a man want his own lady. I've been away so long from my wife that each time it gets more difficult. Take my advice, don't let time slip by you and wish one day that you had spent more by her side."

"General sir, you could not have come closer to how I feel if you tried. She is lovely isn't she? And you know she is just as wonderful on the inside."

"Let's join them," the General took Jean by the arm and walked a few steps toward the couple. "You do not mind," he asked Jean? "It looks as if the two of them are having a far better time than anyone else. Too many people afraid to enjoy themselves I think."

Cisco saw the two headed their way, "Looks as if we are about to have company but before we do, I have to warn you, Edward and Simone have just arrived." Before she had time to reply he was greeting the two men who approached them.

"Jean, General, Tori here is impossible. Jean, your charming wife I'm afraid, is determined to have me introduced to every available female here this evening." Tori only halfway paid attention to the response instead her eyes scanned the room rapidly searching out her enemies. It took only seconds for their eyes to lock. She realized that Simone's hatred still burned within her, carefully concealed behind her demur appearance.

The General too had seen the couple enter and had recognized Simone. Who, after all could forget such a woman. He however could see that she was not the true Southern lady that he had first assumed her to be. She reeked of sexuality and enticement. A deadly combination when used skillfully and by the looks of the woman she knew exactly how. She was a true Delila, straight out of the pages of the Bible. Pity the poor Samson he thought.

Cisco had seen the look Simone shot Tori's way. "Enter the lioness into the arena," he whispered. Tori turned away from Simone's stare and faced the three men her attention turning to Cisco. She was determined not to allow the bitch or her husband ruin this night for her or especially the General.

Jackson's glance at Simone left him cold and angered toward her. He had seen how she covered her glare quickly by coyly turning her eyes toward him. She had smiled briefly at him before turning her attention toward her husband but the fact had remained, she had upset Mrs. Laffite and Cisco's statement had not gone unheard either.

"My dear, I would not let someone like her upset you." The General's hand touched her arm his eyes filled with a wise knowing sort of look about them. The compassion that lay there, also softened his words, giving them an edge of kindness and reassuring strength. "It would seem to this old man's way of thinking, that she is only jealous of you. I have seen such in my lifetime, trust me. That kind is spiteful and vindictive, quite the opposite of you my dear. The woman cannot hope to obtain either your looks or your standing. Tori you are truly woman to be admired. A kind and genteel woman and I am proud to have made your acquaintance. Just you remain as sweet as you are." He turned to Jean then and added, "and you look after her, she has all the qualities of my own dear wife. We are lucky men you and I," he laughed.

Tori joined in the laughter amazed at the man and his charm. His concern was real but his knowledge of the fair sex, was so far off the mark. If only he knew, she thought. Calling her a woman to be admired, now that was funny.

Jean soon found himself chuckling as did Cisco. Their mood which only seconds before, had been on the downslide, was now uplifted and cheerful. People all around them turned to see what was happening.

Simone looked back at Tori herself upon hearing the laughter and misread the whole situation. She in her blind fury thought that they had to be laughing at her. The bitch Tori must have said something awful about her to the General and he must have listened to her believing the filthy lie. She was not about to let her get away with it, not now or ever. "Had I known that this evening was going to include the likes of her and that pirate, I would have turned down the invitation. My it's awful, shameful if you ask me, the way people have conveniently forgotten that Laffite is a wanted man."

Edward agreed with her, as did several men standing around him. Some of the ladies who were still very jealous of Tori and her looks, backed Simone up but only speaking in whispers behind their hands. They feared being overheard by anyone who felt differently. Simone was about to continue with her onslaught of the Jean's reputation and character when the room was called to order by the Governor himself.

"Ladies and Gentlemen before we go in to dinner, I would like to bring your attention to our honored guest and my esteemed friend. The man who saved us all from British rule, General Andrew Jackson."

Everyone applauded, while still others actually cheered, the loudest of which was none other than Dominique You. Some of the ladies giggled like school girls, not sure his actions were appropriate but finding them amusing all the same. All eyes were on the General and his reaction, wondering how he would handle such an outburst.

With no emotion showing on his face, he walked over to the Governor and took his place alongside him, raising his hands in a signal that asked for silence.

"Speech," someone called from the back of the room, quickly joined by the bellow of agreement from Dominique, who once again started applauding. Then just as quickly as his clapping had started, he stopped, calling out for quiet. "Let the General speak. General Jackson sir, please continue," he bowed unsteadily, never taking his eyes off his hero as he spoke.

"That fool is drunk," exclaimed Simone to those around her. "But then what does one expect of a pirate, I ask you?"

The gathering finally fell silent, as everyone waited for Jackson to address the room.

"Ladies and Gentlemen, my fellow Americans, for that is what you all are, regardless of your heritage or background." He looked briefly toward Jean and Tori his lip twitching in an upward motion with what seemed to be the beginning of a smile. He turned then toward the Governor to continue. "I want first to thank my host and hostess," he nodded his head in Cayetana's direction, "for having such a joyous gathering of friends here for this my last evening in New Orleans. I shall miss you and your hospitality greatly. This is a fine and free state, filled with brave and proud citizens." The room exploded into another outburst of applause and cheering, that did not seem to want to stop. The Governor signaled for calm and when the room settled back down he asked the General to proceed.

The General continued. "It is however, not only I, that you should be thanking for the victory that came our way. Thank also the brave men who fought alongside of me. For those few who gave their lives, God rest their souls, so the rest of us could go on developing our grand country in freedom and under our own democratic laws, not under the dictatorship of another country."

Dominique started to cheer again but a sharp look from Jackson rendered him silent. But there is still one more person without whose help we could never have won the battle. Without this fine gentleman's help and that of his men, his supplies and dedication to uphold the American way, you can be assured, that you would be entertaining the British here tonight and not myself. I am of course speaking of Mr. Jean Laffite." He turned and faced Jean pointing in his direction as he did so.

Now Dominique did whistle and cheer as did a few others. Jackson waited for the noise to calm again then he continued, "His patriotic act and heroism has not gone by unnoticed, indeed not. I for one have thanked him and owe him far more than I could ever pay. You too should be proud of your and now my friend. We should honor him tonight as the hero he is."

If the cheering had been loud before, it was dimmed in comparison to the noise which erupted. It was a lusty zealous sort of sound, filling not only the room but the whole house. It grew even louder still as Jean and Tori joined the General and Governor, standing shaking hands and embarrassing each other.

Simone could hardly believe it. Everyone was looking at Tori and Jean like they were gods to be worshipped. They were being treated as if they were royalty, standing there basking in all the glory. What did that stupid General know anyway she asked herself? Jean was a pirate, a common lawbreaker and she for one, would not stand for any of this. It had to end and end right now!

The Governor called for calm once again. He seemed truly pleased with himself, standing between Laffite and Andrew Jackson. A true politician, he was making the most of the situation, placing his arms around both men's shoulders. He looked out into the sea of happy faces before him.

"When we have quiet. Quiet please."

The room hushed but before he could continue, Simone's voice clearly addressed the General and all those present. "Why, General Jackson sir, I'm sure that all of us here agree with you on some of the finer points, your elegant speech touched on. But General sir, is there not a little matter of our hero," she shot Jean a nasty look, "being in danger of being brought up along with his brother and men, on charges of smuggling?" The sound of gasps and people moving uncomfortably rustled about the room. "Or was it piracy? I don't seem to remember which.

Governor you would know tell us please, what was the charge or charges that you issued?"

William looked a might uncomfortable, reaching into his collar with his finger, as if it were to tight around his neck. His other hand had taken a handkerchief from his jacket pocket and he mopped at his brow. The beads of perspiration forming on his face glistened against his now very red complexion.

General Jackson stood motionless and showed no expression one way or the other. He simply stood looking at Simone as her words slid smooth as silk from her mouth. Words, that were as sharp as barbs hitting their mark. He had not liked this woman from the beginning of the evening and now he was more certain than ever that she was trouble. For whatever her reason, it was very evident, that she intended to seek some kind of delight in destroying the Laffite's. It would do his heart good to see her put in her place. Vixens like her, seldom got their comeuppance in public.

Jackson responded immediately, "The Governor has no need to recall whatever Jean did in his past, Madame." He looked toward the Governor and smiled, then turned back to face the crowd and Simone. "I am glad you brought up the difficult subject as I myself did not know quite how to handle the delicate matter. I would not want Mr. Laffite or his beautiful wife Tori, to take offense you know?" The General smiled toward Jean and Tori. "After all he has done for us." He then turned his full attention back to Simone. "Now it was kind of you to approach the matter for me and with it done, I have something here that I would like to read if I may." He reached inside his jacket and removed a letter. "I believe it will clear this problem up. With your permission then?" He looked toward William, who spoke hastily.

"By all means General, please go ahead."

"It is a letter that arrived a few days ago but I had wanted a time such as this, to read it out loud in public. It comes by way of Washington and the President himself." No one spoke or moved as the General read the contents of the document. By the time he finished, it was clear that the President himself had sent the declaration of thanks and gratitude toward Jean, his brother and his men. He had also, for their patriotic acts rendered and terms agreed to, given the Laffite's and all Baratarians full pardons, of all and any past crimes. Not only that, President Madison went on to give each and everyone of the men, full American citizenship.

Andrew Jackson finished reading and turned to hand the letter to Jean. "It is signed by the President himself, James Madison and dated February 6, 1815. Congratulations Jean, you are now a citizen of the United States and a fully pardoned man. I only wish I could do more." He shook Jean's hand and then hugged Tori as laughter escaped from his glowing face.

The room went crazy. People flooded toward the couple flocking to Jean and his lady to offer their congratulations. Simone found herself being pushed aside, as her so-called friends hurried to be included in the mirth and excitement surrounding the very popular pair.

She stood next to Edward and inwardly seethed. Her mouth hung open and as she looked she saw the General smile her way, with a nod of his head and a wink from his eye. The man was obviously pleased at putting her down as he had done. She could not tolerate it and yet she had no choice. What else could she do? They could leave but then that would serve no purpose but to allow victory in the wrong camp. She and Edward could not just stand there, or could they snub the Laffite's. The choice for now, it seemed, had been made for her. She took hold of her husband's hand and made her way toward the throng of well-wisher's.

A line had formed out of nowhere it seemed, each guest stopping and meeting with the hero and his wife, then passing onto meet and wish the American General all the best on his journey home. While she inched forward, step by step, closer to Jean and Tori, her mind raced. They had won again and she had lost but like a snake she would strike and she would see them pay for her humiliation.

Looking at the handsome face of Jean, coming ever closer her way, she found her heart rate quickening. Her lustful desire for him had not dimmed and flashes of nights long ago flickered in her mind's eye. He should have been hers! His arm that protectively clung around Tori's waist should have been around her. His lovemaking had driven her out of her mind. She had risked everything for him and nearly lost it all. But then she had not lost out completely she mused. She was after all Madame Duval, the wife of a very wealthy and respected plantation owner. Laffite, even with his pardon, would always be a pirate. How would Jean feel she wondered if he ever found out that she was the reason that he had lost his chance at becoming a wealthy plantation owner? Maybe, just maybe one day she would tell him.

Edward was offering his congratulations, sounding genuine and sincere. He spoke hastily to Tori, wishing her well and then moved quickly on to the General and William leaving Simone to deal with the sticky situation herself.

Coward she thought, as she watched him slip to William's side. Simone turned her eyes toward Jean's and in a flash she knew her next move. In her most diplomatic manner, she apologized for her actions and accusations, asking for both Jean's and Tori's forgiveness. Many people around them, found her actions to be humbling and truly believable. Her good intentions were very evident and seemed sincere even to the eves-dropping General. They did not for one second fool Tori, who looking at Simone, thought it a shame that Oscars had not been invented yet.

"Madame Laffite, Tori," Simone reached out and took her hand between hers. "I do hope that we may start over and put behind us once and for all any hostilities." She was good, Tori had to give her that much. Not wanting to ruin the General's last night with a scene, Tori smiled and answered her. "Let us try."

"Oh, I am so happy you agree and that you can rise above our past differences. Let us start now shall we not. I for one would love to freshen up before dinner is served. Would you care to join me?" Simone put her head inquisitively to one side her face was that of pure innocence and friendship. Just what she was up to was another question entirely. Cornered as she was, Tori had no choice but to accept the invite.

Edward looked toward his wife. He knew only too well she would never forgive or forget. She was up to something that was for sure. Jean was a little worried as the two ladies excused themselves from their company and headed upstairs. He started to leave himself, to follow his lady, when a hand came on his arm holding him back.

Cisco's voice spoke into his ear softly, "let them go. She can handle herself. It's been coming for sometime you know? I would say, that if I was

Simone right now I would be very careful. Tori can have quite a temper and if my guess is right, she has had about all she can take."

Jean watched as the two ladies disappeared out of sight at the top of the landing, headed for the ladies' parlor. He realized that for the moment there simply was nothing to be done about it but wait and see. Jean turned to join in the conversation going on around him. He would check on Tori if she was gone too long but Cisco was right, Tori could handle herself. His hellcat was more than a handful when angered or pushed too far. Pity Simone indeed.

Edward on the other hand, could not stand the suspense and he wanted to have his say also. Given the chance, he intended to tell that bitch a thing or two. With all the commotion still going on around him, it would be easy enough for him to slip away unnoticed. If anyone did approach him, he would simply explain his need to freshen up. He'd explain away any suspicious actions, such as following those two upstairs. Once on the landing, he quickly looked to see if he had been observed and confident he had not, turned toward the ladies' parlor. Not wanting to be discovered hovering outside the door he entered the darkened and empty room next to it and quietly pushed the adjoining door ajar. It was perfect, he could hear everything and all he had to do now, was wait to make sure they were alone. He stood listening to the two unsuspecting ladies.

Tori sat down in front of the mirror to brush her hair and in a very calm voice spoke to Simone without looking her way. The room was empty except for the two of them, so she had no fear in speaking as she did.

"Come on Simone out with it. All that shit about you wanting a fresh start is just that, shit and I for one like it better when I know just where I stand."

If she had shocked or surprised Simone with her question, it did not outwardly show. Simone remained calm and cool as she retorted, "Your mouth suits the whore that you are. You might have fooled Jean with your ways but not me. I know you for what you really are, a common guttersnipe."

Tori turned, putting the silver hair brush down on the table top. "That's better, all that sweetness was turning my stomach like you do Jean's." Tori watched as her words hit their mark. "After he found you out for the tramp you are, how you mounted any man behind your husband's back and his, he despised you. And just who the hell are you to call me a whore or guttersnipe with a reputation such as you have?"

Simone was not put out by these words, only fired up. "It only bothers you that Jean once loved me. That we slept together and the very words he whispers in your ears now, he told me first."

"Oh don't delude yourself Simone he has told me all about the two of you. About the fact that he never loved you, only enjoyed the sex. The pleasure you two had, he found on other nights in a bed at Rose's, that tell you something? You were just a passing fancy with him and nothing more. It's you who can't stand that he is with me. Now that's more the truth don't you think?"

Simone hated this woman who sat so still in front of her, so calm and poised, so perfect. She had to do something to hurt her, to wipe that smile off her face.

"I think it is you who is the jealous one. I after all am now a respectably married lady of society. I can hold my head up at least. No one will ever doubt my place as they will yours. Jean is nothing more than a common pirate, a broke and penniless one at that I hear. Maybe, if you are really down and out like I think you will be, you could borrow a little something from my dear Edward to get you by."

Edward was about to join in when he stopped himself. His wife was doing a splendid job all by herself. He would wait a while and enjoy listening before putting the crowning glory on moment.

"Why you don't even have any decent jewels. Every lady has them this evening you know? Did you have to sell the few that Jean was able to steal for you?"

This was it, she had reached a sore point. Tori's face was getting flushed and her lips had formed a firm line. Gone was the gloating smile. Simone thought she had found the weakness in Tori's armor and she reveled in the knowledge. She took off a gold bracelet from her wrist and threw it at Tori's feet. It landed inches away from her shoes, laying on the soft carpet, glowing in the lamplight. "Go on! Don't let me stop you from picking it up. Call it a gift of sorts, to start you out on your new life with Jean. Your broke life." She was laughing at her. "I had wanted to destroy Jean and bring you down. Tonight I thought I had lost, now I see I have won. This is far better than anything I or Edward could have come up with. Edward is very influential you know. Your precious Jean will find it hard to get any kind of a decent living in this town and you will live like you started, with nothing."

Tori bent down and slowly picked up the bracelet. She was looking at Simone so strangely. This was perfect, the total degradation of her. Oh the humility she was suffering, Simone laughed even harder. She grabbed at her sides struggling to take in a breath and then looking at Tori she continued. "All the time we planned and tried to ruin you and Jean. Why, I had begun to think that you had that witch Laveau protecting you or something. Did you know for instance among other problems that have befallen your beloved Jean, that it was because of Edward, that Jean was thrown in jail? I see not. That should have worked but oh no he had to go and get out. Still that is all irrelevant now is it not? I will see to it, that you and your husband are slowly blackened in this town. You will come crawling to me and I might, out of the goodness of my heart, get you your old job back at Rose's. Edward will be happy on that event and I really don't mind if he helps himself to your so-called charms. He will return to me after all."

Tori stood up slowly and walked toward Simone stopping a few steps away. She spoke softly and calmly, looking into the burning eyes of her overjoyous foe. The woman before her was truly twisted and she now knew beyond a shadow of a doubt, that there would be no peace for her or Jean, so long as she was around.

"Have you quite finished? Because if you have, I would like to ask you something."

"You can ask all you want, but do hurry up, I'm starving and I would think you would want to eat. Who knows when you will eat again like tonight?"

"Have you been missing something lately? A valuable that you hoped to hang on too?"

Simone looked at her through puzzled eyes. Had Tori gone mad? Had she pushed her too far she wondered?

"I told you keep the bracelet you will need it."

"I am not referring to this," she held out the bracelet and let it fall to the carpet. "No, I am talking about a document that you had hidden behind a certain drawer."

Simone could feel the prickling sensation of something very wrong. What was she talking about? What document hidden where? Then it hit her. My god, was she referring to Leone's will. She had forgotten about it for so long. She had hidden it in her chest of drawers at the back. And those drawers had been sold with everything else in the townhouse.

"I see you are remembering."

"I don't know what you are talking about," snapped Simone, turning to leave. "And if you don't mind, I wish to end this ridiculous conversation and go down for dinner."

"I think not! I think you and I had best finish this once and for all. The document I am talking about is Leone's will and well you know it."

Simone's heart sank. She stood dead still. So it was true, she was referring to the will.

"You had thought maybe that it was lost forever. How very careless of you. When it turned up missing John Grymes thought it was Edward's work and you know, if you had destroyed it, then you would have succeeded."

Simone turned to face Tori hardly believing what she was hearing, and yet knowing it to be the truth. Panic was creeping in.

"But then you did not destroy it did you? I wonder why? Could it be you intended to blackmail your own husband or he you? Well dear Simone, the will is back and Jean will go to court soon to claim what is his. In fact, I think it is you who will be in need of this bracelet not I." Tori kicked it toward Simone. "Oh and one more thing before I go to dinner for I am hungry too. That small income that you had from Adrian, well if you would have been more careful, you could have kept that too but you see my dear Simone, when you married Edward you lost that. Have you not noticed that the payments stopped? No, ah well, you have had a lot on your mind haven't you? I would hope Jean takes pity on you both and allows you to keep what you have bought with his money, it will help you until you find work. Maybe I can put in a good word for you over at Rose's." Tori walked by the shocked Simone who stood frozen to the spot, tears coming to her eyes, tears of anger and frustration.

She was about to physically attack Tori, when the door to the opposite room sprung open. Both ladies turned to face the intruder and found a ghostly white Edward standing with eyes bulging, staring at them.

He looked as if someone had struck him in the face causing a great deal of pain and rage. He had overheard it all and could hardly believe it. Stunned and trembling, he looked from one bitch to the other. He had to do something and fast before he lost everything. His first idea and the only one he would have, sprung into his mind with lightning speed. All he had to do was to grab Tori and hold her for ransom in exchange for the will. He would deal with Simone later.

His idea had come too late. He had waited too long listening behind the open door. Voices were clearly heard coming down the hall toward the parlor and within seconds a grinning Cisco popped his head around the doorway. Behind him was Jean and the General.

"Everything alright up here. You don't look too good Edward my man, something wrong?" Cisco knew that Tori could take care of herself but whatever had gone on here, had to have been one hell of a knockdown drag out with a big punch. No physical evidence of any violence but then Edward looked real bad and Simone who came clearly into view looked no better.

"Everything is fine snarled Edward. You will excuse us, as we are not about to remain in this house one second longer with the likes of this woman and her accusations that have hurt both my wife and myself."

Edward grabbed Simone and pushed past the small group, "You will be hearing from my lawyer; you have not won Laffite. It's not over yet."

Cisco was bursting at the seams, he could hardly contain himself a second longer and the moment he found himself watching Edward's and Simone's backs hastily departing, he popped out the one question on everyone's mind. "Tori, if you don't mind explaining, just what in the hell went on up here anyway?" Tori rolled her eyes and pulled an ugly face at him. She laughed as she then relaxed and answered,

"She got, no they both got what they have had coming to them for a long long time." She smiled at Cisco's grinning face and then looked toward Jean and the General. "Jean, you will have to forgive me, I may have stepped out of bounds on this one but she pushed me to it. That woman can be so infuriating. She just asked for it. I had no idea that Edward was listening. Anyway, I've gone and done it this time." She was looking really worried and the concern in her voice showed clearly on her face.

She briefly told them how and what had happened and when she had finished, it was Andrew Jackson's laughter in the background that broke the silence. He strode up to Tori and placed his arms around her trembling frame, hugging her to him as he would have a child. "Jean, I would say that this little lady here, defended your honor and herself rather well. That Duval woman asked for it from what I can gather. Still all in all you had better go down at once and tell this Grymes fellow, what has transpired and the Governor too. You don't want to lose again what should by all rights be yours, now do you?" His grim face and stern eyes spoke clearly to Jean. He may have just made a suggestion but wished it to be followed as an order.

Jean could see the importance of informing Grymes immediately, knowing Edward and Simone the way he did. It was best to act swiftly, beating them at their own game. "Will you be alright Tori," he asked, love filling his voice as he tenderly spoke? He was not angry at her for spilling the news about Leone's will, rather he was concerned that she had done so alone putting herself in great danger. Jean made a mental note to have a long talk with her on that matter later.

"Tori will be just fine," said Jackson. A good debate always drains one's emotions for a short time. Winning that debate, well that helps towards a fast recovery. Wouldn't you say so my dear?" He held Tori at arms length and laughed.

"That I would indeed," agreed Tori. "Go on ahead Jean, the General and I will follow as soon as I pull myself together. As for you Cisco, I know you, go on with you, get out of here. She won't wait forever you know?"

He all but bounced out of the room, pushing his way ahead of Jean as he did so. "Thanks Tori. And you're wrong you know, about waiting. For me, they always wait!"

"Who's waiting where, what are you talking about?" asked a very puzzled Jean of his wife.

"Nothing for you to worry about, just go and find Grymes and we will join you shortly. I promise to fill you in then. Now go on." She seemed to be her old self again and the General smiled in agreement with her.

"I shall consider it an honor to escort your wife down as soon as she is ready. She will be just fine. You on the other hand had best do as she asks, or like my own wife, I fear she will make you wish you had." He was joking and really enjoying himself, but his point had been clearly made. Jean turned and left smiling. It was nice to know that Andrew Jackson had a love in his life like he had.

Tori looked into the tired face of the General, who was gazing at her with a far-off look in his eyes. "Andrew, is something wrong?"

"No my dear nothing is wrong. I was just thinking of my wife and how very much you remind me of her and of how much I miss her. I have seen so little of her this past year. Always gone as I am, on one campaign or another. It's at times like this, like tonight, that I wonder if it's all worth it?"

Tori took his long boney hand in hers, feeling the cool damp touch of his skin. "General Jackson sir, could we talk for a second in private?"

"Of course we can. You can always feel free to talk to me. If it's about what you just did and how that Jean of yours is going to react. Well now, I would not worry your head over it. I'll talk to him if that's what you want?"

"No sir, what I have to say has nothing to do with that. Please come with me," she took him by the hand over toward the window seat. "Sit here for a second," she let go of his hand and quickly walked to the open door and pushed it closed.

"Please just hear me out. I know you might laugh at me but one day you will remember this conversation and you might just smile then, in fact I know you will." She sat down next to him looking him straight in the face. "I saw a pain in your eyes a moment ago, that most people don't know or have not experienced. It's the wanting to be with someone you love and belong with but can't, because of no fault of your own. I know because I'm in much that same position, in a different sort of a way. But still the pain is the same and I hate to see you hurt like you are. I hate, also to think of you giving up on your dream."

He looked at her silently. Something in her eyes told him she spoke the truth and did understand his agony, his loneliness. The only other person who did that, was his own dear wife, and he surely trusted her.

"What I'm about to tell you, may or may not be the right thing to do but I'm going to any way. General, I am honored to sit here in this room with you. Of having the chance to get to know the kind of man you are and I know that you will make a fine president one day. I should be calling you Mr. President sir, not General. You will be President of this country and you will make a difference. You and your wife will be together in the end. It is all worth it."

The man looked back at her, how could she have known that it was his secret dream to achieve the Office of President? Not even his beloved wife was aware of it. "And what makes you so sure may I ask?" his trembling voice questioned, as his shaking hands took hold of hers.

"It's not what I think will happen, it's what I know will happen. I can't tell you much and time is short but I will try my best to honor your question with a believable explanation if you will allow me?"

Fifteen minutes later Andrew Jackson escorted Madame Laffite into the dining room and seated her next to her husband. He himself was content to sit opposite the pair and though he ate little, his spirits seemed high and his mood joyous. To all at the table, the evening was a grand success and by night's end all admitted they would be sad to see the American General leave. As Tori and Jean walked with Edward Livingston and Jackson toward the General's coach, the mood seemed to dampen. The time for final farewells had arrived.

"We shall say our farewells here, that is unless you intend to rise with the sun as I do?" He was shaking Livingston's hand. "Stay in touch and if you ever need a job, well you will always have one with me." He turned to Jean. "So much I owe you so little can I give you. You have my thanks and my friendship sir." He took Jean's hand and squeezed it with a strength Jean would have thought impossible for such a frail man. Then it was Tori's turn. He bowed low and smiled at her. Madam, thank you. It has been a delight and an honor to meet you." His face was somber and if one looked close, Tori thought they would see the beginnings of tears filling his blue eyes. He reached for her and hugged her to him, as she returned his embrace. Then before she knew it, the General was whispering in her ear, while those around could only guess at what he said, she would never forget it.

"The twenty dollar bill. You did say the twenty dollar bill?"

He held her at arms length then, his face aglow and his eyes laughing. Color was flooding his gray face and he actually seemed to be standing taller, prouder somehow.

"Yes, sir I did." Tori laughed.

"That's what I thought. Gentlemen. Madame. Take care of your lady Mr. Laffite. She is very special. Very special indeed." With that he climbed into his carriage and gave the order to be off.

"Just what was all that about may I ask," questioned Jean once the carriage was on its way?

"You may, but that is something for the General to know and for you to find out, maybe." She pulled at him playfully. "Let's go home shall we?"

"My lady, I thought you would never ask? And maybe I will be able to apply certain methods of torture to learn the secret you and Jackson share."

"You can try Jean, but I can't promise you I'll break," she laughed, linking her arm through his, happily heading home.

Across town, it was a far different atmosphere. A storm was brewing. Two raging personalities on the brink of disaster were about to face off.

Edward had not said one word all the way home. The ride in the carriage had seemed to last a lifetime to them both. Each was going over in their minds all that had just happened. Once back at their townhome, Edward dismissed all the help, a sure sign to Simone that he was furious with her and that she had best keep her wits about her.

He fumbled in the dark hallway, finally lighting a lamp from the smaller one, that was kept burning by the front door. She wished he would say something, anything. They had to think to work together, for they had come too far to let it all be taken away from them now.

He was leading her upstairs, along the hall and into their bedroom. Once inside, he closed the door and sat the lamp down on the dressing table. Then for the first time since they had left that horrible room and Tori, he turned and faced her.

Simone hardly recognized him, his face was twisted up in such a hate filled rage. His eyes were dark and cruel. No reasoning or rationalization lurked behind them. She saw only madness and for the first time in her life she was really terrified.

Speaking through his clenched teeth at first, then spraying spit onto her face as he opened his mouth fully, yelling at her, he demanded answers. He was so close to her, that she could actually feel his hot breath on her face.

Two facts hit her at once. The first being that Edward was stone-cold sober, the second, that he was barely holding control of his temper. She did not know which frightened her the most.

"I have brought you here so we could be alone. So you my dear Simone could explain to me, what in the hell has happened. Just how did that bitch get my brother's will, how?" Edward's vice-like grip had a hold of her arms, his nails digging into her flesh making her grimace with the pain.

Simone started to cry, partly from the pain he was inflicting, partly from the terror that she was experiencing. She could not answer him. The words would not form. Instead she just shook her head.

He shook her violently, screaming "How?" his one word echoing throughout the house.

Simone panicked then and screamed back into his face, "I don't know."

For a split second he seemed to consider believing her and then pushed that thought aside. He raised one hand, holding her firmly with his other. "Don't lie to me. Don't you ever lie to me."

His hand came down across her mouth, knocking her head sideways. Blood from her split lip flew out across the room as a scream of pain left her. "I want to know. I need to know everything, do you hear me?" He took hold of her chin and turned her face up towards his. Then softening his tone and lowering his voice he continued. "Just maybe, if we act right away, somehow we can salvage something." He stroked her face with the back of his hand gently. The old Edward seemed to be back. "But I can't have any more lies."

Simone, too upset not to trust him and shaking from fear of his rage returning, sobbed out a story, leaving out of course, the fact that she had kept the will for her own personal use. Rather she told him, it was in case another will had turned up, they could have forged the one they had, making it look like the newer and updated version. In her mind her quick thinking had saved her from his wrath. In Edward's, things weren't so clear.

He wanted to believe her, but how could he? She had told him that she had destroyed the will, when she in fact had not. One thing was very clear though, if she had done as he asked, they would be safe as Tori had so clearly pointed out. Now they had nothing, nothing at all.

Seeing Edward so quiet, Simone reached out to him. She gently stroked his arm and softly spoke, barely above a whisper she proceeded. "We have to do something. We can say that the will they have is false. The Governor will help us. He is our friend. They can't take this all away from me. I won't let them. You must stop them Edward. You must!"

"And just how do you expect me to do that? I'm afraid my dear, that because of your stupidity and greed you have lost it all for us. You and your scheming ways." He looked right at her speaking very low at first, "You're just like her. Bitch." Then suddenly he yelled at her, "A stupid bitch. Do you here me?"

Simone was angry now, how could he call her stupid? How after all the times she and her plans had saved him from sure disaster? "I am not stupid, or a bitch. If anyone is stupid it's you. You spineless bastard. You had many chances to get Jean and her. You could not even do that right could you? No, I had given you all the support, all the plans, all my love and still you failed. I don't know what I ever saw in you. I should have taken care of Laffite myself." She was shouting at him forgetting herself and her fear completely.

"Yes, you should have. You two deserve each other. You could have taken care of him alright in bed. That's all you are good for. Tori had you right there. I'm the fool here. How I ever married you I don't know. Giving you the Duval name was the biggest mistake of my life."

Simone swung at him and hit him hard. The slap across his cheek was so fierce, that it stung the palm of her hand. She stared at him with a loathing glare and watched as he stood there scrutinizing her, stroking the red welt that crossed half his face.

Never had a woman hit him before. Never and by God, she would not get away with it. He came toward her, his breathing heavy and his eyes narrowing till they were mere slits. A thin line of blood and drool trickled from the corner of his mouth. Edward wiped at his chin with the back of his hand. Looking at it, he saw it came away streaked crimson in color. He realized he had bitten his tongue when she had hit him. He could feel the burn of the bite and taste of his own life's liquid, as the salty blood filled his mouth. He swallowed hard.

Simone could see that she had gone too far. He was beyond reasoning with, she would not even try. She turned and ran to get away from him, until he calmed down.

He was quick, too quick for her. The door was blocked by his twisted body as he turned the key in the lock. His sadistic smile crossing his face, as he spoke, throwing the key across the room. "Going somewhere my love?" She turned and ran to the balcony doors, opening them but not fast enough. His hands were on her, then his fists beat into her head. The ringing in her ears, followed by a sharp pain and a flash of light, forced a strength in her to surface. She fought back and for a brief instant she was free from his grip, but had nowhere to escape to, no place to run. Out on the balcony like a cornered animal she turned to face him.

"Go on, hit me. That's all you're good for anyway. Hitting a woman is just your style you coward. You would never hit a man would you? No. You will never be half the man that Jean is. Do you hear me never?"

Edward reached out with his closed fist and hit her again, this time the blow sent her flying up and backwards, her body landing hard against the wrought iron grilling. The iron work was not yet permanently fixed in place so it gave way easily. Simone could feel it move as she backed against it and knew what was happening. Screaming out in hysteria, one word as she fell to her death, "Edward!"

He could see her going over but try as he might he could not prevent it. In slow motion he watched as she slipped from sight, his name ringing over and over, echoing in his mind. The look on her face pleading with him to save her as she went, her arms reaching out to him repeated in his mind then vanished. Then nothing. Silence and total darkness.

Edward had dropped to his knees and found himself crawling like a child on all fours toward the broken edge of the balcony. His hands grabbed hold of what was left of the grill work, while his eyes looked down to the ground below him. He did not know what he had expected to see, somehow he hoped and prayed that she had survived the fall. His hopes were dashed when he saw his wife, his dear Simone, with her lifeless face staring up at him in the moonlight. How beautiful she looked laying there, smiling up at him with that gentle sort of a look that said I love you. Tears streamed down his agonized face, as heart wrenching sobs escaped with his every breath. Over and over again one word filled the darkness. "Simone." Then nothing. Not a word was uttered, as his brain absorbed the horrendous deed that had befallen him. His Simone was dead and he had killed her. Nothing or no one could change that.

"What have I done!" he screamed into the night, looking up to the dark sky, reaching with his hands toward his God. "Why!" he pleaded, "What have I ever done to deserve this?" His body fell, his head resting between his knees, while his fists pounded at the floor. Then he was still, as his mind rolled and turned inward refusing to accept any part of what he now needed to face. Like a curtain coming down on the last scene of a play, total insanity came down upon his rational mind, ending his life's story. Edward Duval was beyond help. He had no more acts, no more curtain calls, no reason to go on. He only wanted to crawl into that dark void inside his brain and cease to exist.

Seconds passed like hours, creeping by and still he remained lifeless, waiting, listening but for what? He knew only that from a great distance, something or someone was coming. All he had to do was stay still, very still and wait.

Deep down inside Edward gave up struggling. All the goodness that could have been, drowned in the evil sickness of insanity. Dawn filtered into his brain, slowly awakening him. He raised himself stiffly and walked as if in a dream. He did not look at his Simone. Once inside their bedroom, he stood quietly looking into the mirror at his reflection, a reflection that looked back with a vacant stare. Maybe he thought it was nothing more than a nightmare. He had to know! He had to look. The man in the mirror told him to go and see. He turned sharply and moved toward the verandah stopping at the broken edge to look down. Looking at her he laughed. It was a crazy man's laugh.

"Simone don't you know it's not nice to lay like that? Your legs showing and all messed up like that. What will people say my dear? Still you are so tired aren't you? That's fine you just rest. You will wake up feeling a lot better, won't you?"

In his mind, she looked at him and smiled. She spoke softly and lovingly. "Yes, Edward darling. I just need to rest but you have to make them pay. Yes, you do. They must not take your plantation away and they have hurt me. Look, I'm hurt, do you see?"

His eyes left her face and traveled downward, past her twisted neck, they followed the contour of her body and then a scream of rage filled the air, as he saw part of the iron work sticking up out of her lower chest. The dark iron shaft, matched the dried blood staining her once-beautiful gown. He fell backwards, tripping over his own steps, trying to escape the vision. His head turned to face the interior of the house, his hands gripping the side door for support, as he started to fall. Vomit spewed from his mouth, covering his hands and spraying the wall. It did not matter for he did not realize what he was doing. Edward fell on the carpet with the contents of his stomach.

Still her voice was calling to him from the garden. She would not stop! Try as he might to escape her he could not. His hands covered his ears, as he yelled at her madly. When that did not work, he struggled to the bed, ripping at the bedsheets, pulling the pillows down around him. He tried to smother her voice by placing his head between two pillows and crawling under the covers but that failed also. Simone was inside his head, laughing and taunting him, driving him crazy!

"Stop it! he screamed, "Get out, get away!" he pleaded and begged, crying like a baby. Sobbing uncontrollably he begged her to leave him alone. "I'll do what you want. Just stop laughing at me. Stop it, please, please," he cried. It took him several seconds to realize that the noise he was listening to was his own sobs and nothing else. The room was still once again. Her voice was gone.

Edward pulled himself out from under the mass of covers and slowly stood looking once again at the mirror before him. He looked but did not see his reflection, he saw Simone. "You know what must be done. I will see to it that you win. I will never leave you my darling. I'll be with you always." He stepped toward her reaching out with his trembling hand. Then she was gone. His Simone was not there but he knew what had to be done, she was right. She always had been. He moved about the bedroom with a purpose and cared only about listening to Simone's voice, following her directions. There was much to do and so little time. Just so long as she didn't laugh at him he didn't care.

First he had to take some of the covers downstairs and make her comfortable while she rested. She was so cold. Then he would have to give everyone the day off. Yes, that was it. Simone didn't want to be disturbed. She wanted only to talk to him and to rest.

"The key Edward, get the key off the floor. You locked the door remember?"

Oh, she was good. She let no detail go uncovered. He would follow her instructions to the letter. They would all pay for what they had done and his darling Simone was going to make sure they did. First things first. One step at a time. He felt so much better now. Simone was home. She was back safe and sound. They would never hurt her again. "I'm coming my love."

"That's good Edward." She was laughing!

## Chapter 29

Jean left early, his destination was Grymes's office for the purpose of settling Leone's will. Tori and Jean had discussed what to do about their claim against the estate for hours. She had worried over and over in her mind about the latest twist in events and just what it meant. Tori had listened nervously to Jean and his grand plans for settling down and raising a family. While he talked on and on, she had found her mind drifting in alternate directions. She was torn with promises still unkempt and knowledge of things to come. She sat and tried hard to join in his dreams and grand plans for the future but in the end knew he had to be told. He had to know about Galveston.

Tori had waited until they were in bed before approaching the subject. "Jean, we need, I need to talk to you and I'm frightened. I want you to listen and to help. Could you hold me please?" Her voice was shaking and that same haunting look that had filled her for so long, the look he had hoped never to see consume her again, was back. Without even asking, he knew deep down inside his soul what she was about to ask of him and it tore at his heart. Leone's plantation was within their reach and that meant, so was the lake. She might have thought he had forgotten but how could he?

He slipped his arms around her, drawing her close, holding on to her as if she were about to leave him. How could he have forgotten that promise he had made so long ago and the promise she had made herself? He did not utter a word, nor did he want her to talk. He just wanted to hold her, to keep her safe with him.

She broke the silence, "Jean, I have decided to tell you something about yourself, about what is going to happen in the future. Please don't say anything until I've finished because I'm afraid if you do, I'll lose my nerve." His hand stroked her back and reached up slowly into her long hair. He ran his fingers in amongst the soft silky waves and lifted it to his face. The smell of soft summer nights and jasmine filled him. He said nothing. He just waited for her to continue.

"I know that I told you I did not know anything more about what happened to you after the battle. Well I lied." He froze, his heart all but skipped a beat as her words sunk in. What was it she was holding back he wondered? All thoughts of the lake and his promise vanished.

"In history it is written that you don't stay in New Orleans. I don't know exactly when you leave but from what I remember, it was not long after the battle. You and some of your men go off to a place called Galveston." Her voice was soft yet strong as she spoke. "It's an island off the coast of what will one day be the state of Texas. Ironic in a way, that's where I first learned about you, on spring break as a teenager."

He had no idea what this spring break was but dared not disturb her to ask. He would have time later for questions.

"It was South Padre Island or Galveston and money was short, so we went to Galveston. I first read about you and some of your life, while laying on the beach sunbathing. It was a small article in a local paper but I still remember wondering about pirates and buried treasure." She laughed to herself and then gently pushed free of his hold.

"I don't know anything other than that. You leave here and you leave here soon." She did not want to add she knew also that in a few years he would be run off Galveston and once again be a pirate on the high seas.

Jean's face was exploding with relief. He burst out laughing. "You are worried over such a simple and trivial problem as that? Oh, my lady come here," he opened his arms again to her but she did not move.

"Jean this is a problem, don't you see? If you choose to fight for Leone's plantation and win, if you settle down there, you will be changing history."

"I'm sorry my love but I see no problem with settling down and raising a family." He was smiling at her as if nothing she had said mattered. "You yourself, have often told me that from this day on, my life and what happened is a mystery, have you not?"

"True, but..."

"Ah true and no buts. Who is to say that I did not settle down here and live out my life happy and respectable. Maybe you and I wished to remain together, untraceable and unknown?"

"I just don't think so. How could you have stayed and gone to Galveston at the same time?"

"I am not sure myself yet. But I am certain of one thing and that is you. I am a pardoned man. A citizen of America and you and I are destined to live from this day forward together. If not on the plantation, then some place else."

She tried to smile.

"Look at me my love, I don't have any more answers than you do but what I do have, is a love so strong and so full, that I know it to be all that my life needs. He was quiet for a while and then he spoke as if thinking aloud. "You might be right about this Galveston." His mind was racing, plans falling quickly into place, as neatly as one day follows the other. "I know what it is, you wonderful, beautiful lady. It is so simple don't you see?" She did not see but his face was so full of excitement that she felt he did in fact have an answer. "I will leave here," he slapped the side of his leg with his open hand. "I will sail to Galveston but I will not remain there." The astonishment in her eyes told him he was right. "I see that you know this too? He smiled at her. "Once we have my ship and my wealth, although not all at first, this is what we will do together. We will leave here, this house, this city. I will have money from the sale of the land. Grymes and Livingston have already begun to work on claiming back what was confiscated, I'm sure," he frowned. "That will take time and we will have to be careful if we are to vanish."

"Vanish?"

"Disappear, you and I. We will leave Galveston and sail off into the sunset. The island, our island. Together we will remain in paradise and grow old." In his mind he could see it all so clearly and he was so sure he was right. His confidence flowed from him. His happiness and excitement brought back the Jean that she had first known and grown to love. Her Jean was once again the mysterious and scheming privateer.

"You could be right? If you could make it work. Maybe, just maybe."

"No maybe my lady. You have given me the key to my destiny and together we will return to where we began." Flashes of the island and their time together filled her mind with thoughts of long tropical nights and warm lazy days. Could he really have figured it out? Is that really what happened to him, to them?

"I will meet with Grymes first thing in the morning and start things going. So many details have to be arranged and hidden. Sleep is the last thing on my mind and I have so much to do."

She watched him as he moved about the room and dressed, all the time talking and explaining to her about the preparations that had to be made. Then he was gone. He was off downstairs to his study. Suddenly the room was hers, chilled, empty and eerie. Something was not right and she felt it. He made it sound so perfect and it did seem plausible but still Tori's skin prickled with gooseflesh and a shiver caused her to pull the covers up around her. She needed to think and to face what could all too soon be the biggest move of her life.

The last time Jean looked in on Tori, she was fast asleep. Seeing her laying peacefully, curled up on her side, a slight smile tugging at her lips, he relaxed. He had been so worried the past few hours as he worked in his study. The sounds of her walking back and forth upstairs above him, had not stopped until near daybreak. Whether she had finally settled whatever was on her mind, or sheer exhaustion had been the cause, he did not know. Looking at her face and seeing her so tranquil at last, he decided to leave her alone. If he was lucky, by the time she awoke, he would be back with news that would set her mind at ease once and for all.

The morning was young, with the promise of one of those rare clear days ahead. The chill of the past few weeks had passed and now with the warm sun shining brightly, the sky cloudless and the world set right, Cisco felt as if he was walking in a dream. Strange how fate could sneak up on you and change your whole outlook on things, he thought. What he most needed at that moment, was a good strong cup of coffee and to take hold of himself. Seeing Jean walking toward him, was like seeing an answer to his dilemma. He wanted to talk to someone about what had happened to him. He had to share how he felt and who better, than the one man to whom love meant the world.

Jean saw Cisco standing on the corner looking at him, anxiously shifting from foot to foot, while he watched his approach. He noticed also, how the young man was still dressed in the same clothes as the night before. Here was a good indication that he had not been home yet. To Jean, that could only mean one thing. Cisco had spent the night in the arms of some woman and judging by the way he was fidgeting around, that meant trouble.

"Cisco, good morning to you." His face betrayed nothing of his suspicions.

"Jean my man. Just the person I need to talk to. Join me in a cup of coffee won't you?" He had put his arm around Jean's shoulder and was guiding him into the small restaurant. Finding a table so early in the day was no problem. Most of the city was just now coming to life and it would be another hour at least before some of the regulars would stop by for their beignets and fresh brewed coffee.

Cisco placed a quick order and then turned his attention to his companion. "Java. Can't stop shaking with it, can't live without it." He was laughing nervously, running his hands through his hair. "Look, you'll have to bear with me here. I've been up all night and man you know what? Strangest thing, I'm not even tired. Just hit me, that."

"She must have been quite a woman, single I hope?" Cisco shot him a astonished sort of look and then broke into his old familiar grin. "No, she's not married and for your information I did not spend the night with her either. Can you believe it? I can't."

Jean sat back in his chair and frowned. This ought to be good. "You might just have to clarify yourself here. Unlike your Marie, I can't read your mind," he teased.

The two cups of coffee arrived and Cisco's trembling hand picked up his cup, spilling some of the hot liquid down his shirt front. "Damn it!" He put the cup quickly down, then took several seconds frantically wiping at the hot brown stain, before catching Jean's worried look.

"I'm not as bad off as I seem. In fact, I think I have weathered last night well." He gave up with the stain and looked questioningly toward his friend. May I ask you something?"

"Please go ahead don't let me stop you. Knowing you as I do, I'm sure you will ask it anyway."

Cisco just let that remark slide. Something totally uncharacteristic. "Well, I need a man's advice on this one. It's about last night and a young sexy thing that walked into my life. And damn it to hell I just don't know what happened. She turned out to be the prettiest, sweetest person I have ever known. I could have had a real good time, if you get my drift but you know what I did?"

Jean shook his head no.

"Me, the Don Juan of New Orleans, turned down the chance of a lifetime. Instead I made a date for tonight, to take her to the Opera. I hate opera. What in the hell is the matter with me or dare I ask?"

Jean rocked with laughter. He tried several times to stop but each time he looked at Cisco's face he found himself hopelessly breaking up. His young friend had obviously for the first time, fallen in love and with it gained a conscience. The best part was that the young fool was struggling against something that could not be fought.

"Cisco my friend, I think maybe you have become affected by the worst and best illness there is. It's called love my friend, and you will have to face it. Your days of romancing the ladies of this town may indeed be numbered."

Cisco looked back at Jean with a confounded expression. "I was afraid you would say that. I never thought it would happen to me and so damn fast. But how can I be sure?"

"Think about it. What was it you did all last night for one thing?"

He smiled, "I walked the streets after we parted. I walked and thought about her. Of how lovely she is and soft and fragile. And you know what? I don't care if I am about to have to settle for one lady if she is the one. Jean, I just can't get her out of my mind and it scares the hell out of me that I still want her."

"You have your answer Cisco. Take it from a man who knows and hear me, love is the most beautiful of all our emotions. But it can hurt like no other wound. It is like the moth to the flame you see? We can't escape it for it beckons us."

"Ah but see," Cisco's voice went low and somber, "sometimes the moth gets too close and burns."

"That is, true love can consume, but true love meant to be has all the warmth and beauty of the flame, in which the passion can grow, basking in its light. Love, my young friend, is what life is all about and if you have found it, then don't let it slip from your grasp. Take hold and bask in its glow."

Cisco took hold of his cup and sipped from it, looking over the rim at his friend's eyes. He lowered his cup and called for the waiter. "I don't know about you, but I'm really hungry?"

"And calmer by the looks of the way you handled your cup," he laughed. "Love can make you either my friend, hungry or sick at the thought of eating. You are about to see and experience life a whole different way. Never again will you go about each day as you used to." He was beaming, "I am so happy for you and wish you all the best." He raised his cup in a toast, "May you be as happy as my lady and I. Speaking of which she will have to meet this young love of yours once she hears the news. You know how she is and how she feels about you. We shall have you over for dinner." They both chuckled.

"You think she will put the poor girl through the mill?" Cisco quizzed.

"If that means what I think it does, yes. I am sure she will want to know all about her and how she truly feels toward you."

"Well I have no doubt that she will love her as I do. And as far as how she feels toward me, she loves me Jean, I have no doubt in my mind. She loves me, as much as I do her."

The restaurant had filled up as the two friends sat eating and discussing the finer points of love and courtship. Once in a while someone would acknowledge Jean, and polite greetings of the day would be exchanged, but for the most part the two friends sat relatively uninterrupted enjoying each other's company.

Grymes stopped in for his daily breakfast and meeting with friends but upon seeing Jean and Cisco, decided to start his day off with them. Besides he could hardly pass up the chance to see what it was they were so involved in discussing. Cisco looked positively elated.

It took less than five minutes for Jean to tell Grymes about Cisco's latest dilemma, causing another round of joyous laughter and good wishes. Not one of them noticed Edward as he approached the table, followed by a somber looking companion.

"Monsieur Laffite," said Edward in a loud demanding voice, causing a hush to fall all around them. "You have taken from me that which is by birth rightfully mine and you leave me no choice in the matter but to demand satisfaction." His hand came up and the leather gloves he held slapped Jean across the side of his face.

A gasp from another table was the only response. Not a soul moved or talked. Jean stood pushing his chair back across the wooden floor, making a scraping sound as it went. Grymes grabbed a hold of Cisco and without saying a word kept him in his place.

Jean never took his eyes off Edward and as he looked at the man, he knew that the time had come at last, to finish the war that had raged on for so many years. He had no choice now. Edward had seen to that. It had become a matter of honor between Gentlemen.

Without showing any anger, either in his physical appearance or his voice, Jean calmly reached out and took the gloves from Edward's hand. He stood for a second more and then returned the slap. Then he spoke. "It did not have to come to this and yet maybe it did. You have succeeded over the years in hurting those who I care deeply for. You have hurt my lady and your brother who was our dear friend. It saddens me that it has come to this but the choice was yours. It will give me great pleasure to meet your challenge. You however, will have to be the one to name the place and I even give you the choice of weapons. But one word Edward, one word of advice. This is between you and I and no one else. I want Simone and Tori to know nothing of this do you understand? If either of them find out, the whole thing is off." His face darkened, yet the pent-up rage inside of him stayed buried.

Simone was in his head talking softly, telling him to stay calm. "You have my word as a gentlemen. This will remain between us as it should be. As a matter of fact Laffite, I find it in poor taste that you would even consider my actions as a Gentleman to stoop so low as to involve either lady. It sickens me to even have to dirty my hands with the likes of you or your lady. So the sooner we get this over with, the better for all concerned. As for the choice of weapon, I choose pistols and at noon out by the field of Oaks, if that's enough time for you.

"I would be glad to get it over with, as you so elegantly phrased it, but noon is not convenient for me. I have a meeting with John Grymes here," he indicated John with a nod of his head, "a matter of a plantation. You do understand? Is one o'clock fine with you?"

Simone's voice was in his head again, "Easy Edward don't let him get to you my darling. He is just trying to unnerve you. Laffite is frightened that's all. Why else would he delay? You have him now. You have him!"

"If that's the time you choose to meet your death then so be it. I have my second and the doctor has been contacted. You will of course have your second ready, if any will stand for you?"

Cisco breaking free of Grymes's grasp, sprang to his feet. He was disgusted by the audacity of the man. He loathed the very sight of Edward. It would give him a great deal of satisfaction to help end the bastard's miserable life. "I will be Jean's second and believe you me I will see to it that this here duel is a fair one. Do you get what I'm saying?"

Edward hardly noticed let alone listened to him. He had achieved what he came for. "Drink your coffee Laffite, enjoy what's left of your life. I will show the city of New Orleans that a true gentleman such as myself, can overcome the likes of you, the scum of the earth. Or is it sea, being the pirate that you are?" He turned and looked around the restaurant and smiled. He bowed slightly as he spoke, "Good-day gentleman," then he departed.

As the two walked away, Jean noticed for the first time that Edward's second was carrying a long wooden case, it no doubt contained the weapons Edward intended to use.

The sight had not escaped Cisco's attention either. "You aren't going to let him talk you into using his weapons are you? They could be rigged, fixed. You know what I mean. I would not trust him as far as I could throw him."

"Neither would I, and I have no intention of letting him gain the upper hand, no matter how he tries, honest or otherwise. Come on, we have some things to attend to and less than three hours to do it in. One good thing, Tori won't know about this until it's over. Grymes, you'll see to that won't you?"

"Jean I don't like this not one bit. But asking you to not go through with it is useless I suppose?" The look on both Cisco's and Jean's face confirmed it. "I'll do what I can."

"It's called damage control," said a serious Cisco.

"Call it what you want. It won't be easy to keep this from reaching her. I bet half the city knows about it already!"

She could not help the uneasy feeling of dread that hung over her. No matter how she had tried to shake it, the doom and gloom atmosphere continued to make her day dismal. The day had started out all wrong to begin with. What with waking up and finding Jean already out and about. Bessy hadn't been much help in that department either, telling her only that the master said he wouldn't be gone long. Tori had skipped lunch, choosing instead to sit in the warm sun and think about the awful nightmare.

She had been about to sail off with Jean, when a voice had called to her. The voice had been Linni's and then she had found herself at the lake. Kate was there holding out her hands to her telling her to hurry. She had seen it then, the doorway to her time and clearly standing on the other side was her darling little girl, calling for mommy. She had stood there and by the time she moved toward her daughter reaching out to her the nightmare suddenly ended. The dream had been so vivid. But why now? What did it mean? She had almost come to the decision to leave with Jean. To sail off to the islands and accept her destiny, when this happened. How could she let go of her family and her life in the nineties, when she hadn't even tried once to see if she had a chance of getting back?

After all these months of not thinking once about the lake, her family and her trying to return, she now found herself consumed by the overpowering need to at least attempt it. "Maybe that's why I feel so down," she told herself out loud. "I have to ask him to take me there to keep his promise. God, how can I do that? Will he understand?" she asked the sky.

"Don't think God answers out loud, not all the time anyhow. Things happen and then they don't." It was Marie's voice that broke into her privacy.

"Cisco's gone and got his self into a heap of mess. Seen a vision myself last night. I feel, how'd you say just then, Down? Yes sur, that about puts my mood right alongside of yours."

"Well then you had best come and join me, as misery loves company you know?"

"Can't say I do. What I do know ain't good, that be for sure. Trouble all's I feel. It's like you and Cisco. You knowing things but not real clear like.

That's how it is with me most the time. I knows things but ain't always too clear. What I do know is, today ain't a nice day like the sky says it is." Marie looked up and around at the clear sunny heavens. Her face shining in the sunlight, but deeply saddened. She looked at Tori then and walked toward her almost reluctantly. "I ain't sure I should be here but I did hear about something that fit with why I feel this way. Maybe you have a touch of the gift and you be feeling down cause of it too. I guess that you and I have been through the best of times and the worst. You are a good friend and that's the only reason I'm here.

Tori was really starting to get worried. The look on Marie's face was like that when Christopher had gotten sick. She reached out to Marie grabbing her hand and pleaded with her, her voice trembling with apprehension. "Marie, what do you know? What's wrong?"

"There ain't no easy way around this, so I'm just a going to say it as I heard it told to me, not more'n a hour gone. That Edward Duval done gone and called your Jean out. They be all set to duel this here afternoon and Cisco he's gone with him."

Alarmed and horrified Tori dropped Marie's hand and stood staring at her. Her Jean and Cisco in a duel? People died in duels. It would be certain that someone was not going to walk away but which someone?

Bessy called out to Tori from the open doorway, "Mizz Tori, you have a visitor. It be that Mr. Grymes fellow. You want me to show him in?"

Marie shook her head no she didn't need to speak or explain. "No! No Bessy, you tell him I'm resting and not receiving any visitors this afternoon. Go on now you see to it that I'm left alone.

"Yes um, I'll tell him. Don't you worry none, ain't nobody getting by old Bessy." She could still be heard mumbling as she disappeared inside the house.

"I think maybe he came here to keep you from doing what you thinking about doing. You're going to go and stop em ain't you?"

"Your dead right there but where do I go Marie? Do you have any idea where or when this duel was to take place?"

"Didn't at first but then that's what took the time getting here. You best change cause I got you a horse and the directions on how to get there. If you is quick you might get there in time. Cause Lord know's you are the only one that can stop it. The only one that fool Jean is a going to listen to."

Jean and Cisco rode their horses quietly out of town, to the place that was well known to the locals. In years to come, the spot would be replaced by another more convenient location closer to town, called the dueling oaks. Already its reputation for duels and deaths, of foolish hot-blooded young men, was spreading far and wide.

Dueling in Europe had for years, been a way for honorable men to settle their disagreements, to avenge a wrong against one's self or family. The tradition had traveled across the ocean and found a place and acceptance in the homes and lives of the young nation. Unlike Europe though, where the offense was more than often a serious matter, the young men of New Orleans took it and their misplaced honor to new heights. Many a young Creole would lose his life or be severely maimed, over such stupid offenses as a spilled cup of coffee or jealous attentions toward a lady at one of the Quadroon balls. The deadly combination of too much wine and misplaced honor, would be more than enough to trigger the demand of satisfaction, no matter how frivolous the reason. With his honor, his reputation and family name at stake, there would be no other choice for the young gentleman but to duel. The earth beneath the dueling oaks, would be stained forever with needless blood.

Cisco's mood was as gray and dreary as the weather had turned. Dark dismal clouds filled the sky, adding fuel to his somber thoughts. The cold wind to him, felt like the icy fingers of death tugging at his sleeve. He shook himself trying hard not give in further to his melancholy mood. Brighten up he told himself. Death was not looking for him or Jean. It was Edward it called.

Jean saw Edward standing next to his carriage, talking to his second. Three other man were present. He recognized one as the doctor and realized the other two to be the drivers of their carriages. Both blacks stood a short distance away from the area, close to each other and not looking too happy at having to be present at all. All means of etiquette had been observed and met so far as he could tell but still his instinct told him that something was seriously wrong here. He just could not place his finger on what it was.

As they approached walking the horses slowly, he and Cisco surveyed the surrounding area for any possible ambush or set up. "Seems to be as you asked for, no sign of Simone or anyone else for that matter," said Cisco. He raised up in his saddle to better take in the area around him. His nerves were on edge and like Jean, he too had a very uneasy feeling. "Still don't trust the rat. His type just don't fight and when they do the cards are always stacked in their favor. He's got to have something up his sleeve I tell you. That or the man's gone mad."

"I'm sure your right but then the man has been pushed to the brink. After all, he learned last night that he stands to lose everything and a desperate man does desperate acts. Could be that this is just what it is, his only way out!"

They rode their mounts to within a few feet of the carriage where they remained, looking down upon the three men. Edward twisted a smile toward Jean. "Thought you might not show up. Could have sailed on the tide but then you don't have any ships do you? You have nothing but to go after that which is mine and ruin the fine name of my family." His smile vanished as he snarled, "that Laffite will not happen."

"Easy darling, don't push him. He's here and you have him just where you want him. Listen to me my love." Simone was talking so clearly, that Edward was afraid they would hear her. "Shhh." He hissed, putting his finger to his lips, turning away from Laffite, toward his carriage. Cisco caught this action and looked curiously from Edward to his second whose face had a worried sort of fear about it. He observed the doctor look at Jean and then back toward Edward. The doctors face had what Cisco thought could be nothing but pity about it.

The doctor said nothing. What could he say anyway, he knew better. It had gone too far already. Crazy or not and in his opinion the man was out of his mind, Edward was going to duel.

"Show him the pistols, do it now Edward," the voice laughed. Edward reached for the box laying on the back seat. He carefully and tenderly opened the lid, exposing the two pistols that lay side by side. He lifted the container and handed it to his second who in turn, faced Jean.

"If you don't mind Edward, I would like to use one of my own pistols. You may of course inspect the weapon." He unfastened his jacket and reached into his belt, taking out his weapon. He handed it over to Cisco, who held it toward Edward.

"I will do just that and to show no hard feelings you may look at the weapons that I have brought along." He reached and took Jean's pistol from Cisco's hand. As he examined the weapon he continued to talk. "It seems to me, that only a man other than a gentleman, would think that they," he looked toward his second and the box he held, "were anything other than top quality. You will find them in order." His voice had been smooth but laced with disdain. His anger flashed, his voice growling as he snapped his next remark. "Did you think that I would somehow stoop to rendering them inoperable?"

"Oh Edward please, the man's no fool. Stop this and get a hold of yourself." Simone's voice laughed at him. "Of course he would think that of you. It's something that he would do after all. He is not a Duval. He's the scum of the earth, the slayer of women and children. Remember what he did to me after all."

She was right, he had to listen to his Simone. "Yes," he whispered to her. Then he looked directly into Jean's eyes, his mood once again calmer. "Fool. I have no need of meddling with the pistols. That act is beneath me. I am after all, a Duval," he smiled. "I intend to kill you in a fair fight and with honor." His tone was deadly and very serious.

Jean judged that the man actually believed in what he was saying. He also had reached the conclusion, that he had slipped over the edge and that made him a very dangerous and deadly opponent. One that had nothing left to lose was to be feared.

Edward stepped up to Cisco and handed him Jean's weapon and then he looked toward Jean, impatience sounding in his voice. "Don't bother. If you are ready, you may use your pistol. Let us proceed." He turned and walked to his second and took one of the pistols from the box. "Doctor, you have agreed to officiate and as such, may I suggest, that to delay any longer is a waste of our time."

"As you wish." He spoke sounding far more formal and official than he felt. "Monsieur Laffite, if you are ready?"

Jean nodded his head and dismounted, calling to one of the young black boys to come and take his horse. Cisco slid from his saddle and handed the reins of his animal to the young lad and watched as he quickly led them off. He handed Jean his weapon and tried to speak but found that the deadly stare in Jean's dark eyes rendered him helpless. He had only seen one other duel in his life and had never expected to see another. He listened as the doctor spoke to them, laying out the rules and regulations under which the duel would be fought.

"You have a few minutes to confer with your second, at which time I will call for the gentleman to proceed. From that time on neither second may move or be involved until the matter is settled and I myself have examined the outcome. Gentlemen may God have mercy on you both."

Jean and Cisco walked from the meeting, standing a short distance away, just out of hearing range. It was Jean who spoke first, placing his hand upon Cisco's shoulder. "I don't know how this will turn out. God willing, and with a little luck, you and I will ride away together from this place. I have every confidence that I have the upper hand having fought before." His voice trailed off for a second. "I have never had so much at stake, so much to lose and that alone gives Edward an edge."

Cisco quickly added to this last statement, "Yes man, but you have one hell of a reason to win. You have your lady and your love. Nothing could be stronger. Nothing is." He felt like a football coach at half-time, he thought. Giving that last boost to his team that one reason to win.

Jean smiled at his remark. "You're right there she is worth it."

"Besides," added Cisco laughing, "the bastard deserves to die for all he has done and will continue to do, if allowed to live." He would have gone on but the doctors voice rang clear in the afternoon air.

"Gentlemen, take your mark."

Cisco wanted to say good luck but luck would have nothing to do with what was about to happen. It took nerves and skill and a good shot. Instead, "Break a leg." he said softly causing a stunned sort of look from Jean. "I'll explain it to you after this is over," Cisco laughed. "Just don't take it literal." Then he added, "See you soon."

Jean turned and walked toward his opponent. "I pray you are right," he mumbled under his breath. The two men stood inches apart, facing each other, each trying to fathom what the other was thinking. Jean looked at Edward closely. He was either crazy or worse yet sane and very deadly. Something was bothering him he could see it in the man's eyes. The way they stared at him, yet vacant and not really seeing him. It was as if he were not really there at all but off some other place in his mind. Could it be that he was frightened to death, at what was about to take place? Was he thinking about his wife, his life and all that he was risking by this challenge?

Jean could tell him he had no intention of killing him, rather the drawing of blood would be enough. Edward would be disgraced in his own eyes. He would have to face his wife and tell her that he had lost. Jean knew it was obviously their plan to kill him. To try and retain the plantation. Did they not know that it would go to Tori if anything happened to him? Grymes had already drawn up a new will. Grymes had seen to it that Edward and Simone would never again have what Leone had left to Jean's son.

Edward was hardly listening to the doctor as he spoke, telling each man just what to do. Edward turned and faced in the opposite direction of his enemy, feeling Jean's back up against his. Simone was with him. She had stopped laughing and was now whispering instructions, so softly, that he tipped his head to one side slightly trying to hear her voice more clearly.

His face started to twist and twitch, his free hand opening and closing tightly. He was not scared or nervous at all, she had seen to that. He had a deadly purpose and all his concentration was placed in carrying it out. His body trembled with excitement as the seconds drew closer to the inevitable. He would end up with it all. All to the thanks of his beautiful Simone.

But she was dead wasn't she, his own mind's voice asked? No, he answered quickly, blocking that thought. She was just sleeping in the garden, that's all. She had been hurt. She was sick that was it, just like his brother. Yes Leone, had loved him and Edward had loved Leone. It was Laffite's fault, his and his wench's. She would be next to be taken care of. What he had in mind for her, was something far worse than death. She would pay dearly wishing over and over that she had died.

The doctor's voice sounded louder, causing him to pay attention at last. The man had stepped well out of the line of fire, and in so doing was calling out to them. "I will start the count. Remember, ten paces, then turn and fire."

She rode as if the devil himself was after her. All the time trying to think if she had read anything, any book about Jean being killed in a duel, or even fighting one? Could her role in history still be playing out she wondered? Was it now her job to stop this fight before it could alter history. When would the madness end? She did not care about the plantation anymore. All she wanted was Jean's safety.

The cold wind whipped at her hair, brining it down around her shoulders. The top of her blouse was falling to one side, catching the air and bellowing out, tearing the material out of her pant's top. Still, she spurred the horse on. "Please, please dear God in heaven let me be in time. Don't let Edward kill him, not now."

She was praying to herself in her mind, to try and speak out loud would have been impossible, as the wind in her face would have taken her breath away. "Not far, not far to go now." She spurred the animal even harder, pushing it forward, begging it to somehow find the strength and the will to travel faster.

The doctor started the counting, loud and rhythmic in his calling. "One, two, three..."

Edward's twisted smile came on his face. Simone had stopped talking, but he knew she was still with him. All he had to do was wait and listen for her. In a few seconds Jean Laffite would be no more. It was going to be so easy. The fool, all he had to do was turn and fire. Yes, that was all, but not on the count of ten, never! Ten was for fools, lucky number eight was the time. She had spoken. "Eight," Simone's voice had told him.

"Four, five," came the doctors clear call.

"But won't it be cheating he asked her in his mind? I will be accused of murder surely."

"That is if any witnesses were left to tell but there will be none, will there?" she laughed.

"Simone my love, I have done it just as you said. As I kill Laffite, my second will kill his second. The doctor and the Niggers next. Oh how clever you are. I shall win. Jean's men attacked us, but I was strong and I was the victor."

"Seven."

One more step. Now watch my love as he dies!"

Cisco did not trust Edward at all and he was watching him intently. His eyes were riveted on Edward's slow pace. His body language speaking clearly to Cisco's martial arts trained eye. So when he saw the man break stride, and his hand holding the pistol, start an about swing, the indication was clear. Edward had begun to turn on eight and Cisco did not hesitate. His call of warning to Jean, as he raised his own pistol sounded clear and loud.

Jean acted on pure instinct, too late to turn he dropped instead to the ground. As he rolled over he saw Cisco fire his weapon.

The force of being hit, knocked Edward flying. He jerked backward, falling and rolling onto his side. He had felt the red hot burn of the lead, as it ripped into his chest, followed by the explosion of pain, which enveloped his brain, as the bullet tore his insides apart. It's fast deadly trip had pierced his soft flesh easily, then grazing a rib, slowing it down but not stopping it, the bullet finally came to rest, lodged next to his heart. It had cut the main artery as it journeyed to its mark, sealing Edward's fate.

His hand that had been raised at Laffite's back about to fire, flew off to the side as he squeezed the trigger, discharging the gun and missing his mark. He had dropped the weapon upon falling and now his empty hand clutched at his chest, while his face twisted in agony and hate. Simone's name was on his lips, as he struggled to breathe. In his head she was laughing at him. She was laughing hysterically. His eyes followed the ground, looking through the grass toward Jean. His world was on its side. Nothing made much sense to him at first, and it was hard to concentrate with Simone's laughing and all the pain. But still he could see what he longed for, Jean was down.

"Die you bastard," he hissed, satisfied that he had mortally wounded the man. He could understand now why she was laughing. She was happy at last. He started to smile and then unlike himself, who could barely move anymore, he watched in disbelief as Jean started getting up. He stood and looking at him he could not find a mark on him. He was not hit! Once again the bastard would be the winner. His mouth screwed up into a macabre smile as his life blood pumped out of the hole in his chest. Simone's laughter was filling his head even louder than before. She was not happy. She was laughing at him!

"All because of you, you bastard," he tried to yell at Jean. "Damn you to hell. I damn you..." With one last searing pain the world finally went dark. He could not see a thing and the pain was gone, but still he could hear her. He died, listening to Simone's hideous laughter.

Tori had seen the men walking and then the turning of one. The sounds of weapons firing filled the heavens causing a flock of blackbirds to take flight. Dear God she thought, I'm too late, and still she raced the animal toward the scene. Both men had fallen, which one was Jean? To which man should she ride? Closer and closer they rapidly came. Then in a flash she was able to see that the one nearer to her was Jean and he was standing up.

Screaming out his name, over and over she did not slow her pace until she was almost on top of him. Only then did she halt her breakneck pace and jump from the horse's back throwing herself into Jean's arms.

Jean had seen Edward fall but before he could do anything else, Tori's frantic call had made him turn away. He saw her galloping toward him, like a wild woman riding the wind. In seconds she was reining her mount to a stop. Sliding from the foam-covered animal she ran into his arms crying hysterically.

"It's alright," he told her as they clung to each other. "I'm fine. The shot missed me."

She squeezed him tighter in relief and then finding her breath she asked, "Is he dead?" She was afraid of the answer because she wanted him dead for all he had done. But to actually want another human being killed was supposed to be unthinkable.

Jean looked over to where the doctor was examining the body and placing his jacket over Edward's remains. He was dead alright and off behind the doctor, she watched as a very frightened second was running for his carriage.

Edward's friend wanted no further part of this duel or of Edward. He had not been fast enough to stop what had happened, but the doctor had seen what he intended to do and now all he wanted was to get far away, to avoid any questions. The doctor walked over to Jean and Tori. A grim frown was forming deep lines on his forehead, and his lips pursed together in disgust.

"He is dead. Hate these things, such a waste. You know of course he must have been quite deranged. Turning on eight like he did and his second ready to do whatever. He will have some questions to answer will that one. If it hadn't been for your second, calling out as he did, I fear the outcome would have been more deadly for us all."

Tori buried her face still deeper into Jean's shoulder. He had come so close she had almost lost him. She couldn't cry but she couldn't laugh with happiness either.

Jean who had been holding her in his embrace, also realized how very close he had come to being killed. He drew her still tighter into his embrace. A welcome gesture to them both.

Suddenly she felt him stiffen. The change in his body, as he went rigid, alarmed her. But it was his pushing her back from him, his face filled with apprehension and dread that caused her heart to race. She followed his gaze, to see what it was that had caused such a reaction in him. When she found what she was looking for her, world went inside out. Somewhere a voice screamed out, "No!" as she ran toward Cisco and his motionless body. Jean was at his friend's side ahead of her gently turning him over, revealing to them his bloodstained mid section.

"Oh shit," Cisco moaned, when he saw all the blood oozing through his shirt.

"Hush don't talk," Tori told him. Why she said that, she didn't really know? Maybe it was because in all the movies they always said something like it. But hell, this was no movie, he had been shot for real and could be dying. "No," she mumbled looking frantically back toward the doctor. He was conscious and alive, that was a good sign, and they had help.

"Doctor please, it's my friend he's bleeding," she said fearfully looking up into the man's face. "Please help him. Just don't stand there! Do something!" she snapped.

The doctor ignored her anger and bent down by Cisco's side, his hands gently and cautiously feeling under his back. He looked up at Jean, "No, exit wound. Here, I'll need your assistance," he was opening Cisco's shirt, "I'll have to peel away the shirt, here," he pointed to the bloodiest spot, "I want you to be ready to help me halt the bleeding should it be necessary." Jean didn't say a thing. He just knelt by his fallen friend's side ready to aid the doctor in any way he could. While the doctor and Jean made an effort to examine Cisco's wound, Tori held his hand and stroked the side of his face gently.

He forced a smile and even tried to laugh, "I don't understand how this happened."

She could only shake her head. She had no answers for him. The sound of his shirt being ripped away as the doctor worked, brought back memories of the field hospital to Tori's mind. She turned her head to see the damage and watched as the blood began to flow even faster, once the material had been removed and the wound exposed. Jean ripped off his own shirt and the doctor took it, bunching it up quickly. He placed it onto Cisco's stomach and then he asked Jean for his belt. Jean handed it to him and watched as he used it to hold the blood soaked shirt in place, pulling tightly, hoping to stem the flow. For a few seconds it seemed to be working and then they both saw the slow trickle start, running down his side and falling onto the grass. Slowly standing up the doctor looked toward Jean and shook his head from side to side. His face was grim, and his lips were turned down in a helpless scowl.

Tori seeing this and understanding the meaning, spoke with a strength and certain calm in her voice that she knew Jean would not ignore. "Leave us alone. Please go."

The doctor looked at Jean who stood and took him by his arm and walked some distance away. "They are as close as brother and sister. It's only right."

The doctor looked back at the pair and nodded his head. With kindness and understanding in his expression he spoke quietly. "I'll stay just the same. She may need me." "

Tori took Cisco's head in her hands and sitting down she placed him so he could see into her face as she spoke. "Why did you have to go and be so damn brave? You know that now I'm going to have to spend my days nursing you back to health and you are going to be one hell of a patient."

Cisco smiled up at her. She was trying to be so strong, trying to hide from him what he already knew. He had seen the doctor shake of his head.

"Stop it Tori. We both know that I'm not going to stay here with you." He put his lips together and tried to stifle a cough and as he did, the pain caused him to grunt and clench his jaw.

Tori waited helplessly until the pain had passed. She was about to tell him he was wrong, when he reached up and placed his finger on her lips.

"You know it's kind of strange isn't it? Us being here together like this." He shivered in the warm sun that peeked out from behind the wind-driven clouds. "It's cold." His eyes were getting glassy and the pupils were large and not dilating, just like Christopher's had, just before the end.

"Strange, it doesn't hurt any more, always thought it was supposed to hurt like hell, a shot to the gut." Another coughing fit hit then, joined by a funny bubbling sound. His coughing was causing the gaping hole, to express the blood even faster. He squeezed her hand too afraid to let go. "Tori, I guess I was not meant to stay here." He closed his eyes for a second then opened them, a small smile creeping around his mouth, exposing a dimple that only showed when he grinned. He struggled to continue, "I was happy here, wanted to stay. Finally found someone to share my life with. You know? The girl in the taffeta dress?" He was struggling hard to talk, his words dragging slower and slower as they came. "Seems as if I was wrong though. I won't be staying will I?"

Tori just stroked his hand between hers. What could she say? How could she tell him the words that she herself did not want to admit out loud?

Softly, almost a whisper and so quiet that she had to bend her head down to hear him he continued. "I'm going back Tori. I'm going home. It's all been a dream right? Just a dream." A slight breeze blew up and over them. Its gentle touch lifted Tori's hair blowing it over her face. "The wind is calling me. My dream is full of shadows. Was this real, all real? The other dream is now calling me home?"

Tori had tears spilling down her face. They were dropping onto his shoulder. She tried to wipe them from him. "Now you touch me. I should have got shot before," he gave her his last Cisco grin. "You're one hell of a woman." He tried to laugh again. He closed his eyes and lay quiet for a few seconds, then he opened them and looked right at her, "Tori,"

"Yes, what? Anything you want just ask."

"Don't forget me and if you ever go back, well look me up. Can't see you so good, too many shadows. What a dream..." He never finished. His last breath whistled from between his smiling lips, as it left his body. His lifeless eyes looking up to the sky. She reached up gently and closed them.

"I love you my friend. I will never forget you or what you did. You were and always will be my best friend. You saved Jean's life, for that I will cherish your memory." She looked into his handsome face, such a love for life he had had. She would never be able to hear his voice or laughter again and yet she knew that somewhere in time he laughed and joked as he always had.

Jean came to her side. He had seen the slump in her shoulders and the way her head hung low on her chest. He knew that their friend had breathed his last. He got her to let go of Cisco's hand and to stand up and lean against him. She was crying softly, letting the tears fall gently onto Jean's shoulder. There was no need for hysterics or any room for anger. She did not want to leave him that way.

Jean looked down upon the lifeless form of his friend, a man that he owed his life to and much more. How could he comfort his lady in her grief, when he himself had a hard time dealing with it? The sound of horses approaching and voices calling out to them drew their attention away from the tragic sight.

Two riders approached rapidly down the road, followed closely behind by a carriage. Even at the great distance between them, they recognized the driver. It was Cisco's Marie.

John Grymes and Thiac were the first to reach the sad scene and dismounting they walked to Tori and Jean embracing them without speaking. Thiac pulled away from them, looking back at the fast approaching carriage.

"You best leave this to me," he said walking back to meet Marie.

"I won't ask what happened, we'll talk later, said John releasing Jean from his hug and turning toward Tori. "God, I'm so sorry Tori what more can I say? What can I do?"

"Nothing John no one can do anything. It's Marie I'm worried about now."

She watched as Thiac greeted the carriage and talked briefly with its driver. He then helped Marie down and stood aside as she slowly walked toward Cisco's body. She did not take her eyes off him until she stood looking down at his face, then she slowly looked up at Tori and Jean with tear-filled eyes. "I ain't about to mourn him, not like you think I will. I will miss him, as we all will. But it's the living that worry me now," she looked right at Tori. "You'll be a needing some time by yourself you and your man."

"Oh Marie," cried Tori opening her arms to embrace her friend. She walked quickly to her and each clung to the other for a few seconds, before Marie pushed her away.

"I still can't accept it, he's gone, really gone," said Tori shaking her head as she looked at him. And Edward you know, he's gone also."

Marie looked over toward Edward's body and frowned. "Seems he asked for it, if'n you ask me." Tori was shocked by her cold remark and then for the first time she thought about another woman who would be affected by the news. Simone would have to be told and just what her reaction would be, could be anyone's guess. "Who's going to inform Simone?" she asked no one in particular.

"No one," answered Marie. Ain't no need." Again Tori was stunned by the coldness of Marie's voice. She knew she had suffered greatly, like herself, by the loss of Cisco but to be so cruel.

"Well someone has too. Jean? Someone has to tell her."

Marie looked at Tori and shook her head sadly. "Ain't possible. Afore I came here I learned that she was found in her garden. She's dead!"

It was Jean's turn to be stunned now, "Are you sure?"

"Yes em. Best folks can make out is she fell from the balcony above. Found her all covered up with bed covers. My guess is he had something to do with it. People's say how they heard the two fighting real loud, her screaming at him, then it went real quiet. No one would have thought much or found her so soon if'n it hadn't been for a nosy housemaid next door." Marie looked at her Cisco and then back at Jean. He did what he came back to do. Nothing you could have done to change it. That Edward was dead set on killing you, just like he killed his wife. My Cisco he can rest now his job is done. But yours," she looked at Tori, "is not over."

Jean placed his arm around her feeling the fear that swept over her. "Just what do you mean by that? What do you know Marie, what does my lady have left to do?"

"That's up to her. Her destiny is her own choice. I can't help no more. I'll be taking care of Cisco. You two take care of each other." She turned away from them and looking at Thiac spoke softly. "You pick him up for me and put him in my carriage. Then you ride with me you too Mr. John Grymes. The horses are needed elsewhere, for another journey." She did not wait for anyone or any questions. Marie walked behind Thiac, who gently carried Cisco's body to the carriage, as if he were a sleeping child.

John looked at Jean and then kissed Tori on the cheek. "Take all the time you need. You know where I am when you are ready." He shook Jean's hand and followed the others.

The doctor had remained silent up until now. "I'll take Edward's body back with me. You two take the advice of your friends and spend a little time together." He bowed slightly to them, Madame, Monsieur Laffite." With that he walked away, calling to the two black slaves to assist him. Tori looked at Jean and not wanting to remain there a second longer simply stated, "Let's ride."

For an hour they walked the horses slowly, talking of all the good memories they each had about their friend and the way he had affected their lives. Then suddenly Jean stopped his horse looking at his lady quizzically. "Tori, where is it you want to go?"

"Home Jean. I just want to go home and be with you."

There was no funeral for Cisco. Marie chose instead to bury him in a safe and secret spot known only to herself and Thiac. No one questioned her or her reason behind her decision even though it had seemed irrational. As far as the citizens of New Orleans were concerned, the handsome young gentleman had suffered an accident and as per his wishes had been buried quietly.

The weeks had slipped slowly by. The days were filled with meetings with Livingston and Grymes who were trying to restore all that had been confiscated from the Laffite's. Other meetings with Grymes concerned Leone's will and the claim of ownership of the Duval properties. For days Jean and Tori had talked about just what should be done with the plantation. Now that both Edward and Simone were gone the temptation to remain in New Orleans was strong.

"History could be rewritten slightly, couldn't it," he asked her during one of their long talks?

"I don't know Jean. You are asking me to explain and expand on something that I have no idea about. I have asked myself over and over since Cisco's death, just what is my responsibility toward history." She was twisting her gold chain around her finger as she talked. Pulling on the locket, sliding it back and forth as she did so. "Did his death alter anything? Was he meant to return and by not doing so has it now all changed? Or was he meant to die here and by not returning, everything is as it should be? I just don't know anything anymore."

The chain around her neck snapped. The golden clasp had given way to her sharp tugging. Her tone had been a mix between anger and frustration. Now it was filled with dismay and upset. "Oh Jean, look what I have done. It's broken," she cried. The locket was in her tightly clasped fist with its chain dangling free, swinging as she held it out toward him.

"Now I don't even know what I'm doing let alone what I'm saying." She was devastated and broken. The damn had finally burst and all the bottled up emotions flowed free at last. She broke down and cried. Cried for her lost friend, for her love of Jean, for herself and for the decision she knew she had made.

"I'm sorry my love. I never meant to assume that you held the answers. Look," he took the locket from her, "this is a symbol surely? I can have it fixed for you that is easy. I can if you will only let me, fix that which is tearing you apart. Talk to me my lady."

She looked at him through her tears and tried, she really did try to speak, to explain but her tears still came too strongly to allow her more than broken bits and pieces. "I've," she sobbed, "got to decide," she shook her head from side to side. How could she tell him, how could she do it?

Tori listen to me. Calm down. Let me help you. Maybe together we could decide whatever it is, one way or the other, or have you already decided," he asked her with a look of wisdom in his eyes? He knew her so well, she should have guessed she could not hide it from him. "Tori look at me." He lifted her chin up. "You have been so distant these past weeks. Even in your sleep you toss and turn like a ship in unsettled seas. What is it my lady? Come, you can tell me."

She knew the time was now. She could not delay telling him any longer. "I want to go to Leone's house." She took a deep breath and added, "I need to go. That's the only way we will know if we should settle there or not, don't you see?" He did indeed see. It was not just the house on her mind it was the lake. That was the haunting memory that lurked deep behind her eyes. That was the only thing that had and would ever come between them and it was time to face it.

"Are you sure it's just the house and not something more that calls to you," he asked her knowingly?"

"I can't fool you can I? No, it's not just the house, though that is a big part of it. It's the lake and the time door. I asked you years ago to help me return to it. You gave me your word Jean." Her eyes pleaded with him for understanding. "I made myself a promise. I made my family, my daughter a promise. I have to keep that don't you see? I have to try." He pulled her close to him. Fear raced in his heart, at the thought that he could lose her forever, should she succeed and return to her own time. But Cisco had not gone back and Davis was still here, there was no reason to believe that the door worked both ways. This knowledge gave him reason to hope and the courage to give her her answer.

"I am a man of my word you know that. We will leave as soon as can be arranged and one way or the other, we will face whatever awaits us together."

She could hear the pain and hurt in his voice. It killed her to think that he thought it was easy for her to try and leave him, to go back. She was caught in a living hell for she now found herself truly torn between two worlds, two lives and two loves.

"Jean, can't you see. How can I make you understand? Whether I'm to leave for Galveston and the islands, or live on the plantation with you, it does not matter. What matters is I have to do this. So if I do leave with you, it is with my heart clear and my promise kept. Cisco's death made me realize that life is too short and too precious to treat lightly. I have to live with whatever my decision results in, that and my conscience. I made a promise to try to return and you made me a promise once to help me. We can't go on until we have both kept our word."

God help him he did understand and he knew as she did, that it was the last obstacle in their way. Nothing else could or would ever come between them. It had to be done. His only prayer now, was that she failed and he got to keep her with him. If that was wrong, so be it, he would gladly live with it.

By the time the arrangements had been handled and legal documents sorted out, March was into its third week. Grymes had drawn up official documents, showing Jean Laffite to be the new owner of the Duval plantation and properties. The court and its judge had hardly spent any time in its decision, once Leone's last will and testament had been presented. For Jean and Tori it was a bittersweet victory. Neither celebrated or admitted the apprehension they felt growing inside. How long would they remain at the plantation, for a few days or a lifetime, together or be forever separated?

Leone's house and the surrounding grounds had not changed in all the years she had been away. Riding up to the front, Tori half expected Kate to come bustling out, followed closely by Leone and his warmhearted gentle ways. The new overseer was there to meet them and assured them both that he would do all he could to help make the transition an easy one. In return Jean reassured him that his position was secure. He had done a fine job of running the place according to Grymes who had gone over the books carefully. The household servants, some of whom remembered Tori, were only too happy to have the new master and mistress. Their warm and friendly greeting was strengthened by their continued show of willingness to make Jean and his wife feel right at home.

Jean talked with Kate's replacement about the stable and was asking who was in charge there, when Tori slipped away and entered the house, making her way to the one room she felt she had to face alone. Leone's study was the same for the most part. The carpet had been changed, probably because removing the bloody stain had been impossible, she told herself, but his books and his desk sat just as he had left them. She touched the decanter of brandy, thinking back all those years ago, to the time she had shocked him by asking for a good stiff drink. A smile slid across her face. He had loved his brandy and enjoyed her company and their long evenings together.

So much had happened in such a short amount of time. Her run for her life, with his brother and the pain her disappearance had caused him. Kate's death. Her eyes glanced unwanted to the spot on the floor where she had last seen her. Suddenly the room was cold. It had lost its warm and friendly feel. It was a room of death and murder. One that had seen two people fall. One she would always love and miss. The other she hated to even think of. Try another room she thought; this one was not the best place to start after all. Kane's ugly memory, had mixed in with Kate's horrible death. The memories screamed at her from the very walls. She ran out into the hall, slamming the door behind her. It would be the last time she ever set foot in that room again.

Walking down the hall toward her favorite room helped her a little. It was dejavu with so many memories calling to her. In the kitchen, she could still see Kate and hear her as she hummed Tommy's song. The dining room conjured up long dinners and gentle talks with its owner, the staircase where she had first come down dressed as a southern lady. These were happy times and fond memories. But still others darker times lurked behind each turn. Looking out to the garden and the pathway that led to the gazebo, reminded her of her first encounter with Edward. The trail leading to the slave quarters, called up the brutal sick man, who had called himself an overseer. Kane had been nothing more than a racist murdering pig. "Probably the only good thing Edward ever did, killing you," she said out loud, turning back into the kitchen. The house held ghosts both good and bad, that she did not fear and yet neither did she want to face them. It would always be Leone's plantation and if she remained in this time with Jean, she knew she could never live within its walls. Even if everything were different, the lake would always be there, calling to her. She could not live her life always drawn to its shoreline, and that is what would happen. She could not lie to herself about that. She would never stop trying as long as it was within her reach. How could she, she asked herself?

Tori intended to keep her word and visit the spot, while they were here and when she was ready. After that if nothing happened, she would leave this place behind, forever.

Jean came inside and Tori met him, hugging him to her and smiling for the first time in days. "I think I had better show you around and then we can sit down and eat. Did I ever tell you about the first time I came down to eat dinner with Leone?" She was laughing and telling him the story again. He did not mind. Just to see her spirits lifted, made the story fresh and new again for him. By the time they retired for the night, the house had a warmer feeling about it and Tori found herself wondering if she hadn't been too hasty earlier, in thinking about leaving it.

She had wanted to delay for a few days the trip to the lake and Jean saw no problem in doing so. He was like herself, not sure he would ever be really ready to go there. The few days turned into four weeks. First excuses, she wanted to ride around the land and show him all that Leone had shown her. Then she had wanted to change a few things in the slave quarters and main house. Just when she thought she could put it off no longer, the weather changed and wind-driven rain poured down, followed by a freezing cold snap. It was far easier to stay warm and safe by the fire with Jean avoiding the subject.

Finally with May upon them, the sun came out and the whole world seemed to awaken from its long winter sleep. Spring filled the air and with it came the time for them both to decide what was to be done. The planting season would soon be upon them and decisions had to be made. Was this their home or not? Did they plant a crop or leave and sell? As much as he hated to push her, he had to know; they both did. He knew she was once again having nightmares and that she herself knew she could no longer delay it. So it was out of his love for his lady that he made her mind up for her.

That first trip to the lake had been the hardest trip of his life. He had awakened her long before dawn and gently told her that he had their horses waiting for them. She had not said a word, just reached out and clung to him. The look on her face would stay with him the rest of his life. She loved him for that, he had no doubt.

For two days they had arrived at the lake before dawn, leaving the warmth of the house and traveling the short distance to the water's edge. They had sat that first day together looking and waiting, both so tense that neither dared talk. That night they had talked, and for the first time they admitted that it was very unlikely that Tori would ever see her way back to her own time again. Still she had asked to go back. She could not explain it to him or herself, she just had to go. Again nothing happened and again late into the night they talked and held each other close. One thing had become clear to them, she could not make the plantation their home.

Together they had decided to try one last morning and if nothing should happen, they would ride back to New Orleans. They would begin their lives free at last of any guilt holding her to her life in the future. They would sell the plantation and use the money to go and start a new life in the islands.

The morning had been warmer than the last two with the promise of an early summer hanging in the air. In the pre-dawn it was still crisp enough for her to wrap a blanket around her shoulders, as she sat looking out over the calm water. Her mind wandered as she sat there peacefully, then one thought took hold and she knew it to be right. This would be the last time she ever gazed upon the mirror-like surface, the last time she would torture herself with "What if?"

Daybreak had come and gone. The hours had slipped by until at last she could not deny the inevitable any longer. She reached for his hand and without looking at him she spoke lovingly. "Let's go home."

The words rang in his ears and his heart. His prayers had been answered and he swore to God, that he would spend the rest of his days, loving her and making her happy. He knew that a part of her was grieving and wished only that he could ease her pain. Guilt flooded him, as he realized what his happiness was costing her.

"Are you sure, if you wish to try again..."

"No, there is no need. I could come here everyday the rest of my life. I could grow old and gray sitting here, waiting. Waiting for what I ask you? For something that may never happen. Hell, I don't even know what it is I'm supposed to be looking and waiting for." She put her head down on her knees. "Jean, go get the horses. I just need a bit of time alone. I have to say good-bye in my own way."

He did not say anything but just left her side. She was right and he knew it. The most he could do for her at that moment was give her her time and then never leave her side again.

She knew he had gone; she did not need to look to see that. The sound of his footsteps crunching the earth as he left had faded quietly away. Shortly thereafter, she could hear his voice softly calling to the horses off in the distance. The world was hers. The lake and all it held was hers. But she had not unlocked it's secret. What had she expected anyway, she wondered? She raised her head and looked out over the mist-covered shore. She could see the water's edge but beyond that it was shrouded in fog, hiding its glass-like surface and its mystery. The sun was warm on her shoulders and the blanket felt heavy and stifling. She let it fall from her as she stood.

This was it then, the big farewell, the departing of one life to move on to another. The trouble was she didn't know how or what to do. She felt as if she owed Linni and her family more. She owed them her prayers and her hope that they to could be happy and go on with their lives. Without realizing it, she had walked to the water's edge and stood gazing quietly out. It was so peaceful, so still, so perfect. She was so deep in her thoughts that she almost missed it. Almost, but the silence was deafening! It hit her as surely as if a hand had struck her, so overpowering was the sensation.

"It's happening!" was all she could mutter to herself. Without thinking about what she was doing, her hands started tearing at her clothes. She had come naked. She had to return the same way the voice in her head told her. Her top came off in seconds, followed by first one boot and then the other. Falling over, she pulled at her riding pants, which slid down and off faster than she could ever have thought possible. Then naked she stood facing the lake, hesitating briefly. To wait could cost her the one chance. She plunged in.

Jean heard the splash. His head spun around looking back towards the lake. He had covered quite a distance walking the horses while waiting for his lady. But not so far that he couldn't hear her call or worse. There was no denying it, the splash could mean only one thing. His feet started moving before his mind told him he was running.

The water was freezing at first, the shock of it almost took her breath away but still she swam out toward the center of the lake, disappearing into the fog as she went. Long slow strokes digging into the tranquil frigid depths. The icy cold stung her skin, her thoughts screaming at her, asking her just what in the hell was she doing? She swam harder as if trying to outswim her own thoughts. Had she gone crazy? With water this cold hypothermia would not take long to set in and then what?

Jean ran for all he was worth, his heart pounding from both fear and exertion. Somehow in between breaths, he was able to call out Tori's name, over and over he called. To him he traveled at a snail's pace. The lake was just over the small ridge and it seemed to take forever to climb. He just couldn't get there fast enough and then he was there. He was there standing by a fallen blanket, her clothes and the lake. And he was totally alone. She was nowhere to be seen. The water was as still as it had been. Not a ripple or wave touched the shoreline. If anyone was out there swimming, the surface would tell, but the waters were as still as the air.

In one horrible earth-shattering second, he knew. Then the only sound roaring through the heavens like thunder on a summer's storm, was his cry of agony and loss.

She had just made her mind up to turn around and go back, when from what seemed like a great distance away, she heard her name being called. One long agonizing scream of Jean's voice sounding on the breeze, swirling like the mist around her fading fast as the slight wind itself died. Then silence. He must have heard me, she reasoned, but could not risk using what little energy she had left in her freezing body, to return his call. She turned instead and swam back into the mist-covered waters, heading for him and safety.

Her strokes were long and slow. Instead of feeling her body weaken, as she thought it would have, instead of the numbing slow freeze of the icy darkness, she found tepid water hitting her face. Gone was the chill of the air in her lungs. Instead each breath she took now filled her chest with warm muggy air. Her legs hit bottom, scraping her knees on the sand. Still the mist blocked her view, and as it continued to do so until she stood up. Deep down, she already knew what she would see, and as she did rise above the mist, what greeted her eyes took her breath away.

She walked as if in a daze, out of the shallow water, toward the small cove, where Jean should have been standing but where instead, lay a robe and a coffee cup. Her head started spinning as she cautiously walked toward the objects, knowing as she did so, just what they were and where she was.

Tori reached down, her hand trembling as she picked up her robe, her coffee cup rolling over on its side. No one had taken her robe, no woman had stolen them, they were still just where she had left them.

Then a sudden realization hit, a knowing deep inside. Tori knew she was being watched and she knew who was watching her. She turned to look out over the lake and there, way out nearly in the middle, looking back at her was a lone swimmer. By some quirk in time, she found for a brief second, that she was looking back at herself. Then the mist closed in and the image was gone. That Tori, had just begun her journey and this Tori had come full circle. She was back.

She did not know how she walked back to the cabin, or how she looked when Dan saw her coming toward him. She would always remember him looking at her, as if he were seeing a stranger and of how she sat and talked to him for hours, trying to explain what had happened. Nor would she ever forget the moment she was able to prove to him, it had not been a dream...

"You see, Tom it was my hair. I had it tied up in a bandana of sorts. I always rode with it tied up and I had not thought to remove it when I jumped into the lake. It was not until I was back with Dan, trying to explain to him about five years of my life, which had been less than ten minutes here. My proof was my hair. Remember, I told you it was shoulder length and permed. Well in five years it grew and when I let it down, well Dan had to believe me. Then there was the matter of my tan. I did not have one!"

Tom sat there looking at her. Her hair was short and straight. No five years of growth there. She had told him one hell of a story but could he believe it? Any of it?

"Look I know how hard it is and trust me at times, I have had to ask myself if I'm crazy but the simple fact is this. It happened. If you are wondering about my hair, I had it cut again. I tried to erase all ties to him, to that time." She ran her hand through her hair. "Found out you can't erase love or memories."

Tom stood up and walked toward the window. Morning had arrived in the French Quarter. They had been up all night. Strange, he thought he wasn't even tired. He was mixed up though. He wanted to believe her, mostly because of Kate and Leone. It would give him an identity but time travel?

"Tom," she asked "please come here for just a few minutes longer." She watched as he turned toward her. "I did not know until now if telling you was the right thing to do either for you or me. You see even Dan does not know the whole story. Oh sure, he knows most of it but how could I ever tell him about Jean, about Christopher? You are the first and I think the only other person, that will ever know the whole truth. Can you believe that? By me telling you, it's helped heal the pain some but what have I done to you? Have I helped, or do you think my tale the raving of a crazy woman? Have I in some way made it better or not?"

"Tori, Mam," he sat back down by her side. "If I could believe in your story I would have to say that yes, it would help. But Mam you ask me to sit here and tell you something that I can't do. If it helped you to talk, then we should both be glad for that. But the fact remains it's just a story, your story not mine."

His sad face filled her heart. She had made it worse not better. How could she have ever expected him to believe her? "You can talk to Dan. He won't be too happy with me but let me worry about that. He will tell you. You'll believe him won't you?"

"Mam, it's not that. Don't' you see? I need more'n him telling me he believes you." He stood up. "Now if you don't' mind, I think I had best be heading home. You take care of yourself and maybe before you leave, maybe we will talk again. But Tori don't call me, let it be my choice alright?"

Tori would not, could not let it end like this. She wanted him to know that it was the truth, but how? He wanted proof, actual proof.

"Tom! Wait a minute. I have an idea. I know just how to prove it all to you. The question is are you brave enough to face it? If you will give me just a little more of your time and come with me I'll give you your answers, your proof. What do you say? Will you do it?"

Tom turned back to face her. She was serious. She really believed she could prove it to him. A small glimmer of hope took hold inside of him. Who the hell was he to say she couldn't do it, he asked himself? "Well I've spent this much time listening to you, what's a bit more? I guess it's worth it one way or the other."

"Oh Tom, it's worth it. You wait and see. It will all be worth it."

# Chapter 30

Tom sat in his car in front of the hotel, anxiously awaiting Tori to join him. She had said that she needed only thirty minutes to take a quick shower and take care of a few other things. To Tom those thirty minutes had felt more like thirty hours. There was no doubt as to his feelings, but he wanted proof. Yet fear held his emotions in check. If it turned out that the wild story Tori had just finished telling him was true, it would change the way he looked at life. It would forever alter his attitude, not only about himself but about how he lived and would continue to live. If not, well he would handle that later.

True to her word, she had taken only thirty minutes. Watching her walking toward his car, her step lively and her face full of excitement, he found himself gripping the steering wheel. Taking a deep breath he told himself to take it easy.

The car door opened and she slid into the front seat next to him. There was not a hint of fear or doubt in her manner. "Well this is it then," she smiled. "I left a note for Dan, just in case he comes back to the room before we get back. She frowned, her voice going more serious. "I hate lying to him but what choice did I have? I just don't want him to worry and he would never understand this. Anyway, it's best if he thinks me off shopping after an early breakfast."

Tom looked concerned. "You real sure you want to do this, whatever this is? I mean I've been thinking about it while sitting here. I just can't figure out how in the hell you intend to give me concrete evidence." He hated to sound so down, when she seemed to be so sure of herself, but he had to play devil's advocate. Especially if it meant saving them both from a big letdown.

Her smile slipped away as she answered him in a serious tone. "I'm not positive that I can find you concrete evidence as you say, but yes Tom, I really want to do this. If I find what I'm looking for, then you will have no choice but to accept the story for fact. If it's not there, well what I will have attempted to show you, should help convince you."

Tom's mood lifted a little as excitement started to take hold. He felt bad for having put her good spirits in jeopardy and wanted to cheer her up. He wanted to give her back that self-confidence she had had only a few minutes earlier. "Look, when you were telling me the part about my mother last night. I have to tell you that I did have flashes of a dream I used to have as a child and it did sort of fit. What I mean is, the description of that plantation, it could be from a life I had once known. It wasn't much and I thought to myself, this is it, the link but now in the light of day..."

What I have in mind is far more tangible than fleeting memories, wishful thinking or dejavu feelings. I can, I hope, in the next few hours show you something really tangible. Two things to be exact, that will erase all doubts." She touched his arm lightly as if to reassure him that she was certain of what she intended. Then sounding confident once again she asked, "Are you ready? Because if you are, let's get started shall we?"

Tom was more than willing. "As crazy as this seems, I think that I do believe, at least a small part of me does. Still some tangible proof wouldn't hurt any." He started the car. "What did you have in mind?"

"You drive and I'll give you directions. First stop is not far from here and I could use a drink."

He shot her a fearful look. "You mean drink as in drink? It's only ten in the morning. No offense but isn't it a little early to be..."

She laughed at him. "Or a little late, whichever way you look at it. Jean used to say, the sun's setting over the yardarm somewhere. Don't worry Tom, you'll understand in just a few more minutes. Just trust me and go along with me from this point on ok? It's very important that you listen to me and please, just do as I ask."

Once again he told himself he was stupid for going along with her but she seemed so in control, much more than the afternoon before. Something in him did trust her, or at least wanted too. He would just sit back and see.

Her directions took them through the streets of the French Quarter, up one street and down another. She never hesitated once and seemed to know her way around, as if she had lived here all of her life. He wanted to ask her questions about the area and how it had changed, but sat in silence instead.

"Pull over here and park. We will walk the rest of the way," she told him. Tori gave him no chance to question her. As soon as the car stopped, she was out the door. She had to get him to follow her, not allow him one second to change his mind or guess at their destination.

They walked the first block, with Tom looking both ahead in the direction they were headed and then back at Tori. She never faltered in her stride or gave any sign of her emotions. Her face remained blank.

At the corner of Saint Phillip and Bourbon, she finally stood still, looking at him as she dictated her orders. "Just act like a tourist and go along with whatever I ask or tell you to do, ok?"

Before he could answer or question, she was off again, calling over her shoulder, "Come on, stop dawdling." She was headed up Bourbon Street, when suddenly she disappeared into a building.

"It's Laffite's Blacksmith Shop!" he said out loud, following her rapidly inside.

The interior was dimly lit and empty, that was all except for the bartender who was sat on a stool, watching a T.V that hung above him. He was eating what looked like the remains of a hamburger. He didn't even look up at them, until they sat down at the far end of the bar.

"Can I help you folks?" He wiped the corner of his mouth and took a sip of his coffee.

"You sure can, if you can fix a good Bloody Mary," said Tori.

He smiled at them, putting his cup down. "Ain't a bartender that can do it better than me. Fix you right up. And you?" he looked at Tom.

"He'll have the same." She said quickly giving Tom no choice. "Had a great night but boy, are we paying for it now." She laughed putting her hand to her head.

"Know what you mean. This city can do that to you. Where you folks from?"

"I'm from California and my friend here is from the Big Easy. He's been showing me around. I just wanted to come back here for a quick pick-me-up. Loved the place so much last night," she lied easily. "It's got so much atmosphere. Do you mind if I take a look around?"

"Don't mind at all. Most folks, just come in and drink and party. Not many folks know or want to know the history of the place though." He talked, not looking at them, as he mixed their drinks. "Locals know and a few history buffs, s'pect you know?" he looked up at Tom.

"Me, sure. It's Jean Laffite's place, or should say was, right?"

"That's what they say. I did some reading up on the place myself, when I came to work here. If you have any questions, I'd be happy to answer them." He placed the drinks down in front of them, a friendly smile on his face.

"I'm a writer," said Tori. She took a sip of her drink. "Umm, real tasty."

He beamed, proud of his concoction and her compliment, not seeming to care about her statement of writer.

Tom picked his glass up and took a large gulp. Bullshit on the writer crap he thought. Just what game was she playing at here, he asked himself? He was about to try to catch her eye, when she continued her conversation as if he wasn't even there.

"I've written a fiction piece about Laffite and this place. It plays a big role in my story."

"That so?" he seemed pleased.

"My name's Tori, this here is Tom and you are?"

"Trevor's the name."

"Nice to meet you Trevor. It does my heart good to meet someone who knows something about this old place and Laffite. I have read and studied the man and locations connected with him for years but always returned here." She was walking toward the fireplace in the center of the room. "I was told that this was the forge."

"That's what they say. Most of the building is as it was, it's historical you know. Can't change nothing in here, or outside any more."

She smiled to herself, turning away, afraid he might see her expression. If only he knew how much it had changed over the years. True the outside still looked as it had but he was wrong about the inside. For one thing, she could tell him that the floor had all been one level. There had been no step up just past the fireplace. She looked down at the concrete floor and frowned, no such flooring either.

She stepped past the fireplace paying it little attention, when her eye caught the painting facing her on the far wall. Hanging there in all its glory, was what was supposed to be the likeness of Jean Laffite. Now there was something that would have made him furious she thought. It looked nothing like him at all. She walked closer to inspect it, frowning as she did. She had not expected such feelings but they were there just the same. The picture had brought her feelings boiling up. Her temper was close to exploding. Her handsome dashing Jean, had been made to look almost evil. The artist had him all in black and what a stupid expression, if that's what it could be called, she thought. The whole thing was silly and she wouldn't let it get to her. She pushed away the anger. No, she told herself she would be like the real Laffite, who unlike this stern looking image, would have had a sense of humor and roared his head off laughing. "It's just so hard to laugh though," she quietly explained to his ghost and herself. She was angry that the whole world did not know him as she did, nor would they ever. Her anger, gave way rapidly to sadness. Nothing was the same. She had known that it couldn't be, but being in here so soon after remembering it all, was overpowering.

From one end to the other, from the front entrance to the rear, it was nothing but a bar. Small wooden tables, each seating two, were up against the wall, while larger tables filled the interior. Candles, not one lit, sat on each table. There were tables that still needed cleaning and chairs that needed straightening for the new day. What little light did filter in from the open door, or side windows, was just enough to allow her to see the real condition of the establishment. The walls were mere bricks in places, the beams and wooden floor above, darkened with age. That's just it she told herself? The building is old, very old and considering all it must have gone through and seen over the years, it was truly a miracle that it still stood. She looked again and smiled. It was in better condition than she had first allowed herself to admit. Going toward the back end, walking slowly, she continued her exploration. She had to see it both in the past and present state in order to find just what it was she was looking for. The vibrations became stronger as she walked slowly toward the back. It was as if the walls were taking to her. The building was filled with the residue of the past and she could feel it. How many people came here each day to drink and party she wondered? People who would think it nothing more than a funky old pirate's bar, never going beyond their first impressions. And how many would walk toward the back, like she was doing now, hearing the whispers of bygone days, feeling the impressions of its ghosts and really appreciate the history that surrounded them. Not many she figured. Ah but those who did, what an experience, what a trip.

Tori was getting her bearings, she had to be sure of herself first, before she started to retrieve what she had come for. It could only be in one spot. A place so easy to find in the building of the past, but not so easy now. This was not the past and with the interior so altered, that spot would be harder to locate but not impossible. She saw the side door that exited to a small courtyard. In her mind it held so many visions of the bygone era. Now it simply held more empty tables. She tried to open the door only to find it was closed and locked.

"I'll let you have a look out that way, if you'd like?" called Trevor. He had walked from behind the bar and stood by the fireplace all smiles, watching her.

"No, that's all right." she answered. "I'll just take a peek back here and then I'll join you all."

He shrugged his shoulders, "as you like." and walked back to join Tom.

"Like I need to see what's out there," she whispered to herself. She had walked out that door often enough to know what was on the other side. Or what should have been, she reminded herself. At the back of the long-shaped room she was in, stood the piano, surrounded by stools. The rest of the area branched off, to her right, where it ended. The whole interior of the bar formed a large U-shape. The area around the piano was clear, except for a few more tables up against the walls. Half a wall separated this room from the front and directly behind it was the bar. It was in this area, she remembered, that the stairs used to exit, to the upper level. She guessed they were still there, but just not visible from this side. A small area, with large wooden doors was in the darkened corner. Though dimly lit, they were plainly visible and it made her chuckle. The doors were marked Ladies and Gentlemen. Now this was a new addition. "Original my ass," she said out loud. Then quite suddenly she found herself giggling. This would have made Thiac laugh. He had thought the idea of a toilet inside anyone's home was just the sickest thing he could think of.

    Tom called to her from the front of the bar and she left the back area to join him. On her way she turned her head to look over the side wall once again. It's got to be just past that piece of shit artwork she figured. Counting the number of windows and looking back toward the side door, she made a mental note of the approximate location to start her search. Just how to go about it undetected, was going to take a bit of ingenuity on both her's and Tom's part. Step one completed. On to step two she told herself.

    Tom sat sipping his drink, watching her as she approached him. For the life of him, he couldn't see what she hoped to show him here. What proof did she have in mind, he wondered?

    "You know," said Trevor to them both, once Tori had taken her seat next to Tom, "the place is said to be haunted by Laffite. There are those, including myself, that have heard things late at night. Or real early like, when it's deathly quiet. Not so much down here," he looked around, "Mostly upstairs."

    Tori's eyes looked up at him. "Upstairs you say?" So she was right, the stairs still did exist. "Do you think I could take a take a look?" Maybe, it hadn't changed as much up there as down here she thought. And if it had, it would be fun to see just how much.

    Trevor's attitude changed visibly as he looked away quickly. His voice was sharp. "Can't let you do that."

    "I'm sorry, did I say something to offend you?"

    "No Mam. It's just that it's private up there. Just a small apartment of sorts, nothing you would want to see anyway."

    She had the feeling he was hiding something but didn't have a chance to investigate further. His look softened toward her. "But there is this." He pointed to the wall behind the end of the bar. "Now this might be of interest to you. Have you seen it before? The writing that's here?"

    Tori looked to where he was pointing and could not make out any writing, nor did she know what he was talking about. "No, I can't say that I have." She moved closer to see more clearly.

    Trevor smiled and continued. "No one knows who wrote it, or when. It's old though. Been there for years. I had it translated once, being I don't read Italian. Look, I'll shine the flashlight on it for you." He aimed his light up at the spot and slowly Tori could make out the inscription. It says..."

    Her glass fell to the floor, as her recognition of what she was looking at sunk in. Trevor's words stopped halfway through his translation. The sound of shattering glass interrupting his moment of pride.

"Oh, I'm so sorry. It just slipped, God I'm so clumsy."

"Don't worry none. It's nothing that can't be cleaned up. Still got to charge you though," he chuckled. "Fix you another one, if you want?"

"Yes, yes please do. You positively make the very best Bloody Mary I have ever had. You agree Tom?"

He was staring at her and snapped out of his daydream-like state. "Yeh, sure do. Too good to be throwing around like that."

"I fully agree with you," she turned back to Trevor. "I'm so very sorry."

"Like I told you, it's all right. You forget about it. I'll clean it up, just as soon as I fix you another one." He looked back up at the inscription and asked as he did. "You still want to know what it all says?"

"Yes please," she answered excitedly. She waved her hand at Tom, "Come on over hear and take a look at this will you?"

He moved off his stool and joined her, walking around the broken glass and wet floor., his eyes following the direction of the small flashlight beam to the writing in question.

As far as I know it says, "Love passes time. Time passes with love."

Tom held his breath. Now he knew why Tori had dropped her drink with that seen-a-ghost look on her face. She could read the Italian saying before Trevor had had a chance to translate it.

"Interesting saying, what do you think it means?" she asked.

He was back mixing her a fresh drink. "Don't know, but there are those who say Laffite himself put it there, right before he sailed out of here."

"Look, you mind if we take a seat over there," she pointed toward the small table by the side wall. I would like to write that down before I forget it."

"No, go ahead," he handed her the new drink. "I'll clean up the mess and then take care of business. If you have any further questions, I'll be right here."

She took Tom by the arm and led him to the small table. "This should do it." She pulled out the chair and sat down looking around her. "It should be right about here, the problem is getting it without being seen," she told him.

Tom pulled out the opposite chair and sat down, taking a larger swig of his up-until-now, not-wanted drink. "What in the hell are you talking about?" His mind was still swimming around after seeing the inscription. For a few brief seconds, he had considered that she already knew they were written there and it was all apart of an elaborate scheme to fool him. This was something that he rejected though as she had been just as shocked as he was, when shown those words scratched into the brickwork. They could not be what she had come here for though, so what was it and what was she up too?

Tori, those words. I remember you telling me about the locket and the saying inscribed in it. It's the same isn't it?"

"Oh it's the same," she said, her voice breaking a little. "I've no doubt that he wrote it for me to find. He knew about this place becoming what it is and must have known I would come here. It was his way of letting me know..." she stopped talking. Trevor was cleaning up the broken glass and was within hearing range of their conversation.

Tom lowered his voice. "That's not it, is it? What we came here for?"

She shook her head, still watching Trevor clean up. She was pretending to write down notes, biding her time. Finally finishing his mopping up he left, going back to his seat behind the bar.

"No it's not why we are here. What we came for, is behind one of these bricks, right about here." she pointed at the wall down by her side. "The trick is going to be finding it and removing it, without being caught."

Tom looked horrified. "Are you crazy?"

"Nope, not yet anyway. Now all you have to do is keep an eye on our friend over there. I'll do the rest." She was already probing with her fingers, at an exposed area. Her hands were searching frantically, for a certain place on the wall.

What could she be looking for, he wondered again? Then he turned away from what she was up to and kept his eye on the man behind the bar. Thank goodness he seemed more interested in the previous night's receipts and the T.V. than he did with his customers. Tom only hoped it stayed that way, but if Tori didn't stop carrying on as she was and lower her voice, that might not happen.

"Come on be here," she said impatiently. I know it's here."

"Tori, for God's sake lower your voice please," he begged.

She listened to him but still kept whispering to herself. "Sorry, bad habit of mine you know." She looked back at the wall. "Jean damn your hide I need your stash. Even finding the words weren't..."

Suddenly she fell silent. The brick under her hand had moved slightly. The mortar around it was loose and cracked. Some had even fallen away completely. This could be it, she thought. "Oh please let it be," she begged. She pushed a little harder and then reaching into her bag she brought out her nail file. One quick look toward the bar, told her she was still safe. She turned her attention back to the loose brick, pressing the metal blade into the space between the bricks. She pushed and pried at the area. Mortar fell to the floor in small bits and pieces. She scattered it with her foot. Finally the brick was far enough out of the wall for her to grab hold, in a few seconds she would know.

"Damn it," her angry voice snapped. It made Tom jump and Trevor looked over toward them.

"Need two more drinks over here," Tom called out smiling. I'll come and get them, and settle up the tab."

Trevor nodded and went about making two more of his specials. Tom breathed a sigh of relief, then he shot Tori a worried look. "What's wrong? It's not there, wrong spot?" His voice was excited, as his eyes could see for themselves the brick that she was holding in her hand and the open space from which it had come.

"No, I've not looked yet. I just broke a nail."

The two of them laughed, breaking the tension.

"You did what?"

"Broke a nail. Listen to me here. I could be arrested for disfiguring a historical landmark and I'm complaining about my nails."

Her eyes were sparkling, even in the dim light he could tell she was as excited as he was. Only difference, he didn't know what it was he was supposed to be so worked up about. "Don't do a thing till I get back." He got up and taking his wallet from his back pocket walked to the bar. He told himself to remain calm and to act natural. He could not give Trevor any reason to pay them the slightest bit of attention.

Tori watched as he paid the bill and picked up the two drinks along with a piece of paper. She could not hear what was being said between the two but hoped that it was not going to cause any problems or delays. She was so very close. She held the brick at her side out of sight and sat her free hand on her empty glass.

Tom placed the new beverage in front of her, along with the piece of paper. It was a guest receipt and written on it was the translation of the inscription. Tom explained, "I had to tell him something about your outburst. Couldn't really tell the man the truth could I? So I said you were making notes and thought you got the translation backwards. He wrote it down for you."

She looked at her companion. He really surprised her. "Quick thinking. God you're good. Thanks." She took a sip of the drink and looked toward the bar. Trevor had returned to his T.V. show and had turned his back to them.

"Well it's back to work, here goes," she said quietly.

Tom didn't know which one to watch, the bartender or Tori and what she was doing. In the end he flashed his eyes continuously between them both.

She was reaching into the small space and then as her hand disappeared into the hole, she took in a sharp breath. "Thanks Jean, you did remember. I can feel something almost got it." She took in a deep breath and held it. "Got it!" Her hand came out holding a small leather pouch and quickly she dropped it into her open bag. Then she placed the brick back into its original position and kicked at the floor one last time, scattering any visible sign of fallen mortar.

"Drink up," she laughed picking up her glass and downing the contents. "You're going to need it."

Tom did as she said and followed suit. Then before he had time to utter a word, she was on her way outside.

"Thanks," she called back to Trevor.

"Good luck on the book," he answered. "Hey, before you go." They stopped looking back at him. "What's the name of it anyhow?"

Tom looked dumbfounded. Tori just acted as if it was the most natural question to be asked.

"Laffite's Lady." she answered him, "and when it comes out, this place is going to become very popular. Good luck to you!"

Tom and Tori headed for the car walking fast and then running. Tom laughing out loud, waiting until they turned the corner before shouting at her. "And you said I was good. Where in the hell did that come from? I froze, thought he had us." He opened the car door and then went around to his side, climbing in and hitting the lock button before facing her. "You really are good you know? And you weren't kidding were you? I mean you have that pouch and all. Shit it's all true. I mean how in the hell else did you know where to look?" He grabbed her arm, his voice shaking. "My God, do you know what this means? My mother, you knew her and more than that..." His eyes had tears in them as realization hit home and any doubts he had felt washed away.

Tori watched him in silence, letting him express his feelings, letting the belief take hold. "You mean if nothing is in the pouch, you still believe me now, one hundred percent?"

"How in the hell could I not?" he replied. "To tell you the truth, I was afraid that it would turn out a lie. I wanted to believe you."

"Well sitting here like this won't tell us what we have will it. Let's just take a look shall we?" She reached into her bag and removed the pouch, placing it on her lap.

In the daylight, Tom could see that it was made of a thick brown leather. It was gathered at the top by a long strip of cord. It was not a worn or used bag. Rather, it just looked old and dirty but it did not look empty either.

Her fingers pulled at the top, untying the leather cord which at one point snapped easily, as it was so brittle with age. She watched his face, as she turned the pouch upside down, so the contents could fall out. She had no need to see what was falling onto her lap, she already knew what was there.

Tom stared, as the sound of coins broke the silence in the car. His eyes rounded in sheer delight, as a small heap of gold coins mounted up in her hand.

"Holy shit! Will you just look at that. Shit, you're rich, you done gone and won the biggest lottery of all!"

Twenty-five coins had dropped out, shining in the sunlight. Tori picked one up, holding it in her fingers, turning it over slowly she spoke. "You know Tom, up until this moment, it could have all been a dream. I have often wondered if it was not some trick of my mind. If I wasn't in fact crazy. Now I have proof of my own. Look, here it is." She handed the coin to him. "I know you know now also." She looked off into the distance in a daydream-like state. She was remembering something, "God, so long ago and yet for me, it was just over two years ago."

Tom held the coin in his hand afraid almost to look at it. Then he turned it over and over in the palm of his hand examining it closely. "This is an American gold coin. Oh shit, do you know how long it's been since America made gold coins? I've only ever seen one up till now. It was a twenty dollar gold piece, my dad's. I know the date on it, it's 1903. This is much older." He took a look at the rest of the coins, "They're all American, and the dates Tori, they're all before the 1800's. No, here's one dated 1815."

She reached out smiling and took it from him, "That one is mine."

"What are you going to do? I mean these coins are worth a lot in just the weight of gold but much more to collectors I'm sure. They're in mint condition." Then another thought came to mind. "How are you going to tell anyone where you found them and all?"

Tori looked at him and smiled. She already knew what she was going to do with her share. "You can make up your own answer on that question but please come up with a story, other than the truth." She was counting the coins and then she handed him a handful. "I need to let the past go. I don't need a lot of publicity and unwanted questions."

"You mean you are giving these to me?" he sounded disbelieving. "But why?"

"Because in a way they belong to you too. I want you to have them. Call it, paying off a debt I owe to your mother and father. Please I want you to have them. There is only one favor I will ask you in return."

"Name it," he said softly. He loved her so much and not just because of the coins he now held. She had given him so much more than money could buy.

"What is it? Please you can tell me." He didn't like the look coming over her face. It was that tormented look she had the day before and most of the night.

"I want to really break away from the past. I want to put Jean's ghost to rest so to speak. To do that, I have one last place to go and see and now that you know I'm telling you the truth and you know the story, I hope you will help me. I want to go to Christopher's grave. Will you take me?"

He looked at her then, understanding her pain and knowing that she did intend to go because she needed the closure. He decided to support her. She needed a friend to go with her and who better than himself. He knew she could not and would not ask Dan to take her. It had to be him. Tom put the coins into his jeans pocket, never looking away from her pleading stare. He started the car and then grinning asked her, "Where too? You give the directions, I'll take you and now seems the best time don't you think?"

She was talking on Tom's cell phone to the hotel. Dan had not returned as of yet and no messages had been left for her. Tom paid little attention to the rest of her conversation. His attention was on the countryside passing them by. Thoughts and questions rambled around in his head, both intermingling with his emotions. His feelings were just as mixed up as ever.

Tori had finished talking and was sitting silently looking out the side window. Tom could not just ride in silence. "You must be remembering a lot," he said. "I mean this has to be hard for you. I don't know which is harder though. Me not knowing really what it was like, the people, the plantations, the way of life." He looked at her then, taking his eyes off the road ahead briefly. "My mother and father and you. You having to live with the memory and the knowledge, the secret of it all. Have you ever thought of telling anyone else?" He looked back at the road as he continued. "Are you going to tell anyone else besides me that is?"

She nodded her head. "I don't know yet. You see in the beginning, when I first came back, Dan and I wanted to tell someone, just to help me get over the shock and believe you me, it was a hell of a shock. It's like I lived two lives, in two times and died and lost and relived again." She turned to face him. "But the more we talked about it, the more we knew we had no proof of what had happened. Sure my hair was long again overnight, but it could have been that it was never really short in the first place. We could be accused of creating this great big hoax, just for the publicity and the money. The talk shows, magazines and maybe even a tell-all book." she laughed.

Tom frowned and shot her a dirty look.

"We had to think about Linni also. People would have thought me crazy or one big liar, neither of which would look great at a PTA meeting if you understand me?"

"Well you could have gone and got the coins like we just did. They would have had to believe you then."

"I thought of that too and I wasn't sure anything would be there and it was ok, don't you see, they could have said that it was planted there beforehand, by either myself or an accomplice. Sure it would be an expensive hoax but then that's what they would have put it down to in the end. No one wants to believe in time travel. No one really wants to hear from a crazy woman." she whispered, looking back out the car window.

What she had just said made him think. He questioned in his own mind, the idea of her planting the coins. To him it was absurd. He would not allow himself to think along those lines.

"Besides," she continued, "I couldn't do much because of the whole story don't you see? You are the only person besides me that knows the whole damn mess from beginning to end. About Jean and the baby. Something that I have not and will not ever be able to tell Dan. I hate keeping it from him. Really, I'm not ashamed of what I did and how I felt but I just can't hurt him. I can't run the risk of his not understanding why I didn't tell him in the beginning either. He has asked me to marry him and I know he loves me and Linni very much. I know that it has been hard on him but his love for me never let him give up on me. It has to be this way. In a short time, I will cut all ties with the past and Jean. After I see the grave and say my good-byes, it will be over, finished and I will go on with my life."

To Tom she sounded like she was trying to talk herself into believing what she was saying. He felt uncomfortable with the subject, and suddenly, with the trip they were making. But he had to continue with it. He was compelled too, by his need to help her and his own curiosity.

"What was it like back then? I mean this area, this trip we are making now?" he asked her pulling onto the river road. The Mississippi was on his left as they headed North.

"Pretty much as I told you. What has taken us less than an hour, would have taken half a day or more depending on the weather and conditions of the road." She pointed ahead and towards the left. "Slow up, we're almost here. If you'll just pull off to the side in front of Destrehan for a moment, I'll try and describe it to you as it used to be."

He saw the large house and pulled into the small car park on the side. He had never been to this plantation, in particular always choosing instead the more popular and flamboyant plantations such Oak Alley.

"It looks the same on the outside, the house itself, but the grounds have changed and I'm sure that to go inside would break my heart. Marie and J.D. were so proud of their home and the two wings he added, as his family grew. I arrived here after that first Christmas and can tell you it was grand, yet simple. It was a home filled with love and children."

"Do you mind if we just walk around the grounds?" he asked her hopefully. "You could describe it all to me then."

"I really don't want to Tom. It's just so hard to see what has been taken away. For instance, the view of the river is gone. It was never like that." She pointed across the road to the high levee that faced them. "When I used to visit, the driveway curled up and split off just about there," she pointed, "so the carriage could drop off its occupants, either at the front or the back." She was sitting up higher in her seat, as she continued in her description. There used to be a separate kitchen and a storehouse and drying house. The slave cabins, about nineteen of them were down toward the fields. "And there were large sheds that J.D. kept his machinery in. Marie used to play with the children out on the grass among her flower beds. She loved her flowers and on summer evenings we would all sit up there," she indicated the upper balcony, "about halfway along. At the end of the day, we would all sit looking at the river enjoying the different scents carried on the cool breeze." She could see it all so clearly and in the way she was describing it, so could Tom.

"The children were allowed to play in the garden while we sat up there," she smiled to herself. "The whole garden was enclosed by a thick hedge of orange trees, some up to sixteen feet in height, and all the walkways were bordered by large crepe myrtle trees." Her voice had softened and sadly she added, "Gone, it's all gone now."

She shook her head as if trying to remove the sadness and move quickly on to a better memory. "They had their townhouse in the French Quarter as you know, but Marie loved it here the best in the summer and this is where she raised her children. She was a wonderful woman and a great mother you know. Not to mention one of my best and most dear friends. J.D. was in his own right, quite a man also. I could tell you so much about him, more than any of those tour guides could, that's for sure." she chuckled. "Take for instance, the huge marble bathtub off Marie's bedroom. She implied that it had been a gift to them from none other than Napoleon Bonaparte himself."

Tom started to laugh at that statement.

"Don't look at me like that," she laughed out loud. "You wanted to know and I'm not making it up. They knew a lot of important people, both here in this country and in France. Why one of them, the Duc de Orleans, came to stay with them once and he later became King Louis Phillippe of France."

Tom was impressed. He viewed the house with a whole new attitude. If only old homes could talk he thought. There was so much more than just bricks and wood, so much hidden within its walls, in its very history.

"J.D., as I called him, was elected the first State's Senator from Louisiana. That was I think in 1812. Marie hated him being gone so much and him being the family man he was, he resigned without serving out his term. Good thing too, if you ask me. Jackson needed his help. He was one of the men on the committee that helped bridge the gap between the citizens of the city and the General's military. He may have had something to do with Jackson's agreement to meet with Jean, I'm not sure but it wouldn't have surprised me."

"How did those two meet, Jean and J.D. and become friends? After all, they seemed to come from two entirely different worlds if you ask me?"

"Not so different as you think. I never got a straight answer out of either man on that same question but from what I gather, they had met when Jean started using what is called the Harvey Canal. He used it as a shortcut into New Orleans." She grinned at this statement. "It worked out very nicely for all involved for quite a while. Anyway, that's how I think they met, though they could have known each other in France I suppose. Anything is possible."

"You're telling me," he said letting out a large sigh. "I think I will believe nothing is impossible after today."

"Speaking of which, we really need to get going. I still have to see the graveyard and get back before Dan returns."

He started the car up once again and pulled out onto the empty roadway, still heading North, past the grand old home. It came to him then and he spoke with such determination in his voice, that Tori had no doubt he would succeed.

"I'm going to study and I'm going to see to it that more of the past is preserved for the future generations. Tori, I'm going to use the money from the sale of the coins you gave me, to go to college. I will get a degree or whatever it takes, to be able to work to save the past. I'm going to become a historian and maybe even a curator at the museum one day." He turned toward her. "I will keep one gold coin like you and have it mounted. I shall wear it always to remind myself of where I came from."

"You know I think your mother would have liked that. Leone would have been proud of you too. You are a lot like him, determined and strong in your convictions. Yes, they both would have been very proud of you. They were." She looked away from him. He was becoming very emotional. Tears filled his eyes and she didn't need him crying on her right then. She needed his strength for what she was about to face.

Just like everywhere else, the graveyard was no exception, it too had altered over the years. It was still a small cemetery, in contrast to a lot of others, especially those like the St. Louis found in the French Quarter. Also, unlike the above-ground tombs, here the dead lay beneath the ground, among the trees. It was still a peaceful and harmonious place. The only sounds to disturb the hushed atmosphere came from the bird calls over head. Occasionally a noise from the river would be carried on the breeze, to dance among the branches of the moss-draped oaks.

At first glance, the sheer number of headstones, told Tori that many people had joined Christopher since she and Jean had chosen to bury him here. Like them others too had found the place to be one of beauty and tranquillity. It was like having a small slice of heaven on earth. Though rundown and overgrown in places, it was evidently still being taken care of. Some of the closer graves had fresh flowers placed on them and the grass was trimmed and tidy.

Walking through the old iron gate, the two of them could hear the sound of leaves being raked and the hum of someone singing to himself as he worked. Off to the far end of the fence, was an old black man working diligently, stopping only briefly to look up. He nodded his head and smiled brightly, then went back to his work.

Looking around her as she walked toward the far end, Tori could see that some of the older graves, had not been attended to in years. They were long forgotten and left for the grass and time to claim. There were many gray headstones that the rain and weather had worn smooth. Some had weathered the years better, sheltered from the elements and the north blowing winds. But even these stones, could not escape the ravages of time. Their inscriptions were fading with age, erasing the names and dates of those laying beneath them. Stepping carefully among the graves, for there was no clear pathway, Tori and Tom both noticed that quite a few of the old gray stones, were leaning precariously to their sides. They looked as if one good wind would finish the job time had started, and push them over.

Tom looked at Tori and moved closer toward her. He asked the obvious question. "How you going to locate it? I mean the place has had so many new graves since then. Shall we split up and look? You just tell me what to look for."

"That won't be necessary Tom. Don't you remember what I told you? Think. His grave had a tree planted by it and if you follow my gaze, you will see for yourself. Over there, is a large old tree and something tells me, that under its shade, one of those graves is the one I seek."

Tom took her hand, as the two of them made their way over to the tree. Then as if drawn to it like a magnet, Tori walked up to the small marker that lay ingrown in the base of the oak. The roots of the mighty tree had wrapped around the stone and over the years pushed it to an odd angle. Standing there looking at it, one would think the marker was growing out of the wood that encompassed it. It was as if the tree was cradling the small grave and its contents.

The inscription could no longer be made out clearly. Faint in a few places, and completely worn in others. Tori tried to make out the few words that had at one time been inscribed there. "The name could be Christopher," she told Tom. She looked hard at the faint and worn spot, her fingers tracing carefully over the few indents that remained. Her hand moved lower down, where she made out the words, "Taken away from us too soon." Tom knelt down by her side, inspecting the stone closely with her. There was a large blank space after that. Tom's hand ran over the area. It was clear that something had been written there at one time, but nothing at all remained. However at the very bottom, close to the base where it was protected by the tree's roots, some words were still clearly etched. The words brought tears to her eyes as she read them out loud. "Whose memory will always live on in our hearts."

Her hand shook as she touched the top of the headstone. Hello son. I don't know if you know this but he was right, your daddy. You are always in my heart, as I'm sure you were in his." She could feel the stinging of her tears, as a pain burned deep down inside of her. She was crying for far more than just her son. They were tears shed for something, that after this day would be forever buried and left as it should be. A part of history.

Tom sensing that she needed some time alone, walked over to the fence and the old man, who was still working at tidying the grounds.

"Mind if I join you? She needs some time alone." He indicated Tori by looking in her direction.

The old man stopped what he was doing and looked up into Tom's face. His old eyes could see the hidden heritage that lay in his soft features, giving them something in common. Something else told his old bones that he was not the normal curiosity seeker either.

"Ain't been no one buried over there in years. Folks'es these days wants themselves buried fancy like. Got to have themselves laid in some big fancy spot, not run down and old like this is." He spit off to the side and leaned up against the fence. He reached into his pocket and took out a packet of chewing tobacco. The old man offered some to Tom, who politely refused and then he filled his cheek with a fresh wad. He replaced his packet very carefully, paying great attention so as not to spill any. Then once that was taken care of, he looked over at Tori. She was on her knees, cleaning the small area at the base of the tree. It did not take twenty-twenty vision, to tell him that she was crying and that it was a truly personal moment. "Ain't never seen no one come here to take care of no grave like that neither. I been taking care of this place for long as I kin remember. Know every grave. That one, it's too old for any kin. How come she going on like that? Like it some kin of hers or something?"

Tom looked away from Tori and looked into the old man's face, seeing his wary eyes that lay sunken above his hollow cheek bones. Gray stubble clung to the man's chin and his clothes looked old and worn. Yet he had a gentleness about him, a sort of kindness to his face. It had wisdom written in the creases that formed deep furrows in his leather-like skin. He was not a bitter old man. Tom could see that from the way his lips curled upward, the wrinkles permanently making it appear as if he were about to smile. If he were a bitter old codger, then those lines would droop downward in a permanent scowl he told himself. He decided he had the kind of face, that said you could trust.

"If I told you that she did have a claim to the grave, you would only want to know how. So could you just please trust me? And know old man, that soon she will leave and we won't be back. She just has to make peace with herself and her memories."

The old man listened to his words and could see that this kid really cared and that he was not telling him a lie. God had seen to it that he was a good judge of character and he was seldom wrong. He could tell the young man all about his gift, about being able to judge people and all. Like he had earlier. Then he wondered if he should tell him, that they were not the first this day, to pay attention to that grave. He was pondering that very thought, when he saw the figure making his way over to where the woman knelt.

Tori had stopped crying. She was sitting deep in thought, as the sunbeams filtered down among the branches of the tree. She watched as the shadows danced upon the grass. They seemed to play a game of chase, with the golden sunlit spots that would appear and disappear with each breath of wind.

A hand came down upon her shoulder, resting gently as if not wanting to disturb her. The shadow of the person was blocking out the rays of sunlight on Christopher's gravestone. But unlike its dancing partners, this shadow did not move.

Reaching up, she took hold of the hand and held it in hers, never taking her eyes away from the grave. Tom did not utter a word. He was waiting for her to say something first she thought. He was thoughtful and sensitive as always. She was so lucky to have him as a friend, to have him here with her now, so understanding. She could feel the warmth of his skin, the dampness of his palm in hers, as he gently but firmly squeezed hold of her trembling hand. She let herself look away, to gaze at the hand that would help her leave this sad place and all its memories. It came as a shock, when her mind quickly registered the hand she was looking at was not Tom's. This hand was far from young. This hand in hers was that of an old man.

She could not let go of the hand either, for its grasp on hers was as firm as Tom's would have ever been. Had she looked so desperate that some stranger had taken pity on her, she wondered? That may be; he felt she desperately needed his assistance. She turned to face the owner and explained that she was alright, really she was. The words never left her mouth.

The old man standing over her was partially obscured with the sun shining brightly behind him. Squinting, she tried but could not focus on his face at all. His hand held hers even tighter, almost to the point of hurting her and still the stranger did not talk or release her. He slowly walked around to stand at her side. Tori's head followed him, her eyes opening wide, when his face came clearly into view. His dark eyes reached inside of her and spoke to her beyond any description of emotions she had ever experienced. She recognized them immediately. Tori would have known those eyes anywhere and in any time. They were the same eyes that had haunted her dreams every day for years, both in sadness and sheer joy. She let his hand help her up, pulling her to within inches of him and then she was in his arms. She clung to him as he did to her. No words were spoken between them. They were not necessary.

His hair was gray and the heat of a fever pumped out of his thin body. His shirt was soaked from perspiration causing the material to cling to him. The strong shoulders that had once been broad and square, now sagged and seemed to be shuddering weakly. They stood there like that for what seemed like an eternity.

Finally she managed to utter her first words to him. The words that came mixed on her lips, with the taste of salty tears. Tears of both love and fear. "Jean I don't understand, how?" This was all she could utter. She couldn't even bring herself to raise her head from his shoulder.

One of his hands came up to her head and stroked at the side of her face tenderly and still he did not speak.

She pushed back from him a little, trying to get a good look at him, fearing briefly, that she had been mistaken, that this man was not her Jean after all. "Here let me get a better look at you. My God, I'm not dreaming. It is you!"

"That it is my lady," said the old familiar voice. "And it really is you."

She felt him weakening, as they stood only inches apart. "Come and sit over here," she ordered while leading him to the shady side of the tree. "You're exhausted, I can see it and you're not well." Concern filled her voice.

He sat down, finally releasing her hand to do so. Jean leaned his back up against the trunk of the tree for support and then reached out his hand to her. He patted the ground next to him in an invitation to join him.

"My lady, my Tori. You are as I remember you. It seems time has been far kinder to you, than to me. You are as beautiful as the day I first laid eyes on you, or more like night," he laughed hoarsely. "You remember?" His dark eyes flashing at the memory of her in Rose's. Then a sadness filled his face as he added, "As beautiful as the day I lost you."

It was him. His voice was old, the features changed but his spirit was as always, her Jean. So many unanswered questions passed through her mind, so many unfinished thoughts, one overtook the other. The most prominent thought was that he was here, looking at her, still loving her.

He smiled. "It would seem to me, that we both have been brought together once again. And he..." Jean coughed. The conversation was interrupted as his hand grabbed his chest halting his speech.

Tori held his free hand and watched as his breathing became labored for a minute and then it seemed to get easier again.

"Sorry my love, as I was saying, we're together again because of our son and just in time."

"Jean you need a doctor."

"No my lady, what I need is to explain to you what happened. That is why I am here so let me finish. For once just sit and listen." He tried to smile as he tenderly took her hand in his again. "I crossed over three days ago and knew right away I was in the right time. Some future you have here." His face filled with wonder like that of a child's. His eyes flashing and sparkling, as she had so often seen them do. "I have seen for myself all that you told me about, well nearly all," he grinned. "I have seen the carriages that go without horses, the things that fly in the air, the size of the boats, the barges on the river. All as you told me but the city. What did they do to the city? I could not find my way around and people in this time are not so trusting. Not that I blame them overly much, me looking as I do. Some have helped but I was weakening fast and knew only one place I could find. I got here early but left to get some water. When I returned here, I thought myself dead. For you were waiting for me. I could not believe my eyes or my heart. I am not dead am I?" He coughed again, sounding worse than before.

"No Jean, you are not dead. But if we don't get you to a doctor you surely will be."

Just then another voice broke into the conversation. It was Tom. He had come over as soon as he had seen Tori and the stranger sitting together.

"Tori?"

"Tom," she turned to face him. Whether he believed her or not, she would still need his help to get Jean to the car and a doctor. "You won't want to believe me but this old man is Jean, my Jean." His face was blank. "Laffite! she said firmly, than watched as the news hit him.

He did not change the look on his face, his body had stiffened at the news slightly, but he covered that by quickly crouching down. Sure the man was dressed strange but most crazy bums around the city did. Most were eccentric in both actions and manner of clothing. Tom searched the man's face for any sign resembling the description she had given of Laffite. What he saw was the old man scrutinizing him just as closely.

Jean's face lightened, his deep creases relaxing. "Tori, this young man looks a lot like Leone. Can it be, that he is the young Tom you told me of all those years ago?"

Shock registered on Tom's face at this reference to his father. Only the real Laffite could know about Leone. But before he had a chance to respond, Tori was speaking.

"I see your memory is as good as ever. He is the one and the same but you need to stop talking, we have to get you to a doctor."

Jean's hand came up on her arm and he took hold of it, shaking his head as he did so. He pulled himself up to a higher sitting position. "It's not going to do any good I am afraid. I have seen a doctor. True it was a hundred years ago," he laughed, "But I doubt that even your doctors could do anything for me now. Let it be. Let's just sit here for a while and talk. Come join us Tom, I assume that by the look on your face, you know about me and my connection to this lady."

Tom nodded his head, "Yes sir, I know." He ran his hand through his hair, pushing it back. "But before I do, there is something in the car I think we could use." He looked at Tori, "A couple of cokes, yes?"

"That would be great."

He left them without saying another word. He needed to get his head together and they could use a few more minutes to themselves.

Tori moved to Jean's side, sitting with her back leaning up against the tree trunk for added support, so as to allow him the luxury of leaning comfortably against her. She wanted to take him for medical help but knew that to try to do so before he was ready, would be like trying to move a mountain. Once she accepted that, she was able to calmly and rationally talk with him. She told him first of what had happened to her the day she crossed over.

He sat listening to her every word, watching as Tom took his time getting whatever a coke was, from his carriage.

"You know," her voice was gently explaining. "There has not been a day go by, that I have not thought about you, about us." She shifted herself into a more comfortable position. "I even started reading everything I could about those years, about you."

Tom joined them, hesitating at first to sit down and then as if deciding he had no choice, plunked himself down opposite them. "Here," he handed Tori a can of coke, "Sorry it's not ice cold, but beggars can't be choosers I suppose."

Jean said nothing but Tori could see that he found Tom's way of talking amusing. She popped the top of the can and took a swig before handing it over. "Jean try this, it's not what you're used to, but it's wet."

His expression was not so much from the looks of the strange container, but from the way she had opened it and the popping sound it had made. "It seems to me, that if I am to keep you happy, that I must oblige you." He put the can to his parched lips and gingerly took a sip. "Not what I call a man's drink, but then as you say, it's wet." He was grinning as he handed it back to her. He turned to Tom. "Do you know that this here lady, has the damnedest way of always getting her wish? I could tell her one thing, ask her not to do something or other and by God, she would turn right around and get me to do exactly what she wanted."

"I do indeed know what you mean." Tom agreed. "She does have a certain ability in that direction. She got me to bring her here today. It's the last place I would have ever expected to be."

Jean turned back to Tori. "Glad you came," he patted her hand.

"Jean, what happened to you after I left? I mean, I know what happened, you're here but what did you do all those years? I couldn't find one thing in all my reading that told me. I even tried to find a link, anything referring to me, even Christopher here but nothing. His christening records gone. Did you have something to do with that?"

He laughed softly and looked at her with that twinkle of mischief.

Tom could see that he must have been a very handsome man in his prime. Why even now, in the winter of his years, he had a roguish handsome look about him.

Tori half-smiled at Jean. "Don't you go giving me, that who me look Mr. Laffite. You know very well that I can see right through you. Always could, always will. I know some of what you did, or what history said you did. I just want to know, need to know what really happened." She looked at him then and softly pleaded, "Please."

"You talk about knowing me, huh." He looked toward Tom. "That's how she gets you every time. That look of hers, that coy, soft loving appeal, that tugs at your heart so much so, that it becomes a lost battle." He was laughing as he looked back toward her. She had not changed a bit and he was so glad. "I'll try to explain some of what happened but this old mind is not as clear or quick as it once was."

"Liar," she pushed playfully at his side.

"Well then, let's just say I will tell you that which I think is relevant, starting with the most obvious. I take it that you must have gone back to the Cathedral, after all they do keep such good records."

His chuckle made Tom grin and Tori smile. "Oh you devil. You did do something, didn't you? But how on earth? I mean that's the church we're talking about here. I found the records of Pierre's children, they were and are still intact."

"Had no reason to disturb them," he stated simply. "You had told me often enough that in your time there was very little known about my life. I simply chose to help keep it that way. If you will stop interrupting me, I will explain to you what I did."

"I do not interrupt you. You keep avoiding the subject," she said, trying to sound serious.

She was teasing him and he knew it. It was as if time had stood still in their relationship. They were acting as they always had together. His eyes filled with love at the memory.

Tom sat still, watching and seeing the interaction between them both. He understood now, only too clearly, the pain their parting had cost them. Tori's story, her life with this incredible man, had in a flash become very tangible to him.

Jean took the can and another sip of the coke. He did not comment on it this time, just handed it back to her and started to explain. Neither Tori nor Tom spoke a word. They just sat under the shade of the tree and listened to his deep methodical voice.

"You remember our friend Nicholas Girod? The mayor? I see you do." He looked at Tom. "He was not only a friend but the mayor of New Orleans for a while. Very helpful to both my business and myself at times." He looked back at Tori, "more so after you left. He resigned as mayor in the September of 1815. I will not go into detail with his personal life or his dealings with myself. I shall say, that he died a very wealthy gentleman. Let us say, that due to his prospering, thanks to my aid, he owed me a favor. He became church warden of the St. Louis Cathedral, and it was easy enough for him to help me out." Jean had an inscrutable grin covering his face. He was very pleased by the memory of what he had been able to accomplish.

"So that's why the records aren't there. You devil you. You never change do you? Still up to your old tricks. What else did you do?"

"My whole life after you left me, was as you just said, filled with old tricks. That and loneliness." His face saddened as his voice softened. "Now I have to tell you something. I don't know if it is written in your history books or not, but I would not want you to learn of it by reading about it. You shall hear it from my lips." He looked gently at her then. His full attention was on his lady and it was to her that he explained the next part of his life.

"I took a mistress. It is as simple and as complex as that. I will tell you that I never stopped loving you. It does not excuse what I did, but for what it's worth, she never filled my heart, only helped with my loneliness."

Tori's eyes were filled with compassion and understanding beyond anything he could have hoped for.

"Oh my Jean, my love. I could not have expected you to stay alone. I know where I stand. Secure in your heart, a place that will always be mine. Just as you should know, that you are and will forever be in mine."

Jean smiled at this but the smile was fleeting. "There is more. You have a right to know and I have to tell you. It was to Catherine's arms that I went. It was there that I sought refuge from the loneliness, the wanting of you."

"The young Catherine Villars?" Her voice was shaky and sounded a little shocked.

"The one and the same. She was young and had always loved me from afar. Her sister and mother, even my brother Pierre thought the arrangement a good one. Never did I lie to her about you or my love. She never asked for me to love her and for that I will always be a bit ashamed." He lowered his head, wiping at his sweat-filled brow. His fingers squeezing his eyes closed. "We had a child, a boy. He was named after Pierre." He looked up at his lady, pleading in his eyes for forgiveness or at least her understanding.

She reached for him, hugging him to her. She did not utter a word. She did not need to. Then after a few minutes, she sat back and smiled at him. "Did you really go to Galveston?"

"I did." The subject of his mistress and child was now closed as far as he was concerned. He was glad of the change of subject and loved her for doing it. As always, she knew him so well. "When you left, I returned to the City. Not right away, it took me days to leave that lake and you behind." He had looked toward Tom again, bringing him back into the conversation.

"I sat there every morning hoping to join her." He spoke to both of them, looking from one to the other as he continued. "I went to Grymes and had him sell the plantation. My name was not on the deed or the bill of sale. Took some fancy maneuvering, that one did, but Livingston and Grymes, well that's what they got paid so well for. Handling odd requests of mine." He had tapped Tom's leg when he said that.

Tom laughed softly in acknowledgment and clear understanding of his activities with his lawyers.

Jean continued. "Livingston and Grymes both continued to try and reclaim all that was taken away from me. This included my ships as well as merchandise, but as time went by it became only too clear that the tide had turned against me. Knowing about Galveston, I set about arranging with a few close friends, Sauvinet, Girod and Blanque, to purchase my fleet back for me. When I had the ships, not all, but more than enough, my men slowly came to join me once again. I was like a man possessed. I drank, I swore and I set sail with my brother and Dominique. It did not last long but you knew that didn't you?"

She simply nodded her head.

"After that, a storm raged inside of me. I left Catherine and many others on Galveston and tried to return to New Orleans but to no avail. Dominique left my side at this time, choosing to remain in the city. I can't say that I blame him. He did become useful though over the years and always ready and willing to help me. It was at this time, that Marie Laveau reached me and I got a hold of my life. She was a very wise woman and a good friend. Everything I did after that, was with you and your time in mind. It became a game for me, a challenge and one that you have confirmed I won." He coughed hard, buckling over, his hands grabbing his midsection.

Tom helped Tori move him to a more comfortable position once the fit had subsided. He was so exhausted and weak, that it took them both to get him positioned. He lay now, his head in her lap, looking up into her face.

"History did not give up on me, nor would I give up on you. I knew that whatever I did, that you would read about it in your own time and Tori I did not want you to suffer thinking what if. So I simply..." he started coughing again.

She held his head up, holding him until he quieted down. She held the can to his lips and he sipped a small amount, then pushed the can firmly away.

"What does it matter what I did, or where I went. I think that I rather like the mystery man I have created." His dark eyes flashed at her brightly.

Tom spoke to him then. "And you did a damn fine job of it, if I might say so."

"Why thank you sir. I believe I do agree with you there. Still the story is not over is it? I am here after all. I had no intention of ever trying to come to this time, but when I learned that I did not have long left," he took hold of Tori's hand, "well, you and the lake were all I could think of once again." He looked back to Tom, while squeezing her hand. "So I traveled to the lake." He shook his head back and forth in her lap. "I really had no idea that this time thing would work again, let alone to me. But as I sat there, everything went so still. Not a whisper of wind, nothing. Nothing but this loud noise from somewhere up in the sky. When I looked up, I could not see anything, but I could hear it, and without thinking, I stood up and started walking, searching for whatever was making the roaring sound. I walked into the water, trying to follow that sound. Got as deep as my waist, when I finally saw it. The large thing that you had told me of, that flew in the sky. It simply appeared out of the clear blue and I knew I was here, in your time." He closed his eyes and whispered his next remark softly. "Then I found you and that's all I ever wanted to do."

Tori leaned over and took him fully into her embrace, hugging him to her. He had never stopped loving her and now he was once again with her but was it too late? What could she do? What was going to happen now?

A man's cough made the three of them look up. Tom had forgotten about the old black caretaker and now he stood a few feet away from them, staring at them in wonder.

"I been listening behind this old tree and if my ears hear right, I would like a talk with you."

Tori nodded her head affirmatively. She did not really care one way or the other if he joined them. If he had heard what difference would it make, no one would believe this old bum in her arms was Jean Laffite. They would say he was a crazy old man. No, her Jean was still safe.

The caretaker stood by Jean and then he too sat down. "Me old bones ain't doing what they used to. These here young uns don't know of old yet. Here," he reached into his back pocket and pulled out a small flat metal flask. "You need this. It's got more punch than that sugar water. Go on, take a swig."

Jean took it, his hands fumbling with the top, as he opened it. He lifted the flask to his lips, stopping briefly to smell the container under his nose. He smiled and then swallowed a large gulp.

His face reddened, as his eyes watered. "Thank you," his voice sounded horse from whatever it was he had swallowed. "Now that's a man's drink," he added handing the flask back.

The old man's hands took it from him, as he asked seriously the one question on his mind. "You really this Laffite fellow?"

Jean nodded his head. "You can say that whatever is left of this old man is Jean Laffite. May I ask your name my friend?"

The old man looked at Jean and then Tori and Tom. "Well if you are who you say you are, you can prove it by answering a question of mine."

Tom noticed that the old man had not answered Jean's question about his name, but he did not interrupt the conversation to point this out. It seemed trivial to do so.

"Will you do that for me? Answer a question?"

"If I can, I don't mind."

Tori objected, she wanted to get him to the doctor, but Jean shook his head.

"Go ahead, ask your question. I'll just have one more swig from your flask though, in payment." His face held that inscrutable look. He was up to his old tricks again.

The old caretaker handed him the flask. He sat still watching him as his mind raced around in his head. He wanted to know about the story passed down generation to generation in his family. If it were just that a story, then this Jean person would not know of it. And he still might be who he claimed. However, if it were true... he had to know.

"Well there is this here story, one that you might remember. It's after the Battle of New Orleans. Yes sir. The big battle. The story goes that you set a black slave free. A young boy he was. Now can you tell this old man, the name of that there slave? The one that you set free."

Jean looked over at the man, handing him back his flask. He had to think. Yes, he had set a lot of his slaves free over the years. The first, being shortly after he and Tori were at Grand Terre. But, there was one he would never forget, the young boy Thiac had taken under his wing. The boy who had saved his life during the battle. The one that used Jackson's name.

"Can't seem to remember his first name but seems to me the boy you are talking about is Jackson. Is that the one? Used to be so good at names," he whispered.

He was weakening and even his cough sounded different, not as forceful as it had been. Tori hated to see him like that. She looked at him and could see his disappointment in not being able to give the old man the full name. "I think the name was David. Isn't that the boy? You told me about him, the day you sent him to Thiac for a job as a free man."

Jean looked at her, his memory clearing. The fog lifted as the years slipped away and he clearly remembered. "Yes, that is it. It was David Jackson."

They all looked at the caretaker for confirmation that he had the right name. The shock and surprise on this old face, told them before he did, that it was right. "Praise the Lord. You are him! Ain't know one knows that story around here. I don't tell it no more. Folks, they don't care none and anyways they thinks it a lie. Everyone's great, great, great, granddaddy was with you, or knew you, but then I always knew that the story was true. It been handed down like it was till me. I ain't got no one to pass it down to no more. My boy, he got killed over in Nam. Me, I'm the last. Monsieur Laffite, my name's the same as my ancestors, as all the first born boys in our families were called. I'm David Jackson sir and I owe you. My family owes you. Anything I can do to help you, you just name it. Lord, this is just the damnedest thing." Now he was the one to take a large swig from the flask. David was so overcome by emotions, that he pulled out a red piece of cloth that he used for a handkerchief, and blew his nose and wiped at his tear-filled eyes.

Tom got up and walked over to him and helped David get to his feet. "Let's take a short walk. Let them alone for a while. Got anymore of that booze or whatever it is?"

"Sure do, right over that way, in the shed. You just follow old David and we will go and find us some. I think we both needs it."

The two headed off together, Tom looking back over his shoulder and winking. "Won't go far and won't be long. You two behave yourselves."

Tori looked into Jean's weary face. He was staring at her with such a strange smile. "Seems that fate has once again been working. Who would have known? Tori my love. I need to ask you something." He shivered slightly. "I am so tired. So cold."

She moved closer to him, putting his head down in her lap. Flashes of Cisco's death came and went. This was different though she told herself. Jean was not dying, he just needed to see a doctor.

He looked up into her face, forgetting his question for the moment. "Been a long long time since I've been in your arms. It feels good. Feels like I've come home." He closed his tired eyes and rested for a while.

Tori watched his breathing, which was shallow but steady. She waited silently while she studied him. His face looked so peaceful. His skin was tanned, giving him that seafarer's rugged look. You could say he looked weather-beaten, and the lines that ran deeply across his face were etched by the sun and wind, not by old age. His hair was shorter than it had been, but still fell softly below his collar as was the style of so long ago. The gray that was almost like a bluish white, was the only change she could see in that department. She was about to continue with her scrutiny of him when his eyes opened. Looking into them, Tori could see how she could still lose herself in their dark depths.

Jean spoke lovingly, "I am glad that you are in your own time. That you found your Linni and family again. Your life is as it should be while mine is almost over."

Tori looked at him. It sounded like a good-bye speech and she wanted no part of such a thing. "Will you stop talking like that. Look, we are going to get you to a doctor and you will get well. Then I can show you so much. You will see all the things I used to talk about."

He raised his hand up to her face, stroking the side of it. His finger traveled down the side of her cheek, to outline her lips. "So beautiful, so strong. Listen to me now for once, just listen. I am dying and it is right for me to do so. There is not enough time to get me back and I doubt that it was meant to be. I am where I am supposed to be. We are here, you and I, to end what began so long ago." He turned his head away from her and looked over at Christopher's grave. Our son would have loved you so, just like I do." He looked back at her. "He has been alone long enough. Tori see to it, that I join him. Lay me to rest next to him, but no marker. No one must know. I want to be left in peace with our child."

Tori was crying again. She did not want it to end like this. She would not let him go but she would promise him, if only to get him to rest and to a doctor. "You have my word on it Jean, but that's going to be in the future. You just rest now."

Once she had given her word, he relaxed smiling at her. "Please don't cry. You have no need my lady. You have brought me such happiness. Such love. You are here with me now." He lifted her hand to his lips, kissing it lightly. "You did not forget me."

"I will never forget you Jean. How could I?"

"I will always have you in my heart," he placed her hand over his heart, holding it against him.

"And a part of me will always be Laffite's Lady. I love you now and always will."

He smiled up at her. "Remember the good times, the way it was. Here, something for you, it's yours. I carried it all these years." He was struggling, putting his hands behind his neck. Jean was removing a gold chain. The sheer effort started him coughing again and his eyes closed as he struggled to give it to her.

She held out her hand and watched as the small warm locket was placed there. She looked at it and then held it to her lips. The one thing that he could have given her. The one thing that meant more to her than all the money, all the jewels in the world was this simple gold locket. It was the symbol of his love and a memory of their son.

"I hope you will forgive me for taking so long to return it to you?" He smiled weakly. "It is done now. Be happy my lady." He smiled at her. "I am suddenly not so cold, for I am always going to remain warm in the memory of what we have shared." His hand left hers and came up to her face, touching it briefly. Then it fell, knocking hers off his chest as it did. She would not feel his heart stop beneath her hand. She did not have to. She simply knew. Jean Laffite had at last gone home.

Tori let out a stifled cry and then she dropped her head down onto the chest of the man she had loved and shared so much with, her gentleman pirate.

Tom and David ran to her side. It did not take words to explain what had happened. Her face and her actions told them. Tom knelt down and put his arm around her, lifting her off Jean.

"We have to bury him here," was all she said.

"But Tori, I don't know if that can be done. We will see about it later, ok? We will do what we can. Now come with me. David will call someone to take care of him."

"No!" she screamed at him. "You don't understand. I gave my word, I promised him." She looked over at David then. "I said he would be buried next to his son, just as he wanted. I gave him my word. Oh, please David, you have to help me." She turned back to Tom. "You both have to help me."

Tori, I don't know if that can be done. His death has to be reported and a death certificate issued, so much red tape."

Tori shook her head. "I don't give a rat's ass," she yelled angrily. Then she tried to control herself, struggling hard to soften her plea. "He has to be buried here, he has to!" She pushed Tom's arm away and lay her head back down on top of Jean.

It was David who spoke next, kneeling down besides them. "Listen you two, I owe this man a debt. My great, great, great granddaddy never did get to pay him back for what he did. He saved his life and set him free and he always said that he owed him. Our whole family owed this man. The story, it been going a long time and now, well it seems to me, that this is how the debt is a going to be paid. I know some folk and I know how we can git this here done. It going to take some money. If you willing, I kin git him buried right where you want, this here very day. I will see to it that the Jackson family that's left, it being me of course, finally pays back the debt." He scratched his head. "Seems it was meant to be anyway. Like God his self is giving me a chance to even the score. Why else do you suppose I be here. I ask you, if not for this?"

Tori raised up and smiled gently at him. "I think maybe you are so right there. If I have come to realize something in the past few years and my travels, it's that everything happens for a good reason. Don't you worry about the money, you can have whatever it takes to get the job done and then some."

The sun hung low on the horizon. The hot summer air was cooling down. The long day was giving gracefully away to the blanket of nightfall. Tori was ending her day holding on to Tom and David's hands. The three of them were alone, standing in front of a fresh unmarked grave.

"I owe you David. Without you this could not have happened."

"You don't owe me nothing, no Mam. I will be joining him along with my family in a few years, God willing. I'm going to be a hero. Yes siree. I was the one that put things right. My ancestor, he's a going to be very pleased with me. Yes Mam, pleased is not the word. Don't you go a worrying about this here little secret that we got neither. I ain't a going to be telling no one. Hell, ain't anyone ever going to believe me no how and I ain't a going to do nothing but keep an eye on things round here, till the good Lord calls me."

Tori hugged the old man to her. "Thank you."

David was quite taken with this and a little embarrassed. "You have my address. Write me sometime. Let me know how you are doing. Who knows, maybe we will talk sometime when things are healed some. Maybe we can just sit and talk." He nodded to her and moved off slowly humming the same tune that he had when they first arrived that morning.

Tori looked at the grave. Strange, she thought. She was not as sad now as she had been. She knew that he was finally at peace and she herself could go on, free at last. She had her answers.

Tom had gone to get the car, he would be here in a few minutes and she would leave this place, never to return. Tori took the locket out of her purse and looked at it closely for the first time since Jean had given it back to her. She opened it and there inside, was the small lock of Christopher's hair which curled around the words "Christopher, forever our son." And opposite this, on the other open half was the saying. "Love passes time. Time passes with love." She stood so still, remembering the first time he had given it to her.

"Want some help putting it on?" Dan's voice asked breaking the silence.

She turned to look into his face, what could she say? How did he find her here?

Dan walked toward her and reached out his arms. Come here. Seems to me you need a hug." Seeing she didn't move he added, "It's alright. I know what's happened. I've talked with Tom. He called me and I came right away. Oh my darling what a shock. You should have called me. I would have helped you. Don't you know by now that I love you? That I would do anything for you."

She fell into his arms. He was so good to her, but would he understand if he knew the whole story? She would have to tell him now. The locket would tell him if nothing else, but how?

Standing there holding her, he looked over her shoulder to the fresh grave. He would have liked to have met the man that lay beneath the soil. The man who had helped his darling Tori. Then his eyes went to the small gravestone nestled in amongst the tree roots. He noticed that someone had tidied it up and put fresh flowers on it. He thought nothing of it. His main concern was Tori. He stepped back and took the open locket from her hand. She did not try to stop him, only watched as he briefly looked inside and then closed it. There was no reaction one way or the other. Maybe he had not seen the inscription she thought.

Dan put his hands around her neck, putting the locket on and fastened the chain. All the time his eyes were flashing between the locket and the small grave behind her. The whole story came clear to him. The missing pieces fell into place. This was what she had held back from him. This was the thing that she had feared he would not understand, that would hurt him. The fact that she had had another man's child! A child that they had undoubtedly lost shortly thereafter, if his guess was right. That was what the small gravestone was next to Laffite's grave. My God, what she had gone through. He held her back from him to look into the face of the woman he loved. "I love you, as he must have. I understand that. You two shared so much but you are free now, free to tell me the whole story. That is, when you are ready. And Tori, you can tell me all about the child."

Tori looked at him, shock on her face, fear in her eyes. He knew!

Seeing the questioning look behind her eyes, Dan reached her arm and turned her around to face the grave. He pointed at the small headstone and then touched the locket gently with his fingers, lifting it up for a second, then letting it fall back against her skin. He kissed her tenderly and held her face gently between his hands. "You must have hurt so bad. Why didn't you trust my love enough to tell me? I would have listened and understood. After all, he loved you as I do. We had that in common if nothing else. And you really loved him." His words caught in his throat. "The pain of not thinking you could share this with me. No wonder the sleepless nights. My poor baby." He held her closer and tighter.

She was crying softly, speaking barely above a whisper. "I do love you Dan. I do. It's just that I didn't want you to doubt that. When I came back and told you in bits and pieces what had happened to me, it was just easier to leave out, at first, the parts that were so painful. Then as time went by, I just couldn't tell you out of fear. I had grown so close to you and needed you. Then I fell in love with you and I just couldn't." She fell silent and took in a couple of deep breaths. "It's true a part of me did, does love Jean, but believe me when I tell you, I love you. Now I just need time to come to grips with all this."

"I know that, you silly girl. And you will have all the time you need. His eyes were filling with tears. If he had thought he loved her before beyond what mere words could describe, he knew he loved her even more now. She had been living a lie to protect him and his feelings. What more proof did he need to know how she really felt about him. "We can talk and heal your soul. Look Tori, I know that you will always think of him, that is only natural. But sweetheart, what we have is so strong, it will carry us forever, don't doubt that."

She wiped the tears from his cheeks, first with her hands then with gentle kisses.

Dan smiled at her, a compassionate, understanding expression. "In time we will talk of him and your life with him, all of it. When you are ready to share, I'll be waiting."

The two of them walked together hand in hand, out of the little iron gate, to Dan's car.

Tom waved at them from his and then called out to them both. "I'll call you at the hotel tomorrow. We will get together then. Take care of each other, he would have wanted that." Then he started his car and pulled onto the road.

Dan and Tori climbed into the car. Looking outside, she saw the sun had set, leaving the sky a delicate pink. The soft light shed a warm glow across the land. The shadows of the day were giving way to the soft blanket of nightfall. And as they pulled away, Tori looked toward the graveyard one last time. There for a fleeting second, she thought she saw Jean. A young Jean and her son waving happily at her. But then she knew her eyes were clouded by her silent tears and wishful thinking. She blinked and found the image had gone. But not so her tears. They were a different kind of tears, for they were shed out of love, not sadness. She knew in her heart all was as it all should be. Tori took a hold of Dan's hand and squeezed it gently. She had her place with her Dan, as Jean had with history and his son. She remembered his words, and smiled at the thought of the secret that lay buried behind them. Jean had said, "I rather like the mystery man I have become." And so did she.

# Epilogue

Tori and Dan returned home where they were finally able to live with all that had happened. A year later they were married and Dan adopted Linni shortly thereafter. Tori no longer suffered from depression or the haunting nightmares that had controlled her life for so long, but still felt something was missing. It was Dan who suggested that she research what had happened to her friends after she returned from the year 1815. His reason being, that all her ghosts needed to be put to rest. Here then is what she learned and today is documented historical fact for all to read. For Tori, it was the final key to her peace of mind.

Jean Laffite:

Truly a mystery. Some say he was born in France still others claim Santo Domingo. Even the years differ. 1780 or 1782. I believe the correct date of birth to be April 22, 1782. Place, Port-au-Prince. He was the youngest of eight children and was said to speak Spanish, French, Italian and English with ease. Jean arrived in New Orleans around 1809 and sailed away to Galveston sometime after The Battle of New Orleans. President James Madison did pardon him and his men for patriotic services but Jean never got all his property returned. He disappeared from public view in the early 1820's. It was said that he died, while still others claimed he changed his name to John Lafflin, married and moved North. John Lafflin died in 1854, leaving behind a widow and two sons. There are so many myths mixed in with truth it leaves one wondering. The more you read of this man, the more you realize he truly is an enigma. Whatever he did and wherever he went we should all be thankful for having had him cross our shores. To this very day there is no known grave for this American Hero.

Pierre Laffite:

Elder brother of Jean. Born possibly in Bordeaux 1770 by one report. I believe he was born in Port-au Prince, October 21, 1779. He arrived in New Orleans around the same time as his brother Jean. He was married to the daughter of Jean Baptiste Sel, an artist known for his miniature portraits. They had seven children. Pierre had two black mistresses in his lifetime. Adelaide Maselari was the first. They had two children. Marie Villars came next. She was the daughter of a white man and a quadroon mother. Together they had seven children. He and his brother Jean were for years, the talk of New Orleans and between them ran the largest smuggling operation of its time. He left New Orleans with Jean and from there many tales are told of what he did next. It is said that in later years he lived with and was cared for by his son Eugene in the small Missouri town of Crevecoeur. At the age of 65, on March 9th 1844 he died and was buried in the Wesleyan Cemetery of St. Louis.

Dominique You:
    His real name is Alexandre Frederic Laffite. Born April 14, 1771. Port-au-Prince. He was the older brother of Jean and Pierre. Why he chose to be called Dominique You is not clear, nor is his reason for hiding his family ties. He was known only to New Orleans as one of Jean's Captains. His expertise with the cannon during the Battle of New Orleans allowed him to out shoot the British He ended his years in New Orleans, married and operating a tavern in the French Quarter. He died on November 14, 1830. His burial the next day was quite an affair. The city paid all expenses and flags were lowered to half-staff. Businesses closed and the newspaper published notices asking for all friends of the deceased to attend. He is buried in a small tomb in St. Louis No 2 Cemetery.

John Davis:
    Born Paris, France 1773 arrived New Orleans 1809. Not much was known about him until he purchased Tremoulet's Hotel and renamed it the United States Hotel. He owned and operated the first of its kind gambling casino. Davis had gambling establishments both on Bayou St. John and in Manderville. He ran his casino's just like modern day Las Vegas, only 120 years ahead of his time. Croupeirs and dealers worked four-hour shifts around the clock and there was no betting limit. Free food and drink were given to those who played. He helped introduce the game of poker and the deck of cards we use today. He spoke French, Spanish and English. It is difficult to find any portrait of this man and is said he would not allow any likeness of himself to be made. After 1815 he went on to run the famous ballroom Orleans, home of the quadroon balls. He also owned and ran The New Orleans Opera Company. He married Marie Fleicite Meunier, a native of Tours France. He died in New Orleans June 13, 1839. His wake was held at the Orleans Ballroom. He is buried in St. Louis Cemetery, No 1.

John Randolph Grymes:
    Born December 14, 1786. Virginia. Appointed U.S. district attorney for Louisiana 1811. Law partner and friend to Edward Livingston. Served as counsel to General Andrew Jackson during The Battle of New Orleans. He was Jean Laffite's attorney in secret until he resigned his elected position to represent the Laffite brothers openly. He was involved in several duels and known to love the good life. He lived elegantly and had a taste for gambling. He married on December 1, 1822 to Cayetana Claiborne, the widow of Governor William Claiborne. They had two children. John Grymes died on December 3, 1854.

William C.C. Claiborne:
    Born 1775, Virginia. Married 3 times. His last wife was Cayetana Susana Bosque. They had two children. This marriage improved his standing among the native population and got him appointed first Governor of Louisiana. As Governor he tried many times to destroy Jean Laffite and his smuggling

activities. He left office in November 1816 to be chosen on January 13, 1817 as U.S. Senator. Before he could take the job he died in New Orleans. November 23, 1817. Buried in St.Louis Cemetery. Later reinterred Metairie Cemetery.

Marie Laveau:

Born 1794 a free woman of color. She is known as the Voodoo Queen. She married a mulatto freedman, Jacques Paris. He died three years later and apparently she then lived with a Christophe Glapion. It is unclear if they were ever married. Together they had fifteen children. She started her career as a hairdresser in the homes of the rich. It is true that Marie was given her home on St. Ann Street by a grateful client. In later years she turned away from voodoo but too late to destroy the image she had created. She died in 1881 and burial was in St. Louis Cemetery No 1. Many people still visit her tomb.

Nicolas Girod:

Born 1747 in France. Arrived Louisiana in the late 1770's. He became Mayor of New Orleans September 12, 1812. He resigned September 4, 1815 to salvage his waning personal finances. He served as city alderman, 1824-1825, and as church warden of the St. Louis Cathedral. He like Laffite, was linked to an alleged plot to rescue Napoleon from St. Helena in the 1820's. He never married. Died on September 1, 1840 and left several hundred thousand dollars to various close friends and New Orleans charities.

Thiac:

Little is known about this man other than he was a blacksmith. He was a free man of color, most likely from Santo Domingo. Friend of both Laffite's. He had a bad reputation with the authorities. Arrested for receiving stolen goods and for harboring stolen slaves at his smithy.

Beluch:

Born New Orleans, December 15, 1780. Captain of several merchant vessels out of New Orleans. He became one of Laffite's men. He narrowly avoided capture when Barataria was destroyed. He enlisted in the American forces defending New Orleans and commanded one of the 24-pounders with Dominique. After the battle he settled in Puerto Cabell and resumed his old ways. He died October 4, 1860.

Jean Noel Destrehan:

Born 1754. He was the first Deputy Mayor of New Orleans. His home, the Destrehan Plantation still stands today on the river road in the town of Destrehan. It is possible that he knew Laffite and it is said that Laffite's treasure is buried somewhere on the grounds of the plantation. Destrehan helped plan and defend the city against the British. He married Marie Celeste de Logny in 1787. He died on October 9, 1823 and was buried in a cemetery that was known as The Little Red Church.

Marie Celeste Destrehan:

Born 1786, she was the loving and devoted wife of Jean Noel Destrehan. Together they had fourteen children and added the two extra wings onto the house to make room for them all. She died September 3, 1824 in Boston, Mass.

Edward Livingston:

Born N.Y. State 1764. Practiced law and was elected to Congress 1795. In 1801 President Jefferson made him United States Attorney. He then became Mayor of New York City. He resigned his position in 1803 and went to New Orleans. He was a leading figure in many famous legal cases. His partner was John Grymes. Edward was appointed Jackson's military secretary. They were old friends. He died in 1836.

Andrew Jackson:

Born March 15, 1767. Married 1791 to Rachel Donelson. He was a man known for his fierce sense of justice and fairness and his high integrity. In his lifetime he fought six duels. One left a bullet lodged close to his heart for the rest of his life. His men began calling him "Old Hickory" around 1813, after the toughest wood they knew. He was a tough man who would not give up a fight. He arrived in New Orleans December 2, 1814, and soon met with Jean Laffite in secret, making a deal with him. He accepted Jean's help of guns, ammunition and manpower. It was fact that the man was ill when he arrived to face the British. He was hailed as a hero after the battle and true to his word was able to hand over the pardons to Laffite and his men from the President. Jackson went on to become President himself in the year 1828 and yes, as we all know, he is on the twenty dollar bill. He died in the year 1845.